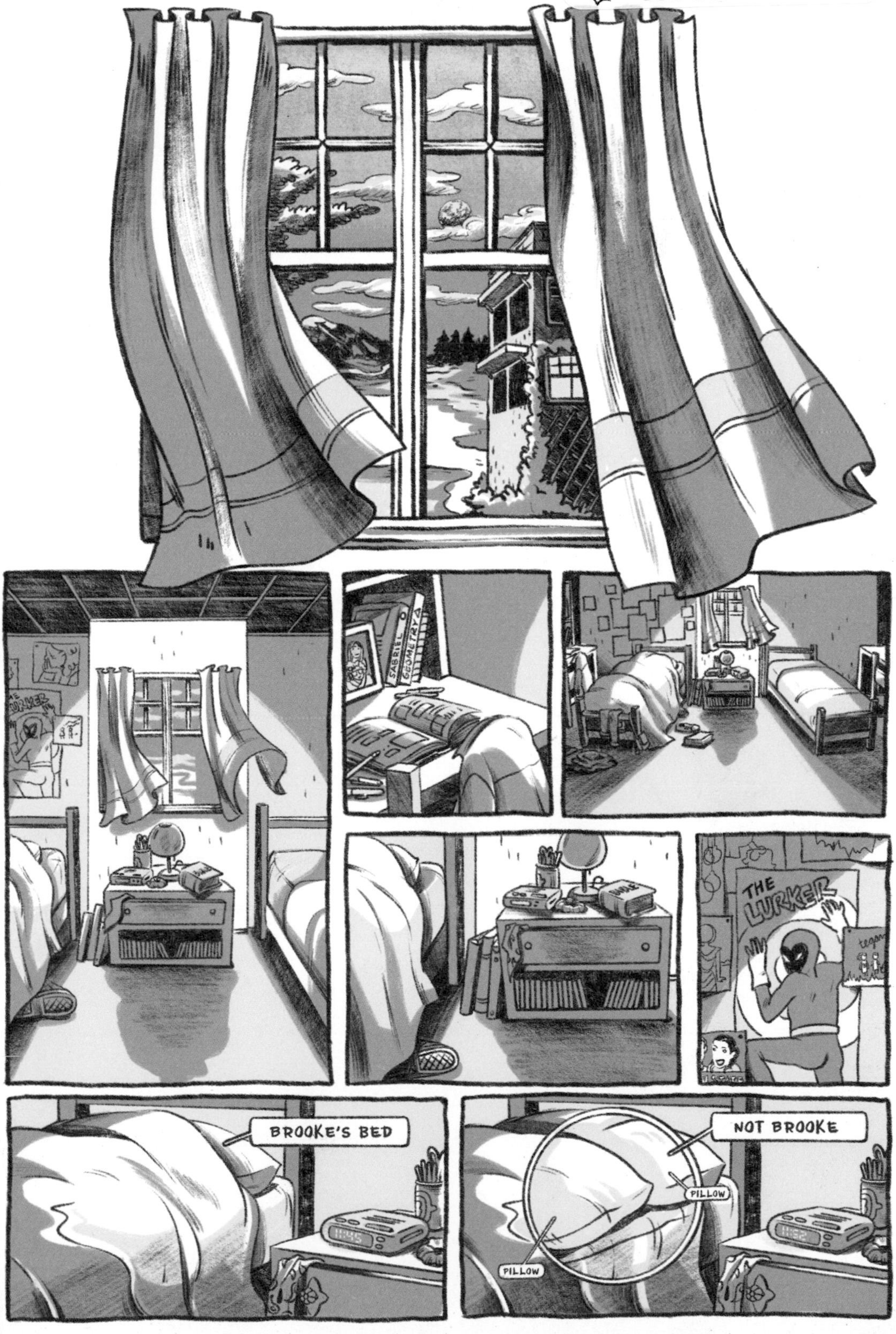
SABRIEL
GEOMETRY
THE LURKER
BROOKE'S BED
NOT BROOKE
PILLOW
PILLOW

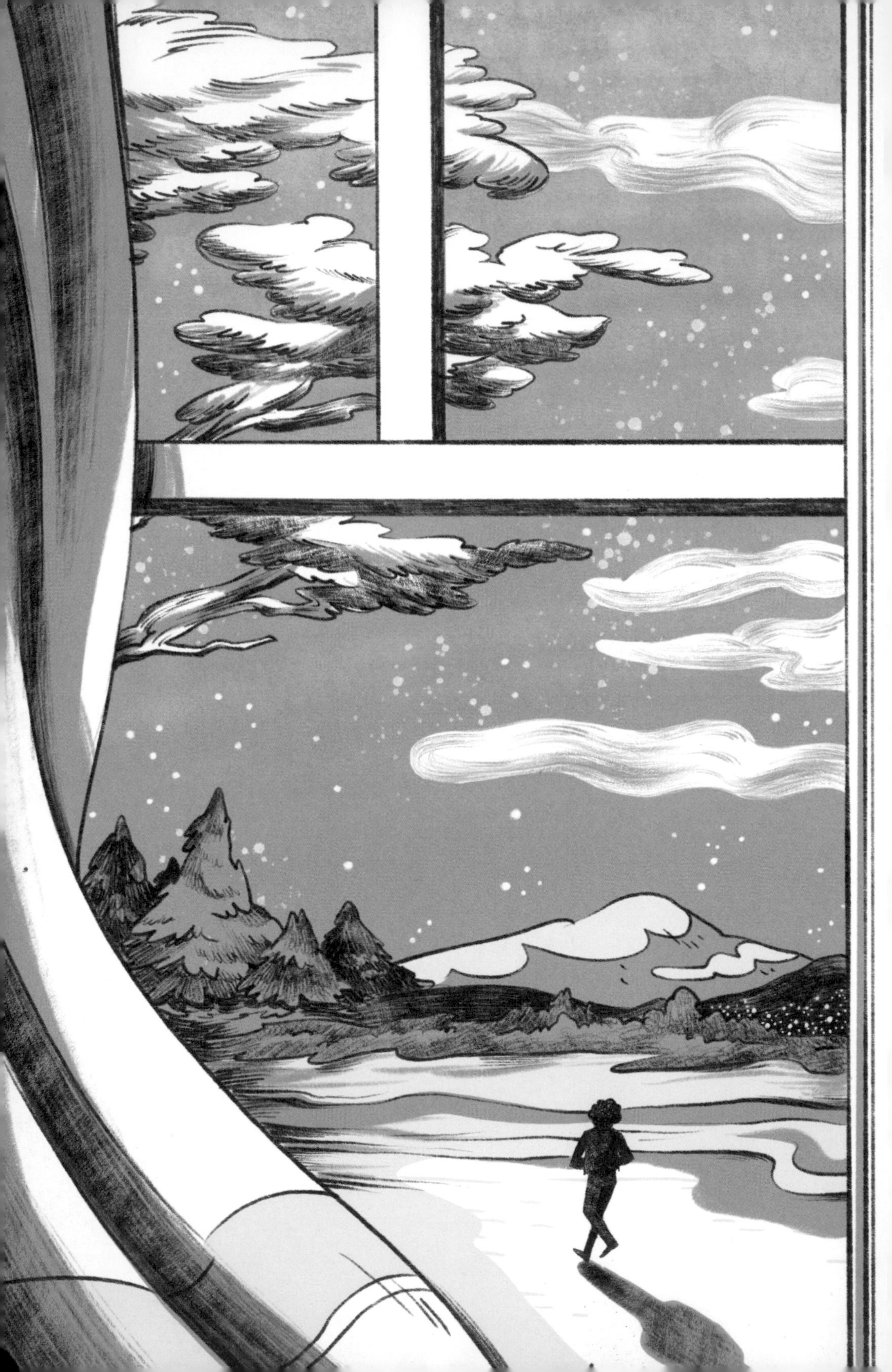

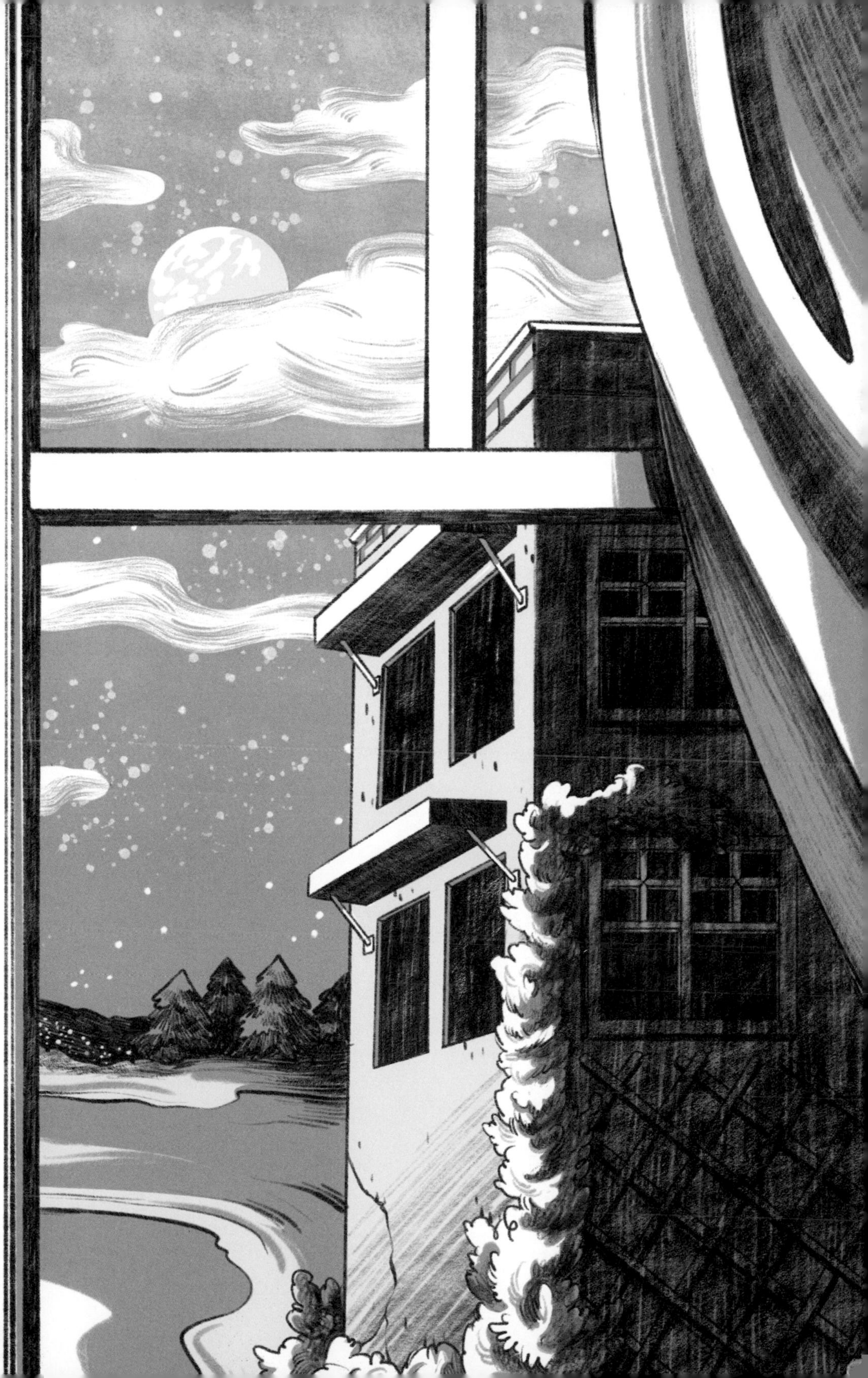

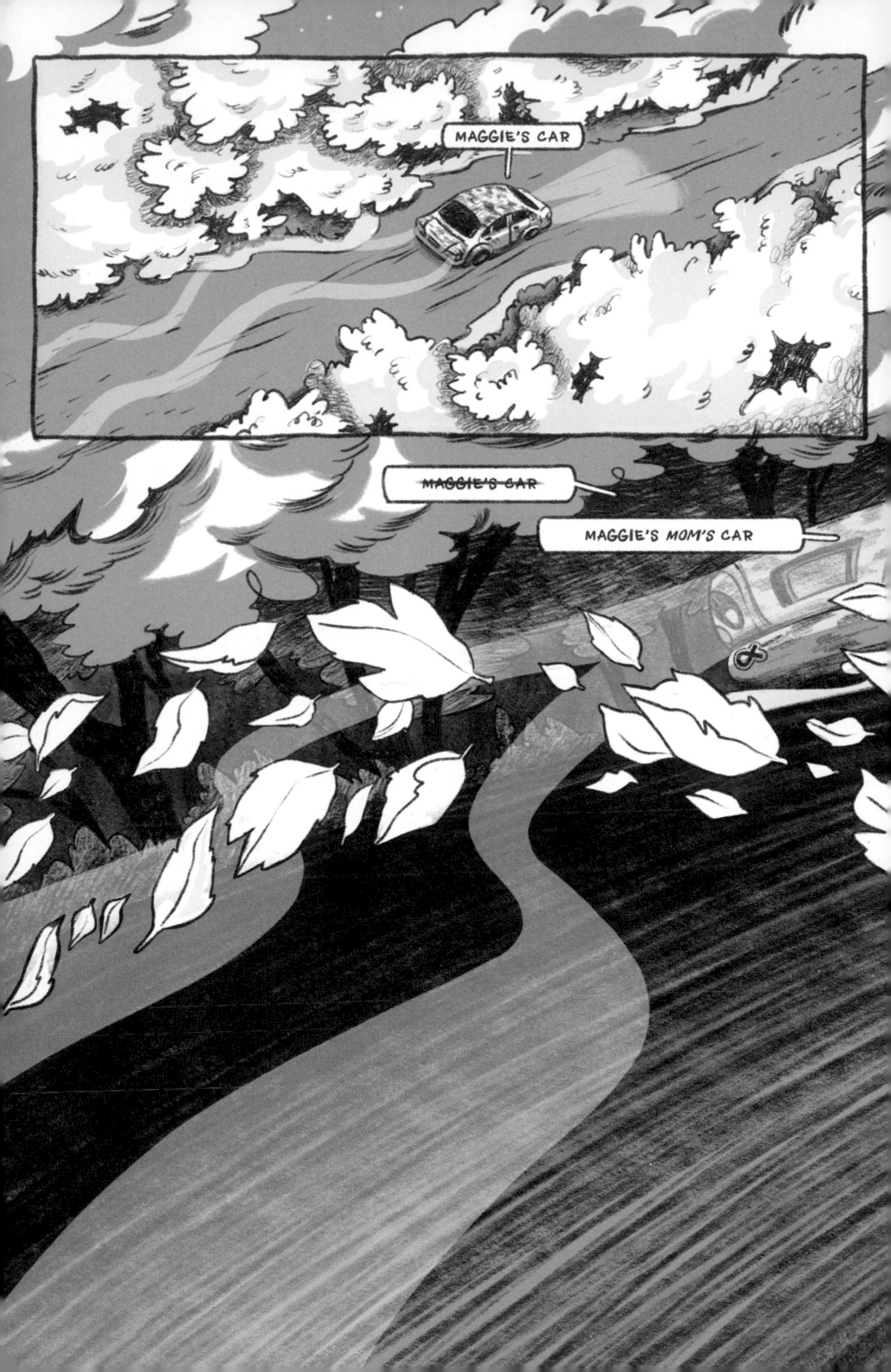
MAGGIE'S CAR
~~MAGGIE'S CAR~~
MAGGIE'S *MOM'S* CAR

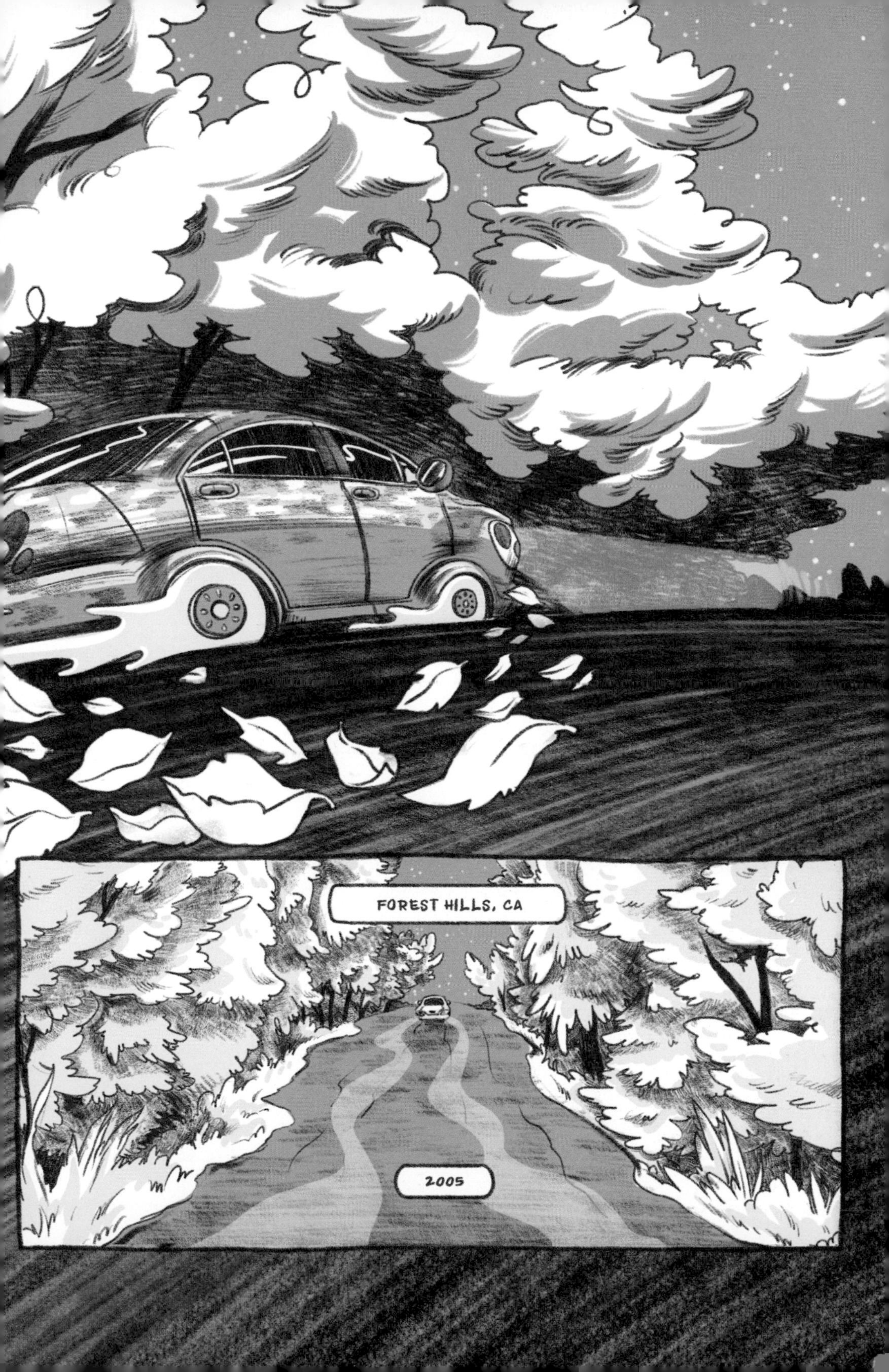
FOREST HILLS, CA
2005

Forest Bootleg

NICOLE GOUX

Atheneum NEW YORK LONDON TORONTO SYDNEY NEW DELHI

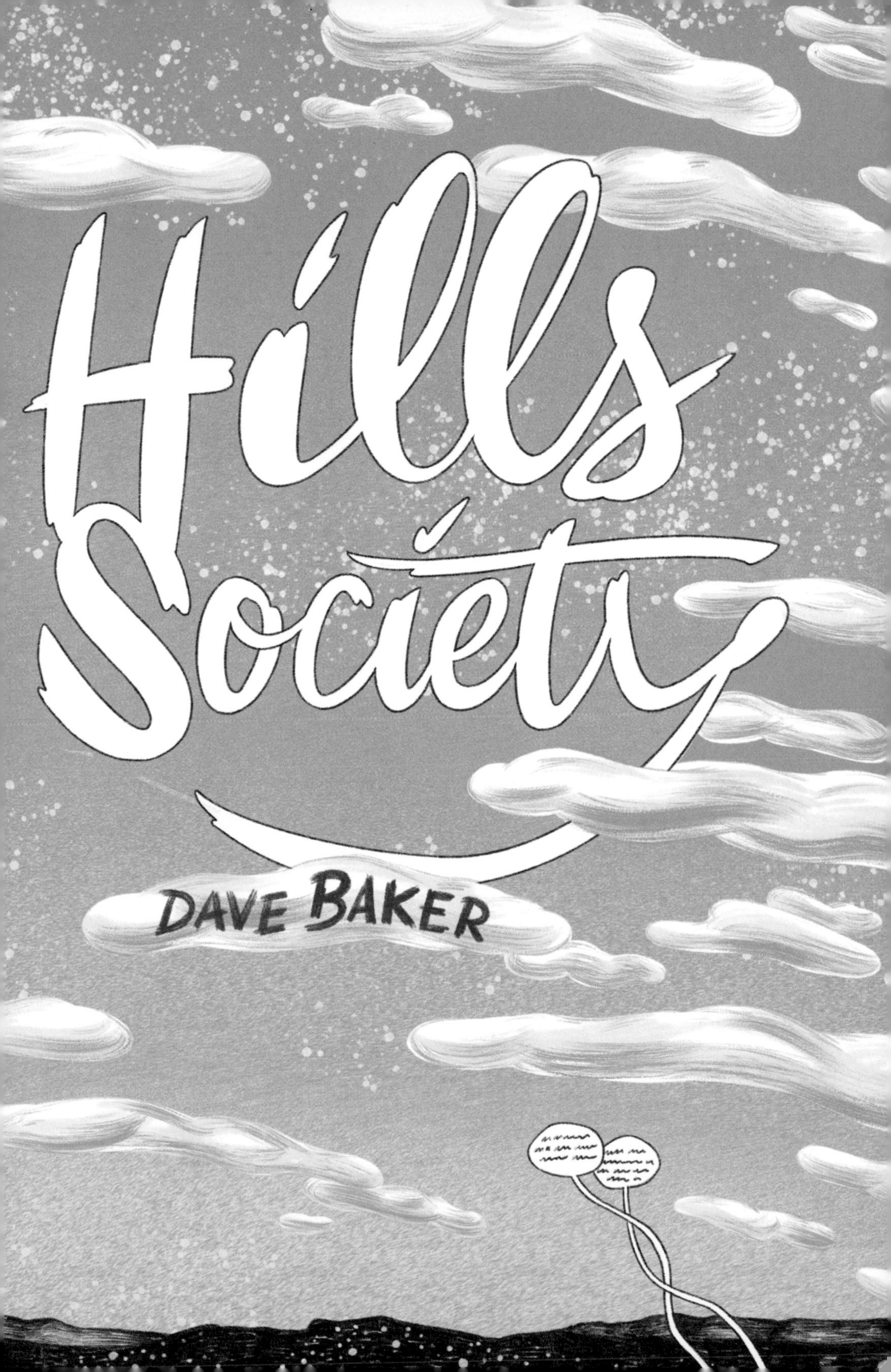
Hills Society
DAVE BAKER

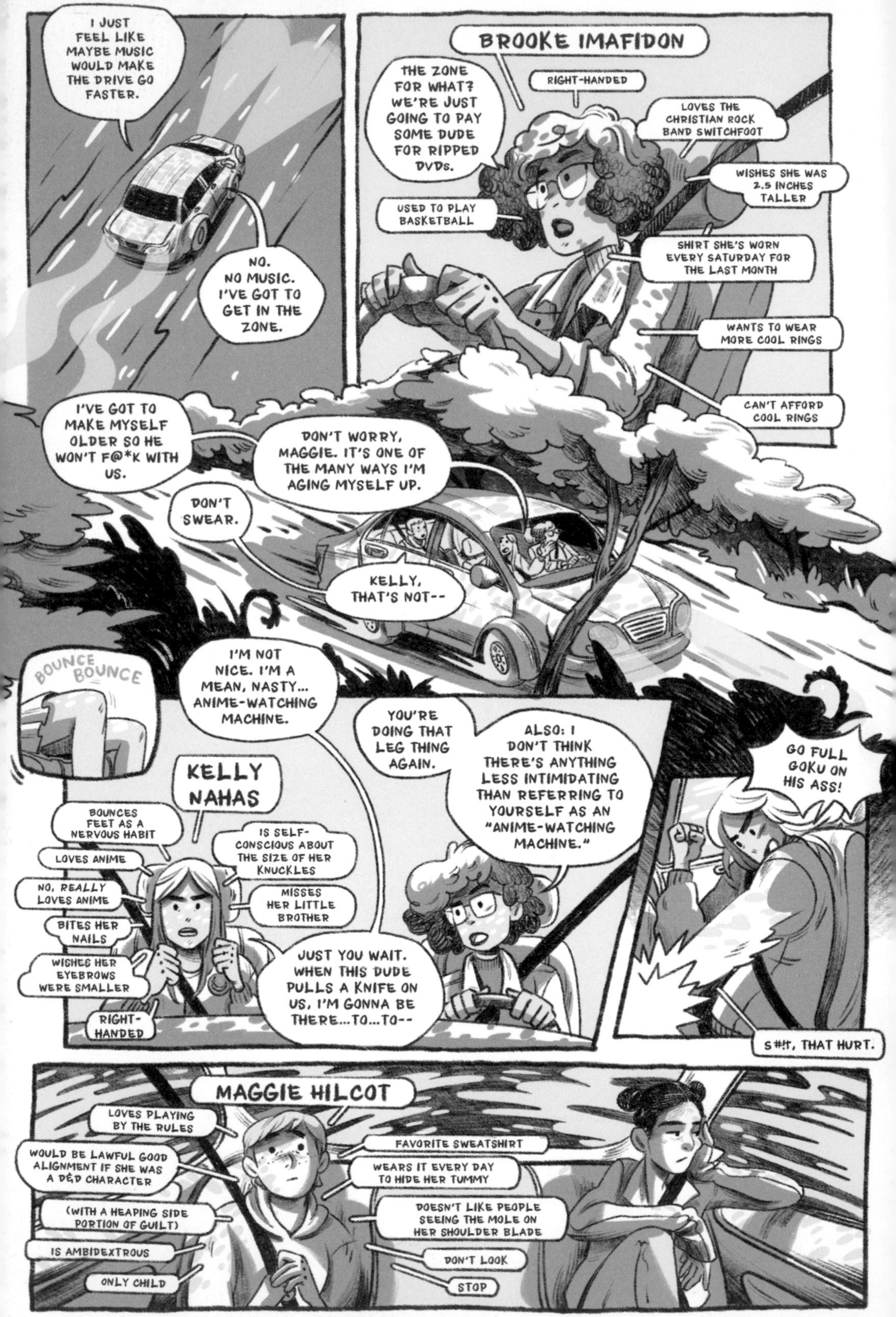
I JUST FEEL LIKE MAYBE MUSIC WOULD MAKE THE DRIVE GO FASTER.
NO. NO MUSIC. I'VE GOT TO GET IN THE ZONE.
BROOKE IMAFIDON
THE ZONE FOR WHAT? WE'RE JUST GOING TO PAY SOME DUDE FOR RIPPED DVDs.
RIGHT-HANDED
LOVES THE CHRISTIAN ROCK BAND SWITCHFOOT
WISHES SHE WAS 2.5 INCHES TALLER
USED TO PLAY BASKETBALL
SHIRT SHE'S WORN EVERY SATURDAY FOR THE LAST MONTH
WANTS TO WEAR MORE COOL RINGS
CAN'T AFFORD COOL RINGS
I'VE GOT TO MAKE MYSELF OLDER SO HE WON'T F@*K WITH US.
DON'T WORRY, MAGGIE. IT'S ONE OF THE MANY WAYS I'M AGING MYSELF UP.
DON'T SWEAR.
KELLY, THAT'S NOT--
BOUNCE BOUNCE
I'M NOT NICE. I'M A MEAN, NASTY... ANIME-WATCHING MACHINE.
KELLY NAHAS
BOUNCES FEET AS A NERVOUS HABIT
LOVES ANIME
NO, REALLY LOVES ANIME
BITES HER NAILS
WISHES HER EYEBROWS WERE SMALLER
RIGHT-HANDED
IS SELF-CONSCIOUS ABOUT THE SIZE OF HER KNUCKLES
MISSES HER LITTLE BROTHER
JUST YOU WAIT. WHEN THIS DUDE PULLS A KNIFE ON US, I'M GONNA BE THERE...TO...TO--
YOU'RE DOING THAT LEG THING AGAIN.
ALSO: I DON'T THINK THERE'S ANYTHING LESS INTIMIDATING THAN REFERRING TO YOURSELF AS AN "ANIME-WATCHING MACHINE."
GO FULL GOKU ON HIS ASS!
S#!T, THAT HURT.
MAGGIE HILCOT
LOVES PLAYING BY THE RULES
WOULD BE LAWFUL GOOD ALIGNMENT IF SHE WAS A D&D CHARACTER
(WITH A HEAPING SIDE PORTION OF GUILT)
IS AMBIDEXTROUS
ONLY CHILD
FAVORITE SWEATSHIRT
WEARS IT EVERY DAY TO HIDE HER TUMMY
DOESN'T LIKE PEOPLE SEEING THE MOLE ON HER SHOULDER BLADE
DON'T LOOK
STOP

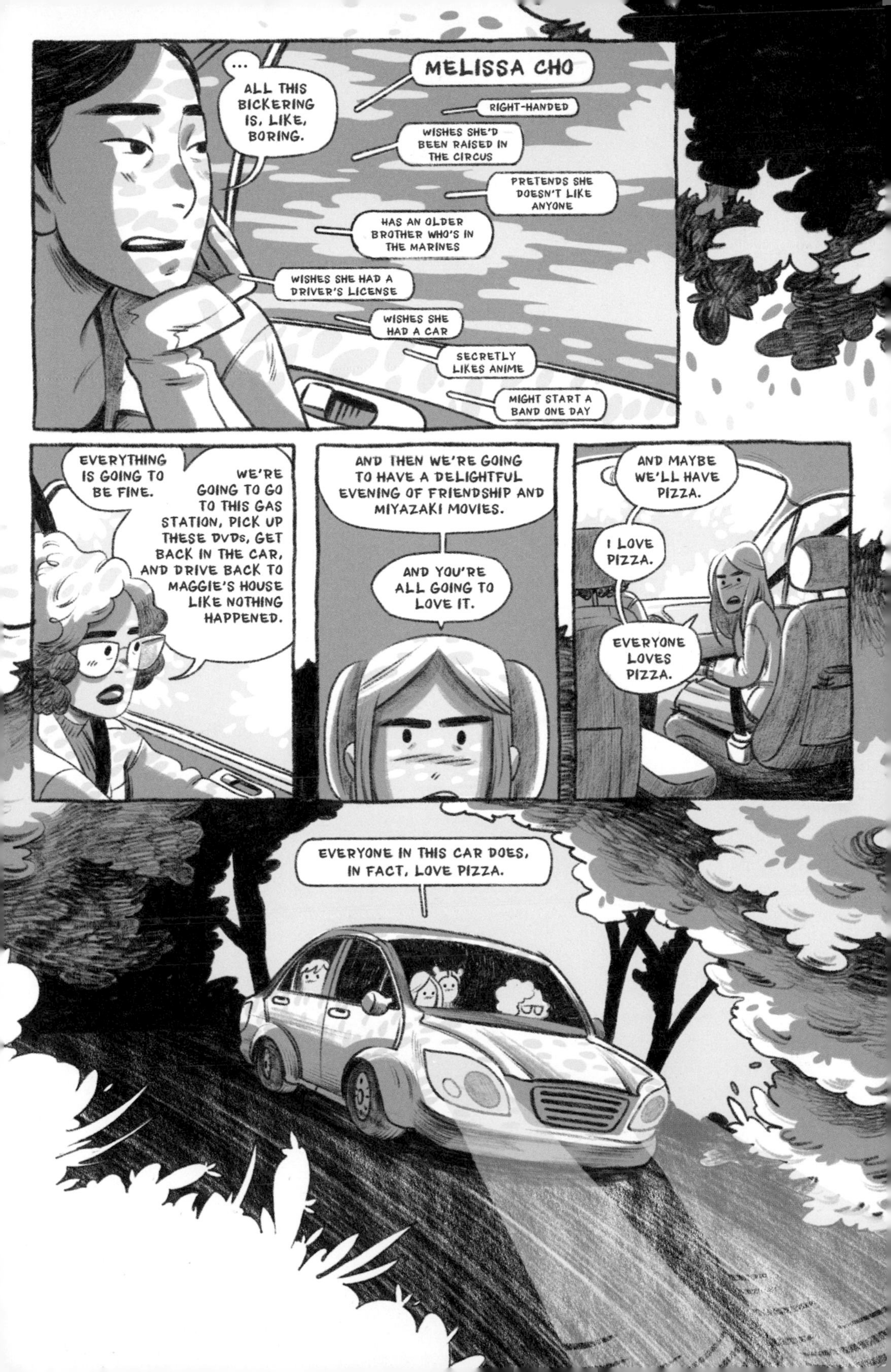
...
ALL THIS BICKERING IS, LIKE, BORING.
MELISSA CHO
RIGHT-HANDED
WISHES SHE'D BEEN RAISED IN THE CIRCUS
PRETENDS SHE DOESN'T LIKE ANYONE
HAS AN OLDER BROTHER WHO'S IN THE MARINES
WISHES SHE HAD A DRIVER'S LICENSE
WISHES SHE HAD A CAR
SECRETLY LIKES ANIME
MIGHT START A BAND ONE DAY
EVERYTHING IS GOING TO BE FINE.
WE'RE GOING TO GO TO THIS GAS STATION, PICK UP THESE DVDs, GET BACK IN THE CAR, AND DRIVE BACK TO MAGGIE'S HOUSE LIKE NOTHING HAPPENED.
AND THEN WE'RE GOING TO HAVE A DELIGHTFUL EVENING OF FRIENDSHIP AND MIYAZAKI MOVIES.
AND YOU'RE ALL GOING TO LOVE IT.
AND MAYBE WE'LL HAVE PIZZA.
I LOVE PIZZA.
EVERYONE LOVES PIZZA.
EVERYONE IN THIS CAR DOES, IN FACT, LOVE PIZZA.

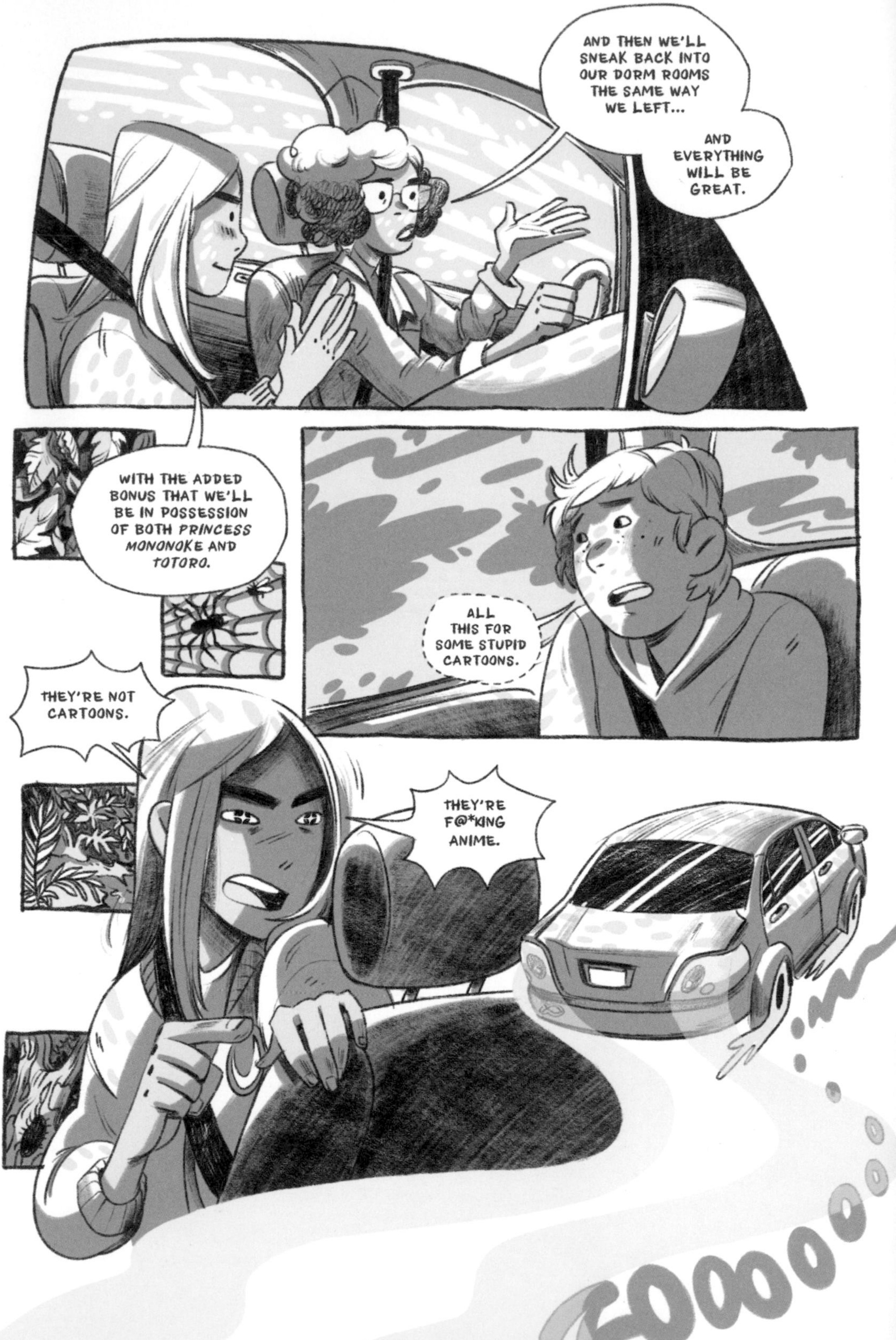
AND THEN WE'LL SNEAK BACK INTO OUR DORM ROOMS THE SAME WAY WE LEFT...
AND EVERYTHING WILL BE GREAT.
WITH THE ADDED BONUS THAT WE'LL BE IN POSSESSION OF BOTH *PRINCESS MONONOKE* AND *TOTORO*.
ALL THIS FOR SOME STUPID CARTOONS.
THEY'RE NOT CARTOONS.
THEY'RE F@*KING ANIME.
ZOOOOO

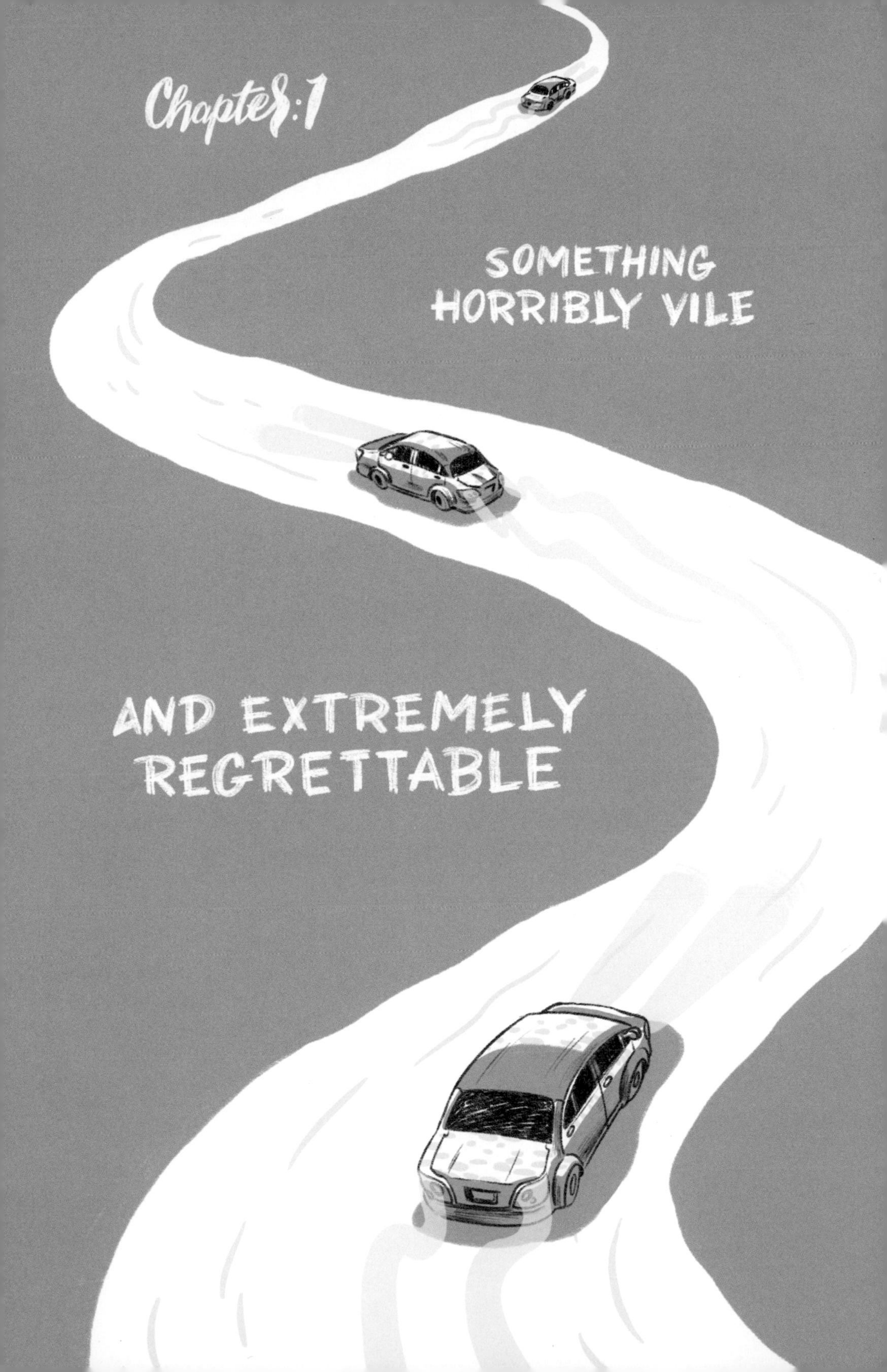
Chapter 1
SOMETHING
HORRIBLY VILE
AND EXTREMELY
REGRETTABLE

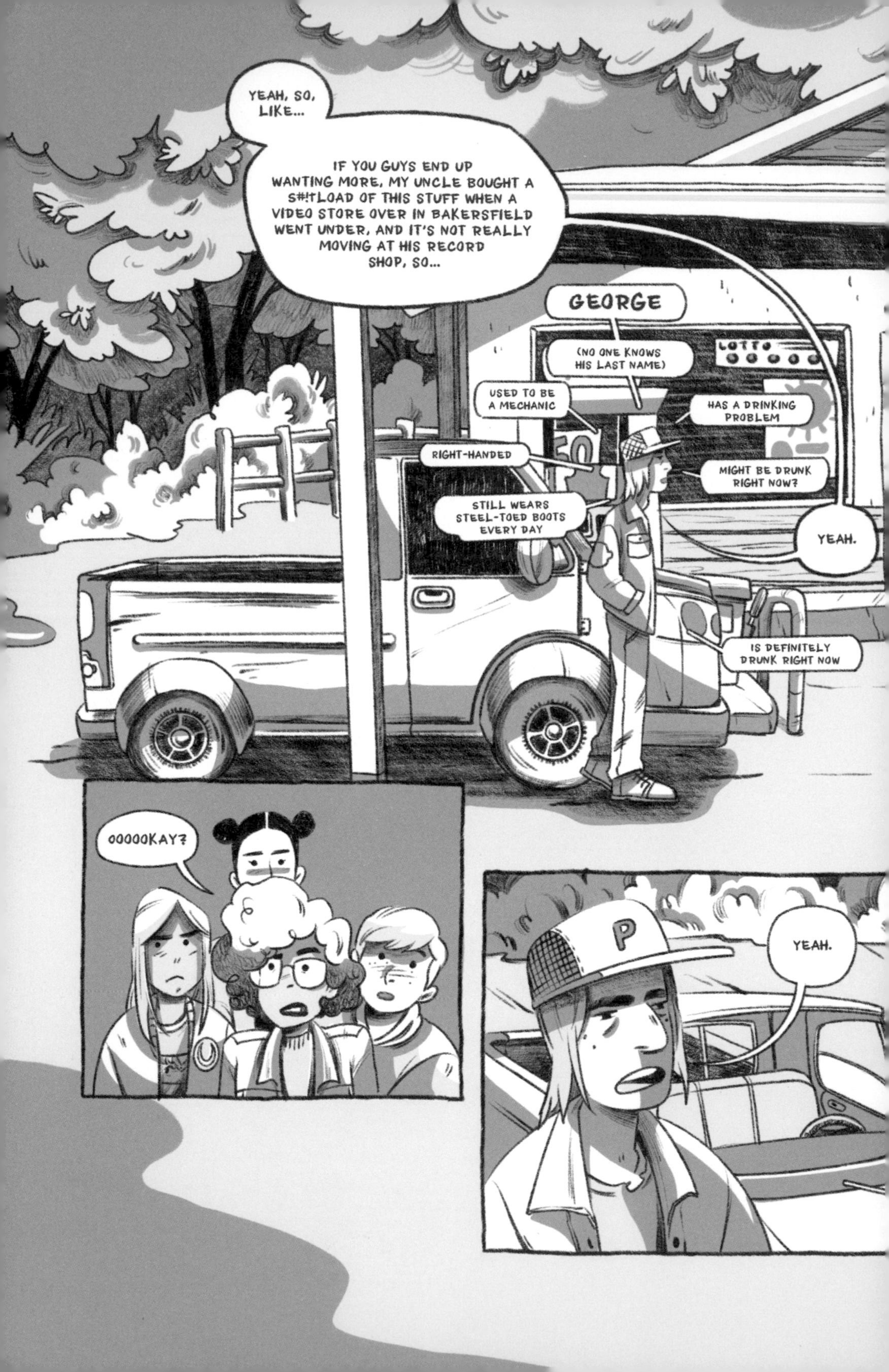
YEAH, SO, LIKE...
IF YOU GUYS END UP WANTING MORE, MY UNCLE BOUGHT A S#!TLOAD OF THIS STUFF WHEN A VIDEO STORE OVER IN BAKERSFIELD WENT UNDER, AND IT'S NOT REALLY MOVING AT HIS RECORD SHOP, SO...
GEORGE
(NO ONE KNOWS HIS LAST NAME)
USED TO BE A MECHANIC
HAS A DRINKING PROBLEM
RIGHT-HANDED
MIGHT BE DRUNK RIGHT NOW?
STILL WEARS STEEL-TOED BOOTS EVERY DAY
YEAH.
IS DEFINITELY DRUNK RIGHT NOW
LOTTO
OOOOOKAY?
YEAH.

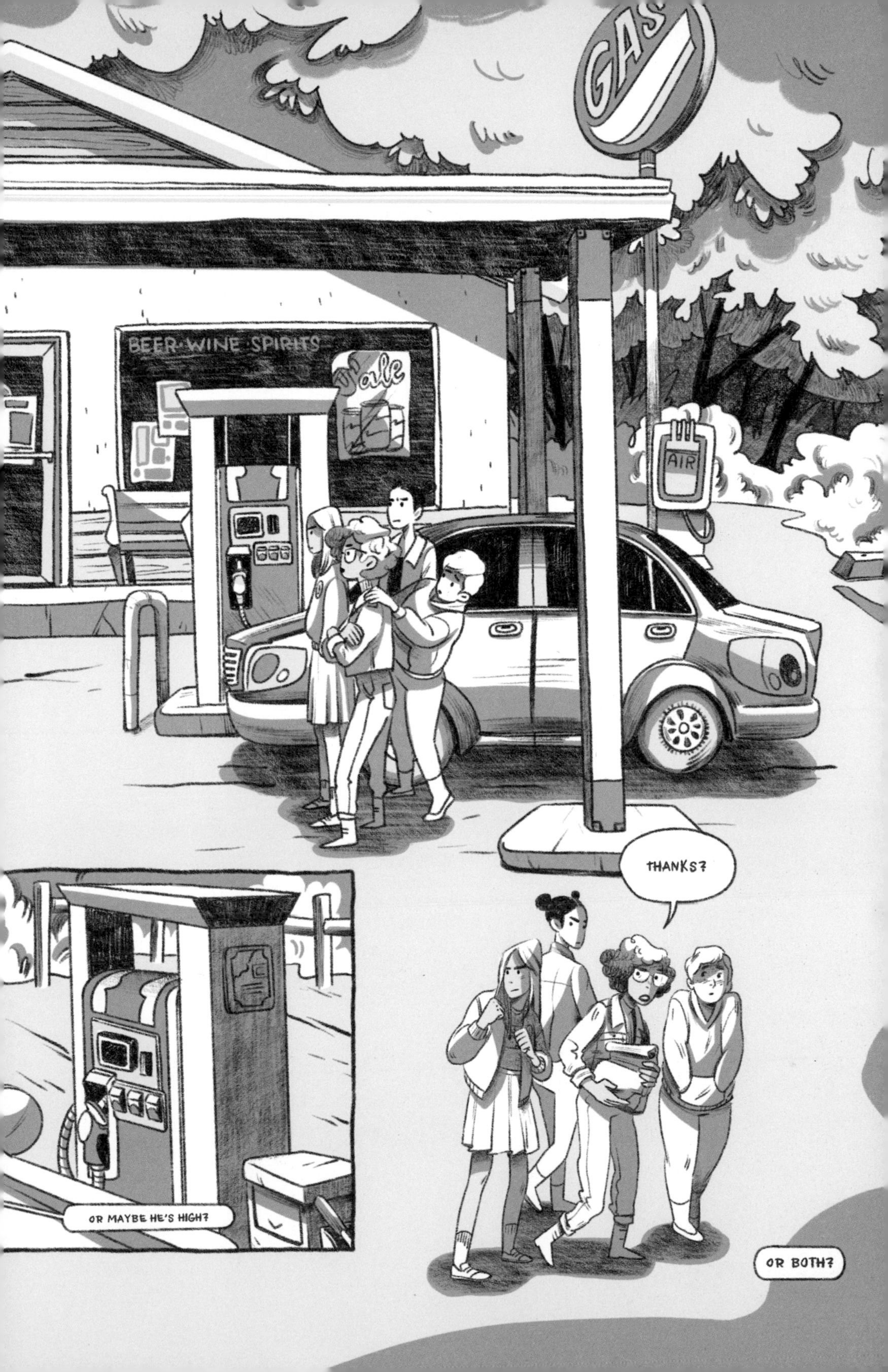
BEER·WINE·SPIRITS
Sale
AIR
GAS
THANKS?
OR MAYBE HE'S HIGH?
OR BOTH?

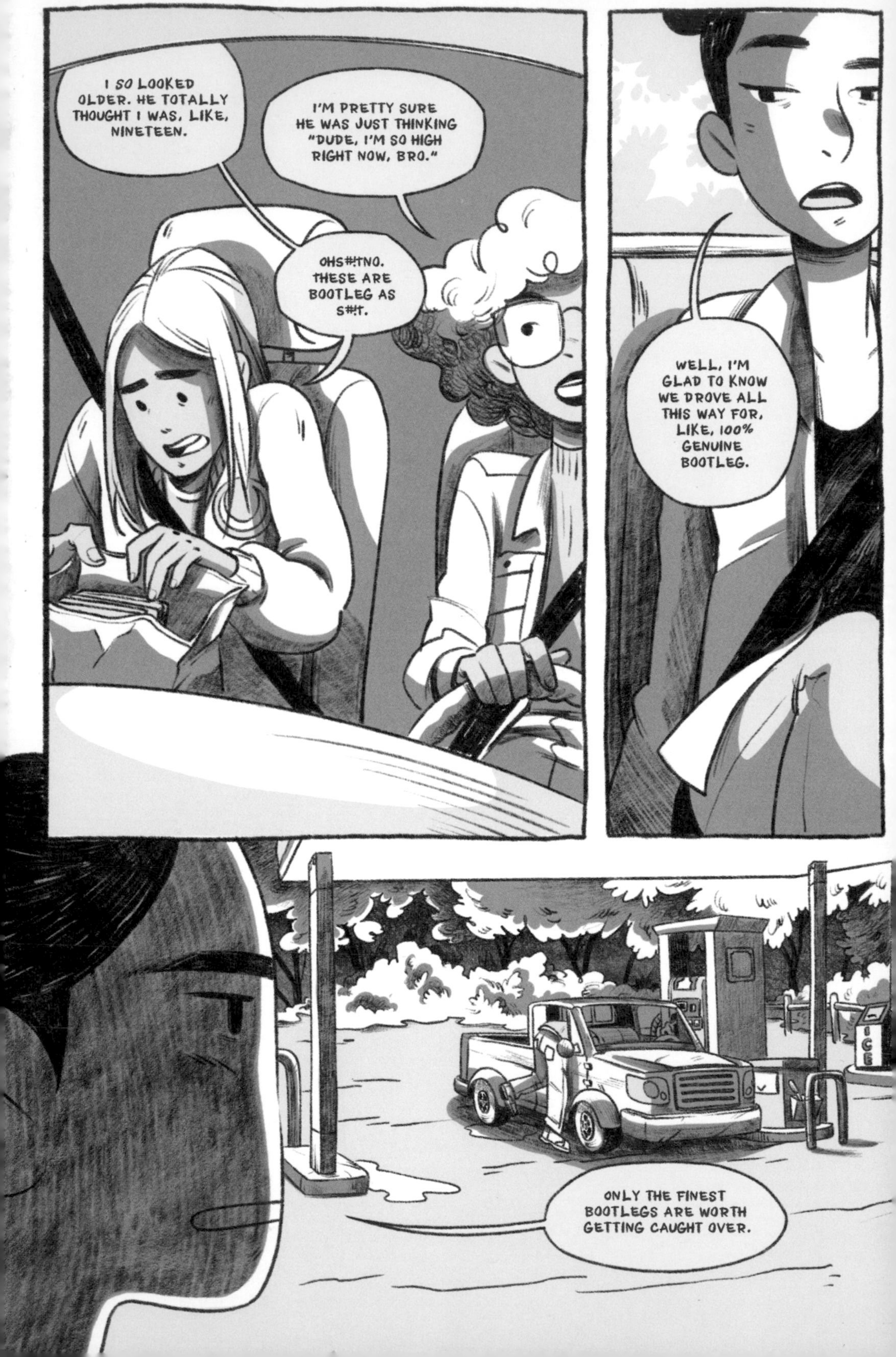
I SO LOOKED OLDER. HE TOTALLY THOUGHT I WAS, LIKE, NINETEEN.
I'M PRETTY SURE HE WAS JUST THINKING "DUDE, I'M SO HIGH RIGHT NOW, BRO."
OHS#!TNO. THESE ARE BOOTLEG AS S#!T.
WELL, I'M GLAD TO KNOW WE DROVE ALL THIS WAY FOR, LIKE, 100% GENUINE BOOTLEG.
ICE
ONLY THE FINEST BOOTLEGS ARE WORTH GETTING CAUGHT OVER.

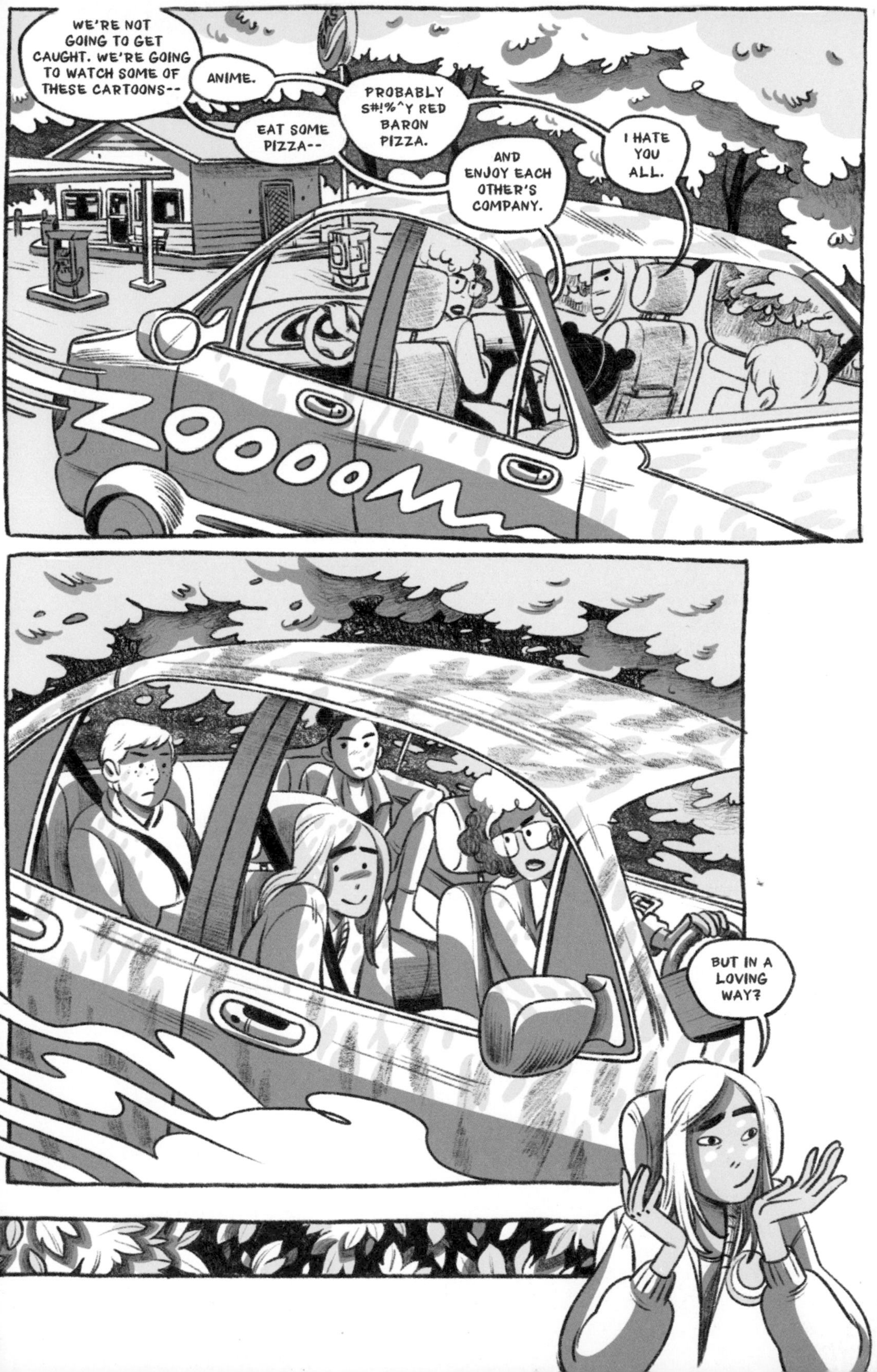
WE'RE NOT GOING TO GET CAUGHT. WE'RE GOING TO WATCH SOME OF THESE CARTOONS--
ANIME.
EAT SOME PIZZA--
PROBABLY S#!%^Y RED BARON PIZZA.
AND ENJOY EACH OTHER'S COMPANY.
I HATE YOU ALL.
ZOOOOM
BUT IN A LOVING WAY?

A BRIEF HISTORY OF KELLY'S OBSESSION WITH ANIME

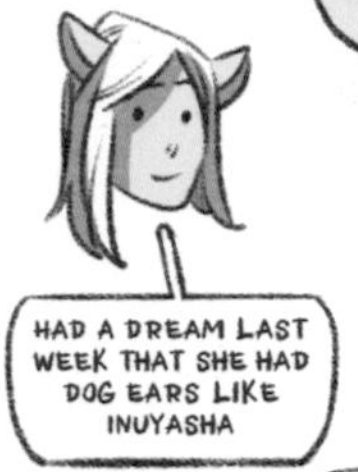
HAD A DREAM LAST WEEK THAT SHE HAD DOG EARS LIKE INUYASHA

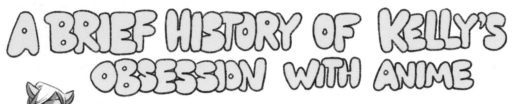

KELLY FIRST DISCOVERED ANIME FROM HER COUSIN HAROLD, WHO WAS IN AN ANIME VHS TAPE TRADE-BY-MAIL GROUP. HER INITIAL EXPOSURE TOOK SHAPE IN THE FORM OF HIGHLY DEGRADED COPIES OF *BATTLE OF THE PLANETS/GATCHAMAN*. SHE DIDN'T INITIALLY CONNECT WITH THE MATERIAL.

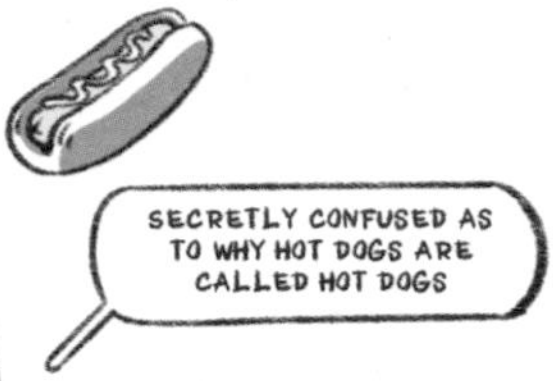
SECRETLY CONFUSED AS TO WHY HOT DOGS ARE CALLED HOT DOGS

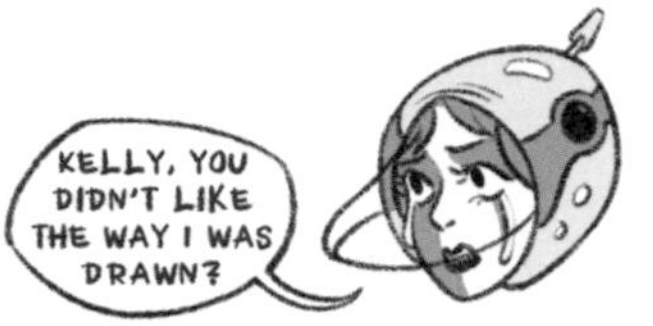
KELLY, YOU DIDN'T LIKE THE WAY I WAS DRAWN?

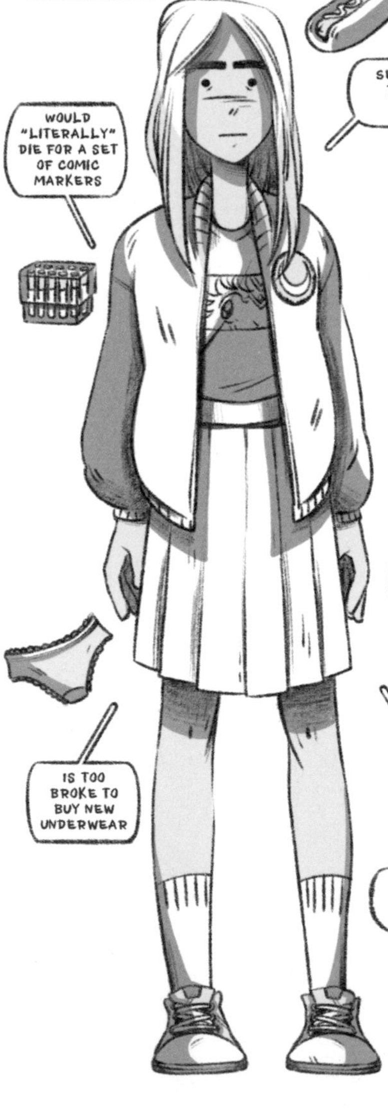
WOULD "LITERALLY" DIE FOR A SET OF COMIC MARKERS
IS TOO BROKE TO BUY NEW UNDERWEAR

A FEW YEARS LATER SHE RAN ACROSS *METROPOLIS*. (NO, NOT THE GERMAN EXPRESSIONIST MOVIE, THE ANIME BY RINTARO AND KATSUHIRO OTOMO.) TO SAY IT SPARKED AN OBSESSION WOULD BE A GRAVE UNDERSTATEMENT.

SINCE THEN, SHE'S BEEN FEVERISHLY WATCHING AND COLLECTING ANIME. (NO, SHE DOESN'T LIKE MANGA THAT MUCH. IT'S TOO MUCH MONEY FOR HOW QUICKLY SHE READS THEM.)

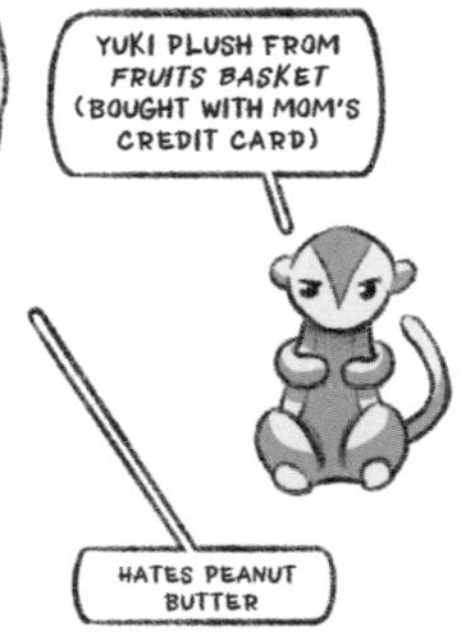
YUKI PLUSH FROM *FRUITS BASKET* (BOUGHT WITH MOM'S CREDIT CARD)
HATES PEANUT BUTTER

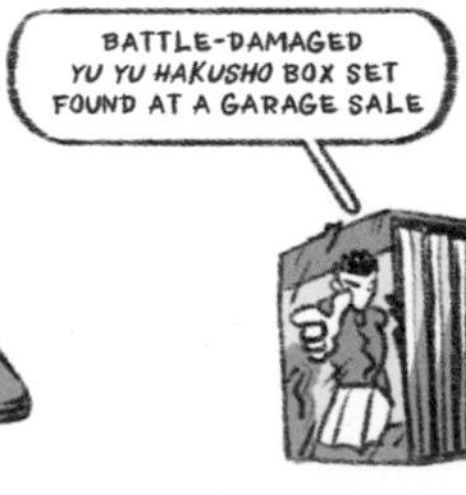
BATTLE-DAMAGED *YU YU HAKUSHO* BOX SET FOUND AT A GARAGE SALE

CURRENTLY, SHE'S OBSESSED WITH *DRAGON BALL* AND HAYAO MIYAZAKI MOVIES.

SHE THINKS THE BURNED DVDs SHE'S JUST BOUGHT ARE *MY NEIGHBOR TOTORO* AND *PRINCESS MONONOKE*.

WHAT SHE DOESN'T KNOW IS THAT THEY'RE ACTUALLY...

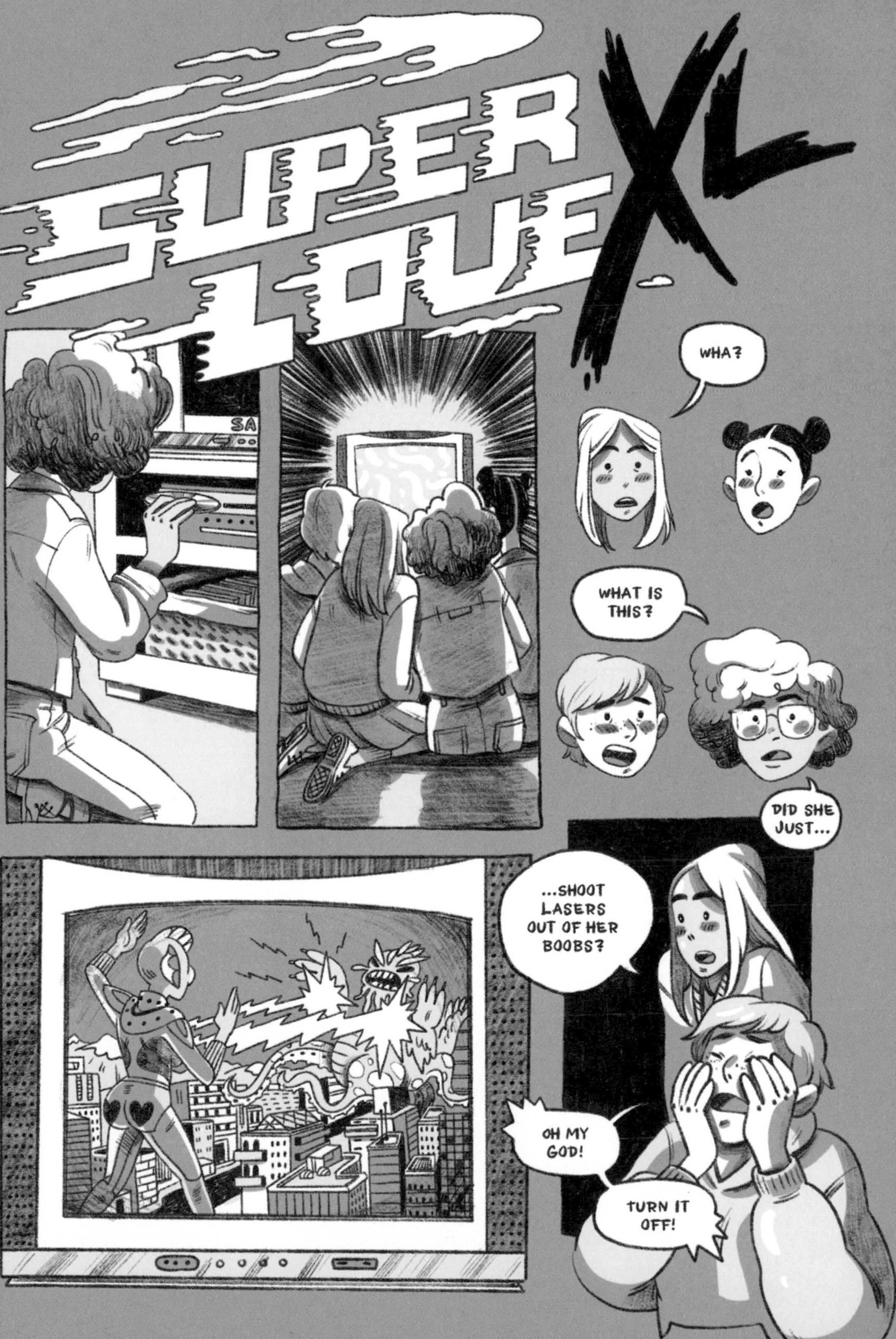
SUPER LOVE XL
SA
WHA?
WHAT IS THIS?
DID SHE JUST...
...SHOOT LASERS OUT OF HER BOOBS?
OH MY GOD!
TURN IT OFF!

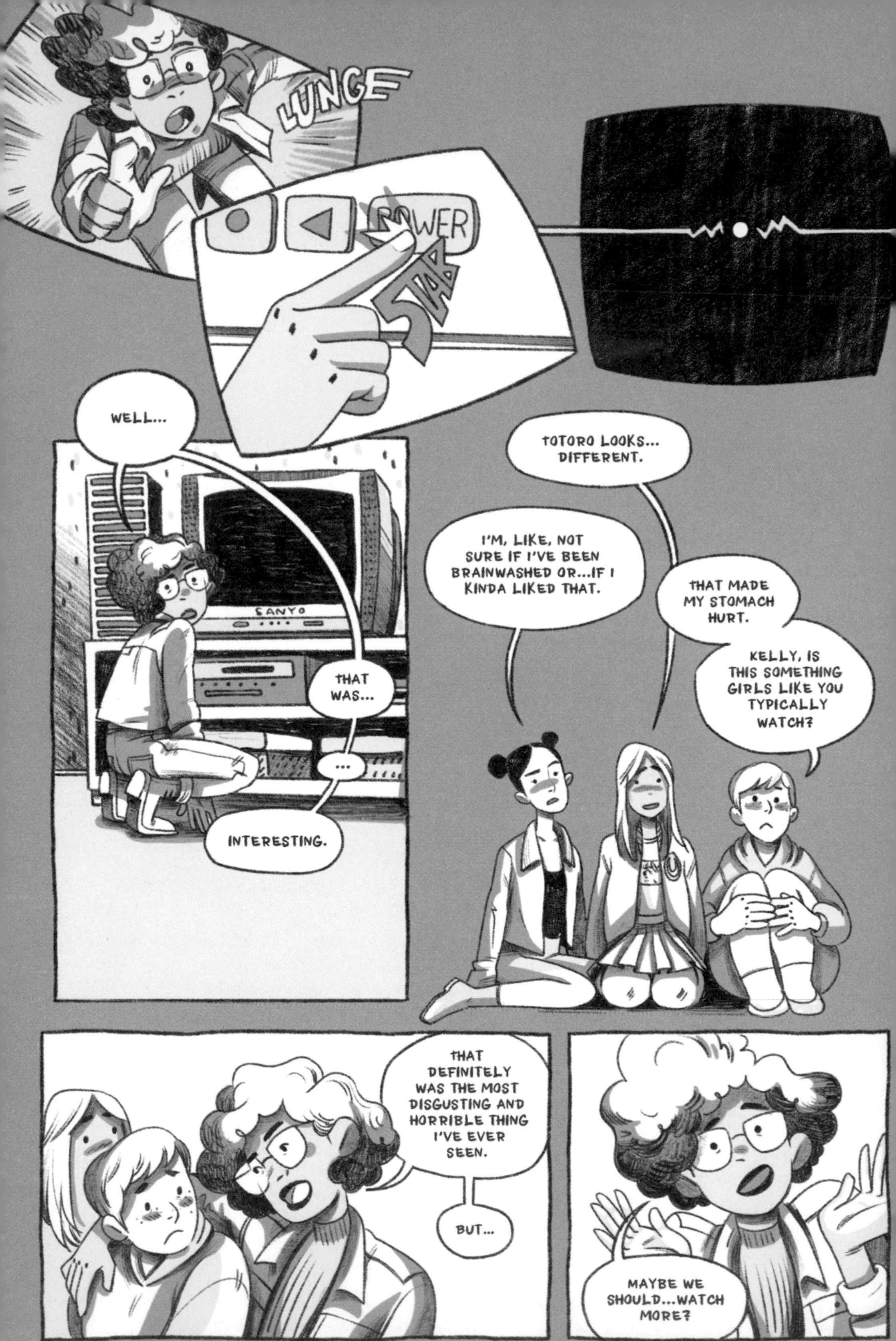
LUNGE
POWER
STAB
WELL...
THAT WAS...
...
INTERESTING.
TOTORO LOOKS... DIFFERENT.
I'M, LIKE, NOT SURE IF I'VE BEEN BRAINWASHED OR...IF I KINDA LIKED THAT.
THAT MADE MY STOMACH HURT.
KELLY, IS THIS SOMETHING GIRLS LIKE YOU TYPICALLY WATCH?
THAT DEFINITELY WAS THE MOST DISGUSTING AND HORRIBLE THING I'VE EVER SEEN.
BUT...
MAYBE WE SHOULD...WATCH MORE?

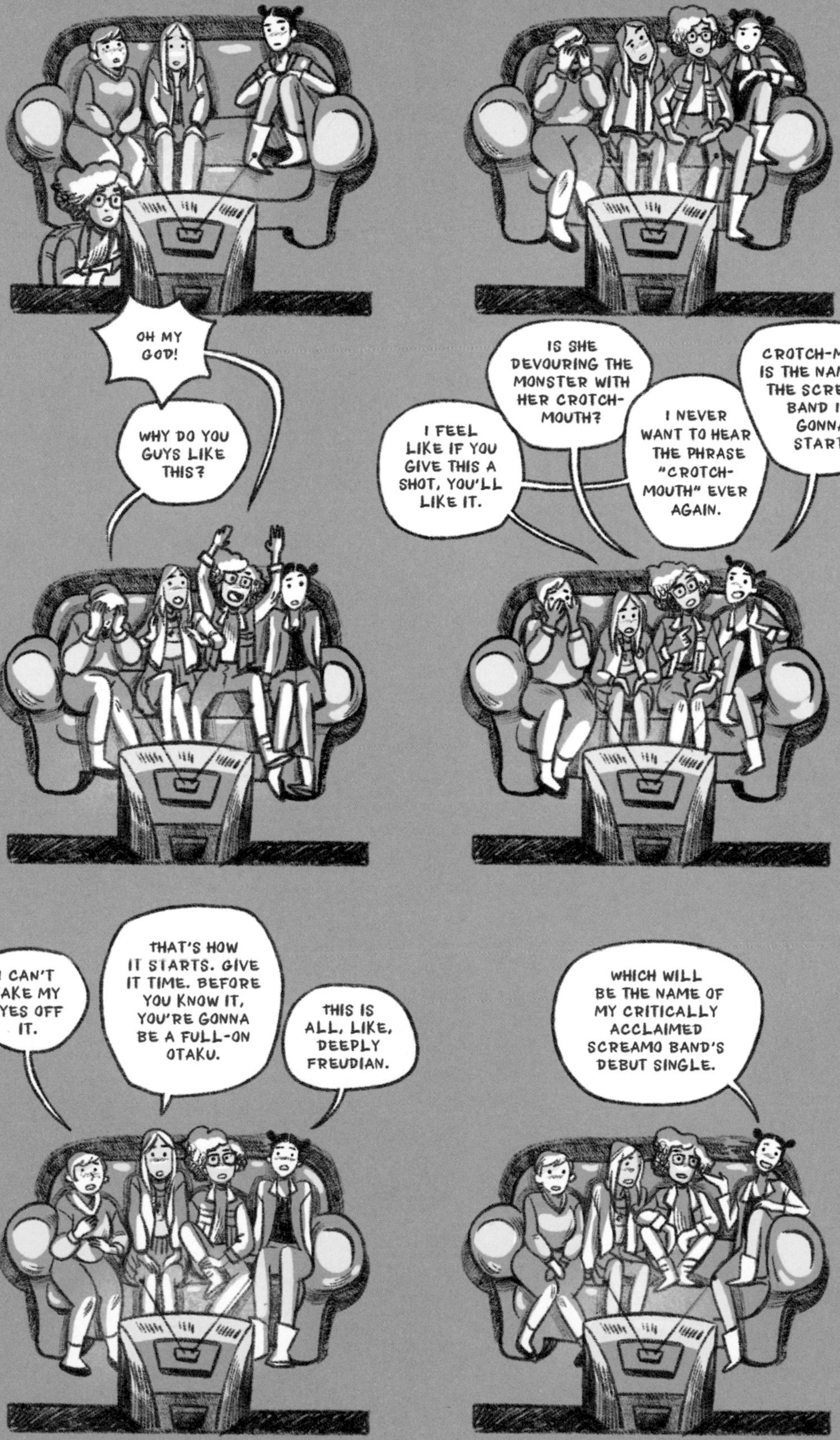
OH MY GOD!
WHY DO YOU GUYS LIKE THIS?
IS SHE DEVOURING THE MONSTER WITH HER CROTCH-MOUTH?
I FEEL LIKE IF YOU GIVE THIS A SHOT, YOU'LL LIKE IT.
I NEVER WANT TO HEAR THE PHRASE "CROTCH-MOUTH" EVER AGAIN.
CROTCH-MOUTH IS THE NAME OF THE SCREAMO BAND I'M GONNA START.
I CAN'T TAKE MY EYES OFF IT.
THAT'S HOW IT STARTS. GIVE IT TIME. BEFORE YOU KNOW IT, YOU'RE GONNA BE A FULL-ON OTAKU.
THIS IS ALL, LIKE, DEEPLY FREUDIAN.
WHICH WILL BE THE NAME OF MY CRITICALLY ACCLAIMED SCREAMO BAND'S DEBUT SINGLE.

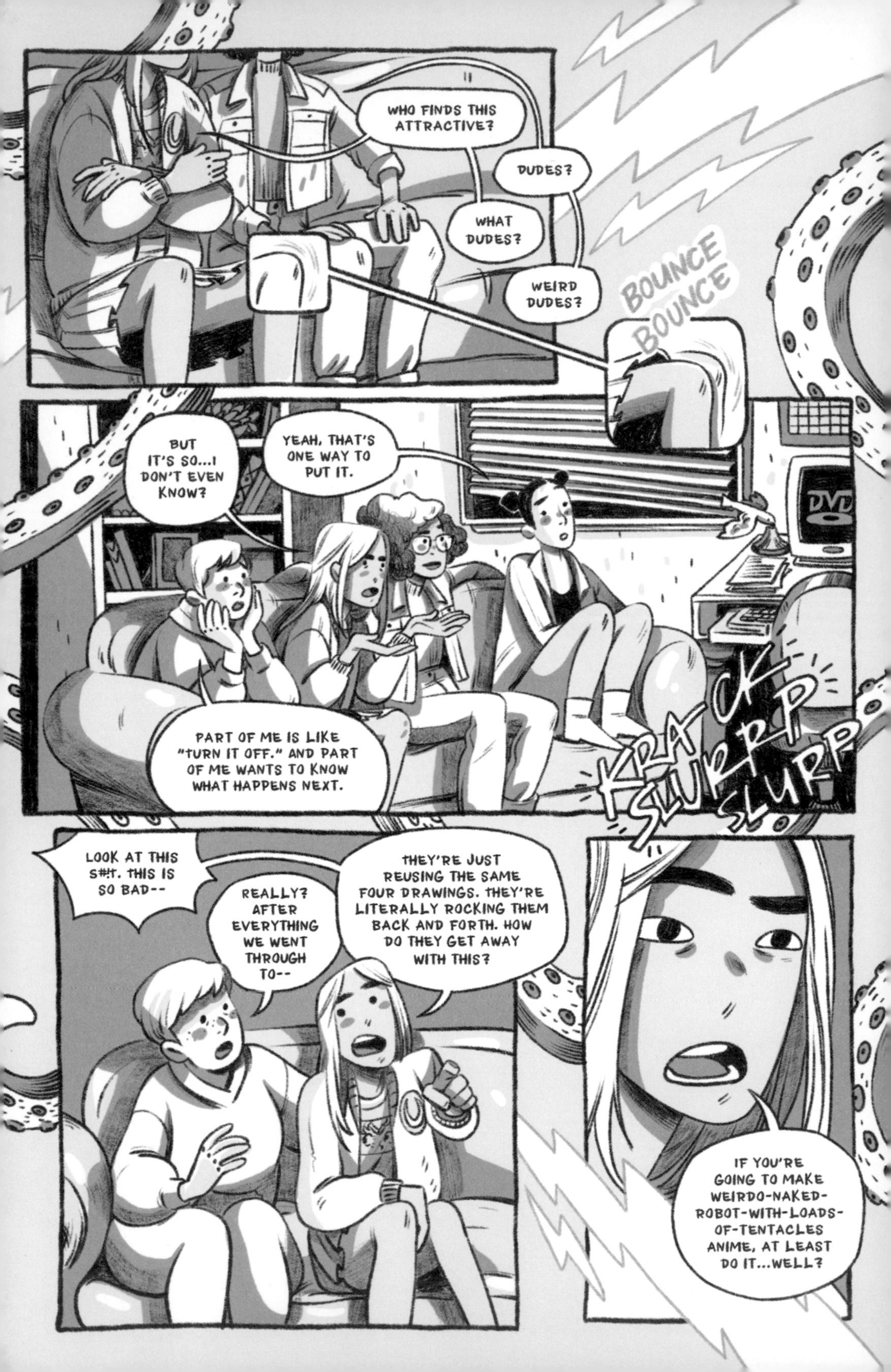
WHO FINDS THIS ATTRACTIVE?
DUDES?
WHAT DUDES?
WEIRD DUDES?
BOUNCE BOUNCE
BUT IT'S SO...I DON'T EVEN KNOW?
YEAH, THAT'S ONE WAY TO PUT IT.
DVD
PART OF ME IS LIKE "TURN IT OFF." AND PART OF ME WANTS TO KNOW WHAT HAPPENS NEXT.
KRACK
SLURP SLURP
LOOK AT THIS S#!T. THIS IS SO BAD--
REALLY? AFTER EVERYTHING WE WENT THROUGH TO--
THEY'RE JUST REUSING THE SAME FOUR DRAWINGS. THEY'RE LITERALLY ROCKING THEM BACK AND FORTH. HOW DO THEY GET AWAY WITH THIS?
IF YOU'RE GOING TO MAKE WEIRDO-NAKED-ROBOT-WITH-LOADS-OF-TENTACLES ANIME, AT LEAST DO IT...WELL?

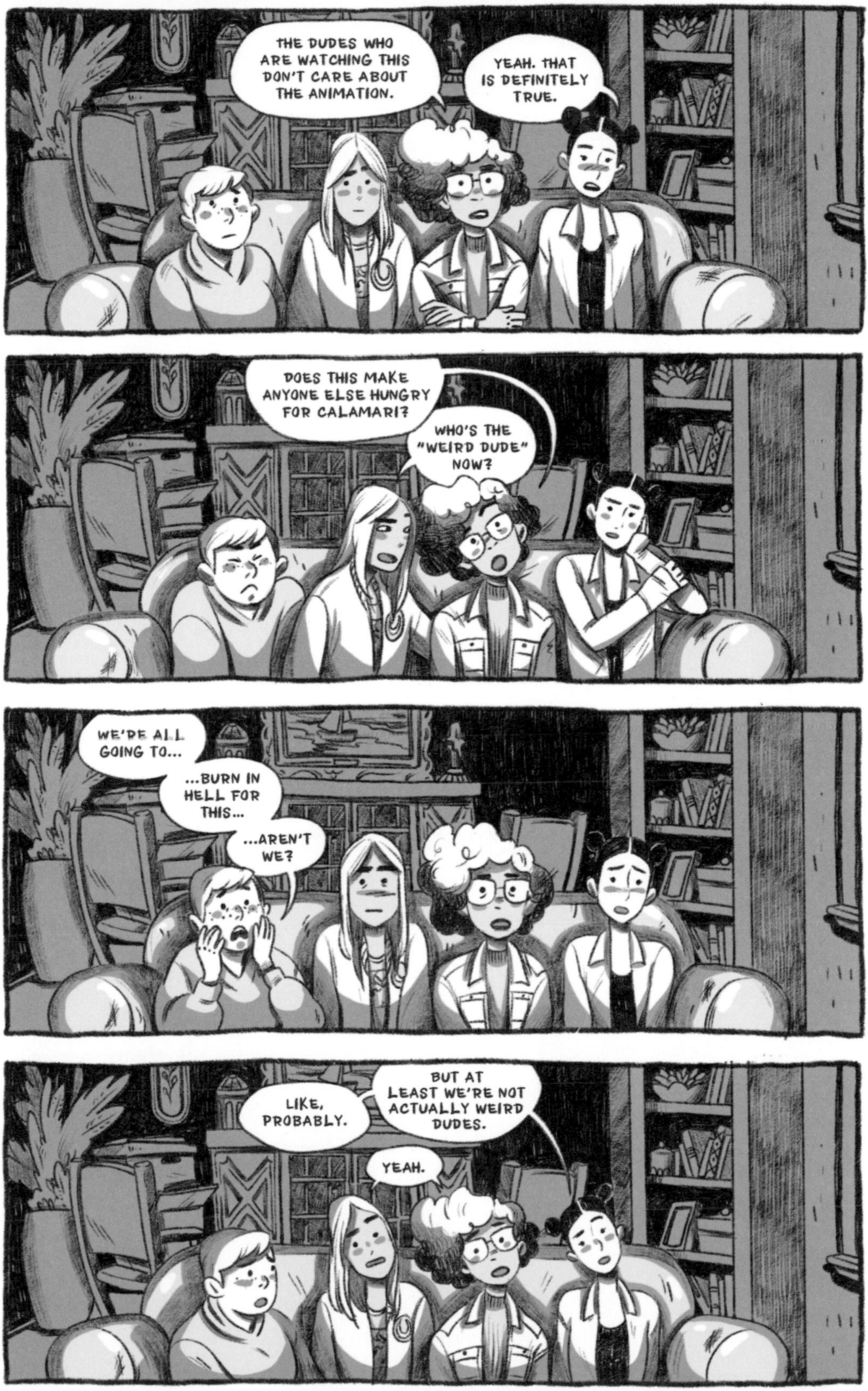
THE DUDES WHO ARE WATCHING THIS DON'T CARE ABOUT THE ANIMATION.
YEAH. THAT IS DEFINITELY TRUE.
DOES THIS MAKE ANYONE ELSE HUNGRY FOR CALAMARI?
WHO'S THE "WEIRD DUDE" NOW?
WE'RE ALL GOING TO...
...BURN IN HELL FOR THIS...
...AREN'T WE?
LIKE, PROBABLY.
BUT AT LEAST WE'RE NOT ACTUALLY WEIRD DUDES.
YEAH.

A BRIEF HISTORY OF EVERY TIME BROOKE HAS THOUGHT ABOUT BURNING IN HELL

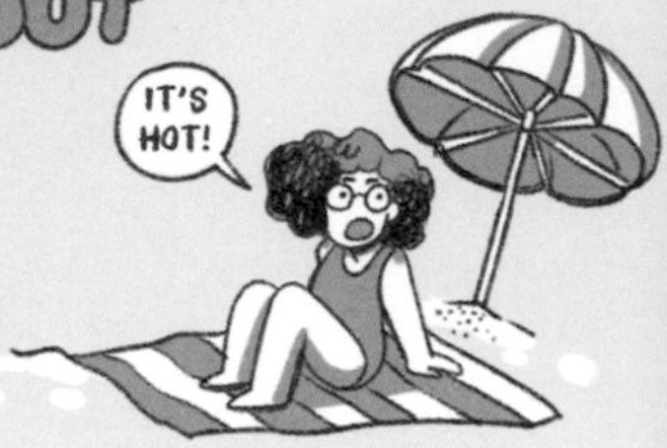

IT'S HOT!

BROOKE IMIFADON IS NOT FROM FOREST HILLS. SHE'S A PRODUCT OF SOUTHERN CALIFORNIA THROUGH AND THROUGH. THAT BEING SAID, HER UPBRINGING WASN'T THE AVERAGE CALIFORNIAN'S EXPERIENCE.

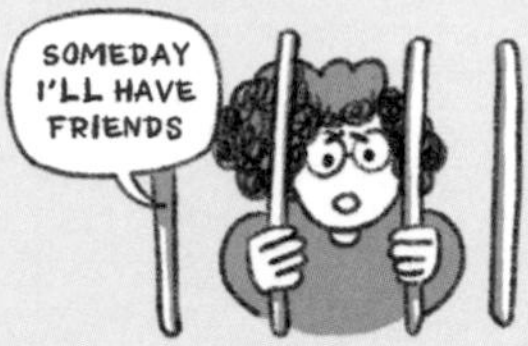

SOMEDAY I'LL HAVE FRIENDS

BROOKE'S FATHER, GABRIEL, WAS...WELL, THERE'S NO NICE WAY TO PUT THIS, SO WE'LL JUST COME OUT AND SAY IT. HE WAS IN A CULT. SO BROOKE WAS RAISED UNDER A VERY STRICT CHRISTIAN DOCTRINE. WHEN SHE TURNED FOURTEEN, SHE WAS TAKEN FROM HER FATHER'S CUSTODY AND GIVEN TO HER MOTHER...WHO *ALSO* HAS A VERY STRICT PERSONALITY.

BROOKE'S MOTHER, HAZEL JOHNSTON, IS AN INTELLECTUAL PROPERTY LAWYER. SHE'S A NO-NONSENSE WOMAN WHO AT TIMES SEEMS LIKE SHE ISN'T VERY HAPPY TO BE BROOKE'S MOTHER. TO SAY THEY HAVE A ROCKY RELATIONSHIP IS PUTTING IT LIGHTLY.

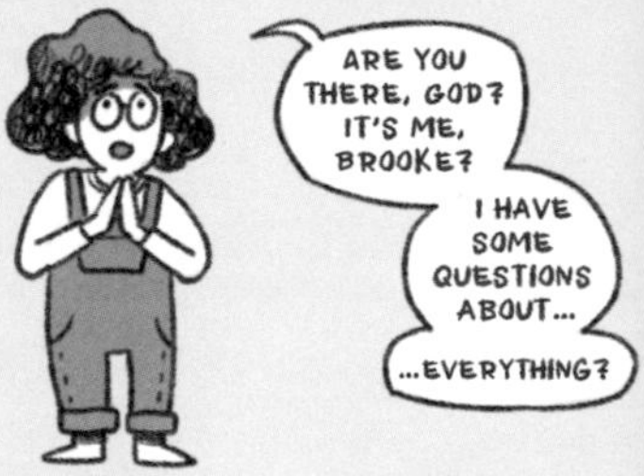

ARE YOU THERE, GOD? IT'S ME, BROOKE?
I HAVE SOME QUESTIONS ABOUT...
...EVERYTHING?

AFTER GOING THROUGH A ROUGH PATCH, BROOKE DECIDED SHE DIDN'T WANT TO GO TO PUBLIC SCHOOL. WHAT HAPPENED NEXT WAS NOT AT ALL WHAT BROOKE HAD ANTICIPATED. HER CONSERVATIVE CHRISTIAN GRANDMOTHER OFFERED TO PAY FOR HER TO ATTEND FOREST HILLS CHRISTIAN ACADEMY. A BOARDING SCHOOL FOR YOUNG PEOPLE...*OF FAITH.*

HAZEL DECIDED BROOKE WOULD ATTEND. IT WOULD PROVIDE HER WITH STRUCTURE AND BRING HER CLOSER TO GOD.

HAS ANY OF THAT HAPPENED?

WELL, SHE'S SITTING ON A COUCH WATCHING A SEVENTY-FOOT-TALL METAL WOMAN FIRE LASERS OUT OF HER BREASTS TO SAVE A CITY FROM BIZARRELY PHALLIC-LOOKING SQUID MONSTERS...

SO...

YOU BE THE JUDGE.

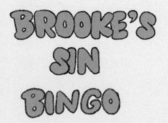

BROOKE'S SIN BINGO

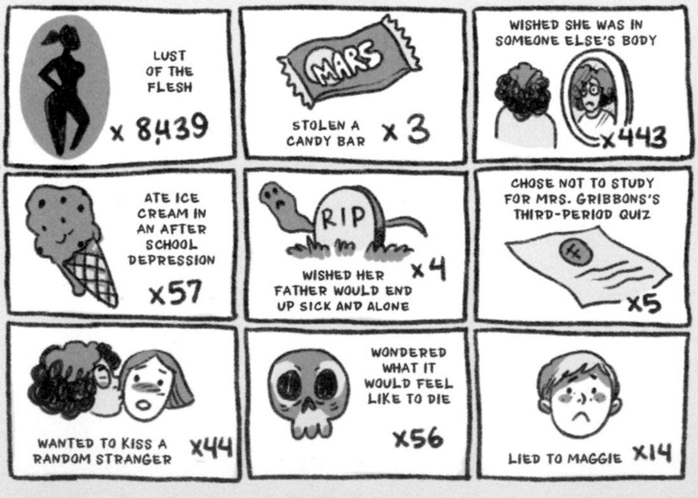

LUST OF THE FLESH
x 8,439
MARS
STOLEN A CANDY BAR
x 3
WISHED SHE WAS IN SOMEONE ELSE'S BODY
x443
ATE ICE CREAM IN AN AFTER SCHOOL DEPRESSION
x57
RIP
WISHED HER FATHER WOULD END UP SICK AND ALONE
x4
CHOSE NOT TO STUDY FOR MRS. GRIBBONS'S THIRD-PERIOD QUIZ
x5
WANTED TO KISS A RANDOM STRANGER
x44
WONDERED WHAT IT WOULD FEEL LIKE TO DIE
x56
LIED TO MAGGIE
x14

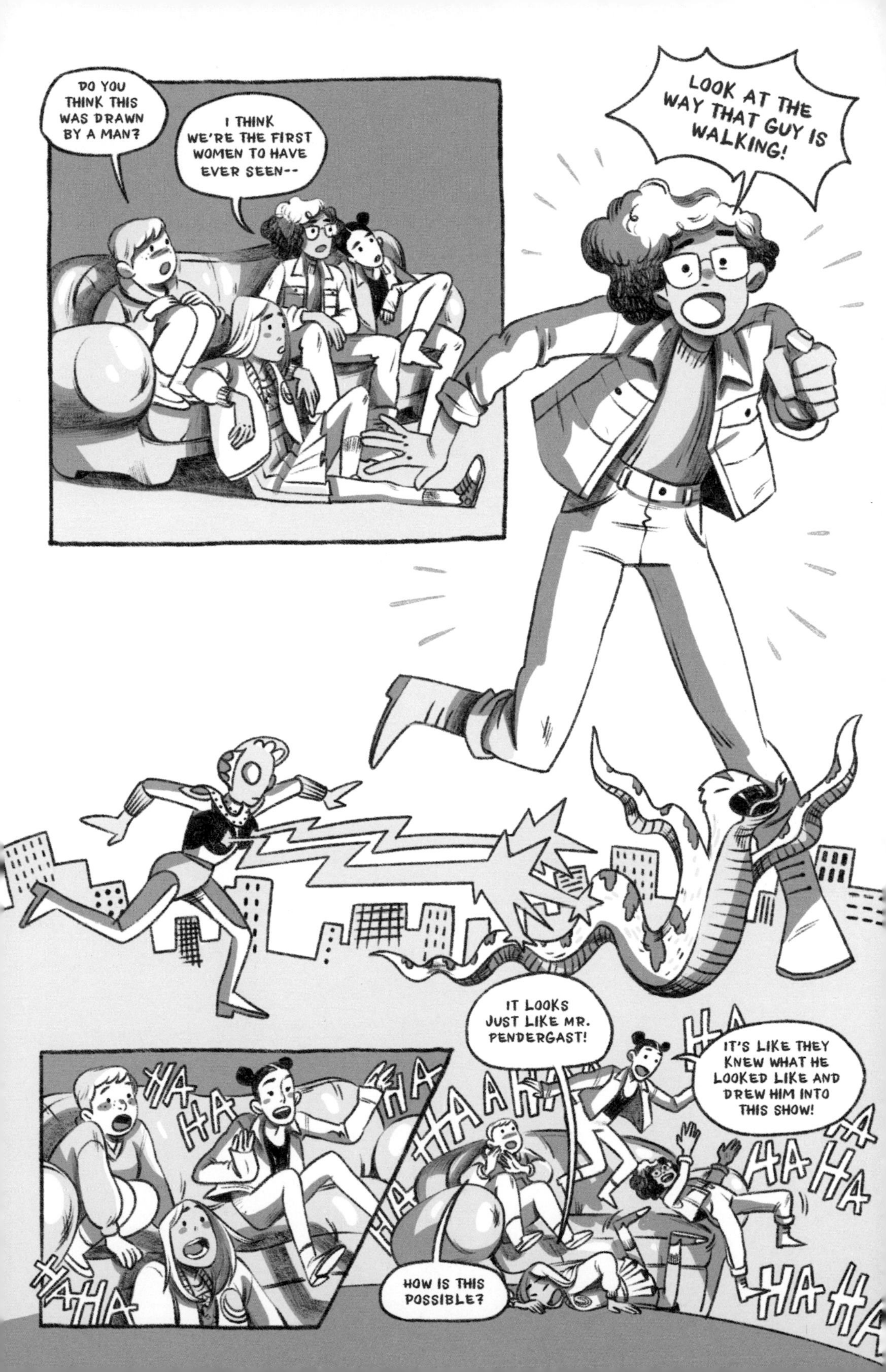
DO YOU THINK THIS WAS DRAWN BY A MAN?
I THINK WE'RE THE FIRST WOMEN TO HAVE EVER SEEN--
LOOK AT THE WAY THAT GUY IS WALKING!
HA HA HA HA
HAHA
IT LOOKS JUST LIKE MR. PENDERGAST!
IT'S LIKE THEY KNEW WHAT HE LOOKED LIKE AND DREW HIM INTO THIS SHOW!
HAHAHA
HA HA HA HA
HOW IS THIS POSSIBLE?
HAHA

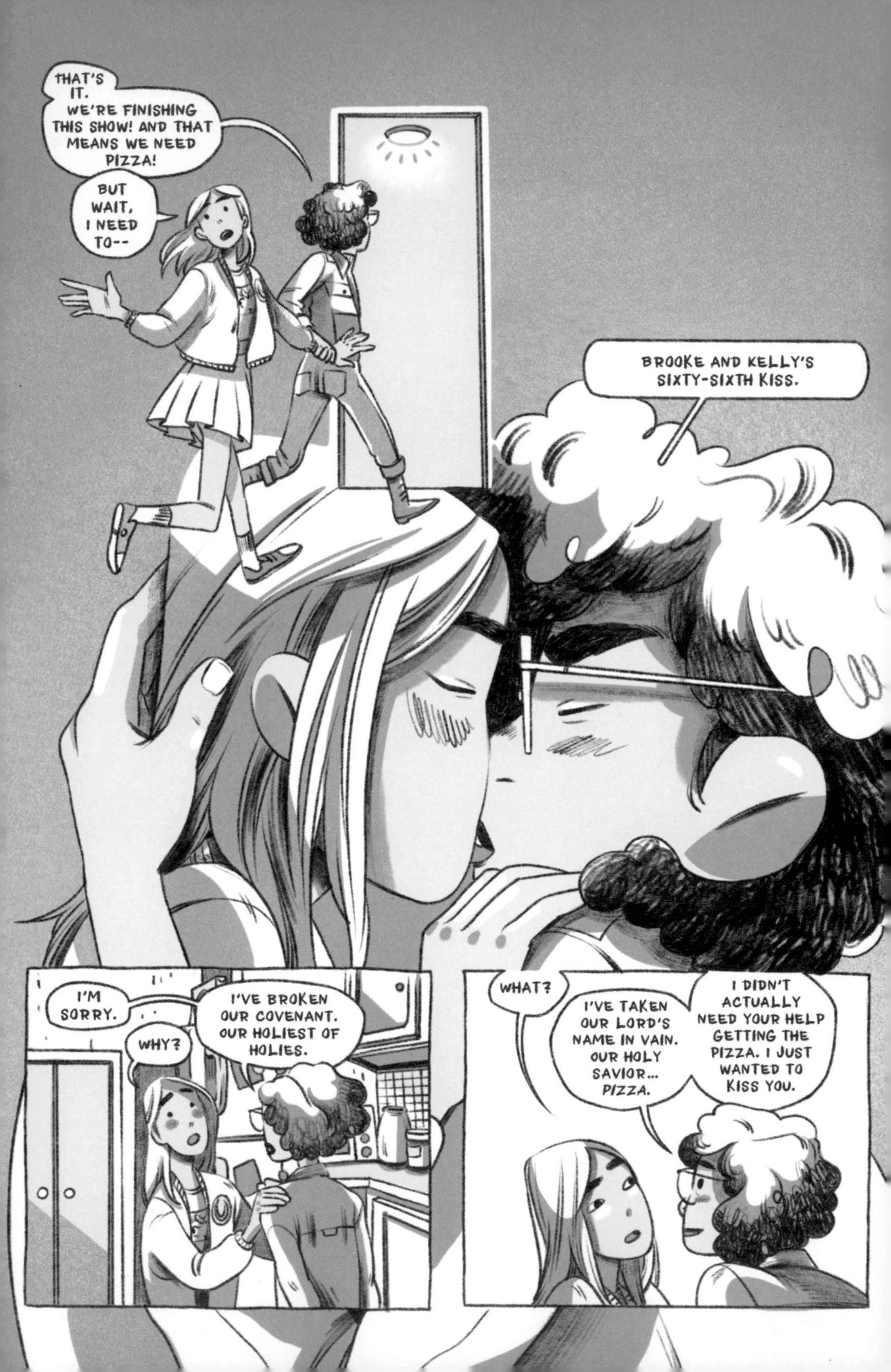
THAT'S IT. WE'RE FINISHING THIS SHOW! AND THAT MEANS WE NEED PIZZA!
BUT WAIT, I NEED TO--
BROOKE AND KELLY'S SIXTY-SIXTH KISS.
I'M SORRY.
WHY?
I'VE BROKEN OUR COVENANT. OUR HOLIEST OF HOLIES.
WHAT?
I'VE TAKEN OUR LORD'S NAME IN VAIN. OUR HOLY SAVIOR... PIZZA.
I DIDN'T ACTUALLY NEED YOUR HELP GETTING THE PIZZA. I JUST WANTED TO KISS YOU.

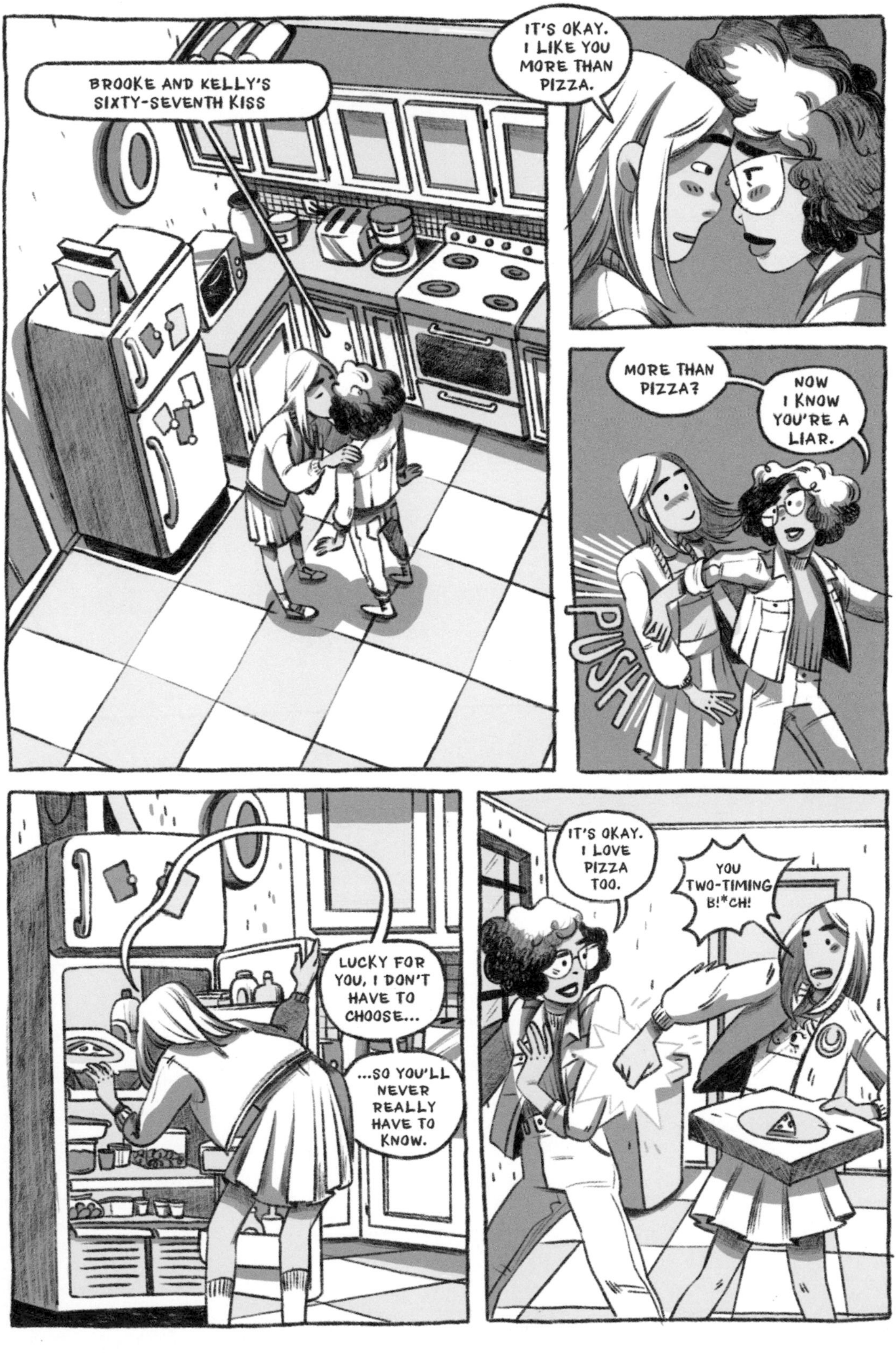
BROOKE AND KELLY'S SIXTY-SEVENTH KISS
IT'S OKAY. I LIKE YOU MORE THAN PIZZA.
MORE THAN PIZZA?
NOW I KNOW YOU'RE A LIAR.
PUSH
LUCKY FOR YOU, I DON'T HAVE TO CHOOSE...
...SO YOU'LL NEVER REALLY HAVE TO KNOW.
IT'S OKAY. I LOVE PIZZA TOO.
YOU TWO-TIMING B!*CH!

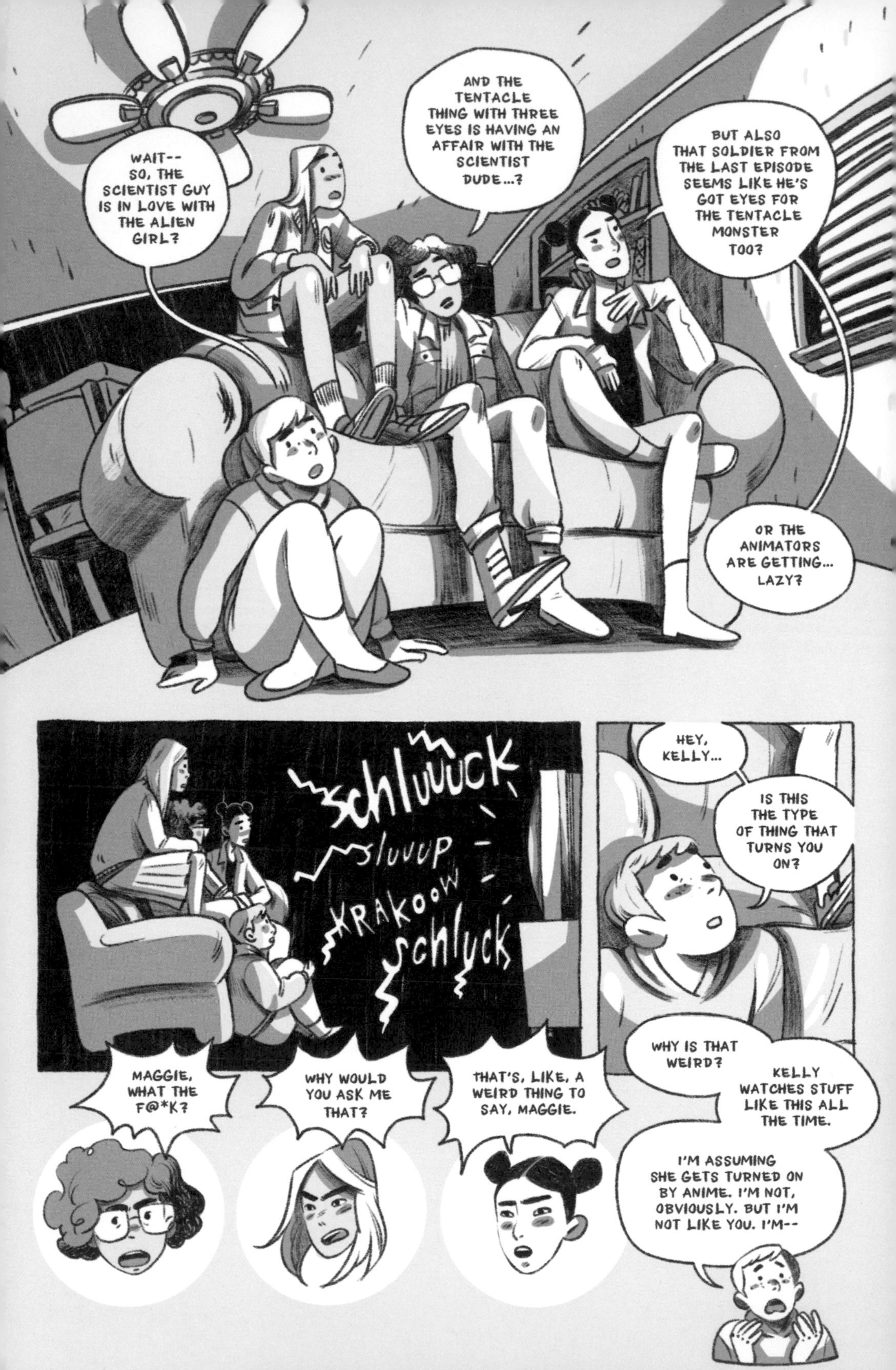
WAIT-- SO, THE SCIENTIST GUY IS IN LOVE WITH THE ALIEN GIRL?
AND THE TENTACLE THING WITH THREE EYES IS HAVING AN AFFAIR WITH THE SCIENTIST DUDE...?
BUT ALSO THAT SOLDIER FROM THE LAST EPISODE SEEMS LIKE HE'S GOT EYES FOR THE TENTACLE MONSTER TOO?
OR THE ANIMATORS ARE GETTING... LAZY?
SCHLUUUCK
SLUUUP
KRAKOOW
SCHLUCK
HEY, KELLY...
IS THIS THE TYPE OF THING THAT TURNS YOU ON?
MAGGIE, WHAT THE F@*K?
WHY WOULD YOU ASK ME THAT?
THAT'S, LIKE, A WEIRD THING TO SAY, MAGGIE.
WHY IS THAT WEIRD?
KELLY WATCHES STUFF LIKE THIS ALL THE TIME.
I'M ASSUMING SHE GETS TURNED ON BY ANIME. I'M NOT, OBVIOUSLY. BUT I'M NOT LIKE YOU. I'M--

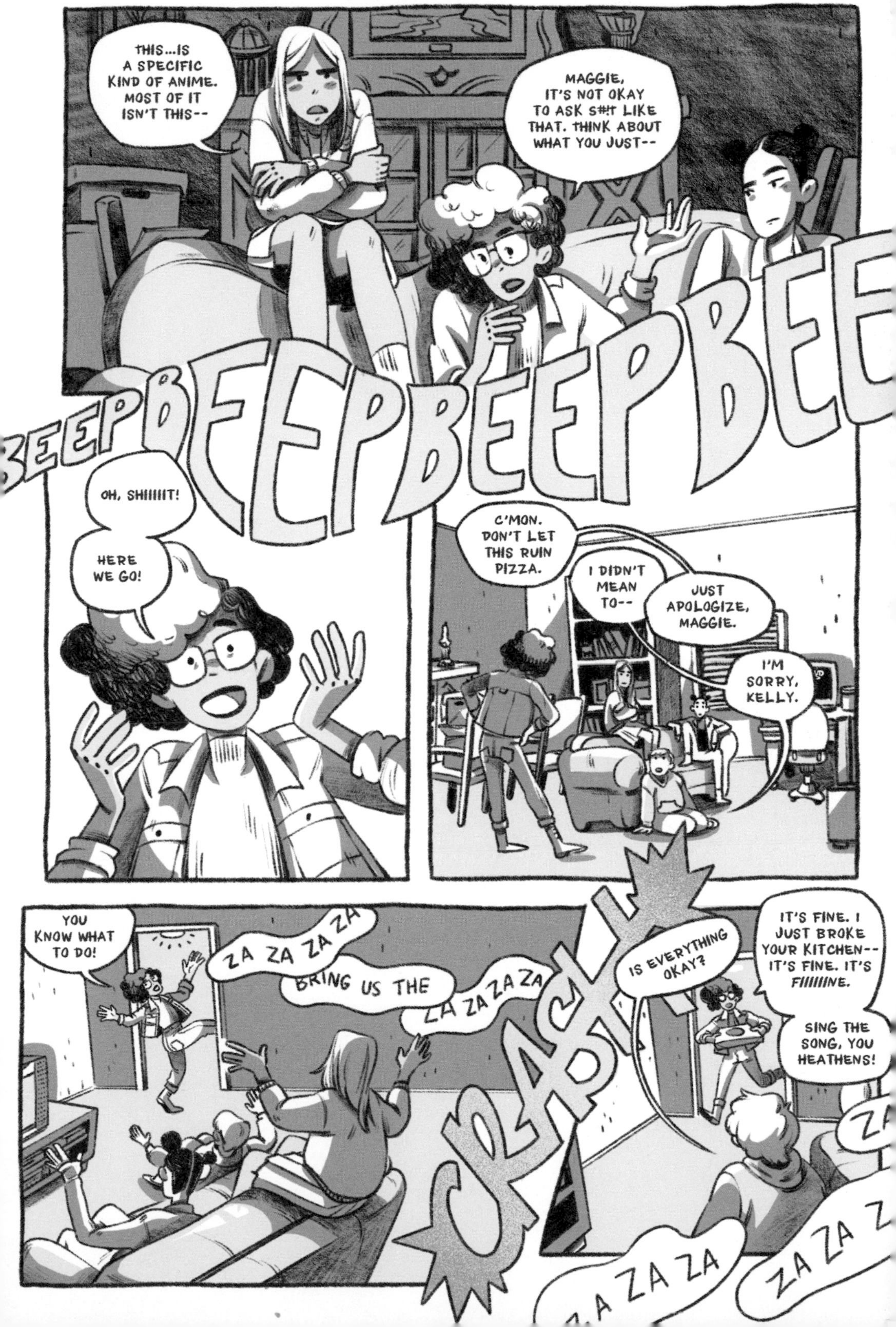
THIS...IS A SPECIFIC KIND OF ANIME. MOST OF IT ISN'T THIS--
MAGGIE, IT'S NOT OKAY TO ASK S#!t LIKE THAT. THINK ABOUT WHAT YOU JUST--
BEEPBEEPBEEPBEEPBEE
OH, SHIIIIIT!
HERE WE GO!
C'MON. DON'T LET THIS RUIN PIZZA.
I DIDN'T MEAN TO--
JUST APOLOGIZE, MAGGIE.
I'M SORRY, KELLY.
YOU KNOW WHAT TO DO!
ZA ZA ZA ZA
BRING US THE
ZA ZA ZA ZA
IS EVERYTHING OKAY?
CRASH
IT'S FINE. I JUST BROKE YOUR KITCHEN-- IT'S FINE. IT'S FIIIIINE.
SING THE SONG, YOU HEATHENS!
ZA ZA ZA
ZA ZA ZA

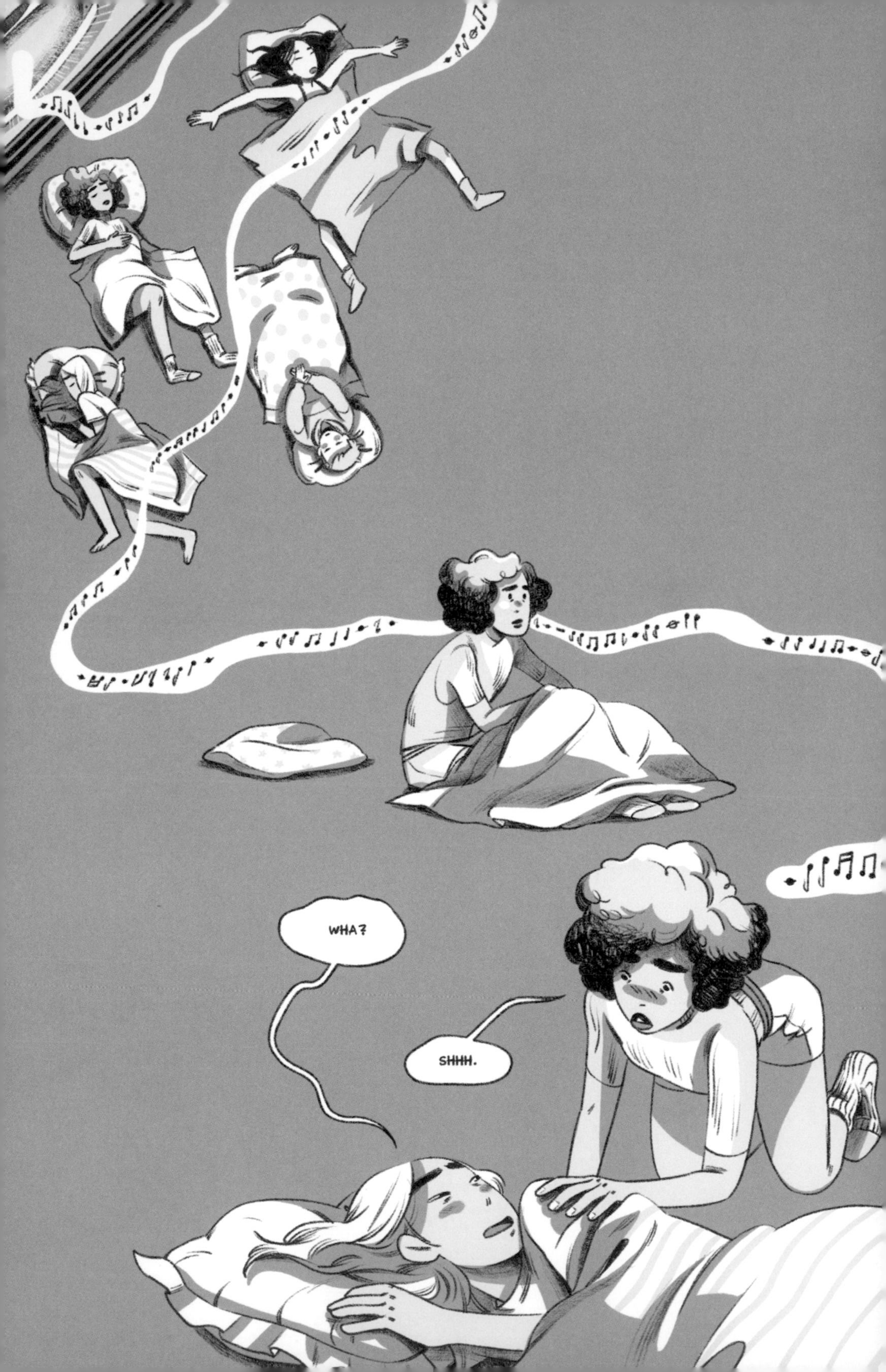
WHA?
SHHH.

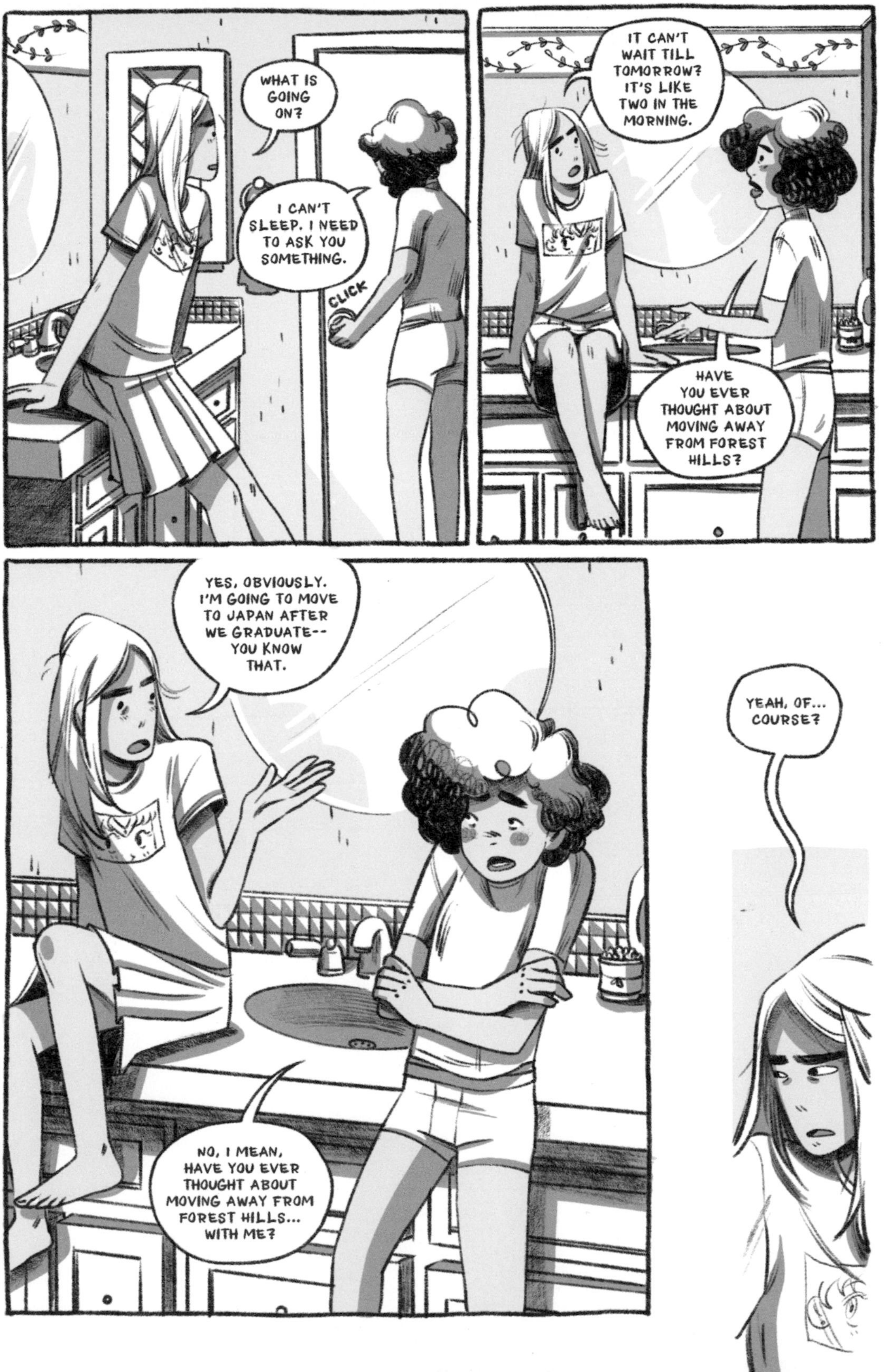
WHAT IS GOING ON?
I CAN'T SLEEP. I NEED TO ASK YOU SOMETHING.
CLICK
IT CAN'T WAIT TILL TOMORROW? IT'S LIKE TWO IN THE MORNING.
HAVE YOU EVER THOUGHT ABOUT MOVING AWAY FROM FOREST HILLS?
YES, OBVIOUSLY. I'M GOING TO MOVE TO JAPAN AFTER WE GRADUATE-- YOU KNOW THAT.
NO, I MEAN, HAVE YOU EVER THOUGHT ABOUT MOVING AWAY FROM FOREST HILLS... WITH ME?
YEAH, OF... COURSE?

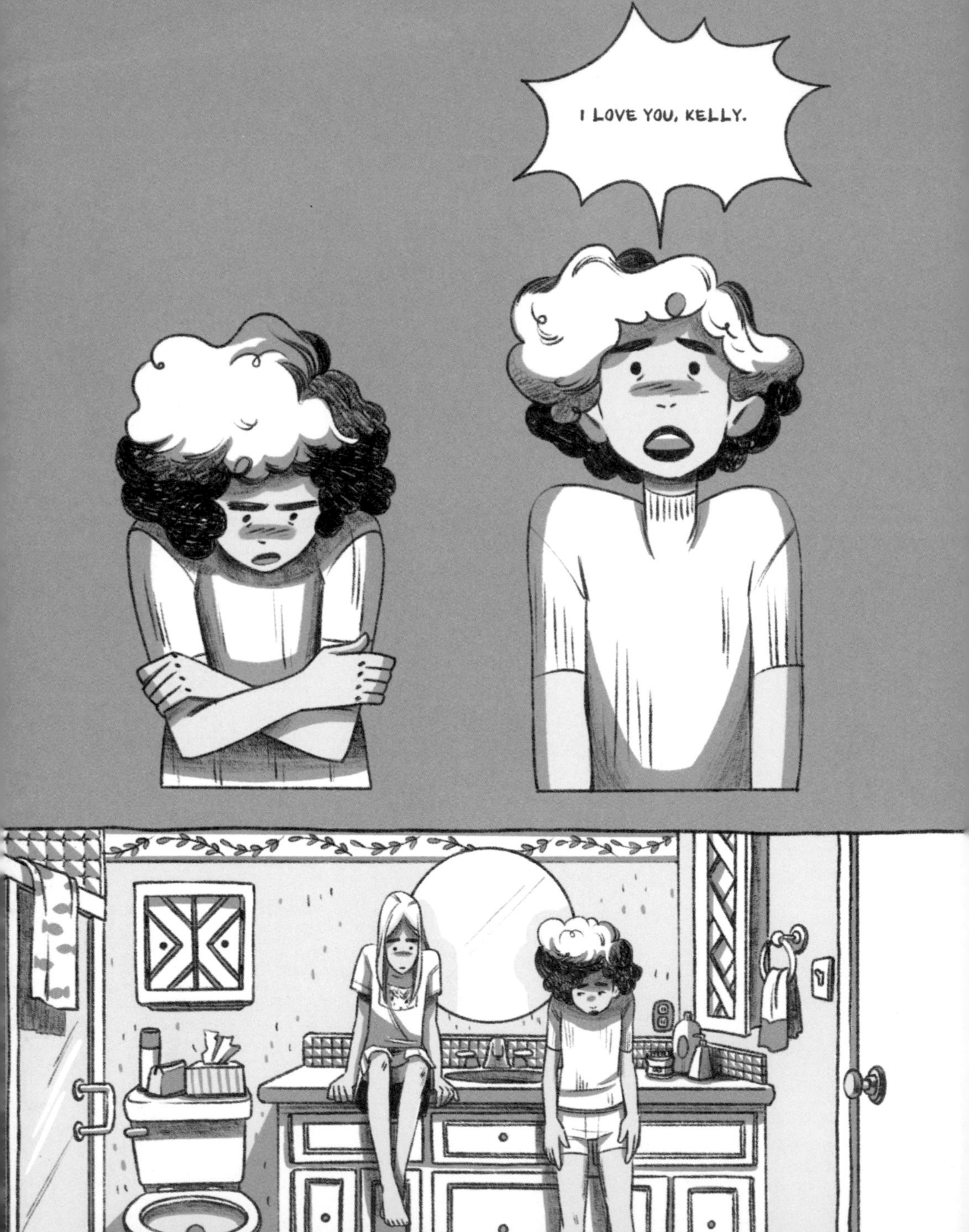
I LOVE YOU, KELLY.

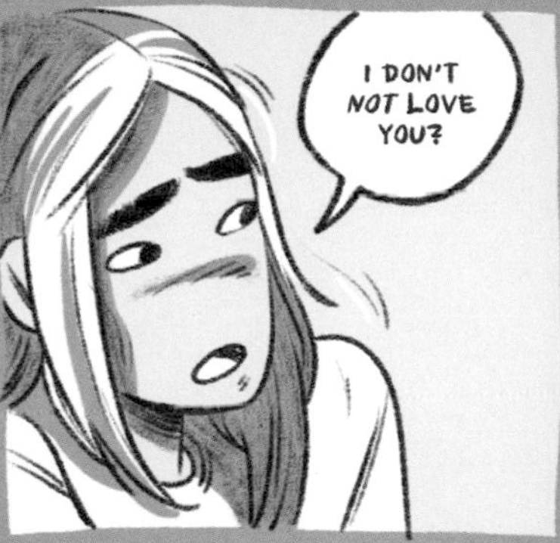
I DON'T *NOT* LOVE YOU?

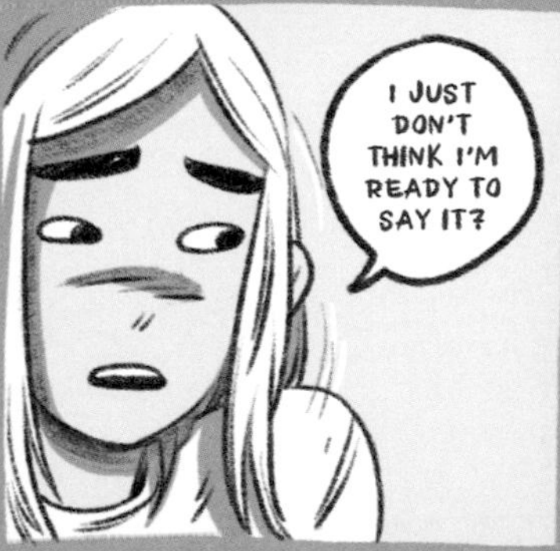
I JUST DON'T THINK I'M READY TO SAY IT?

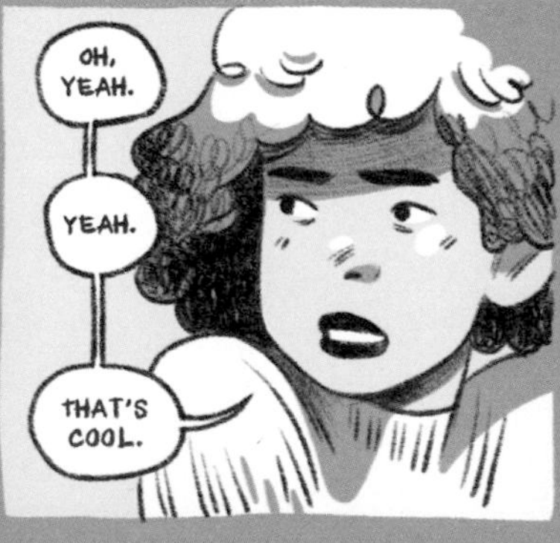
OH, YEAH.
YEAH.
THAT'S COOL.

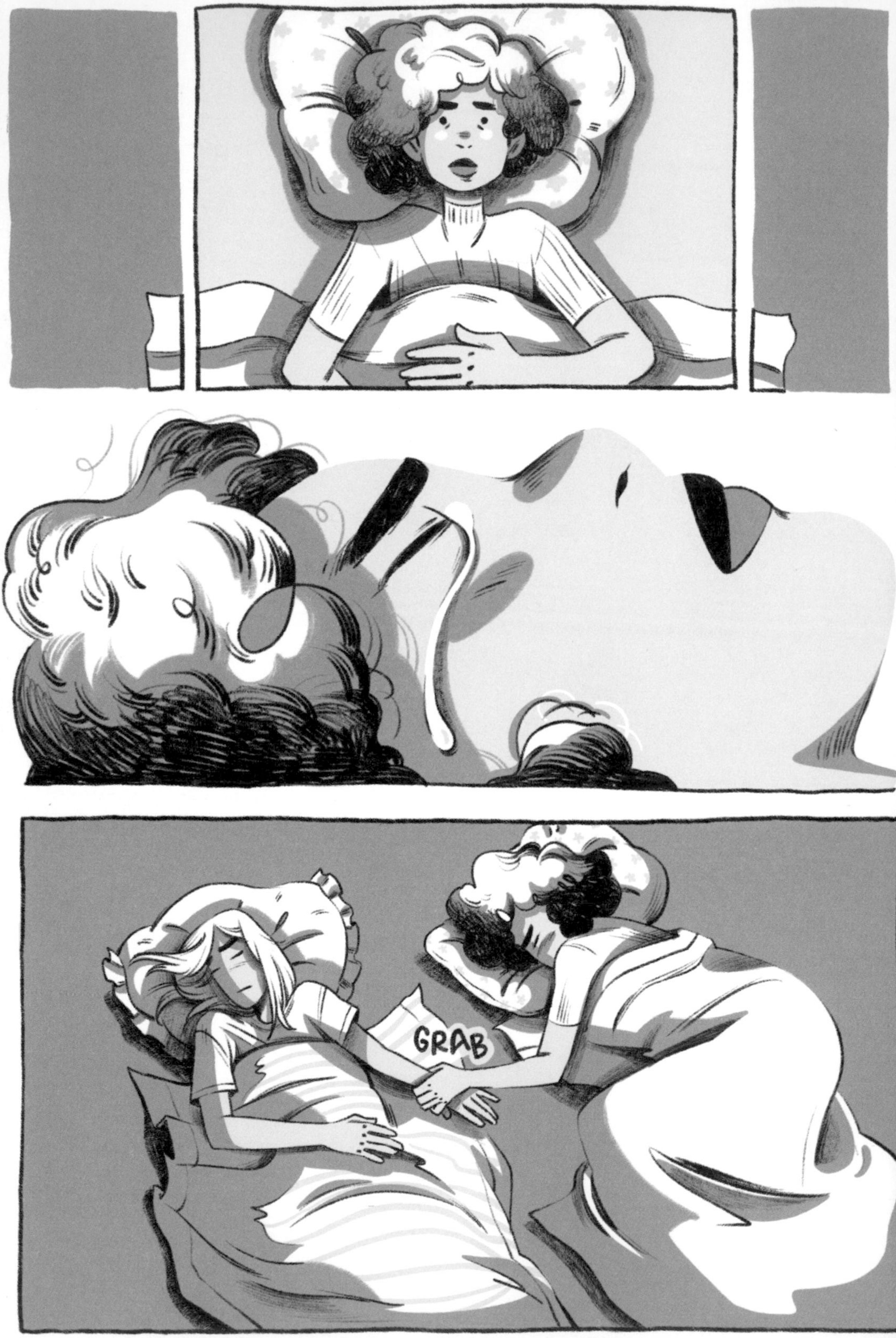
GRAB

A BRIEF HISTORY OF BROOKE'S LONELINESS

BROOKE HAS KNOWN SHE WAS A LESBIAN SINCE SHE WAS 7 AND 4/7 YEARS OLD. SHE WAS SITTING IN CHURCH WITH HER FATHER WHEN THE REALIZATION CAME. SHE COULDN'T TAKE HER EYES OFF OF MRS. CHATTERJEE. SHE WAS THE MOST BEAUTIFUL WOMAN BROOKE HAD EVER SEEN.

BROOKE DIDN'T EVEN HAVE A CONCEPT OF SEXUAL IDENTITY YET, BUT SHE KNEW DEEP IN HER BONES THAT SHE WANTED TO BE AS CLOSE TO MRS. CHATTERJEE AS SHE COULD. SHE ALSO FELT VERY ALONE IN THIS MOMENT, BECAUSE SHE UNDERSTOOD THAT MRS. CHATTERJEE WOULD NEVER FEEL THE SAME WAY ABOUT HER.

ON HER NINTH BIRTHDAY, BROOKE WANTED A PAIR OF OVERALLS. HER FATHER SAID NO, BECAUSE PANTS WERE MEANT FOR MEN. SHE DIDN'T KNOW HOW TO PARSE THIS AT THE TIME, BUT SHE KNEW THAT HER FATHER'S WORDS HAD A MEANING SHE WAS NOT FULLY GRASPING.

THEY WOULDN'T SPEAK OF THIS AGAIN UNTIL BROOK WAS THIRTEEN, WHEN HER DAD FOUND A FOLDER UNDER HER BED FILLED WITH MAGAZINE CUTOUTS OF SWIMSUIT MODELS. SHE TRIED TO EXPLAIN, BUT BEFORE SHE COULD FINISH...HE BURST INTO TEARS AND LEFT THE ROOM.

THIS WAS THE ONLY TIME SHE'D EVER SEE HIM CRY.

BROOKE TRIED TO CONVINCE HERSELF SHE WASN'T GAY AFTER THAT. SHE PERFORMATIVELY TALKED ABOUT BOYS IN FRONT OF HER FATHER. THIS WORKED ABOUT AS WELL AS YOU'D EXPECT.

AND THEN, BEFORE SHE KNEW IT...SHE WAS LIVING WITH HER MOM...AND LIFE WAS VERY DIFFERENT, IN BOTH GOOD AND BAD WAYS.

WHEN BROOKE WAS FIRST KISSED BY HENRY VICENTE OUTSIDE THE REC CENTER FOUR SUMMERS AGO, IT WAS EMPTY AND BIZARRELY WET. LIKE HE JUST LICKED HER FACE. SHE DID NOT FEEL ANY HUMAN CONNECTION IN THAT MOMENT.

TO SAY THAT A PERVADING FEELING OF ISOLATION HAS BEEN THE ONE CONSTANT IN BROOKE'S LIFE WOULD BE PRETTY ACCURATE.

AND THIS MOMENT. RIGHT NOW. DESPITE DATING KELLY FOR OVER FOUR MONTHS AND BEING FRIENDS WITH HER FOR WHO-KNOWS-HOW-LONG AND LOVING HER MORE THAN LIFE ITSELF... BROOKE FEELS AS THOUGH HER PHYSICAL PRESENCE ON EARTH MATTERS TO A GRAND TOTAL OF ZERO PEOPLE.

BUT ALSO PIZZA IS PRETTY COOL, SO, WHAT-THE-F@*K-EVER.

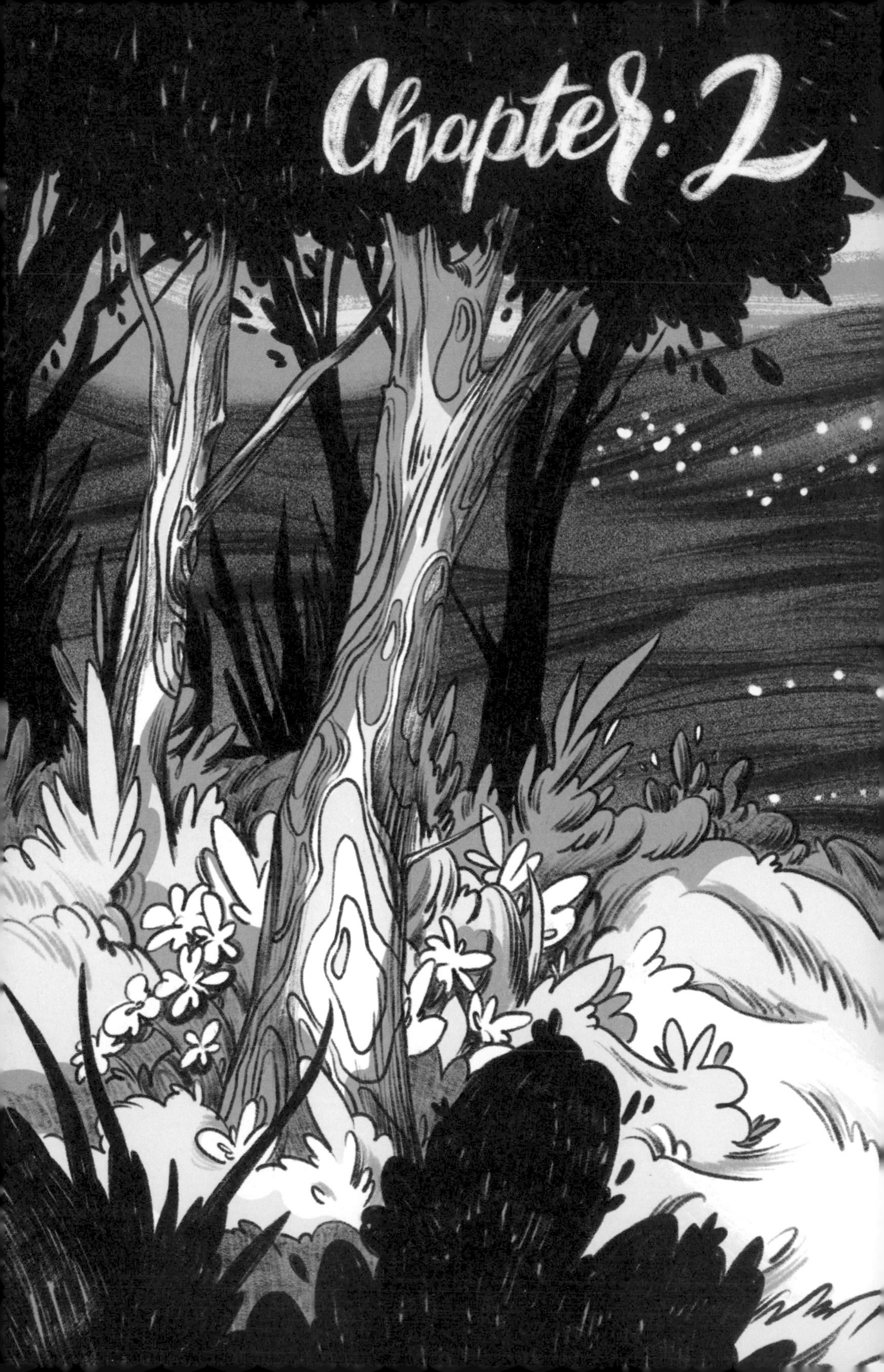
Chapter: 2

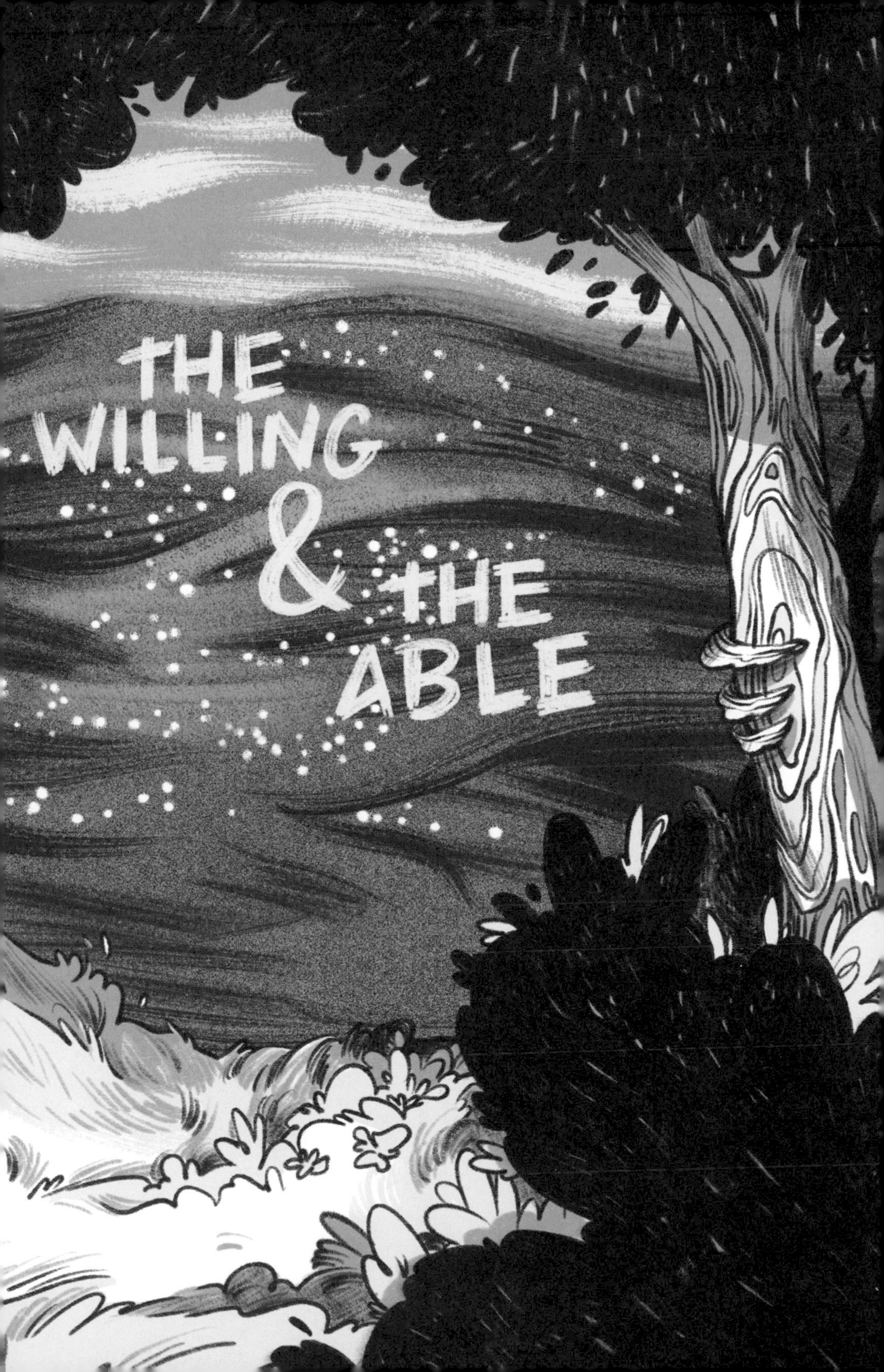
THE WILLING & THE ABLE

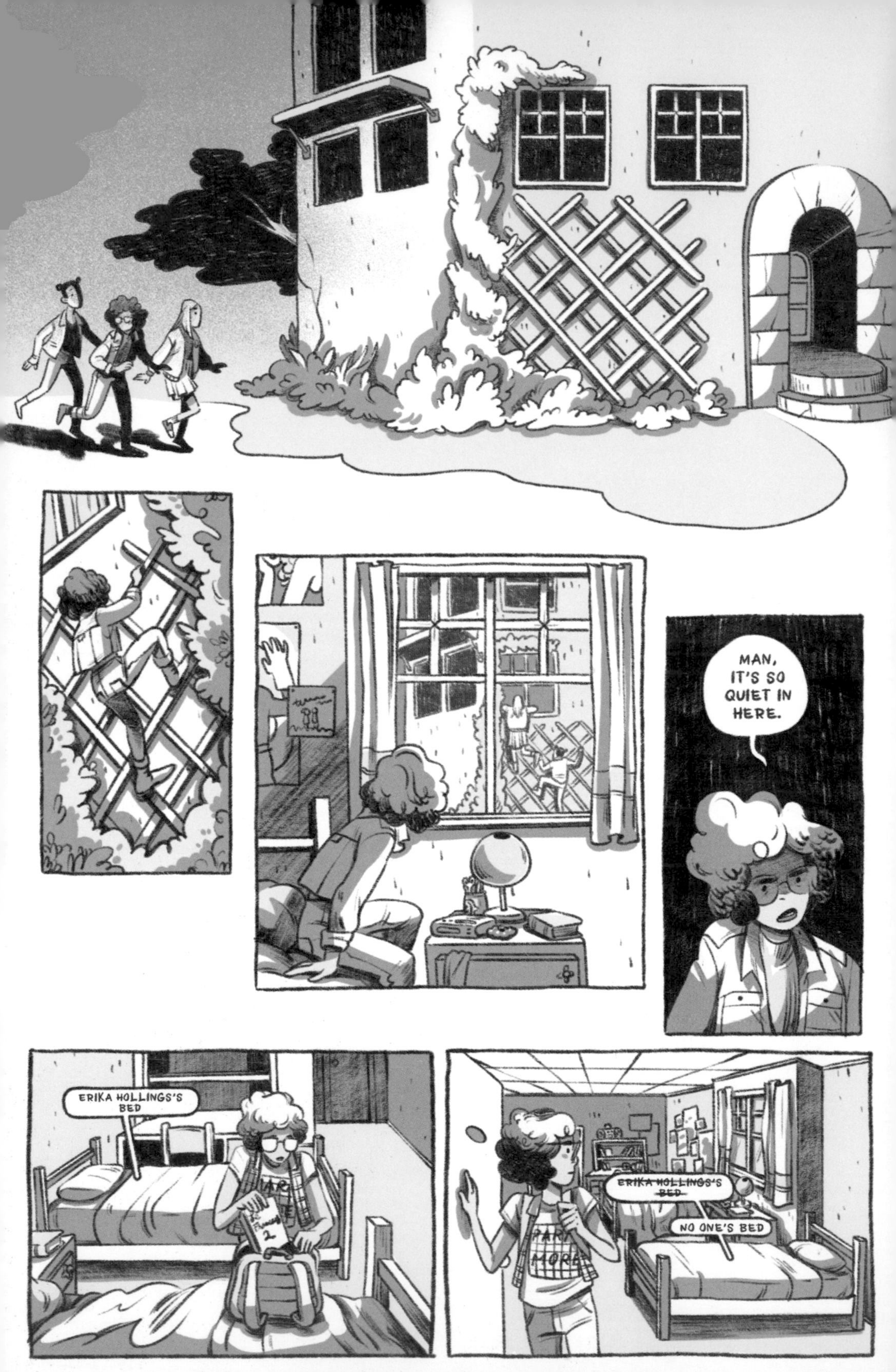
MAN, IT'S SO QUIET IN HERE.
ERIKA HOLLINGS'S BED
ERIKA HOLLINGS'S BED
NO ONE'S BED

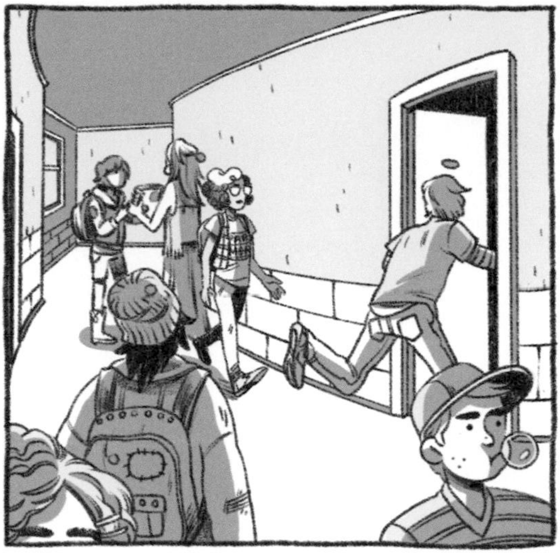

ERIKA HOLLINGS WAS BROOKE'S ROOMMATE. SHE COMMITTED SUICIDE IN THE GYM SHOWERS, STILL IN HER CLOTHES. BROOKE DOESN'T LIKE TO TALK ABOUT IT.

ERIKA WAS A QUARRELSOME PERSON WHO COULD HAVE FOUND A REASON TO PICK A FIGHT WITH ANYONE.

BROOKE LIKED THIS ABOUT HER. SHE ENJOYED THE BACK-AND-FORTH.

MOST OF THE TIME.

THE WEIRDEST PART IS HOW QUICKLY EVERYONE HAS MOVED ON. YES, IT WAS AT THE BEGINNING OF THE YEAR, BUT IT'S ALMOST LIKE IT NEVER HAPPENED.

EXCEPT THERE'S AN EMPTY BED IN BROOKE'S ROOM.

ALL THE PEOPLE WHO DIDN'T KNOW ERIKA PRETENDED THAT SHE MEANT SO MUCH TO THEM...

ALL THE TEACHERS CHECKED IN ON BROOKE, AS IF SHE HAD BEEN ERIKA'S FAMILY...

THEY WERE ROOMMATES FOR SIX WEEKS.

BROOKE STILL DOESN'T KNOW WHY ERIKA KILLED HERSELF.

ALL SHE DOES KNOW IS THAT SHE'S GLAD THE GRIEF COUNSELORS AND FORCED MOURNING ARE OVER.

TO COMPOUND THINGS, MRS. GRAHAM, THE LIVE-IN DORMS SUPERVISOR, DIED TWO MONTHS AGO.

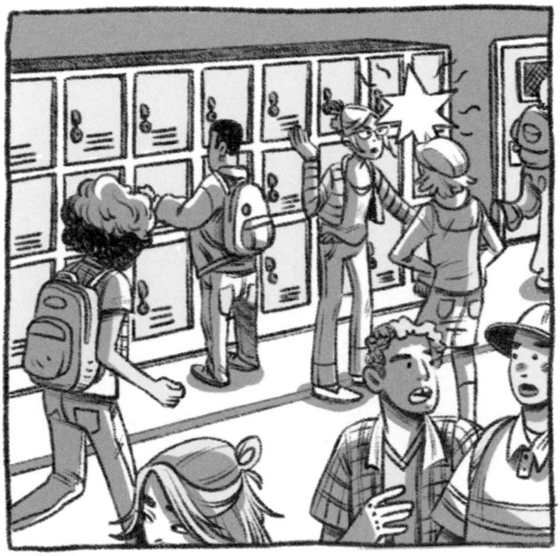

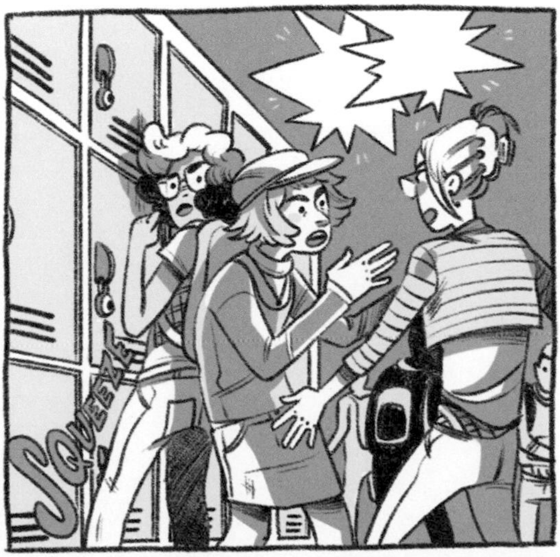
SQUEEZE

FOREST HILLS CHRISTIAN ACADEMY IS STILL SEARCHING FOR A REPLACEMENT...

IF YOU'RE A WOMAN OF FAITH WHO HAS TWO TO FIVE YEARS' EXPERIENCE WORKING WITH TEENAGERS AND WANT FREE ROOM AND BOARD ON TOP OF A TEACHER'S SALARY... APPLICATIONS ARE WELCOME.

FOREST HILLS, CA

POPULATION 9,003

FOUNDED IN 1881

A MINING TOWN UNTIL THE 1970S, FOREST HILLS WAS REBORN WHEN THE CHRISTIAN BOARDING SCHOOL WAS NEWLY ESTABLISHED.

IT'S FAIR TO SAY THAT FOREST HILLS EXISTS TO SERVICE THE SCHOOL. THE ONLY OTHER HIGH SCHOOL IN THE AREA, GEORGE EL CAMINO HIGH, IS A SEVEN-TOWN SCHOOL.

THE MOST EXCITING THING THAT HAPPENS IN FOREST HILLS IS WHEN THE ACADEMY FOOTBALL TEAM PLAYS THE EL CAMINO HIGH FOOTBALL TEAM.

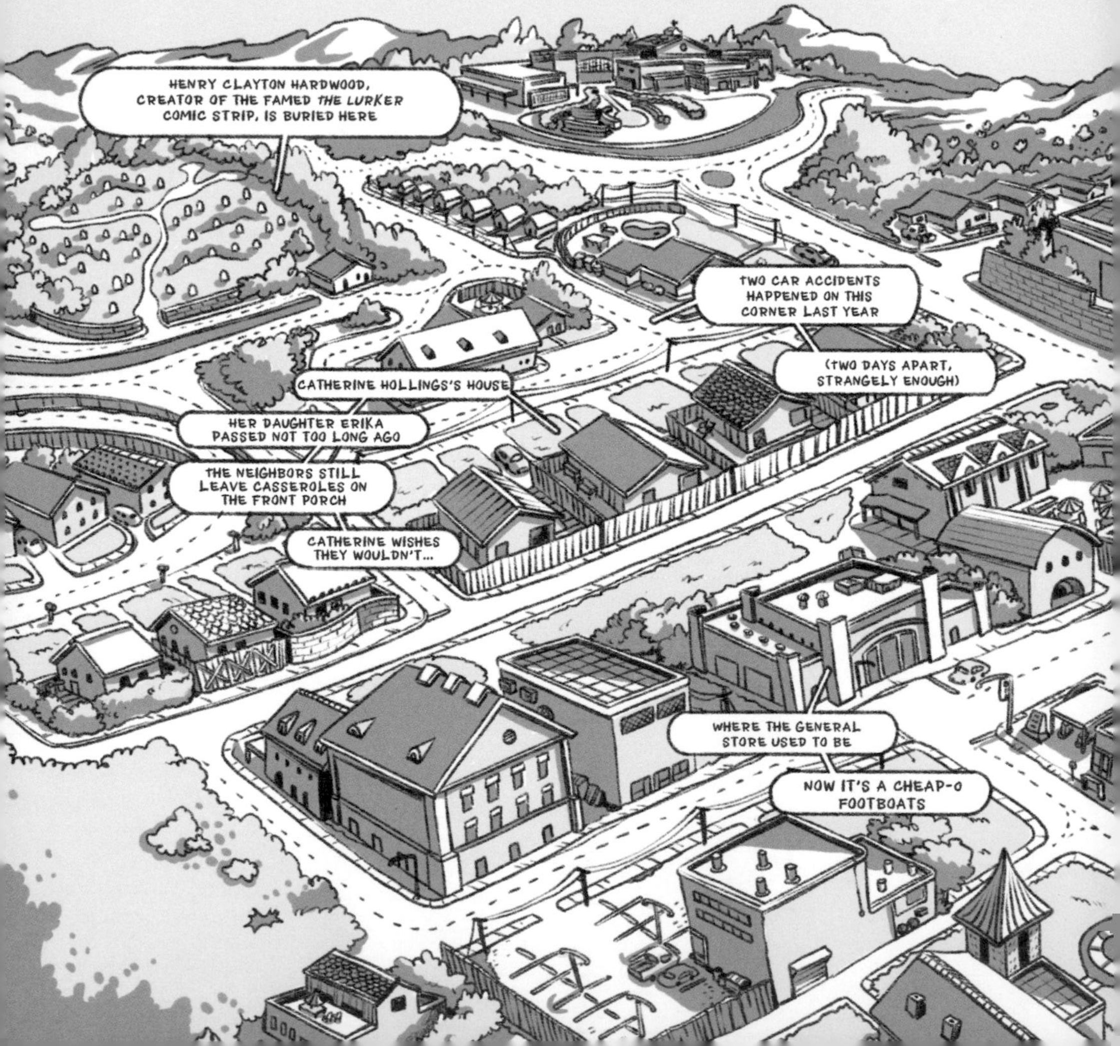
HENRY CLAYTON HARDWOOD, CREATOR OF THE FAMED *THE LURKER* COMIC STRIP, IS BURIED HERE
TWO CAR ACCIDENTS HAPPENED ON THIS CORNER LAST YEAR
(TWO DAYS APART, STRANGELY ENOUGH)
CATHERINE HOLLINGS'S HOUSE
HER DAUGHTER ERIKA PASSED NOT TOO LONG AGO
THE NEIGHBORS STILL LEAVE CASSEROLES ON THE FRONT PORCH
CATHERINE WISHES THEY WOULDN'T...
WHERE THE GENERAL STORE USED TO BE
NOW IT'S A CHEAP-O FOOTBOATS

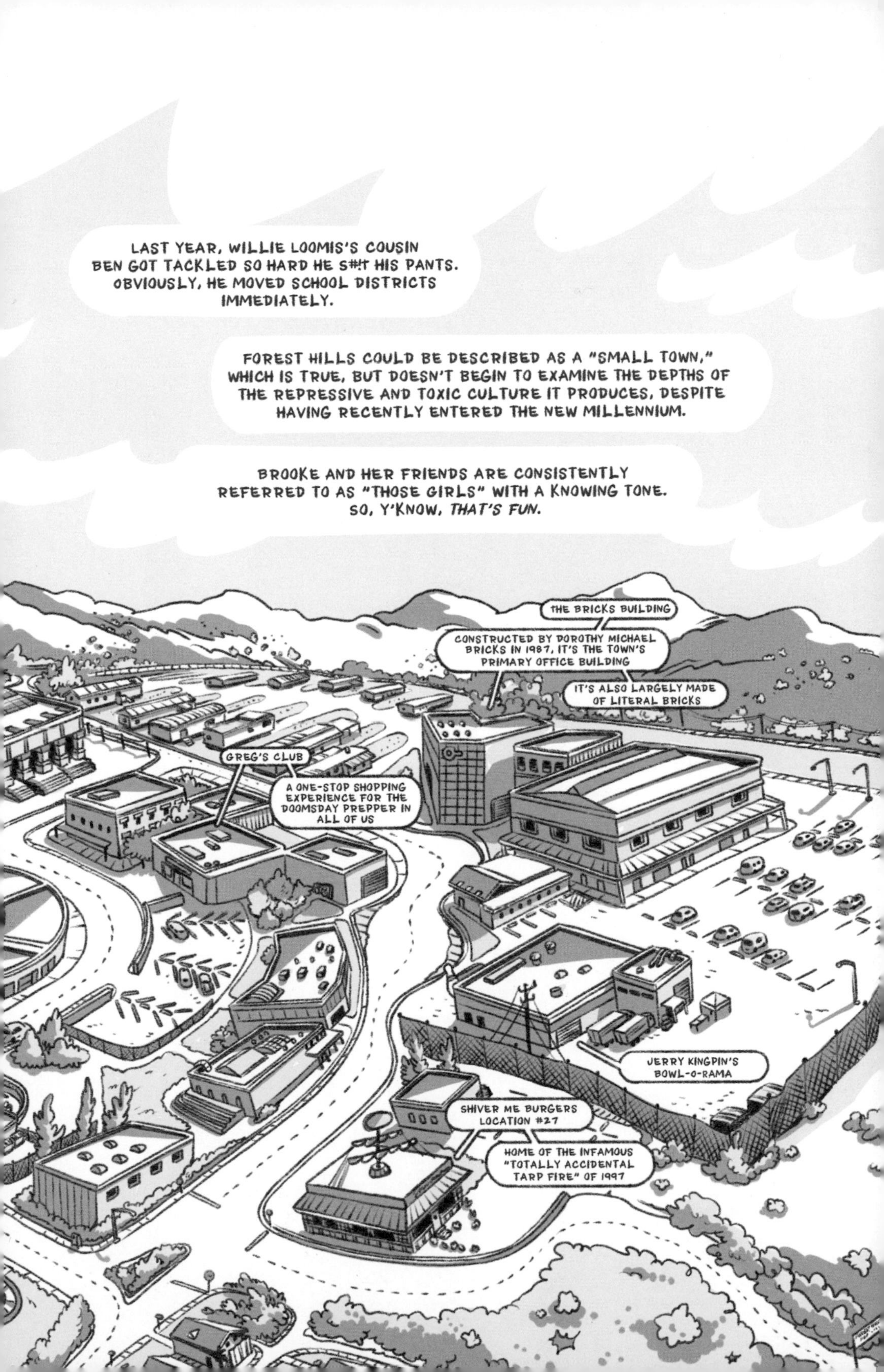
LAST YEAR, WILLIE LOOMIS'S COUSIN BEN GOT TACKLED SO HARD HE S#!T HIS PANTS. OBVIOUSLY, HE MOVED SCHOOL DISTRICTS IMMEDIATELY.
FOREST HILLS COULD BE DESCRIBED AS A "SMALL TOWN," WHICH IS TRUE, BUT DOESN'T BEGIN TO EXAMINE THE DEPTHS OF THE REPRESSIVE AND TOXIC CULTURE IT PRODUCES, DESPITE HAVING RECENTLY ENTERED THE NEW MILLENNIUM.
BROOKE AND HER FRIENDS ARE CONSISTENTLY REFERRED TO AS "THOSE GIRLS" WITH A KNOWING TONE. SO, Y'KNOW, *THAT'S FUN.*
THE BRICKS BUILDING
CONSTRUCTED BY DOROTHY MICHAEL BRICKS IN 1987, IT'S THE TOWN'S PRIMARY OFFICE BUILDING
IT'S ALSO LARGELY MADE OF LITERAL BRICKS
GREG'S CLUB
A ONE-STOP SHOPPING EXPERIENCE FOR THE DOOMSDAY PREPPER IN ALL OF US
JERRY KINGPIN'S BOWL-O-RAMA
SHIVER ME BURGERS LOCATION #27
HOME OF THE INFAMOUS "TOTALLY ACCIDENTAL TARP FIRE" OF 1997

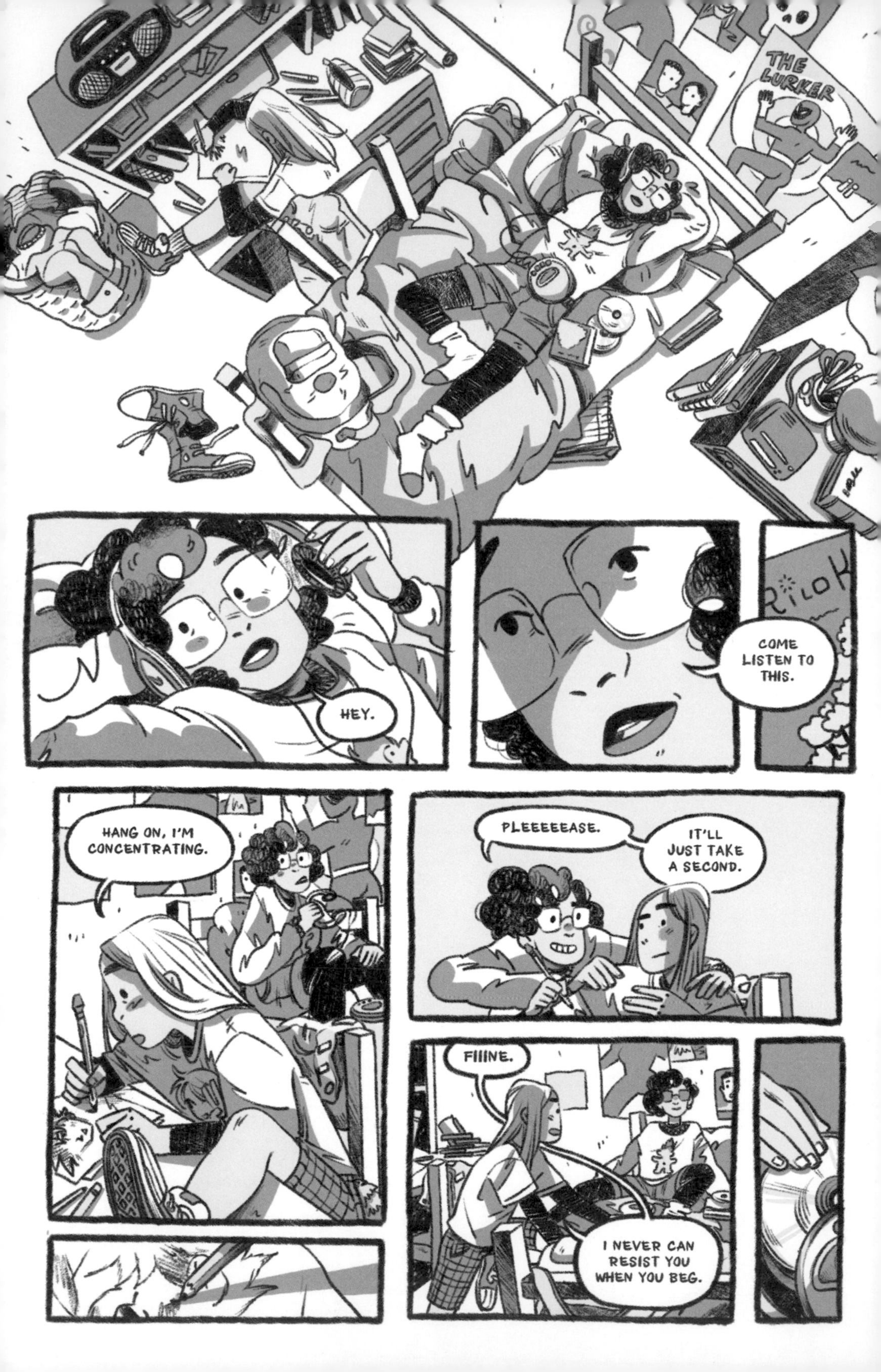
THE LURKER
HEY.
COME LISTEN TO THIS.
HANG ON, I'M CONCENTRATING.
PLEEEEEASE.
IT'LL JUST TAKE A SECOND.
FIIINE.
I NEVER CAN RESIST YOU WHEN YOU BEG.

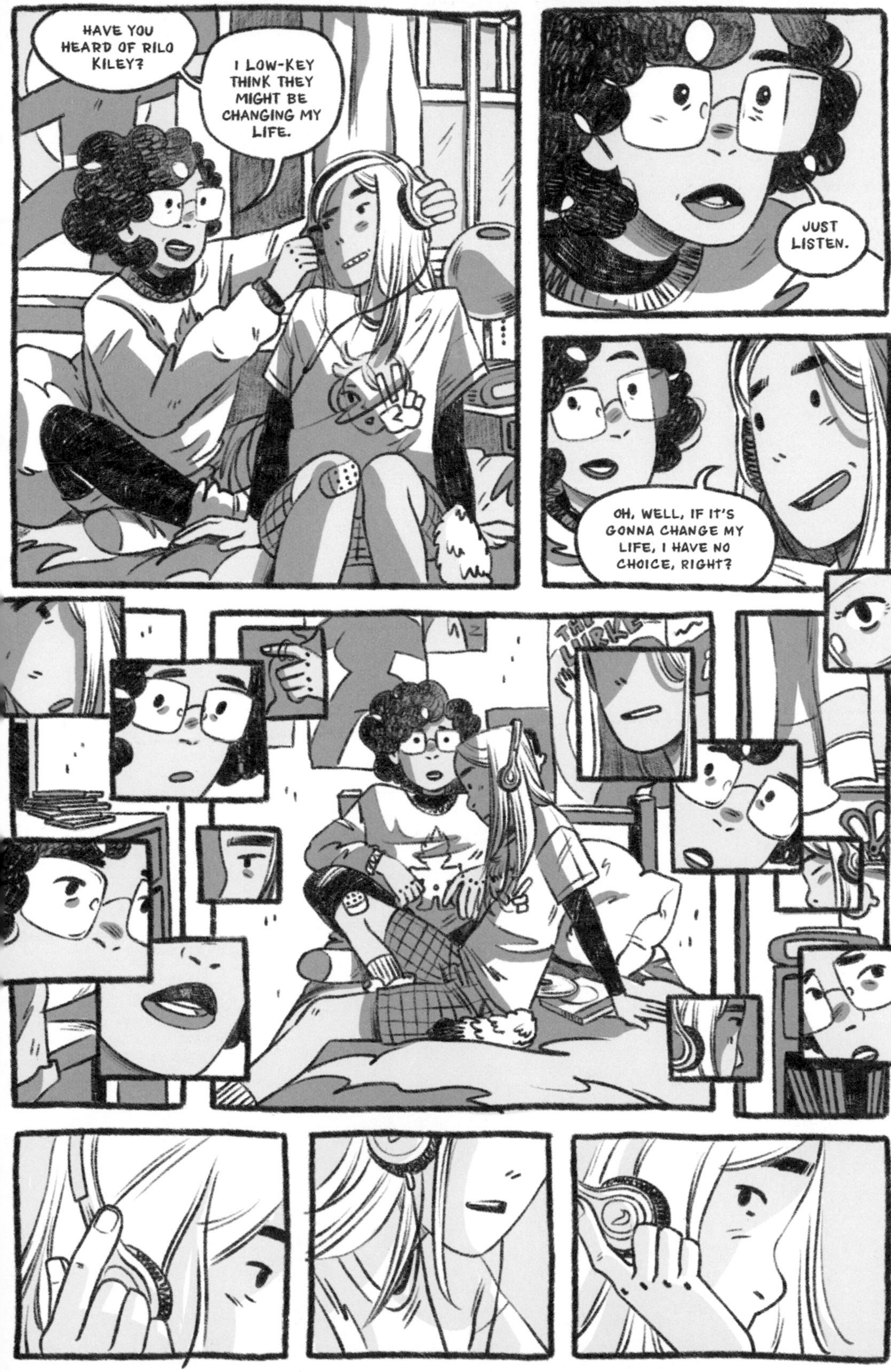
HAVE YOU HEARD OF RILO KILEY?
I LOW-KEY THINK THEY MIGHT BE CHANGING MY LIFE.
JUST LISTEN.
OH, WELL, IF IT'S GONNA CHANGE MY LIFE, I HAVE NO CHOICE, RIGHT?

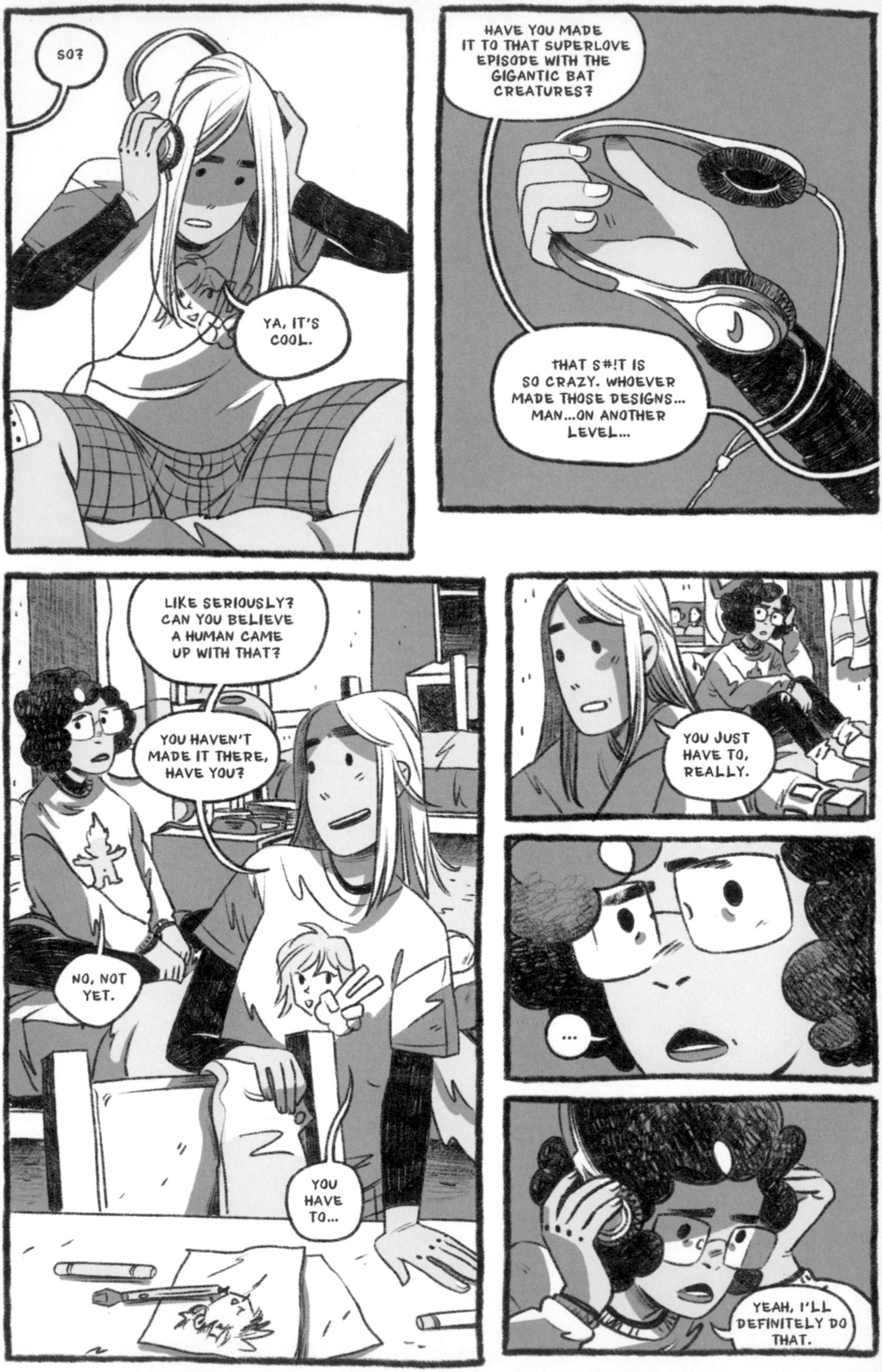
SO?
YA, IT'S COOL.
HAVE YOU MADE IT TO THAT SUPERLOVE EPISODE WITH THE GIGANTIC BAT CREATURES?
THAT S#!T IS SO CRAZY. WHOEVER MADE THOSE DESIGNS... MAN...ON ANOTHER LEVEL...
LIKE SERIOUSLY? CAN YOU BELIEVE A HUMAN CAME UP WITH THAT?
YOU HAVEN'T MADE IT THERE, HAVE YOU?
NO, NOT YET.
YOU HAVE TO...
YOU JUST HAVE TO, REALLY.
...
YEAH, I'LL DEFINITELY DO THAT.

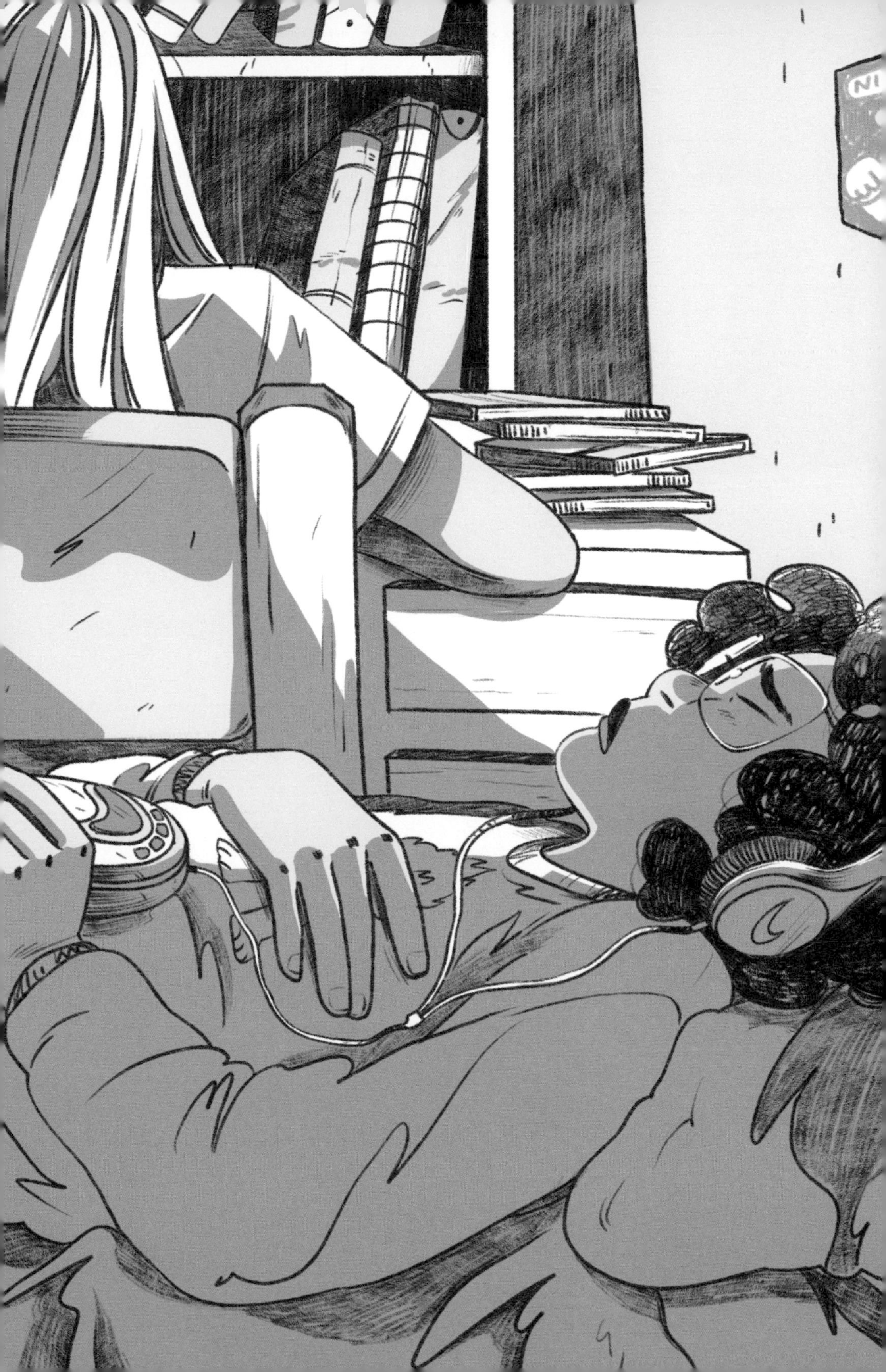

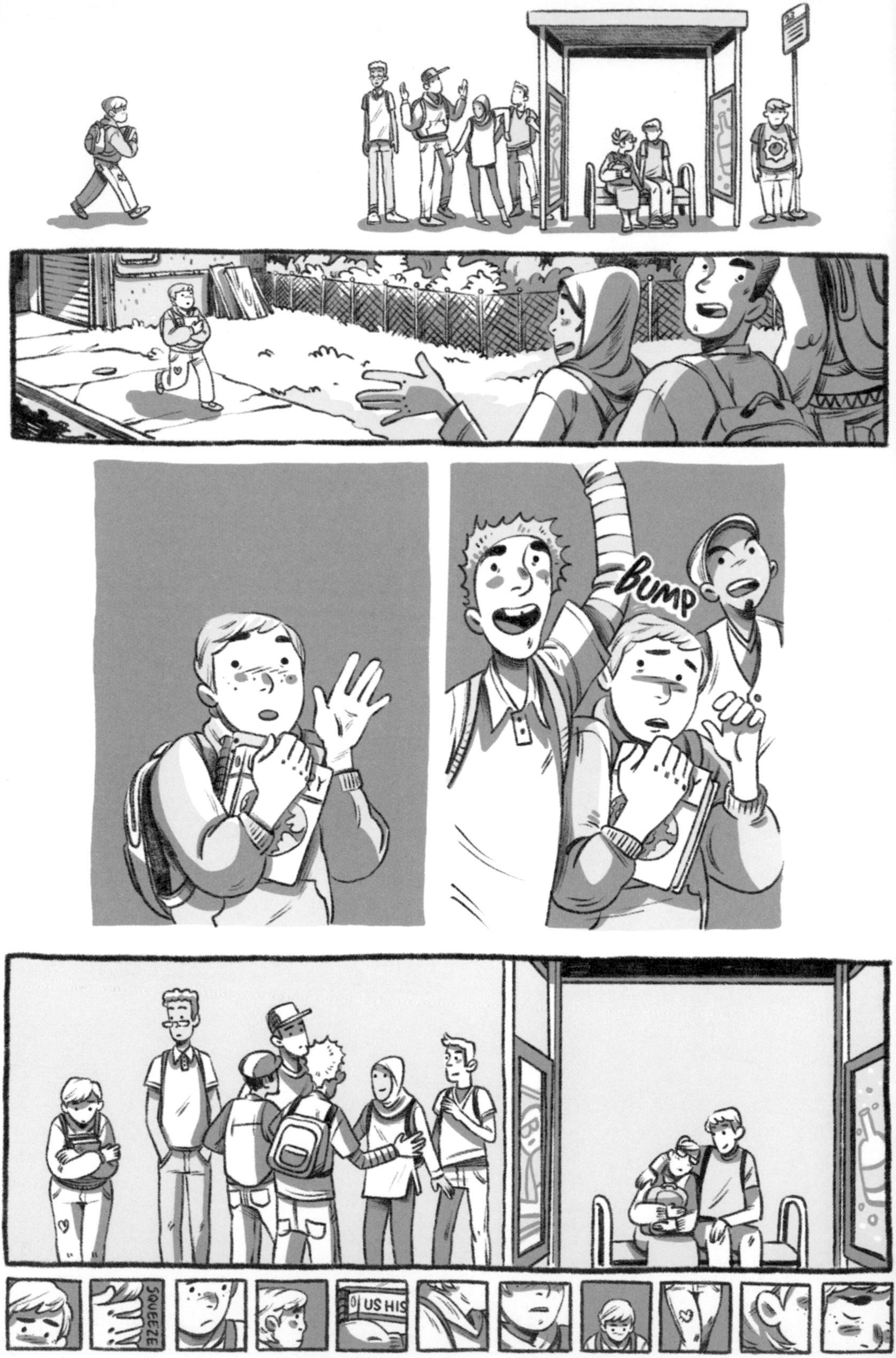
BUMP
SQUEEZE
US HIS

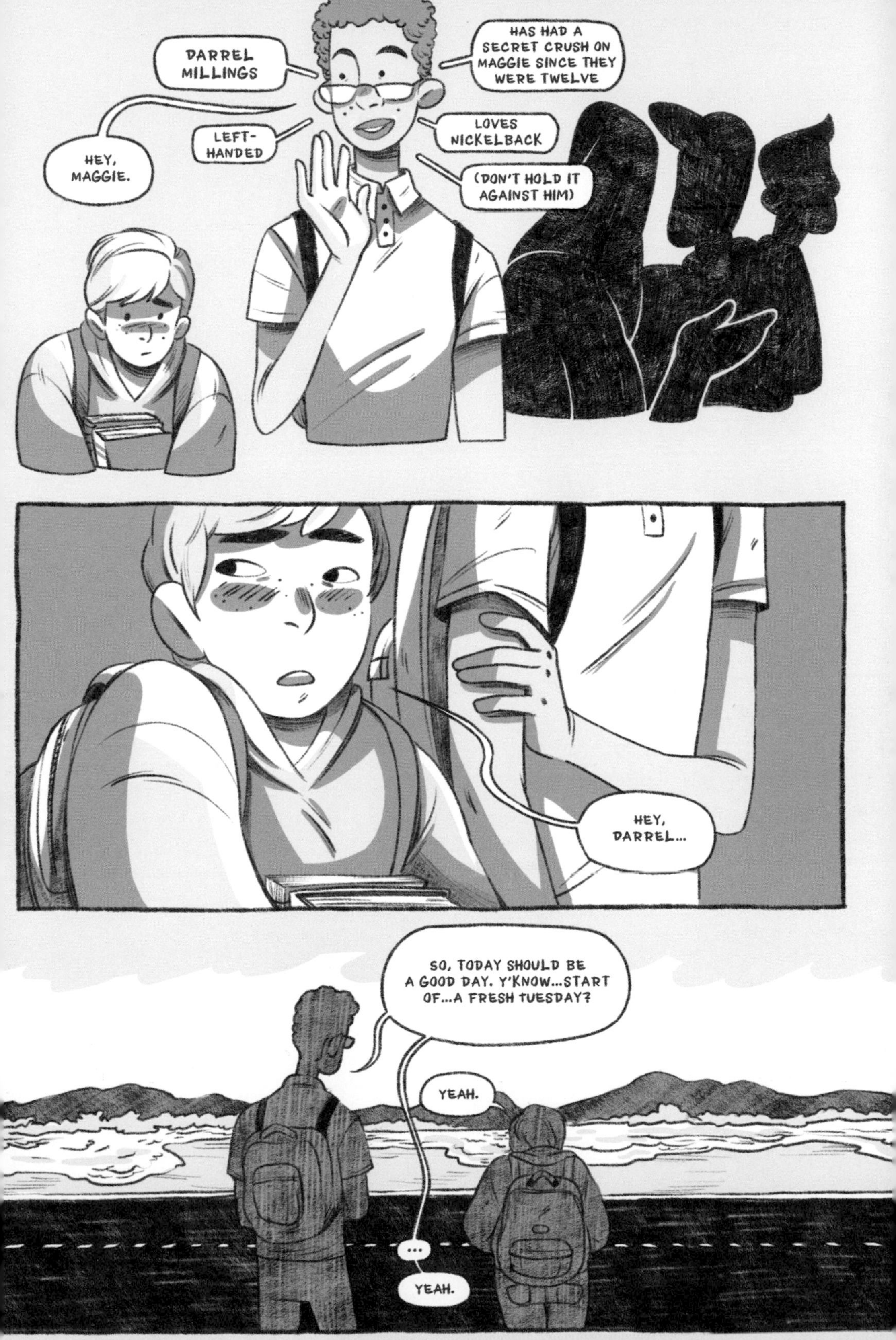
DARREL MILLINGS
HAS HAD A SECRET CRUSH ON MAGGIE SINCE THEY WERE TWELVE
LEFT-HANDED
LOVES NICKELBACK
(DON'T HOLD IT AGAINST HIM)
HEY, MAGGIE.
HEY, DARREL...
SO, TODAY SHOULD BE A GOOD DAY. Y'KNOW...START OF...A FRESH TUESDAY?
YEAH.
...
YEAH.

A BRIEF HISTORY OF THE SMALL LIFE OF MAGGIE HILCOT

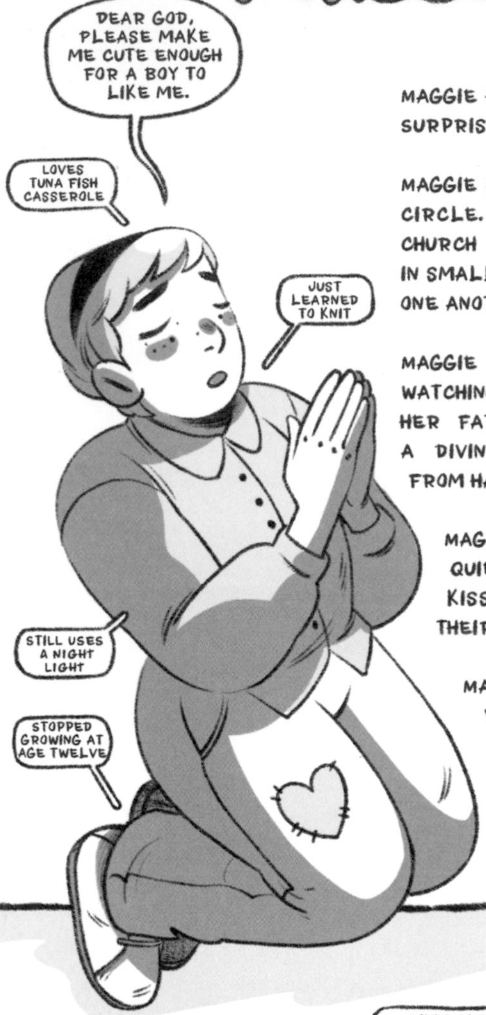
DEAR GOD, PLEASE MAKE ME CUTE ENOUGH FOR A BOY TO LIKE ME.
LOVES TUNA FISH CASSEROLE
JUST LEARNED TO KNIT
STILL USES A NIGHT LIGHT
STOPPED GROWING AT AGE TWELVE

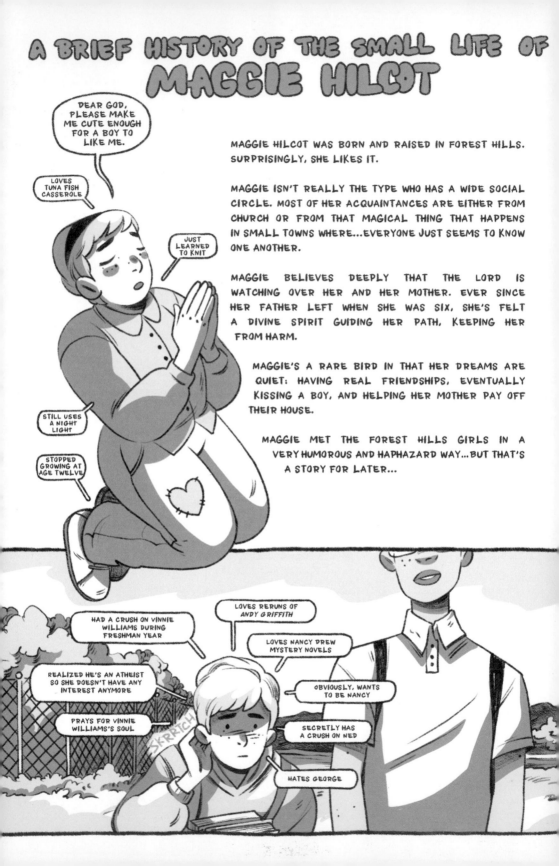

MAGGIE HILCOT WAS BORN AND RAISED IN FOREST HILLS. SURPRISINGLY, SHE LIKES IT.

MAGGIE ISN'T REALLY THE TYPE WHO HAS A WIDE SOCIAL CIRCLE. MOST OF HER ACQUAINTANCES ARE EITHER FROM CHURCH OR FROM THAT MAGICAL THING THAT HAPPENS IN SMALL TOWNS WHERE...EVERYONE JUST SEEMS TO KNOW ONE ANOTHER.

MAGGIE BELIEVES DEEPLY THAT THE LORD IS WATCHING OVER HER AND HER MOTHER. EVER SINCE HER FATHER LEFT WHEN SHE WAS SIX, SHE'S FELT A DIVINE SPIRIT GUIDING HER PATH, KEEPING HER FROM HARM.

MAGGIE'S A RARE BIRD IN THAT HER DREAMS ARE QUIET: HAVING REAL FRIENDSHIPS, EVENTUALLY KISSING A BOY, AND HELPING HER MOTHER PAY OFF THEIR HOUSE.

MAGGIE MET THE FOREST HILLS GIRLS IN A VERY HUMOROUS AND HAPHAZARD WAY...BUT THAT'S A STORY FOR LATER...

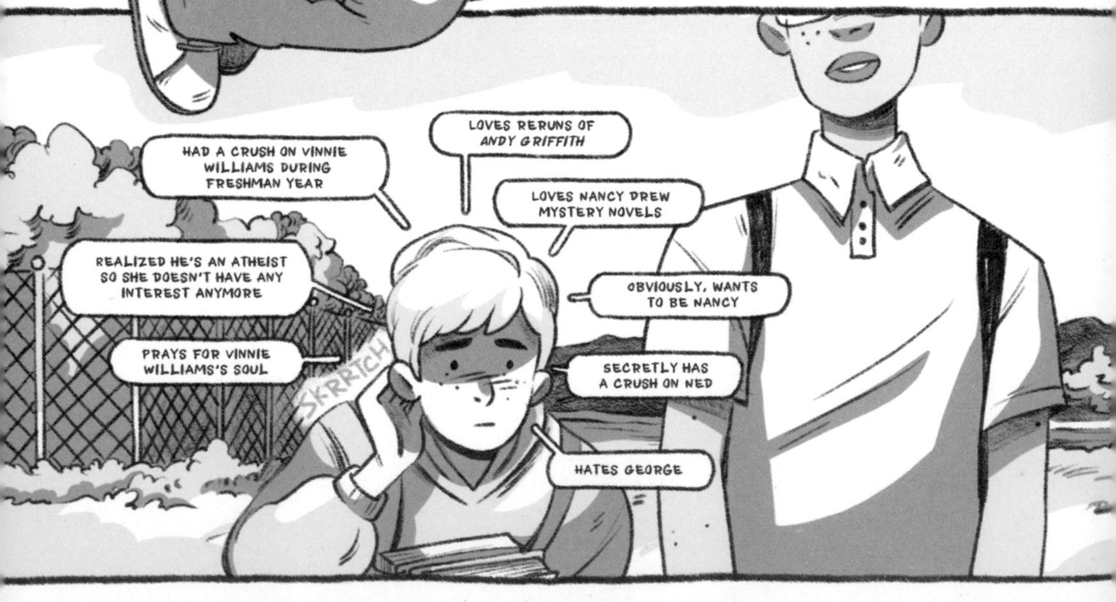
HAD A CRUSH ON VINNIE WILLIAMS DURING FRESHMAN YEAR
LOVES RERUNS OF *ANDY GRIFFITH*
LOVES NANCY DREW MYSTERY NOVELS
REALIZED HE'S AN ATHEIST SO SHE DOESN'T HAVE ANY INTEREST ANYMORE
OBVIOUSLY, WANTS TO BE NANCY
PRAYS FOR VINNIE WILLIAMS'S SOUL
SKRRTCH
SECRETLY HAS A CRUSH ON NED
HATES GEORGE

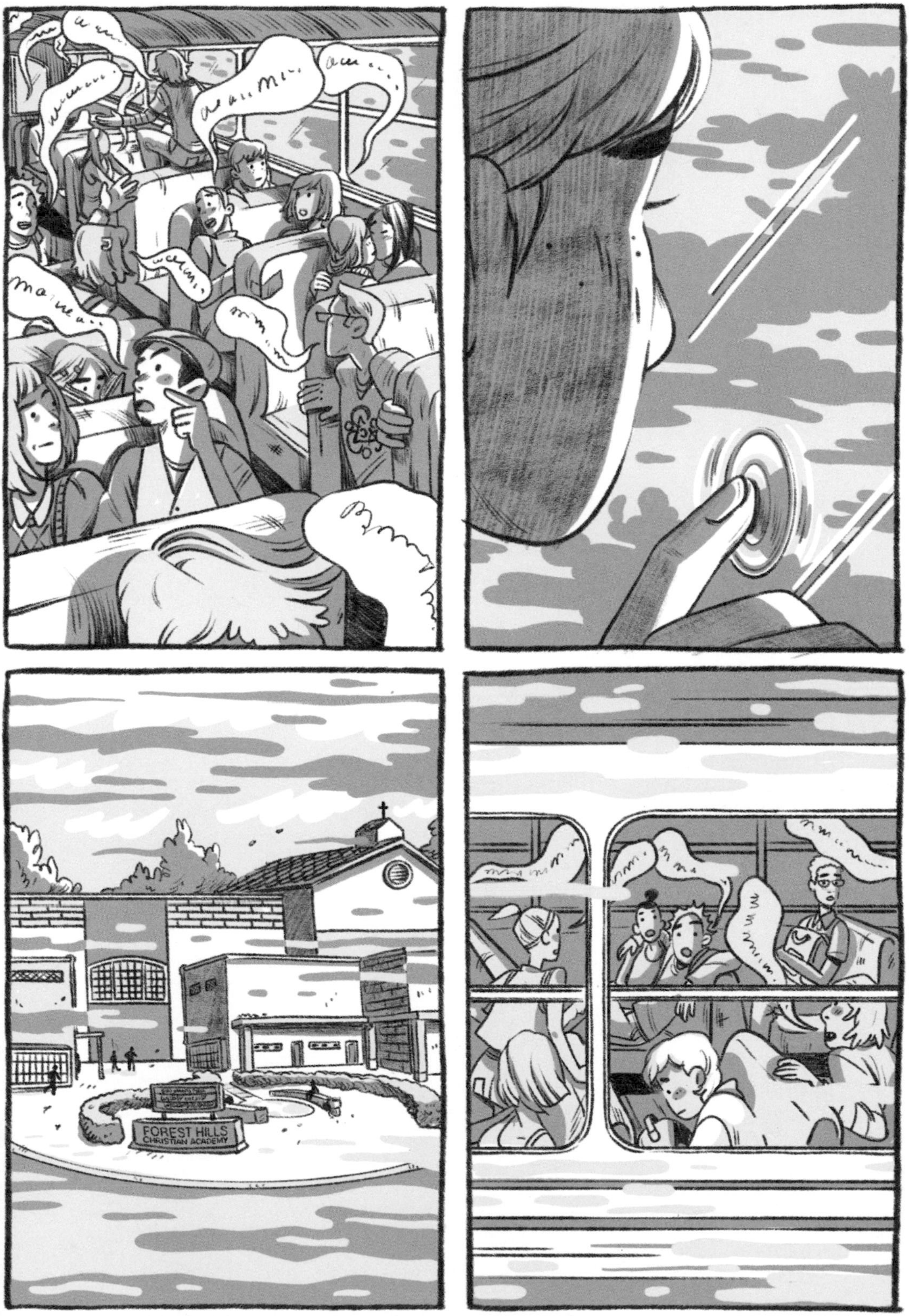
FOREST HILLS
CHRISTIAN ACADEMY

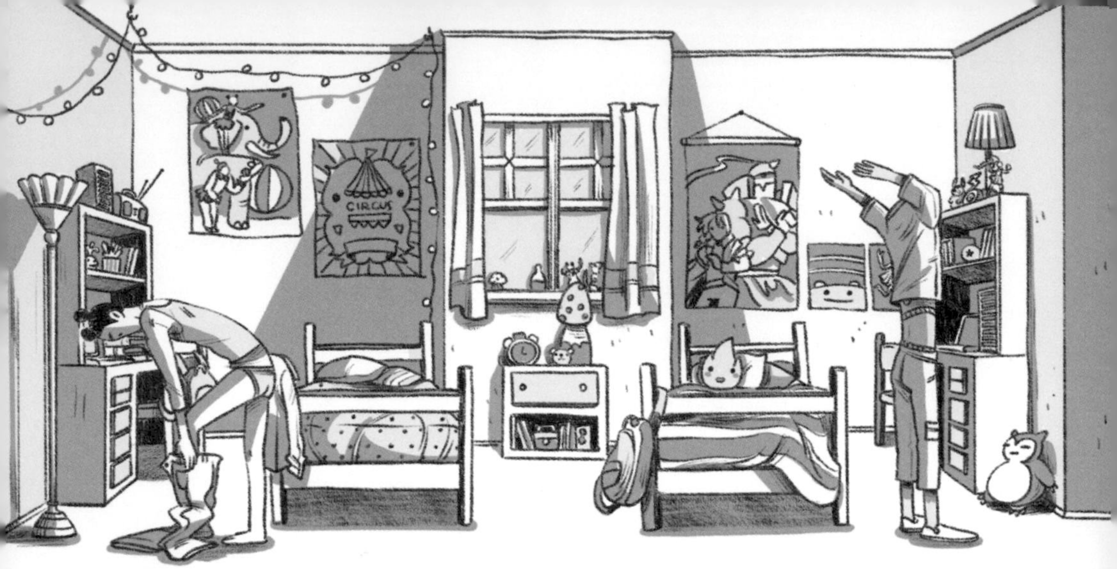
CIRCUS

A BRIEF HISTORY OF MELISSA CHO'S LEFT SOCK

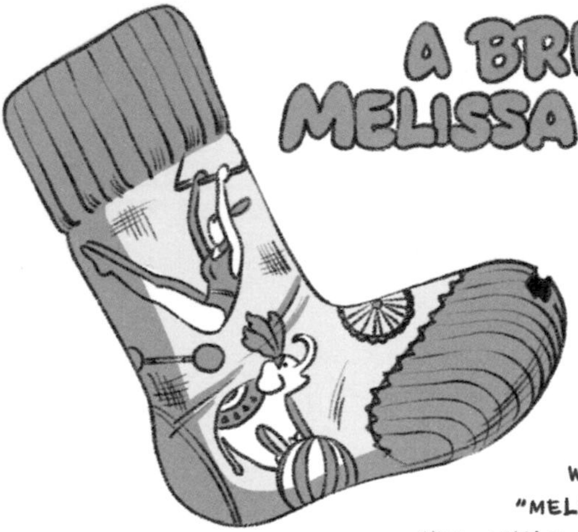

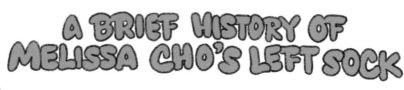

MELISSA'S FAMILY MOVED AROUND A LOT WHEN SHE WAS LITTLE. AND WHEN WE SAY "MELISSA'S FAMILY," WE LITERALLY MEAN HER WHOLE FAMILY. HER GRANDPARENTS, HER FATHER, MOTHER, AND OLDER BROTHER MOVED FOUR TIMES BETWEEN WHEN MELISSA WAS FOUR TO ELEVEN.

MELISSA'S MOTHER, JOAN, IS THE BREADWINNER IN THE FAMILY. SHE WORKS IN THE HIGH-STAKES WORLD OF PAPER CLIP MANUFACTURING. JOAN IS A BRIGHT WOMAN WHO OVERSEES MANUFACTURING PLANT REHABILITATIONS.

MELISSA NEVER REALLY BONDED WITH HER MOTHER OVER ANY COMMON INTERESTS. SHE SPENT MOST OF HER TIME ALONE, OR WITH HER GRANDFATHER, WHO DIDN'T TALK MUCH. HOWEVER, ON HER THIRTEENTH BIRTHDAY, HE GIFTED MELISSA WITH A PAIR OF CIRCUS-BRANDED SOCKS. MOST GIRLS HER AGE WOULD HAVE THOUGHT THEY WERE FOR LITTLE KIDS, BUT MELISSA'S LOVE OF THE TRAPEZE TRIUMPHED. SHE STILL HAS THEM TO THIS DAY.

WELL, ONE OF THEM, ANYWAY...

SHE'S CURRENTLY WEARING IT...

...ON HER LEFT FOOT.

YOU READY?

YEAH, RIGHT BEHIND YOU.

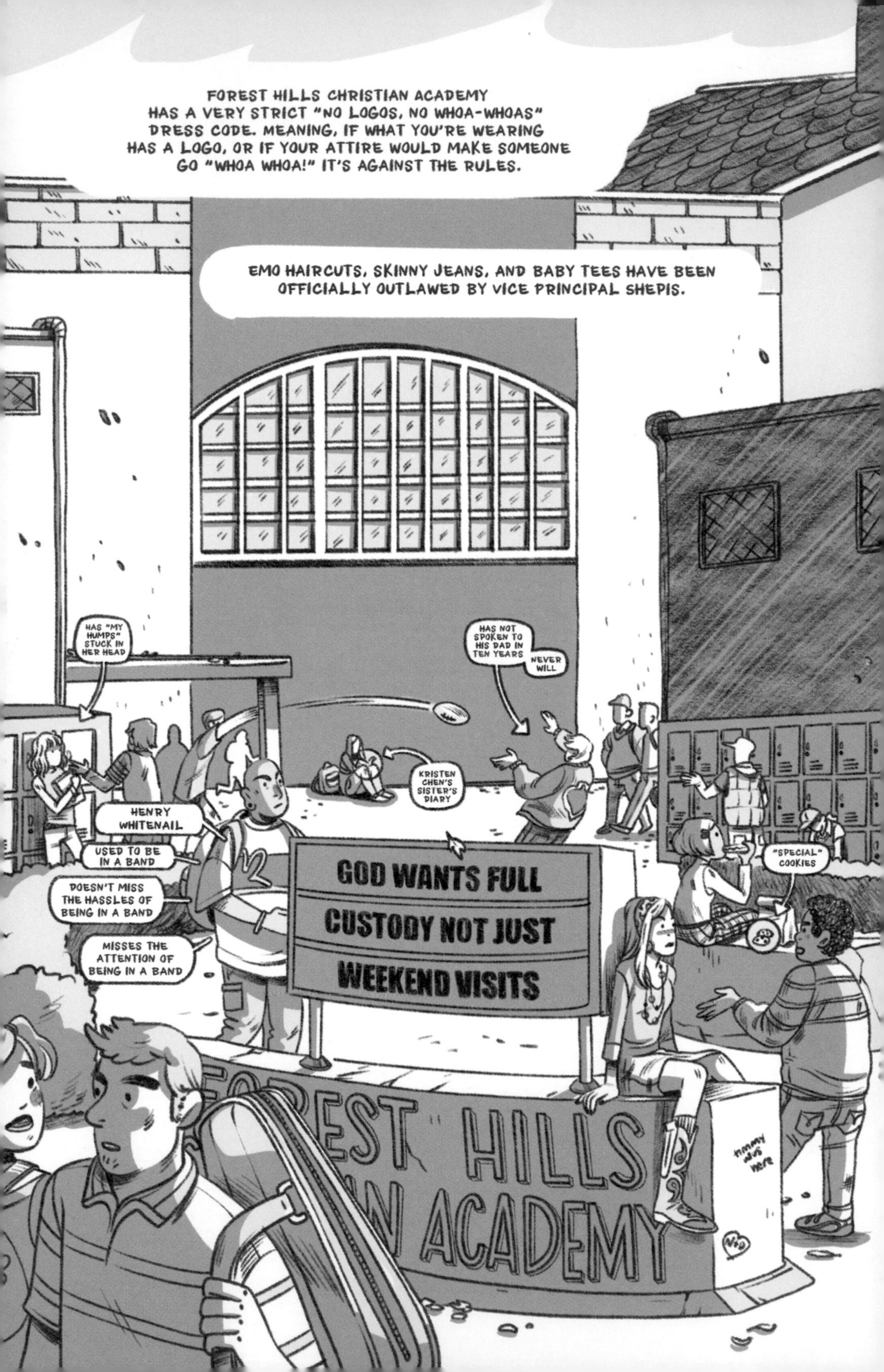
FOREST HILLS CHRISTIAN ACADEMY HAS A VERY STRICT "NO LOGOS, NO WHOA-WHOAS" DRESS CODE. MEANING, IF WHAT YOU'RE WEARING HAS A LOGO, OR IF YOUR ATTIRE WOULD MAKE SOMEONE GO "WHOA WHOA!" IT'S AGAINST THE RULES.
EMO HAIRCUTS, SKINNY JEANS, AND BABY TEES HAVE BEEN OFFICIALLY OUTLAWED BY VICE PRINCIPAL SHEPIS.
HAS "MY HUMPS" STUCK IN HER HEAD
HAS NOT SPOKEN TO HIS DAD IN TEN YEARS
NEVER WILL
KRISTEN CHEN'S SISTER'S DIARY
HENRY WHITENAIL
USED TO BE IN A BAND
DOESN'T MISS THE HASSLES OF BEING IN A BAND
MISSES THE ATTENTION OF BEING IN A BAND
GOD WANTS FULL
CUSTODY NOT JUST
WEEKEND VISITS
"SPECIAL" COOKIES
HILLS
ACADEMY
timmy was here

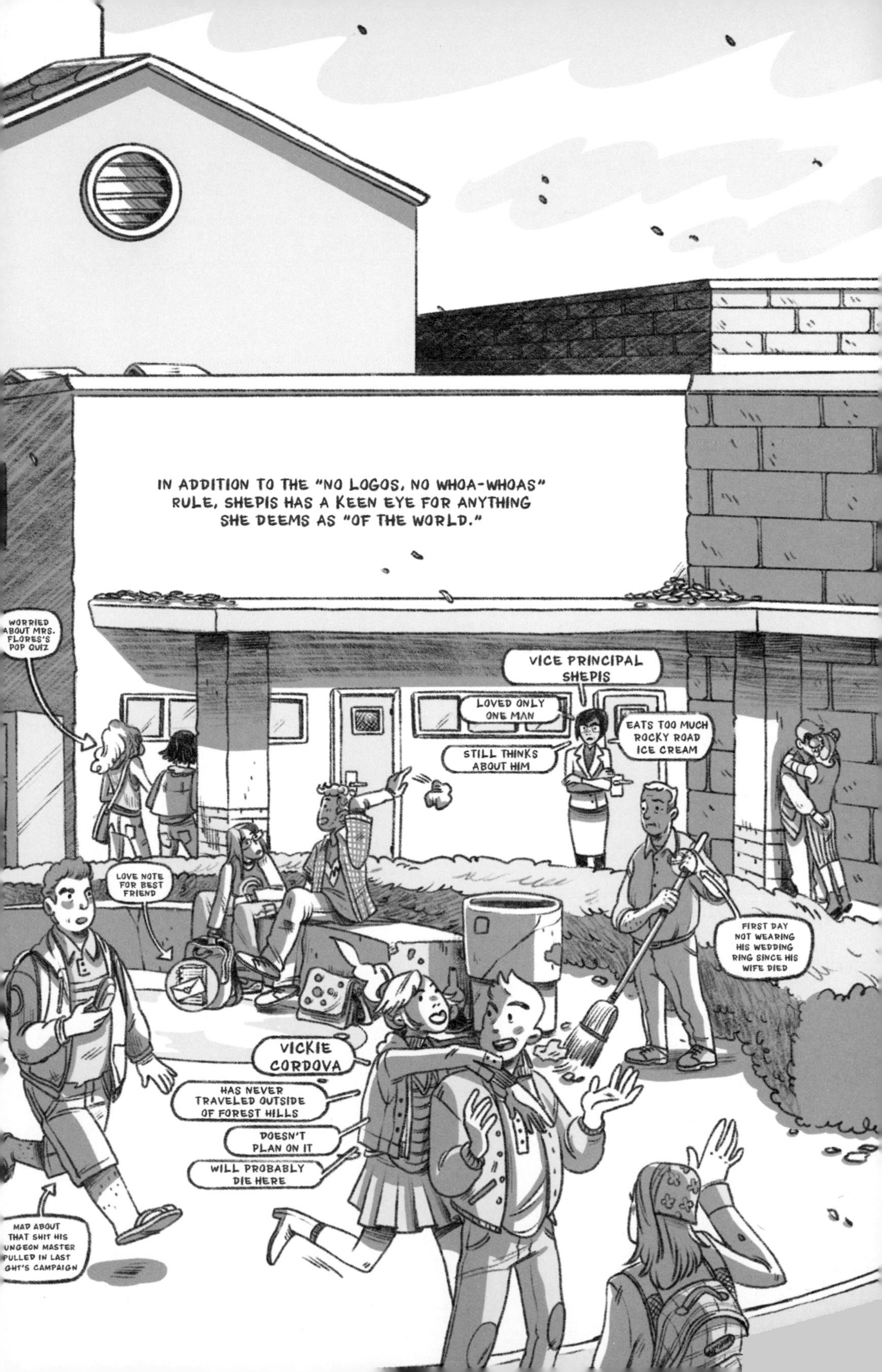
IN ADDITION TO THE "NO LOGOS, NO WHOA-WHOAS" RULE, SHEPIS HAS A KEEN EYE FOR ANYTHING SHE DEEMS AS "OF THE WORLD."
WORRIED ABOUT MRS. FLORES'S POP QUIZ
VICE PRINCIPAL SHEPIS
LOVED ONLY ONE MAN
STILL THINKS ABOUT HIM
EATS TOO MUCH ROCKY ROAD ICE CREAM
LOVE NOTE FOR BEST FRIEND
FIRST DAY NOT WEARING HIS WEDDING RING SINCE HIS WIFE DIED
VICKIE CORDOVA
HAS NEVER TRAVELED OUTSIDE OF FOREST HILLS
DOESN'T PLAN ON IT
WILL PROBABLY DIE HERE
MAD ABOUT THAT SHIT HIS UNGEON MASTER PULLED IN LAST GHT'S CAMPAIGN

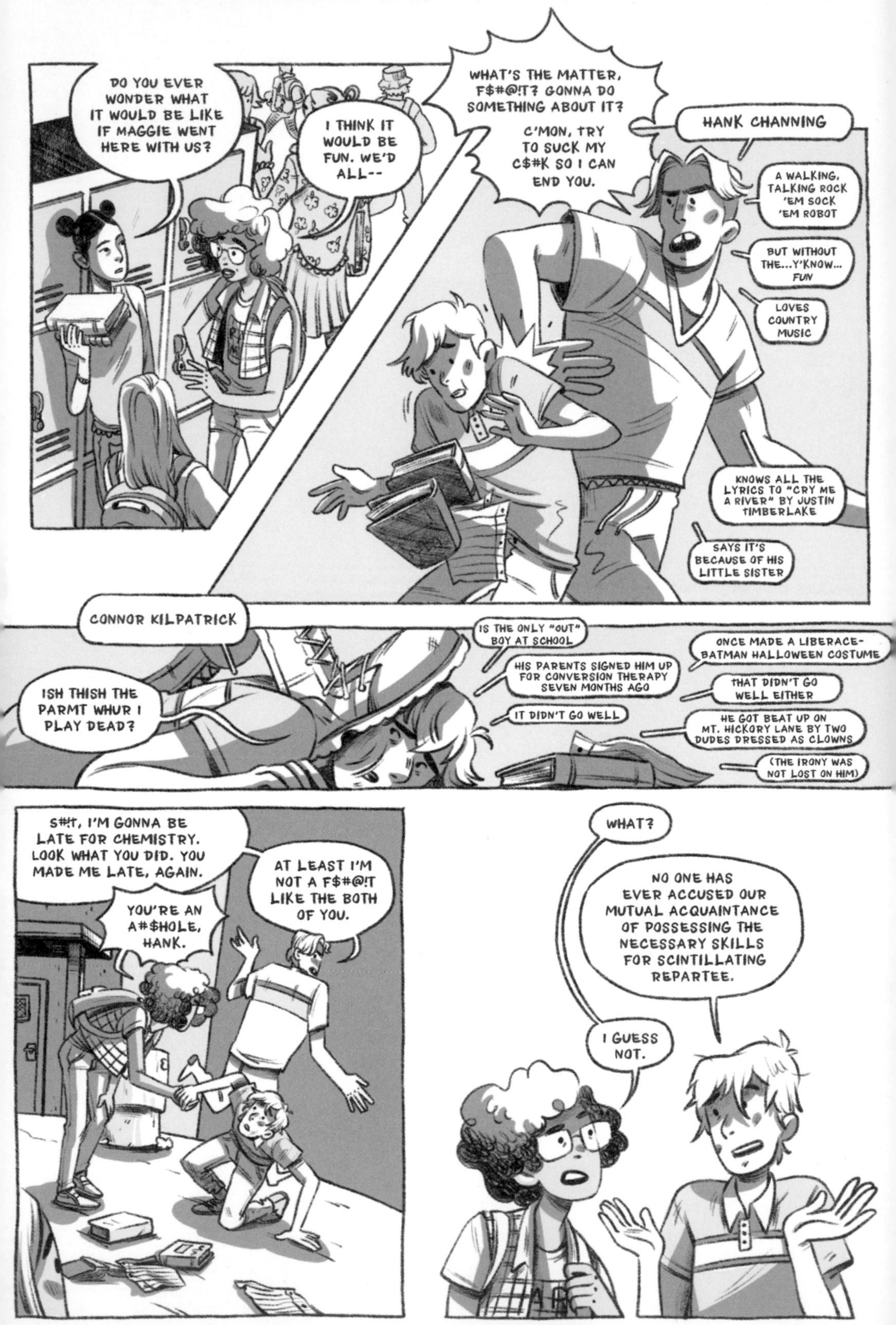
DO YOU EVER WONDER WHAT IT WOULD BE LIKE IF MAGGIE WENT HERE WITH US?
I THINK IT WOULD BE FUN. WE'D ALL--
WHAT'S THE MATTER, F$#@!T? GONNA DO SOMETHING ABOUT IT?
C'MON, TRY TO SUCK MY C$#K SO I CAN END YOU.
HANK CHANNING
A WALKING, TALKING ROCK 'EM SOCK 'EM ROBOT
BUT WITHOUT THE...Y'KNOW... FUN
LOVES COUNTRY MUSIC
KNOWS ALL THE LYRICS TO "CRY ME A RIVER" BY JUSTIN TIMBERLAKE
SAYS IT'S BECAUSE OF HIS LITTLE SISTER
CONNOR KILPATRICK
ISH THISH THE PARMT WHUR I PLAY DEAD?
IS THE ONLY "OUT" BOY AT SCHOOL
HIS PARENTS SIGNED HIM UP FOR CONVERSION THERAPY SEVEN MONTHS AGO
IT DIDN'T GO WELL
ONCE MADE A LIBERACE-BATMAN HALLOWEEN COSTUME
THAT DIDN'T GO WELL EITHER
HE GOT BEAT UP ON MT. HICKORY LANE BY TWO DUDES DRESSED AS CLOWNS
(THE IRONY WAS NOT LOST ON HIM)
S#!T, I'M GONNA BE LATE FOR CHEMISTRY. LOOK WHAT YOU DID. YOU MADE ME LATE, AGAIN.
YOU'RE AN A#$HOLE, HANK.
AT LEAST I'M NOT A F$#@!T LIKE THE BOTH OF YOU.
WHAT?
NO ONE HAS EVER ACCUSED OUR MUTUAL ACQUAINTANCE OF POSSESSING THE NECESSARY SKILLS FOR SCINTILLATING REPARTEE.
I GUESS NOT.

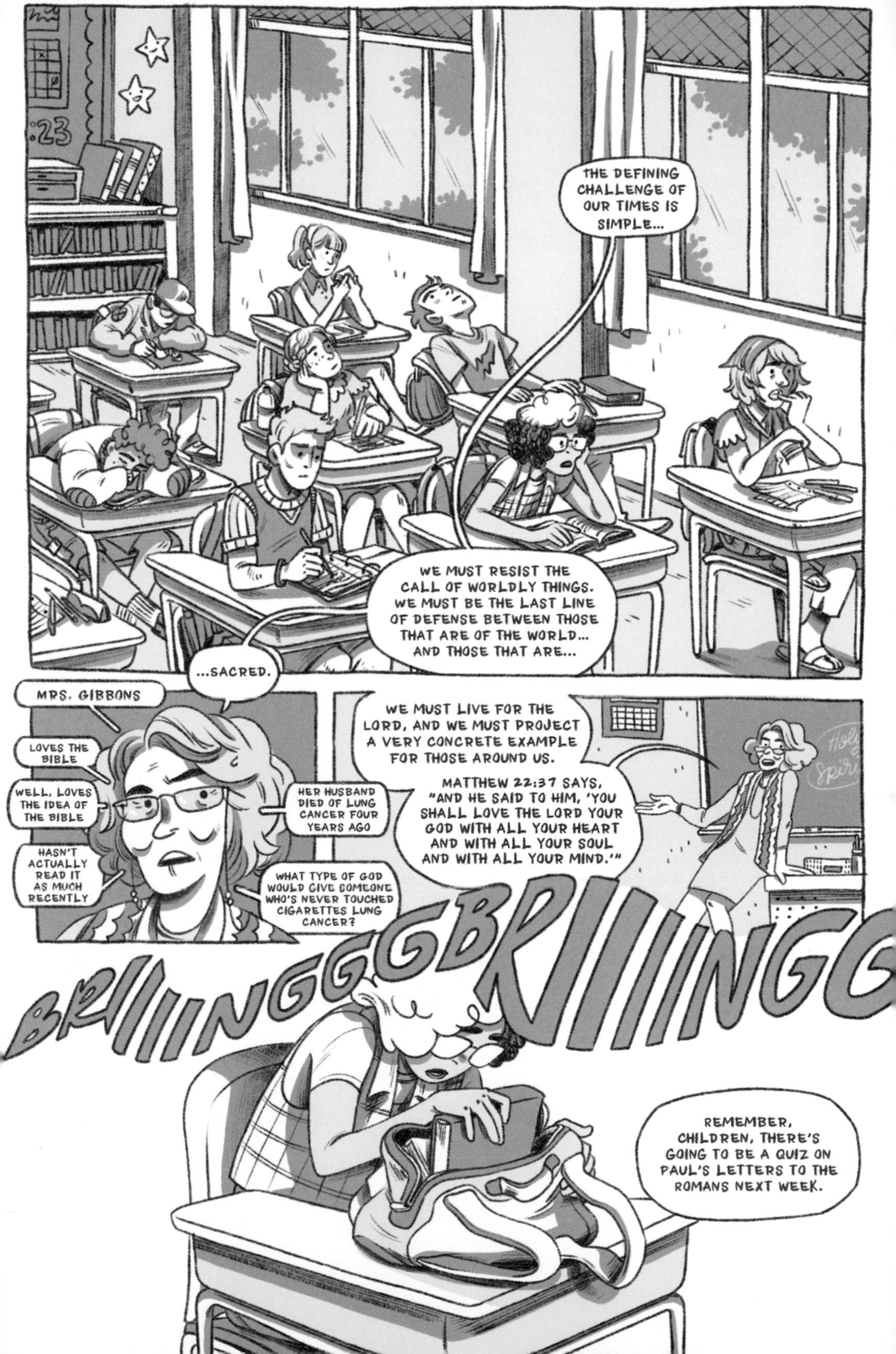
THE DEFINING CHALLENGE OF OUR TIMES IS SIMPLE...
WE MUST RESIST THE CALL OF WORLDLY THINGS. WE MUST BE THE LAST LINE OF DEFENSE BETWEEN THOSE THAT ARE OF THE WORLD... AND THOSE THAT ARE...
...SACRED.
MRS. GIBBONS
LOVES THE BIBLE
WELL, LOVES THE IDEA OF THE BIBLE
HASN'T ACTUALLY READ IT AS MUCH RECENTLY
HER HUSBAND DIED OF LUNG CANCER FOUR YEARS AGO
WHAT TYPE OF GOD WOULD GIVE SOMEONE WHO'S NEVER TOUCHED CIGARETTES LUNG CANCER?
WE MUST LIVE FOR THE LORD, AND WE MUST PROJECT A VERY CONCRETE EXAMPLE FOR THOSE AROUND US.
MATTHEW 22:37 SAYS, "AND HE SAID TO HIM, 'YOU SHALL LOVE THE LORD YOUR GOD WITH ALL YOUR HEART AND WITH ALL YOUR SOUL AND WITH ALL YOUR MIND.'"
BRIIIINGGGBRIIIINGG
REMEMBER, CHILDREN, THERE'S GOING TO BE A QUIZ ON PAUL'S LETTERS TO THE ROMANS NEXT WEEK.

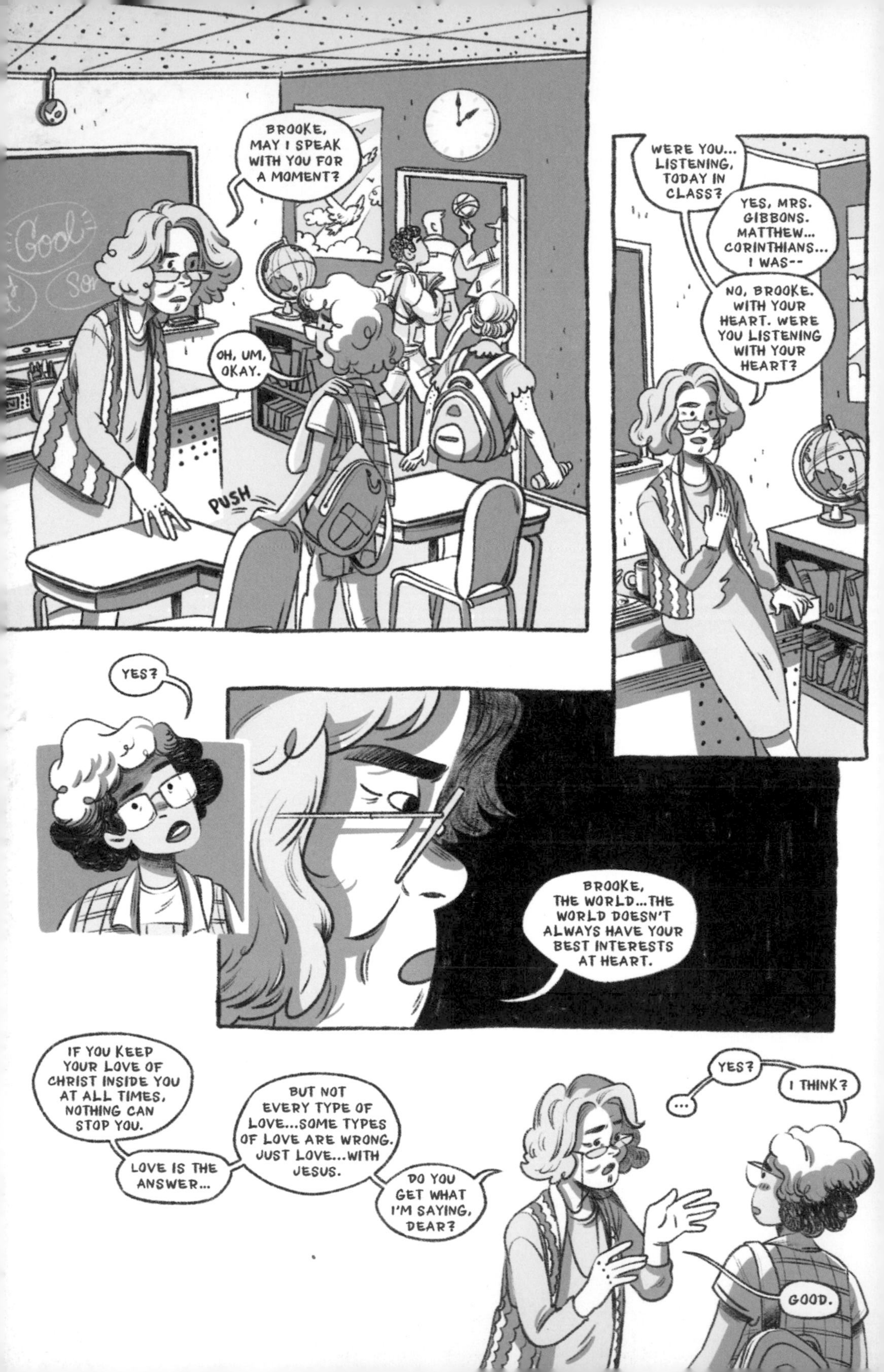
BROOKE, MAY I SPEAK WITH YOU FOR A MOMENT?
OH, UM, OKAY.
PUSH
WERE YOU... LISTENING, TODAY IN CLASS?
YES, MRS. GIBBONS. MATTHEW... CORINTHIANS... I WAS--
NO, BROOKE. WITH YOUR HEART. WERE YOU LISTENING WITH YOUR HEART?
YES?
BROOKE, THE WORLD...THE WORLD DOESN'T ALWAYS HAVE YOUR BEST INTERESTS AT HEART.
IF YOU KEEP YOUR LOVE OF CHRIST INSIDE YOU AT ALL TIMES, NOTHING CAN STOP YOU.
LOVE IS THE ANSWER...
BUT NOT EVERY TYPE OF LOVE...SOME TYPES OF LOVE ARE WRONG. JUST LOVE...WITH JESUS.
DO YOU GET WHAT I'M SAYING, DEAR?
...
YES?
I THINK?
GOOD.

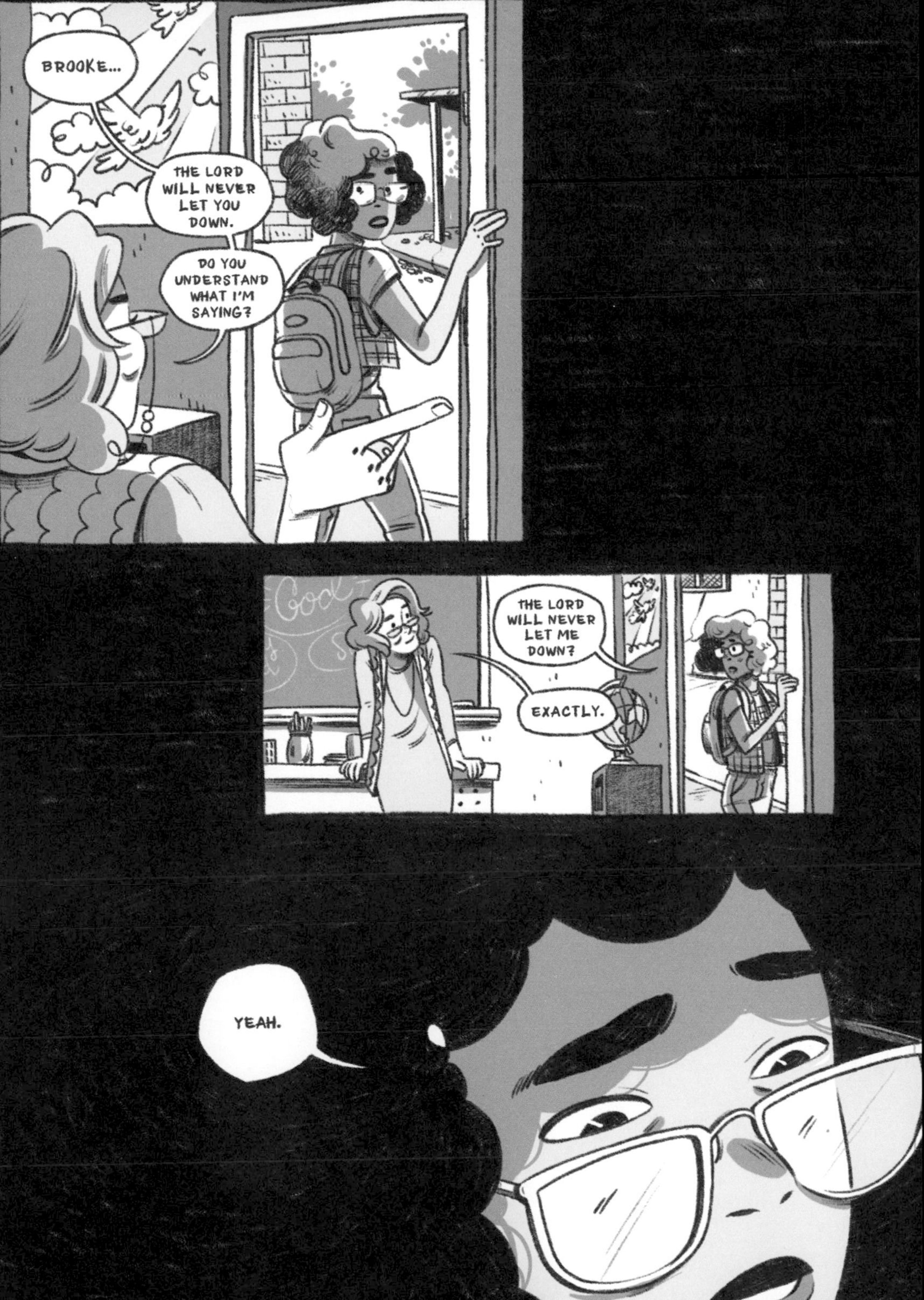
BROOKE...
THE LORD WILL NEVER LET YOU DOWN.
DO YOU UNDERSTAND WHAT I'M SAYING?
THE LORD WILL NEVER LET ME DOWN?
EXACTLY.
YEAH.

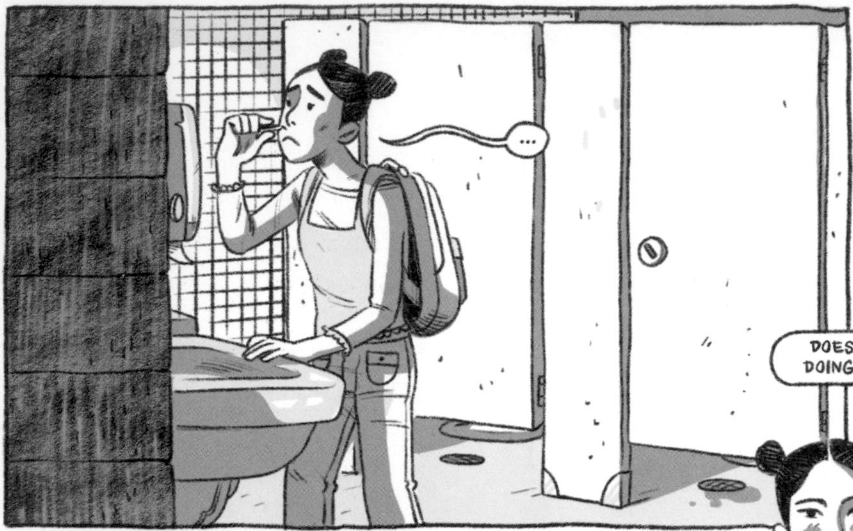
...

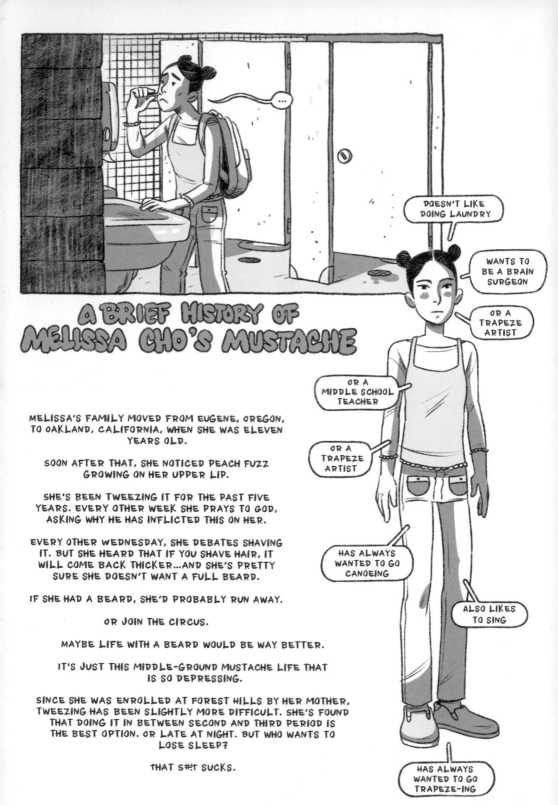

A BRIEF HISTORY OF MELISSA CHO'S MUSTACHE

MELISSA'S FAMILY MOVED FROM EUGENE, OREGON, TO OAKLAND, CALIFORNIA, WHEN SHE WAS ELEVEN YEARS OLD.

SOON AFTER THAT, SHE NOTICED PEACH FUZZ GROWING ON HER UPPER LIP.

SHE'S BEEN TWEEZING IT FOR THE PAST FIVE YEARS. EVERY OTHER WEEK SHE PRAYS TO GOD, ASKING WHY HE HAS INFLICTED THIS ON HER.

EVERY OTHER WEDNESDAY, SHE DEBATES SHAVING IT. BUT SHE HEARD THAT IF YOU SHAVE HAIR, IT WILL COME BACK THICKER...AND SHE'S PRETTY SURE SHE DOESN'T WANT A FULL BEARD.

IF SHE HAD A BEARD, SHE'D PROBABLY RUN AWAY.

OR JOIN THE CIRCUS.

MAYBE LIFE WITH A BEARD WOULD BE WAY BETTER.

IT'S JUST THIS MIDDLE-GROUND MUSTACHE LIFE THAT IS SO DEPRESSING.

SINCE SHE WAS ENROLLED AT FOREST HILLS BY HER MOTHER, TWEEZING HAS BEEN SLIGHTLY MORE DIFFICULT. SHE'S FOUND THAT DOING IT IN BETWEEN SECOND AND THIRD PERIOD IS THE BEST OPTION. OR LATE AT NIGHT. BUT WHO WANTS TO LOSE SLEEP?

THAT S#!T SUCKS.

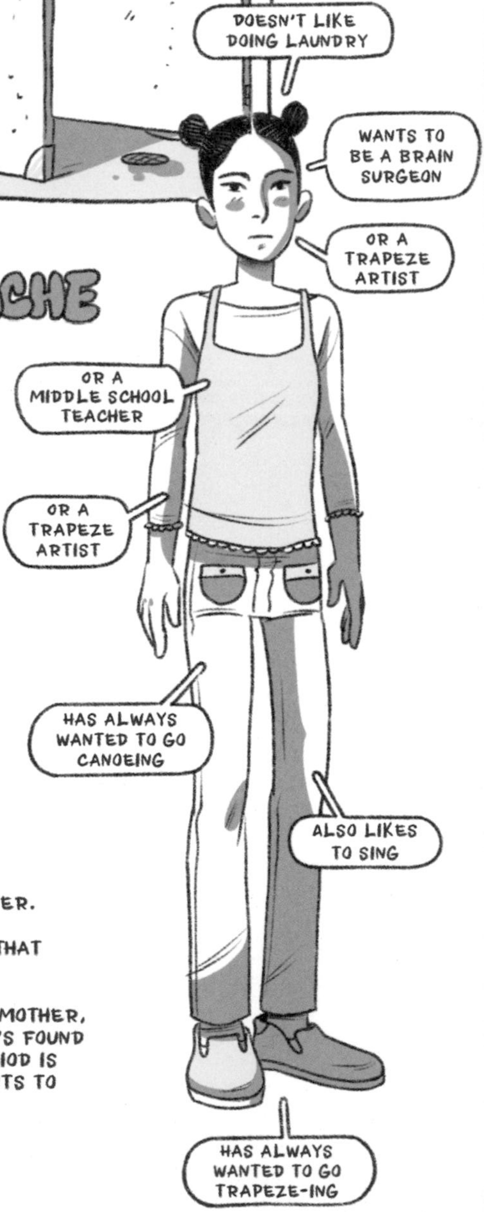
DOESN'T LIKE DOING LAUNDRY
WANTS TO BE A BRAIN SURGEON
OR A TRAPEZE ARTIST
OR A MIDDLE SCHOOL TEACHER
OR A TRAPEZE ARTIST
HAS ALWAYS WANTED TO GO CANOEING
ALSO LIKES TO SING
HAS ALWAYS WANTED TO GO TRAPEZE-ING

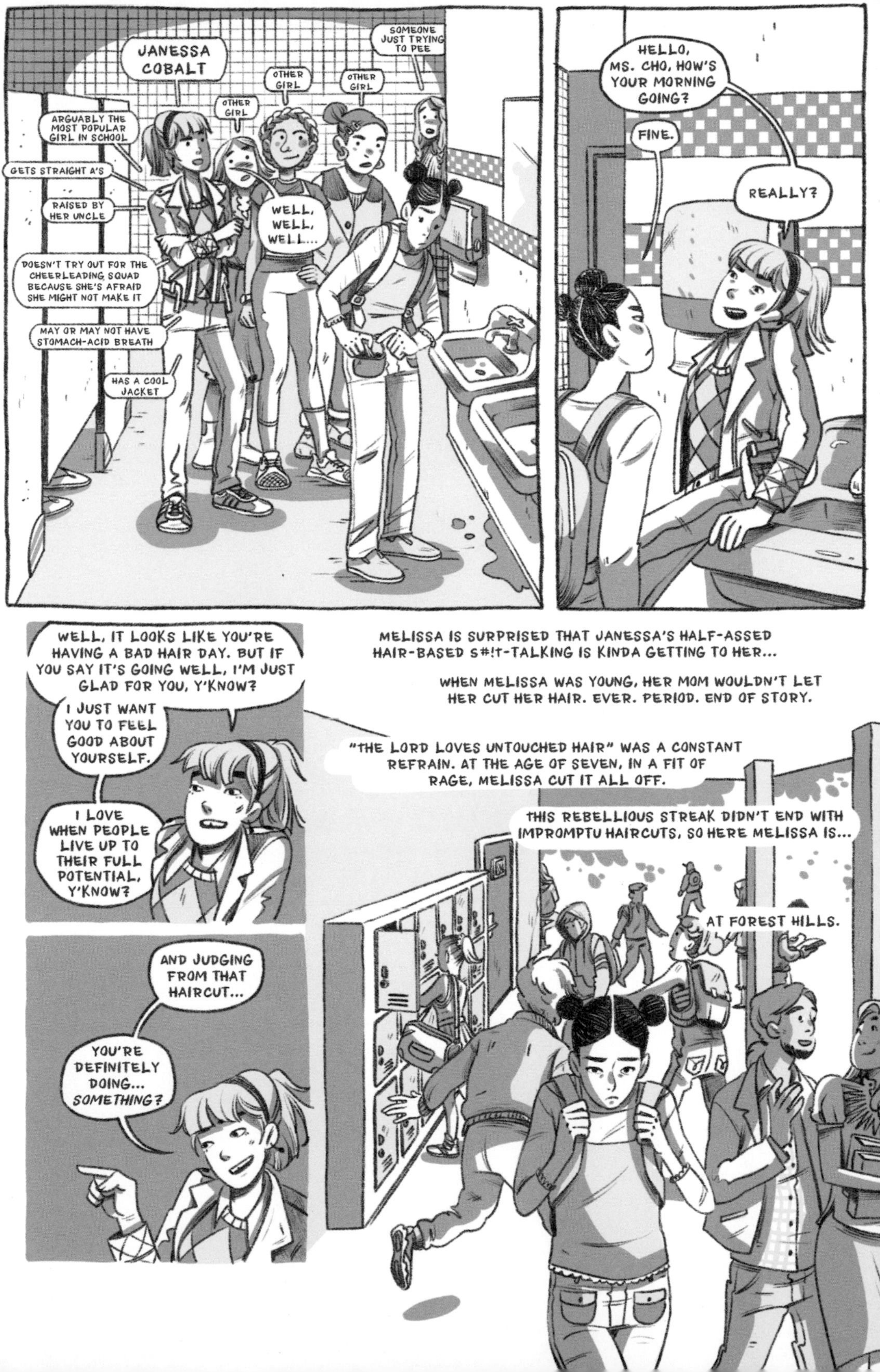
JANESSA COBALT
ARGUABLY THE MOST POPULAR GIRL IN SCHOOL
GETS STRAIGHT A'S
RAISED BY HER UNCLE
DOESN'T TRY OUT FOR THE CHEERLEADING SQUAD BECAUSE SHE'S AFRAID SHE MIGHT NOT MAKE IT
MAY OR MAY NOT HAVE STOMACH-ACID BREATH
HAS A COOL JACKET
OTHER GIRL
OTHER GIRL
OTHER GIRL
SOMEONE JUST TRYING TO PEE
WELL, WELL, WELL...
HELLO, MS. CHO, HOW'S YOUR MORNING GOING?
FINE.
REALLY?
WELL, IT LOOKS LIKE YOU'RE HAVING A BAD HAIR DAY. BUT IF YOU SAY IT'S GOING WELL, I'M JUST GLAD FOR YOU, Y'KNOW?
I JUST WANT YOU TO FEEL GOOD ABOUT YOURSELF.
I LOVE WHEN PEOPLE LIVE UP TO THEIR FULL POTENTIAL, Y'KNOW?
AND JUDGING FROM THAT HAIRCUT...
YOU'RE DEFINITELY DOING... SOMETHING?
MELISSA IS SURPRISED THAT JANESSA'S HALF-ASSED HAIR-BASED S#!T-TALKING IS KINDA GETTING TO HER...
WHEN MELISSA WAS YOUNG, HER MOM WOULDN'T LET HER CUT HER HAIR. EVER. PERIOD. END OF STORY.
"THE LORD LOVES UNTOUCHED HAIR" WAS A CONSTANT REFRAIN. AT THE AGE OF SEVEN, IN A FIT OF RAGE, MELISSA CUT IT ALL OFF.
THIS REBELLIOUS STREAK DIDN'T END WITH IMPROMPTU HAIRCUTS, SO HERE MELISSA IS...
AT FOREST HILLS.

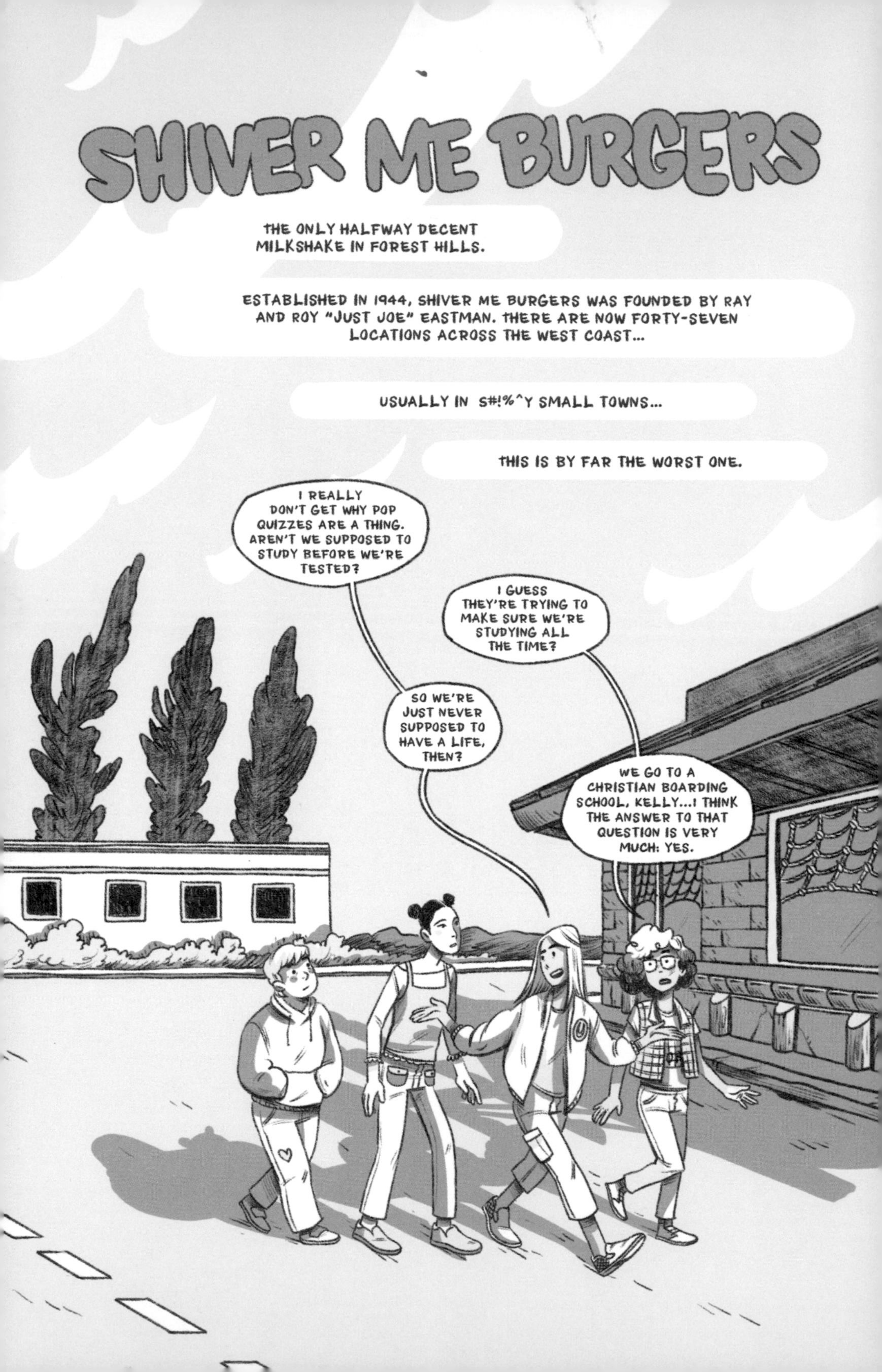
SHIVER ME BURGERS
THE ONLY HALFWAY DECENT MILKSHAKE IN FOREST HILLS.
ESTABLISHED IN 1944, SHIVER ME BURGERS WAS FOUNDED BY RAY AND ROY "JUST JOE" EASTMAN. THERE ARE NOW FORTY-SEVEN LOCATIONS ACROSS THE WEST COAST...
USUALLY IN S#!%^Y SMALL TOWNS...
THIS IS BY FAR THE WORST ONE.
I REALLY DON'T GET WHY POP QUIZZES ARE A THING. AREN'T WE SUPPOSED TO STUDY BEFORE WE'RE TESTED?
I GUESS THEY'RE TRYING TO MAKE SURE WE'RE STUDYING ALL THE TIME?
SO WE'RE JUST NEVER SUPPOSED TO HAVE A LIFE, THEN?
WE GO TO A CHRISTIAN BOARDING SCHOOL, KELLY...I THINK THE ANSWER TO THAT QUESTION IS VERY MUCH: YES.

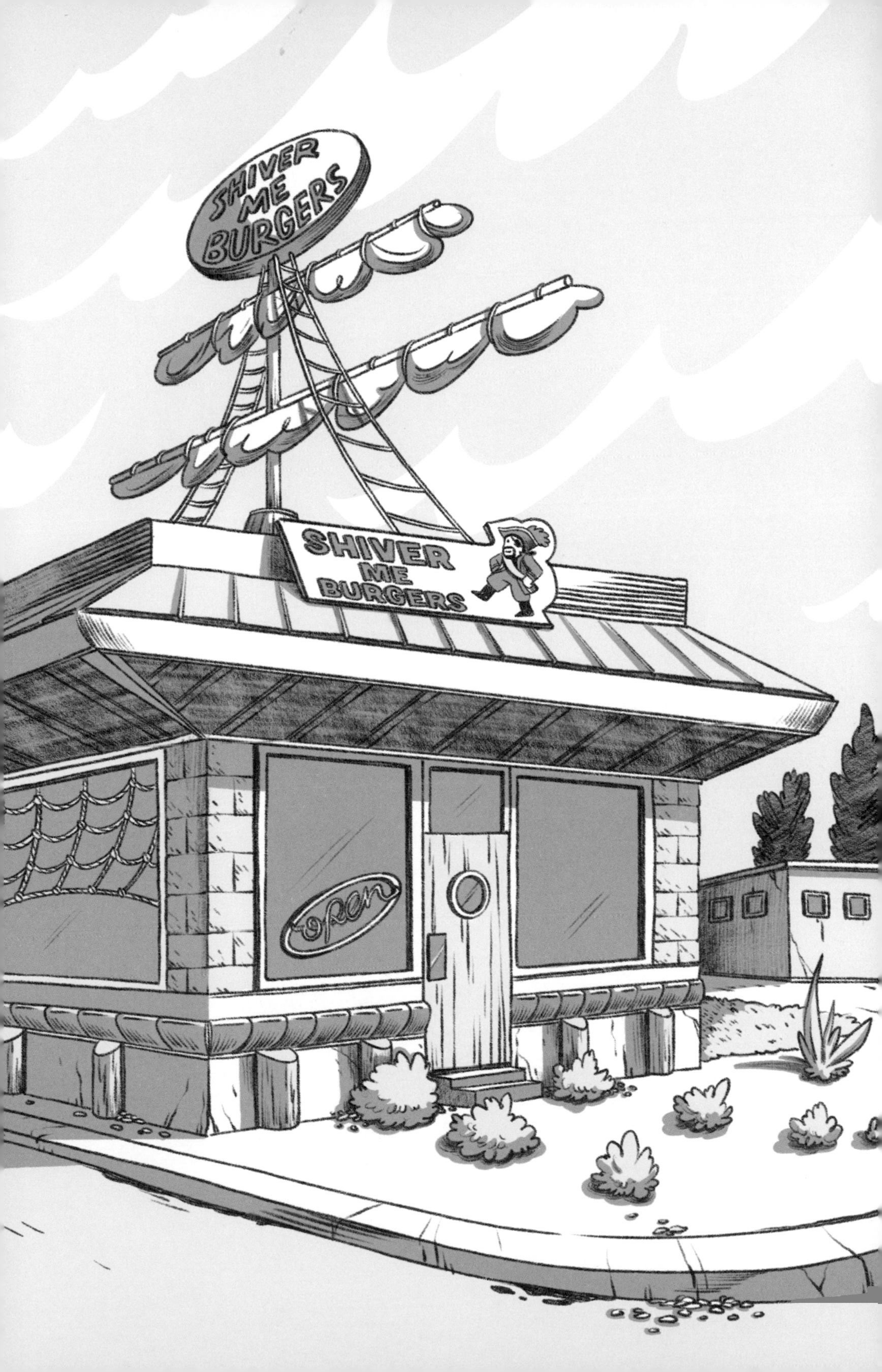
SHIVER ME BURGERS
SHIVER ME BURGERS
OPEN

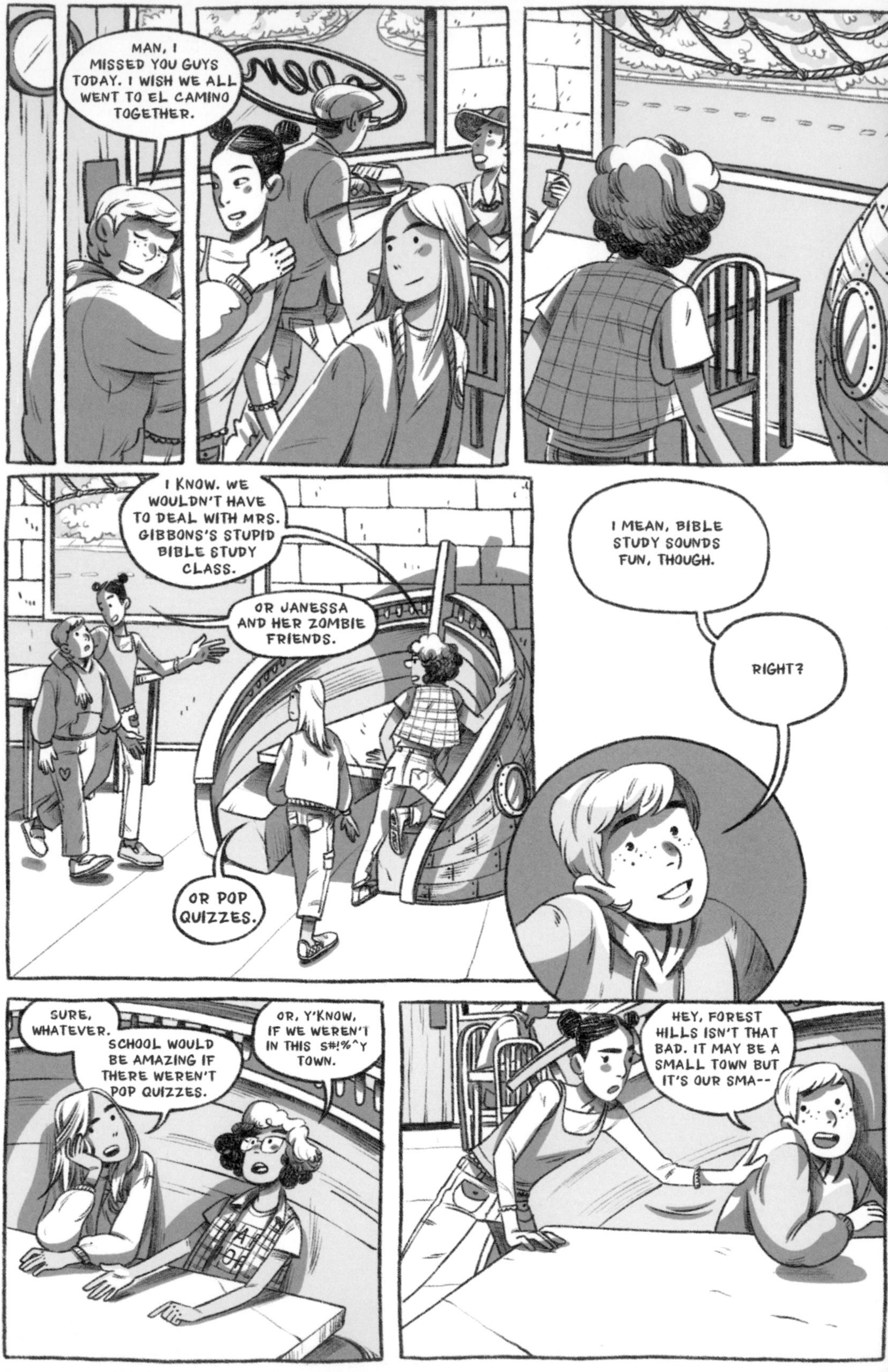
MAN, I MISSED YOU GUYS TODAY. I WISH WE ALL WENT TO EL CAMINO TOGETHER.
I KNOW. WE WOULDN'T HAVE TO DEAL WITH MRS. GIBBONS'S STUPID BIBLE STUDY CLASS.
OR JANESSA AND HER ZOMBIE FRIENDS.
OR POP QUIZZES.
I MEAN, BIBLE STUDY SOUNDS FUN, THOUGH.
RIGHT?
SURE, WHATEVER.
SCHOOL WOULD BE AMAZING IF THERE WEREN'T POP QUIZZES.
OR, Y'KNOW, IF WE WEREN'T IN THIS S#!%^Y TOWN.
HEY, FOREST HILLS ISN'T THAT BAD. IT MAY BE A SMALL TOWN BUT IT'S OUR SMA--

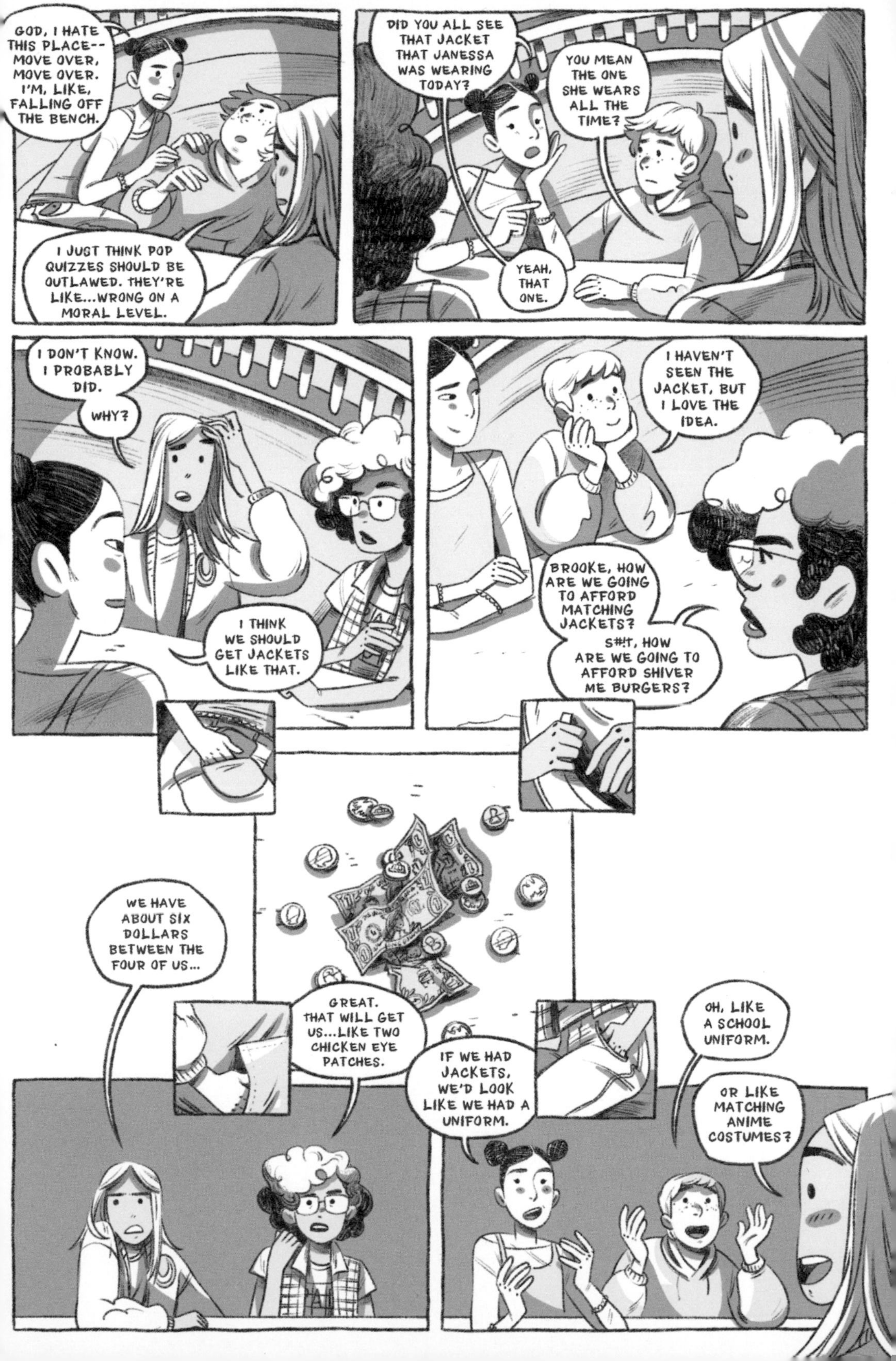
GOD, I HATE THIS PLACE-- MOVE OVER, MOVE OVER. I'M, LIKE, FALLING OFF THE BENCH.
I JUST THINK POP QUIZZES SHOULD BE OUTLAWED. THEY'RE LIKE...WRONG ON A MORAL LEVEL.
DID YOU ALL SEE THAT JACKET THAT JANESSA WAS WEARING TODAY?
YOU MEAN THE ONE SHE WEARS ALL THE TIME?
YEAH, THAT ONE.
I DON'T KNOW. I PROBABLY DID.
WHY?
I THINK WE SHOULD GET JACKETS LIKE THAT.
I HAVEN'T SEEN THE JACKET, BUT I LOVE THE IDEA.
BROOKE, HOW ARE WE GOING TO AFFORD MATCHING JACKETS?
S#!T, HOW ARE WE GOING TO AFFORD SHIVER ME BURGERS?
WE HAVE ABOUT SIX DOLLARS BETWEEN THE FOUR OF US...
GREAT. THAT WILL GET US...LIKE TWO CHICKEN EYE PATCHES.
IF WE HAD JACKETS, WE'D LOOK LIKE WE HAD A UNIFORM.
OH, LIKE A SCHOOL UNIFORM.
OR LIKE MATCHING ANIME COSTUMES?

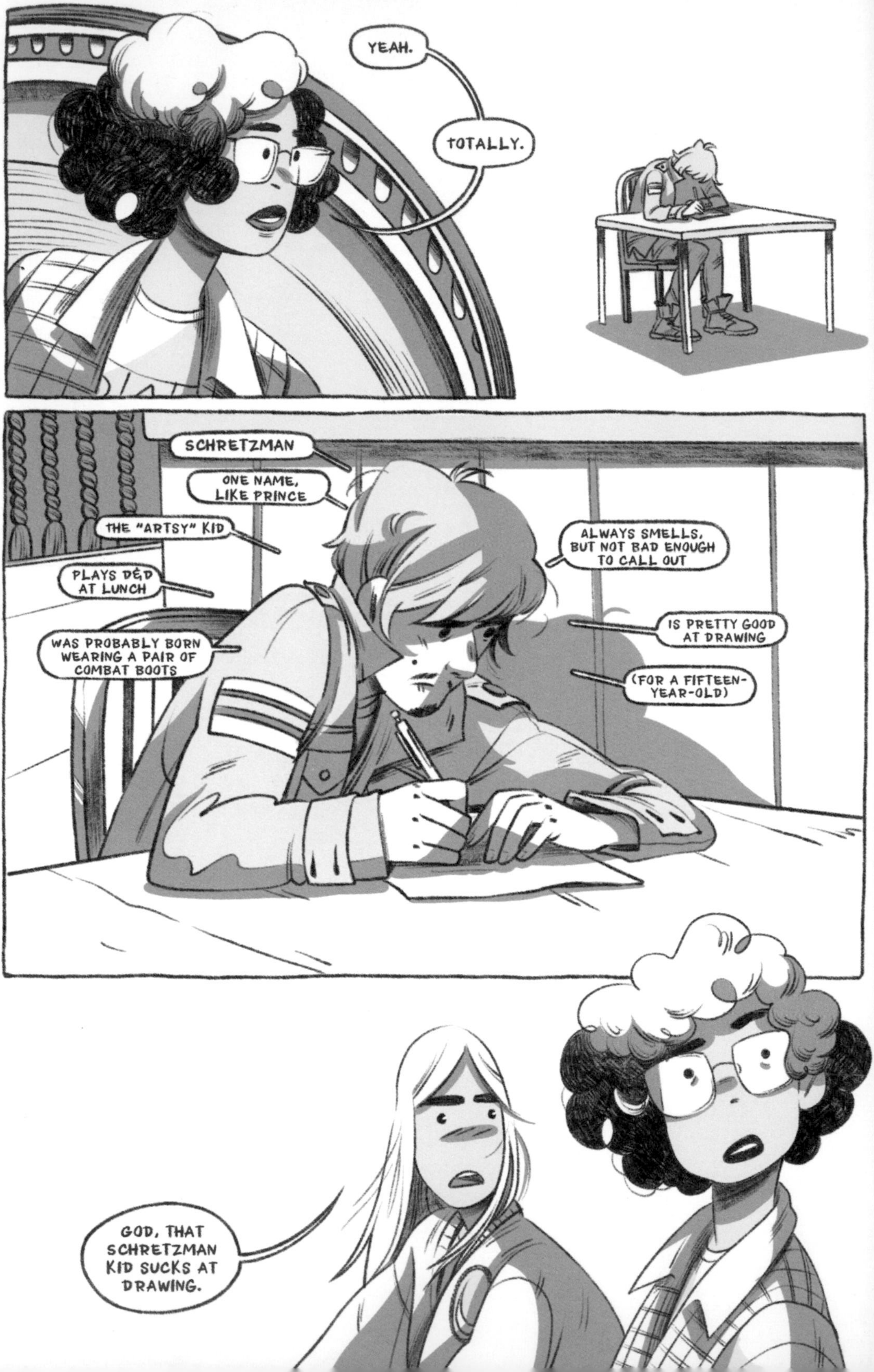
YEAH.
TOTALLY.
SCHRETZMAN
ONE NAME, LIKE PRINCE
THE "ARTSY" KID
PLAYS D&D AT LUNCH
WAS PROBABLY BORN WEARING A PAIR OF COMBAT BOOTS
ALWAYS SMELLS, BUT NOT BAD ENOUGH TO CALL OUT
IS PRETTY GOOD AT DRAWING
(FOR A FIFTEEN-YEAR-OLD)
GOD, THAT SCHRETZMAN KID SUCKS AT DRAWING.

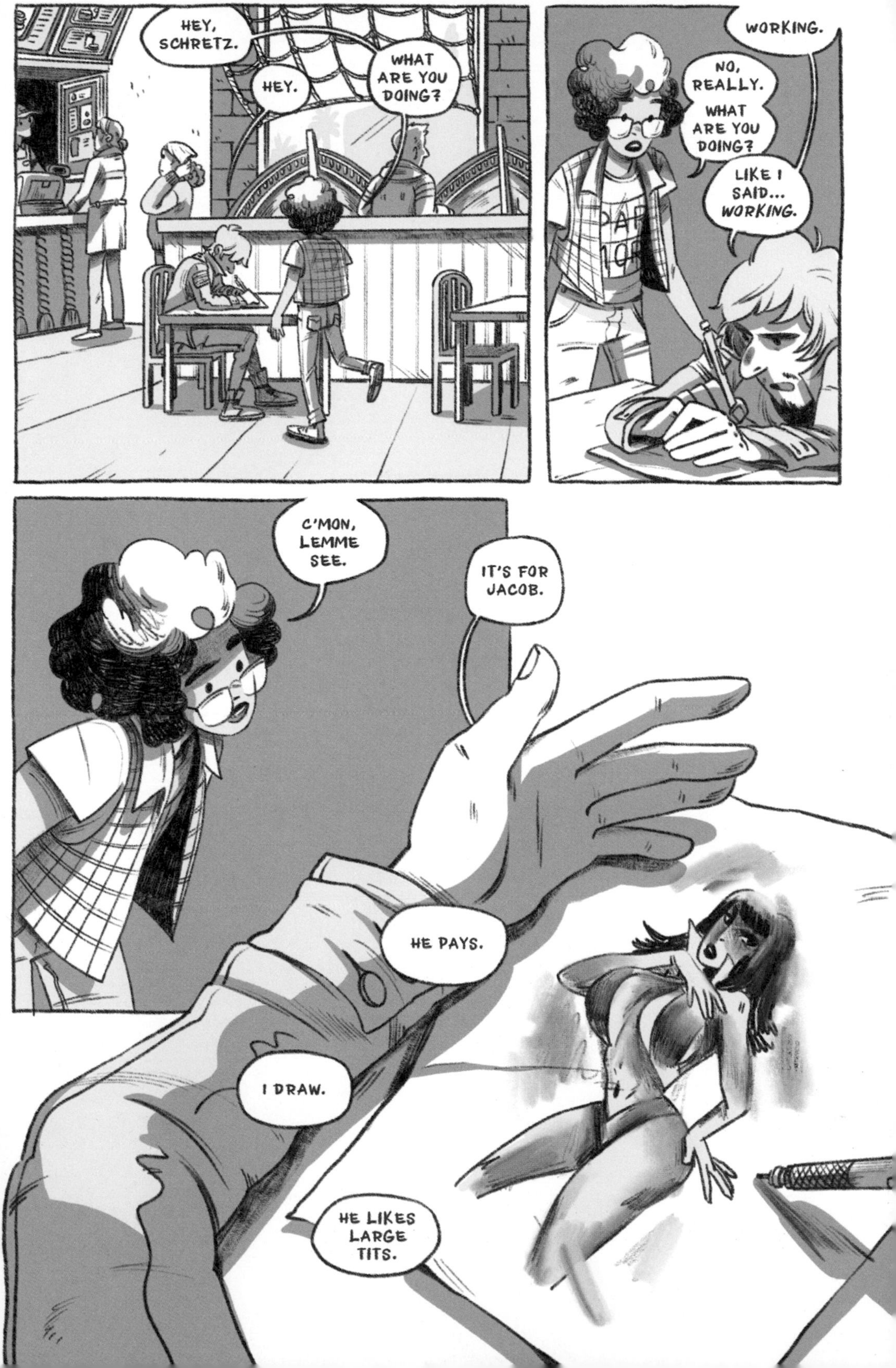
HEY, SCHRETZ.
HEY.
WHAT ARE YOU DOING?
WORKING.
NO, REALLY.
WHAT ARE YOU DOING?
LIKE I SAID... WORKING.
C'MON, LEMME SEE.
IT'S FOR JACOB.
HE PAYS.
I DRAW.
HE LIKES LARGE TITS.

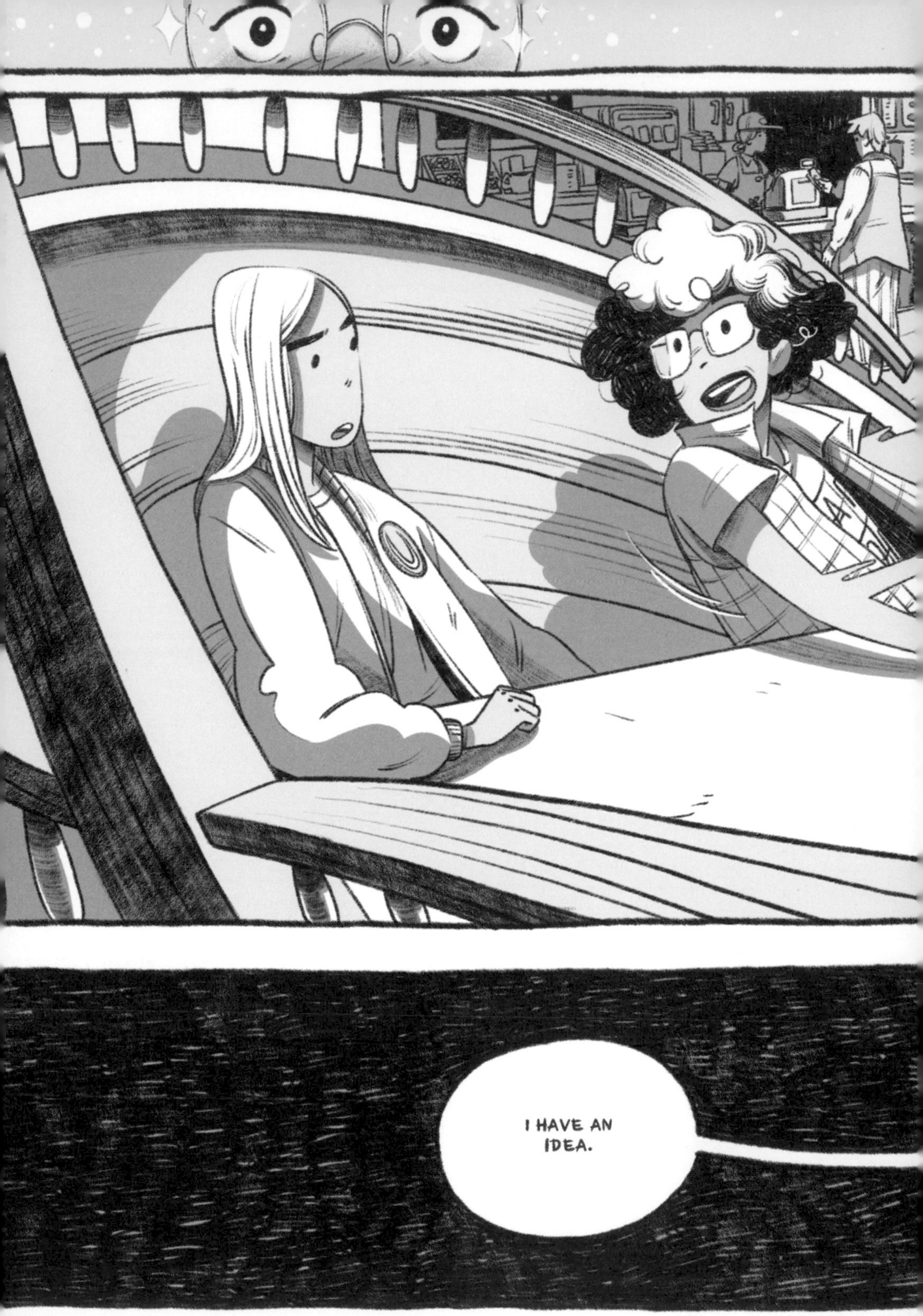
I HAVE AN IDEA.

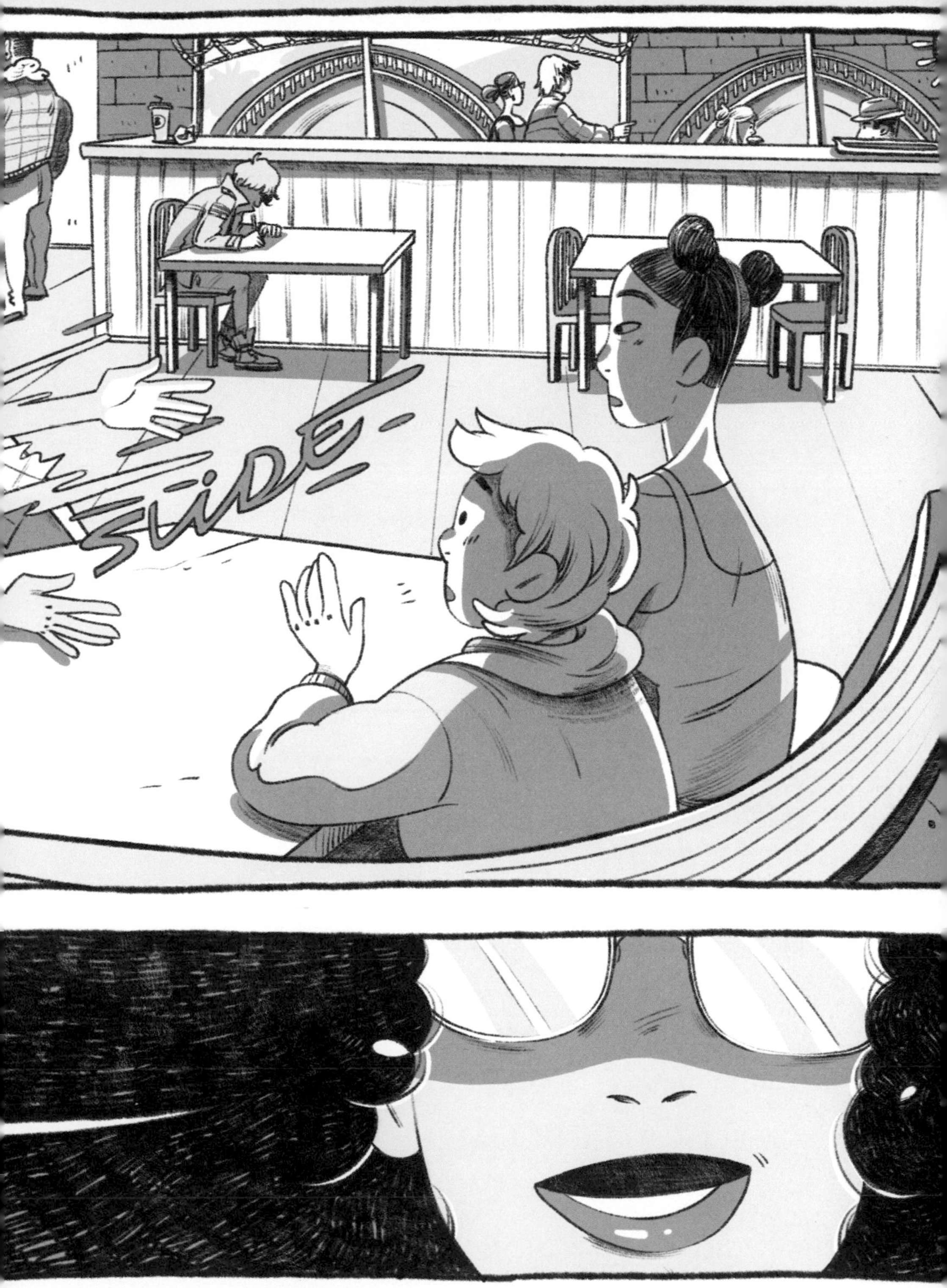
SLIDE

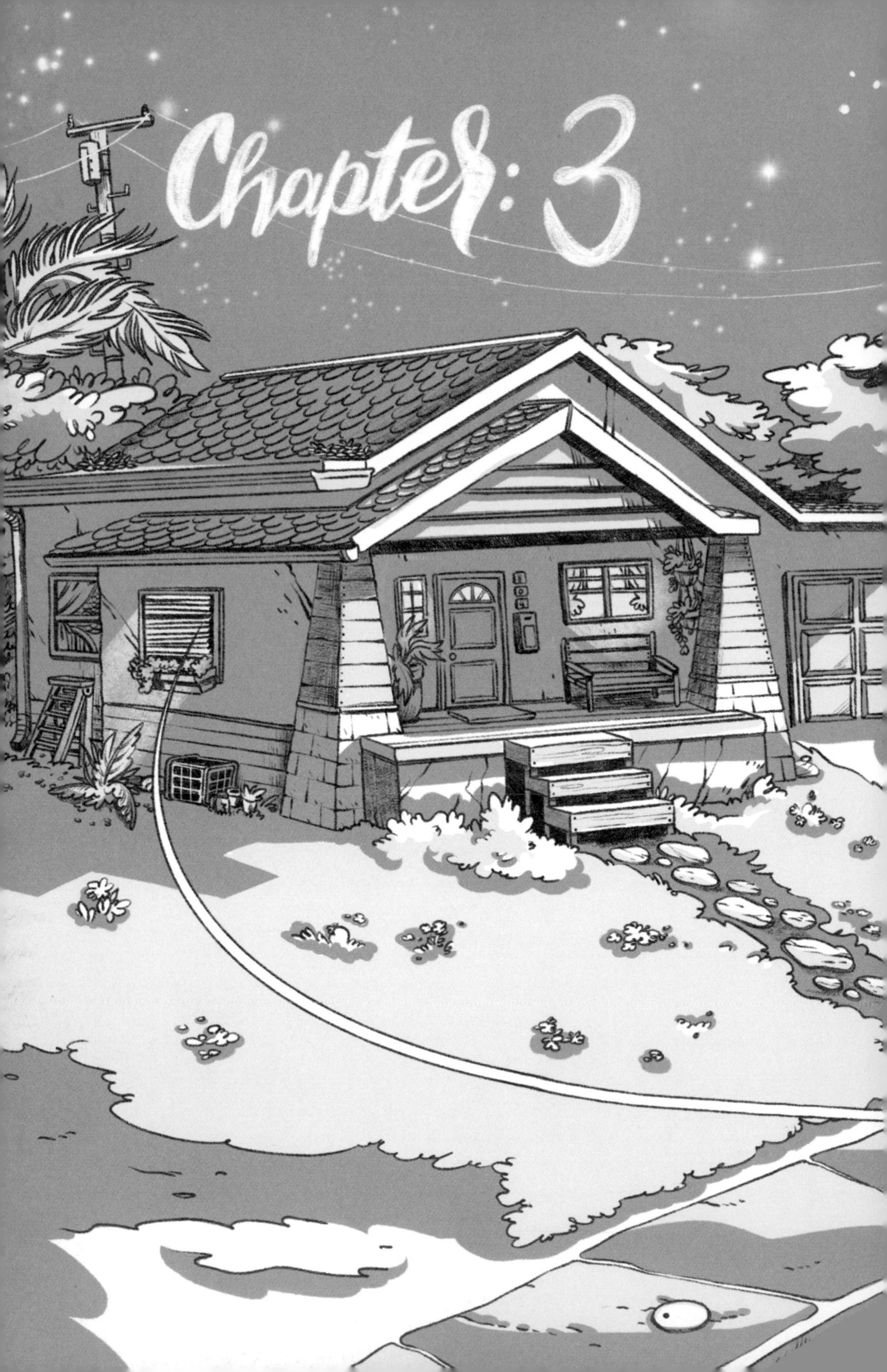
Chapter: 3

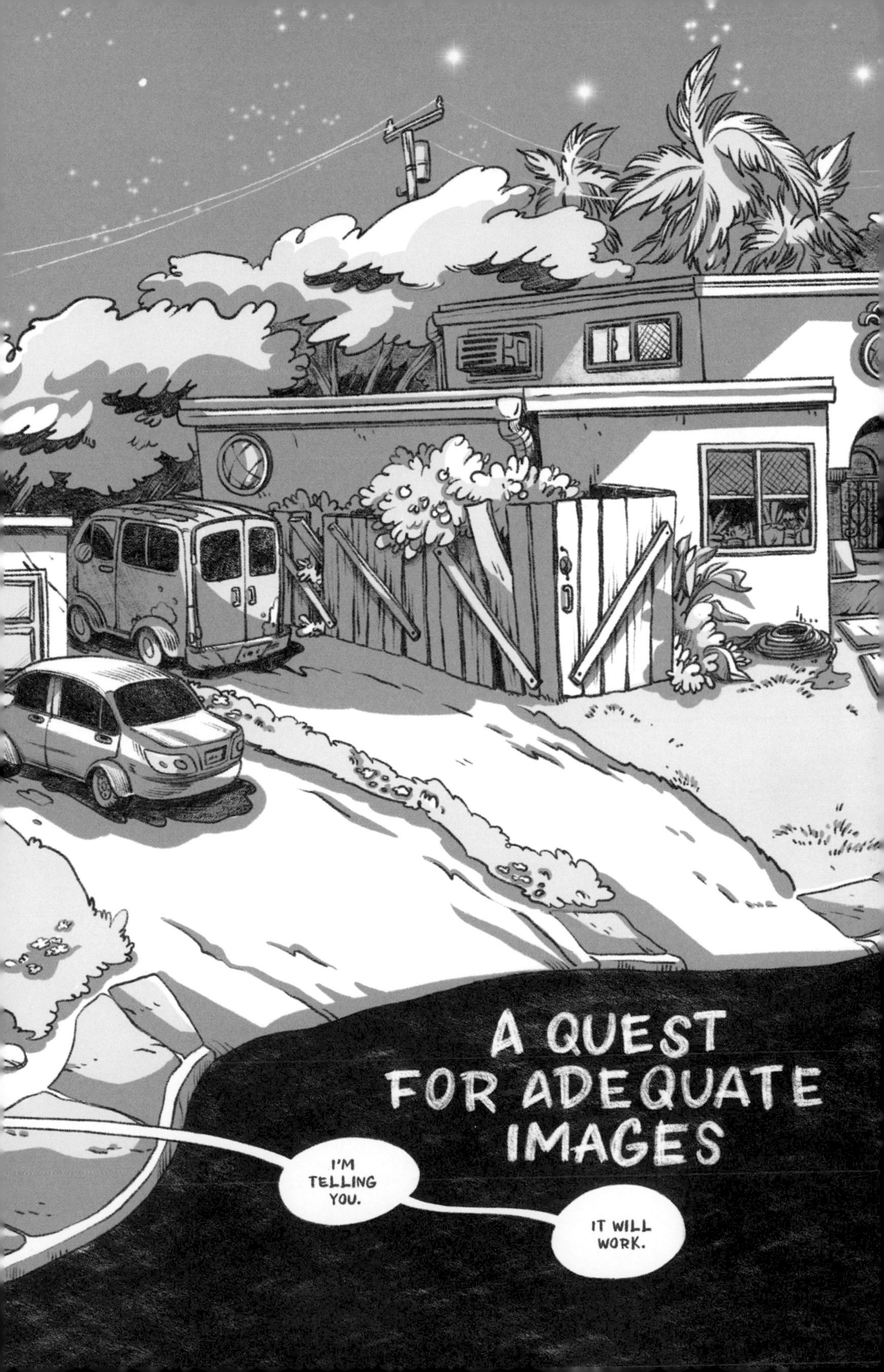
A QUEST FOR ADEQUATE IMAGES
I'M TELLING YOU.
IT WILL WORK.

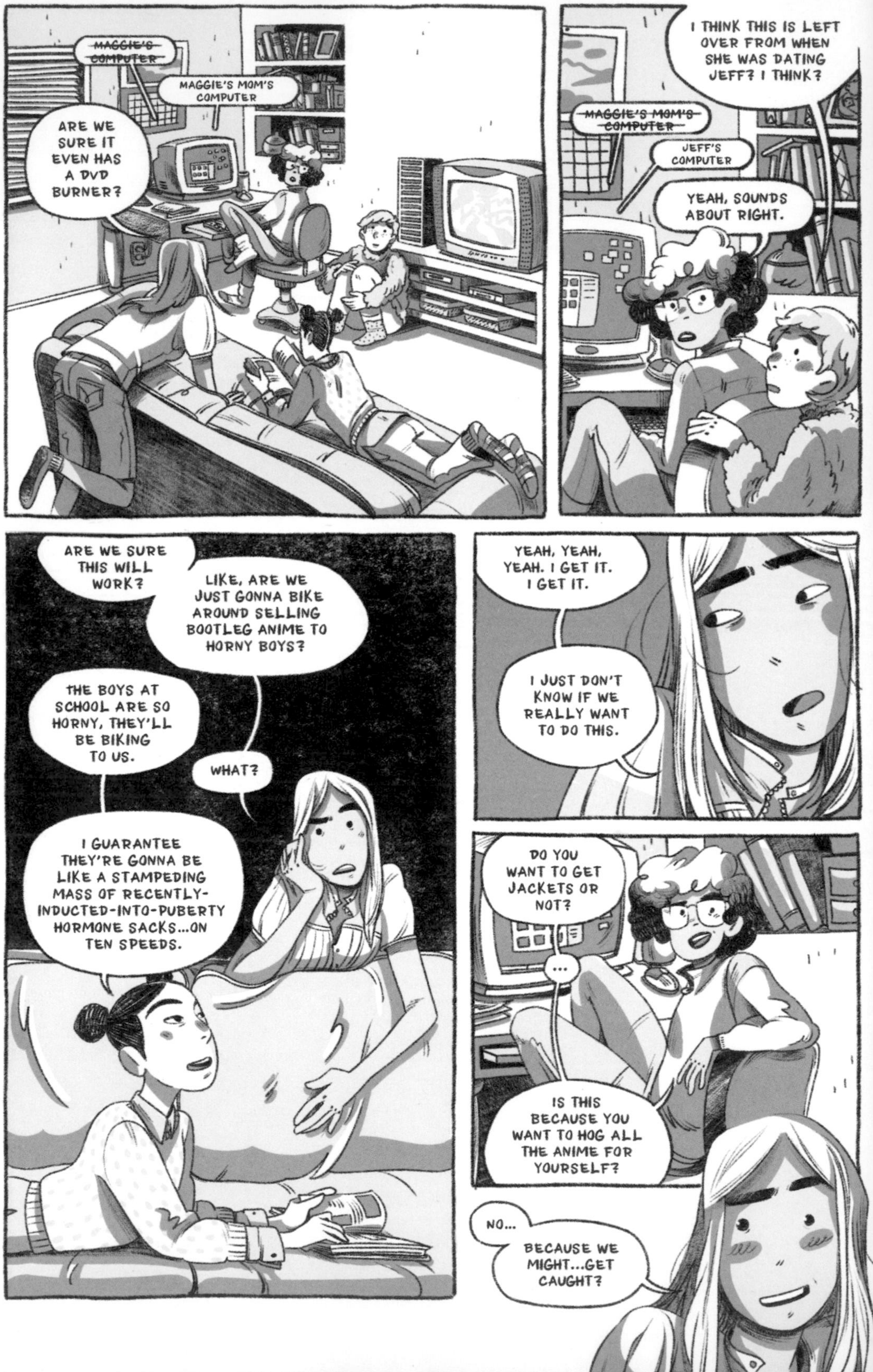

MAGGIE'S COMPUTER
MAGGIE'S MOM'S COMPUTER
ARE WE SURE IT EVEN HAS A DVD BURNER?
I THINK THIS IS LEFT OVER FROM WHEN SHE WAS DATING JEFF? I THINK?
MAGGIE'S MOM'S COMPUTER
JEFF'S COMPUTER
YEAH, SOUNDS ABOUT RIGHT.
ARE WE SURE THIS WILL WORK?
LIKE, ARE WE JUST GONNA BIKE AROUND SELLING BOOTLEG ANIME TO HORNY BOYS?
THE BOYS AT SCHOOL ARE SO HORNY, THEY'LL BE BIKING TO US.
WHAT?
I GUARANTEE THEY'RE GONNA BE LIKE A STAMPEDING MASS OF RECENTLY-INDUCTED-INTO-PUBERTY HORMONE SACKS...ON TEN SPEEDS.
YEAH, YEAH, YEAH. I GET IT. I GET IT.
I JUST DON'T KNOW IF WE REALLY WANT TO DO THIS.
DO YOU WANT TO GET JACKETS OR NOT?
...
IS THIS BECAUSE YOU WANT TO HOG ALL THE ANIME FOR YOURSELF?
NO...
BECAUSE WE MIGHT...GET CAUGHT?

A BRIEF HISTORY OF KELLY'S COMPLEX RELATIONSHIP WITH CHRISTIANITY ✝

KELLY WAS RAISED AS A CHRISTIAN. A METHODIST, TO BE EXACT. WHEN HER PATERNAL GRANDPARENTS IMMIGRATED FROM SAUDI ARABIA, THEY BEFRIENDED A GROUP OF METHODISTS IN NORTH DAKOTA. HER FATHER BECAME DEEPLY INVOLVED IN THE CHURCH AND PASSED THAT ON TO KELLY. IT WAS GOOD SOMETIMES...AND NOT GOOD OTHER TIMES.

ATTENDING FOREST HILLS HAS BEEN GOOD FOR KELLY BECAUSE IT'S NON-DENOMINATIONAL. IT'S ALLOWED HER A BIT MORE ELASTICITY THAN SHE PREVIOUSLY WAS ALLOWED IN HER FATHER'S STRICT HOUSEHOLD.

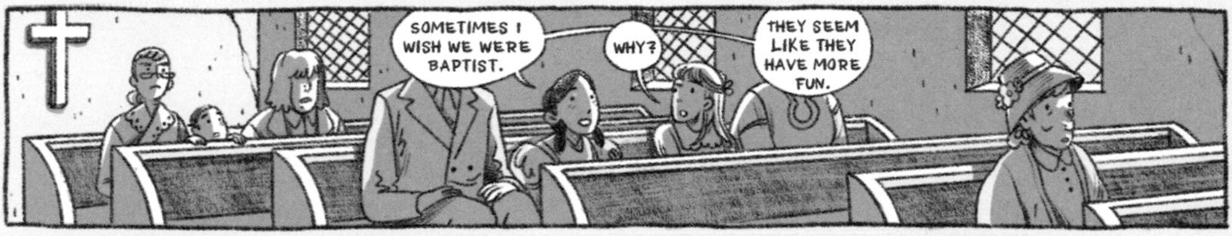
SOMETIMES I WISH WE WERE BAPTIST.
WHY?
THEY SEEM LIKE THEY HAVE MORE FUN.

THESE DAYS KELLY TRIES NOT TO THINK ABOUT GOD. AS MUCH AS YOU CAN IN A SCHOOL THAT'S ALL ABOUT...WELL, GOD. OCCASIONALLY, SHE STILL GETS PANGS OF GUILT FOR SWEARING, KISSING BROOKE, AND EVEN...WATCHING ANIME.

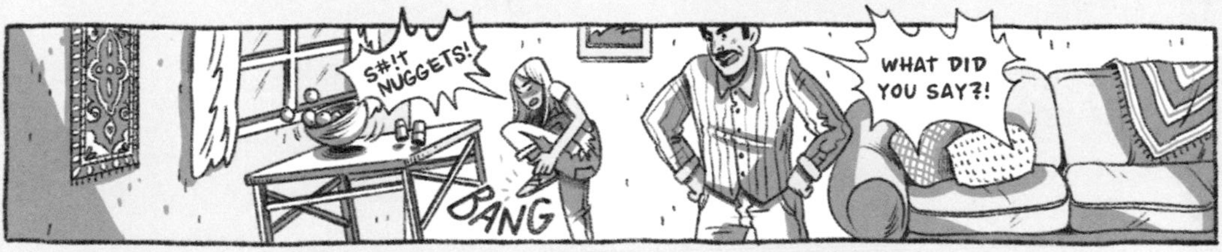
S#!T NUGGETS!
BANG
WHAT DID YOU SAY?!

THE BIGGEST TURNING POINT FOR KELLY WAS WHEN SHE FIRST KISSED HELEN MACGUIRE IN EIGHTH GRADE...AND THE WORLD DIDN'T END.

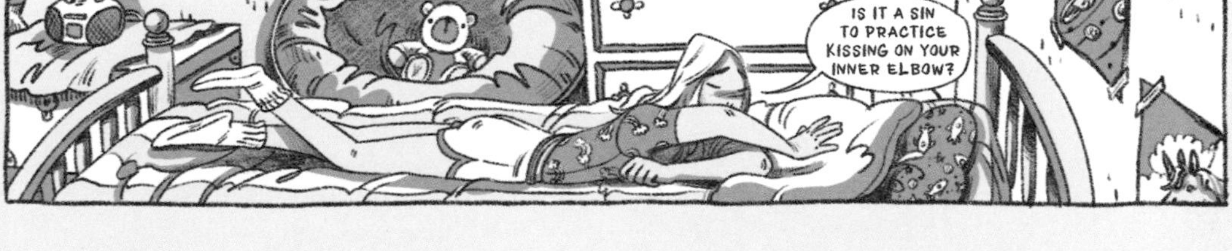
IS IT A SIN TO PRACTICE KISSING ON YOUR INNER ELBOW?

THERE'S STILL A DARK NIGHT OR TWO WHERE SHE PRAYS TO THE BIG G, BUT THE ONE THING SHE'S CERTAIN IS THAT HE, SHE, OR IT DOESN'T GIVE TWO S#!TS IF SHE HAS PREMARITAL SEX.

ALSO: SHE WANTS TO HOG ALL THE ANIME FOR HERSELF...*JUST A LITTLE.*

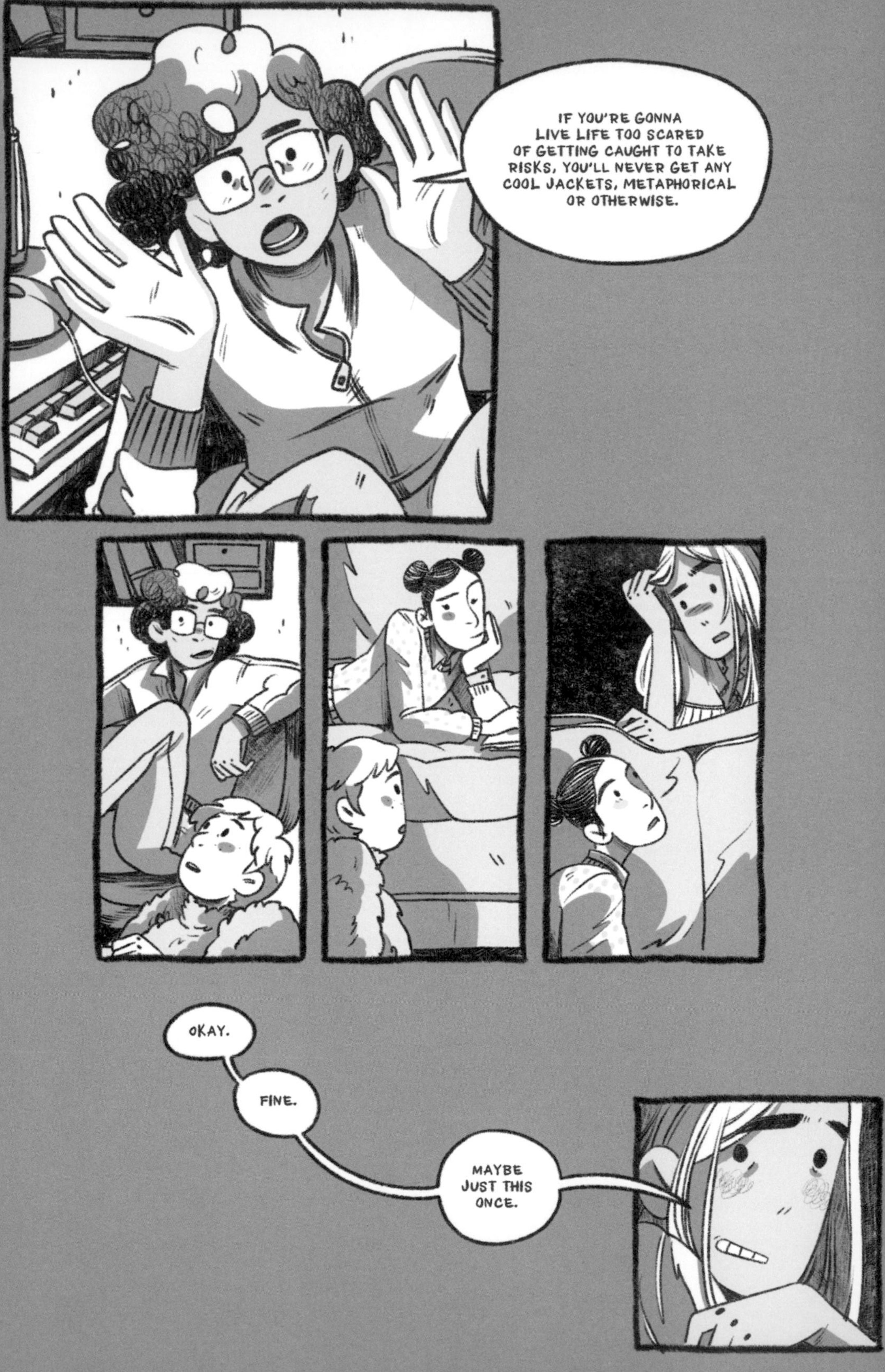
IF YOU'RE GONNA LIVE LIFE TOO SCARED OF GETTING CAUGHT TO TAKE RISKS, YOU'LL NEVER GET ANY COOL JACKETS, METAPHORICAL OR OTHERWISE.
OKAY.
FINE.
MAYBE JUST THIS ONCE.

BURN TO MEDIA - {DISC}
BURN OPTIONS
BURN PROGESS
BURN SPEED: 16X(22, 160 KB/S)
NUMBER OF COPIES 1
BURN METHOD
DISC AT ONCE
SESSION AT ONCE
BURN OPTIONS
USE BUFFER PROTECTION
SIMULATE BURNING PROCESS
MODE2XA INSTEAD OF MODE 1
CACHE COMPILATION BEFORE BURNING
SHUTDOWN COMPUTER AFTER COMPLETION
FINALIZE DISC
EJECT DISC AFTER BURNING
VERIFY DATA AFTER BURNING
BURN DISC
CANCEL
CLICK

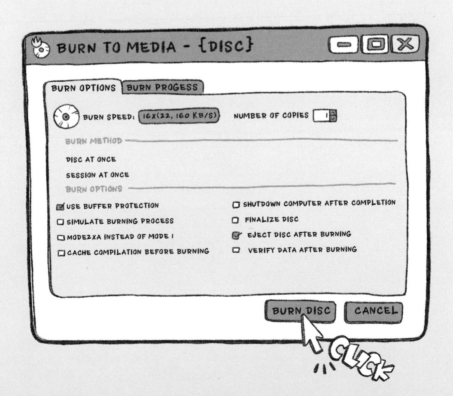

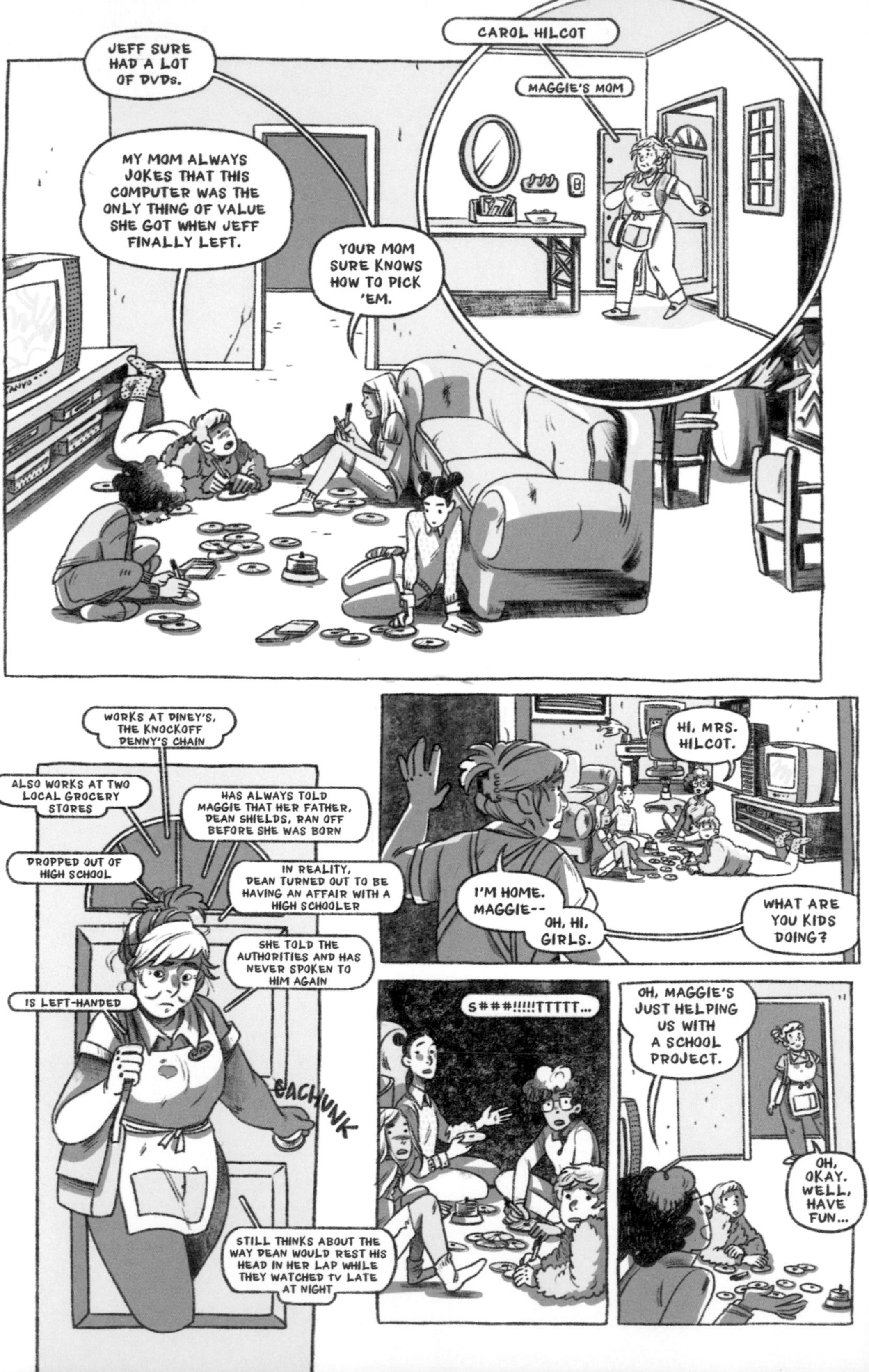
JEFF SURE HAD A LOT OF DVDs.
MY MOM ALWAYS JOKES THAT THIS COMPUTER WAS THE ONLY THING OF VALUE SHE GOT WHEN JEFF FINALLY LEFT.
YOUR MOM SURE KNOWS HOW TO PICK 'EM.
CAROL HILCOT
MAGGIE'S MOM
WORKS AT DINEY'S, THE KNOCKOFF DENNY'S CHAIN
ALSO WORKS AT TWO LOCAL GROCERY STORES
HAS ALWAYS TOLD MAGGIE THAT HER FATHER, DEAN SHIELDS, RAN OFF BEFORE SHE WAS BORN
DROPPED OUT OF HIGH SCHOOL
IN REALITY, DEAN TURNED OUT TO BE HAVING AN AFFAIR WITH A HIGH SCHOOLER
SHE TOLD THE AUTHORITIES AND HAS NEVER SPOKEN TO HIM AGAIN
IS LEFT-HANDED
CACHUNK
STILL THINKS ABOUT THE WAY DEAN WOULD REST HIS HEAD IN HER LAP WHILE THEY WATCHED TV LATE AT NIGHT
HI, MRS. HILCOT.
I'M HOME. MAGGIE--
OH, HI, GIRLS.
WHAT ARE YOU KIDS DOING?
S###!!!!!TTTTT...
OH, MAGGIE'S JUST HELPING US WITH A SCHOOL PROJECT.
OH, OKAY. WELL, HAVE FUN...

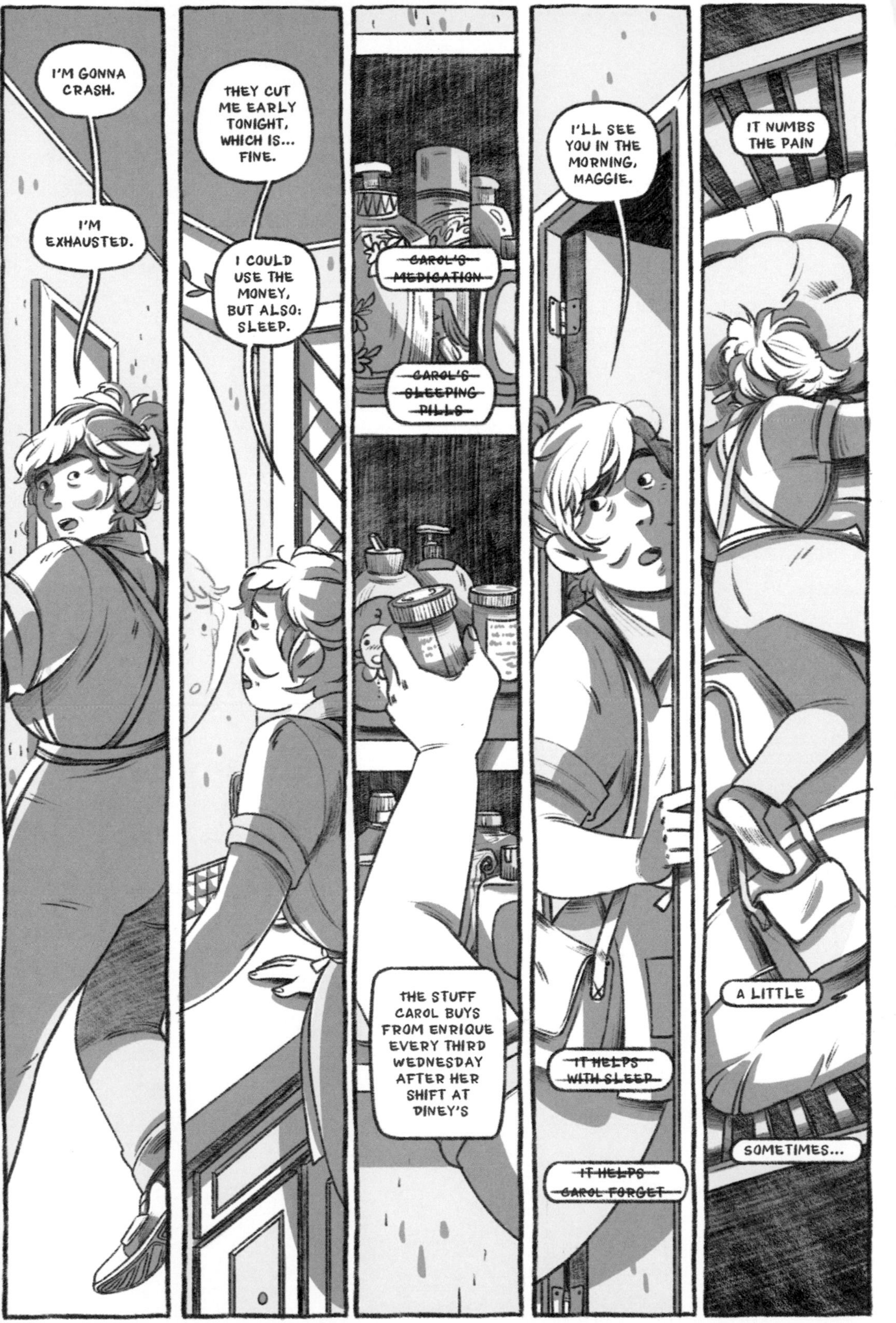

I'M GONNA CRASH.
I'M EXHAUSTED.
THEY CUT ME EARLY TONIGHT, WHICH IS... FINE.
I COULD USE THE MONEY, BUT ALSO: SLEEP.
~~CAROL'S MEDICATION~~
~~CAROL'S SLEEPING PILLS~~
THE STUFF CAROL BUYS FROM ENRIQUE EVERY THIRD WEDNESDAY AFTER HER SHIFT AT DINEY'S
I'LL SEE YOU IN THE MORNING, MAGGIE.
~~IT HELPS WITH SLEEP~~
~~IT HELPS CAROL FORGET~~
IT NUMBS THE PAIN
A LITTLE
SOMETIMES...

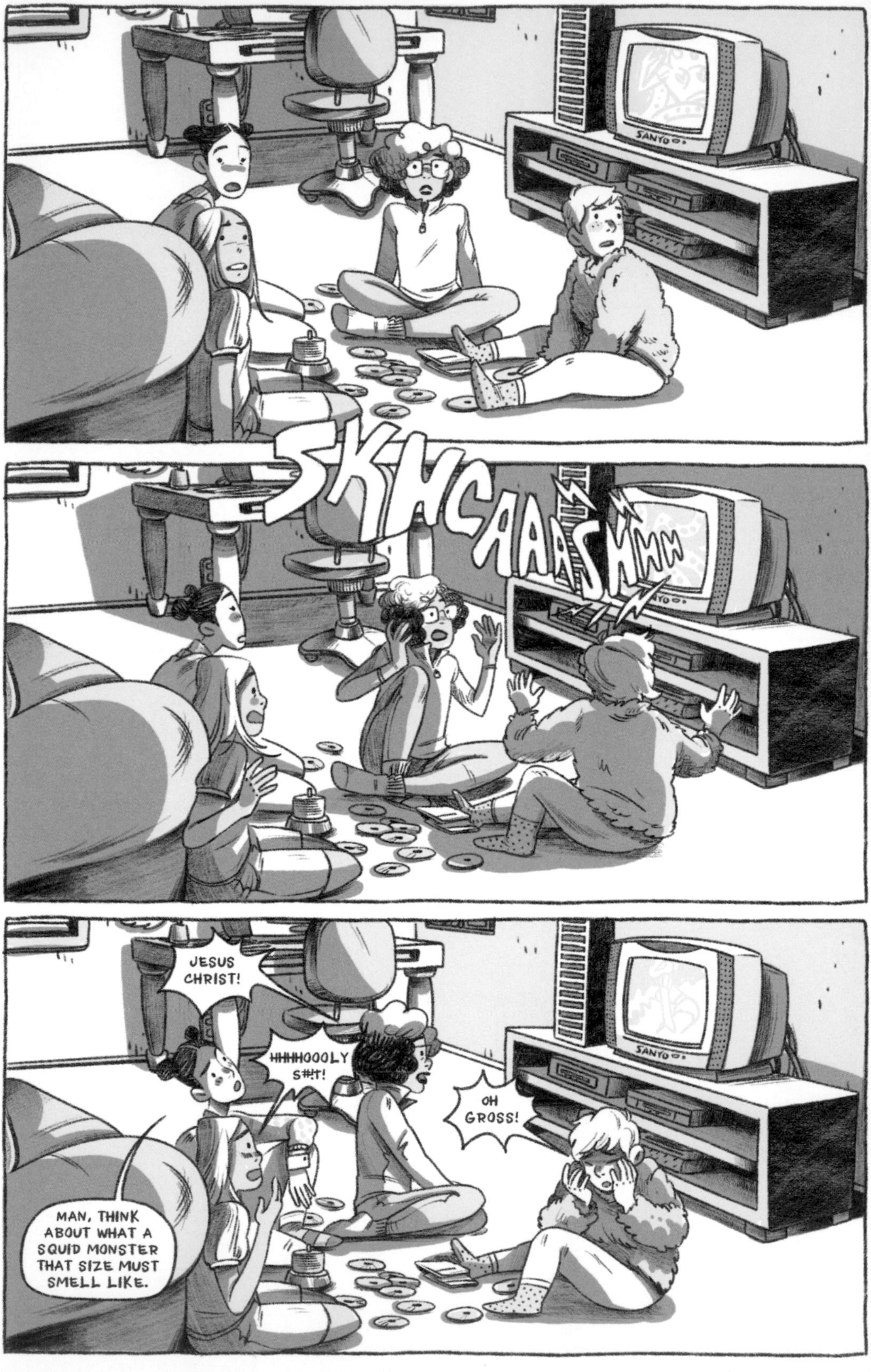
SKNCAAASHHH
JESUS CHRIST!
HHHHOOOLY S#!T!
OH GROSS!
MAN, THINK ABOUT WHAT A SQUID MONSTER THAT SIZE MUST SMELL LIKE.

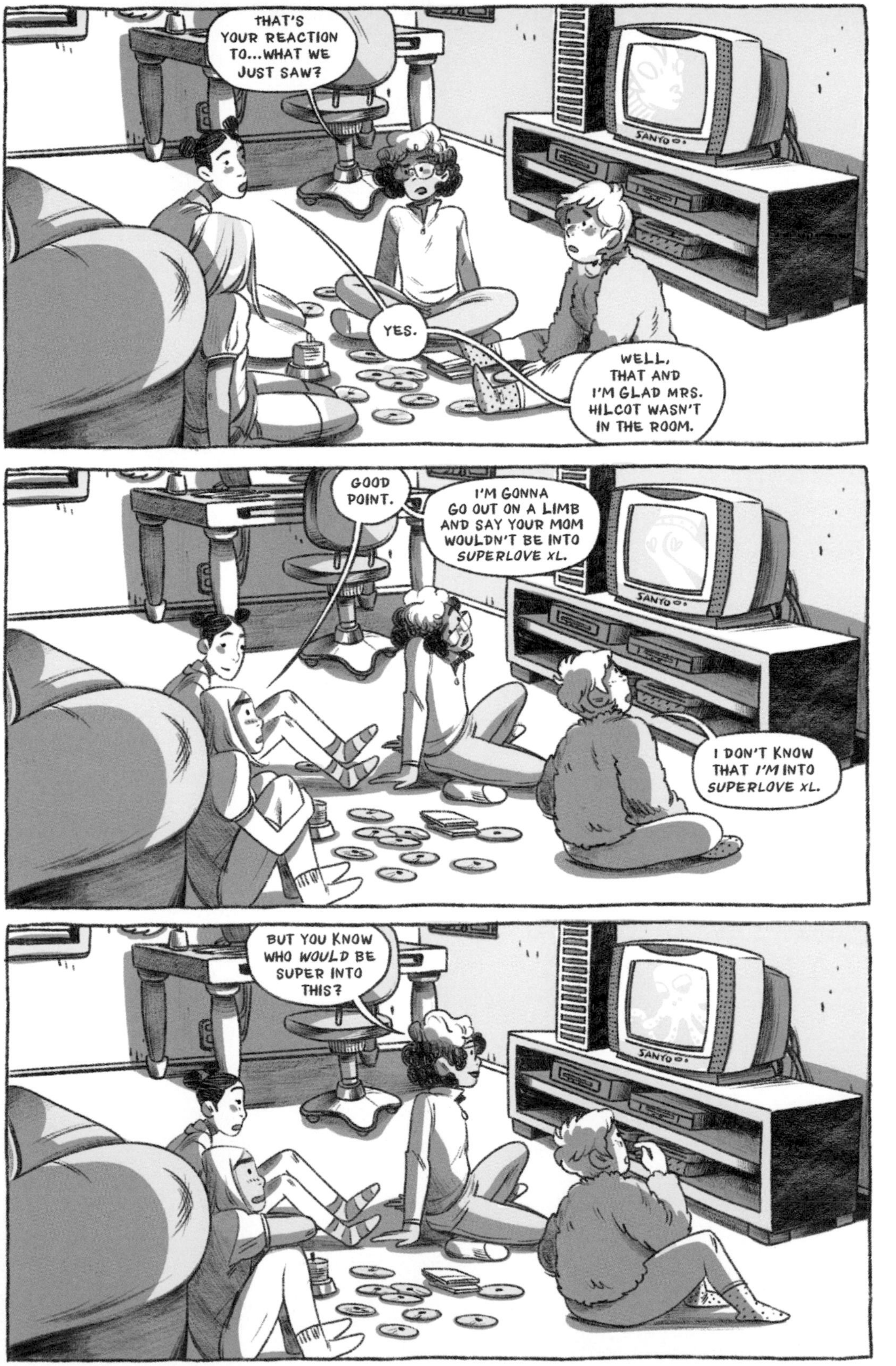
THAT'S YOUR REACTION TO...WHAT WE JUST SAW?
YES.
WELL, THAT AND I'M GLAD MRS. HILCOT WASN'T IN THE ROOM.
GOOD POINT.
I'M GONNA GO OUT ON A LIMB AND SAY YOUR MOM WOULDN'T BE INTO *SUPERLOVE XL*.
I DON'T KNOW THAT *I'M* INTO *SUPERLOVE XL*.
BUT YOU KNOW WHO *WOULD* BE SUPER INTO THIS?
SANYO

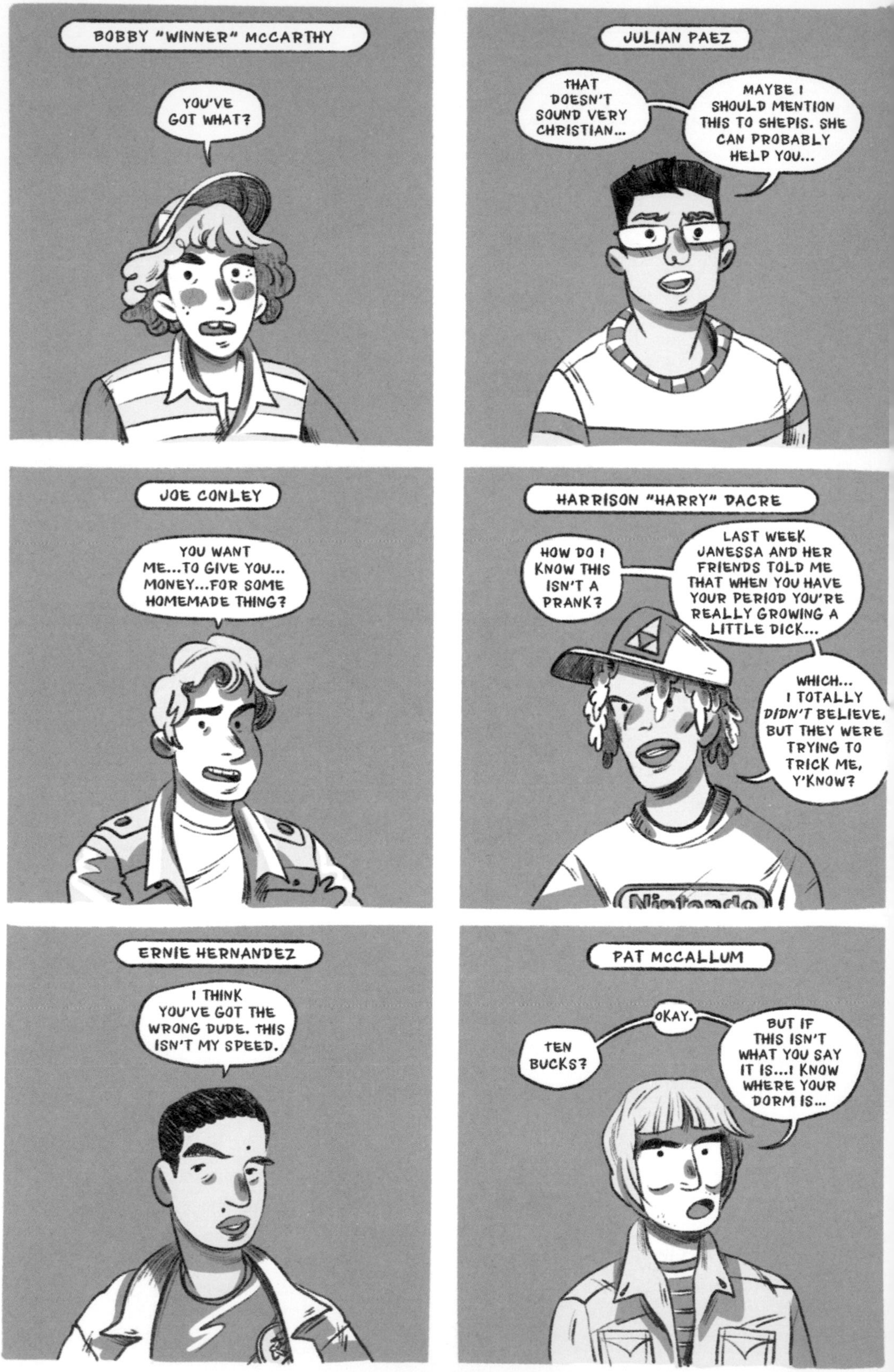
BOBBY "WINNER" McCARTHY
YOU'VE GOT WHAT?
JULIAN PAEZ
THAT DOESN'T SOUND VERY CHRISTIAN...
MAYBE I SHOULD MENTION THIS TO SHEPIS. SHE CAN PROBABLY HELP YOU...
JOE CONLEY
YOU WANT ME...TO GIVE YOU... MONEY...FOR SOME HOMEMADE THING?
HARRISON "HARRY" DACRE
HOW DO I KNOW THIS ISN'T A PRANK?
LAST WEEK JANESSA AND HER FRIENDS TOLD ME THAT WHEN YOU HAVE YOUR PERIOD YOU'RE REALLY GROWING A LITTLE DICK...
WHICH... I TOTALLY *DIDN'T* BELIEVE, BUT THEY WERE TRYING TO TRICK ME, Y'KNOW?
ERNIE HERNANDEZ
I THINK YOU'VE GOT THE WRONG DUDE. THIS ISN'T MY SPEED.
PAT McCALLUM
TEN BUCKS?
OKAY.
BUT IF THIS ISN'T WHAT YOU SAY IT IS...I KNOW WHERE YOUR DORM IS...

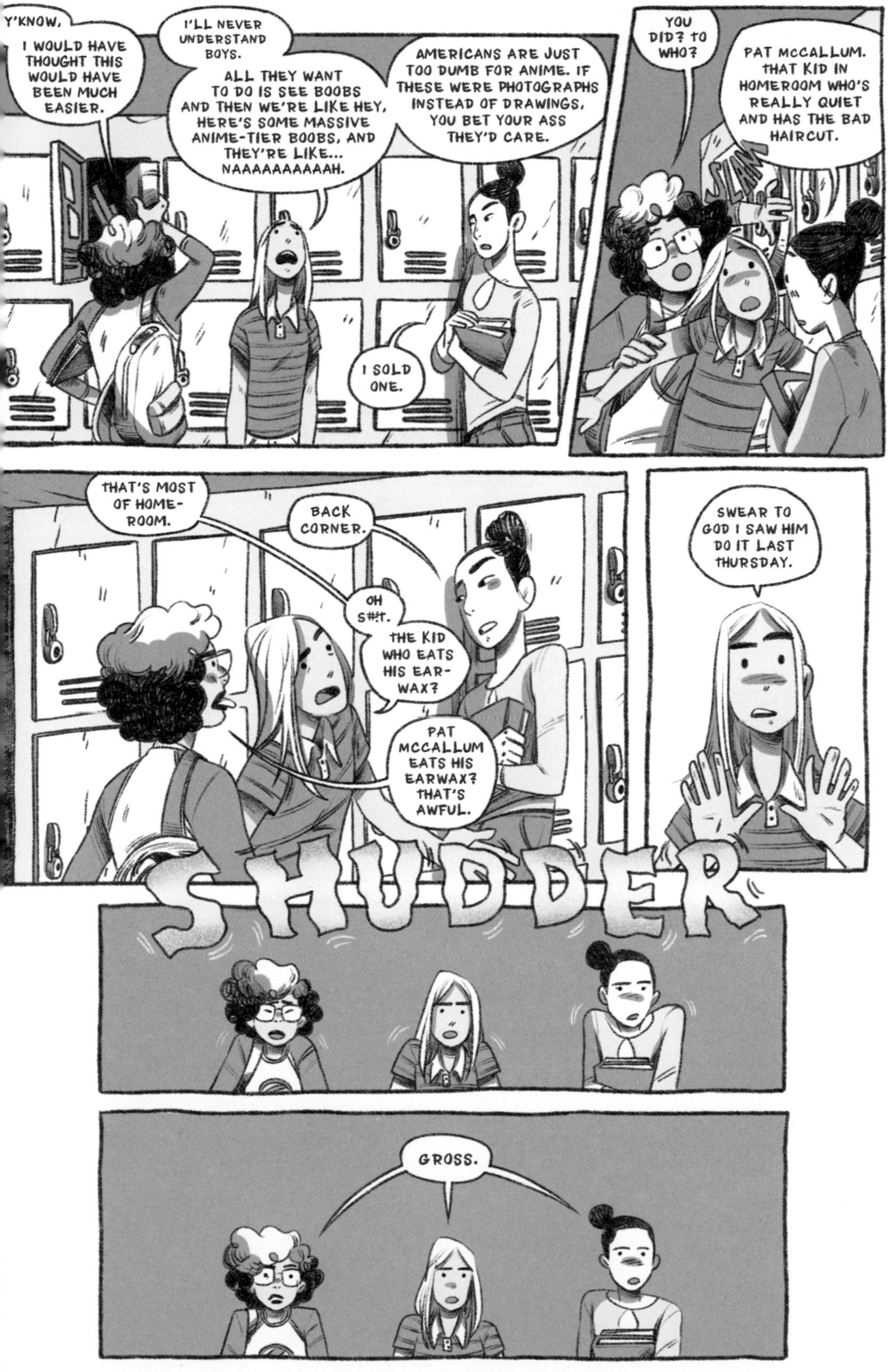
Y'KNOW,
I WOULD HAVE THOUGHT THIS WOULD HAVE BEEN MUCH EASIER.
I'LL NEVER UNDERSTAND BOYS.
ALL THEY WANT TO DO IS SEE BOOBS AND THEN WE'RE LIKE HEY, HERE'S SOME MASSIVE ANIME-TIER BOOBS, AND THEY'RE LIKE... NAAAAAAAAAAH.
AMERICANS ARE JUST TOO DUMB FOR ANIME. IF THESE WERE PHOTOGRAPHS INSTEAD OF DRAWINGS, YOU BET YOUR ASS THEY'D CARE.
I SOLD ONE.
YOU DID? TO WHO?
SLAM
PAT McCALLUM. THAT KID IN HOMEROOM WHO'S REALLY QUIET AND HAS THE BAD HAIRCUT.
THAT'S MOST OF HOME-ROOM.
BACK CORNER.
OH S#!T.
THE KID WHO EATS HIS EAR-WAX?
PAT McCALLUM EATS HIS EARWAX? THAT'S AWFUL.
SWEAR TO GOD I SAW HIM DO IT LAST THURSDAY.
SHUDDER
GROSS.

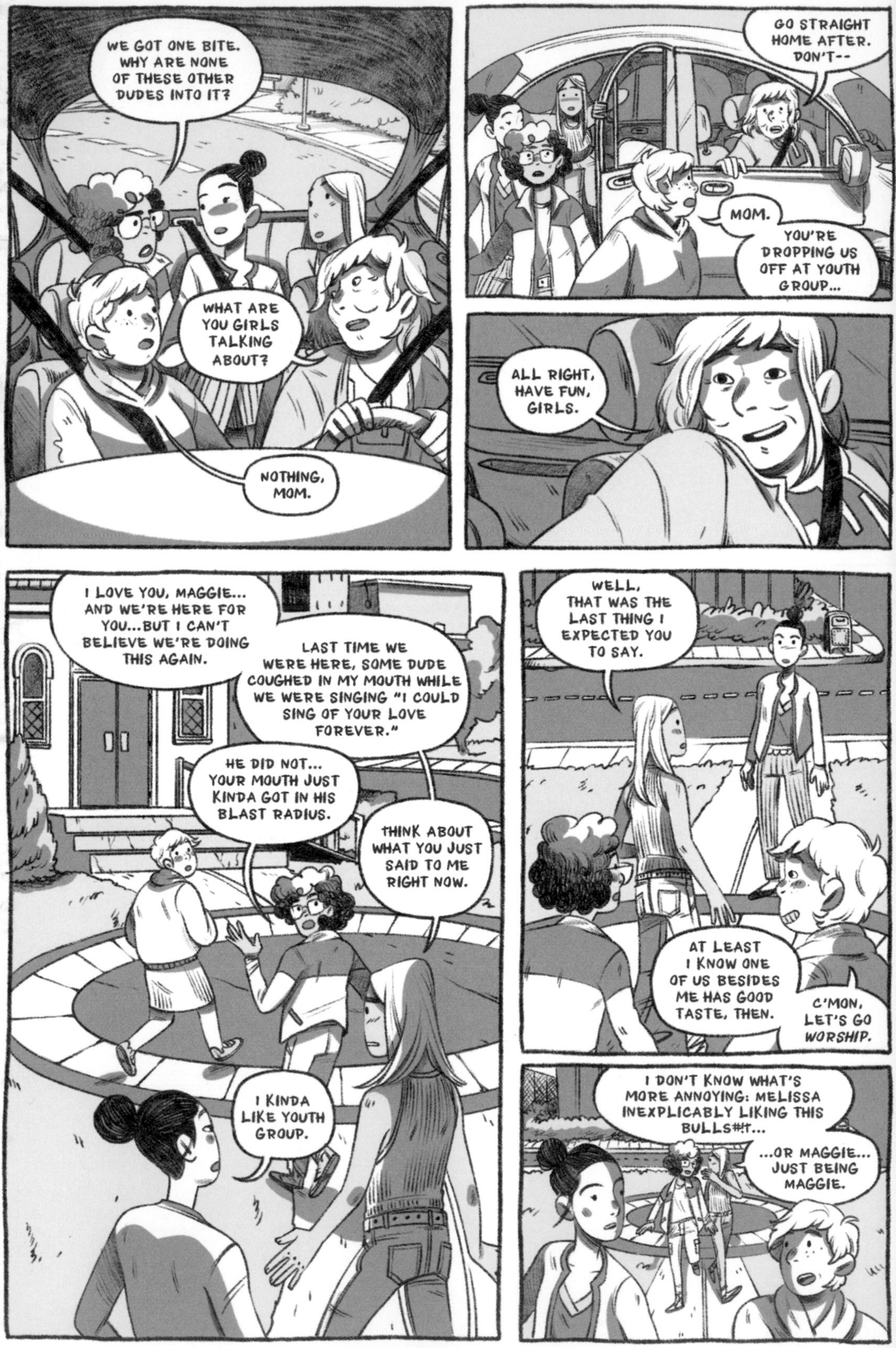
WE GOT ONE BITE. WHY ARE NONE OF THESE OTHER DUDES INTO IT?
WHAT ARE YOU GIRLS TALKING ABOUT?
NOTHING, MOM.
GO STRAIGHT HOME AFTER. DON'T--
MOM.
YOU'RE DROPPING US OFF AT YOUTH GROUP...
ALL RIGHT, HAVE FUN, GIRLS.
I LOVE YOU, MAGGIE... AND WE'RE HERE FOR YOU...BUT I CAN'T BELIEVE WE'RE DOING THIS AGAIN.
LAST TIME WE WERE HERE, SOME DUDE COUGHED IN MY MOUTH WHILE WE WERE SINGING "I COULD SING OF YOUR LOVE FOREVER."
HE DID NOT... YOUR MOUTH JUST KINDA GOT IN HIS BLAST RADIUS.
THINK ABOUT WHAT YOU JUST SAID TO ME RIGHT NOW.
I KINDA LIKE YOUTH GROUP.
WELL, THAT WAS THE LAST THING I EXPECTED YOU TO SAY.
AT LEAST I KNOW ONE OF US BESIDES ME HAS GOOD TASTE, THEN.
C'MON, LET'S GO *WORSHIP.*
I DON'T KNOW WHAT'S MORE ANNOYING: MELISSA INEXPLICABLY LIKING THIS BULLS#!T...
...OR MAGGIE... JUST BEING MAGGIE.

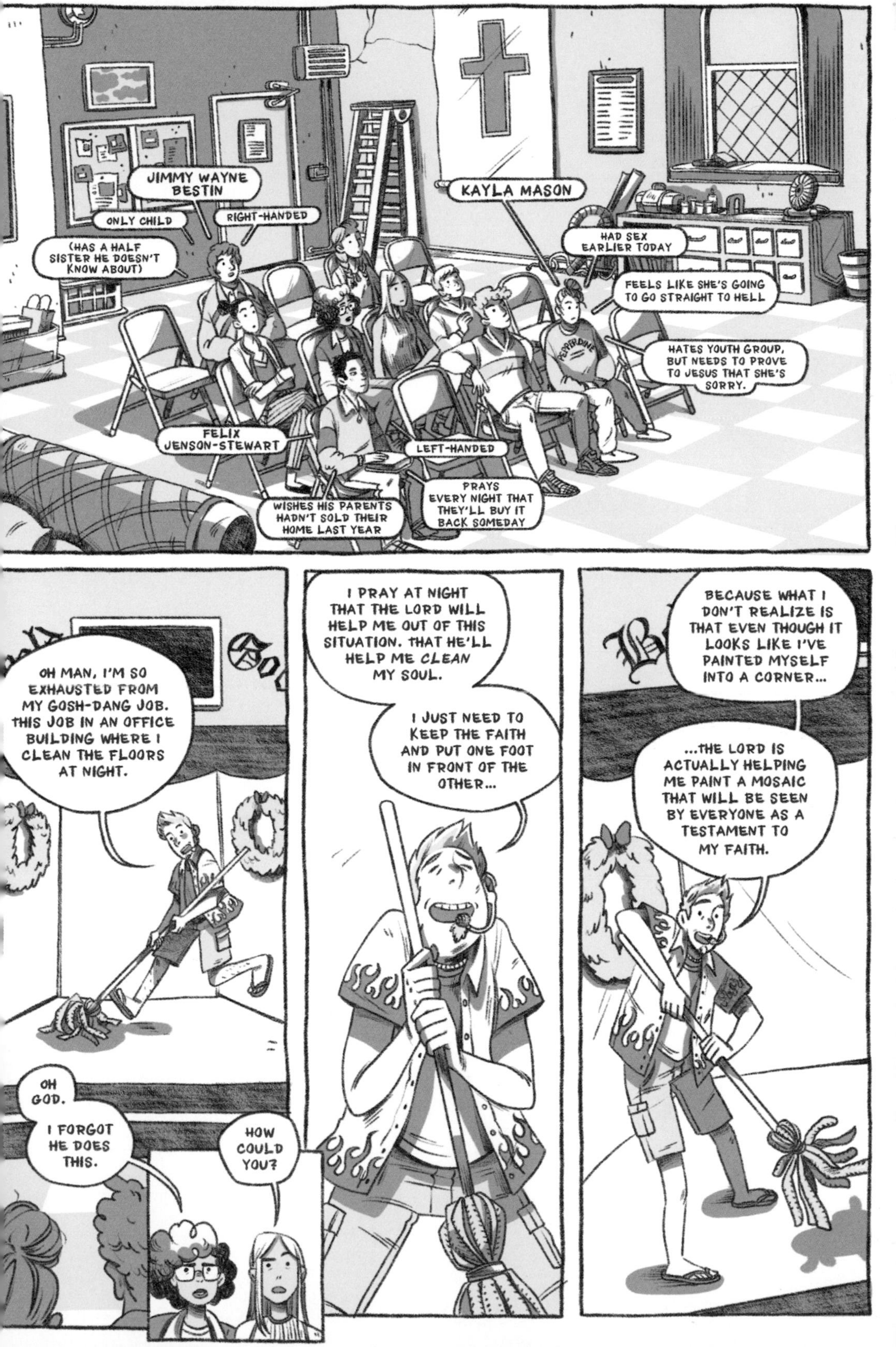
JIMMY WAYNE BESTIN
ONLY CHILD
(HAS A HALF SISTER HE DOESN'T KNOW ABOUT)
RIGHT-HANDED
KAYLA MASON
HAD SEX EARLIER TODAY
FEELS LIKE SHE'S GOING TO GO STRAIGHT TO HELL
HATES YOUTH GROUP, BUT NEEDS TO PROVE TO JESUS THAT SHE'S SORRY.
PEPPERDINE
FELIX JENSON-STEWART
LEFT-HANDED
WISHES HIS PARENTS HADN'T SOLD THEIR HOME LAST YEAR
PRAYS EVERY NIGHT THAT THEY'LL BUY IT BACK SOMEDAY
OH MAN, I'M SO EXHAUSTED FROM MY GOSH-DANG JOB. THIS JOB IN AN OFFICE BUILDING WHERE I CLEAN THE FLOORS AT NIGHT.
OH GOD.
I FORGOT HE DOES THIS.
HOW COULD YOU?
I PRAY AT NIGHT THAT THE LORD WILL HELP ME OUT OF THIS SITUATION. THAT HE'LL HELP ME *CLEAN* MY SOUL.
I JUST NEED TO KEEP THE FAITH AND PUT ONE FOOT IN FRONT OF THE OTHER...
BECAUSE WHAT I DON'T REALIZE IS THAT EVEN THOUGH IT LOOKS LIKE I'VE PAINTED MYSELF INTO A CORNER...
...THE LORD IS ACTUALLY HELPING ME PAINT A MOSAIC THAT WILL BE SEEN BY EVERYONE AS A TESTAMENT TO MY FAITH.

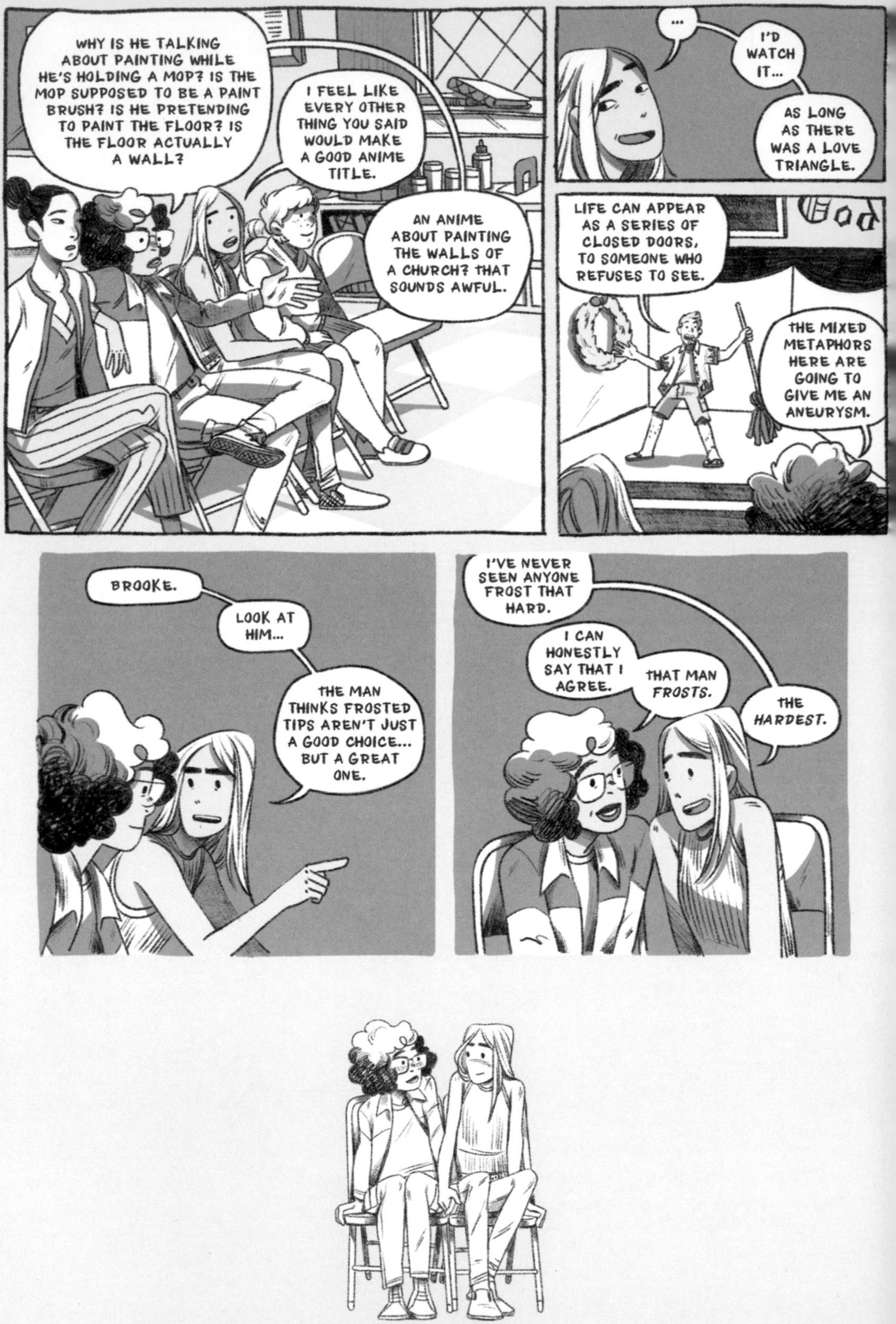
WHY IS HE TALKING ABOUT PAINTING WHILE HE'S HOLDING A MOP? IS THE MOP SUPPOSED TO BE A PAINT BRUSH? IS HE PRETENDING TO PAINT THE FLOOR? IS THE FLOOR ACTUALLY A WALL?
I FEEL LIKE EVERY OTHER THING YOU SAID WOULD MAKE A GOOD ANIME TITLE.
AN ANIME ABOUT PAINTING THE WALLS OF A CHURCH? THAT SOUNDS AWFUL.
...
I'D WATCH IT...
AS LONG AS THERE WAS A LOVE TRIANGLE.
LIFE CAN APPEAR AS A SERIES OF CLOSED DOORS, TO SOMEONE WHO REFUSES TO SEE.
THE MIXED METAPHORS HERE ARE GOING TO GIVE ME AN ANEURYSM.
BROOKE.
LOOK AT HIM...
THE MAN THINKS FROSTED TIPS AREN'T JUST A GOOD CHOICE... BUT A GREAT ONE.
I'VE NEVER SEEN ANYONE FROST THAT HARD.
I CAN HONESTLY SAY THAT I AGREE.
THAT MAN *FROSTS*.
THE *HARDEST*.

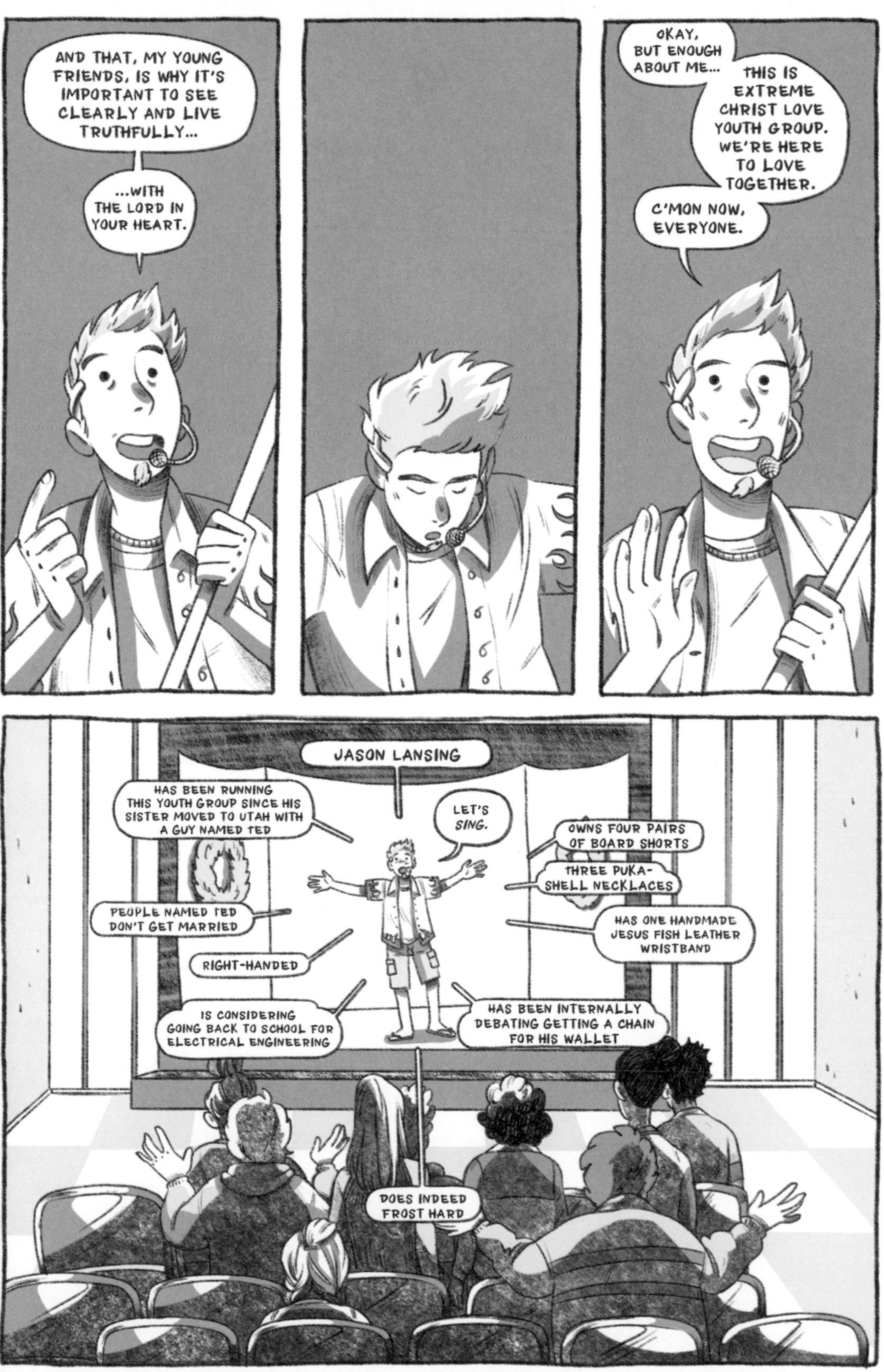
AND THAT, MY YOUNG FRIENDS, IS WHY IT'S IMPORTANT TO SEE CLEARLY AND LIVE TRUTHFULLY...
...WITH THE LORD IN YOUR HEART.
OKAY, BUT ENOUGH ABOUT ME...
THIS IS EXTREME CHRIST LOVE YOUTH GROUP. WE'RE HERE TO LOVE TOGETHER.
C'MON NOW, EVERYONE.
JASON LANSING
HAS BEEN RUNNING THIS YOUTH GROUP SINCE HIS SISTER MOVED TO UTAH WITH A GUY NAMED TED
LET'S SING.
OWNS FOUR PAIRS OF BOARD SHORTS
THREE PUKA-SHELL NECKLACES
PEOPLE NAMED TED DON'T GET MARRIED
HAS ONE HANDMADE JESUS FISH LEATHER WRISTBAND
RIGHT-HANDED
IS CONSIDERING GOING BACK TO SCHOOL FOR ELECTRICAL ENGINEERING
HAS BEEN INTERNALLY DEBATING GETTING A CHAIN FOR HIS WALLET
DOES INDEED FROST HARD

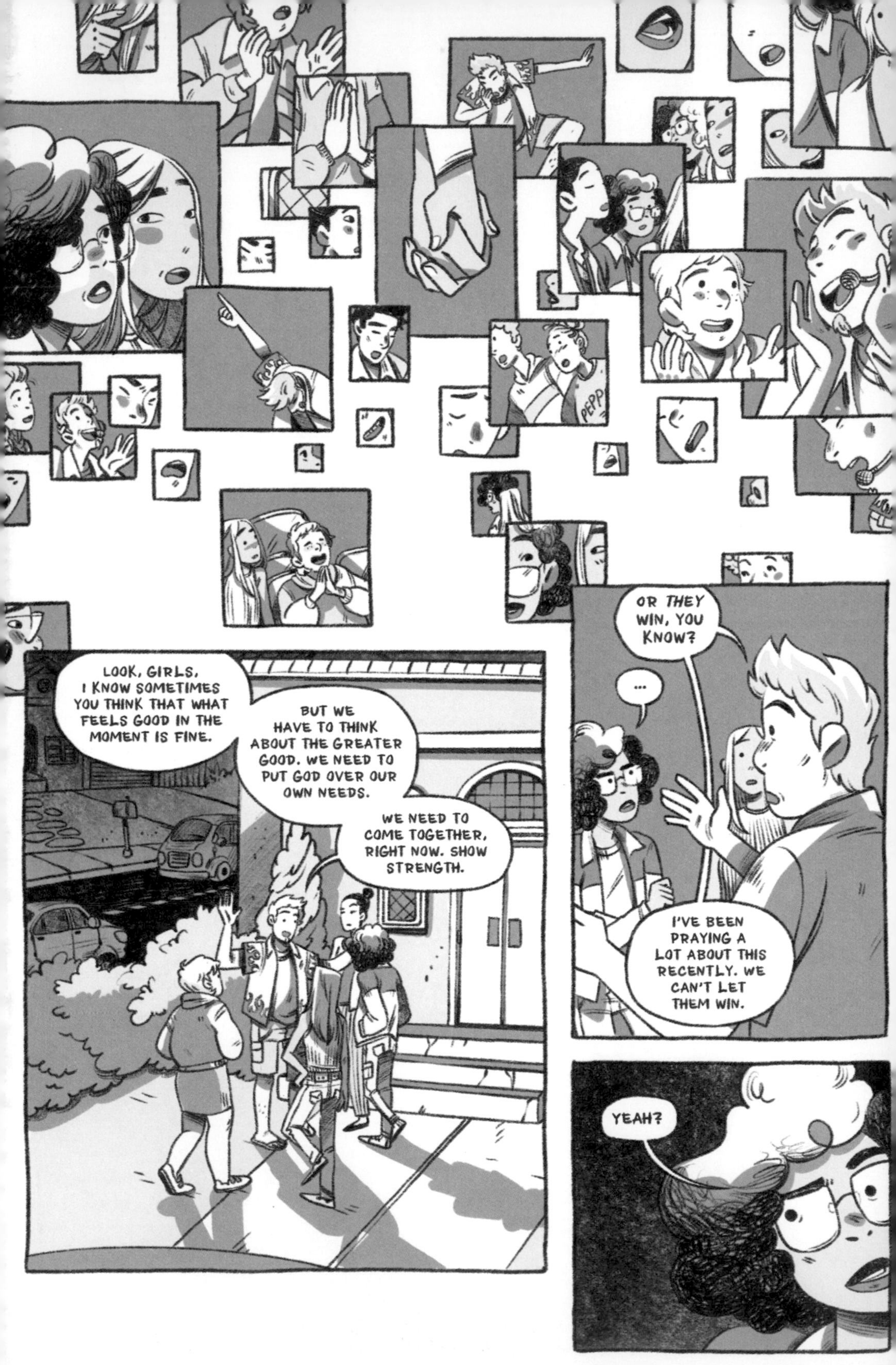
LOOK, GIRLS, I KNOW SOMETIMES YOU THINK THAT WHAT FEELS GOOD IN THE MOMENT IS FINE.
BUT WE HAVE TO THINK ABOUT THE GREATER GOOD. WE NEED TO PUT GOD OVER OUR OWN NEEDS.
WE NEED TO COME TOGETHER, RIGHT NOW. SHOW STRENGTH.
...
I'VE BEEN PRAYING A LOT ABOUT THIS RECENTLY. WE CAN'T LET THEM WIN.
OR *THEY* WIN, YOU KNOW?
YEAH?

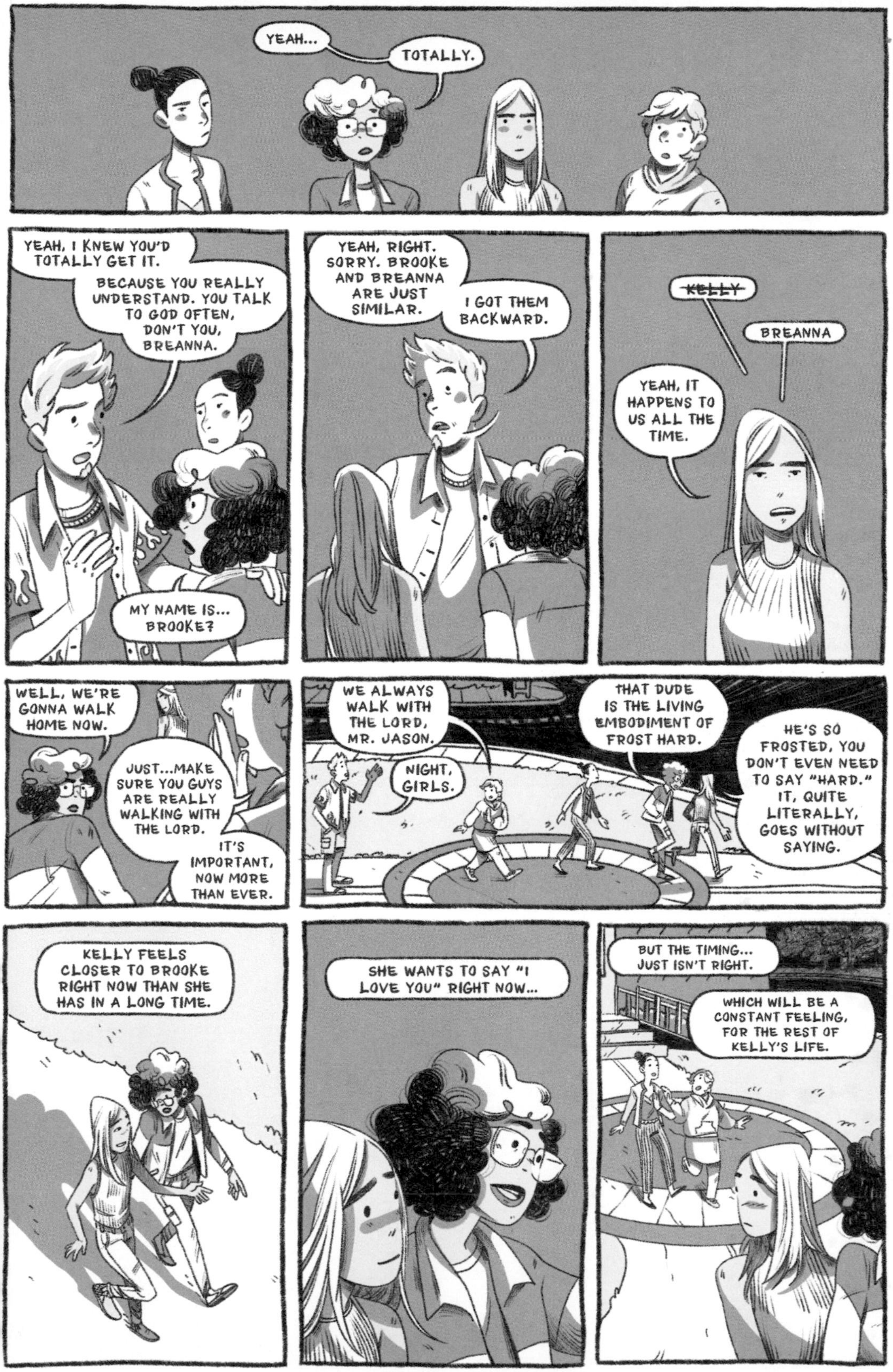
YEAH...
TOTALLY.
YEAH, I KNEW YOU'D TOTALLY GET IT.
BECAUSE YOU REALLY UNDERSTAND. YOU TALK TO GOD OFTEN, DON'T YOU, BREANNA.
MY NAME IS... BROOKE?
YEAH, RIGHT. SORRY. BROOKE AND BREANNA ARE JUST SIMILAR.
I GOT THEM BACKWARD.
~~KELLY~~
BREANNA
YEAH, IT HAPPENS TO US ALL THE TIME.
WELL, WE'RE GONNA WALK HOME NOW.
JUST...MAKE SURE YOU GUYS ARE REALLY WALKING WITH THE LORD.
IT'S IMPORTANT, NOW MORE THAN EVER.
WE ALWAYS WALK WITH THE LORD, MR. JASON.
NIGHT, GIRLS.
THAT DUDE IS THE LIVING EMBODIMENT OF FROST HARD.
HE'S SO FROSTED, YOU DON'T EVEN NEED TO SAY "HARD." IT, QUITE LITERALLY, GOES WITHOUT SAYING.
KELLY FEELS CLOSER TO BROOKE RIGHT NOW THAN SHE HAS IN A LONG TIME.
SHE WANTS TO SAY "I LOVE YOU" RIGHT NOW...
BUT THE TIMING... JUST ISN'T RIGHT.
WHICH WILL BE A CONSTANT FEELING, FOR THE REST OF KELLY'S LIFE.

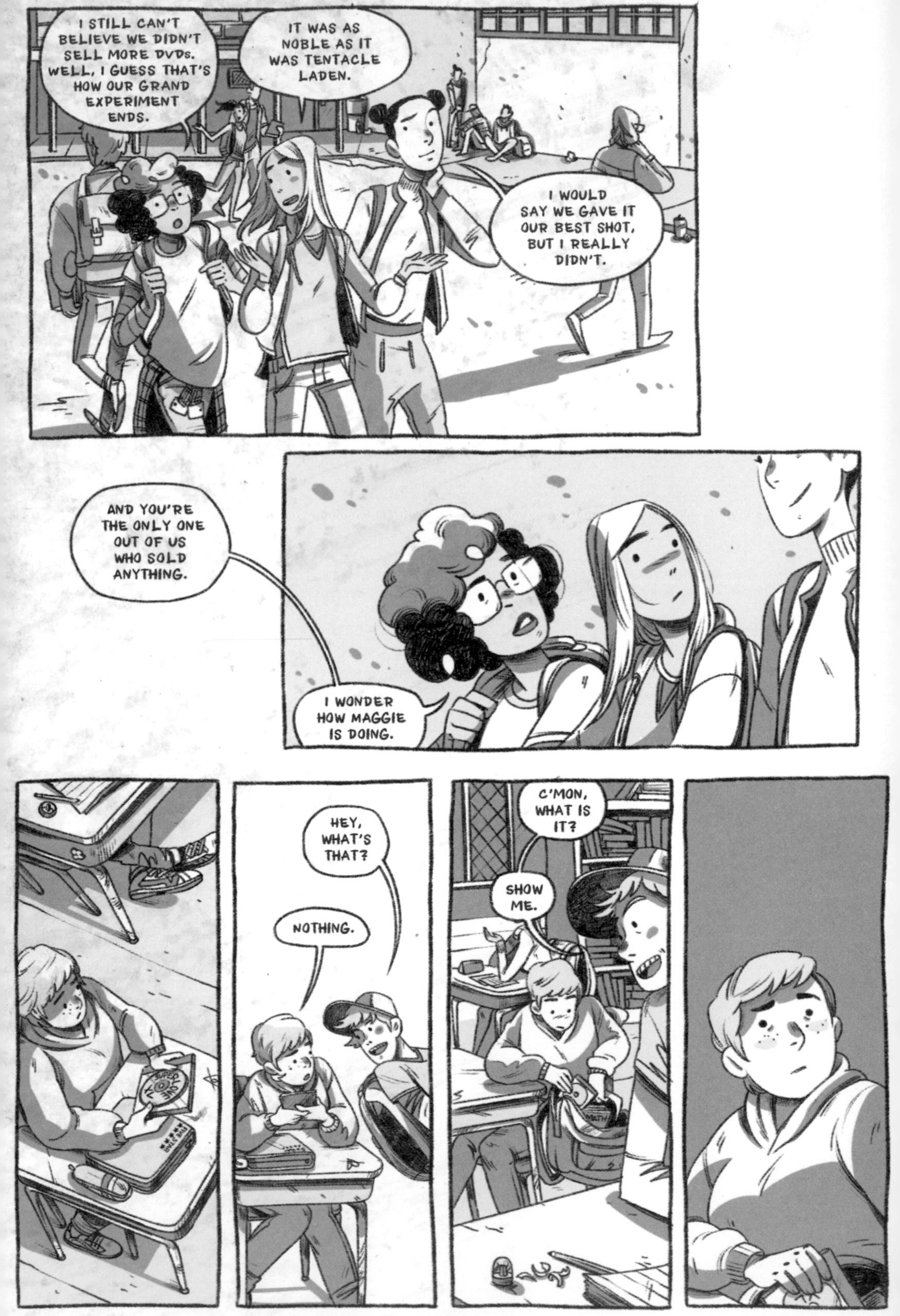
I STILL CAN'T BELIEVE WE DIDN'T SELL MORE DVDs. WELL, I GUESS THAT'S HOW OUR GRAND EXPERIMENT ENDS.
IT WAS AS NOBLE AS IT WAS TENTACLE LADEN.
I WOULD SAY WE GAVE IT OUR BEST SHOT, BUT I REALLY DIDN'T.
AND YOU'RE THE ONLY ONE OUT OF US WHO SOLD ANYTHING.
I WONDER HOW MAGGIE IS DOING.
HEY, WHAT'S THAT?
NOTHING.
C'MON, WHAT IS IT?
SHOW ME.

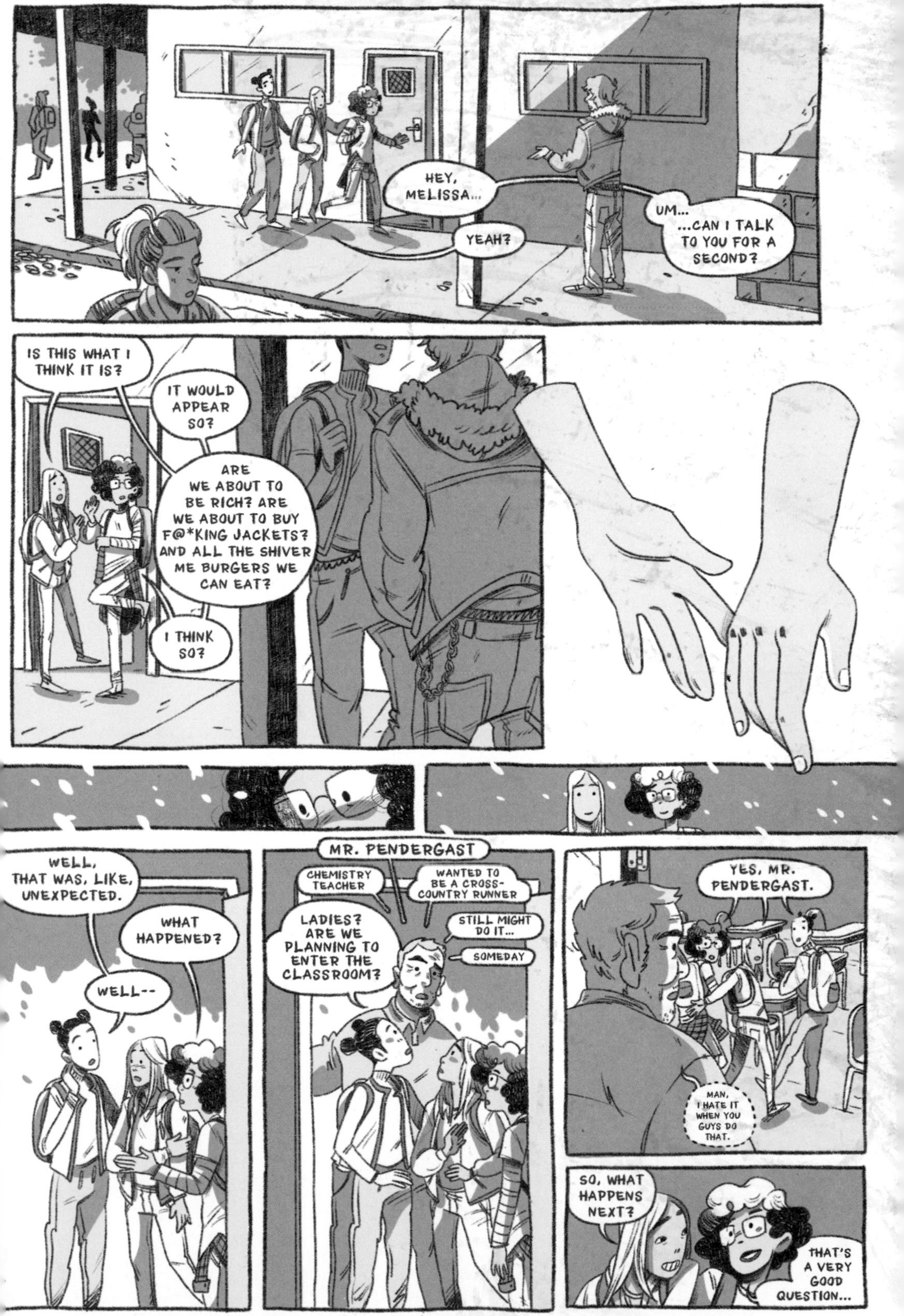
HEY, MELISSA...
YEAH?
UM... ...CAN I TALK TO YOU FOR A SECOND?
IS THIS WHAT I THINK IT IS?
IT WOULD APPEAR SO?
ARE WE ABOUT TO BE RICH? ARE WE ABOUT TO BUY F@*KING JACKETS? AND ALL THE SHIVER ME BURGERS WE CAN EAT?
I THINK SO?
WELL, THAT WAS, LIKE, UNEXPECTED.
WHAT HAPPENED?
WELL--
MR. PENDERGAST
CHEMISTRY TEACHER
WANTED TO BE A CROSS-COUNTRY RUNNER
STILL MIGHT DO IT...
SOMEDAY
LADIES? ARE WE PLANNING TO ENTER THE CLASSROOM?
YES, MR. PENDERGAST.
MAN, I HATE IT WHEN YOU GUYS DO THAT.
SO, WHAT HAPPENS NEXT?
THAT'S A VERY GOOD QUESTION...

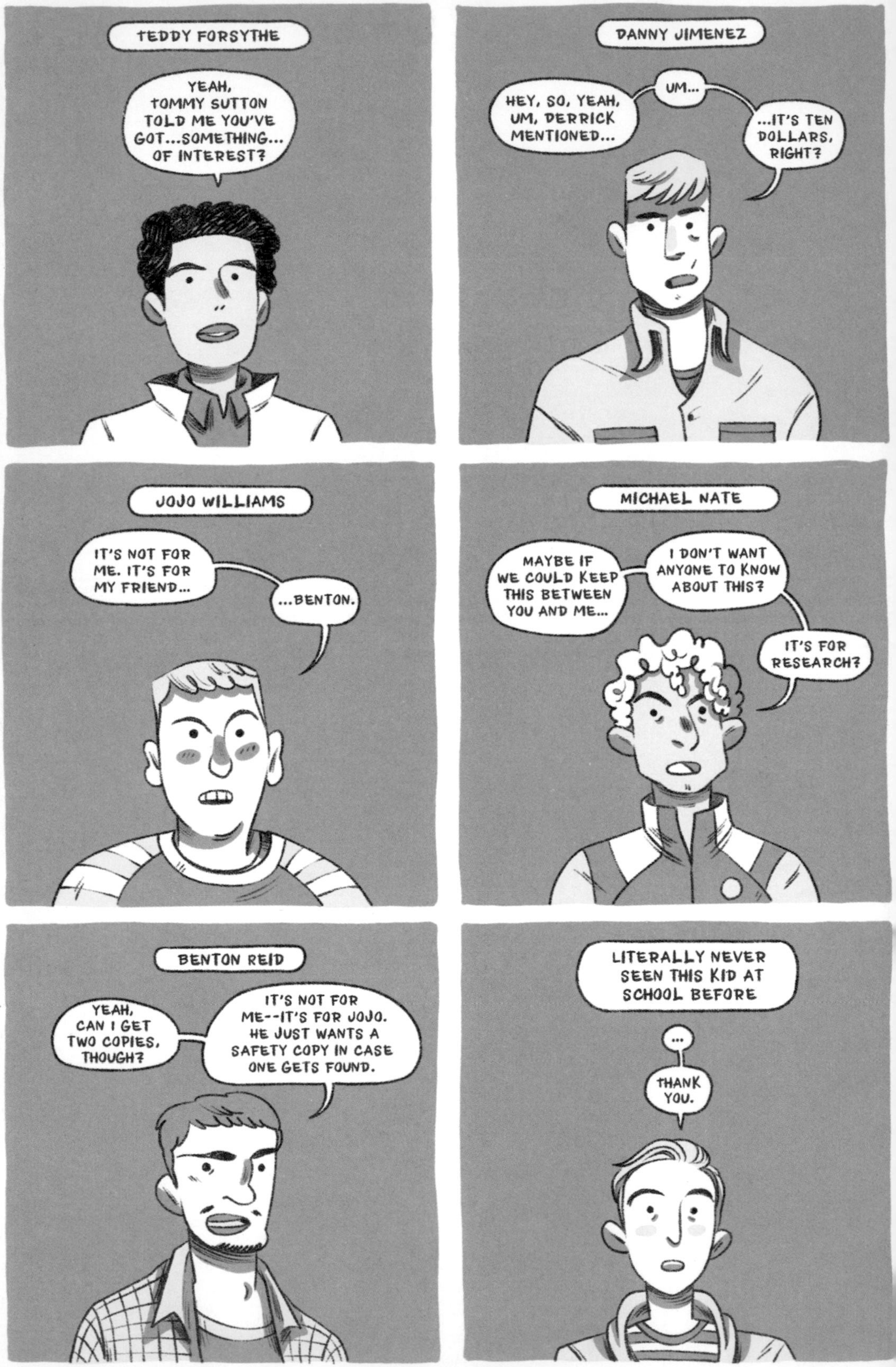
TEDDY FORSYTHE
YEAH, TOMMY SUTTON TOLD ME YOU'VE GOT...SOMETHING... OF INTEREST?
DANNY JIMENEZ
HEY, SO, YEAH, UM, DERRICK MENTIONED...
UM...
...IT'S TEN DOLLARS, RIGHT?
JOJO WILLIAMS
IT'S NOT FOR ME. IT'S FOR MY FRIEND...
...BENTON.
MICHAEL NATE
MAYBE IF WE COULD KEEP THIS BETWEEN YOU AND ME...
I DON'T WANT ANYONE TO KNOW ABOUT THIS?
IT'S FOR RESEARCH?
BENTON REID
YEAH, CAN I GET TWO COPIES, THOUGH?
IT'S NOT FOR ME--IT'S FOR JOJO. HE JUST WANTS A SAFETY COPY IN CASE ONE GETS FOUND.
LITERALLY NEVER SEEN THIS KID AT SCHOOL BEFORE
...
THANK YOU.

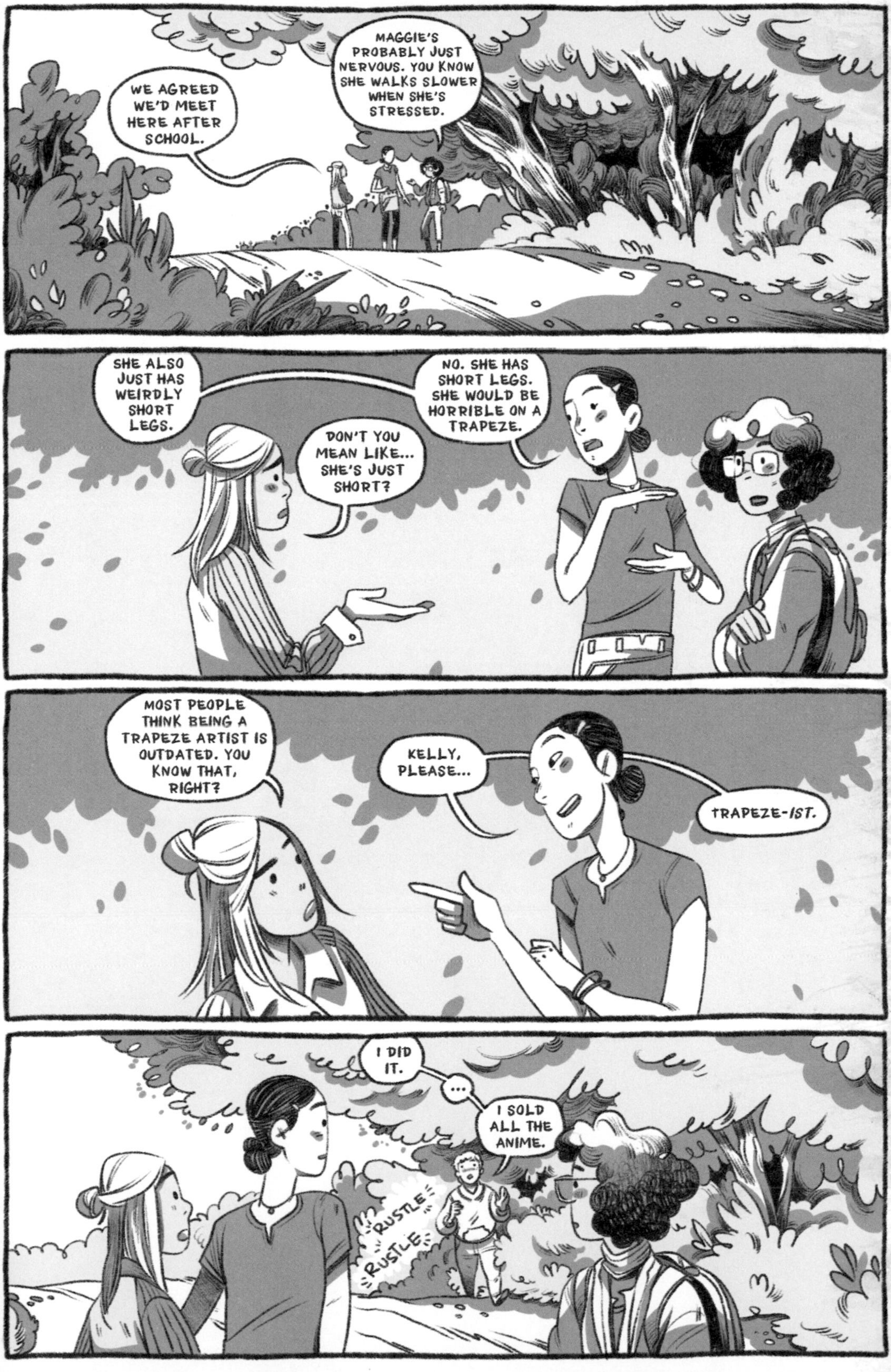
WE AGREED WE'D MEET HERE AFTER SCHOOL.
MAGGIE'S PROBABLY JUST NERVOUS. YOU KNOW SHE WALKS SLOWER WHEN SHE'S STRESSED.
SHE ALSO JUST HAS WEIRDLY SHORT LEGS.
DON'T YOU MEAN LIKE... SHE'S JUST SHORT?
NO. SHE HAS SHORT LEGS. SHE WOULD BE HORRIBLE ON A TRAPEZE.
MOST PEOPLE THINK BEING A TRAPEZE ARTIST IS OUTDATED. YOU KNOW THAT, RIGHT?
KELLY, PLEASE...
TRAPEZE-IST.
I DID IT.
...
I SOLD ALL THE ANIME.
RUSTLE
RUSTLE

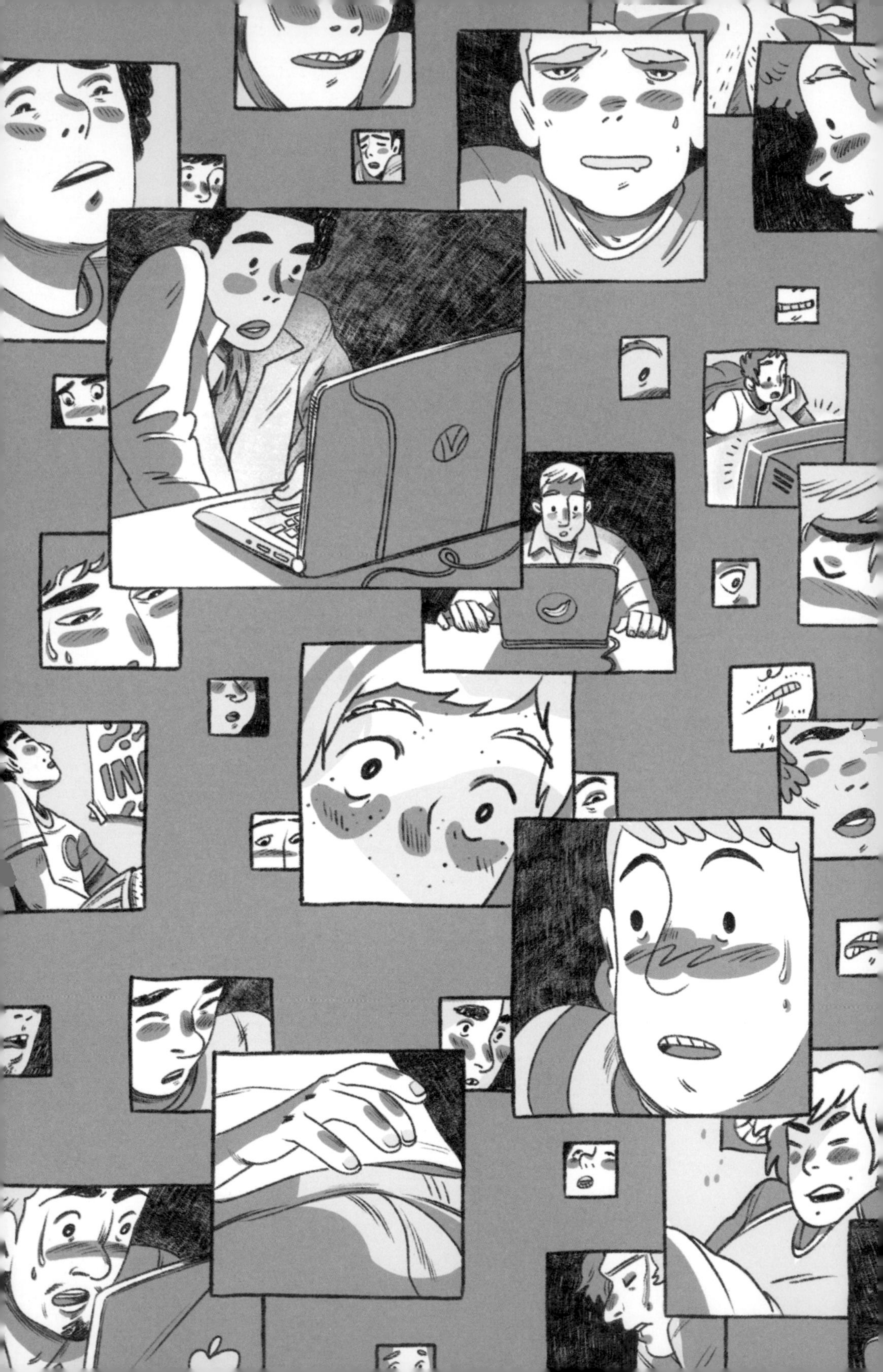

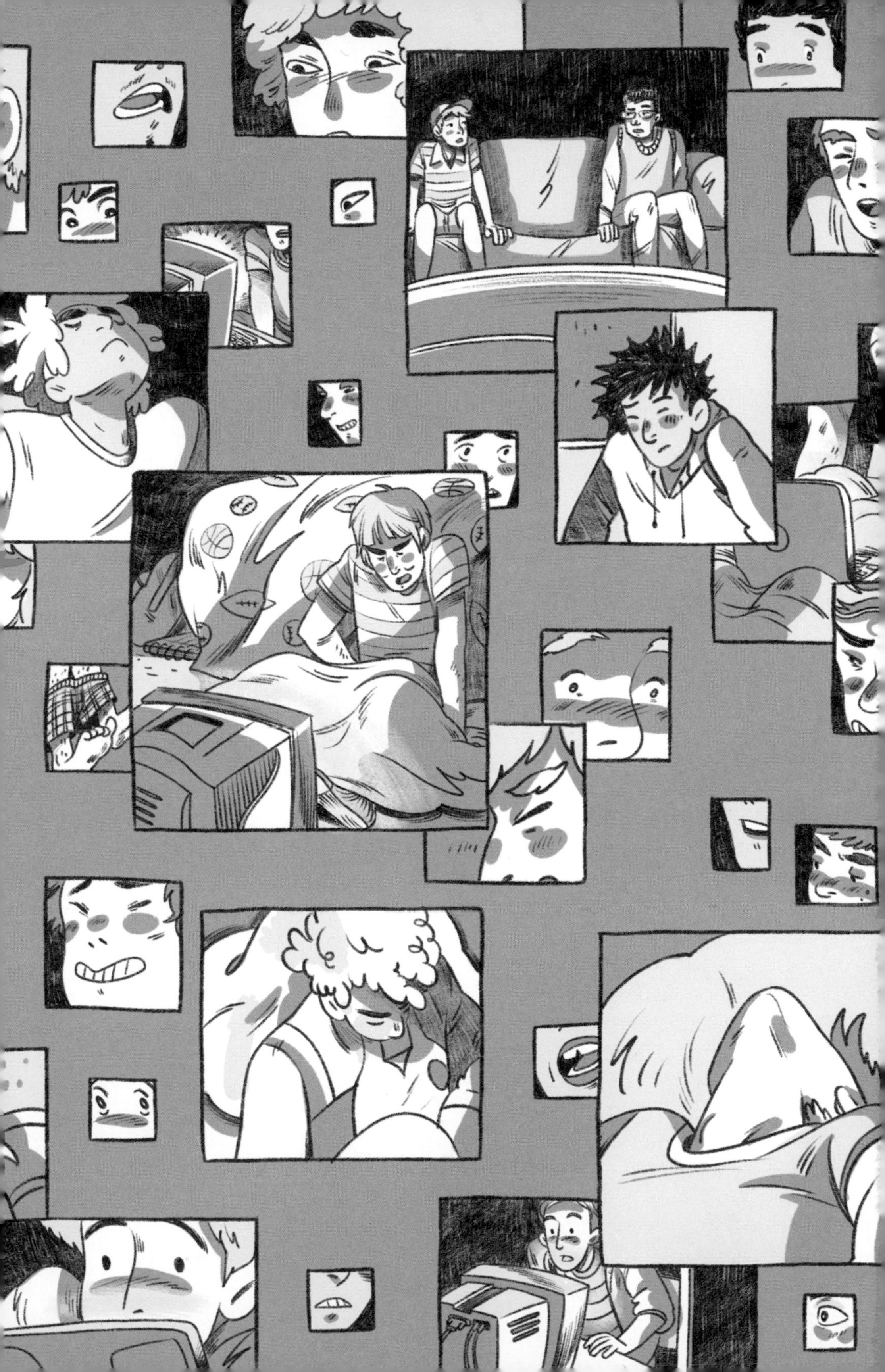

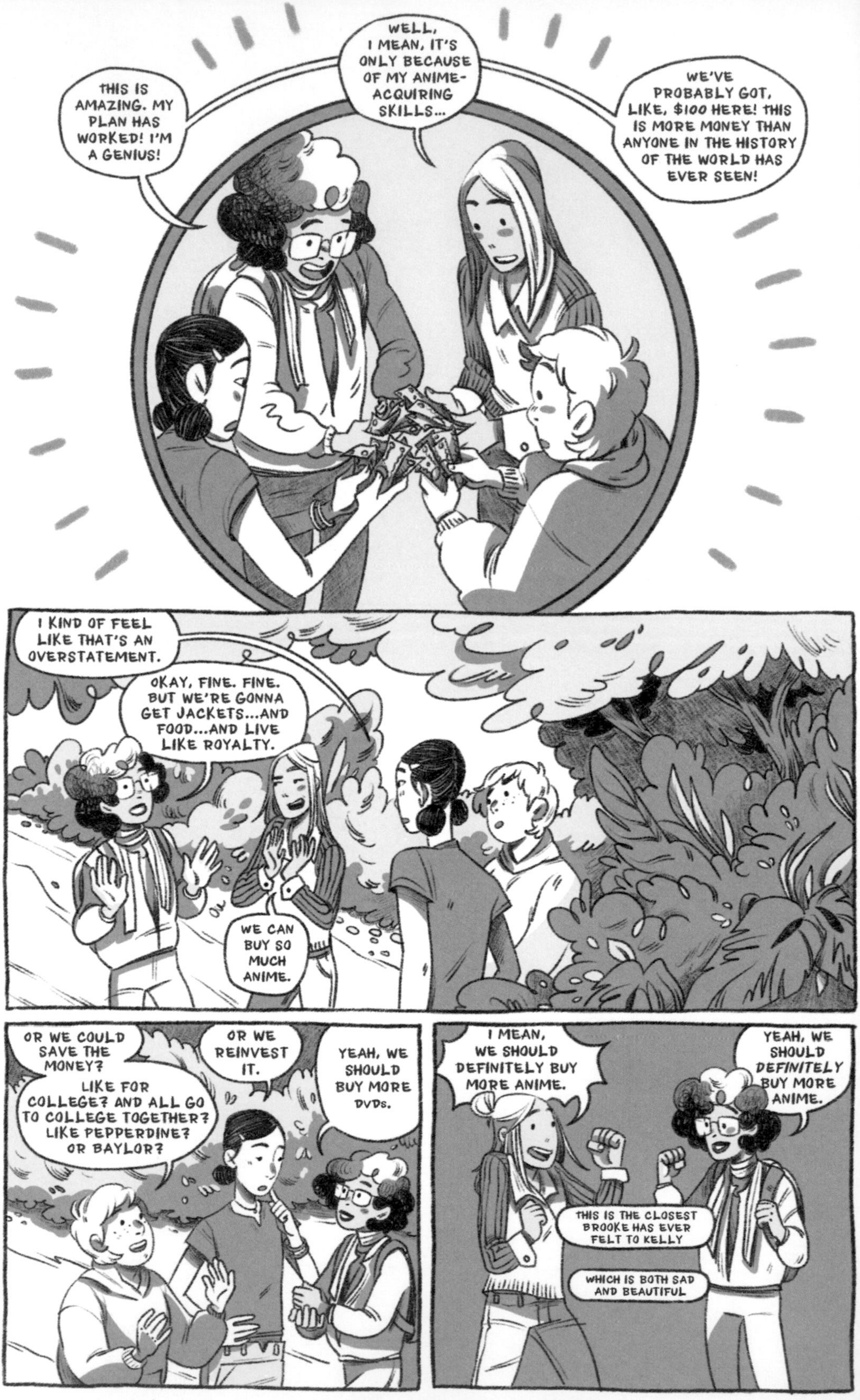
THIS IS AMAZING. MY PLAN HAS WORKED! I'M A GENIUS!
WELL, I MEAN, IT'S ONLY BECAUSE OF MY ANIME-ACQUIRING SKILLS...
WE'VE PROBABLY GOT, LIKE, $100 HERE! THIS IS MORE MONEY THAN ANYONE IN THE HISTORY OF THE WORLD HAS EVER SEEN!
I KIND OF FEEL LIKE THAT'S AN OVERSTATEMENT.
OKAY, FINE. FINE. BUT WE'RE GONNA GET JACKETS...AND FOOD...AND LIVE LIKE ROYALTY.
WE CAN BUY SO MUCH ANIME.
OR WE COULD SAVE THE MONEY?
LIKE FOR COLLEGE? AND ALL GO TO COLLEGE TOGETHER? LIKE PEPPERDINE? OR BAYLOR?
OR WE REINVEST IT.
YEAH, WE SHOULD BUY MORE DVDs.
I MEAN, WE SHOULD DEFINITELY BUY MORE ANIME.
YEAH, WE SHOULD *DEFINITELY* BUY MORE ANIME.
THIS IS THE CLOSEST BROOKE HAS EVER FELT TO KELLY
WHICH IS BOTH SAD AND BEAUTIFUL

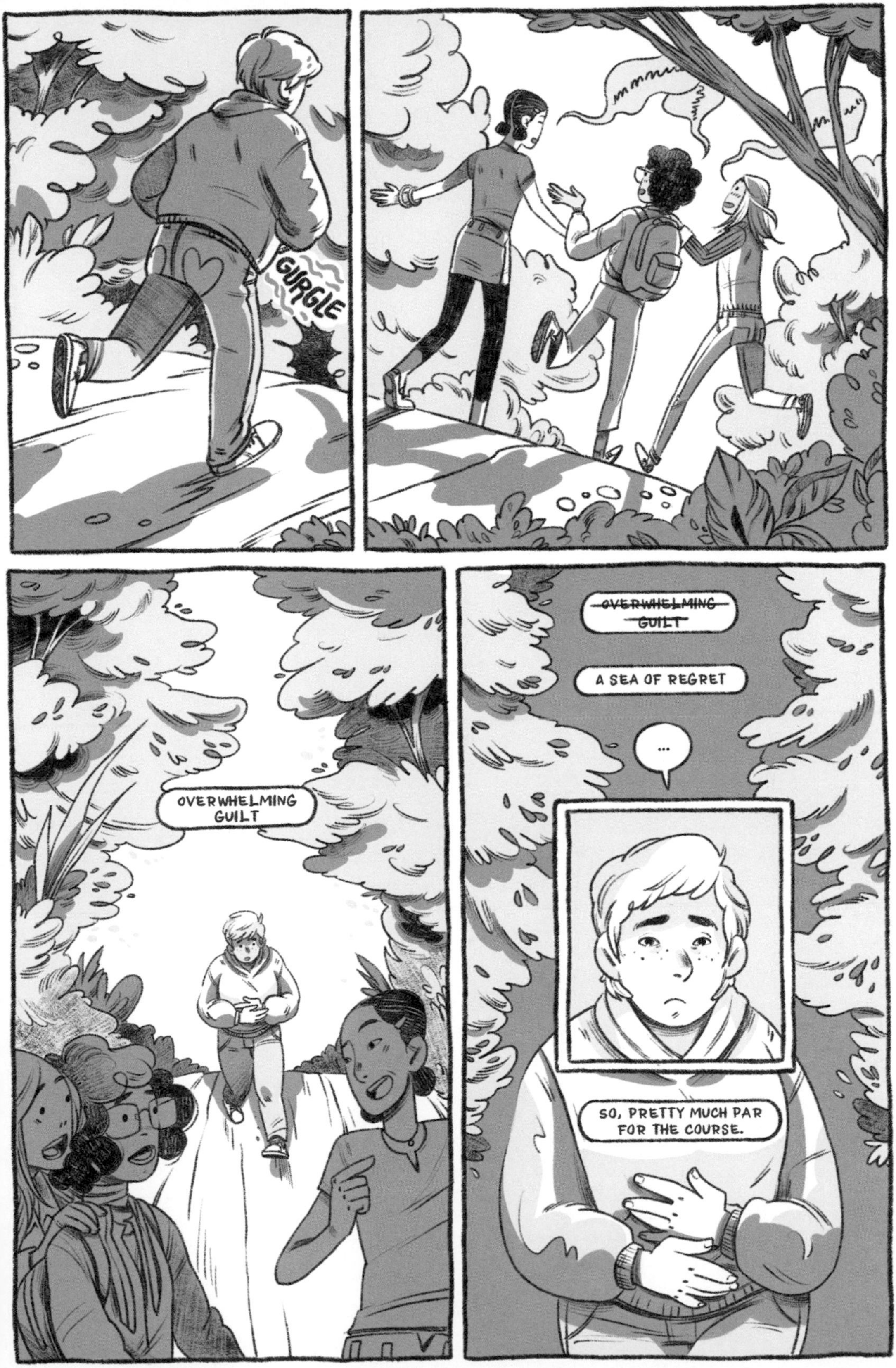
GURGLE
OVERWHELMING GUILT
~~OVERWHELMING GUILT~~
A SEA OF REGRET
...
SO, PRETTY MUCH PAR FOR THE COURSE.

A BRIEF HISTORY OF MAGGIE'S UNFULFILLED DESIRES

ALL MAGGIE WANTS IN THE WORLD IS TO BE ENROLLED AT FOREST HILLS CHRISTIAN ACADEMY. SHE'S BEEN BEGGING HER MOM TO SEND HER THERE FOR THE LAST YEAR AND A HALF, BUT THE TUITION IS JUST TOO EXPENSIVE. CAROL'S CONSTANT REFRAIN IS "WHY WOULD I SEND YOU TO A BOARDING SCHOOL THAT'S IN THE SAME TOWN WE LIVE IN?"

MAGGIE NEVER HAS A GOOD ANSWER FOR THAT QUESTION. SHE DOESN'T HAVE THE WORDS TO COMMUNICATE THE SENSE OF BELONGING AND STRENGTH SHE FINDS IN HER FRIENDS. SHE STUMBLES WHEN TRYING TO RELAY THAT THE SCHOOL IS BETTER SUITED FOR HER BECAUSE IT WILL DEEPEN HER CONNECTION WITH GOD.

EVERY TIME THEY HAVE THIS CONVERSATION, CAROL KNOWS HOW TO POKE HOLES IN MAGGIE'S ARGUMENTS. "WHEN YOU WERE IN FIFTH GRADE AND BECKY WILLIAMS GOT BRACES, YOU WANTED BRACES." "TWO SUMMERS AGO, YOU TRIED OUT FOR SWIM TEAM BECAUSE YOU WENT TO A SLEEPOVER AT MEGAN HITCHENS'S HOUSE, AND THEY HAD A POOL."

SOMETIMES MAGGIE SITS ALONE AT NIGHT AND FEELS EMPTY. NOT LONELY OR DEPRESSED, JUST EMPTY. LIKE A BARREN WASTELAND OF ABSENCE AND WANT.

MAGGIE KNOWS THAT HER MOTHER THINKS SHE'S COMFORTABLE IN THE ROLE OF A FOLLOWER. MAGGIE KNOWS THAT HER MOTHER DOESN'T LIKE THIS BECAUSE IT REMINDS HER OF THE WORST PARTS OF HERSELF.

AND, YES...ON A BAD DAY, MAGGIE IS COMFORTABLE AS A FOLLOWER. BUT ULTIMATELY, SHE'S JUST LOOKING FOR SOMETHING TO HELP HER THROUGH THE DAY...BESIDES HER FAITH. BECAUSE AS MUCH AS SHE HESITATES TO ADMIT IT...SOMETIMES, FAITH ISN'T ENOUGH FOR MAGGIE.

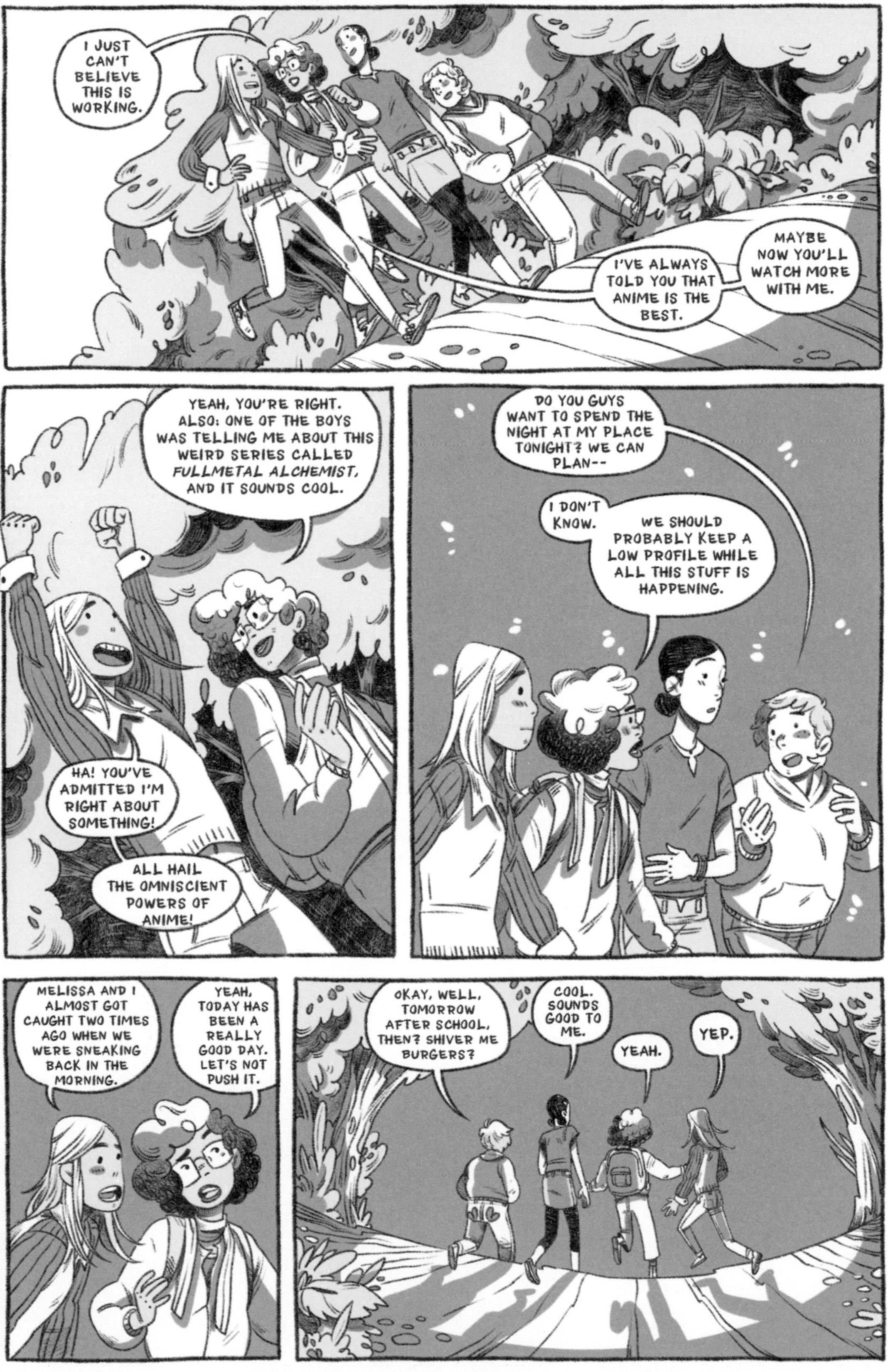
I JUST CAN'T BELIEVE THIS IS WORKING.
I'VE ALWAYS TOLD YOU THAT ANIME IS THE BEST.
MAYBE NOW YOU'LL WATCH MORE WITH ME.
YEAH, YOU'RE RIGHT. ALSO: ONE OF THE BOYS WAS TELLING ME ABOUT THIS WEIRD SERIES CALLED *FULLMETAL ALCHEMIST*, AND IT SOUNDS COOL.
HA! YOU'VE ADMITTED I'M RIGHT ABOUT SOMETHING!
ALL HAIL THE OMNISCIENT POWERS OF ANIME!
DO YOU GUYS WANT TO SPEND THE NIGHT AT MY PLACE TONIGHT? WE CAN PLAN--
I DON'T KNOW.
WE SHOULD PROBABLY KEEP A LOW PROFILE WHILE ALL THIS STUFF IS HAPPENING.
MELISSA AND I ALMOST GOT CAUGHT TWO TIMES AGO WHEN WE WERE SNEAKING BACK IN THE MORNING.
YEAH, TODAY HAS BEEN A REALLY GOOD DAY. LET'S NOT PUSH IT.
OKAY, WELL, TOMORROW AFTER SCHOOL, THEN? SHIVER ME BURGERS?
COOL. SOUNDS GOOD TO ME.
YEAH.
YEP.

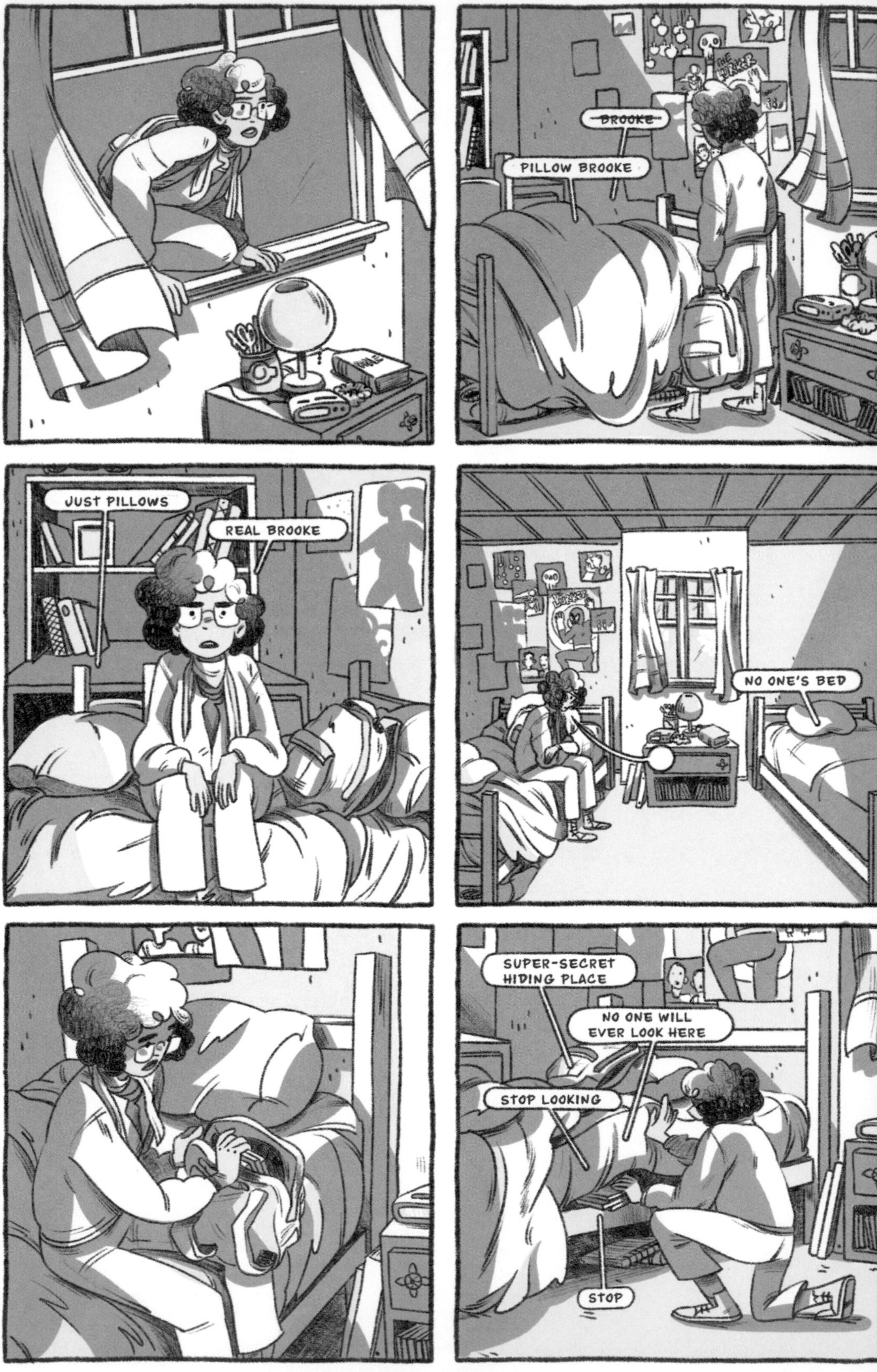
~~BROOKE~~
PILLOW BROOKE
JUST PILLOWS
REAL BROOKE
NO ONE'S BED
SUPER-SECRET HIDING PLACE
NO ONE WILL EVER LOOK HERE
STOP LOOKING
STOP

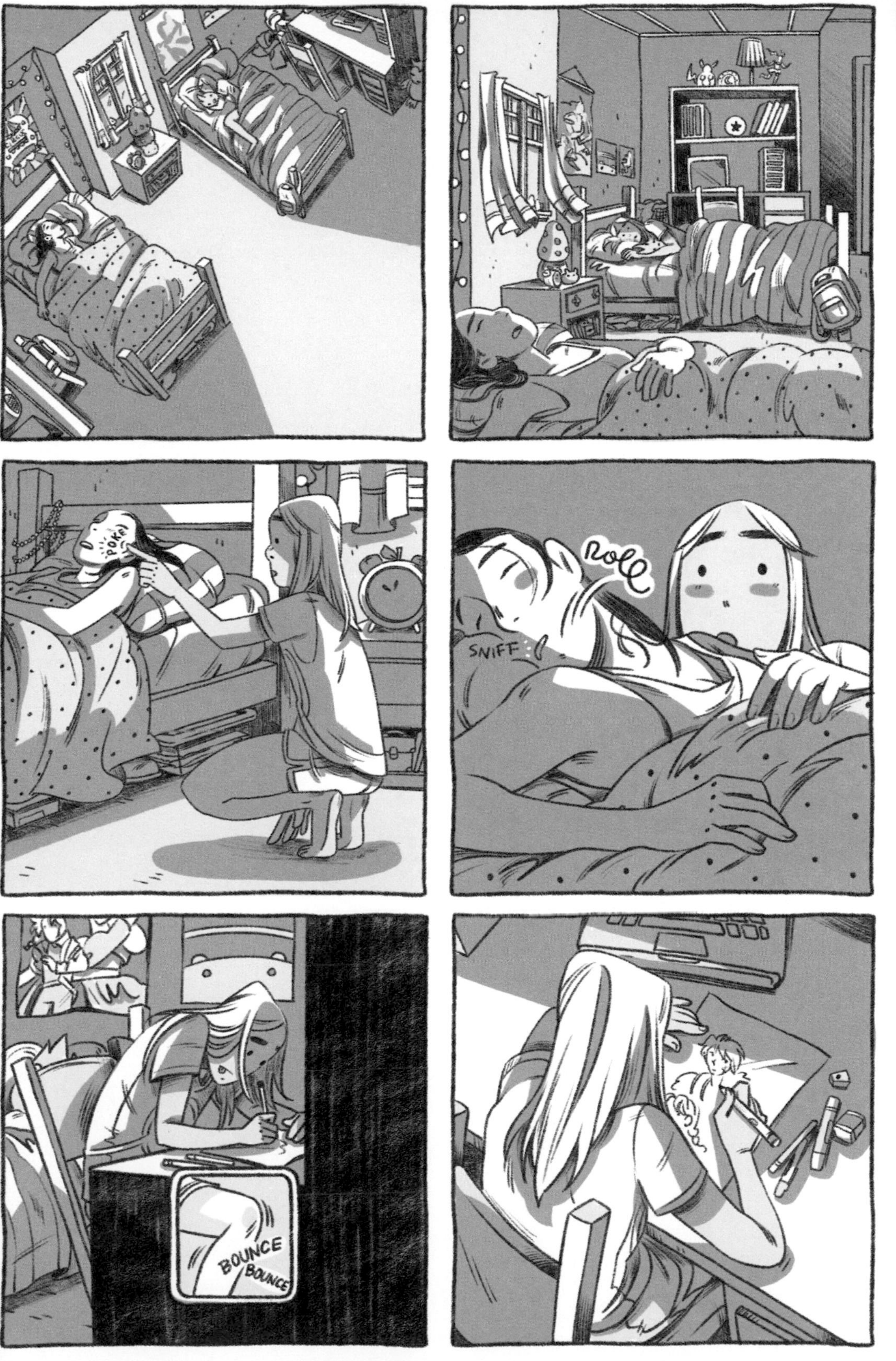
POKE!
ROLL
SNIFF
BOUNCE
BOUNCE

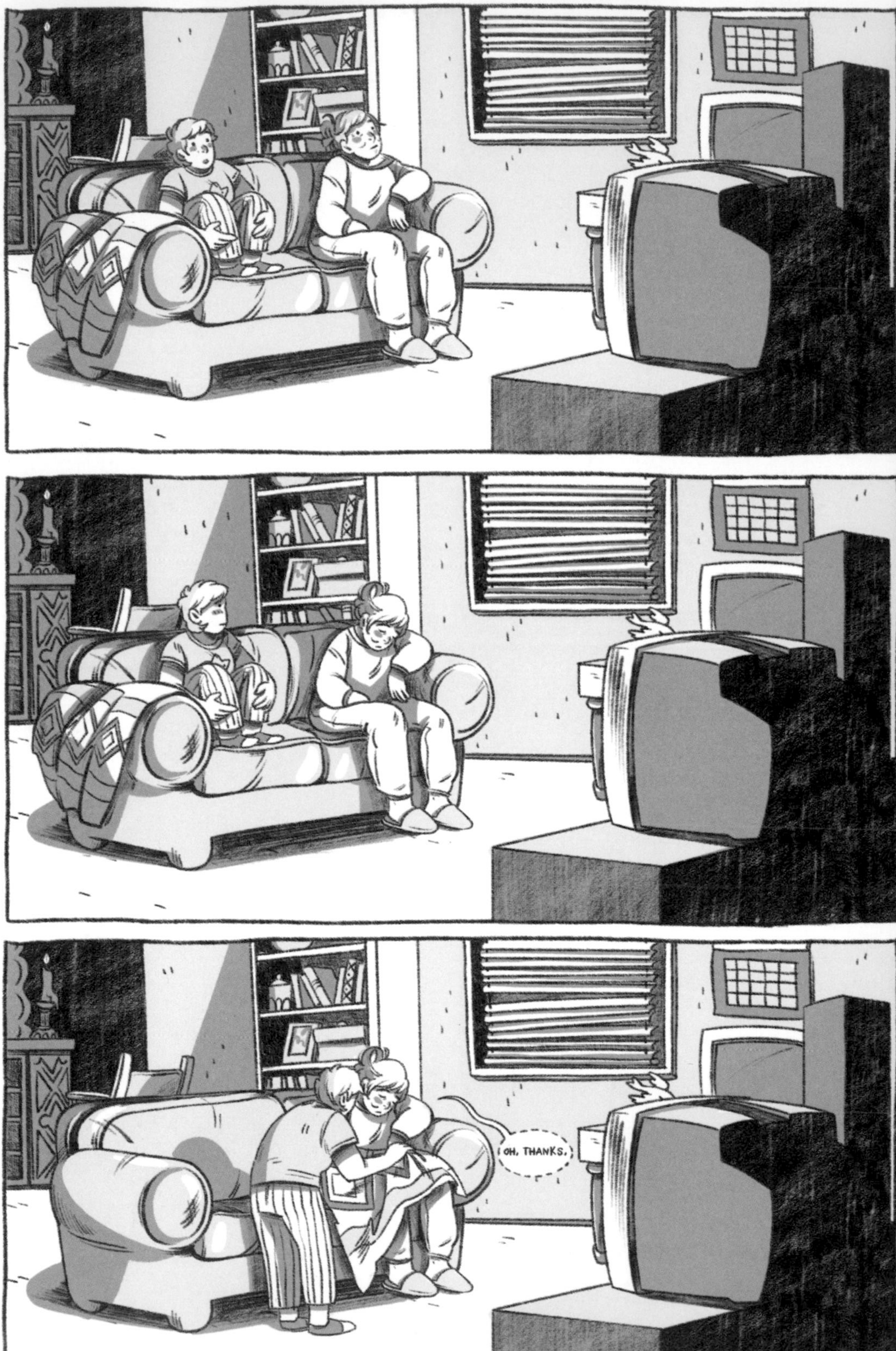
OH, THANKS.

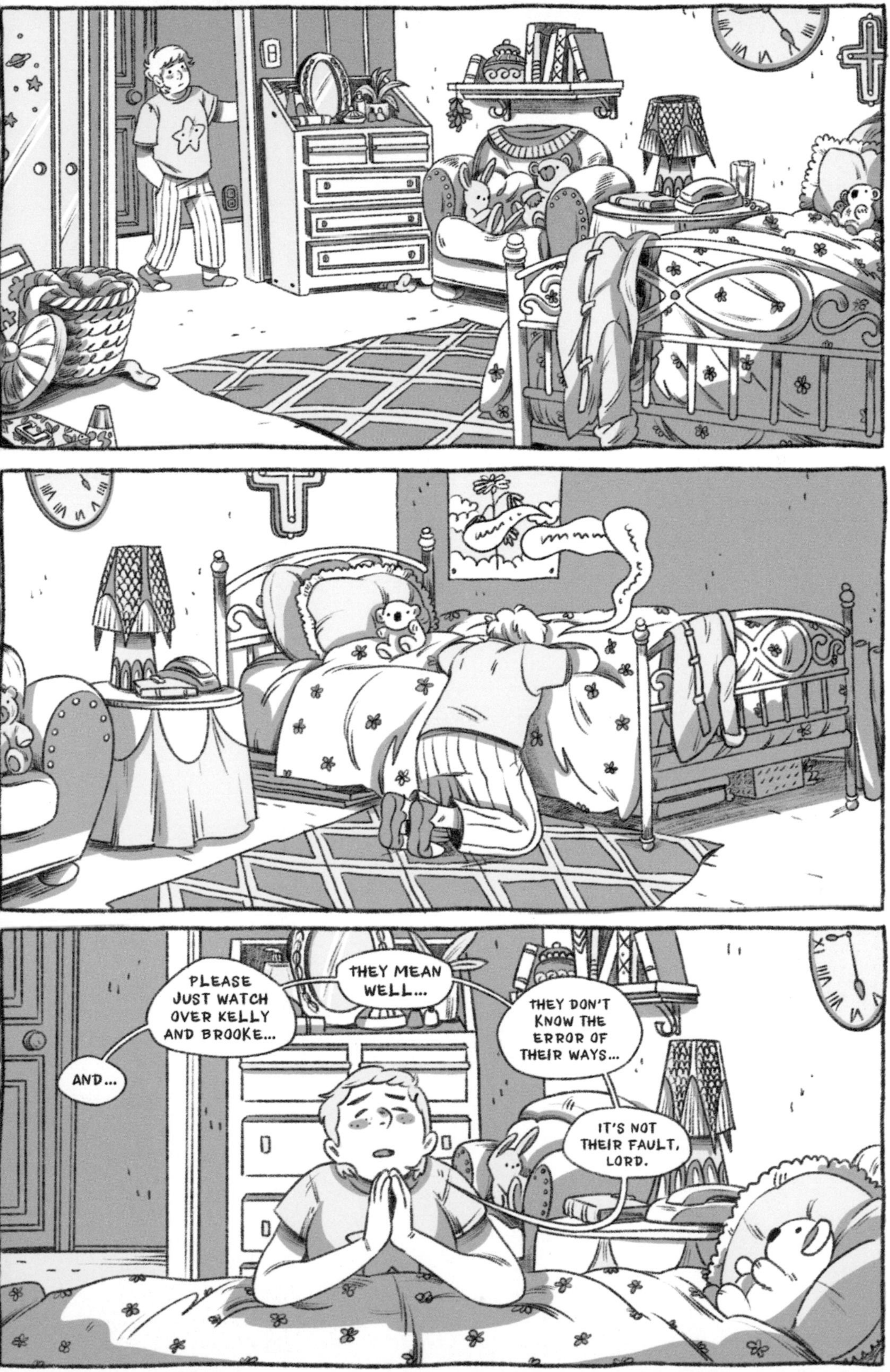
AND...
PLEASE JUST WATCH OVER KELLY AND BROOKE...
THEY MEAN WELL...
THEY DON'T KNOW THE ERROR OF THEIR WAYS...
IT'S NOT THEIR FAULT, LORD.

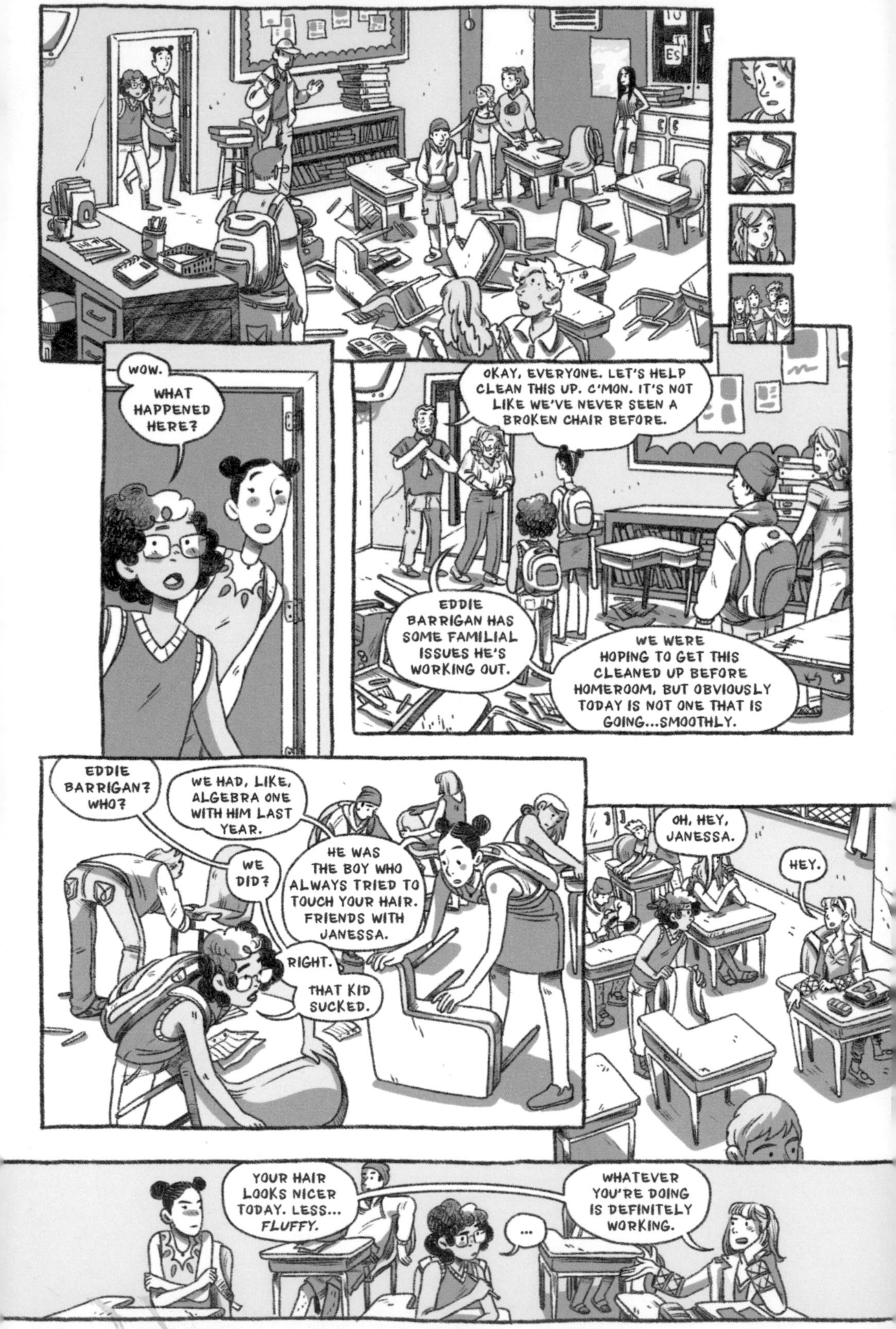
WOW.
WHAT HAPPENED HERE?
OKAY, EVERYONE. LET'S HELP CLEAN THIS UP. C'MON. IT'S NOT LIKE WE'VE NEVER SEEN A BROKEN CHAIR BEFORE.
EDDIE BARRIGAN HAS SOME FAMILIAL ISSUES HE'S WORKING OUT.
WE WERE HOPING TO GET THIS CLEANED UP BEFORE HOMEROOM, BUT OBVIOUSLY TODAY IS NOT ONE THAT IS GOING...SMOOTHLY.
EDDIE BARRIGAN? WHO?
WE HAD, LIKE, ALGEBRA ONE WITH HIM LAST YEAR.
WE DID?
HE WAS THE BOY WHO ALWAYS TRIED TO TOUCH YOUR HAIR. FRIENDS WITH JANESSA.
RIGHT.
THAT KID SUCKED.
OH, HEY, JANESSA.
HEY.
YOUR HAIR LOOKS NICER TODAY. LESS... *FLUFFY.*
WHATEVER YOU'RE DOING IS DEFINITELY WORKING.
...

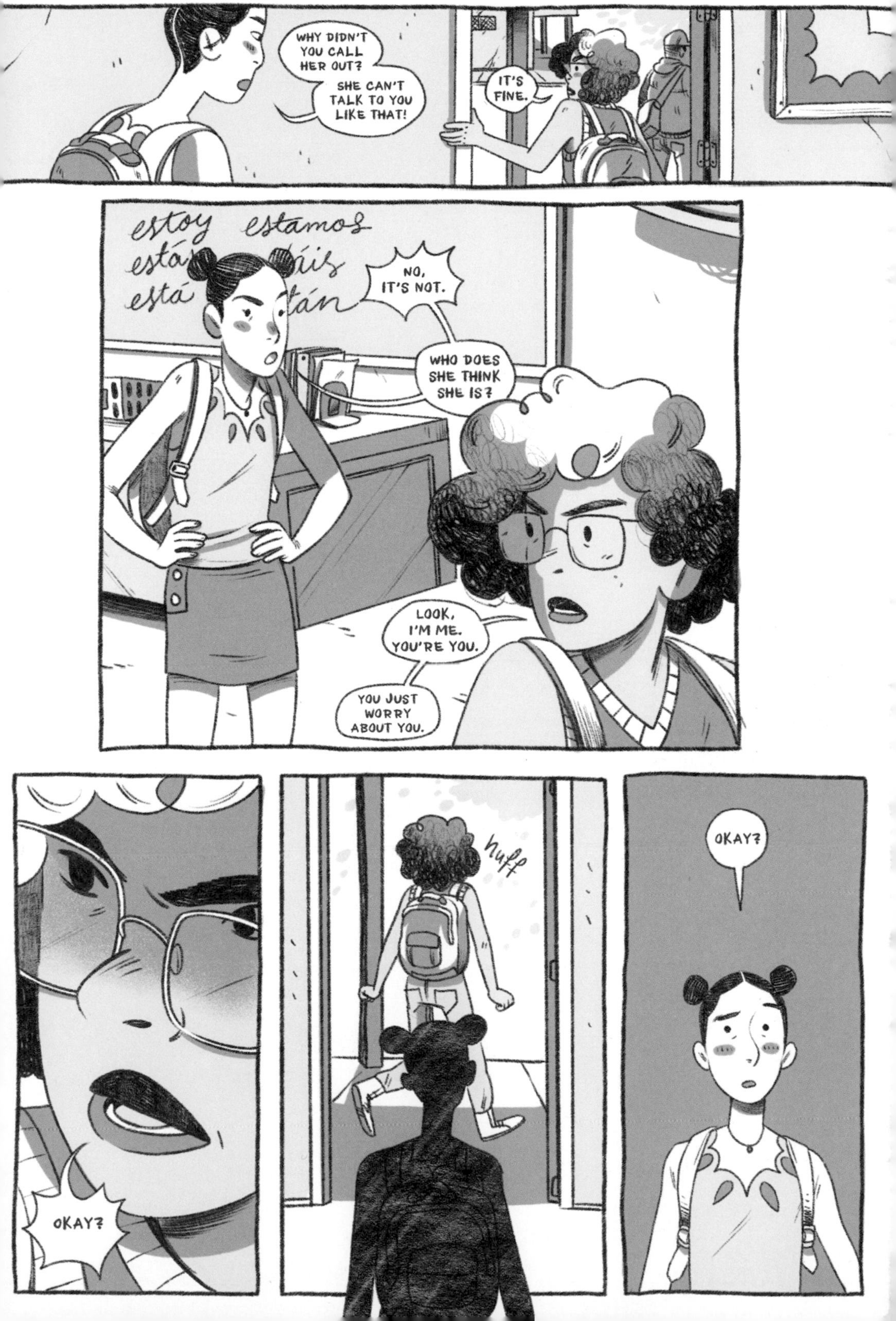
WHY DIDN'T YOU CALL HER OUT?
SHE CAN'T TALK TO YOU LIKE THAT!
IT'S FINE.
estoy estamos
está
está
NO, IT'S NOT.
WHO DOES SHE THINK SHE IS?
LOOK, I'M ME. YOU'RE YOU.
YOU JUST WORRY ABOUT YOU.
OKAY?
huff
OKAY?

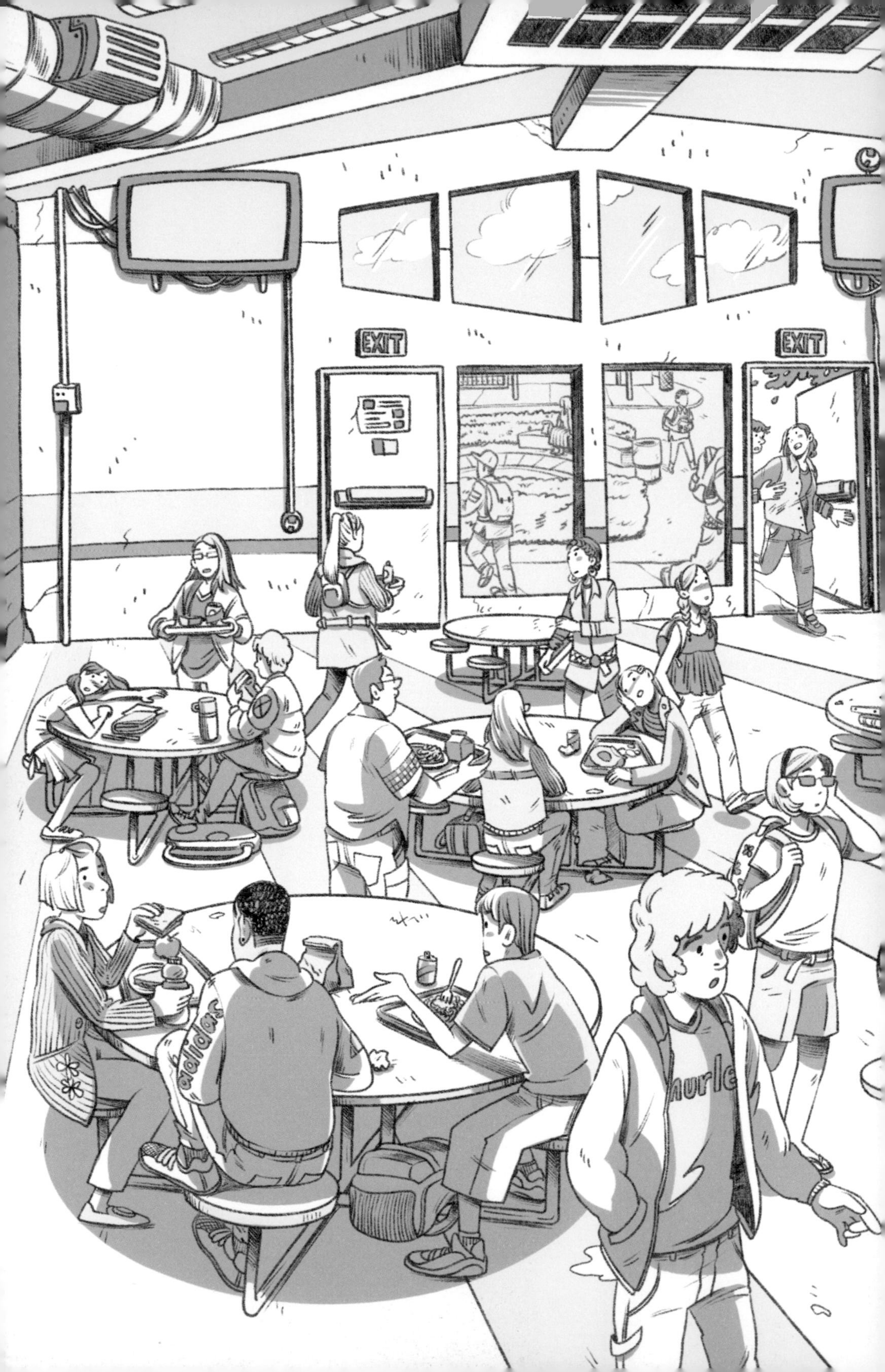
EXIT
EXIT
adidas
hurle

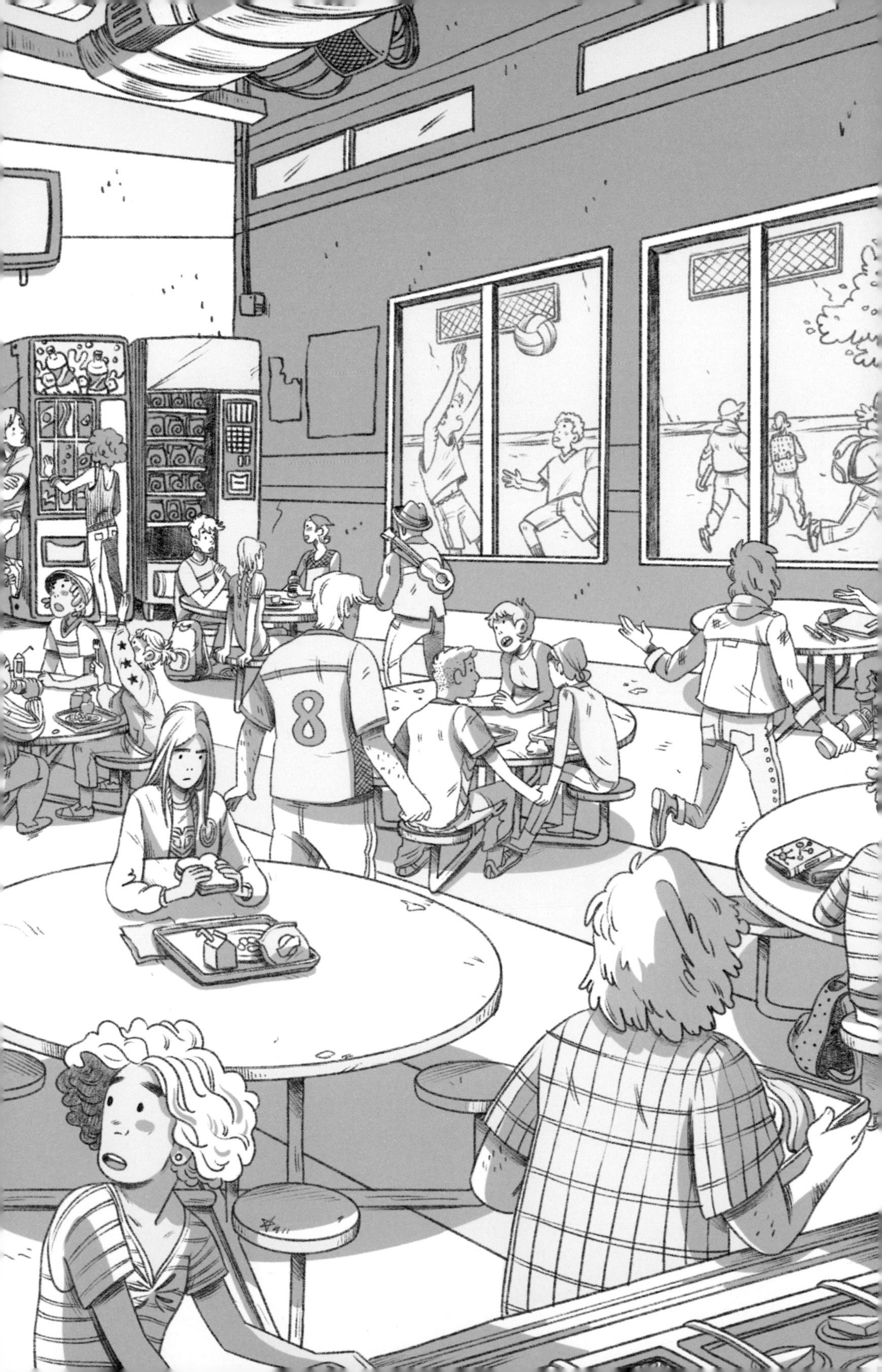

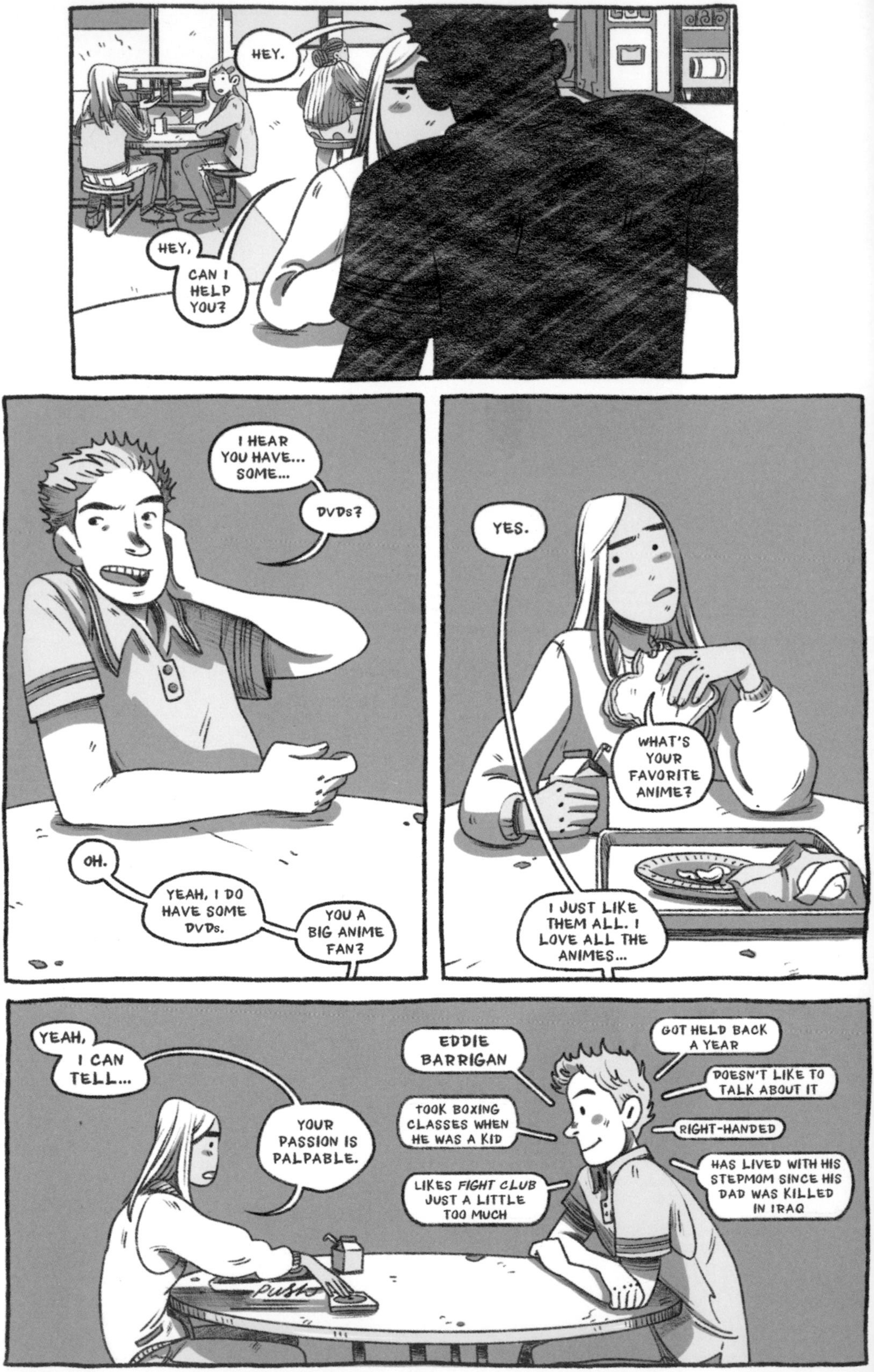
HEY.
HEY,
CAN I HELP YOU?
I HEAR YOU HAVE... SOME...
DVDs?
OH.
YEAH, I DO HAVE SOME DVDs.
YOU A BIG ANIME FAN?
YES.
WHAT'S YOUR FAVORITE ANIME?
I JUST LIKE THEM ALL. I LOVE ALL THE ANIMES...
YEAH, I CAN TELL...
YOUR PASSION IS PALPABLE.
EDDIE BARRIGAN
GOT HELD BACK A YEAR
DOESN'T LIKE TO TALK ABOUT IT
TOOK BOXING CLASSES WHEN HE WAS A KID
RIGHT-HANDED
LIKES *FIGHT CLUB* JUST A LITTLE TOO MUCH
HAS LIVED WITH HIS STEPMOM SINCE HIS DAD WAS KILLED IN IRAQ

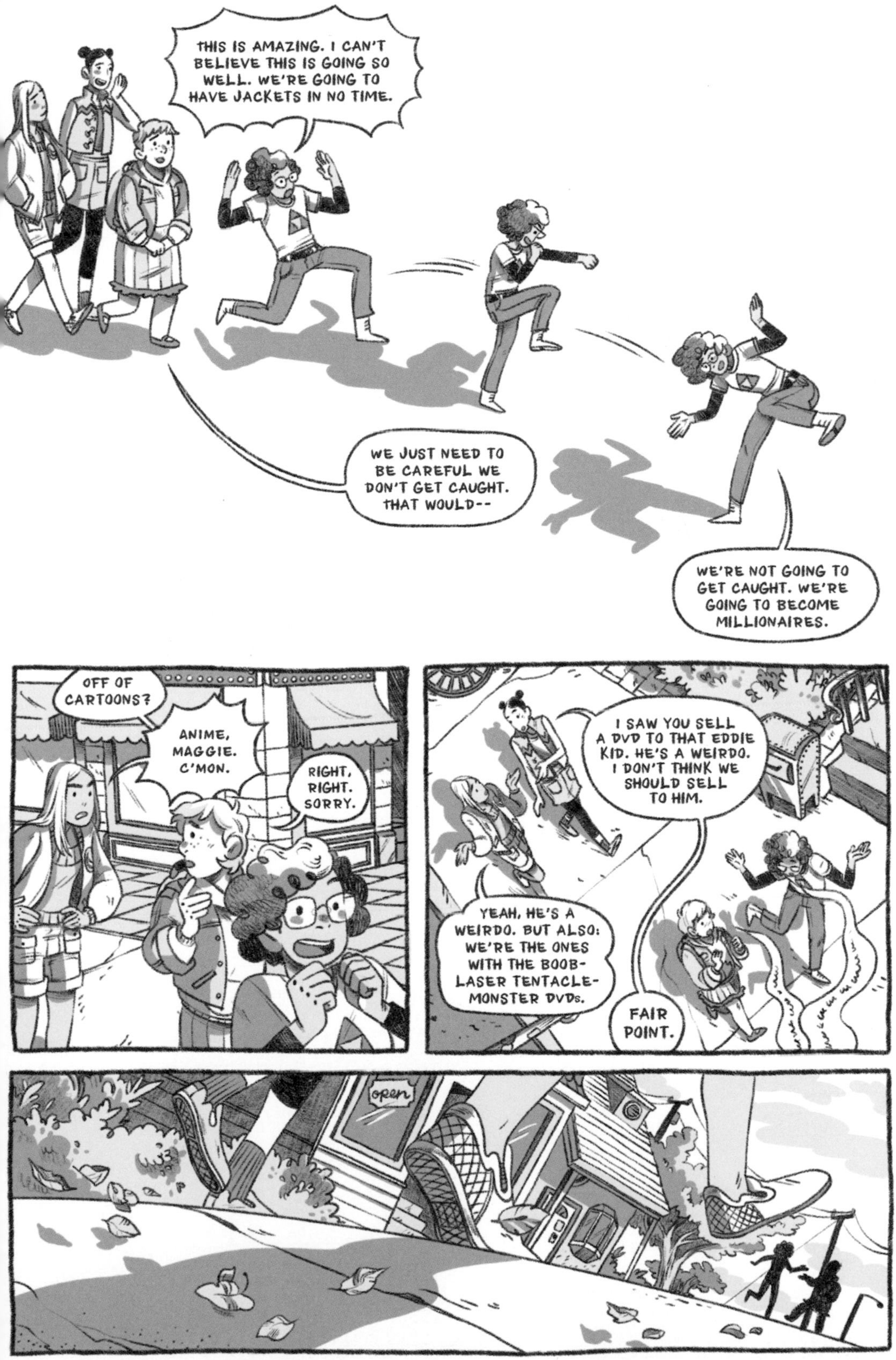
THIS IS AMAZING. I CAN'T BELIEVE THIS IS GOING SO WELL. WE'RE GOING TO HAVE JACKETS IN NO TIME.
WE JUST NEED TO BE CAREFUL WE DON'T GET CAUGHT. THAT WOULD--
WE'RE NOT GOING TO GET CAUGHT. WE'RE GOING TO BECOME MILLIONAIRES.
OFF OF CARTOONS?
ANIME, MAGGIE. C'MON.
RIGHT, RIGHT. SORRY.
I SAW YOU SELL A DVD TO THAT EDDIE KID. HE'S A WEIRDO. I DON'T THINK WE SHOULD SELL TO HIM.
YEAH, HE'S A WEIRDO. BUT ALSO: WE'RE THE ONES WITH THE BOOB-LASER TENTACLE-MONSTER DVDs.
FAIR POINT.
open

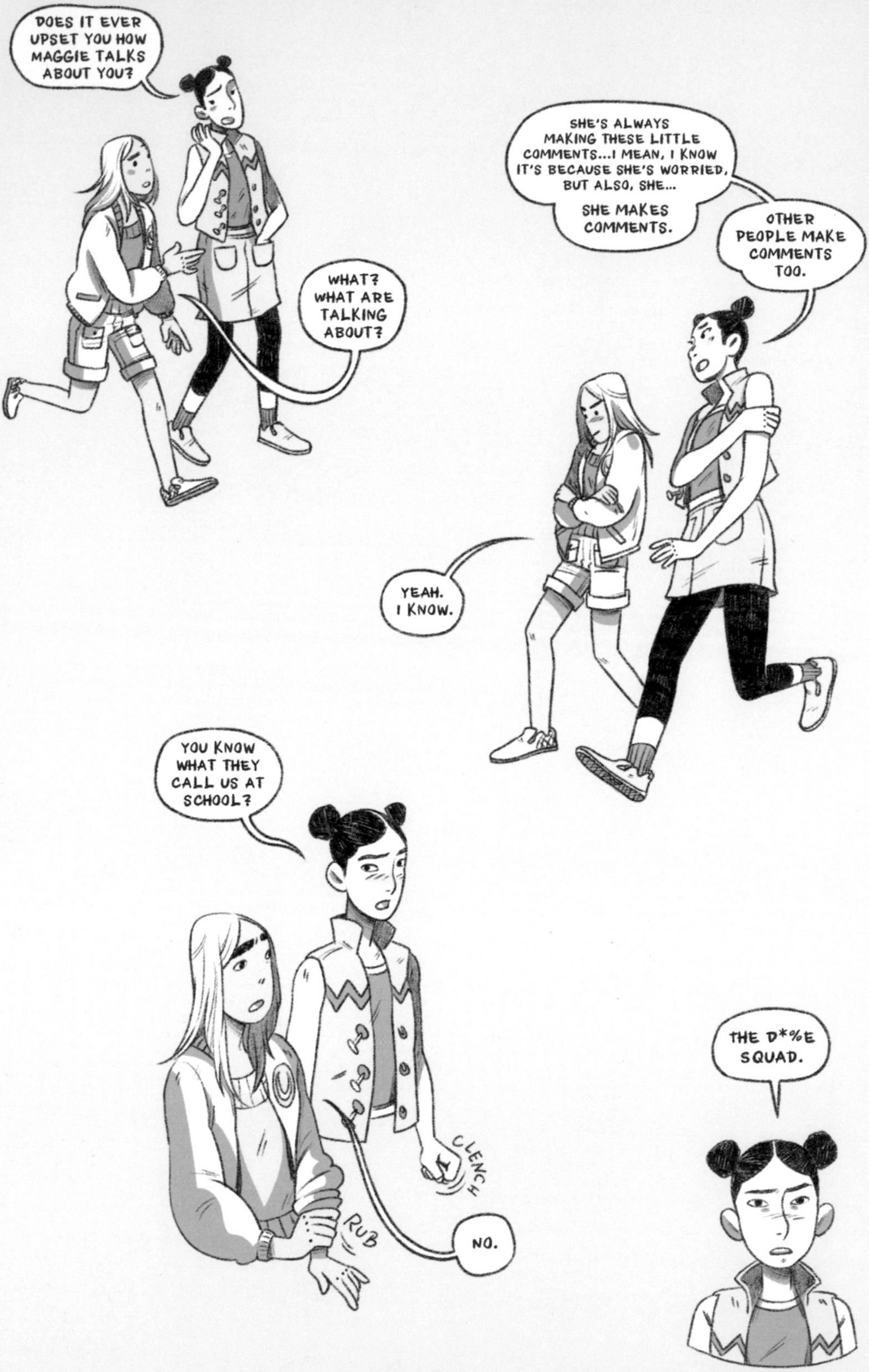
DOES IT EVER UPSET YOU HOW MAGGIE TALKS ABOUT YOU?
WHAT? WHAT ARE TALKING ABOUT?
SHE'S ALWAYS MAKING THESE LITTLE COMMENTS...I MEAN, I KNOW IT'S BECAUSE SHE'S WORRIED, BUT ALSO, SHE...
SHE MAKES COMMENTS.
OTHER PEOPLE MAKE COMMENTS TOO.
YEAH. I KNOW.
YOU KNOW WHAT THEY CALL US AT SCHOOL?
CLENCH
RUB
NO.
THE D*%E SQUAD.

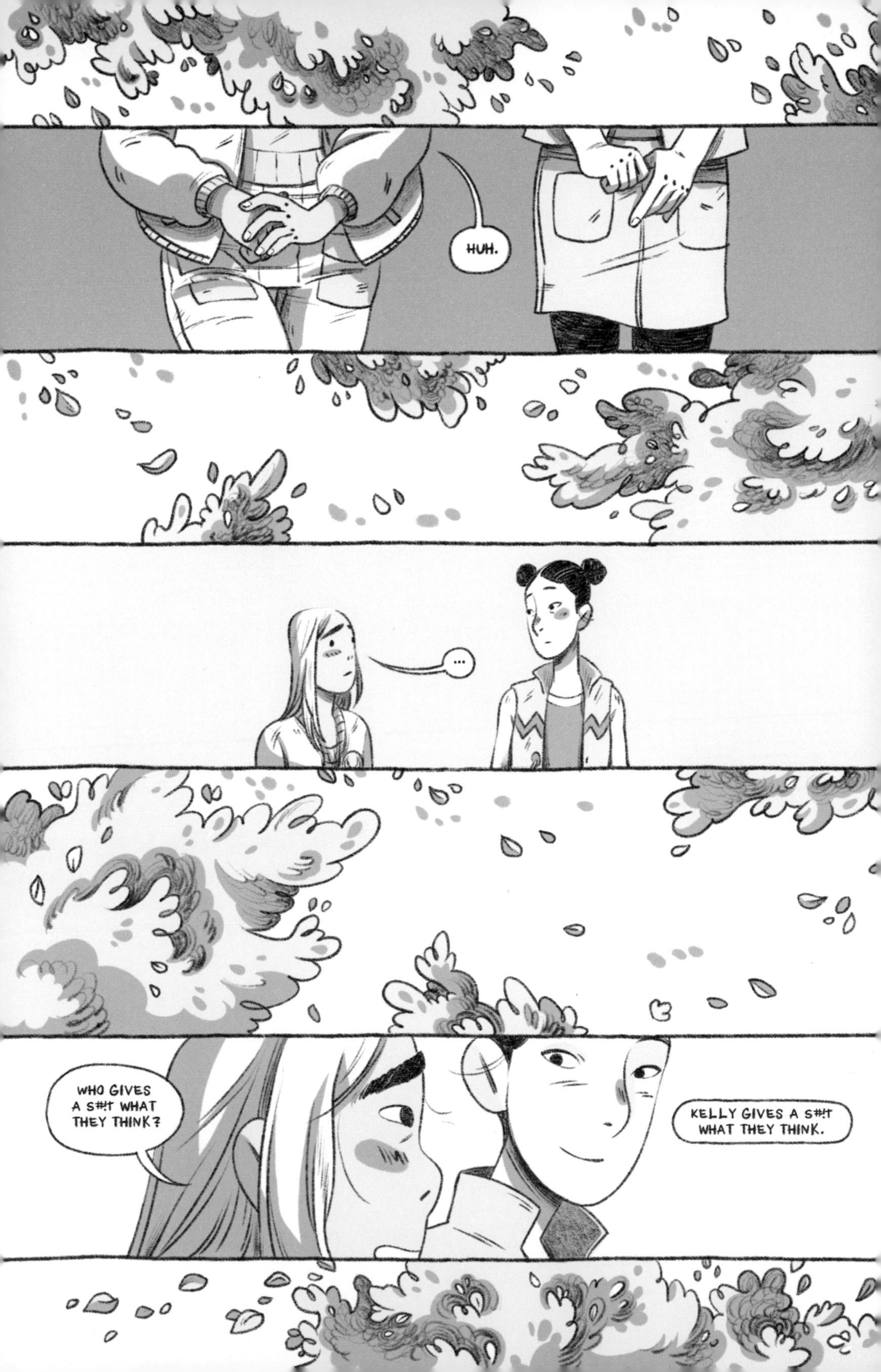
HUH.
...
WHO GIVES A S#!T WHAT THEY THINK?
KELLY GIVES A S#!T WHAT THEY THINK.

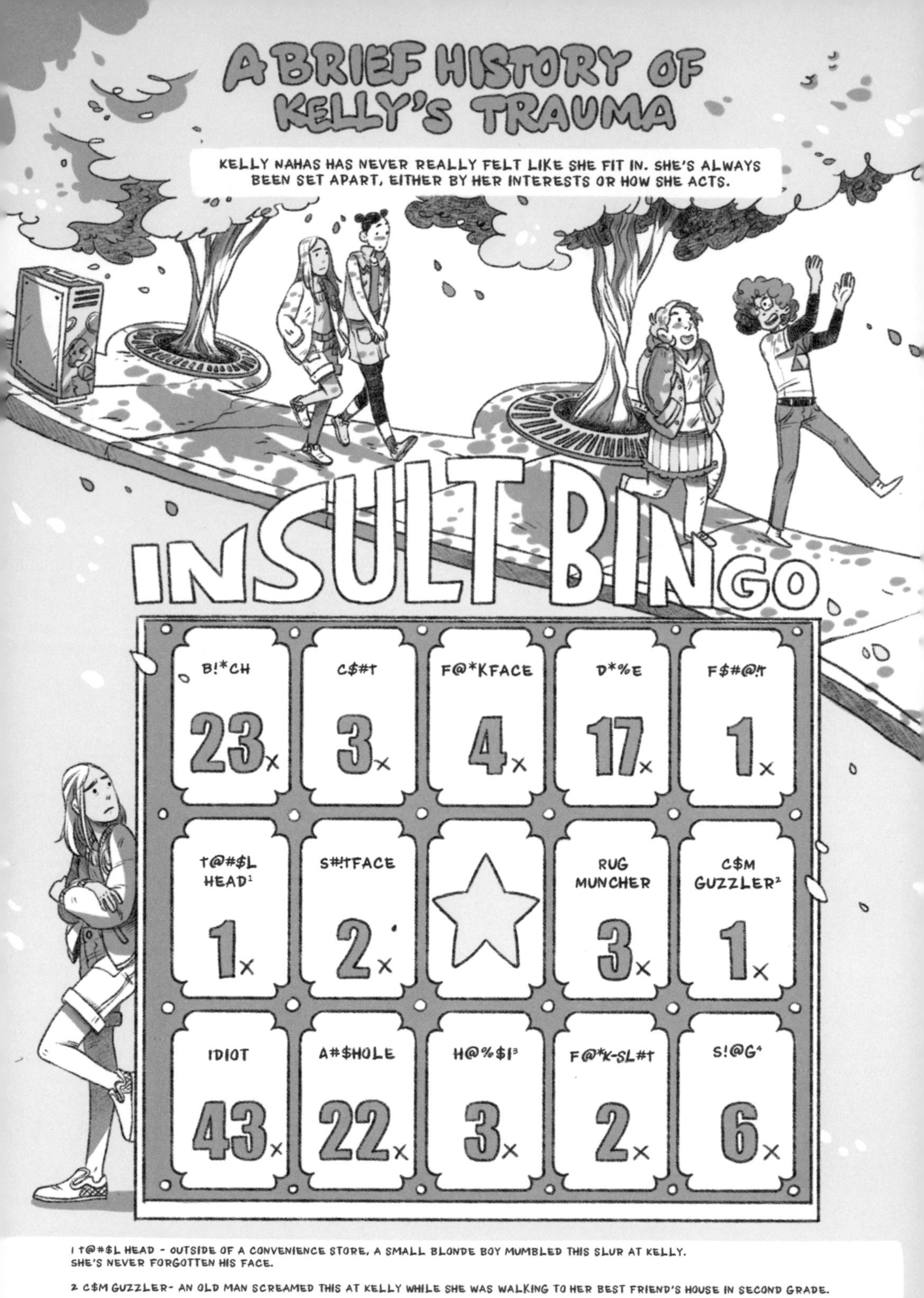
A BRIEF HISTORY OF KELLY'S TRAUMA
KELLY NAHAS HAS NEVER REALLY FELT LIKE SHE FIT IN. SHE'S ALWAYS BEEN SET APART, EITHER BY HER INTERESTS OR HOW SHE ACTS.
INSULT BINGO
B!*CH 23x
C$#T 3x
F@*KFACE 4x
D*%E 17x
F$#@!T 1x
T@#$L HEAD[1] 1x
S#!TFACE 2x
RUG MUNCHER 3x
C$M GUZZLER[2] 1x
IDIOT 43x
A#$HOLE 22x
H@%$I[3] 3x
F@*K-SL#T 2x
S!@G[4] 6x

1 T@#$L HEAD - OUTSIDE OF A CONVENIENCE STORE, A SMALL BLONDE BOY MUMBLED THIS SLUR AT KELLY. SHE'S NEVER FORGOTTEN HIS FACE.

2 C$M GUZZLER- AN OLD MAN SCREAMED THIS AT KELLY WHILE SHE WAS WALKING TO HER BEST FRIEND'S HOUSE IN SECOND GRADE.

3 H@%$I - TWO OLDER GIRLS KEPT REFERRING TO KELLY BY THIS WHEN SHE FIRST GOT TO FOREST HILLS. SHE THOUGHT IT WAS A NICKNAME, UNTIL ONE OF THE TEACHERS REPRIMANDED THE OLDER GIRLS.

4 KELLY'S STILL NOT SURE WHAT THE NAME IS IN REFERENCE TO. SOMETHING ABOUT A CARTOON? LIKE NOT AN ANIME?

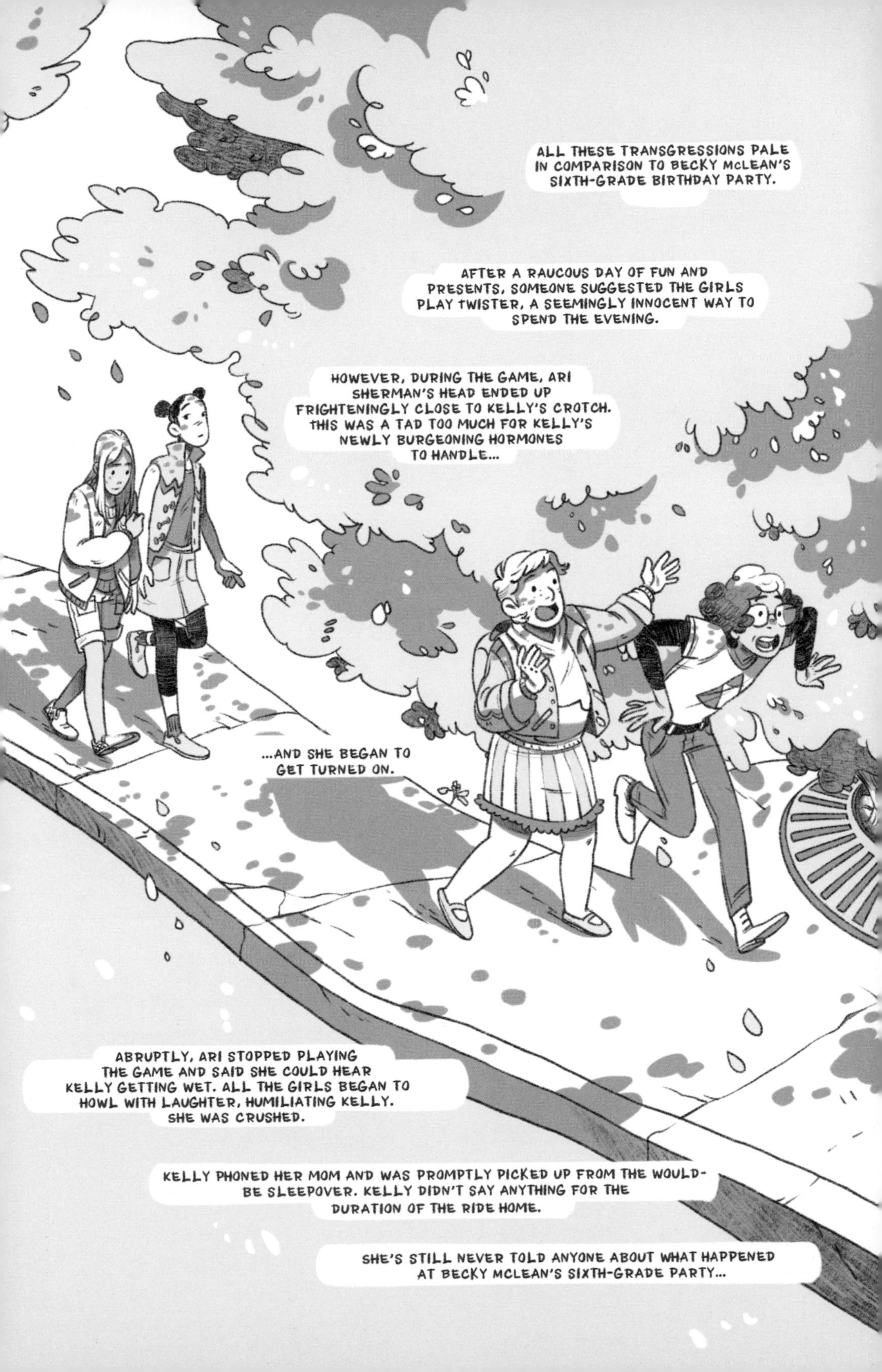
ALL THESE TRANSGRESSIONS PALE IN COMPARISON TO BECKY McLEAN'S SIXTH-GRADE BIRTHDAY PARTY.
AFTER A RAUCOUS DAY OF FUN AND PRESENTS, SOMEONE SUGGESTED THE GIRLS PLAY TWISTER, A SEEMINGLY INNOCENT WAY TO SPEND THE EVENING.
HOWEVER, DURING THE GAME, ARI SHERMAN'S HEAD ENDED UP FRIGHTENINGLY CLOSE TO KELLY'S CROTCH. THIS WAS A TAD TOO MUCH FOR KELLY'S NEWLY BURGEONING HORMONES TO HANDLE...
...AND SHE BEGAN TO GET TURNED ON.
ABRUPTLY, ARI STOPPED PLAYING THE GAME AND SAID SHE COULD HEAR KELLY GETTING WET. ALL THE GIRLS BEGAN TO HOWL WITH LAUGHTER, HUMILIATING KELLY. SHE WAS CRUSHED.
KELLY PHONED HER MOM AND WAS PROMPTLY PICKED UP FROM THE WOULD-BE SLEEPOVER. KELLY DIDN'T SAY ANYTHING FOR THE DURATION OF THE RIDE HOME.
SHE'S STILL NEVER TOLD ANYONE ABOUT WHAT HAPPENED AT BECKY McLEAN'S SIXTH-GRADE PARTY...

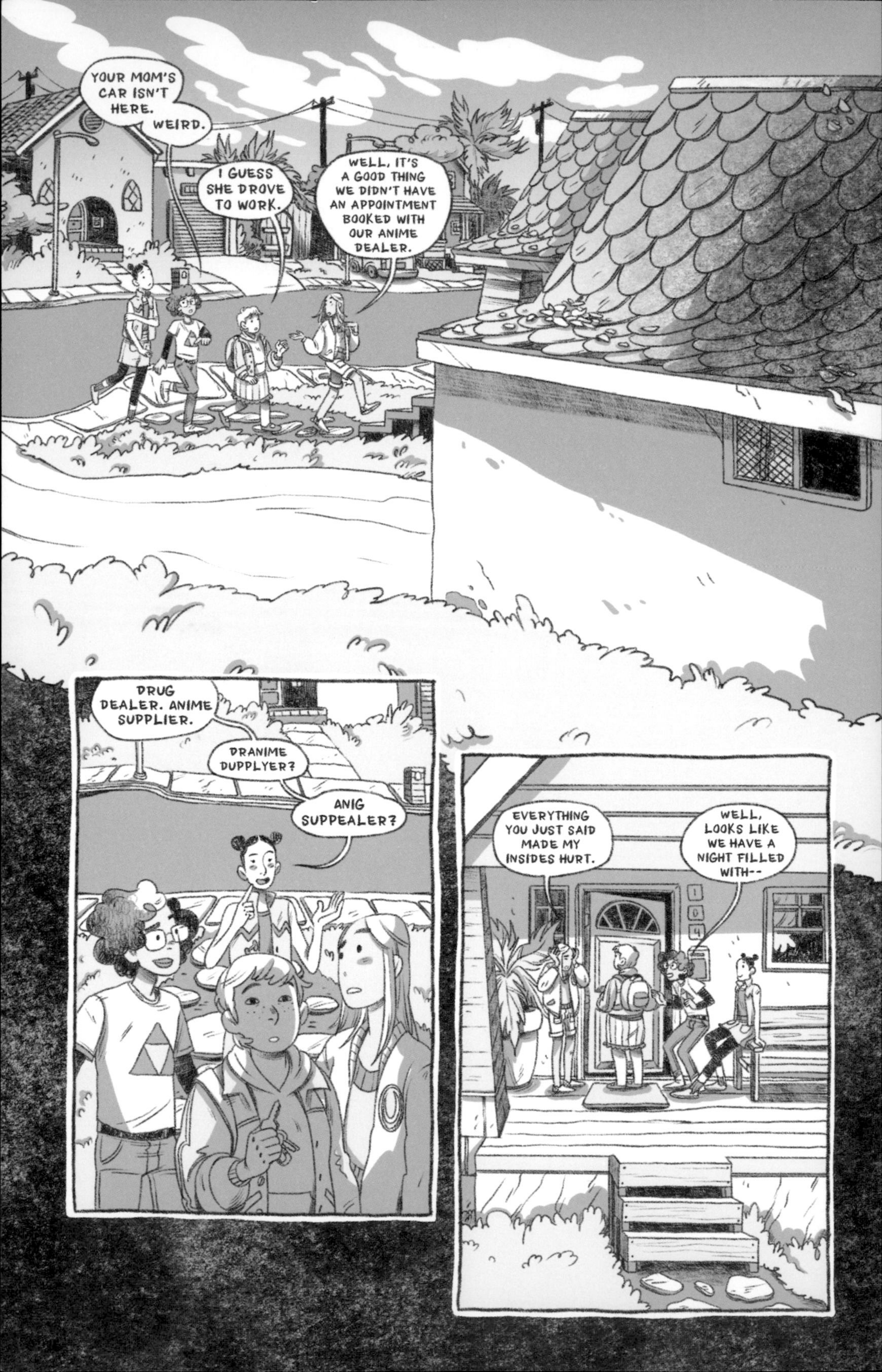
YOUR MOM'S CAR ISN'T HERE.
WEIRD.
I GUESS SHE DROVE TO WORK.
WELL, IT'S A GOOD THING WE DIDN'T HAVE AN APPOINTMENT BOOKED WITH OUR ANIME DEALER.
DRUG DEALER. ANIME SUPPLIER.
DRANIME DUPPLYER?
ANIG SUPPEALER?
EVERYTHING YOU JUST SAID MADE MY INSIDES HURT.
WELL, LOOKS LIKE WE HAVE A NIGHT FILLED WITH--
104

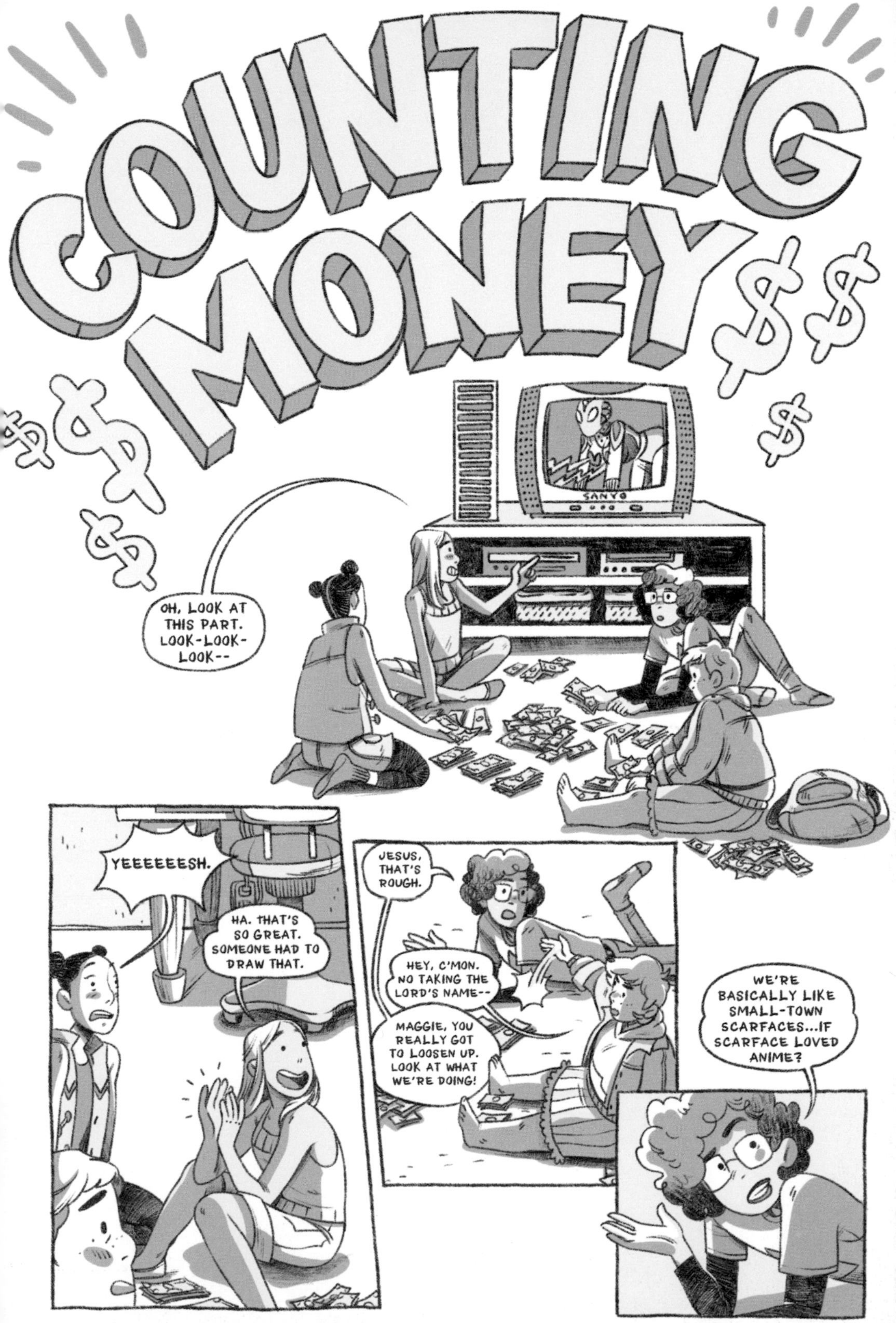
COUNTING MONEY
SANYO
OH, LOOK AT THIS PART. LOOK-LOOK-LOOK--
YEEEEEESH.
HA. THAT'S SO GREAT. SOMEONE HAD TO DRAW THAT.
JESUS, THAT'S ROUGH.
HEY, C'MON. NO TAKING THE LORD'S NAME--
MAGGIE, YOU REALLY GOT TO LOOSEN UP. LOOK AT WHAT WE'RE DOING!
WE'RE BASICALLY LIKE SMALL-TOWN SCARFACES...IF SCARFACE LOVED ANIME?

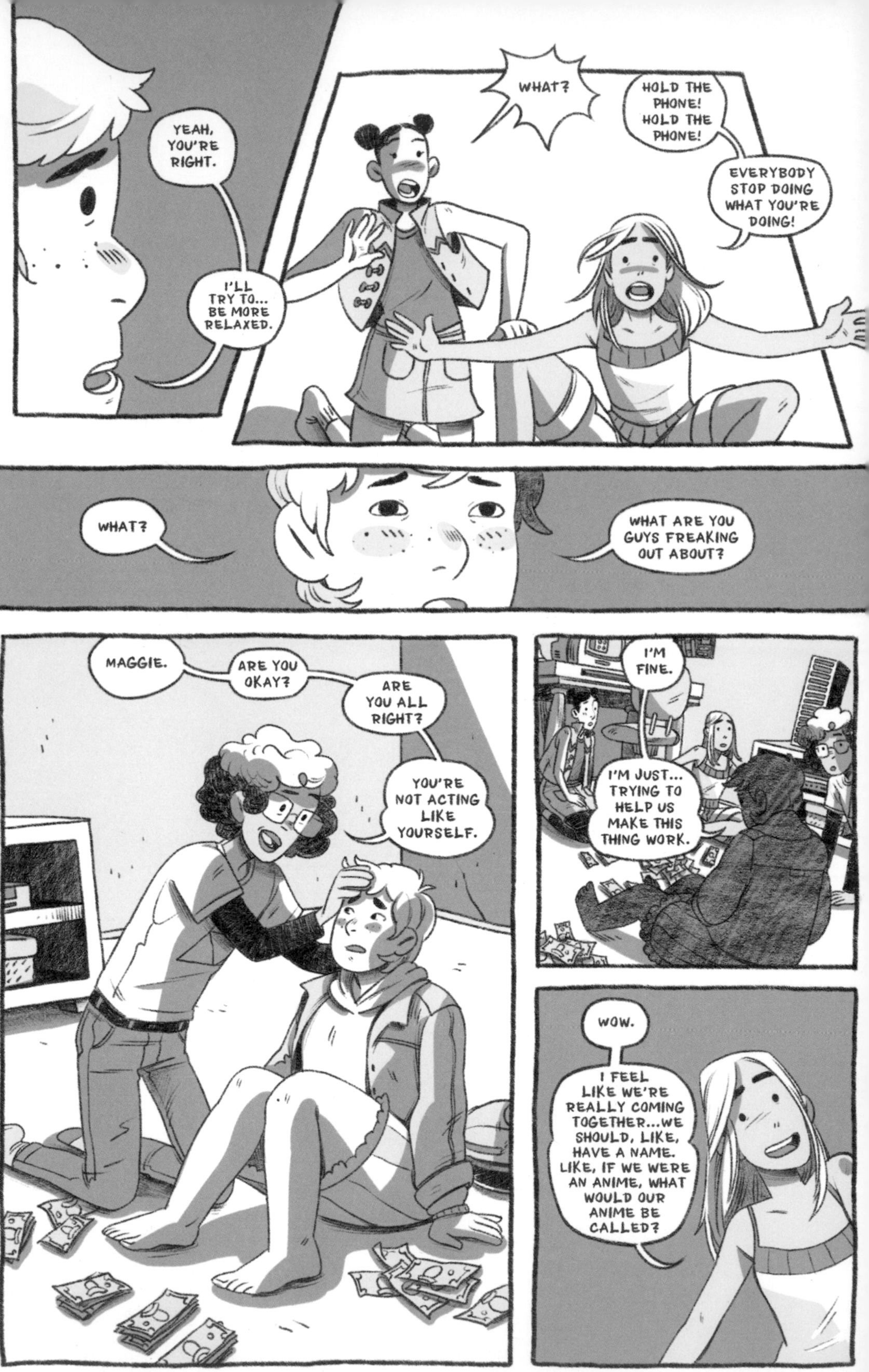
YEAH, YOU'RE RIGHT.
I'LL TRY TO... BE MORE RELAXED.
WHAT?
HOLD THE PHONE! HOLD THE PHONE!
EVERYBODY STOP DOING WHAT YOU'RE DOING!
WHAT?
WHAT ARE YOU GUYS FREAKING OUT ABOUT?
MAGGIE.
ARE YOU OKAY?
ARE YOU ALL RIGHT?
YOU'RE NOT ACTING LIKE YOURSELF.
I'M FINE.
I'M JUST... TRYING TO HELP US MAKE THIS THING WORK.
WOW.
I FEEL LIKE WE'RE REALLY COMING TOGETHER...WE SHOULD, LIKE, HAVE A NAME. LIKE, IF WE WERE AN ANIME, WHAT WOULD OUR ANIME BE CALLED?

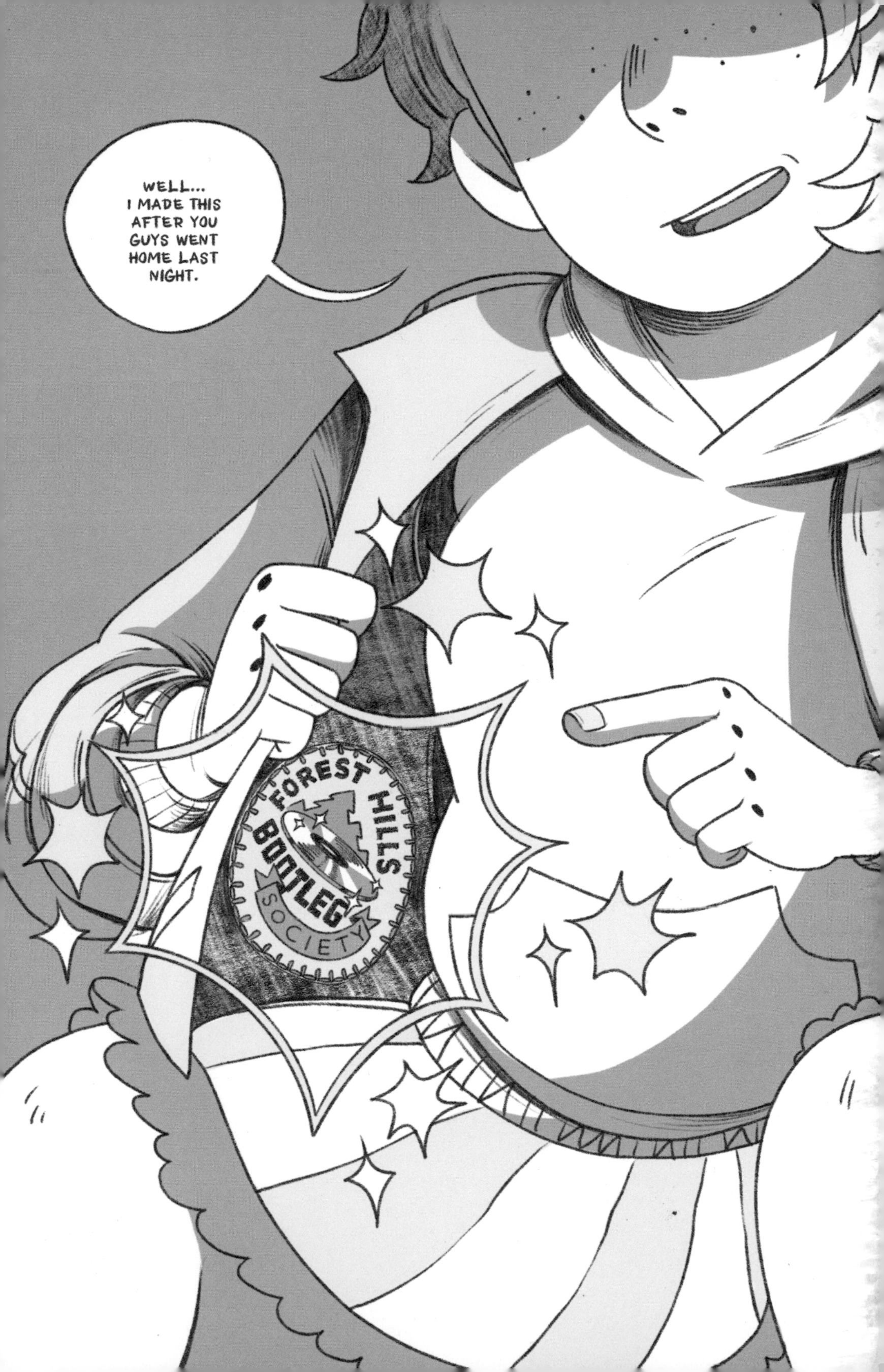
WELL... I MADE THIS AFTER YOU GUYS WENT HOME LAST NIGHT.
FOREST HILLS BOOTLEG SOCIETY

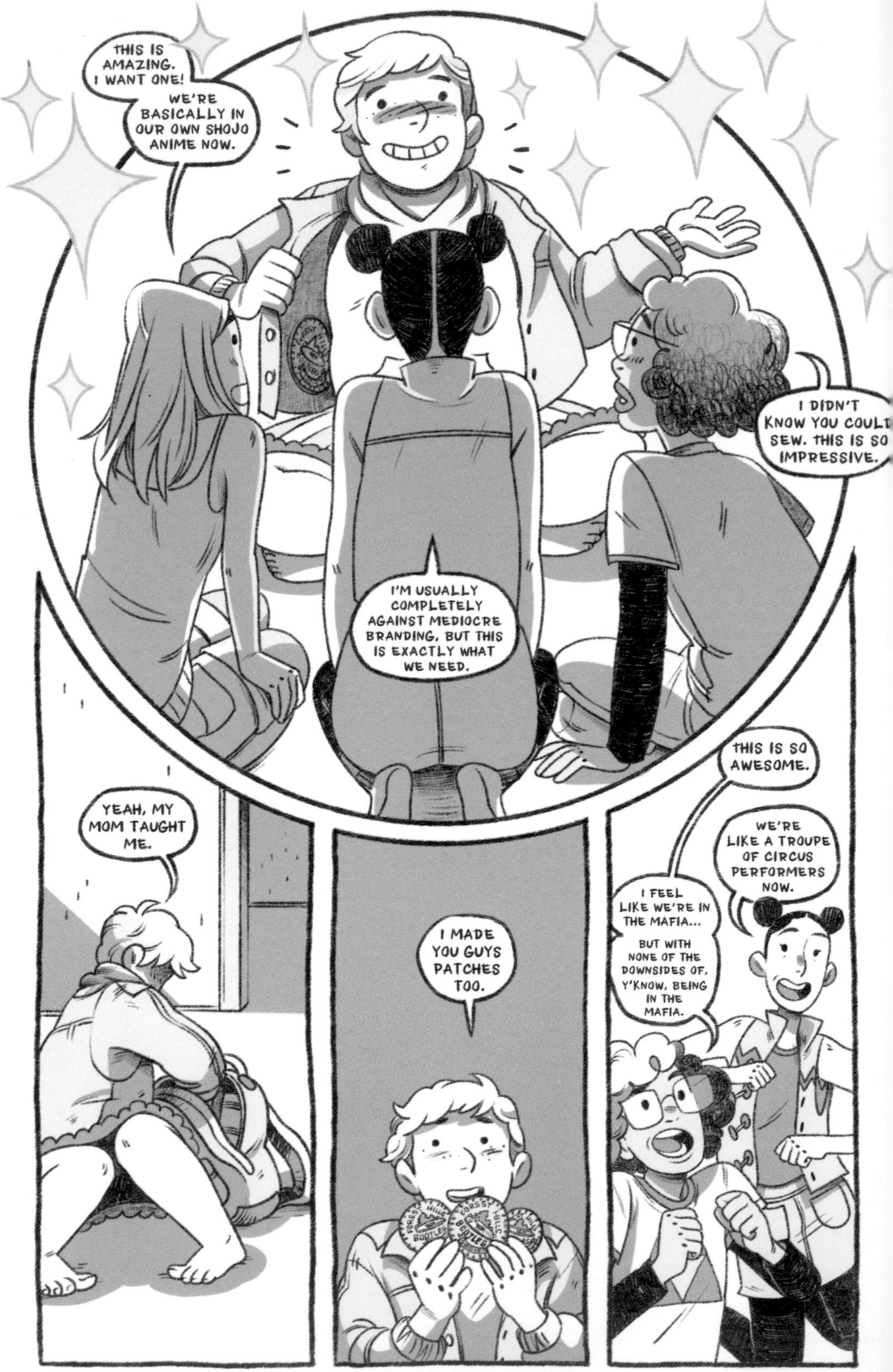
THIS IS AMAZING. I WANT ONE!
WE'RE BASICALLY IN OUR OWN SHOJO ANIME NOW.
I DIDN'T KNOW YOU COULD SEW. THIS IS SO IMPRESSIVE.
I'M USUALLY COMPLETELY AGAINST MEDIOCRE BRANDING, BUT THIS IS EXACTLY WHAT WE NEED.
YEAH, MY MOM TAUGHT ME.
I MADE YOU GUYS PATCHES TOO.
FOREST HILLS BOOTLEG
THIS IS SO AWESOME.
WE'RE LIKE A TROUPE OF CIRCUS PERFORMERS NOW.
I FEEL LIKE WE'RE IN THE MAFIA...
BUT WITH NONE OF THE DOWNSIDES OF, Y'KNOW, BEING IN THE MAFIA.

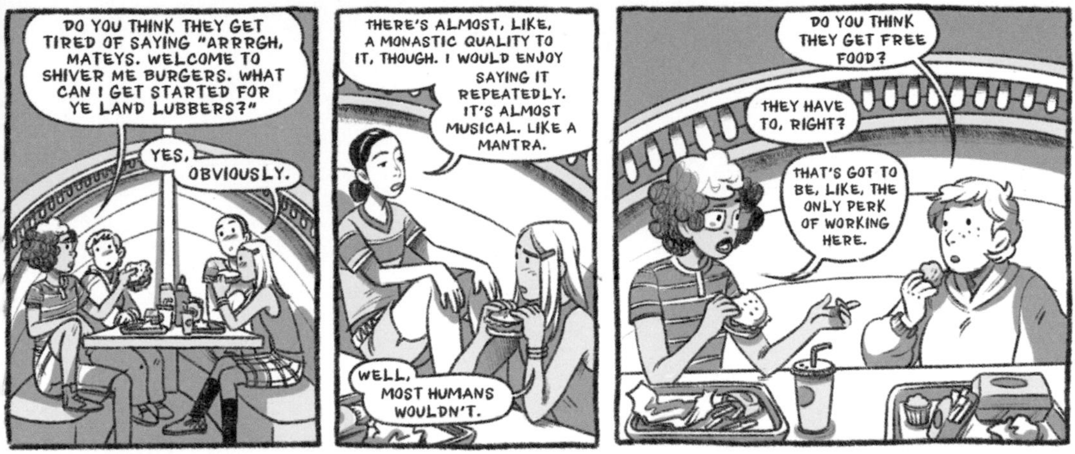
DO YOU THINK THEY GET TIRED OF SAYING "ARRRGH, MATEYS. WELCOME TO SHIVER ME BURGERS. WHAT CAN I GET STARTED FOR YE LAND LUBBERS?"
YES, OBVIOUSLY.
THERE'S ALMOST, LIKE, A MONASTIC QUALITY TO IT, THOUGH. I WOULD ENJOY SAYING IT REPEATEDLY. IT'S ALMOST MUSICAL. LIKE A MANTRA.
WELL, MOST HUMANS WOULDN'T.
DO YOU THINK THEY GET FREE FOOD?
THEY HAVE TO, RIGHT?
THAT'S GOT TO BE, LIKE, THE ONLY PERK OF WORKING HERE.

A BRIEF HISTORY OF A TEXTILES MANUFACTURING PLANT

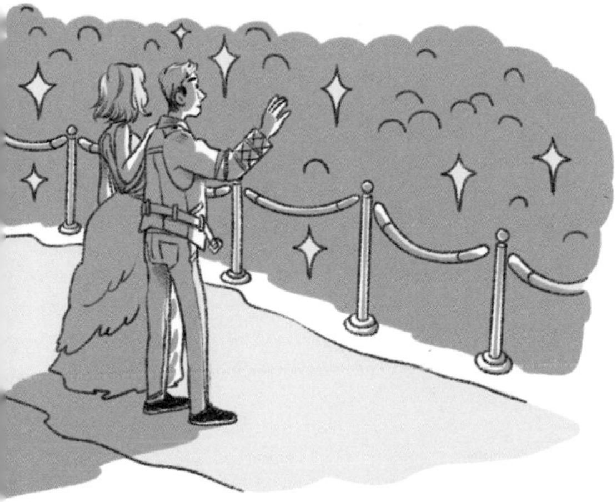

EVER SINCE TEEN HEARTTHROB GEORGIO SIMONE WAS SPOTTED ON THE RED CARPET SPORTING A MERZO SPEED FREAK DOWN JACKET TWO NEW YORK FASHION WEEKS AGO, YOUNG PEOPLE ACROSS THE COUNTRY HAVE BEEN CLAMORING FOR THE GARMENT TO BE AVAILABLE COMMERCIALLY.

HOWEVER, THE $529.99 RETAIL PRICE WAS A RED FLAG FOR MOST U.S.-BASED RETAIL-CHAIN BUYERS. THUS, THE COMPANY MERZO FASHION LLC. STEPPED UP TO THE CHALLENGE.

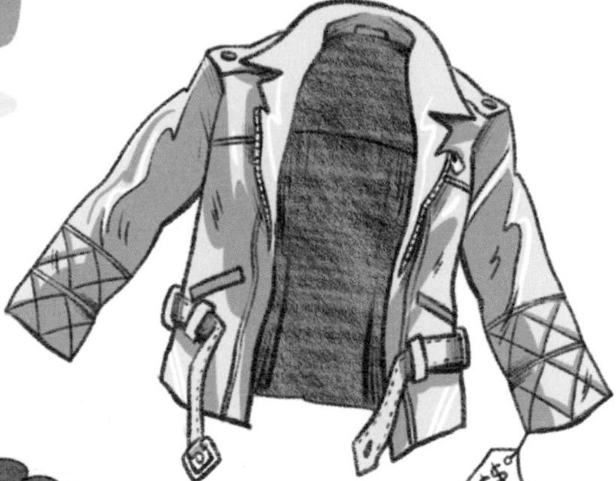
$$$

WITH THEIR NEW MANUFACTURING PLANT OVERSEAS, THEY'VE BEEN PRODUCING NEARLY IDENTICAL JACKETS FOR A QUARTER OF THE RETAIL PRICE. BIG BOX RETAIL CHAINS ACROSS THE COUNTRY HAVE BEEN SUPPLYING MERZO HEADQUARTERS WITH ORDERS BY THE DUMP-TRUCK LOAD.

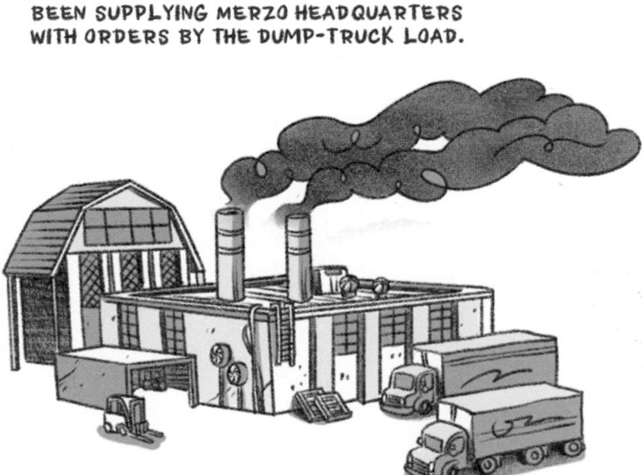

MOST PEOPLE DON'T KNOW THAT THEIR NEW JACKETS ARE PRODUCED BY WORKERS PAID CENTS ON THE DOLLAR, THAT THEY'RE FORCED TO ENDURE GRUELING SCHEDULES, AND THAT FOUR FACTORY WORKERS PASSED AWAY LAST WINTER FROM A GAS LEAK.

THEY ONLY CARE ABOUT THE JACKETS, WELL...BECAUSE THEY JUST LOOK COOL.

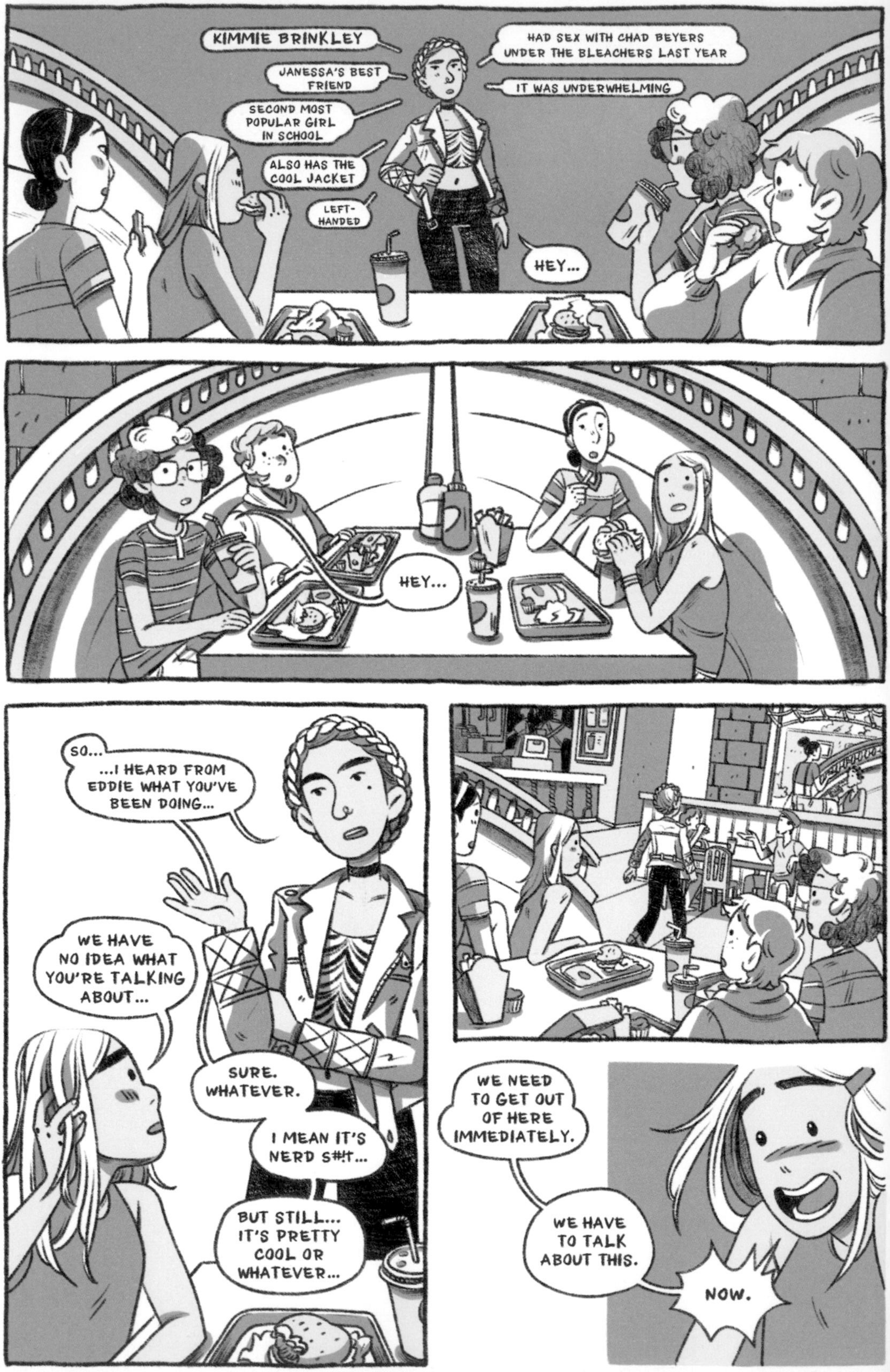
KIMMIE BRINKLEY
JANESSA'S BEST FRIEND
SECOND MOST POPULAR GIRL IN SCHOOL
ALSO HAS THE COOL JACKET
LEFT-HANDED
HAD SEX WITH CHAD BEYERS UNDER THE BLEACHERS LAST YEAR
IT WAS UNDERWHELMING
HEY...
HEY...
SO...
...I HEARD FROM EDDIE WHAT YOU'VE BEEN DOING...
WE HAVE NO IDEA WHAT YOU'RE TALKING ABOUT...
SURE. WHATEVER.
I MEAN IT'S NERD S#!T...
BUT STILL... IT'S PRETTY COOL OR WHATEVER...
WE NEED TO GET OUT OF HERE IMMEDIATELY.
WE HAVE TO TALK ABOUT THIS.
NOW.

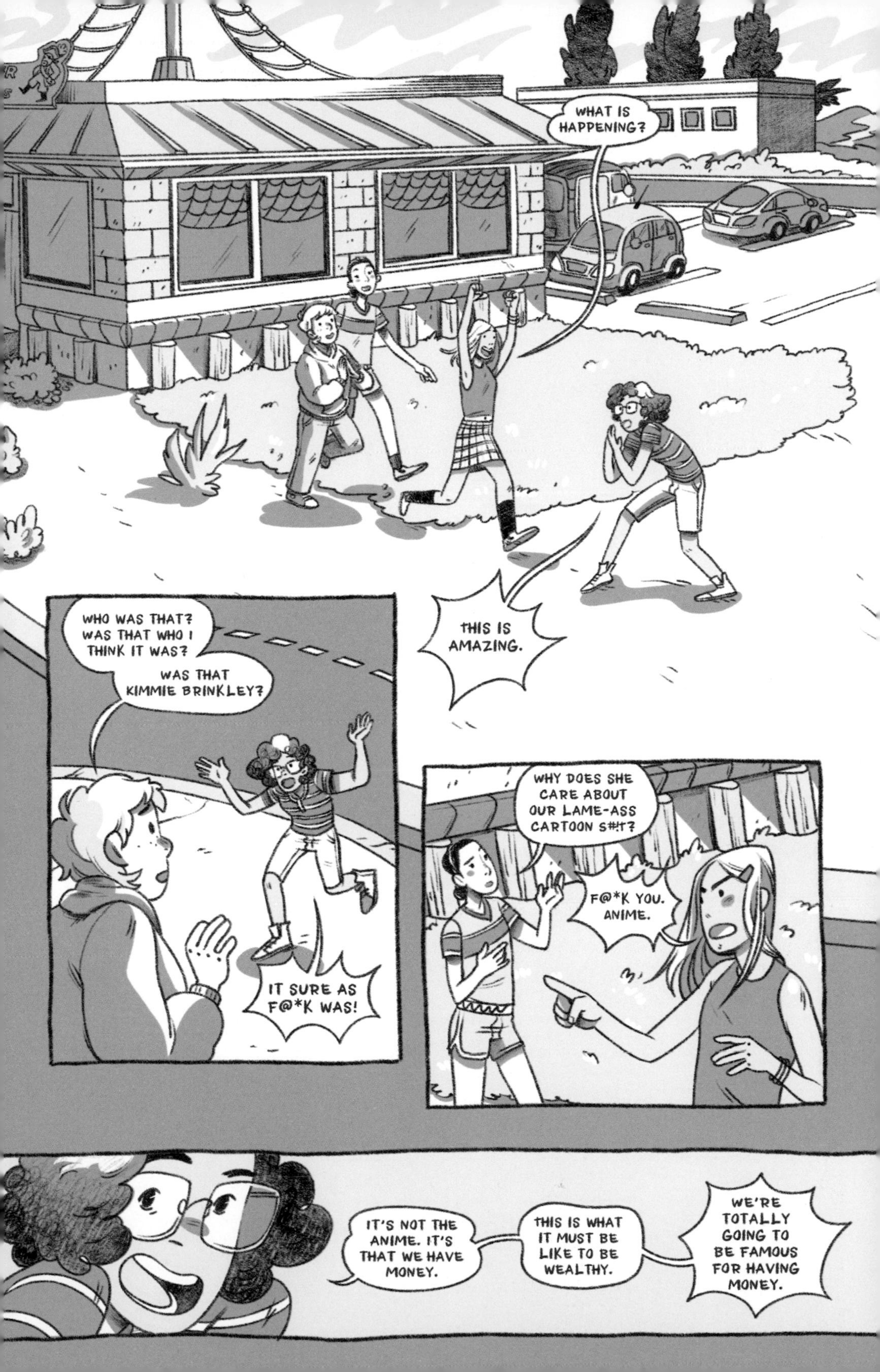
WHAT IS HAPPENING?
THIS IS AMAZING.
WHO WAS THAT? WAS THAT WHO I THINK IT WAS?
WAS THAT KIMMIE BRINKLEY?
IT SURE AS F@*K WAS!
WHY DOES SHE CARE ABOUT OUR LAME-ASS CARTOON S#!T?
F@*K YOU. ANIME.
IT'S NOT THE ANIME. IT'S THAT WE HAVE MONEY.
THIS IS WHAT IT MUST BE LIKE TO BE WEALTHY.
WE'RE TOTALLY GOING TO BE FAMOUS FOR HAVING MONEY.

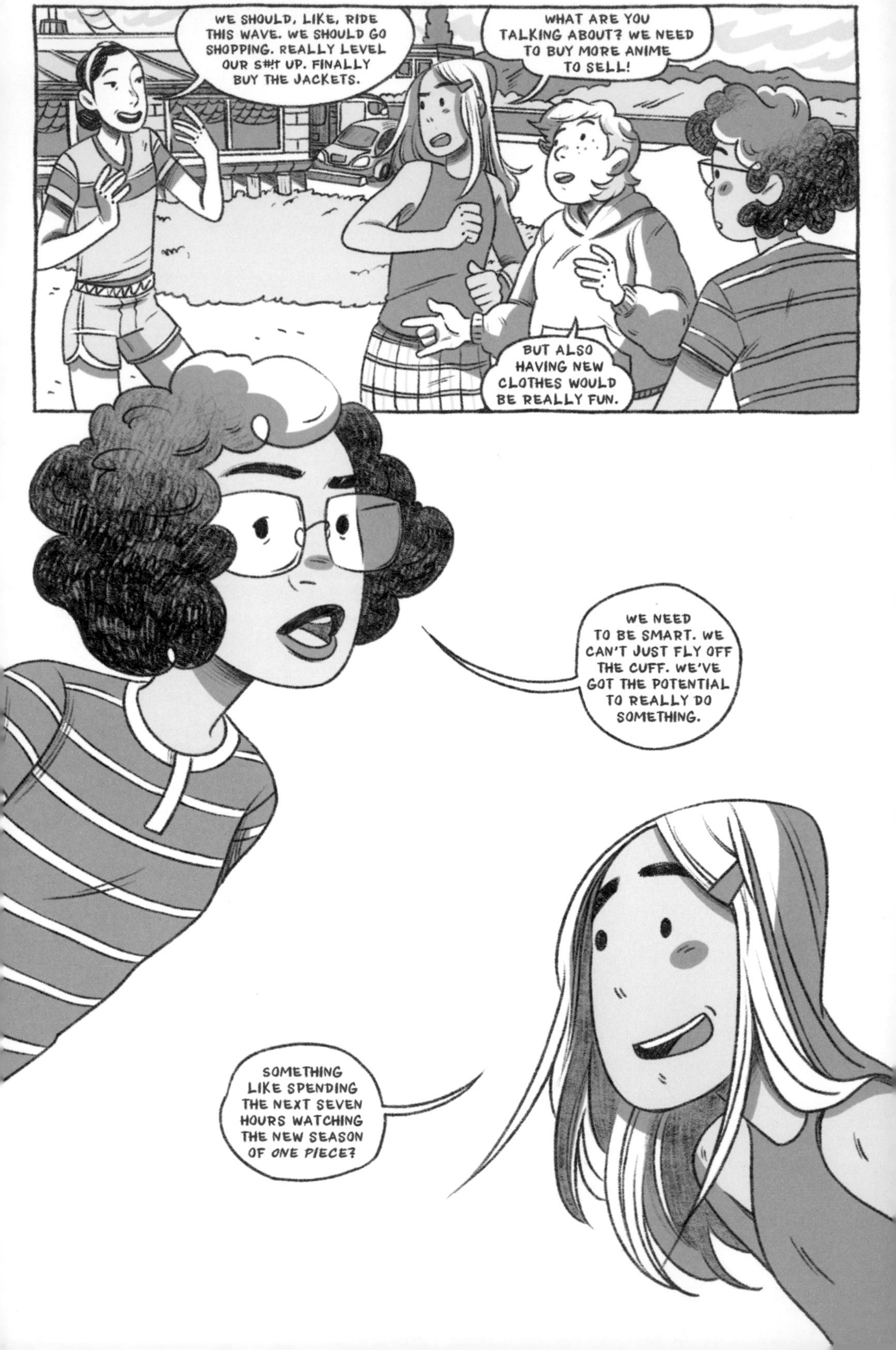
WE SHOULD, LIKE, RIDE THIS WAVE. WE SHOULD GO SHOPPING. REALLY LEVEL OUR S#!T UP. FINALLY BUY THE JACKETS.
WHAT ARE YOU TALKING ABOUT? WE NEED TO BUY MORE ANIME TO SELL!
BUT ALSO HAVING NEW CLOTHES WOULD BE REALLY FUN.
WE NEED TO BE SMART. WE CAN'T JUST FLY OFF THE CUFF. WE'VE GOT THE POTENTIAL TO REALLY DO SOMETHING.
SOMETHING LIKE SPENDING THE NEXT SEVEN HOURS WATCHING THE NEW SEASON OF *ONE PIECE*?

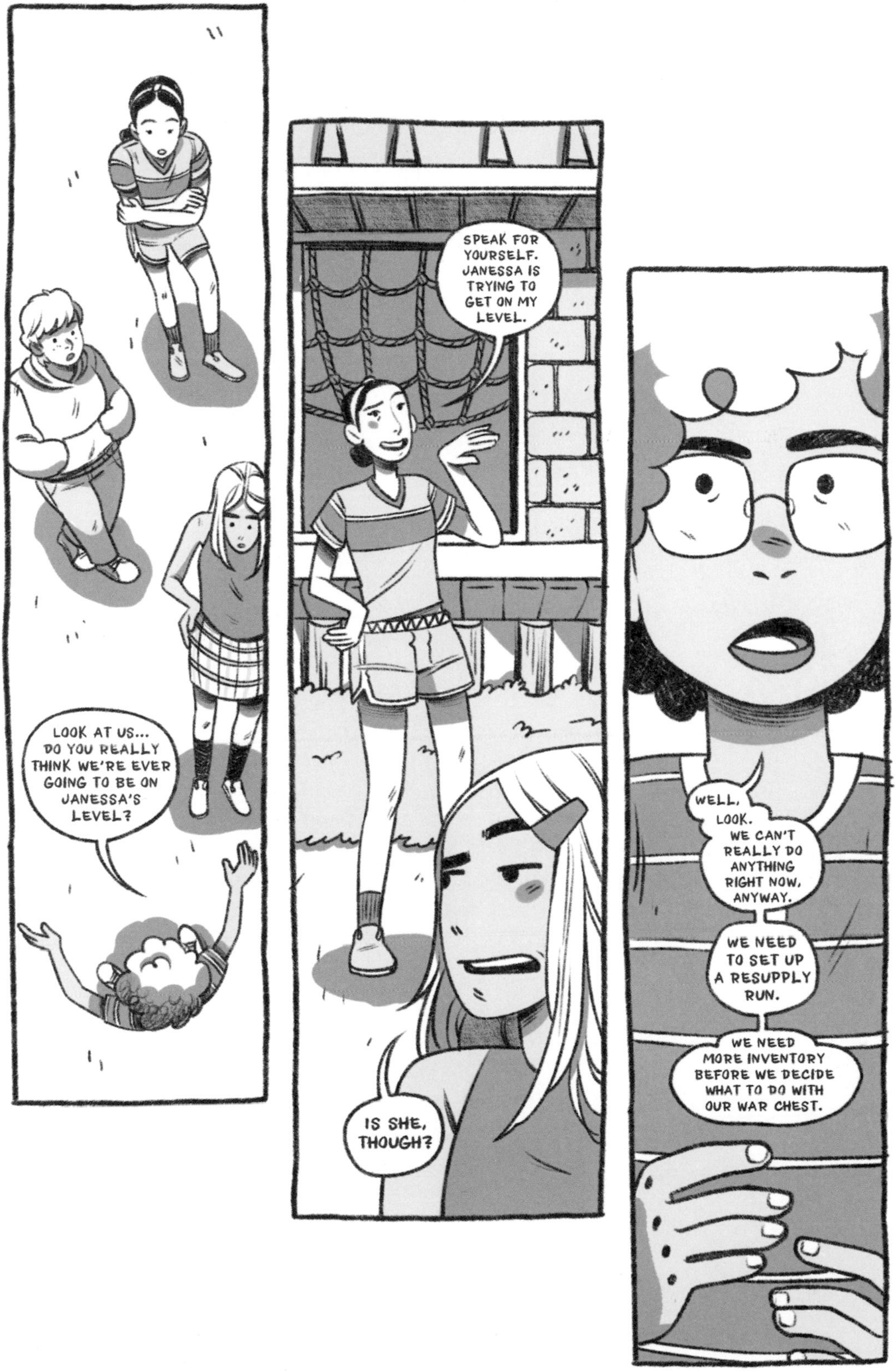
LOOK AT US... DO YOU REALLY THINK WE'RE EVER GOING TO BE ON JANESSA'S LEVEL?
SPEAK FOR YOURSELF. JANESSA IS TRYING TO GET ON MY LEVEL.
IS SHE, THOUGH?
WELL, LOOK.
WE CAN'T REALLY DO ANYTHING RIGHT NOW, ANYWAY.
WE NEED TO SET UP A RESUPPLY RUN.
WE NEED MORE INVENTORY BEFORE WE DECIDE WHAT TO DO WITH OUR WAR CHEST.

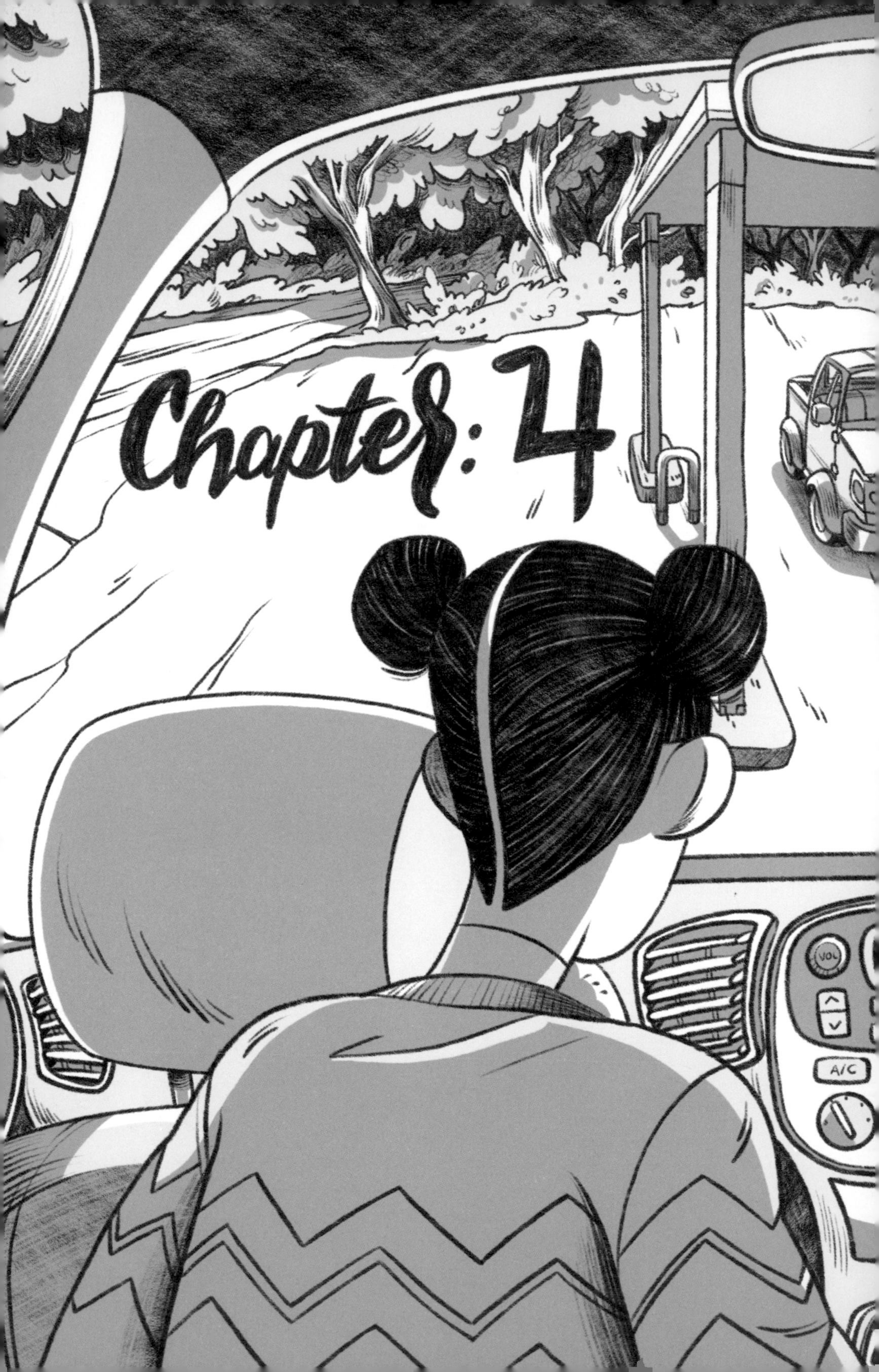
Chapter: 4
VOL
A/C

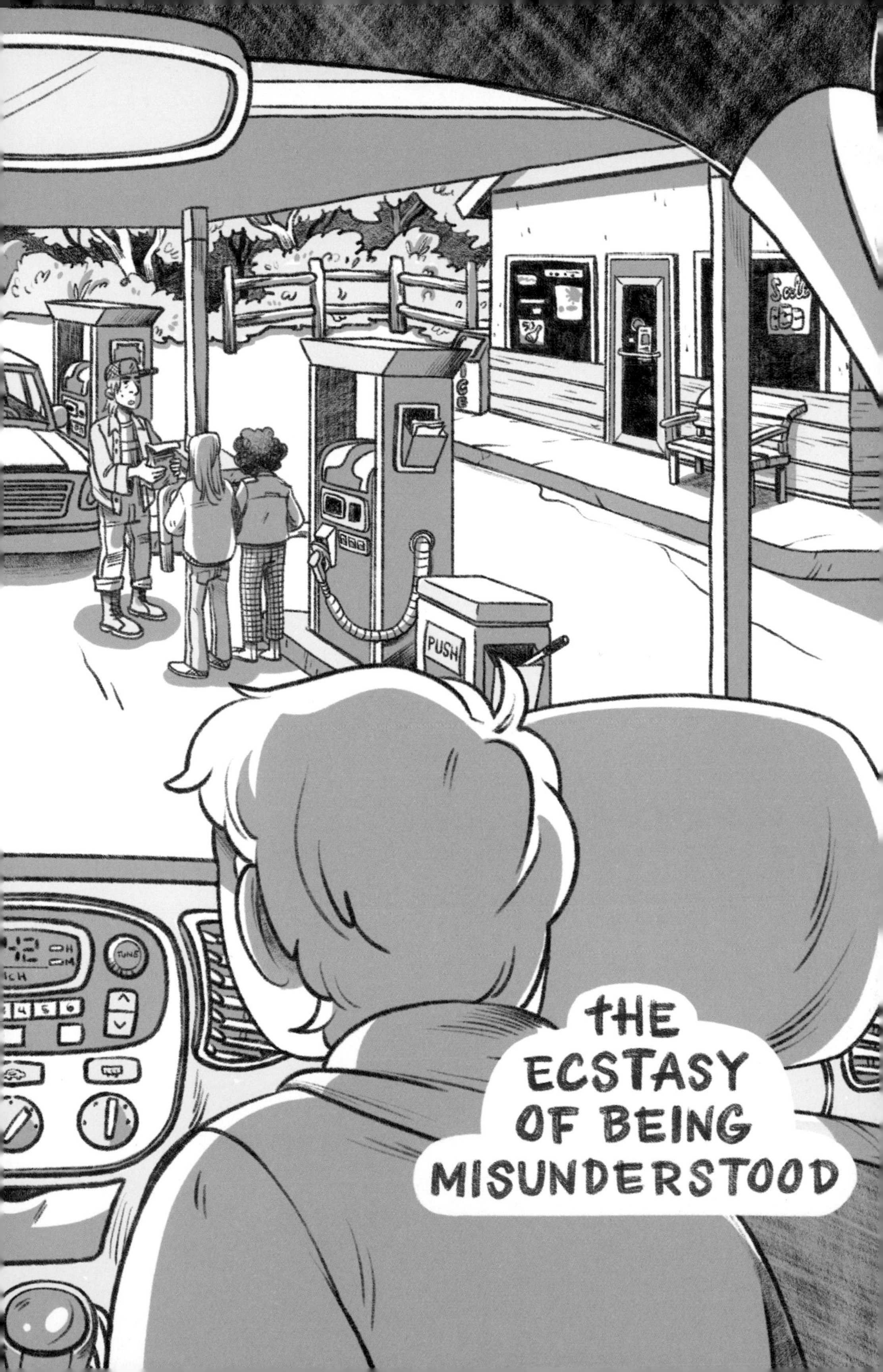
PUSH
THE ECSTASY OF BEING MISUNDERSTOOD

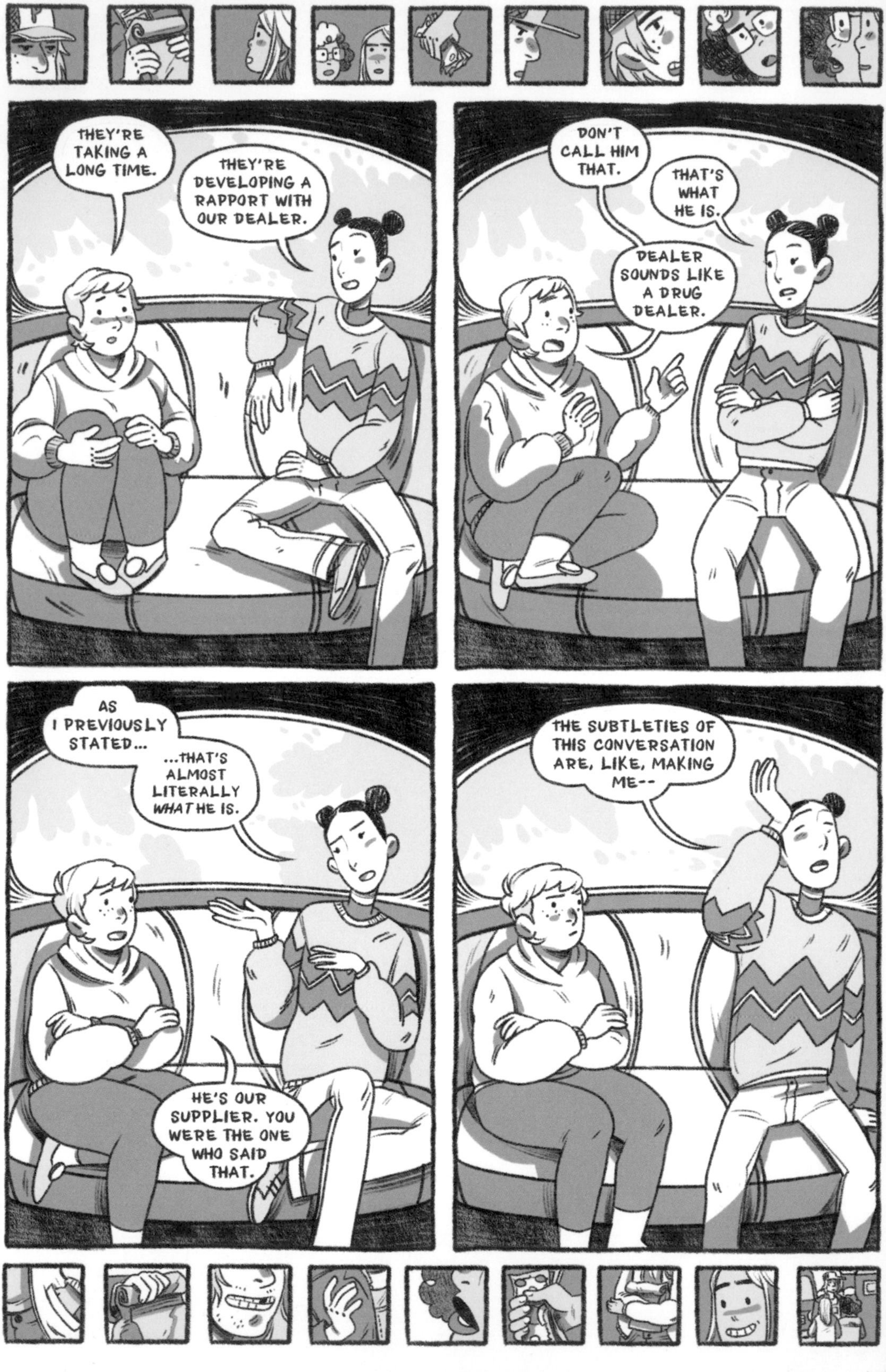
THEY'RE TAKING A LONG TIME.
THEY'RE DEVELOPING A RAPPORT WITH OUR DEALER.
DON'T CALL HIM THAT.
THAT'S WHAT HE IS.
DEALER SOUNDS LIKE A DRUG DEALER.
AS I PREVIOUSLY STATED...
...THAT'S ALMOST LITERALLY *WHAT* HE IS.
HE'S OUR SUPPLIER. YOU WERE THE ONE WHO SAID THAT.
THE SUBTLETIES OF THIS CONVERSATION ARE, LIKE, MAKING ME--

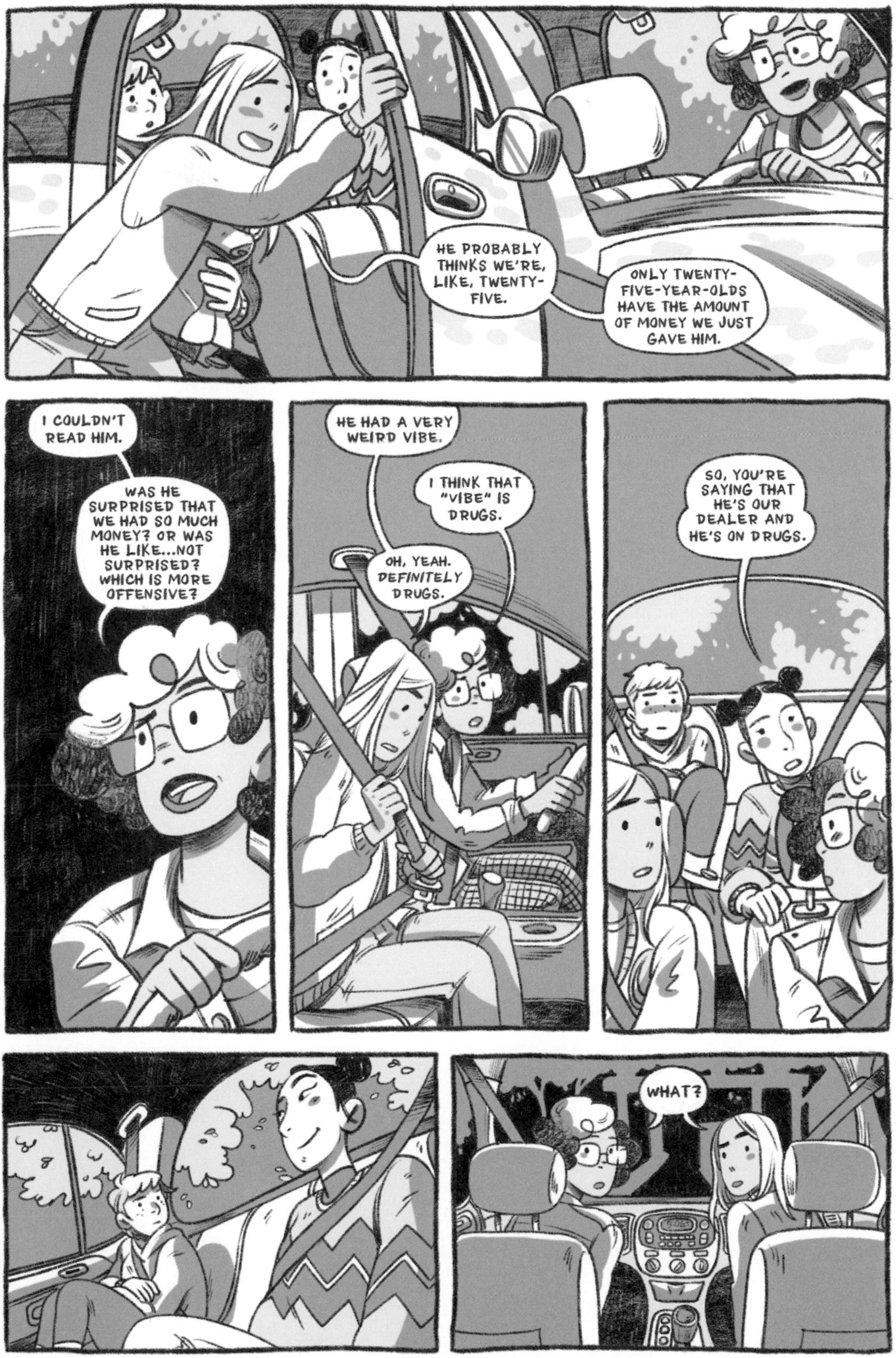
HE PROBABLY THINKS WE'RE, LIKE, TWENTY-FIVE.
ONLY TWENTY-FIVE-YEAR-OLDS HAVE THE AMOUNT OF MONEY WE JUST GAVE HIM.
I COULDN'T READ HIM.
WAS HE SURPRISED THAT WE HAD SO MUCH MONEY? OR WAS HE LIKE...NOT SURPRISED? WHICH IS MORE OFFENSIVE?
HE HAD A VERY WEIRD VIBE.
I THINK THAT "VIBE" IS DRUGS.
OH, YEAH. *DEFINITELY* DRUGS.
SO, YOU'RE SAYING THAT HE'S OUR DEALER AND HE'S ON DRUGS.
WHAT?

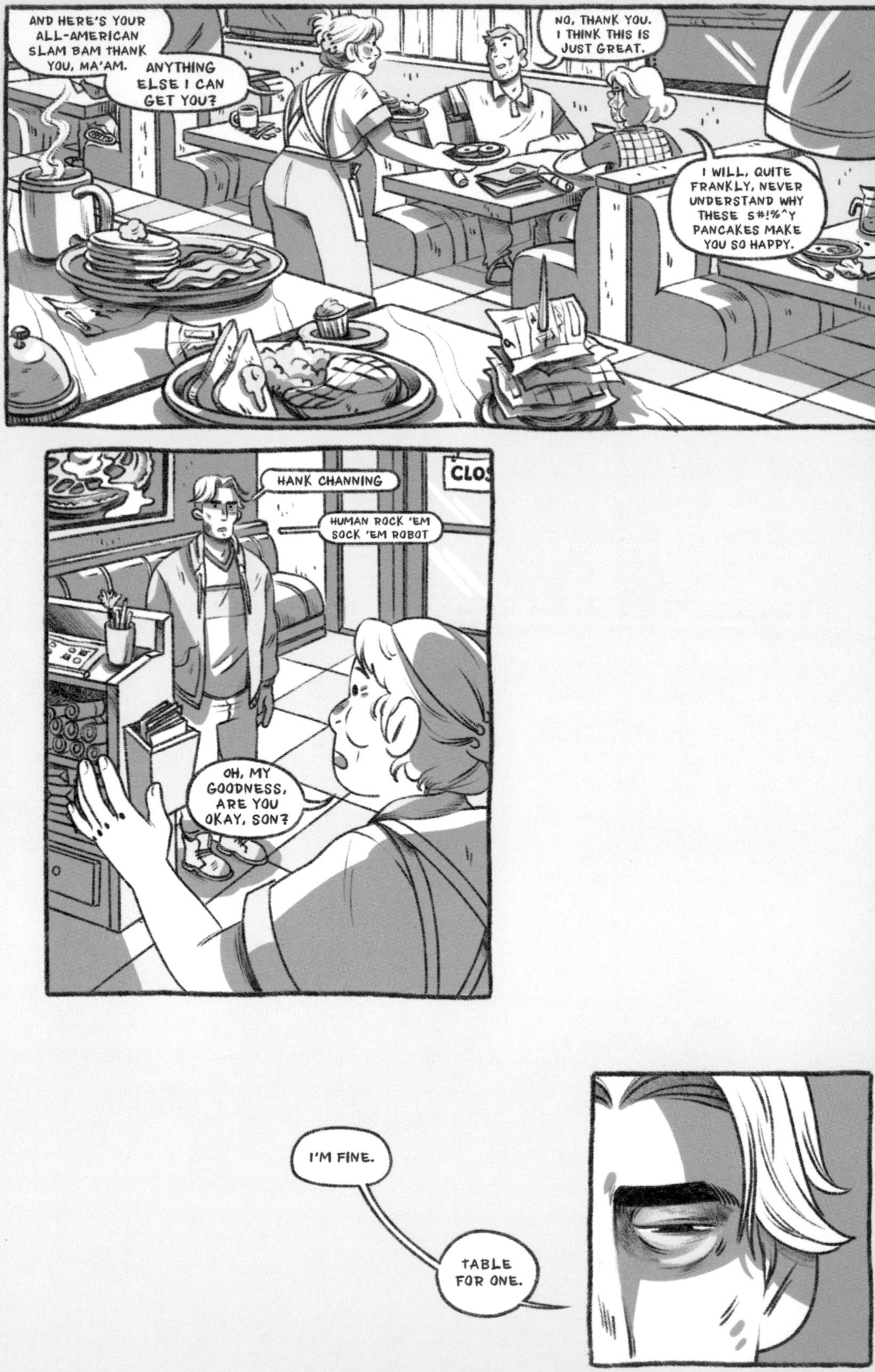
AND HERE'S YOUR ALL-AMERICAN SLAM BAM THANK YOU, MA'AM.
ANYTHING ELSE I CAN GET YOU?
NO, THANK YOU. I THINK THIS IS JUST GREAT.
I WILL, QUITE FRANKLY, NEVER UNDERSTAND WHY THESE S#!%^Y PANCAKES MAKE YOU SO HAPPY.
CLOS
HANK CHANNING
HUMAN ROCK 'EM SOCK 'EM ROBOT
OH, MY GOODNESS, ARE YOU OKAY, SON?
I'M FINE.
TABLE FOR ONE.

CAN I GET YOU ANYTHING?

MAYBE LATER. I JUST WANT TO SIT HERE RIGHT NOW IF THAT'S OKAY.

OVER THE YEARS, CAROL HAS HAD FLEETING DAYDREAMS OF RAISING A SON.

IN THIS MOMENT, SHE IS COMPLETELY LOST. SHE HAS NO IDEA HOW TO CONNECT WITH THIS POOR, OBVIOUSLY HURTING BOY.

HANK DOESN'T WANT CAROL'S SYMPATHY.

HE JUST WANTS TO FEEL FINE.

FOR ONCE...

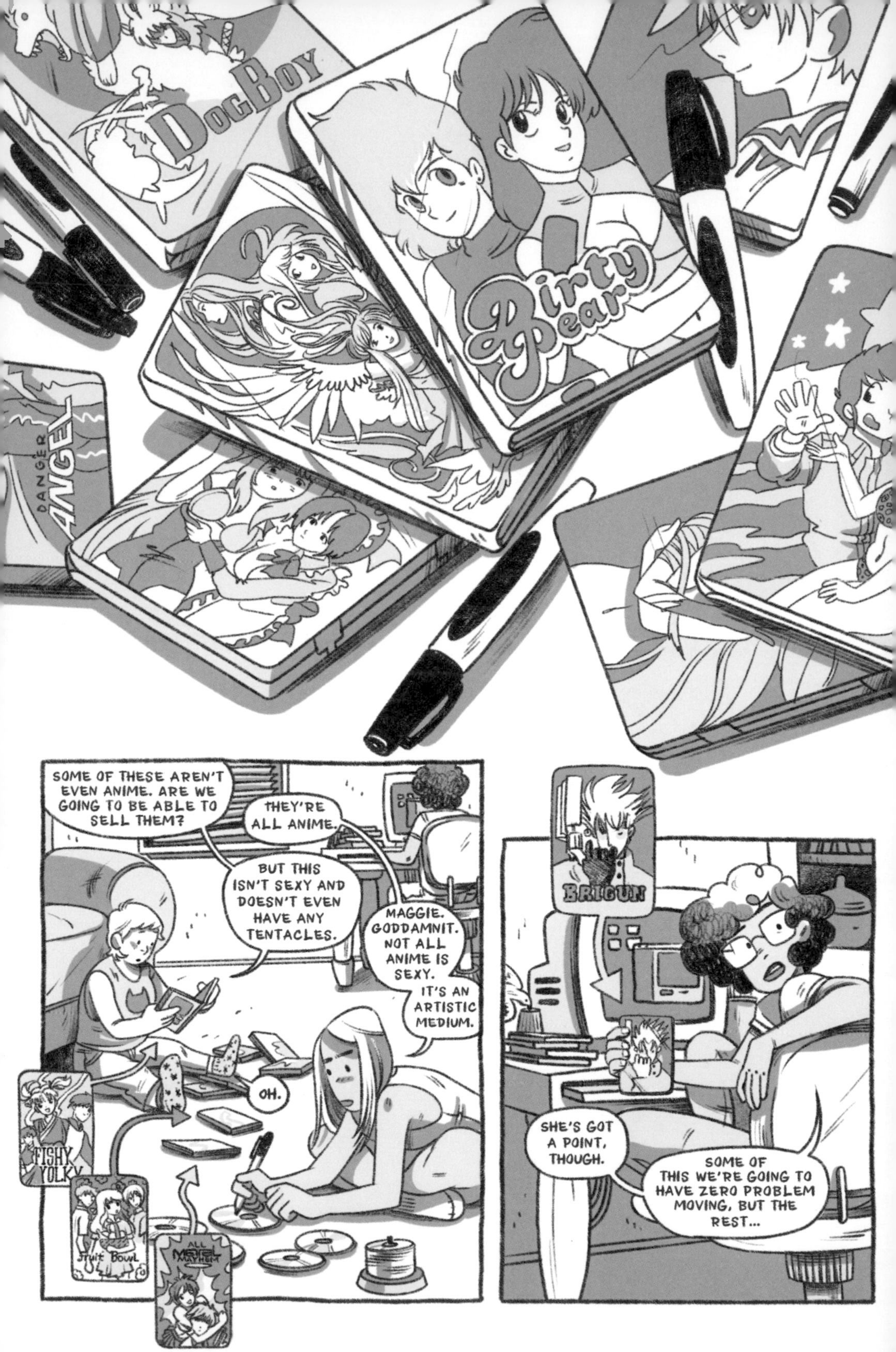
DOGBOY
Dirty Bear
DANGER ANGEL
SOME OF THESE AREN'T EVEN ANIME. ARE WE GOING TO BE ABLE TO SELL THEM?
THEY'RE ALL ANIME.
BUT THIS ISN'T SEXY AND DOESN'T EVEN HAVE ANY TENTACLES.
MAGGIE. GODDAMNIT. NOT ALL ANIME IS SEXY.
IT'S AN ARTISTIC MEDIUM.
OH.
FISHY YOLKY
Fruit Bowl
ALL METAL MAYHEM
BRIGUN
SHE'S GOT A POINT, THOUGH.
SOME OF THIS WE'RE GOING TO HAVE ZERO PROBLEM MOVING, BUT THE REST...

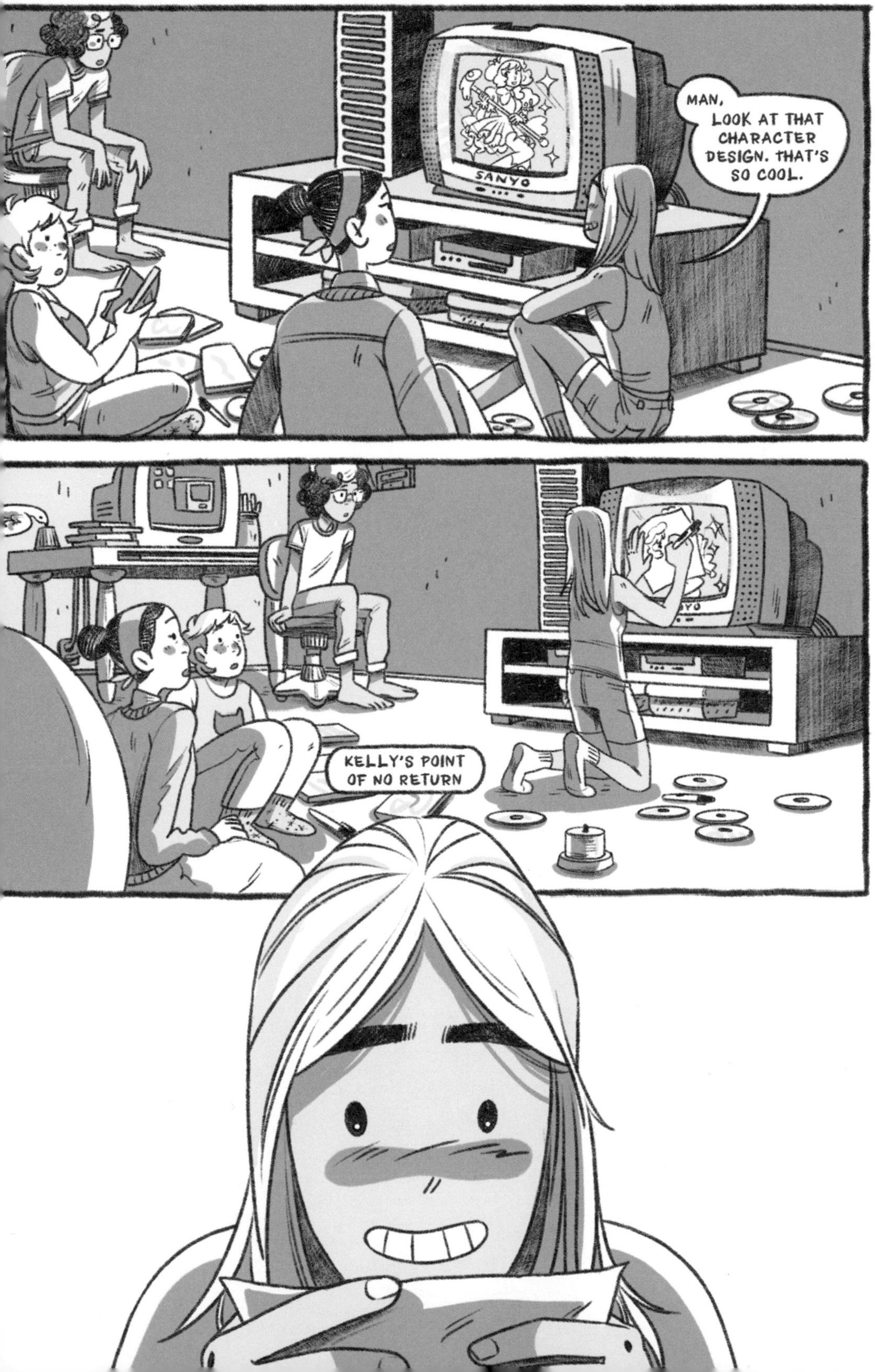
MAN,
LOOK AT THAT CHARACTER DESIGN. THAT'S SO COOL.
SANYO
KELLY'S POINT OF NO RETURN

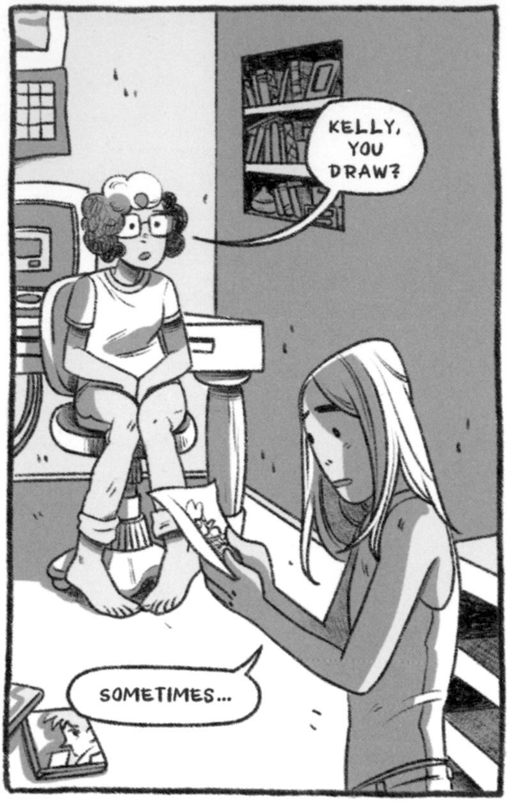
KELLY, YOU DRAW?
SOMETIMES...

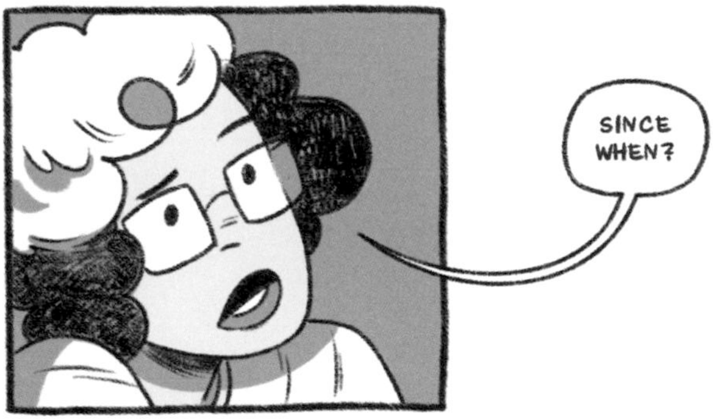
SINCE WHEN?

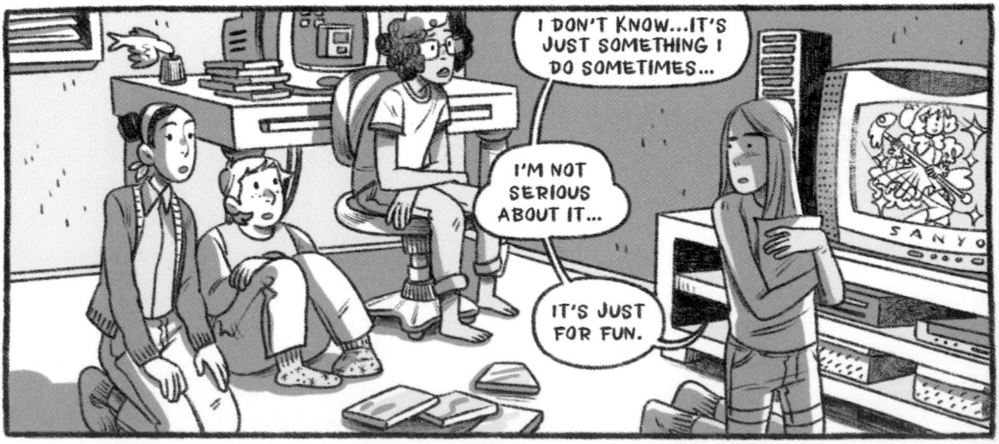
I DON'T KNOW...IT'S JUST SOMETHING I DO SOMETIMES...
I'M NOT SERIOUS ABOUT IT...
IT'S JUST FOR FUN.
SANYO

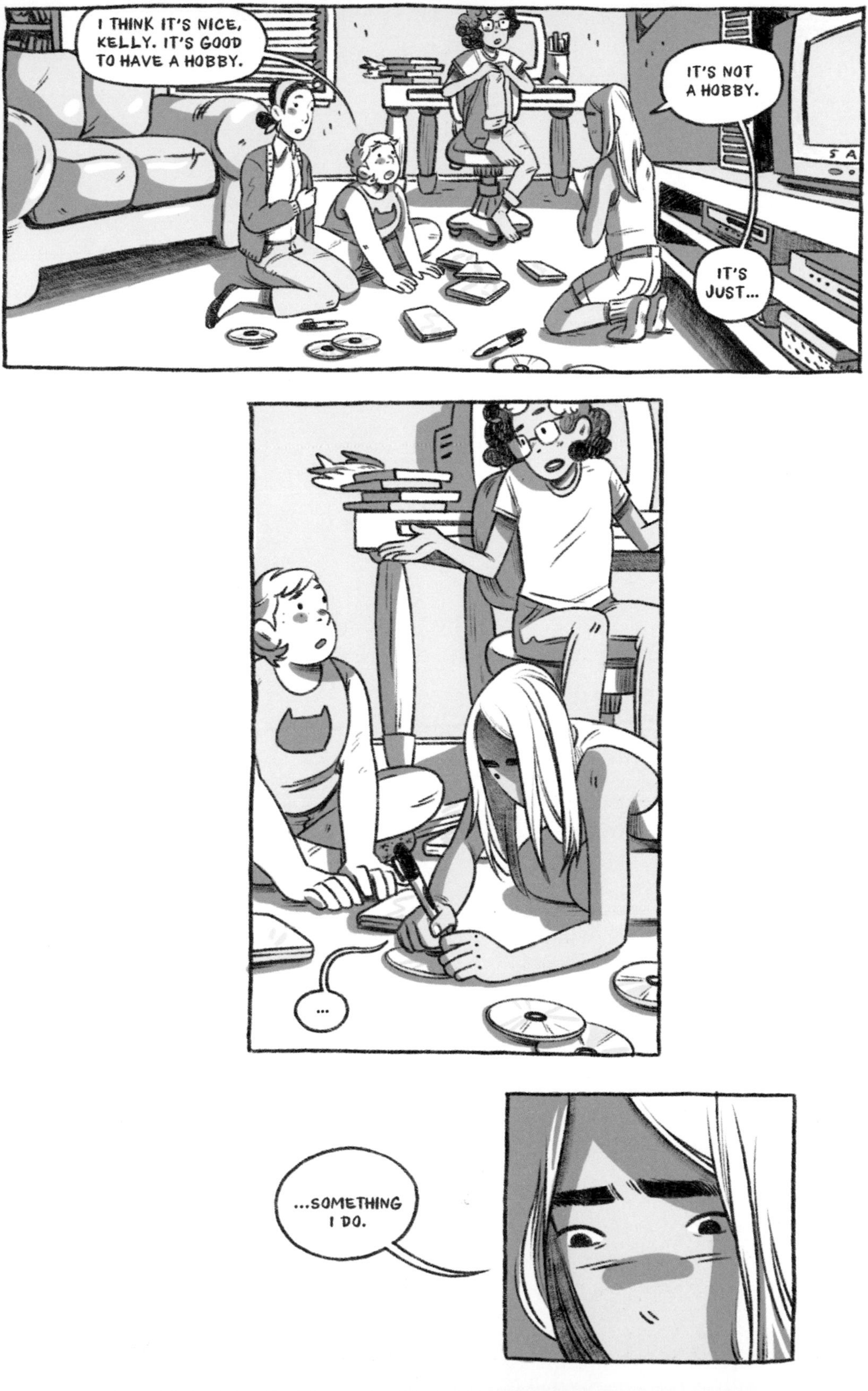
I THINK IT'S NICE, KELLY. IT'S GOOD TO HAVE A HOBBY.
IT'S NOT A HOBBY.
IT'S JUST...
...
...SOMETHING I DO.

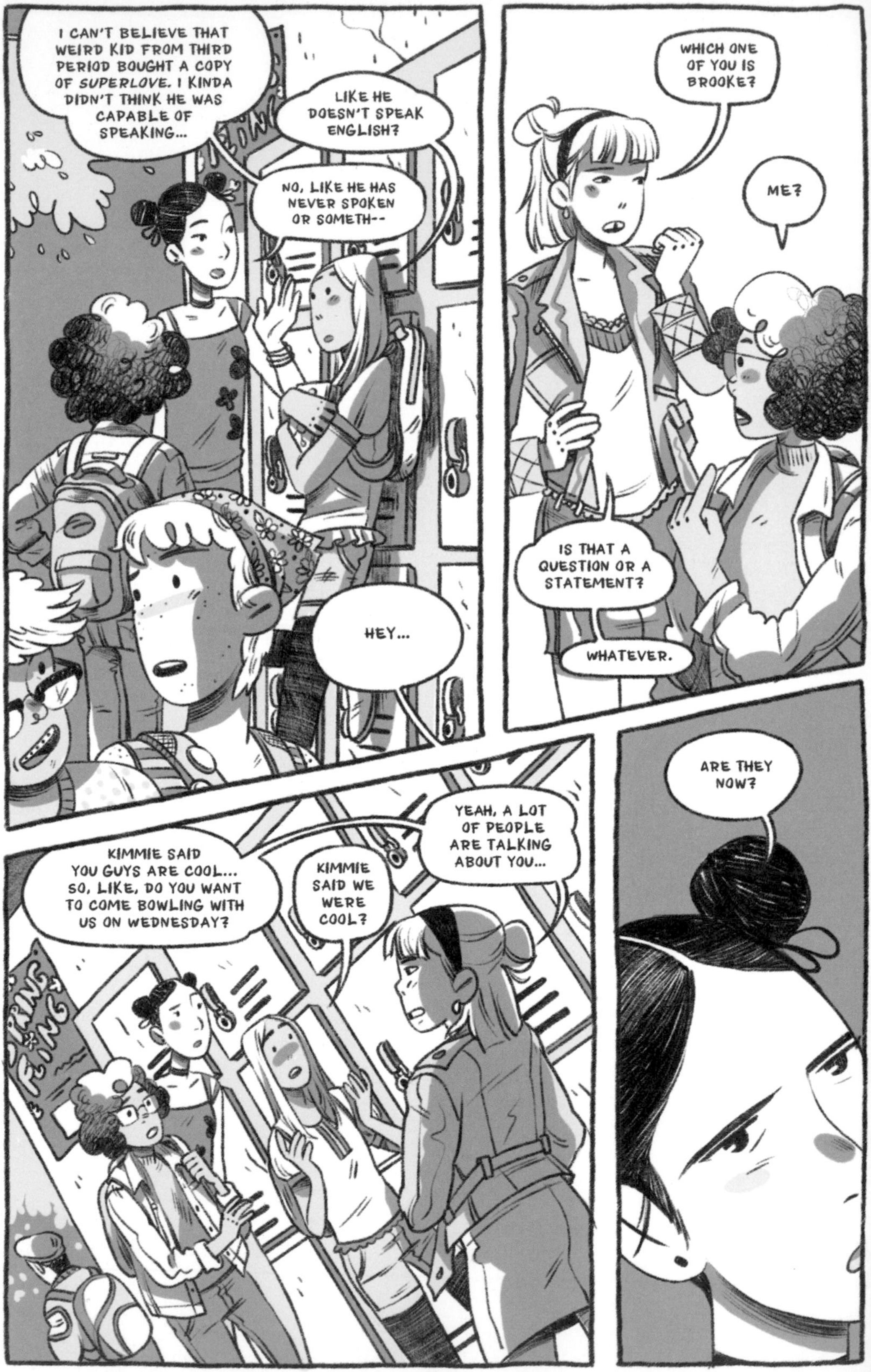
I CAN'T BELIEVE THAT WEIRD KID FROM THIRD PERIOD BOUGHT A COPY OF *SUPERLOVE*. I KINDA DIDN'T THINK HE WAS CAPABLE OF SPEAKING...
LIKE HE DOESN'T SPEAK ENGLISH?
NO, LIKE HE HAS NEVER SPOKEN OR SOMETH--
HEY...
WHICH ONE OF YOU IS BROOKE?
ME?
IS THAT A QUESTION OR A STATEMENT?
WHATEVER.
KIMMIE SAID YOU GUYS ARE COOL... SO, LIKE, DO YOU WANT TO COME BOWLING WITH US ON WEDNESDAY?
KIMMIE SAID WE WERE COOL?
YEAH, A LOT OF PEOPLE ARE TALKING ABOUT YOU...
ARE THEY NOW?

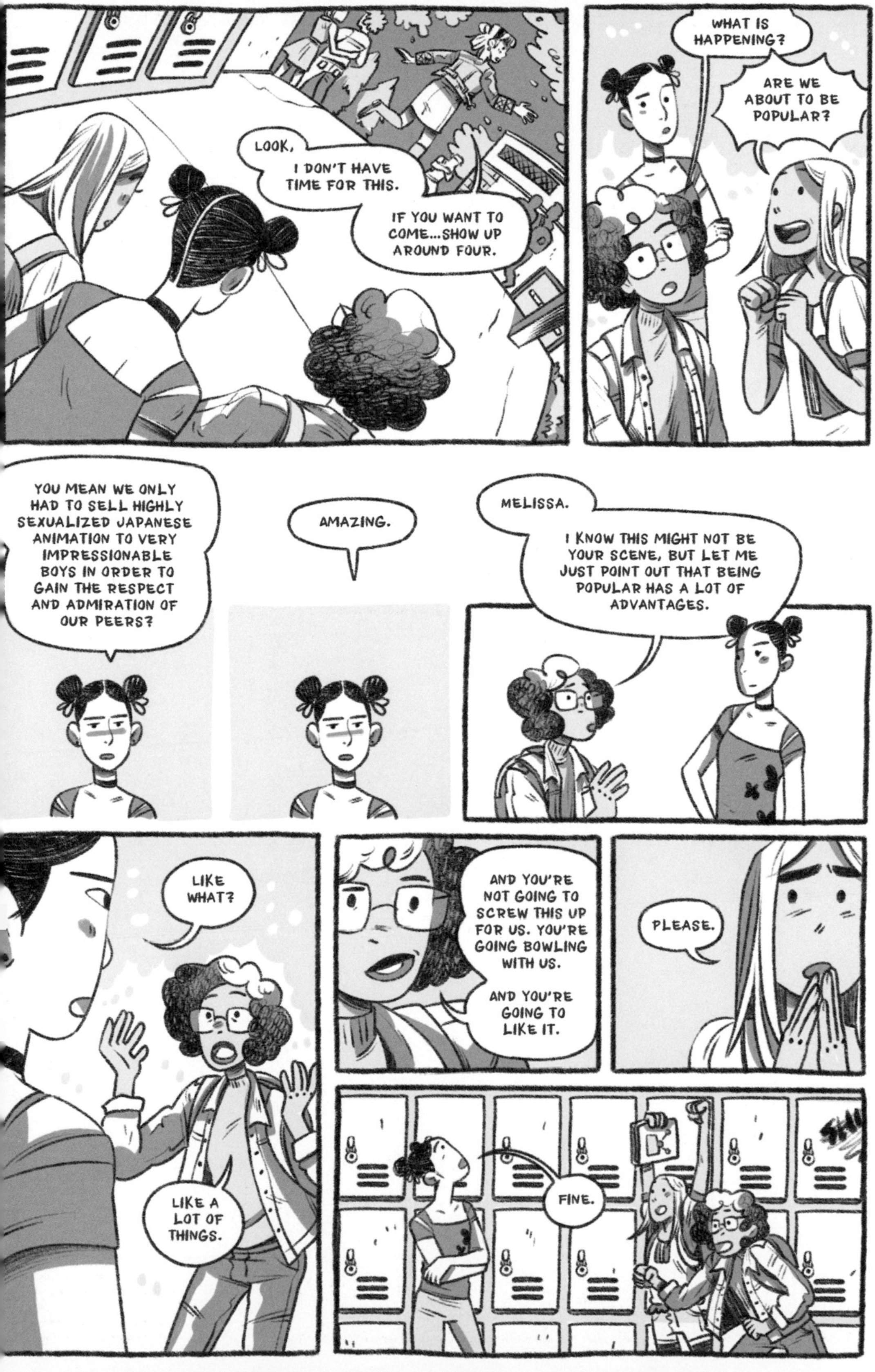
LOOK,
I DON'T HAVE TIME FOR THIS.
IF YOU WANT TO COME...SHOW UP AROUND FOUR.
WHAT IS HAPPENING?
ARE WE ABOUT TO BE POPULAR?
YOU MEAN WE ONLY HAD TO SELL HIGHLY SEXUALIZED JAPANESE ANIMATION TO VERY IMPRESSIONABLE BOYS IN ORDER TO GAIN THE RESPECT AND ADMIRATION OF OUR PEERS?
AMAZING.
MELISSA.
I KNOW THIS MIGHT NOT BE YOUR SCENE, BUT LET ME JUST POINT OUT THAT BEING POPULAR HAS A LOT OF ADVANTAGES.
LIKE WHAT?
LIKE A LOT OF THINGS.
AND YOU'RE NOT GOING TO SCREW THIS UP FOR US. YOU'RE GOING BOWLING WITH US.
AND YOU'RE GOING TO LIKE IT.
PLEASE.
FINE.

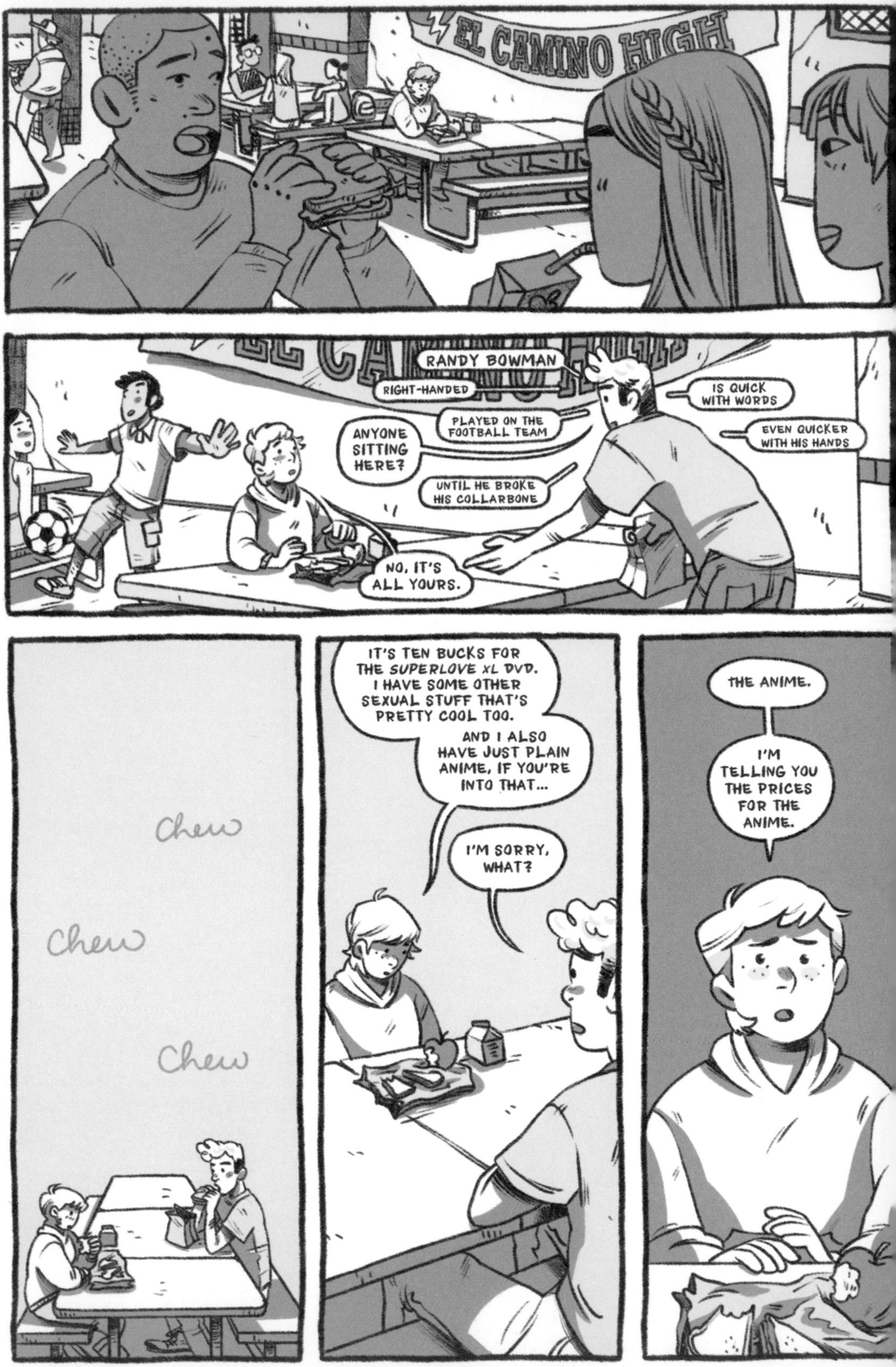
EL CAMINO HIGH
RANDY BOWMAN
RIGHT-HANDED
PLAYED ON THE FOOTBALL TEAM
UNTIL HE BROKE HIS COLLARBONE
IS QUICK WITH WORDS
EVEN QUICKER WITH HIS HANDS
ANYONE SITTING HERE?
NO, IT'S ALL YOURS.
Chew
Chew
Chew
IT'S TEN BUCKS FOR THE *SUPERLOVE XL* DVD. I HAVE SOME OTHER SEXUAL STUFF THAT'S PRETTY COOL TOO.
AND I ALSO HAVE JUST PLAIN ANIME, IF YOU'RE INTO THAT...
I'M SORRY, WHAT?
THE ANIME.
I'M TELLING YOU THE PRICES FOR THE ANIME.

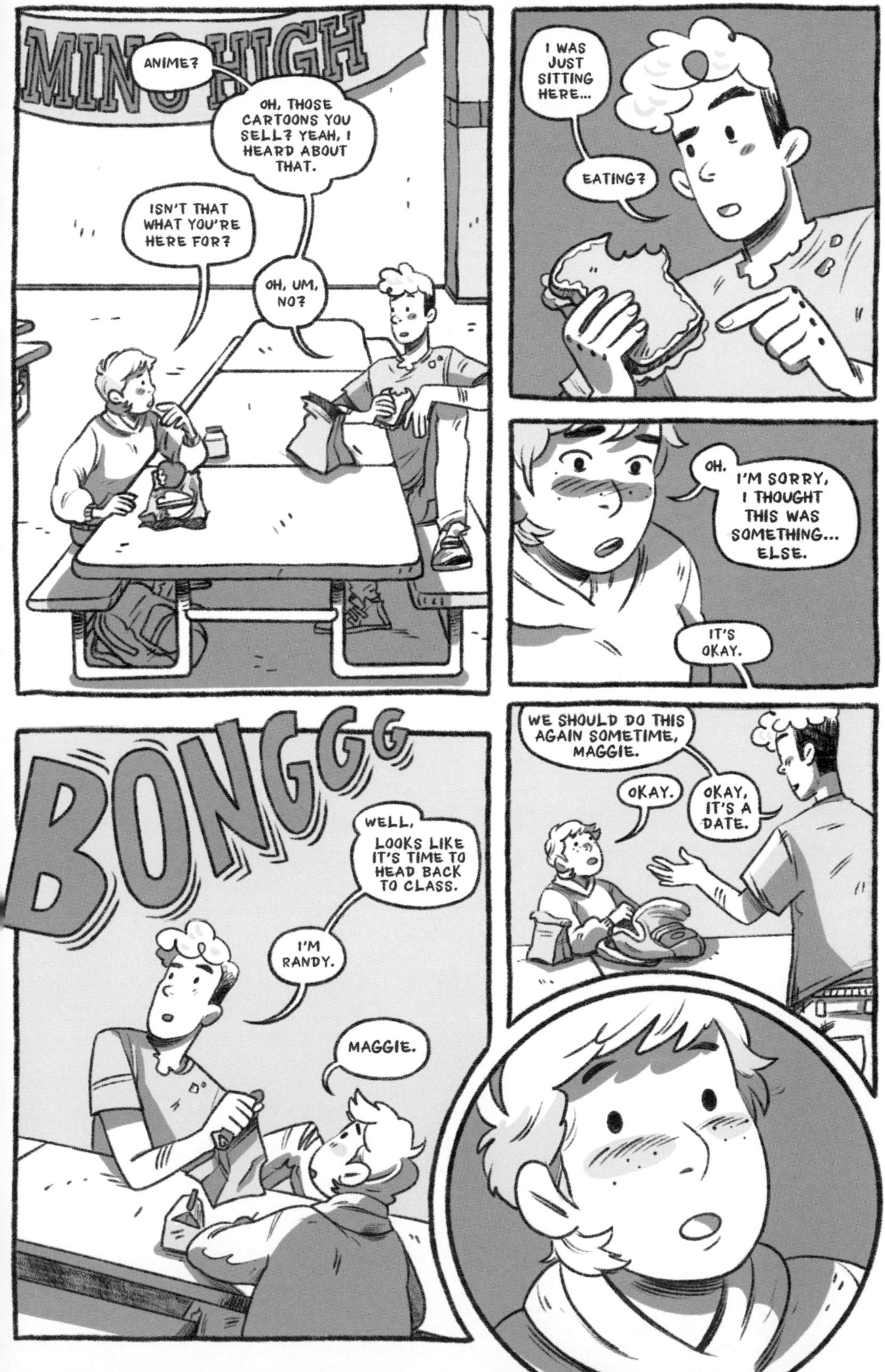
MINO HIGH
ANIME?
OH, THOSE CARTOONS YOU SELL? YEAH, I HEARD ABOUT THAT.
ISN'T THAT WHAT YOU'RE HERE FOR?
OH, UM, NO?
I WAS JUST SITTING HERE...
EATING?
OH.
I'M SORRY, I THOUGHT THIS WAS SOMETHING... ELSE.
IT'S OKAY.
BONGGG
WELL,
LOOKS LIKE IT'S TIME TO HEAD BACK TO CLASS.
I'M RANDY.
MAGGIE.
WE SHOULD DO THIS AGAIN SOMETIME, MAGGIE.
OKAY.
OKAY, IT'S A DATE.

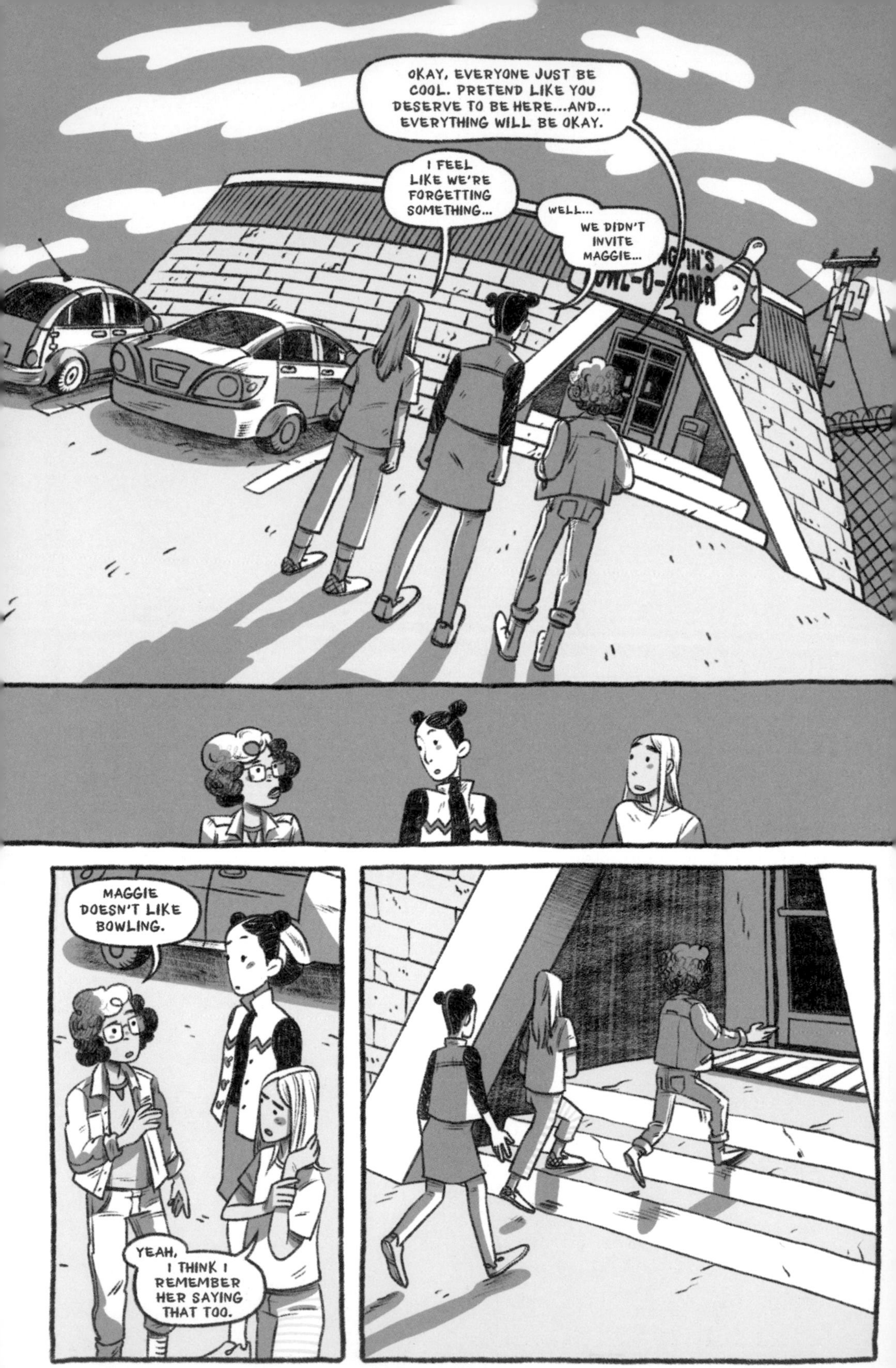
OKAY, EVERYONE JUST BE COOL. PRETEND LIKE YOU DESERVE TO BE HERE...AND... EVERYTHING WILL BE OKAY.
I FEEL LIKE WE'RE FORGETTING SOMETHING...
WELL...
WE DIDN'T INVITE MAGGIE...
MAGGIE DOESN'T LIKE BOWLING.
YEAH, I THINK I REMEMBER HER SAYING THAT TOO.

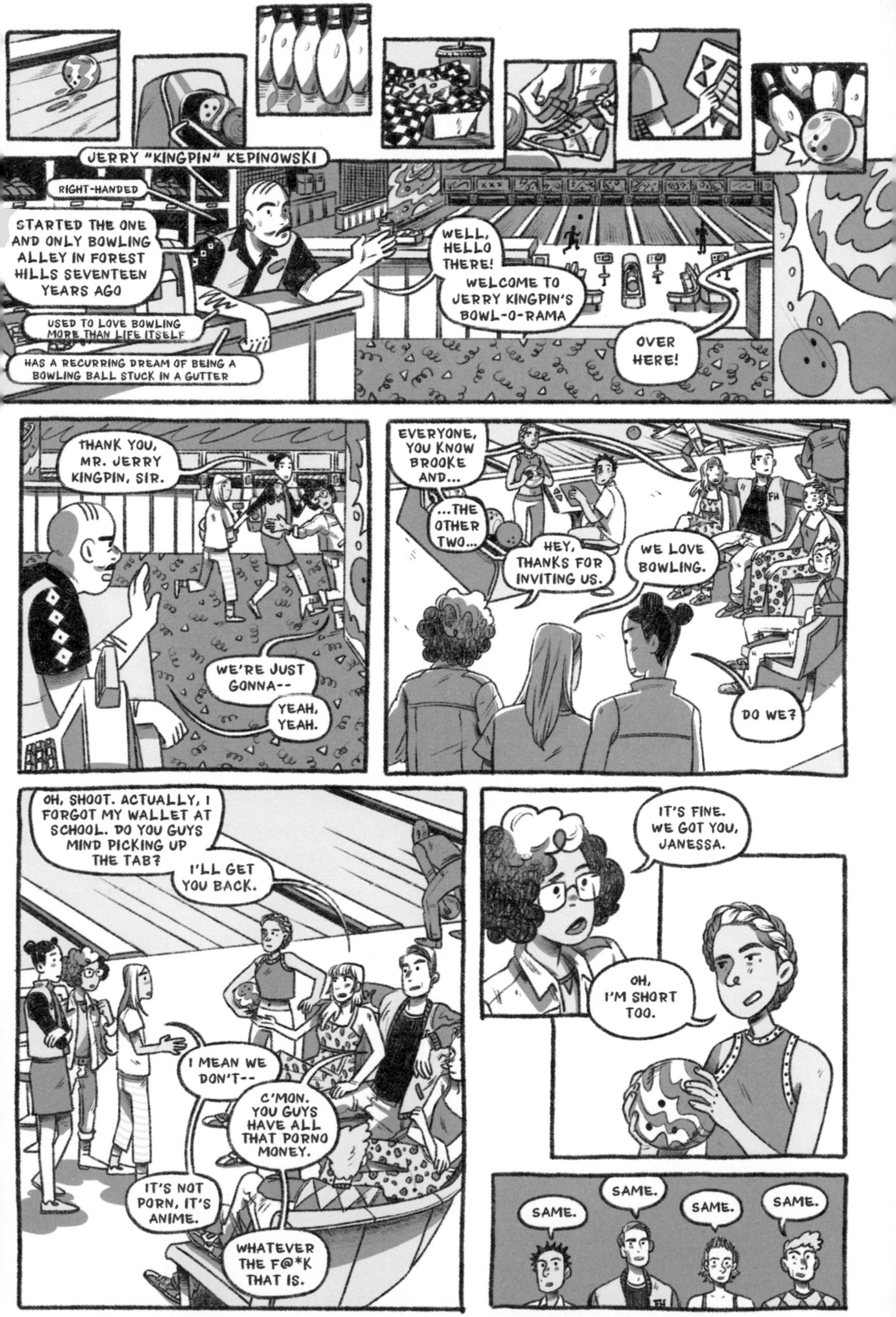
JERRY "KINGPIN" KEPINOWSKI
RIGHT-HANDED
STARTED THE ONE AND ONLY BOWLING ALLEY IN FOREST HILLS SEVENTEEN YEARS AGO
USED TO LOVE BOWLING MORE THAN LIFE ITSELF
HAS A RECURRING DREAM OF BEING A BOWLING BALL STUCK IN A GUTTER
WELL, HELLO THERE!
WELCOME TO JERRY KINGPIN'S BOWL-O-RAMA
OVER HERE!
THANK YOU, MR. JERRY KINGPIN, SIR.
WE'RE JUST GONNA--
YEAH, YEAH.
EVERYONE, YOU KNOW BROOKE AND...
...THE OTHER TWO...
HEY, THANKS FOR INVITING US.
WE LOVE BOWLING.
DO WE?
OH, SHOOT. ACTUALLY, I FORGOT MY WALLET AT SCHOOL. DO YOU GUYS MIND PICKING UP THE TAB?
I'LL GET YOU BACK.
I MEAN WE DON'T--
C'MON. YOU GUYS HAVE ALL THAT PORNO MONEY.
IT'S NOT PORN, IT'S ANIME.
WHATEVER THE F@*K THAT IS.
IT'S FINE. WE GOT YOU, JANESSA.
OH, I'M SHORT TOO.
SAME.
SAME.
SAME.
SAME.

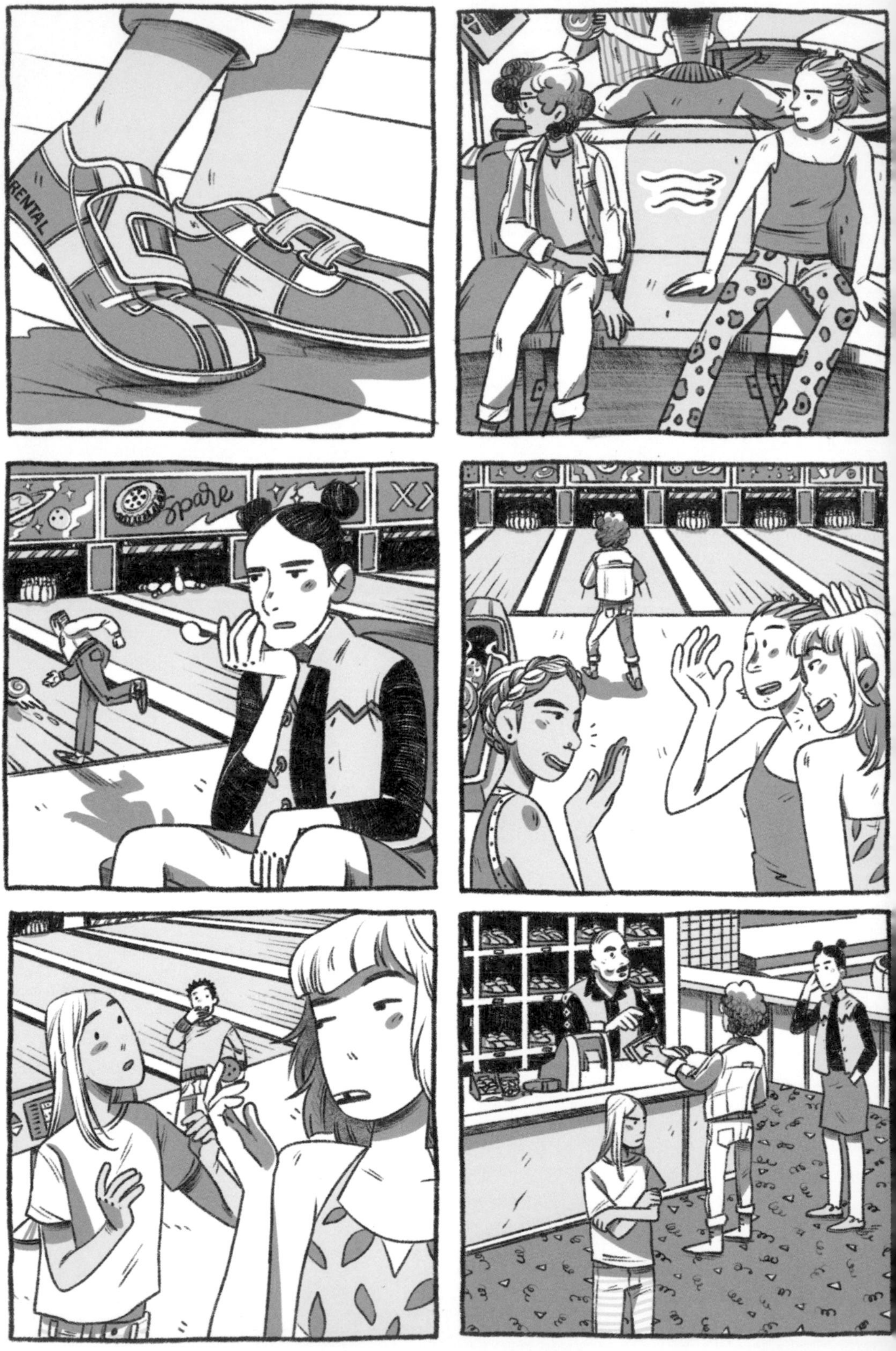
RENTAL
spare

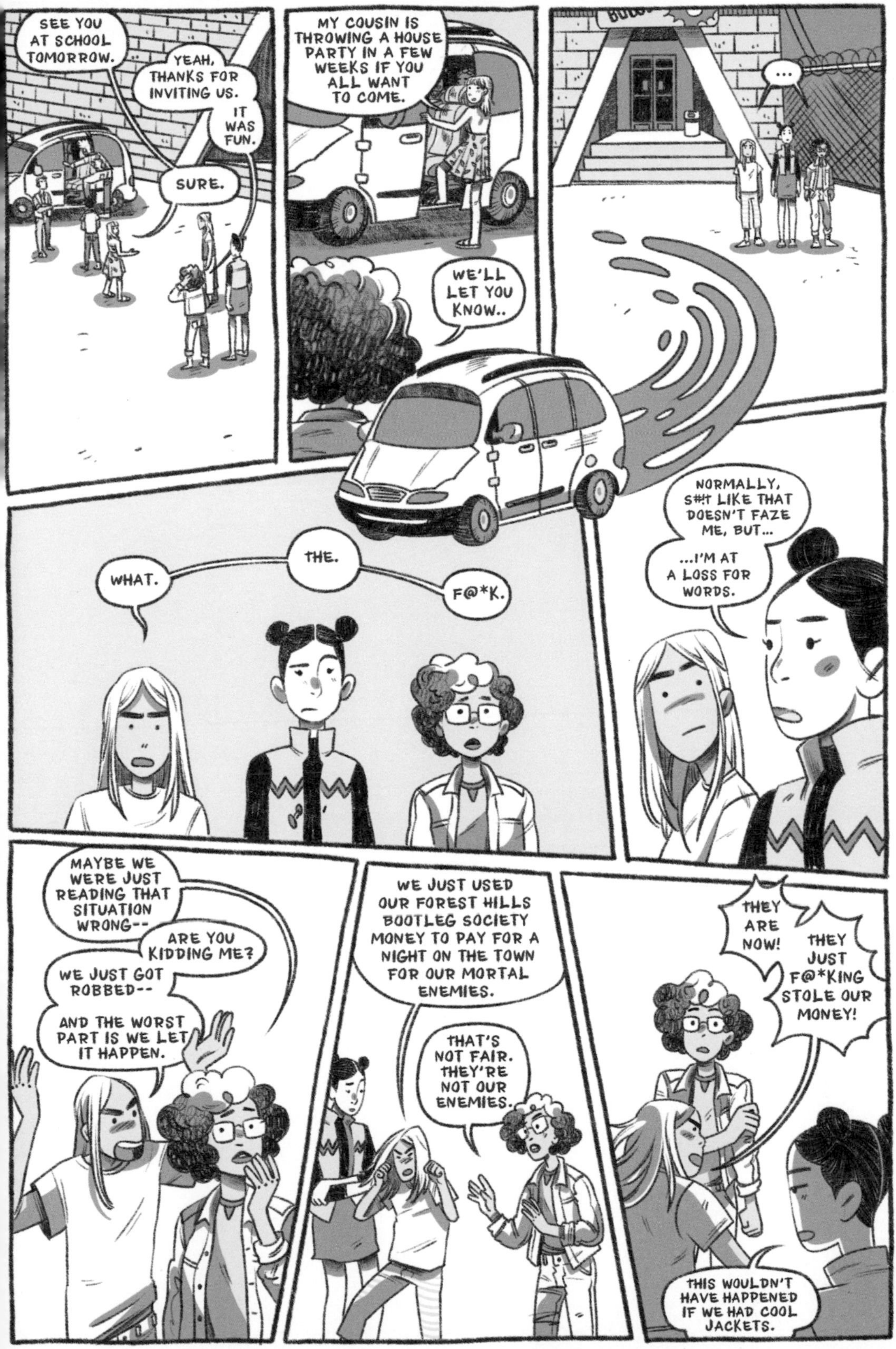
SEE YOU AT SCHOOL TOMORROW.
YEAH, THANKS FOR INVITING US.
IT WAS FUN.
SURE.
MY COUSIN IS THROWING A HOUSE PARTY IN A FEW WEEKS IF YOU ALL WANT TO COME.
WE'LL LET YOU KNOW..
...
WHAT.
THE.
F@*K.
NORMALLY, S#!T LIKE THAT DOESN'T FAZE ME, BUT...
...I'M AT A LOSS FOR WORDS.
MAYBE WE WERE JUST READING THAT SITUATION WRONG--
ARE YOU KIDDING ME?
WE JUST GOT ROBBED--
AND THE WORST PART IS WE LET IT HAPPEN.
WE JUST USED OUR FOREST HILLS BOOTLEG SOCIETY MONEY TO PAY FOR A NIGHT ON THE TOWN FOR OUR MORTAL ENEMIES.
THAT'S NOT FAIR. THEY'RE NOT OUR ENEMIES.
THEY ARE NOW!
THEY JUST F@*KING STOLE OUR MONEY!
THIS WOULDN'T HAVE HAPPENED IF WE HAD COOL JACKETS.

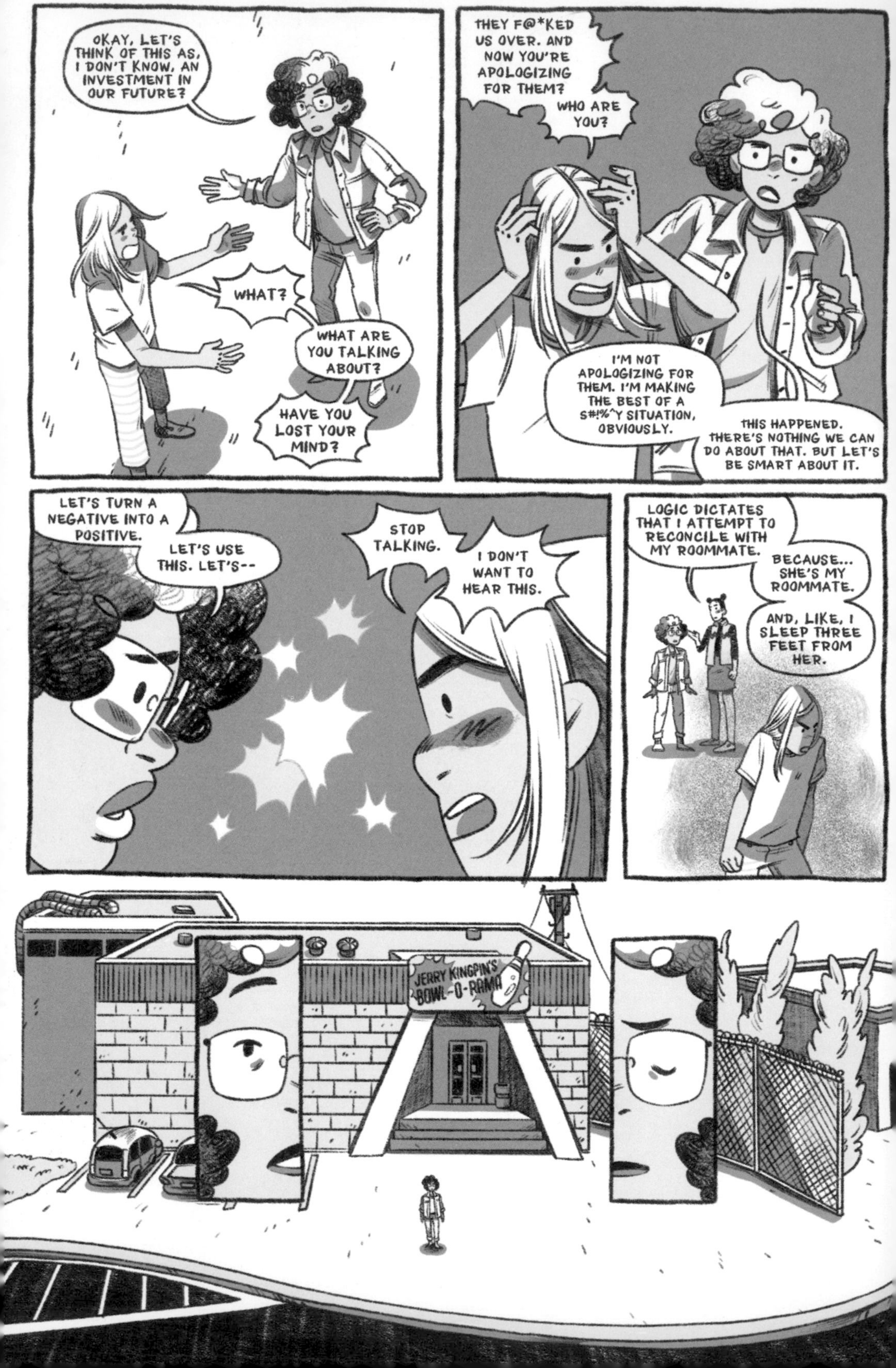
OKAY, LET'S THINK OF THIS AS, I DON'T KNOW, AN INVESTMENT IN OUR FUTURE?
WHAT?
WHAT ARE YOU TALKING ABOUT?
HAVE YOU LOST YOUR MIND?
THEY F@*KED US OVER. AND NOW YOU'RE APOLOGIZING FOR THEM?
WHO ARE YOU?
I'M NOT APOLOGIZING FOR THEM. I'M MAKING THE BEST OF A S#!%^Y SITUATION, OBVIOUSLY.
THIS HAPPENED. THERE'S NOTHING WE CAN DO ABOUT THAT. BUT LET'S BE SMART ABOUT IT.
LET'S TURN A NEGATIVE INTO A POSITIVE.
LET'S USE THIS. LET'S--
STOP TALKING.
I DON'T WANT TO HEAR THIS.
LOGIC DICTATES THAT I ATTEMPT TO RECONCILE WITH MY ROOMMATE.
BECAUSE... SHE'S MY ROOMMATE.
AND, LIKE, I SLEEP THREE FEET FROM HER.
JERRY KINGPIN'S BOWL-O-RAMA

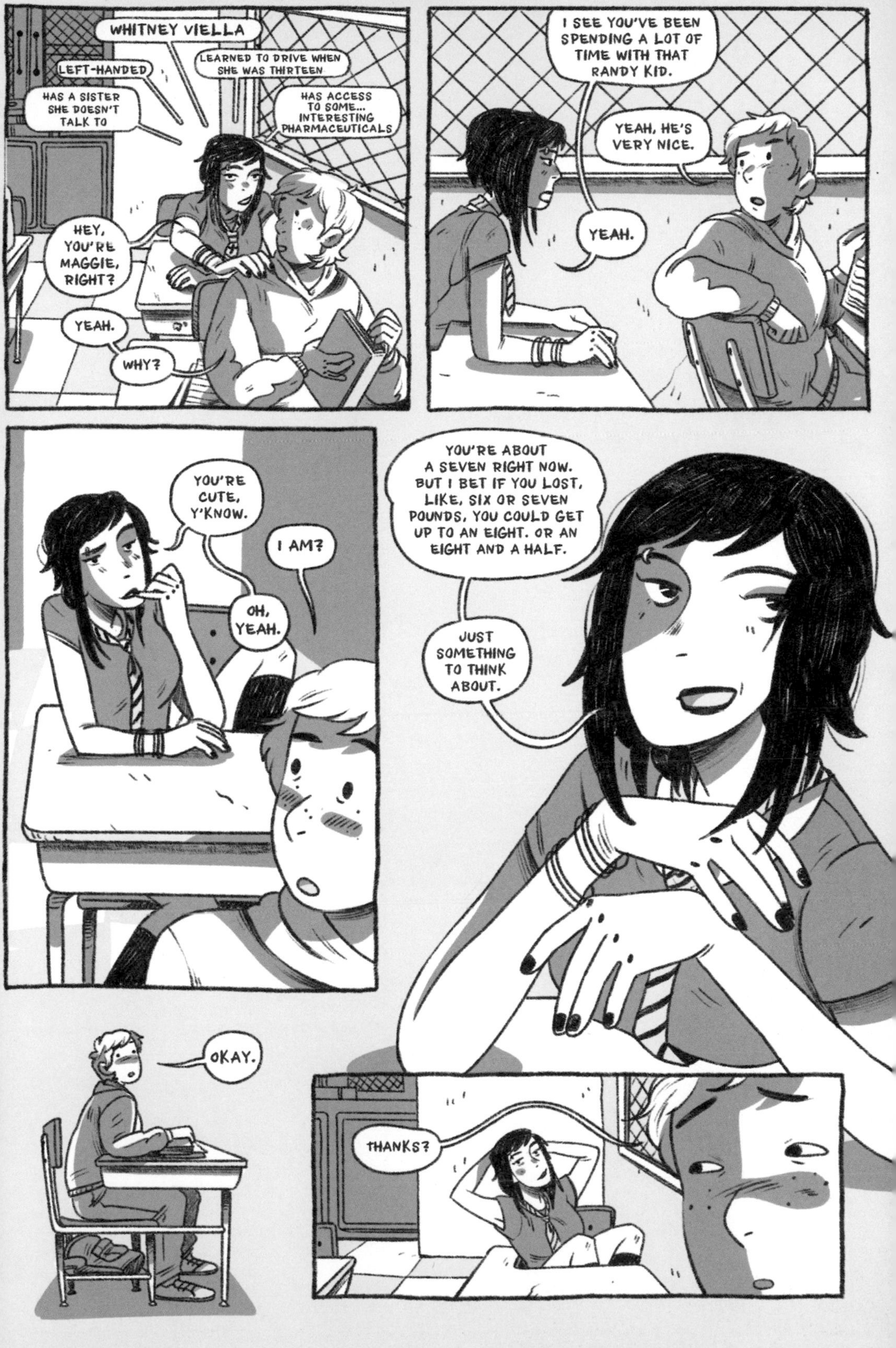
WHITNEY VIELLA
LEFT-HANDED
LEARNED TO DRIVE WHEN SHE WAS THIRTEEN
HAS A SISTER SHE DOESN'T TALK TO
HAS ACCESS TO SOME... INTERESTING PHARMACEUTICALS
HEY, YOU'RE MAGGIE, RIGHT?
YEAH.
WHY?
I SEE YOU'VE BEEN SPENDING A LOT OF TIME WITH THAT RANDY KID.
YEAH, HE'S VERY NICE.
YEAH.
YOU'RE CUTE, Y'KNOW.
I AM?
OH, YEAH.
YOU'RE ABOUT A SEVEN RIGHT NOW. BUT I BET IF YOU LOST, LIKE, SIX OR SEVEN POUNDS, YOU COULD GET UP TO AN EIGHT. OR AN EIGHT AND A HALF.
JUST SOMETHING TO THINK ABOUT.
OKAY.
THANKS?

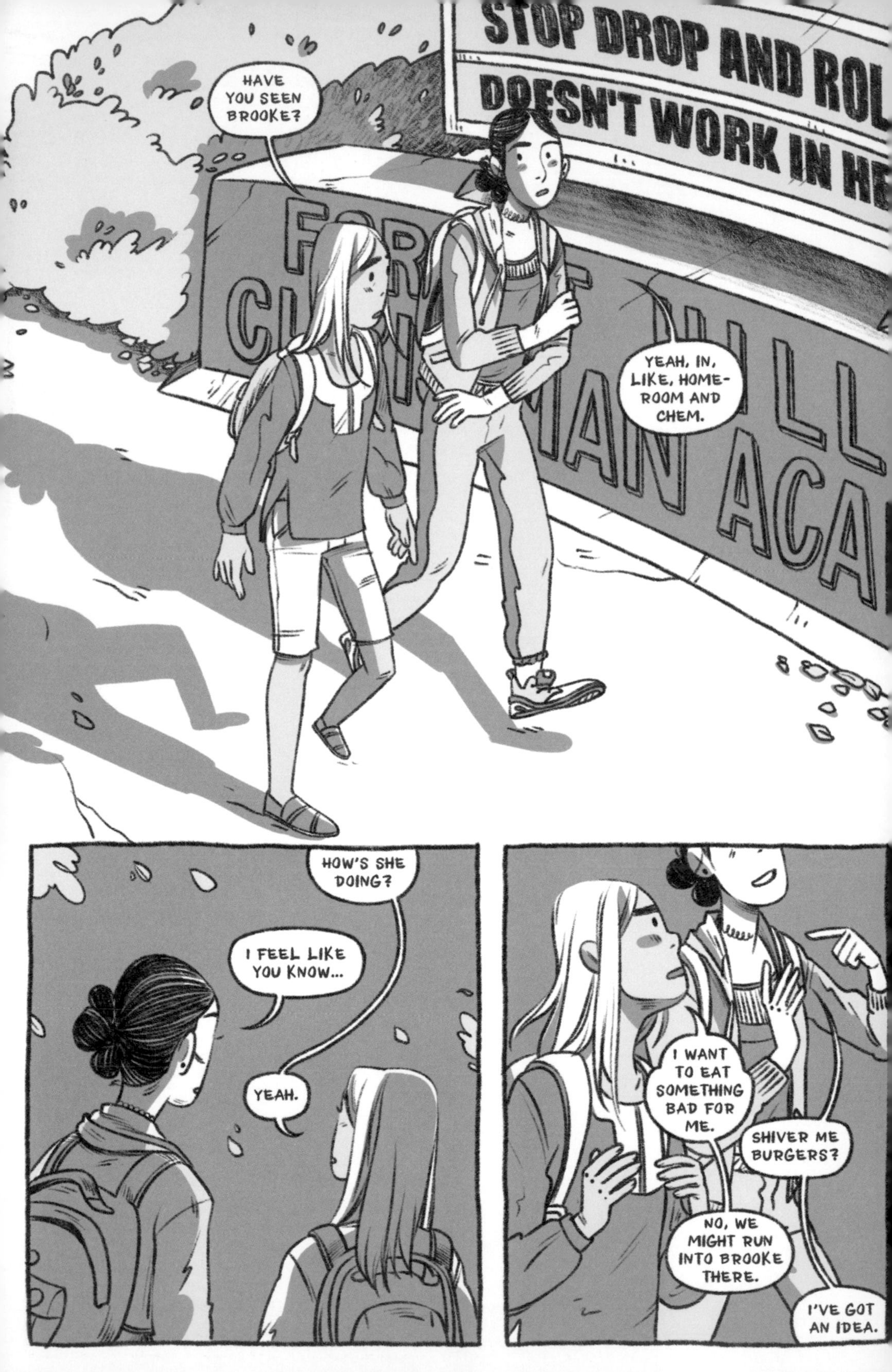
STOP DROP AND ROL
DOESN'T WORK IN HE
HAVE YOU SEEN BROOKE?
YEAH, IN, LIKE, HOME-ROOM AND CHEM.
HOW'S SHE DOING?
I FEEL LIKE YOU KNOW...
YEAH.
I WANT TO EAT SOMETHING BAD FOR ME.
SHIVER ME BURGERS?
NO, WE MIGHT RUN INTO BROOKE THERE.
I'VE GOT AN IDEA.

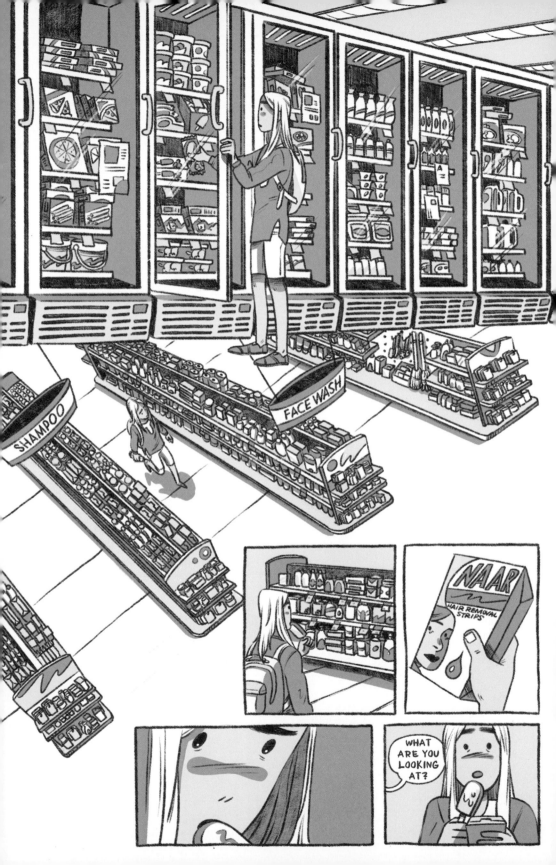

SHAMPOO

FACE WASH

NAAR
HAIR REMOVAL STRIPS

WHAT ARE YOU LOOKING AT?

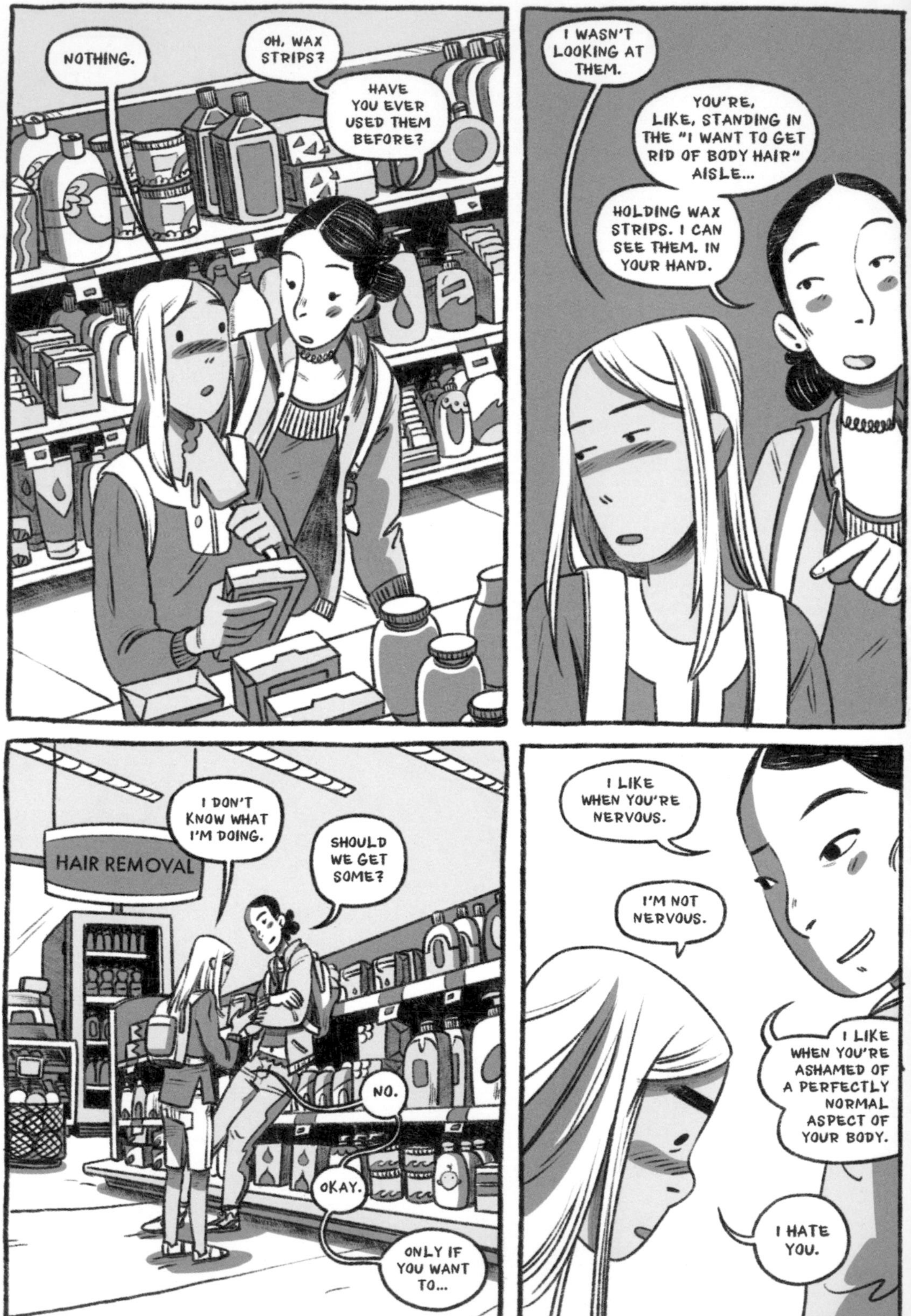
NOTHING.
OH, WAX STRIPS?
HAVE YOU EVER USED THEM BEFORE?
I WASN'T LOOKING AT THEM.
YOU'RE, LIKE, STANDING IN THE "I WANT TO GET RID OF BODY HAIR" AISLE...
HOLDING WAX STRIPS. I CAN SEE THEM. IN YOUR HAND.
HAIR REMOVAL
I DON'T KNOW WHAT I'M DOING.
SHOULD WE GET SOME?
NO.
OKAY.
ONLY IF YOU WANT TO...
I LIKE WHEN YOU'RE NERVOUS.
I'M NOT NERVOUS.
I LIKE WHEN YOU'RE ASHAMED OF A PERFECTLY NORMAL ASPECT OF YOUR BODY.
I HATE YOU.

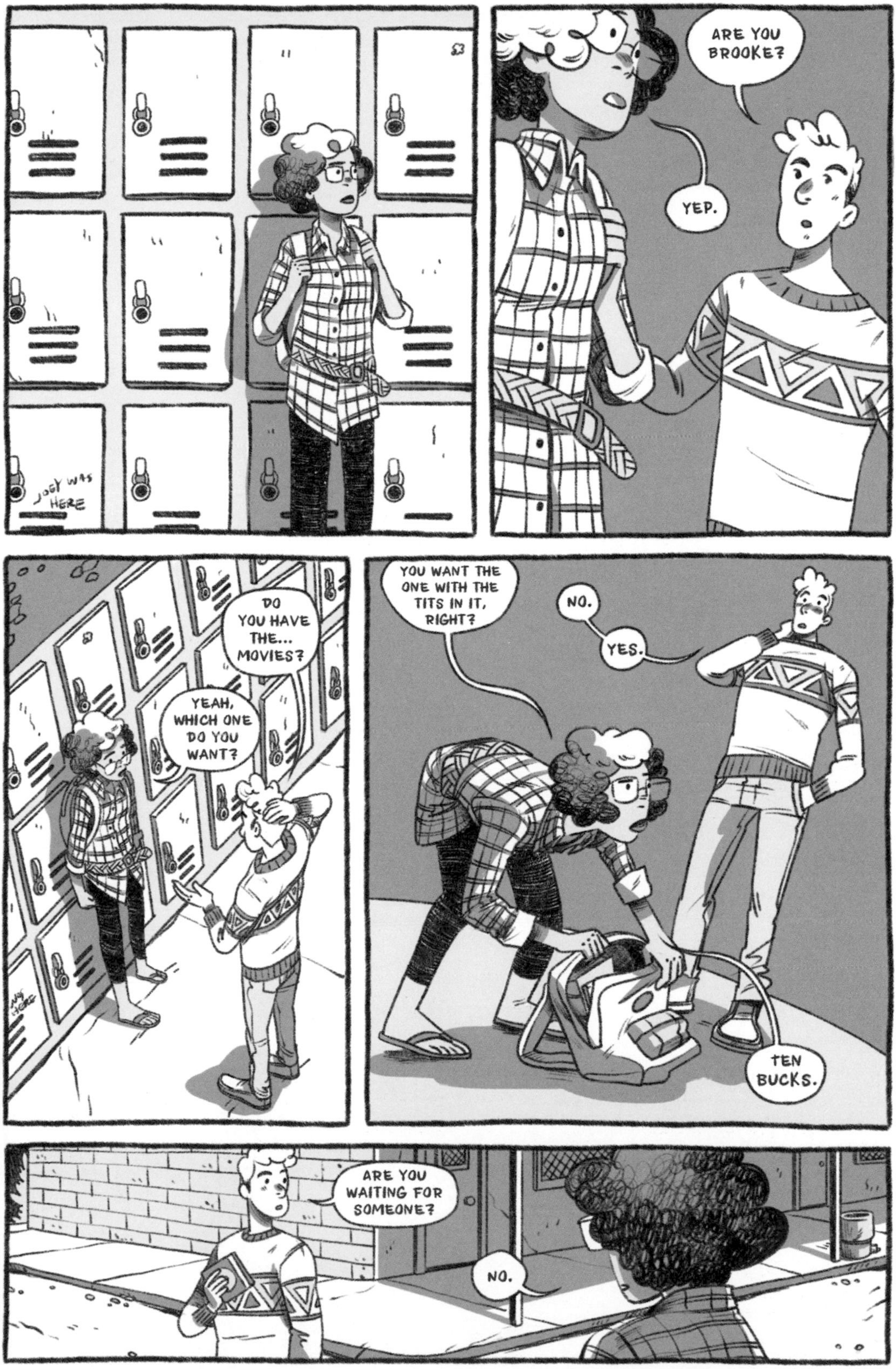

JOEY WAS HERE
ARE YOU BROOKE?
YEP.
DO YOU HAVE THE... MOVIES?
YEAH, WHICH ONE DO YOU WANT?
YOU WANT THE ONE WITH THE TITS IN IT, RIGHT?
NO.
YES.
TEN BUCKS.
ARE YOU WAITING FOR SOMEONE?
NO.

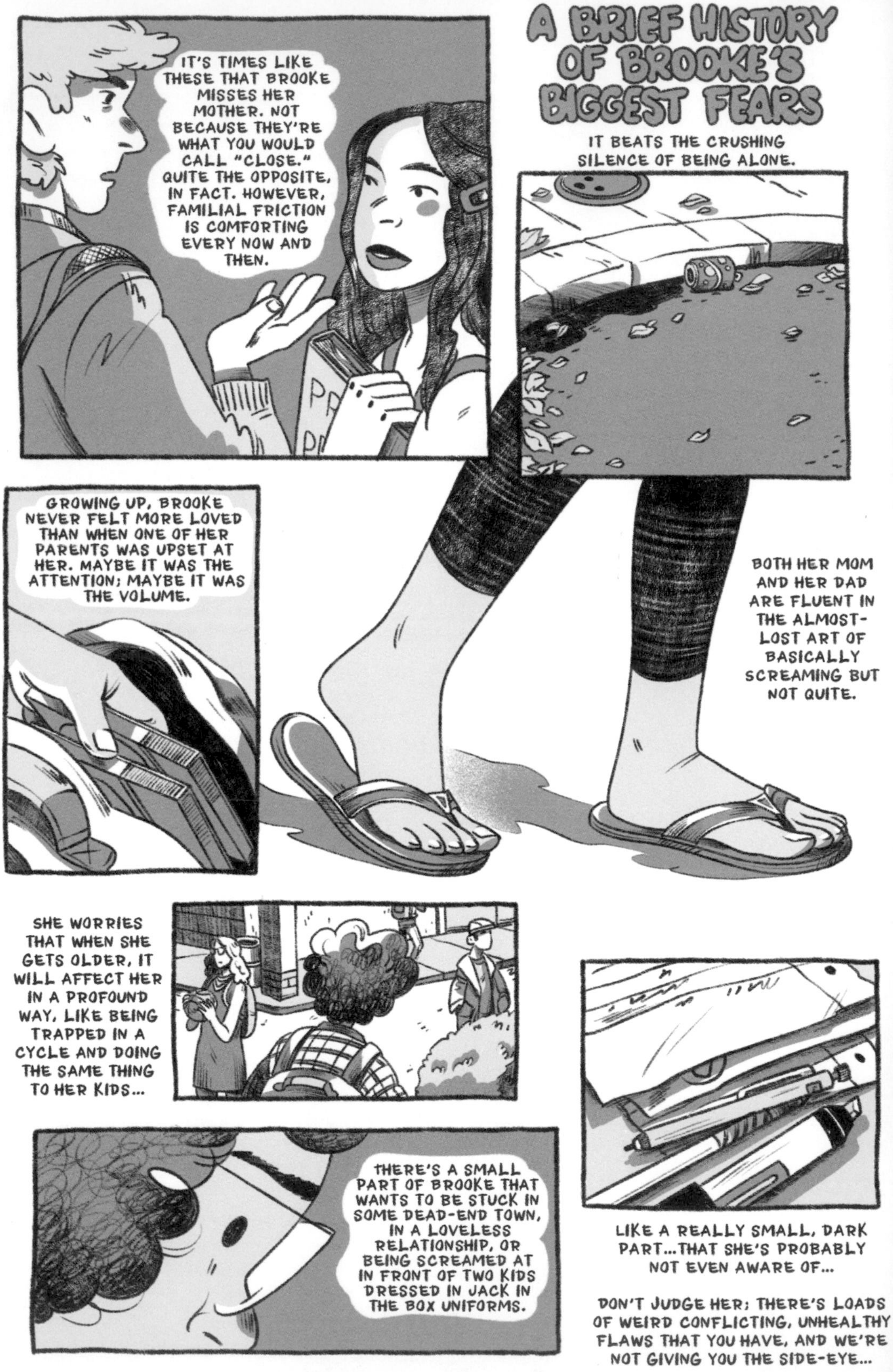
A BRIEF HISTORY OF BROOKE'S BIGGEST FEARS
IT'S TIMES LIKE THESE THAT BROOKE MISSES HER MOTHER. NOT BECAUSE THEY'RE WHAT YOU WOULD CALL "CLOSE." QUITE THE OPPOSITE, IN FACT. HOWEVER, FAMILIAL FRICTION IS COMFORTING EVERY NOW AND THEN.
IT BEATS THE CRUSHING SILENCE OF BEING ALONE.
GROWING UP, BROOKE NEVER FELT MORE LOVED THAN WHEN ONE OF HER PARENTS WAS UPSET AT HER. MAYBE IT WAS THE ATTENTION; MAYBE IT WAS THE VOLUME.
BOTH HER MOM AND HER DAD ARE FLUENT IN THE ALMOST-LOST ART OF BASICALLY SCREAMING BUT NOT QUITE.
SHE WORRIES THAT WHEN SHE GETS OLDER, IT WILL AFFECT HER IN A PROFOUND WAY, LIKE BEING TRAPPED IN A CYCLE AND DOING THE SAME THING TO HER KIDS...
THERE'S A SMALL PART OF BROOKE THAT WANTS TO BE STUCK IN SOME DEAD-END TOWN, IN A LOVELESS RELATIONSHIP, OR BEING SCREAMED AT IN FRONT OF TWO KIDS DRESSED IN JACK IN THE BOX UNIFORMS.
LIKE A REALLY SMALL, DARK PART...THAT SHE'S PROBABLY NOT EVEN AWARE OF...
DON'T JUDGE HER; THERE'S LOADS OF WEIRD CONFLICTING, UNHEALTHY FLAWS THAT YOU HAVE, AND WE'RE NOT GIVING YOU THE SIDE-EYE...

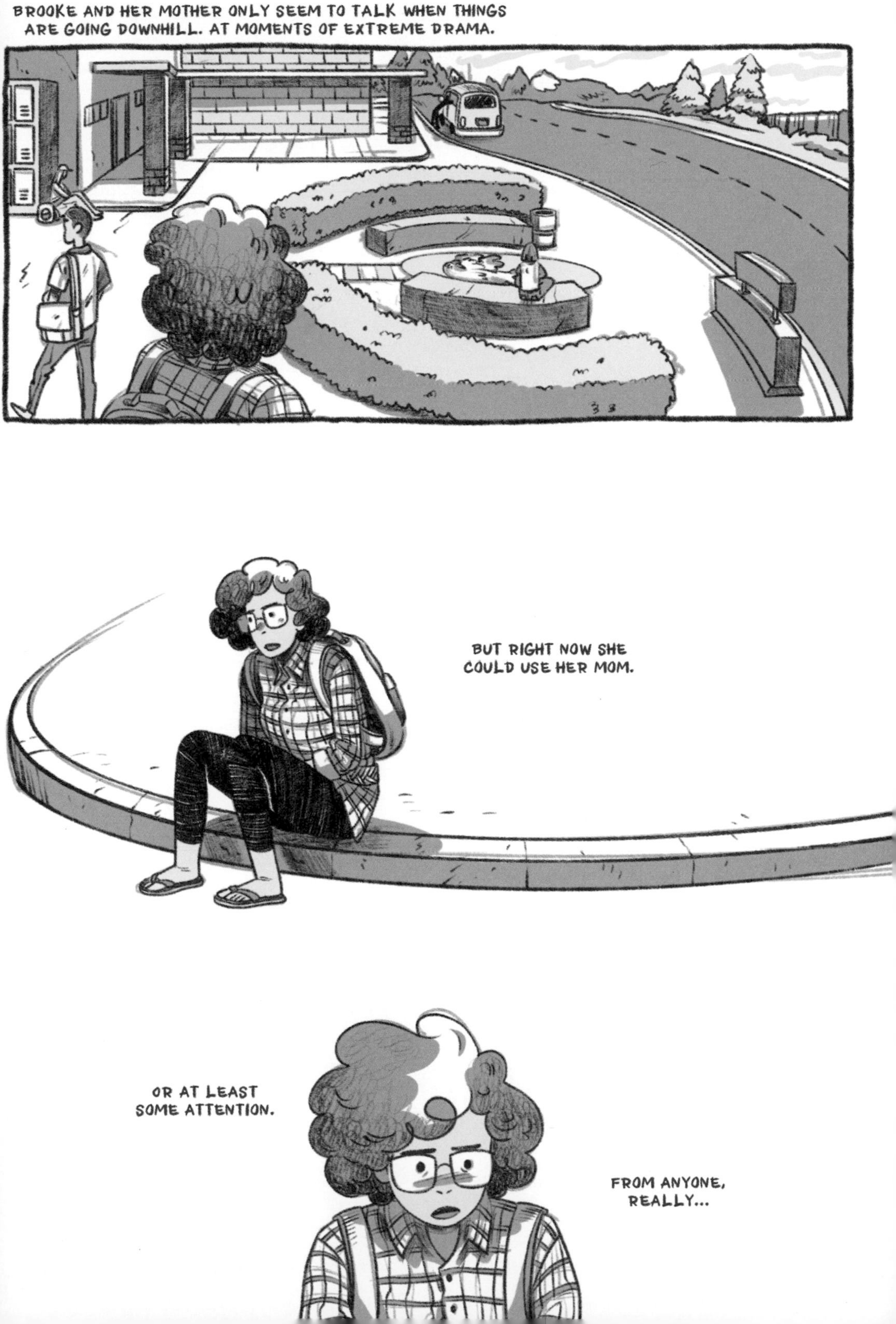
BROOKE AND HER MOTHER ONLY SEEM TO TALK WHEN THINGS ARE GOING DOWNHILL. AT MOMENTS OF EXTREME DRAMA.
BUT RIGHT NOW SHE COULD USE HER MOM.
OR AT LEAST SOME ATTENTION.
FROM ANYONE, REALLY...

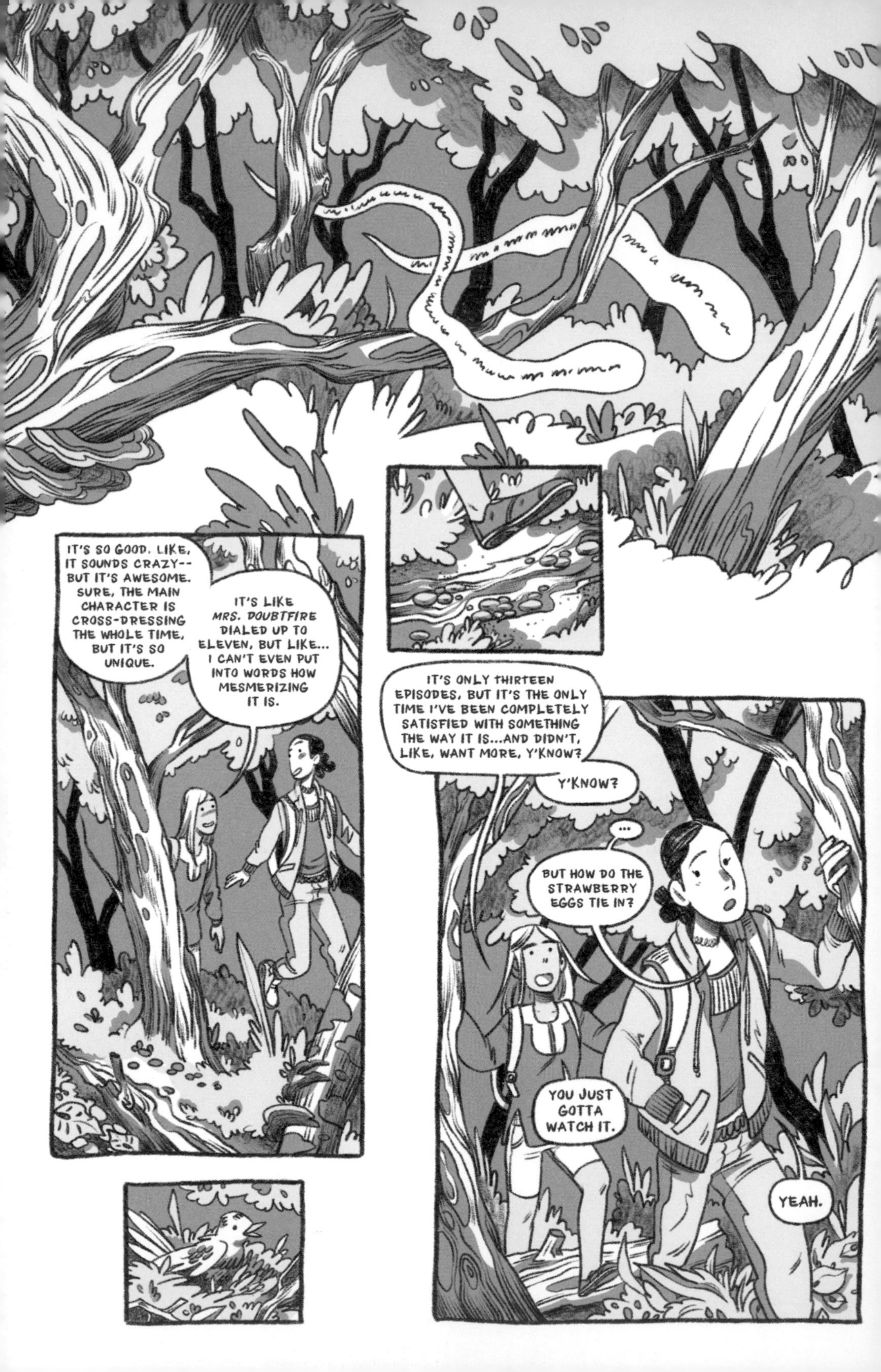
IT'S SO GOOD. LIKE, IT SOUNDS CRAZY--BUT IT'S AWESOME. SURE, THE MAIN CHARACTER IS CROSS-DRESSING THE WHOLE TIME, BUT IT'S SO UNIQUE.
IT'S LIKE *MRS. DOUBTFIRE* DIALED UP TO ELEVEN, BUT LIKE... I CAN'T EVEN PUT INTO WORDS HOW MESMERIZING IT IS.
IT'S ONLY THIRTEEN EPISODES, BUT IT'S THE ONLY TIME I'VE BEEN COMPLETELY SATISFIED WITH SOMETHING THE WAY IT IS...AND DIDN'T, LIKE, WANT MORE, Y'KNOW?
Y'KNOW?
...
BUT HOW DO THE STRAWBERRY EGGS TIE IN?
YOU JUST GOTTA WATCH IT.
YEAH.

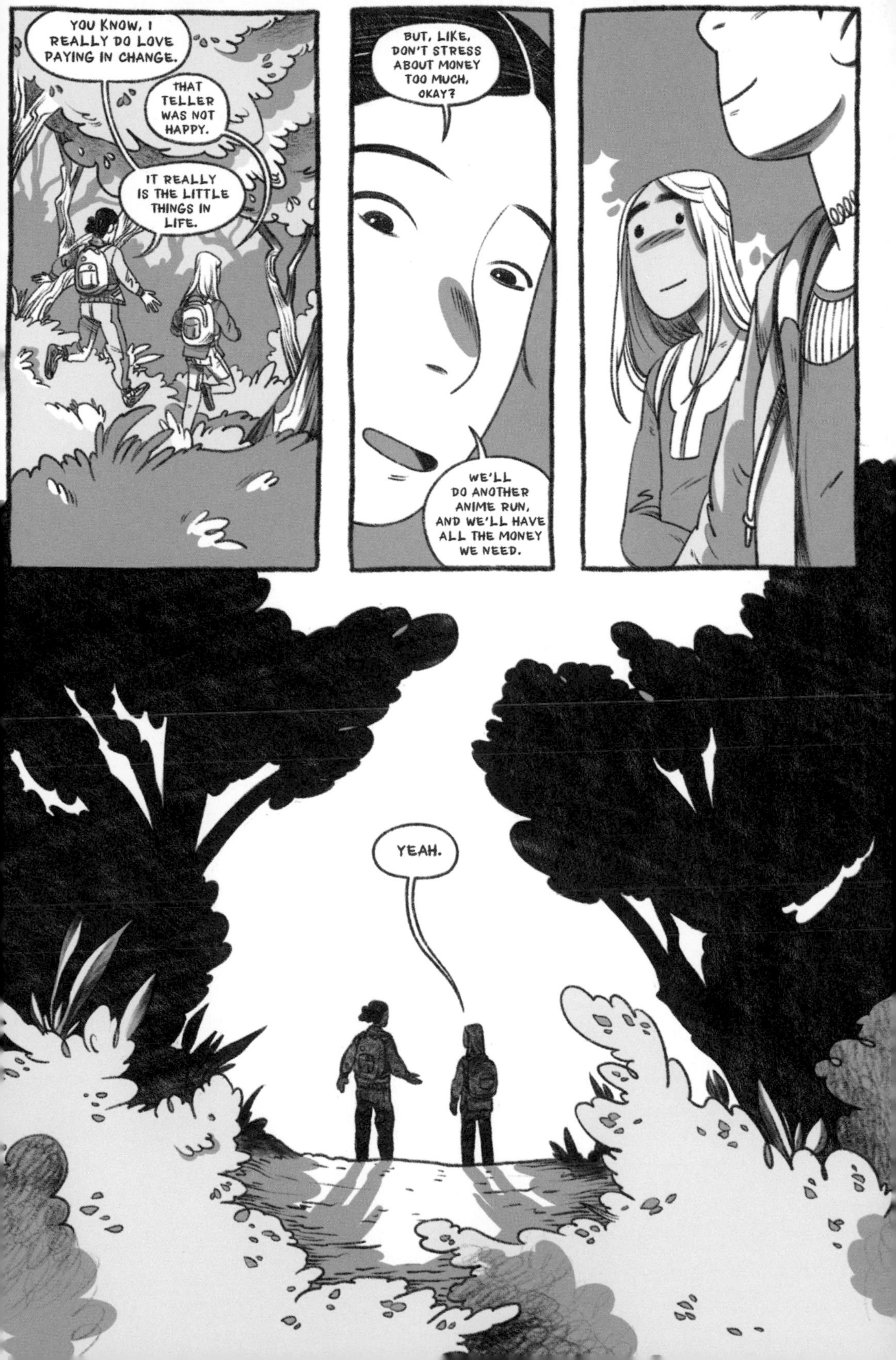
YOU KNOW, I REALLY DO LOVE PAYING IN CHANGE.
THAT TELLER WAS NOT HAPPY.
IT REALLY IS THE LITTLE THINGS IN LIFE.
BUT, LIKE, DON'T STRESS ABOUT MONEY TOO MUCH, OKAY?
WE'LL DO ANOTHER ANIME RUN, AND WE'LL HAVE ALL THE MONEY WE NEED.
YEAH.

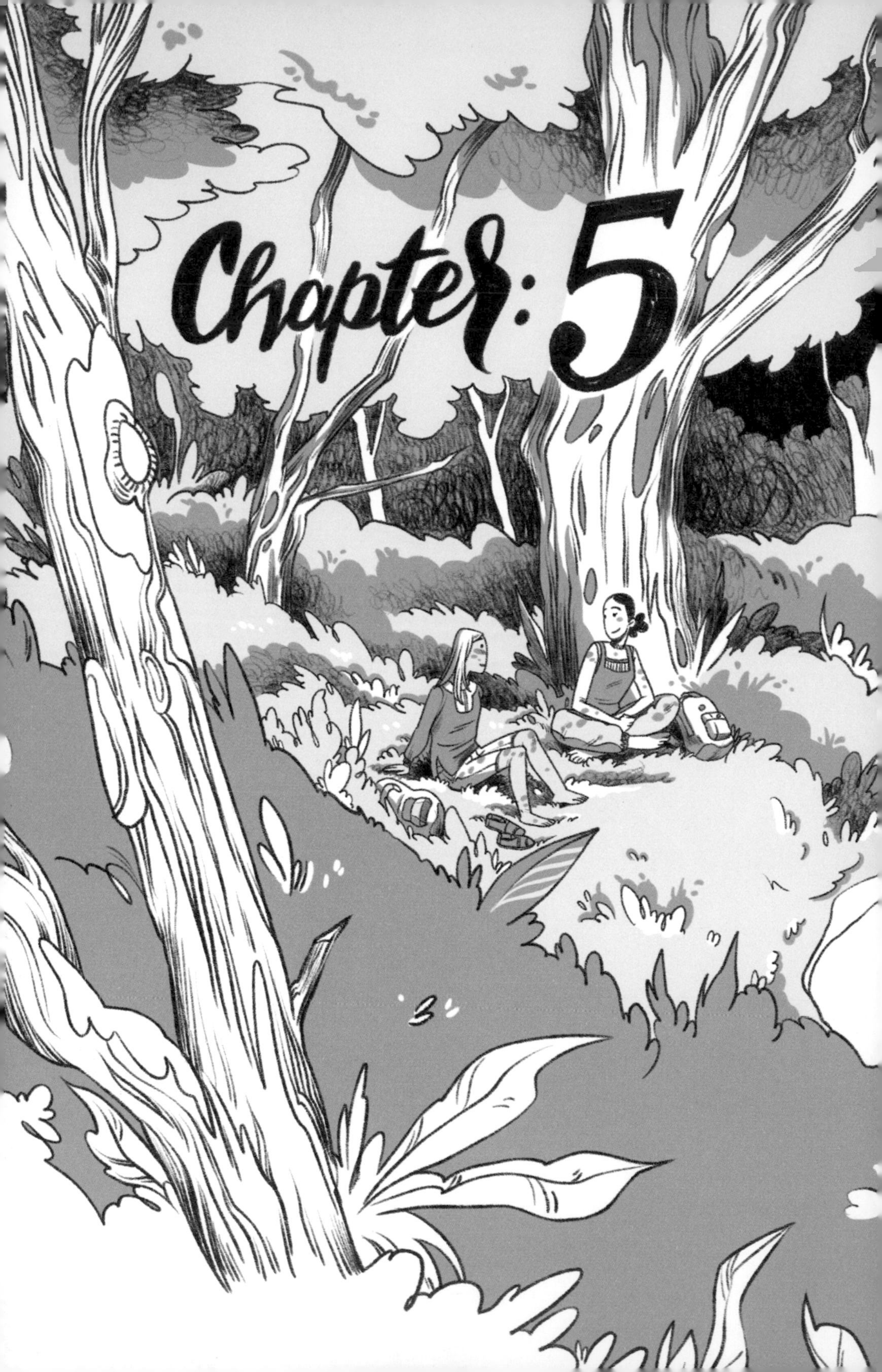
Chapter 5

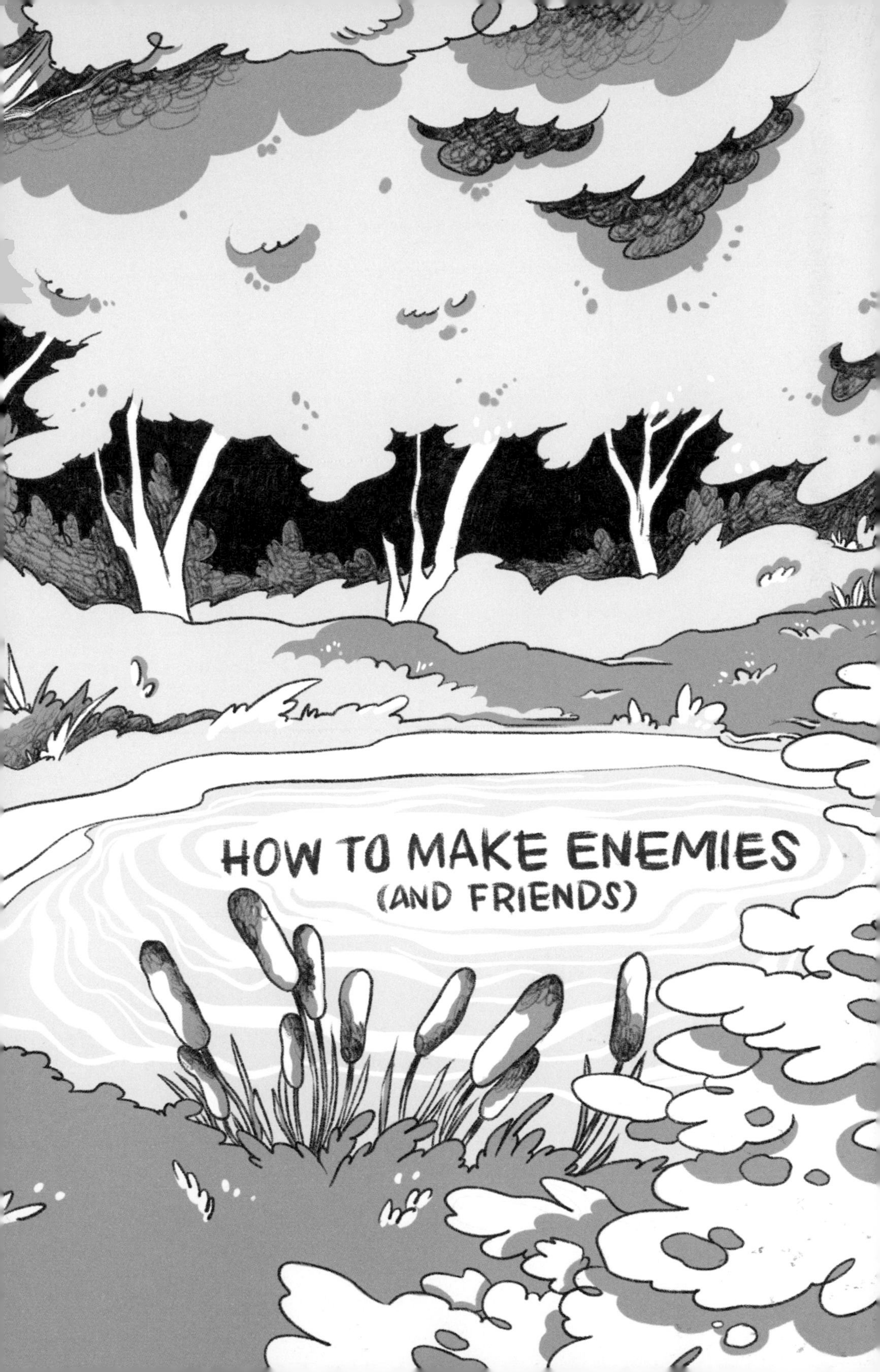
HOW TO MAKE ENEMIES
(AND FRIENDS)

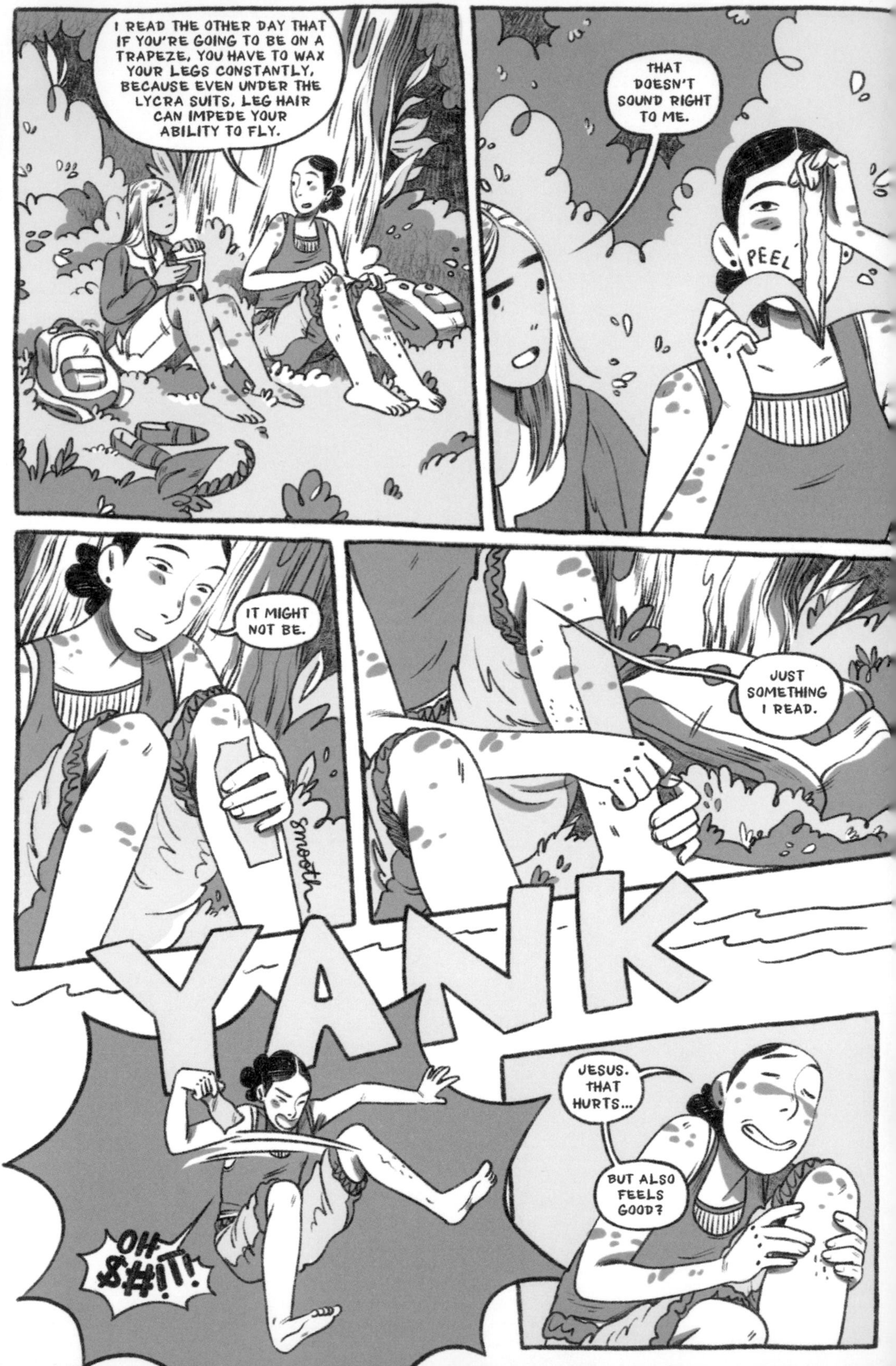
I READ THE OTHER DAY THAT IF YOU'RE GOING TO BE ON A TRAPEZE, YOU HAVE TO WAX YOUR LEGS CONSTANTLY, BECAUSE EVEN UNDER THE LYCRA SUITS, LEG HAIR CAN IMPEDE YOUR ABILITY TO FLY.
THAT DOESN'T SOUND RIGHT TO ME.
PEEL
IT MIGHT NOT BE.
smooth
JUST SOMETHING I READ.
YANK
OH $#!T!
JESUS. THAT HURTS...
BUT ALSO FEELS GOOD?

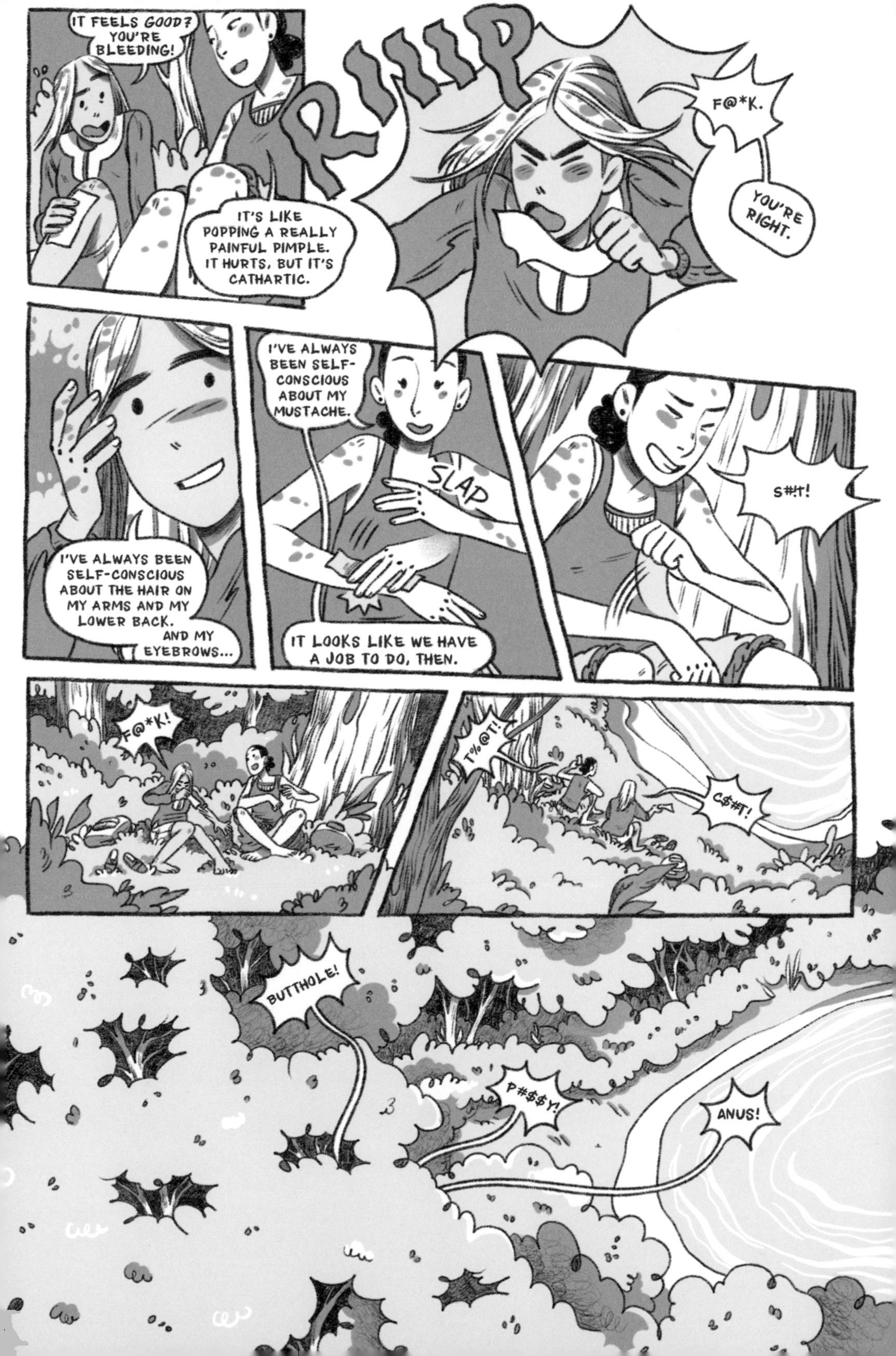

IT FEELS GOOD? YOU'RE BLEEDING!
IT'S LIKE POPPING A REALLY PAINFUL PIMPLE. IT HURTS, BUT IT'S CATHARTIC.
RIIIIP
F@*K.
YOU'RE RIGHT.
I'VE ALWAYS BEEN SELF-CONSCIOUS ABOUT THE HAIR ON MY ARMS AND MY LOWER BACK.
AND MY EYEBROWS...
I'VE ALWAYS BEEN SELF-CONSCIOUS ABOUT MY MUSTACHE.
SLAP
IT LOOKS LIKE WE HAVE A JOB TO DO, THEN.
S#!T!
F@*K!
T%@T!
C$#T!
BUTTHOLE!
P#$$Y!
ANUS!

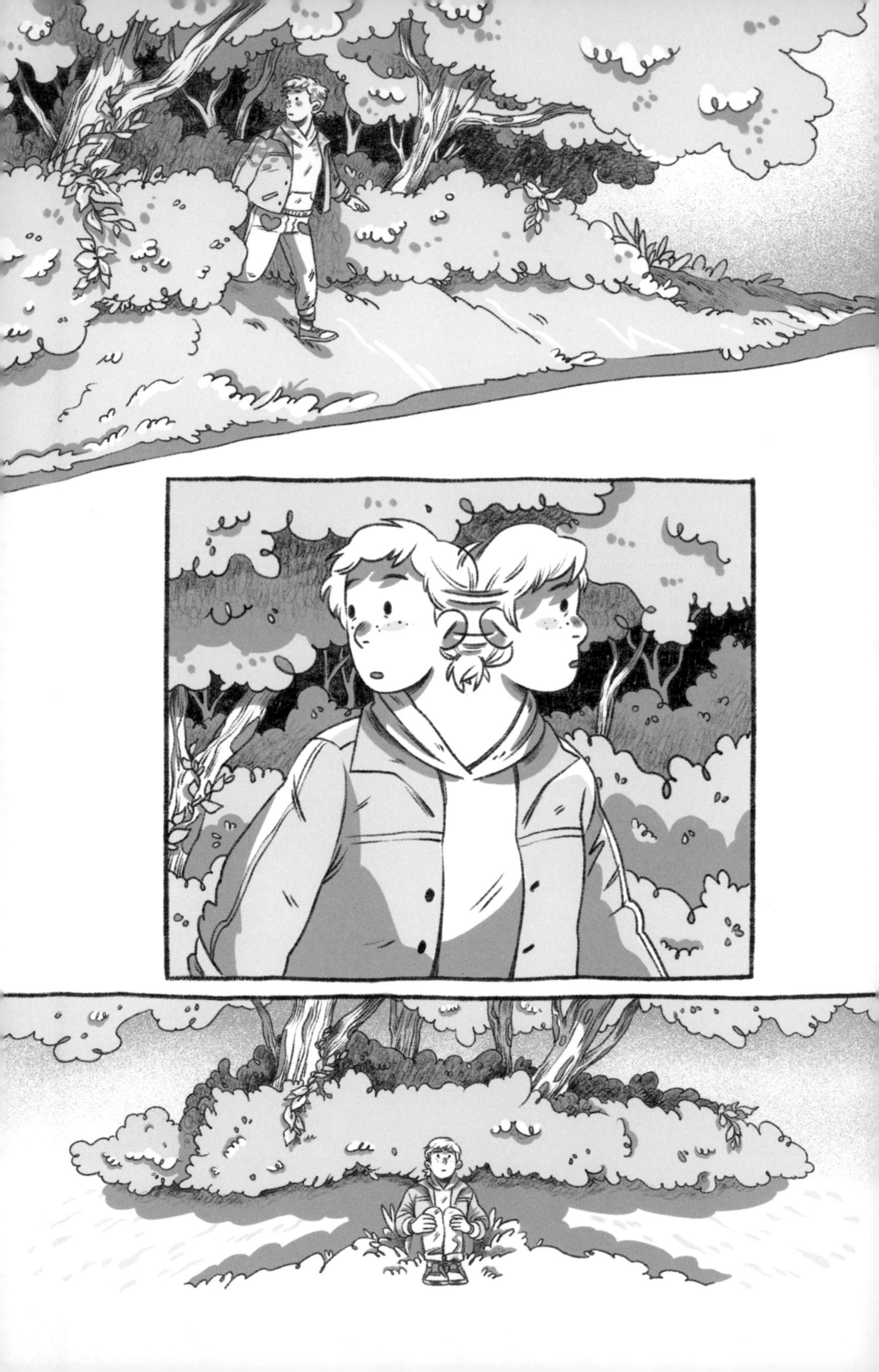

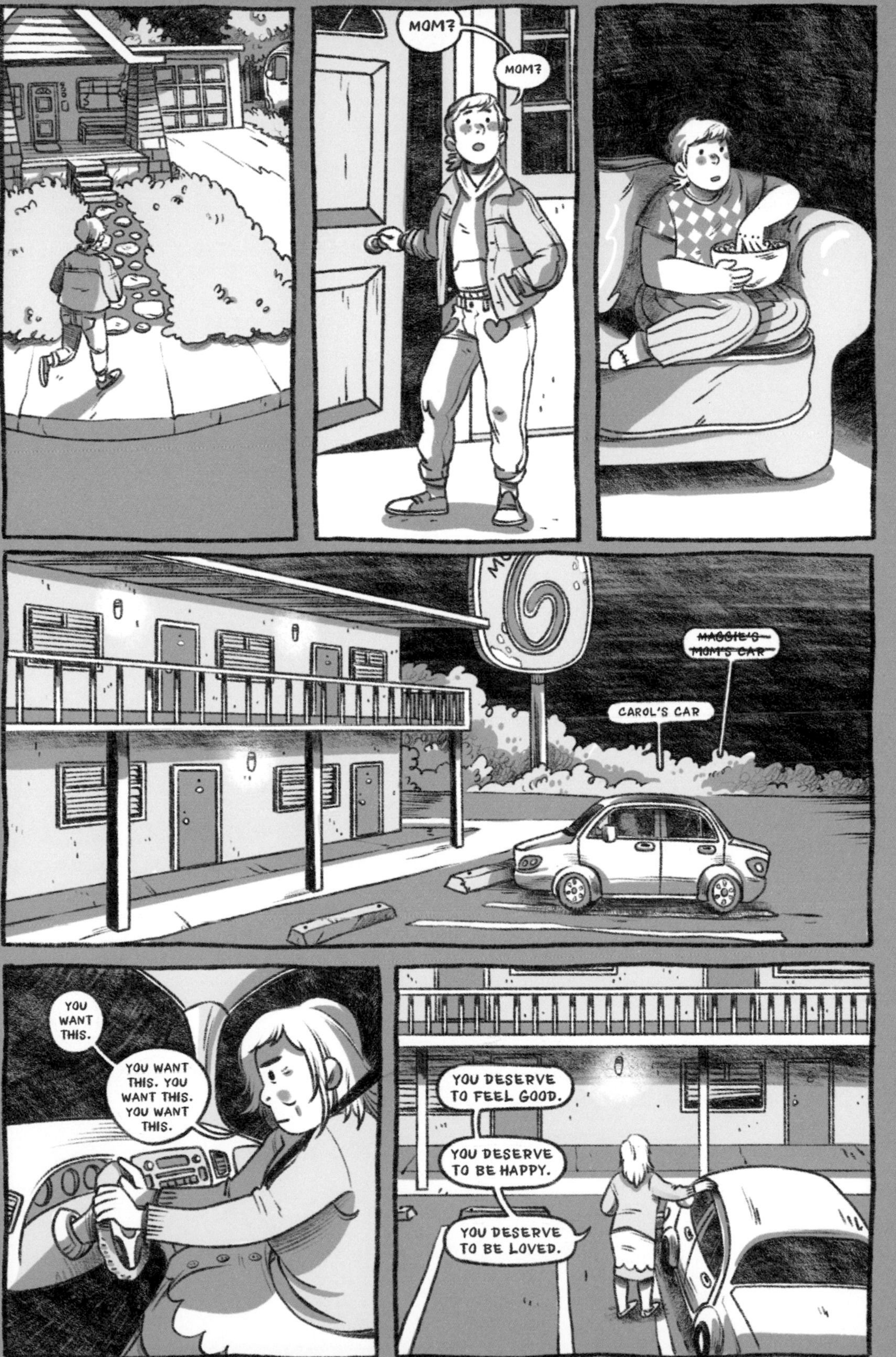
MOM?
MOM?
~~MAGGIE'S MOM'S CAR~~
CAROL'S CAR
YOU WANT THIS.
YOU WANT THIS. YOU WANT THIS. YOU WANT THIS.
YOU DESERVE TO FEEL GOOD.
YOU DESERVE TO BE HAPPY.
YOU DESERVE TO BE LOVED.

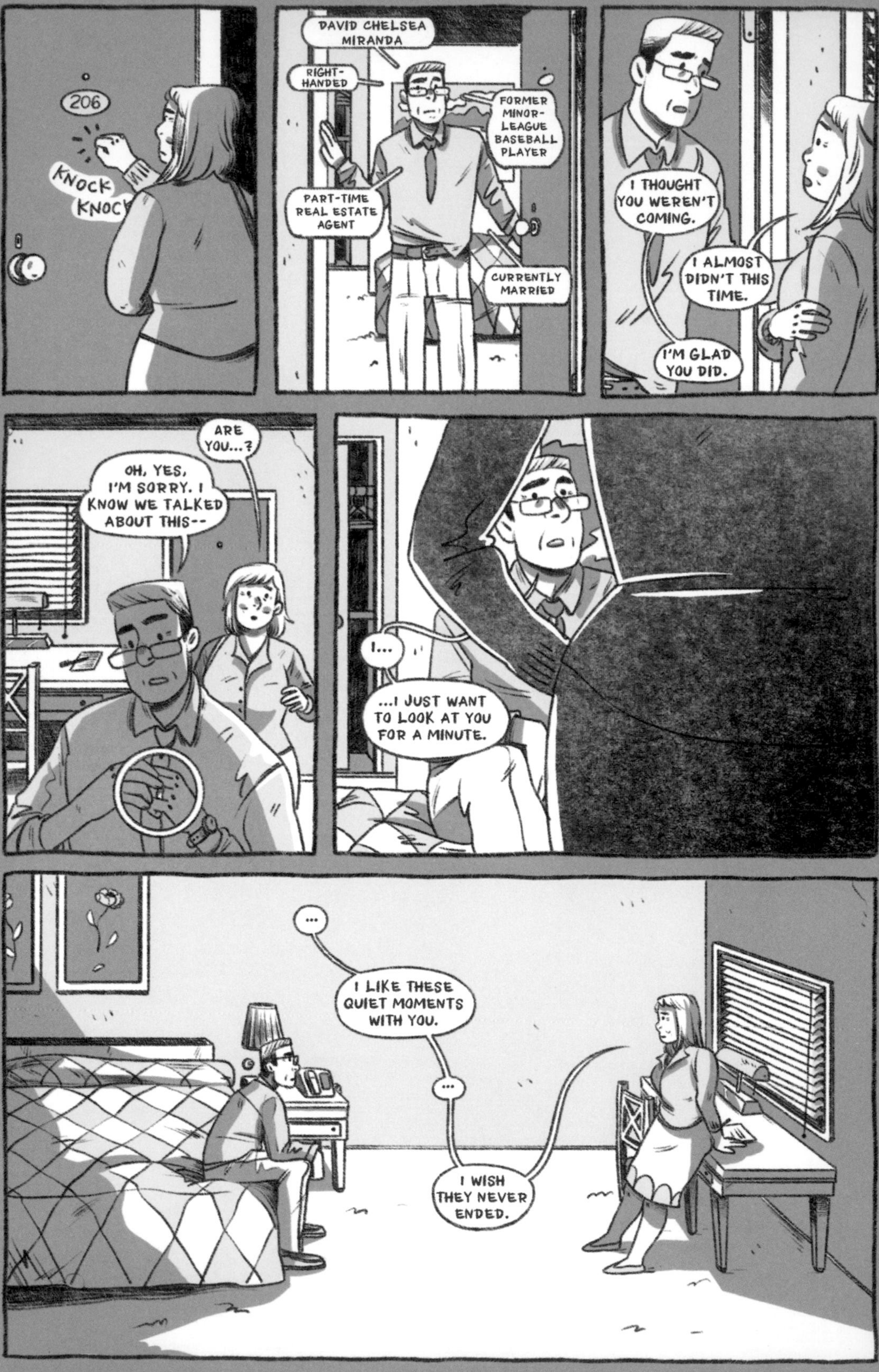
206
KNOCK KNOCK
DAVID CHELSEA MIRANDA
RIGHT-HANDED
FORMER MINOR-LEAGUE BASEBALL PLAYER
PART-TIME REAL ESTATE AGENT
CURRENTLY MARRIED
I THOUGHT YOU WEREN'T COMING.
I ALMOST DIDN'T THIS TIME.
I'M GLAD YOU DID.
ARE YOU...?
OH, YES, I'M SORRY. I KNOW WE TALKED ABOUT THIS--
I...
...I JUST WANT TO LOOK AT YOU FOR A MINUTE.
...
I LIKE THESE QUIET MOMENTS WITH YOU.
...
I WISH THEY NEVER ENDED.

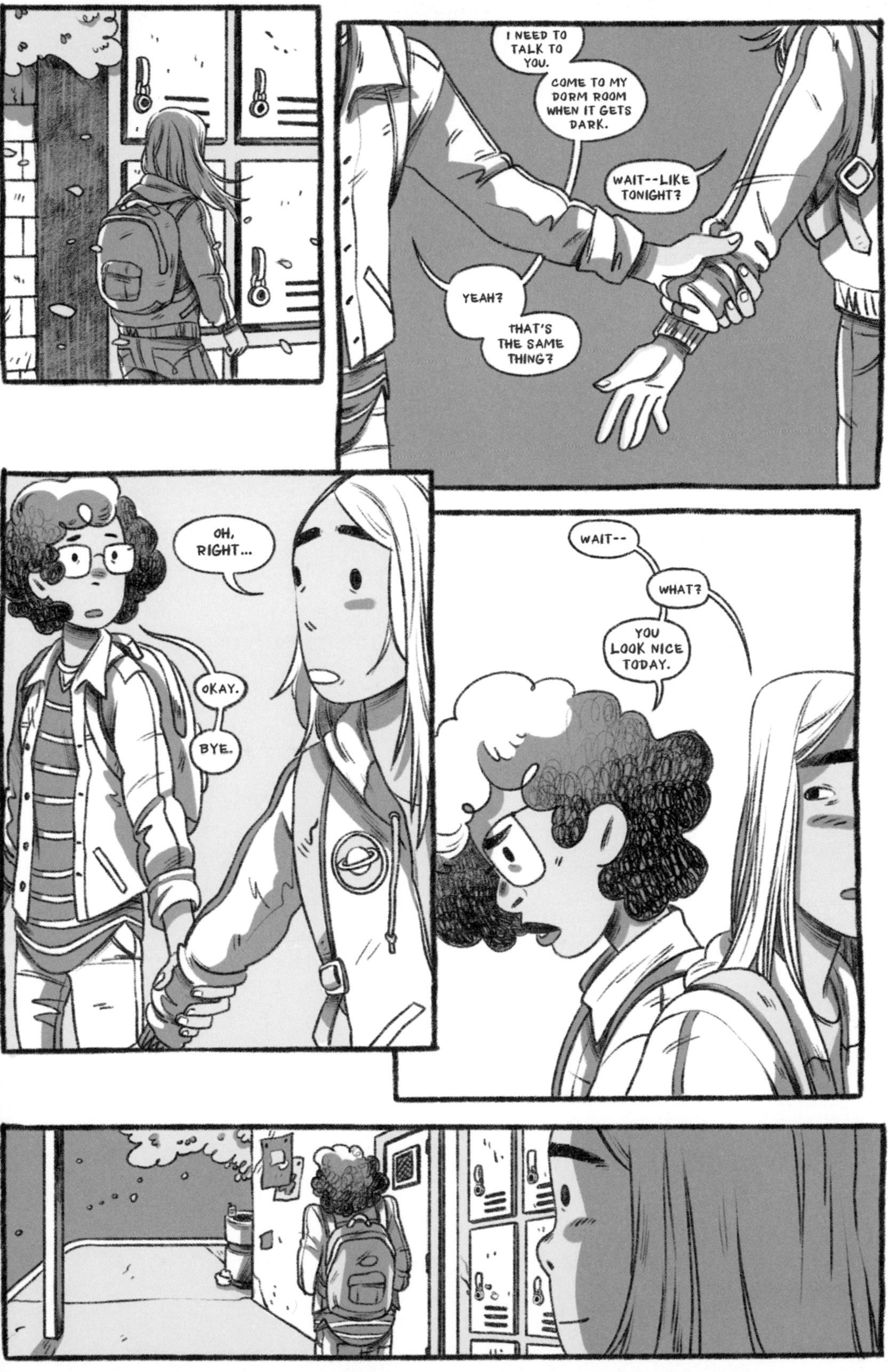
I NEED TO TALK TO YOU.
COME TO MY DORM ROOM WHEN IT GETS DARK.
WAIT--LIKE TONIGHT?
YEAH?
THAT'S THE SAME THING?
OH, RIGHT...
OKAY.
BYE.
WAIT--
WHAT?
YOU LOOK NICE TODAY.

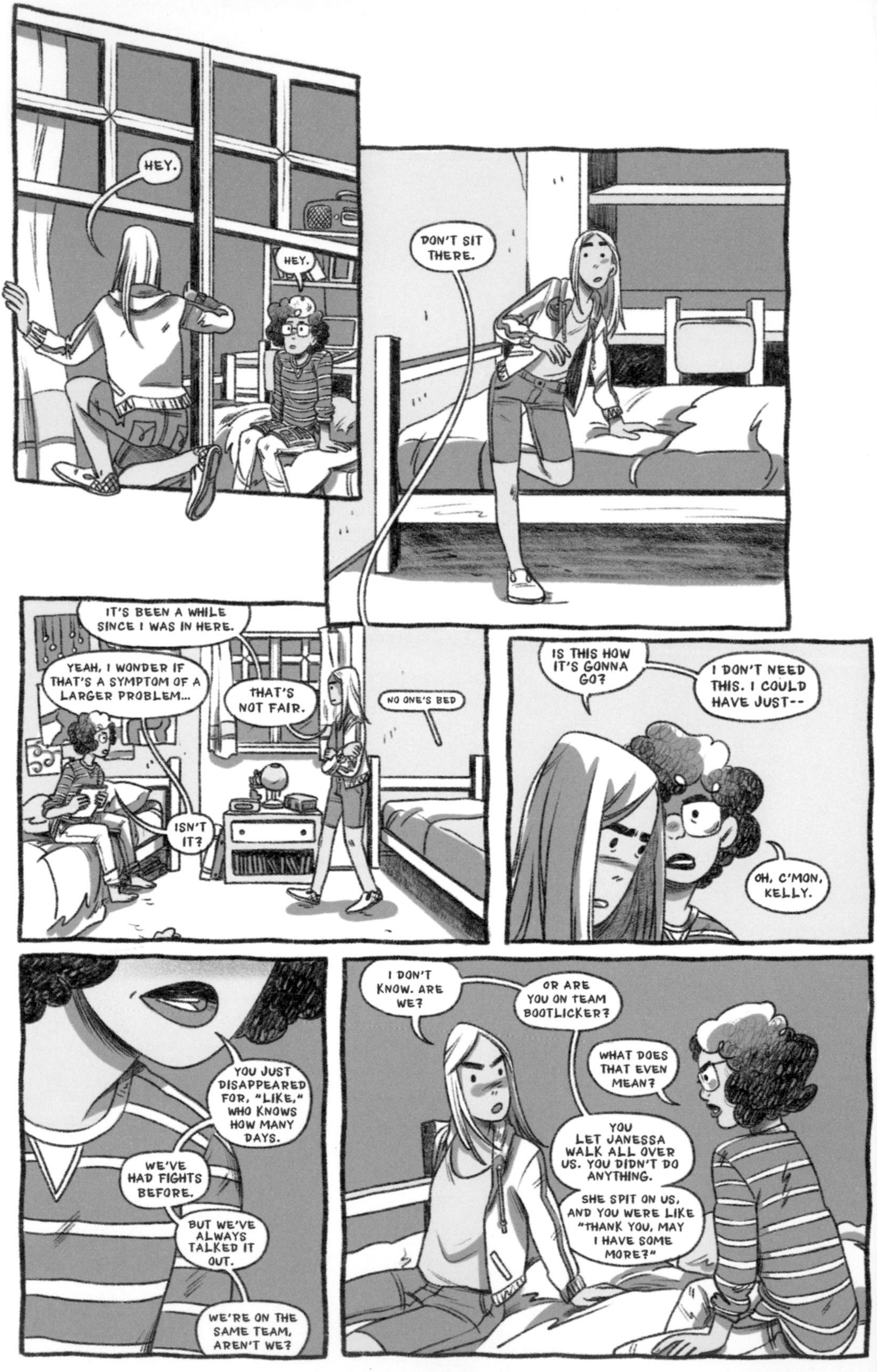
HEY.
HEY.
DON'T SIT THERE.
IT'S BEEN A WHILE SINCE I WAS IN HERE.
YEAH, I WONDER IF THAT'S A SYMPTOM OF A LARGER PROBLEM...
THAT'S NOT FAIR.
ISN'T IT?
NO ONE'S BED
IS THIS HOW IT'S GONNA GO?
I DON'T NEED THIS. I COULD HAVE JUST--
OH, C'MON, KELLY.
YOU JUST DISAPPEARED FOR, "LIKE," WHO KNOWS HOW MANY DAYS.
WE'VE HAD FIGHTS BEFORE.
BUT WE'VE ALWAYS TALKED IT OUT.
WE'RE ON THE SAME TEAM, AREN'T WE?
I DON'T KNOW. ARE WE?
OR ARE YOU ON TEAM BOOTLICKER?
WHAT DOES THAT EVEN MEAN?
YOU LET JANESSA WALK ALL OVER US. YOU DIDN'T DO ANYTHING.
SHE SPIT ON US, AND YOU WERE LIKE "THANK YOU, MAY I HAVE SOME MORE?"

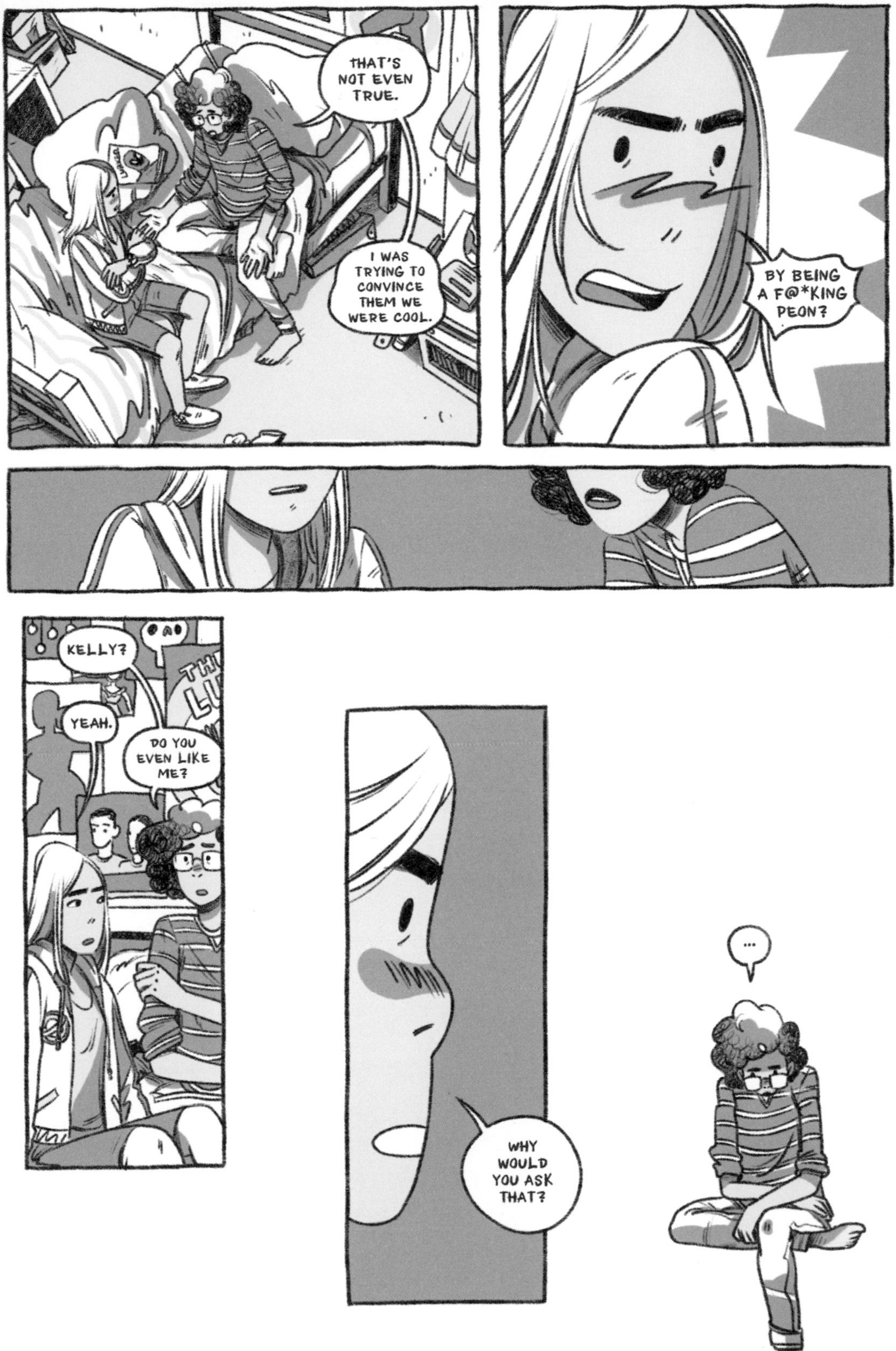
THAT'S NOT EVEN TRUE.
I WAS TRYING TO CONVINCE THEM WE WERE COOL.
BY BEING A F@*KING PEON?
KELLY?
YEAH.
DO YOU EVEN LIKE ME?
WHY WOULD YOU ASK THAT?
...

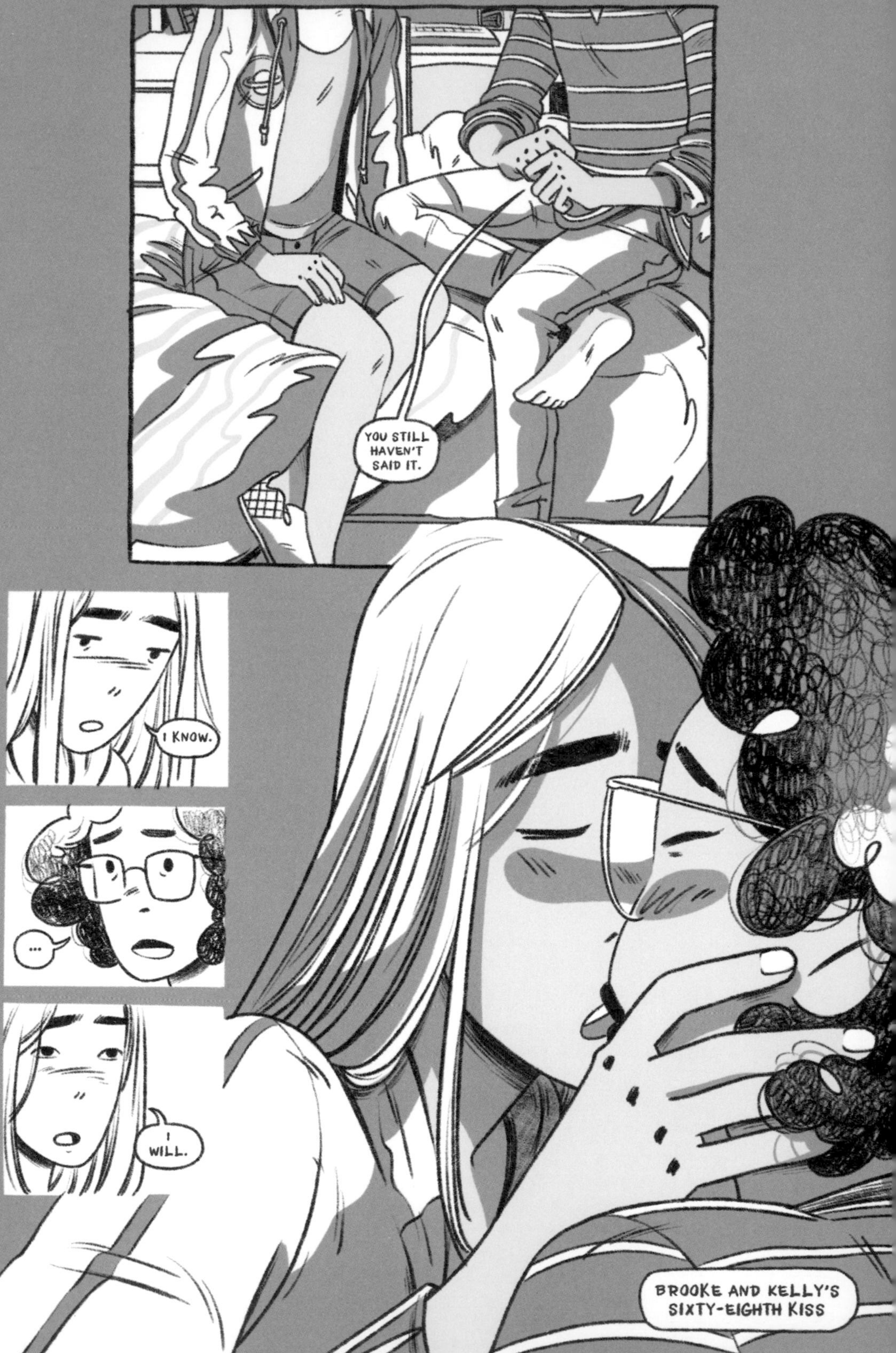
YOU STILL HAVEN'T SAID IT.
I KNOW.
...
I WILL.
BROOKE AND KELLY'S SIXTY-EIGHTH KISS

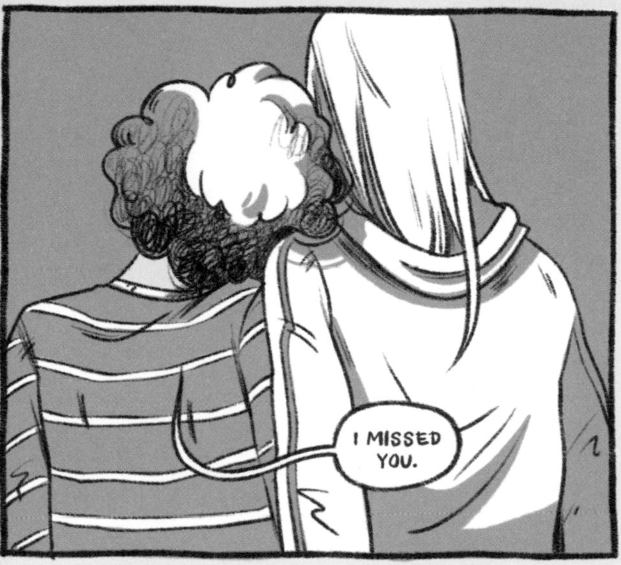
I MISSED YOU.
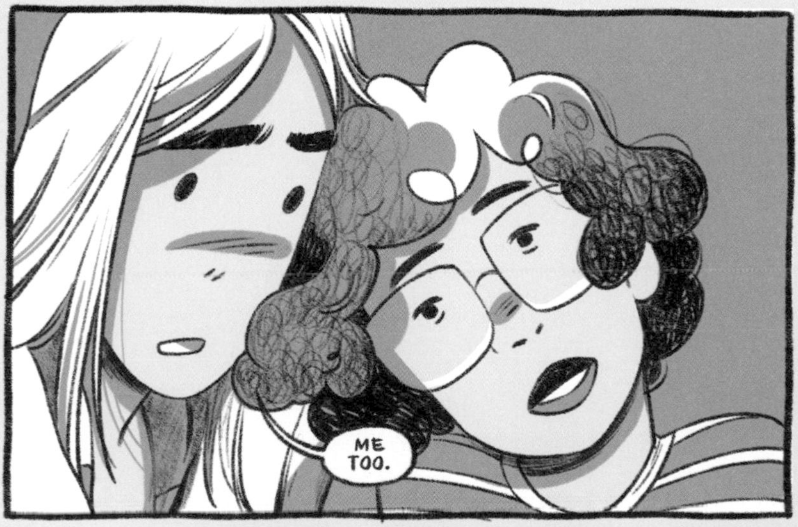
ME TOO.
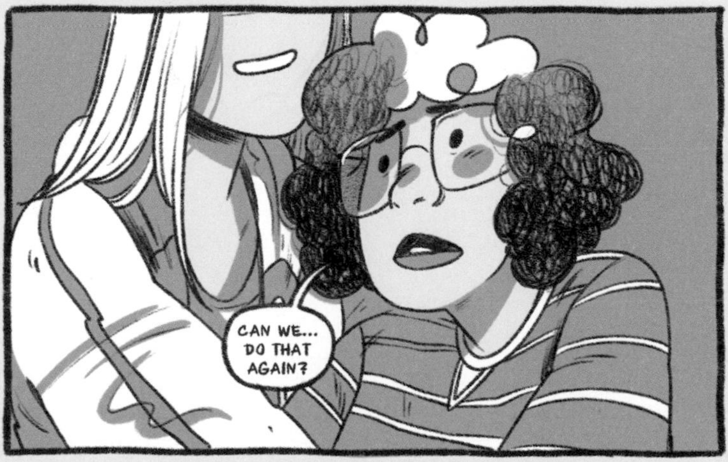
CAN WE... DO THAT AGAIN?

MELISSA'S POINT OF NO RETURN

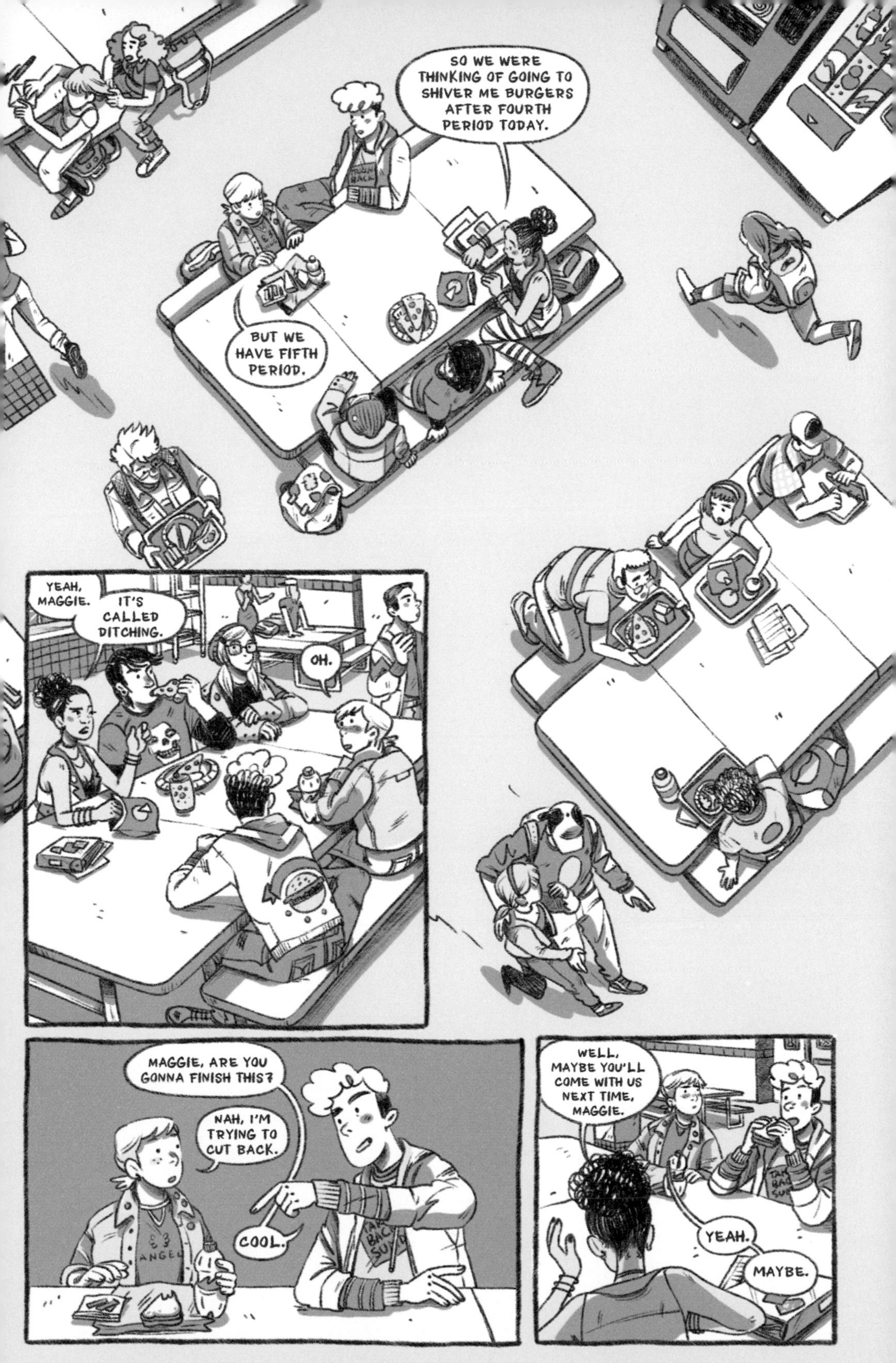
SO WE WERE THINKING OF GOING TO SHIVER ME BURGERS AFTER FOURTH PERIOD TODAY.
BUT WE HAVE FIFTH PERIOD.
YEAH, MAGGIE.
IT'S CALLED DITCHING.
OH.
MAGGIE, ARE YOU GONNA FINISH THIS?
NAH, I'M TRYING TO CUT BACK.
COOL.
WELL, MAYBE YOU'LL COME WITH US NEXT TIME, MAGGIE.
YEAH.
MAYBE.

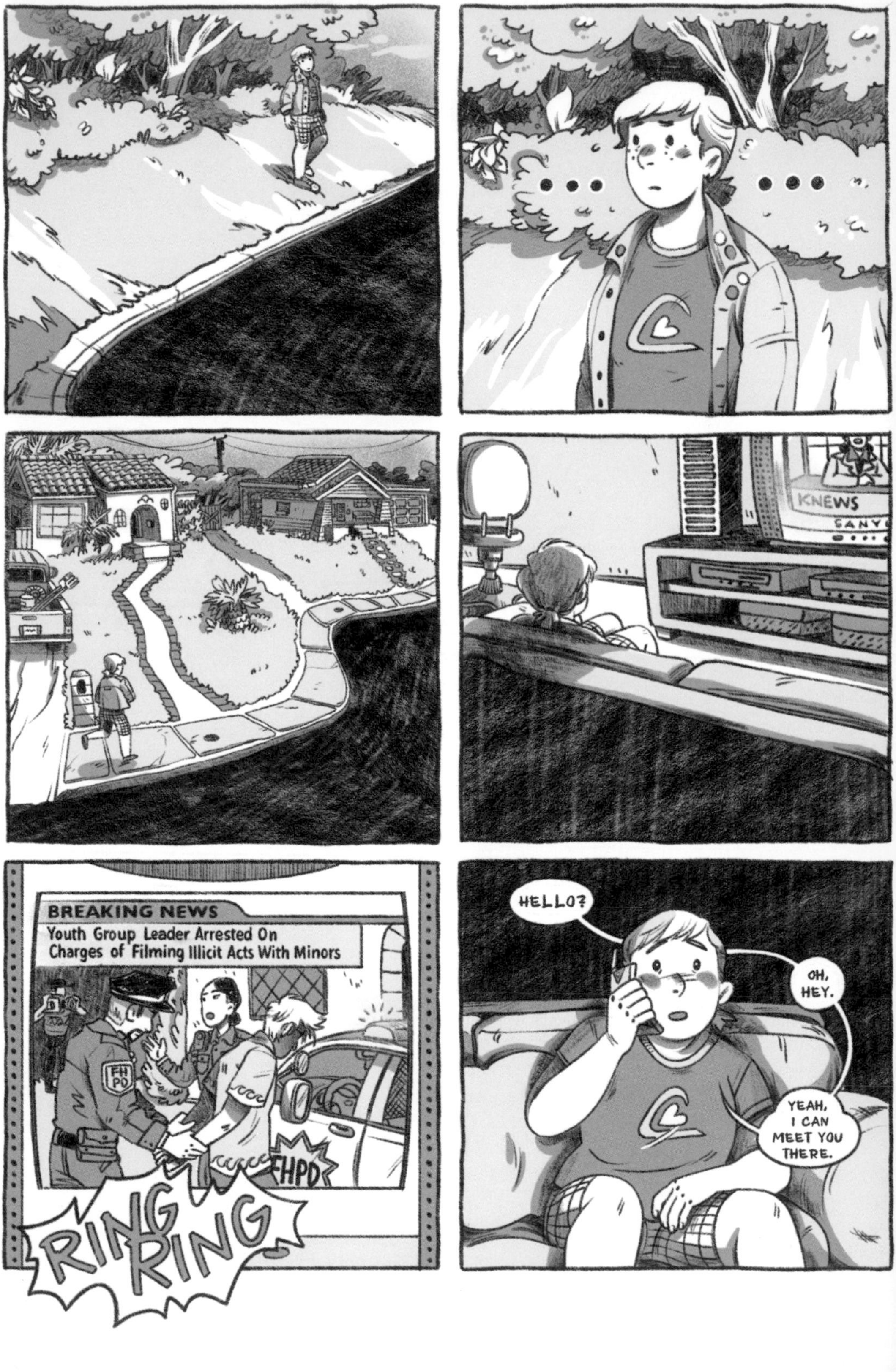
KNEWS
SANY
BREAKING NEWS
Youth Group Leader Arrested On
Charges of Filming Illicit Acts With Minors
FH PD
FHPD
RING RING
HELLO?
OH, HEY.
YEAH, I CAN MEET YOU THERE.

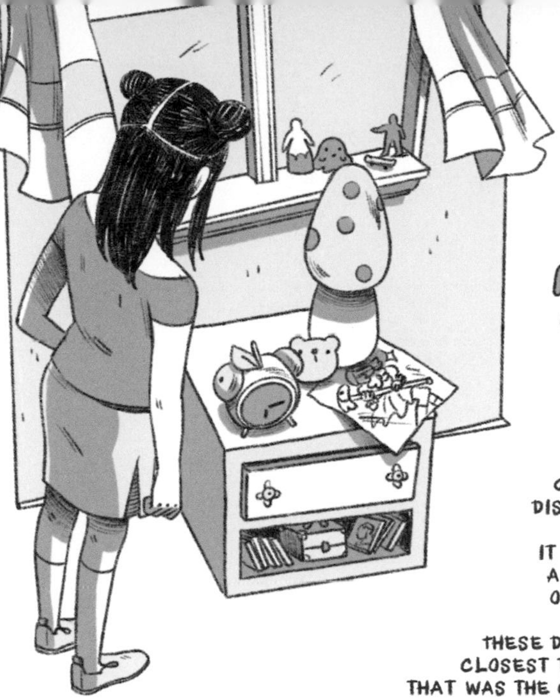

A BRIEF HISTORY OF MELISSA CHO'S RECENT CONFLICTING EMOTIONS

ON HER NINTH BIRTHDAY, MELISSA FOUND A DISPOSABLE CAMERA THAT HER GRANDFATHER HAD LEFT OUT BY MISTAKE. SHE TOOK IT AND KEPT IT UNDER HER BED FOR TWO AND A HALF YEARS. SHE HAD PLANNED TO USE IT ONE DAY. TO CAPTURE SOMETHING SPECIAL.

THESE DAYS, MELISSA FINDS HERSELF FEELING THE CLOSEST THING SHE'S FELT TO HAPPY. OR AT LEAST THAT WAS THE CASE...Y'KNOW...WHEN BROOKE AND KELLY WEREN'T SPEAKING TO EACH OTHER.

MELISSA HAS NEVER FELT LIKE THIS ABOUT SOMEONE. THERE'S A CACOPHONY OF CONFLICTING AND OPPOSING EMOTIONS THAT ARE ALL SWIRLING INSIDE HER. SHE'S NOT SURE WHAT TO DO WITH THEM. SO SHE'S JUST GOING TO IGNORE THEM FOR THE TIME BEING.

SHE'S STARTED PRAYING AT NIGHT FOR ANOTHER MOMENT LIKE THE ONE IN THE WOODS. SHE'S DREADING THE DAY WHEN HER LEG HAIR HAS GROWN OUT, BECAUSE IT WILL BE A DEFINITIVE END TO THE SOLACE SHE FOUND IN THAT QUIET INTIMACY SHE SHARED WITH KELLY.

MELISSA'S BEEN HAVING A RECURRING DAYDREAM ABOUT FINDING THAT OLD DISPOSABLE CAMERA AND TAKING A PICTURE OF KELLY.

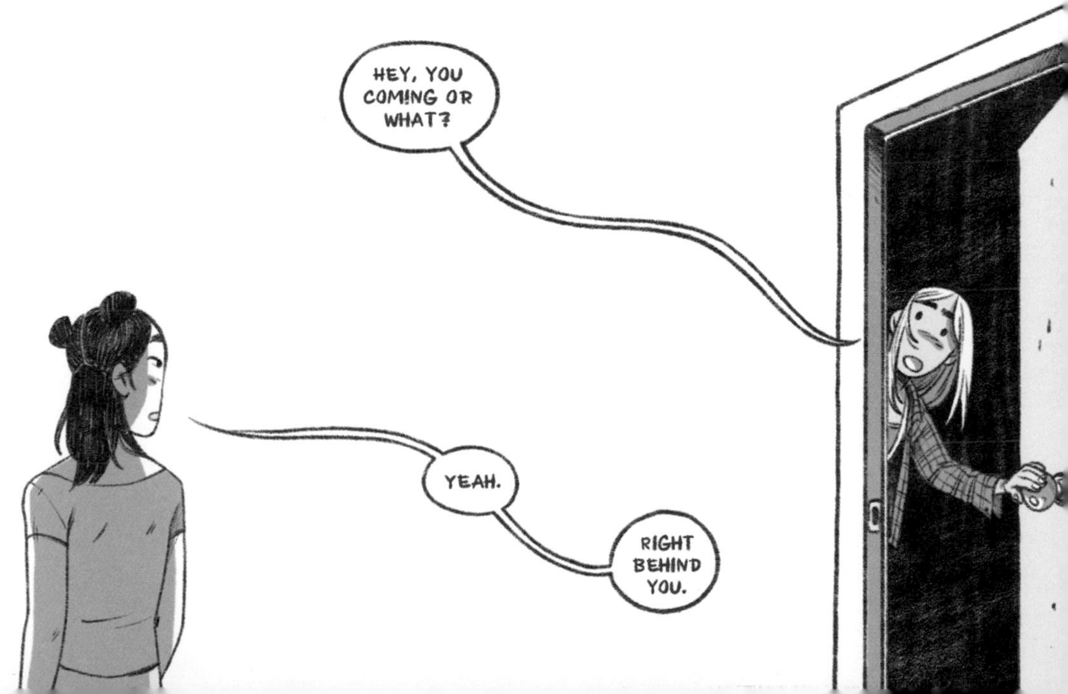
HEY, YOU COMING OR WHAT?
YEAH.
RIGHT BEHIND YOU.

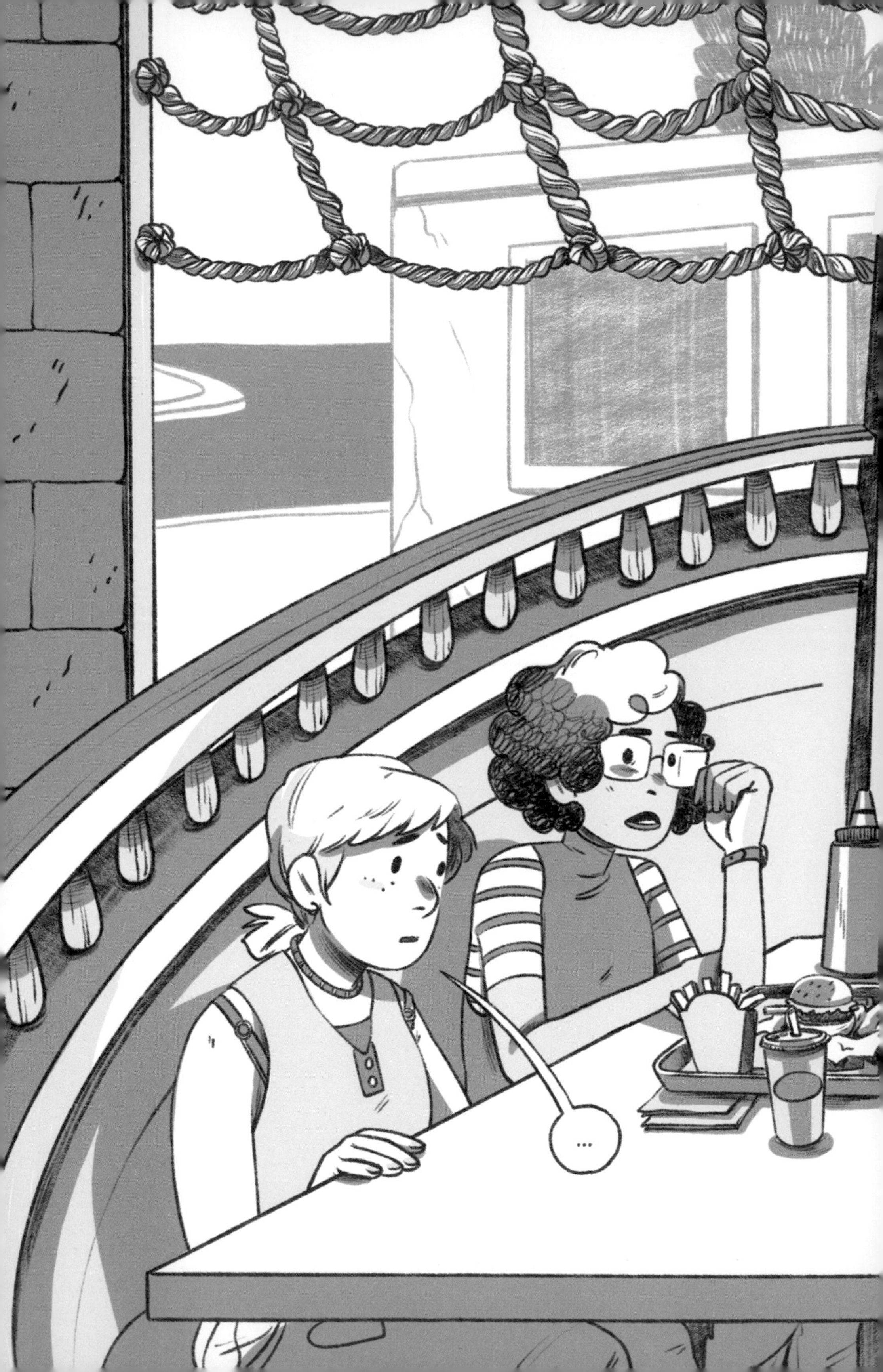
...

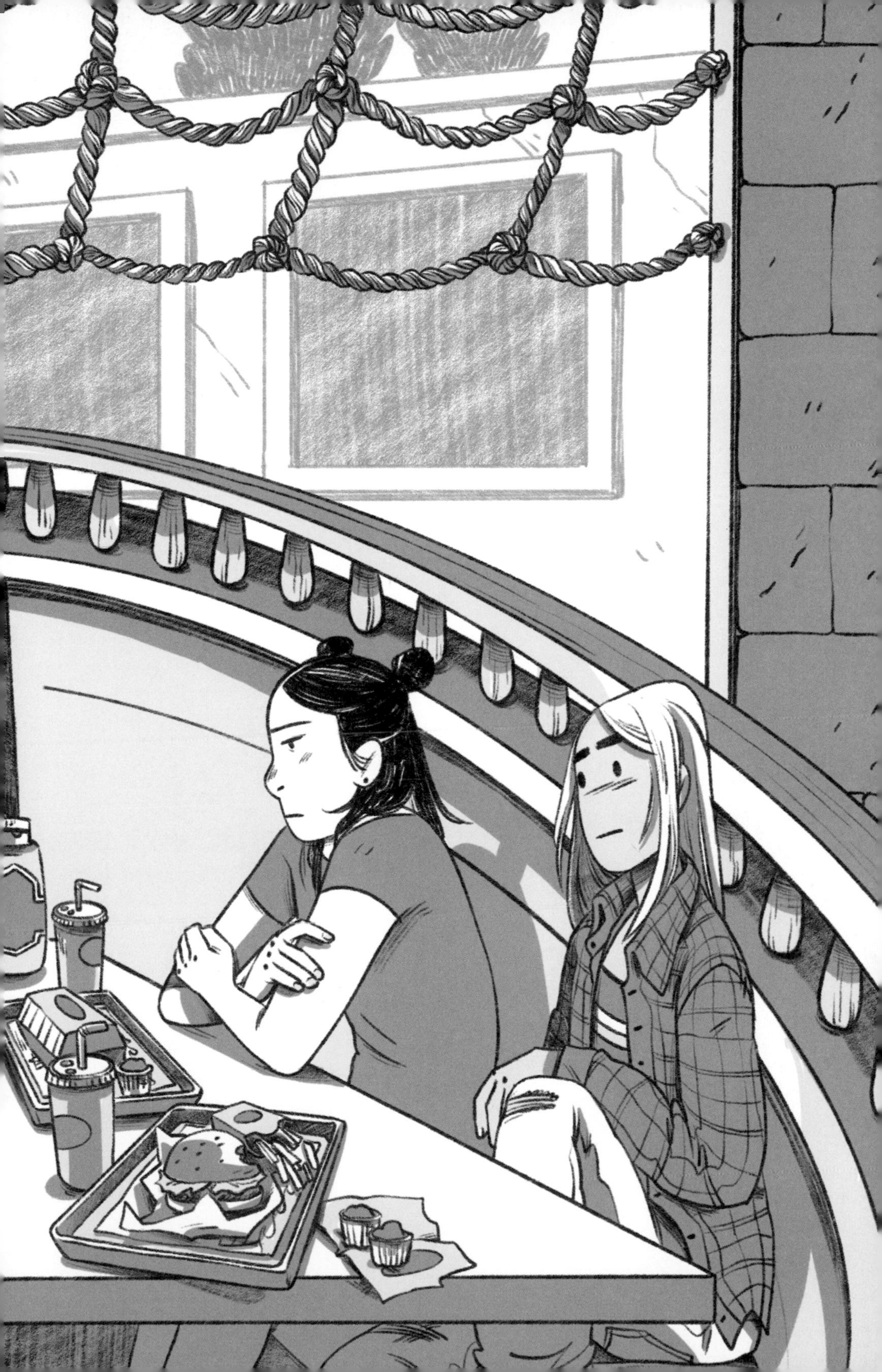

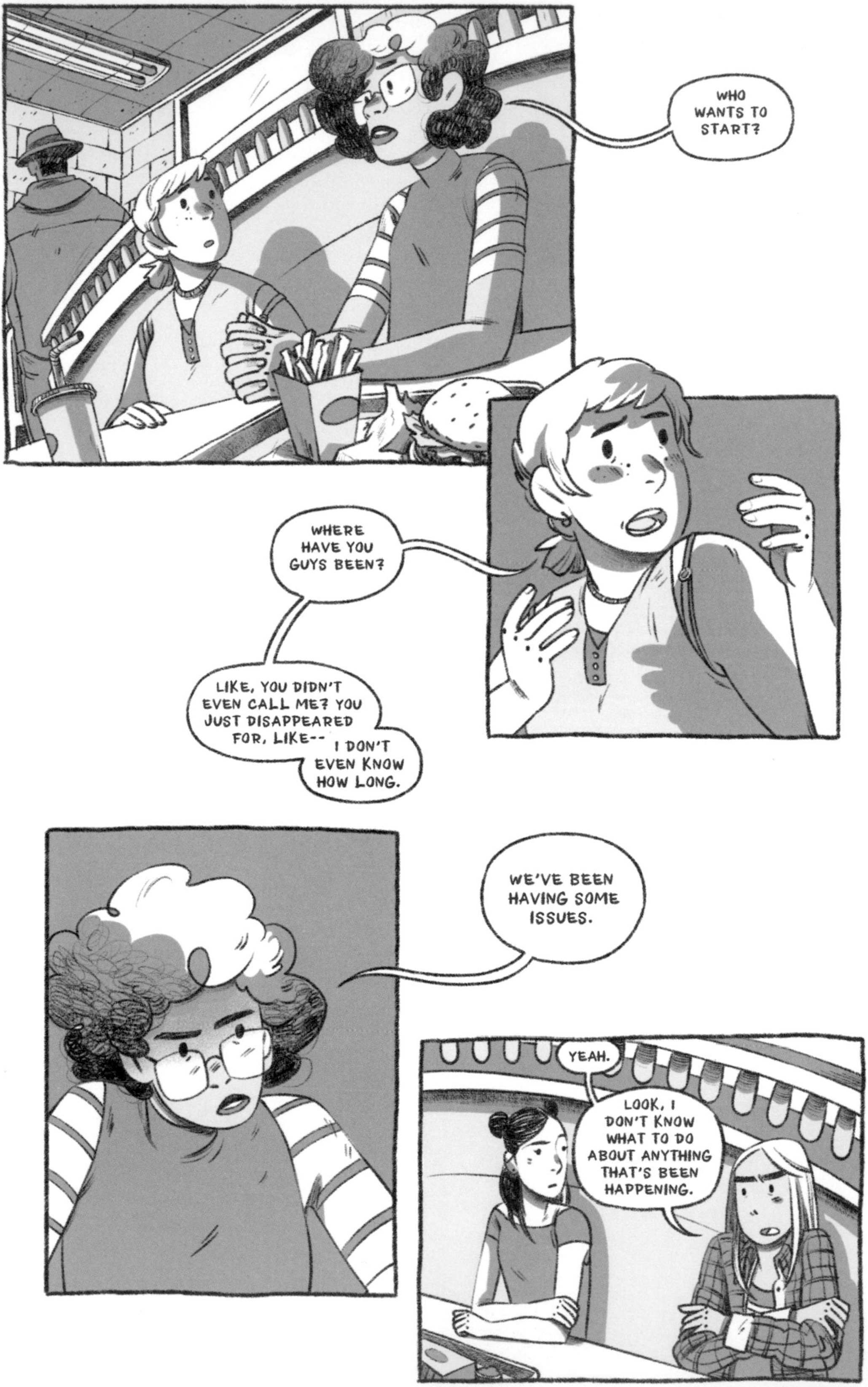
WHO WANTS TO START?
WHERE HAVE YOU GUYS BEEN?
LIKE, YOU DIDN'T EVEN CALL ME? YOU JUST DISAPPEARED FOR, LIKE--
I DON'T EVEN KNOW HOW LONG.
WE'VE BEEN HAVING SOME ISSUES.
YEAH.
LOOK, I DON'T KNOW WHAT TO DO ABOUT ANYTHING THAT'S BEEN HAPPENING.

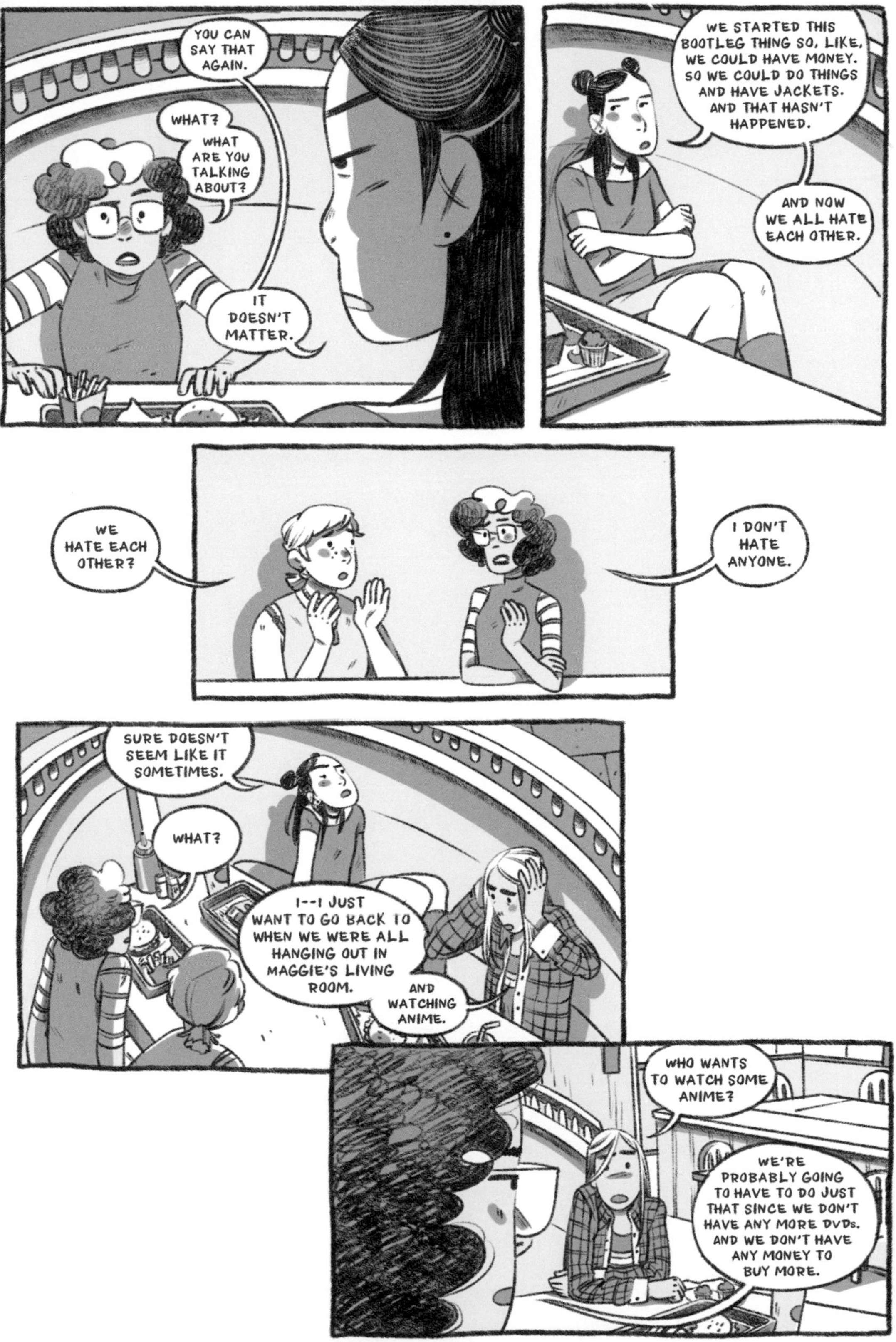
YOU CAN SAY THAT AGAIN.
WHAT?
WHAT ARE YOU TALKING ABOUT?
IT DOESN'T MATTER.
WE STARTED THIS BOOTLEG THING SO, LIKE, WE COULD HAVE MONEY. SO WE COULD DO THINGS AND HAVE JACKETS. AND THAT HASN'T HAPPENED.
AND NOW WE ALL HATE EACH OTHER.
WE HATE EACH OTHER?
I DON'T HATE ANYONE.
SURE DOESN'T SEEM LIKE IT SOMETIMES.
WHAT?
I--I JUST WANT TO GO BACK TO WHEN WE WERE ALL HANGING OUT IN MAGGIE'S LIVING ROOM.
AND WATCHING ANIME.
WHO WANTS TO WATCH SOME ANIME?
WE'RE PROBABLY GOING TO HAVE TO DO JUST THAT SINCE WE DON'T HAVE ANY MORE DVDs. AND WE DON'T HAVE ANY MONEY TO BUY MORE.

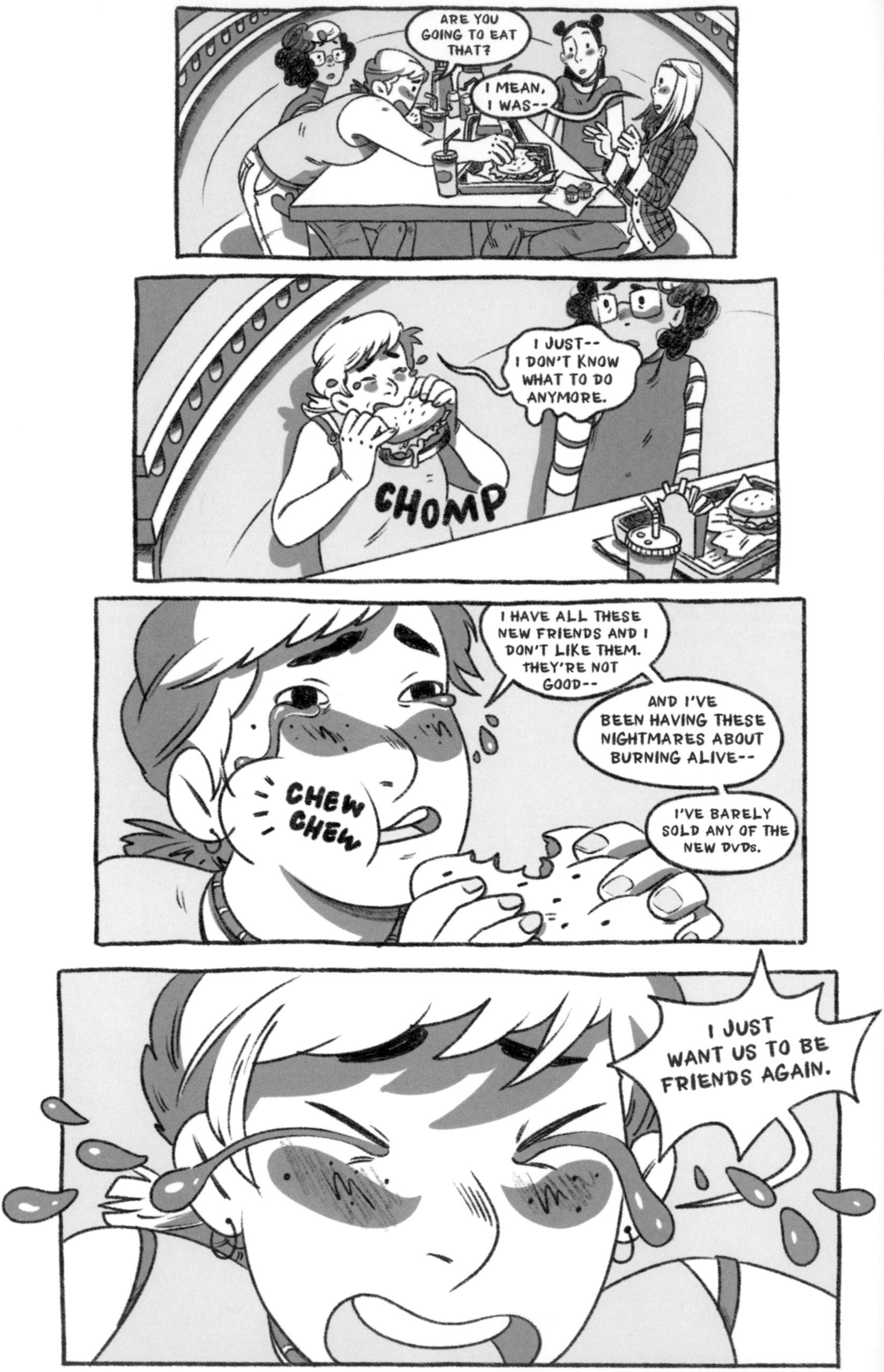
ARE YOU GOING TO EAT THAT?
I MEAN, I WAS--
I JUST-- I DON'T KNOW WHAT TO DO ANYMORE.
CHOMP
I HAVE ALL THESE NEW FRIENDS AND I DON'T LIKE THEM. THEY'RE NOT GOOD--
AND I'VE BEEN HAVING THESE NIGHTMARES ABOUT BURNING ALIVE--
I'VE BARELY SOLD ANY OF THE NEW DVDs.
CHEW CHEW
I JUST WANT US TO BE FRIENDS AGAIN.

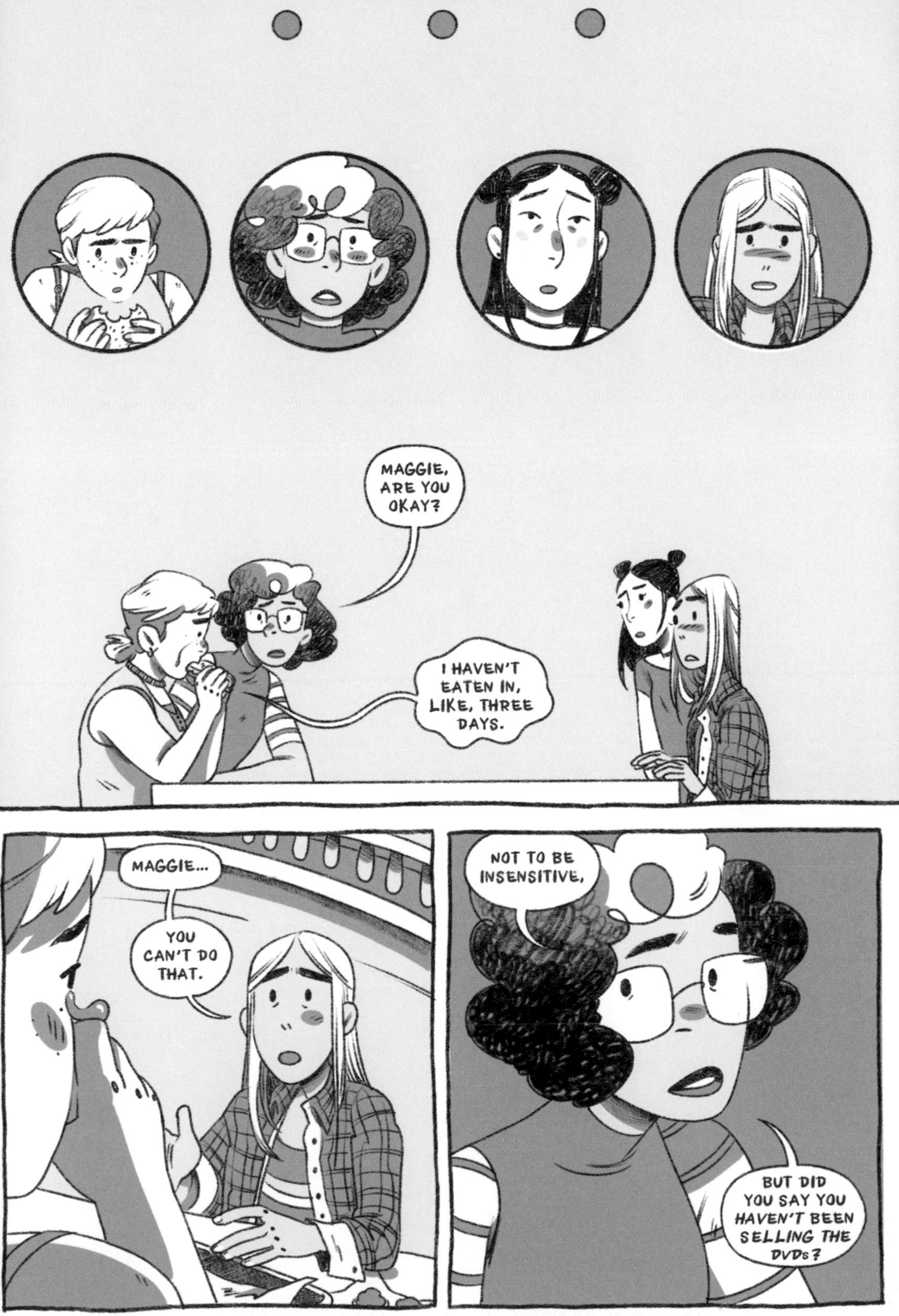
MAGGIE, ARE YOU OKAY?
I HAVEN'T EATEN IN, LIKE, THREE DAYS.
MAGGIE...
YOU CAN'T DO THAT.
NOT TO BE INSENSITIVE,
BUT DID YOU SAY YOU HAVEN'T BEEN SELLING THE DVDs?

Chapter: 7

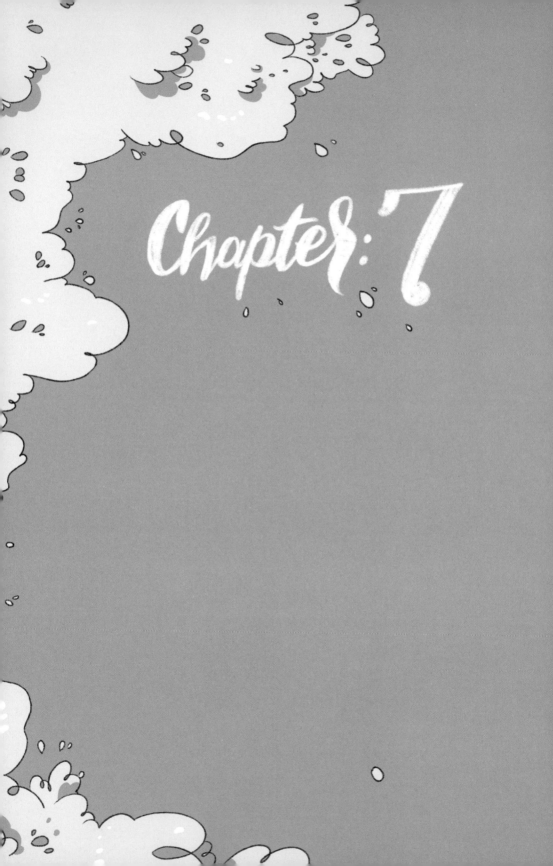

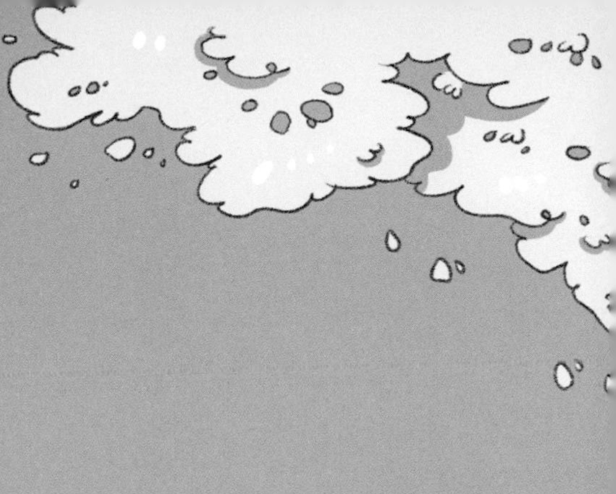

HALF-STEP ECHOES

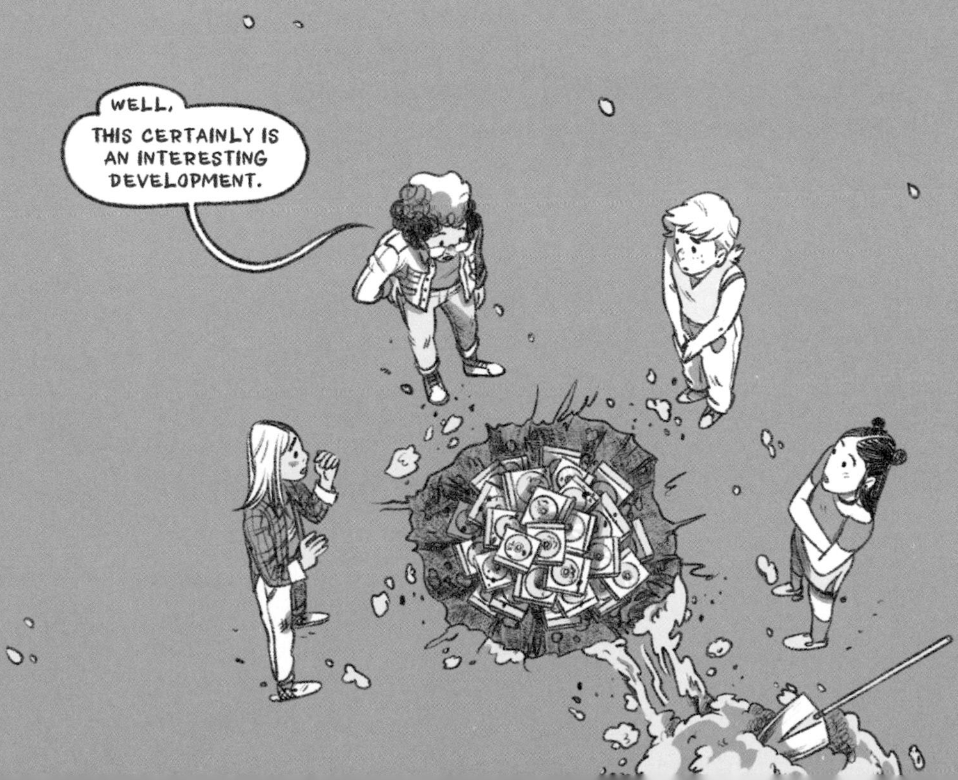
WELL, THIS CERTAINLY IS AN INTERESTING DEVELOPMENT.

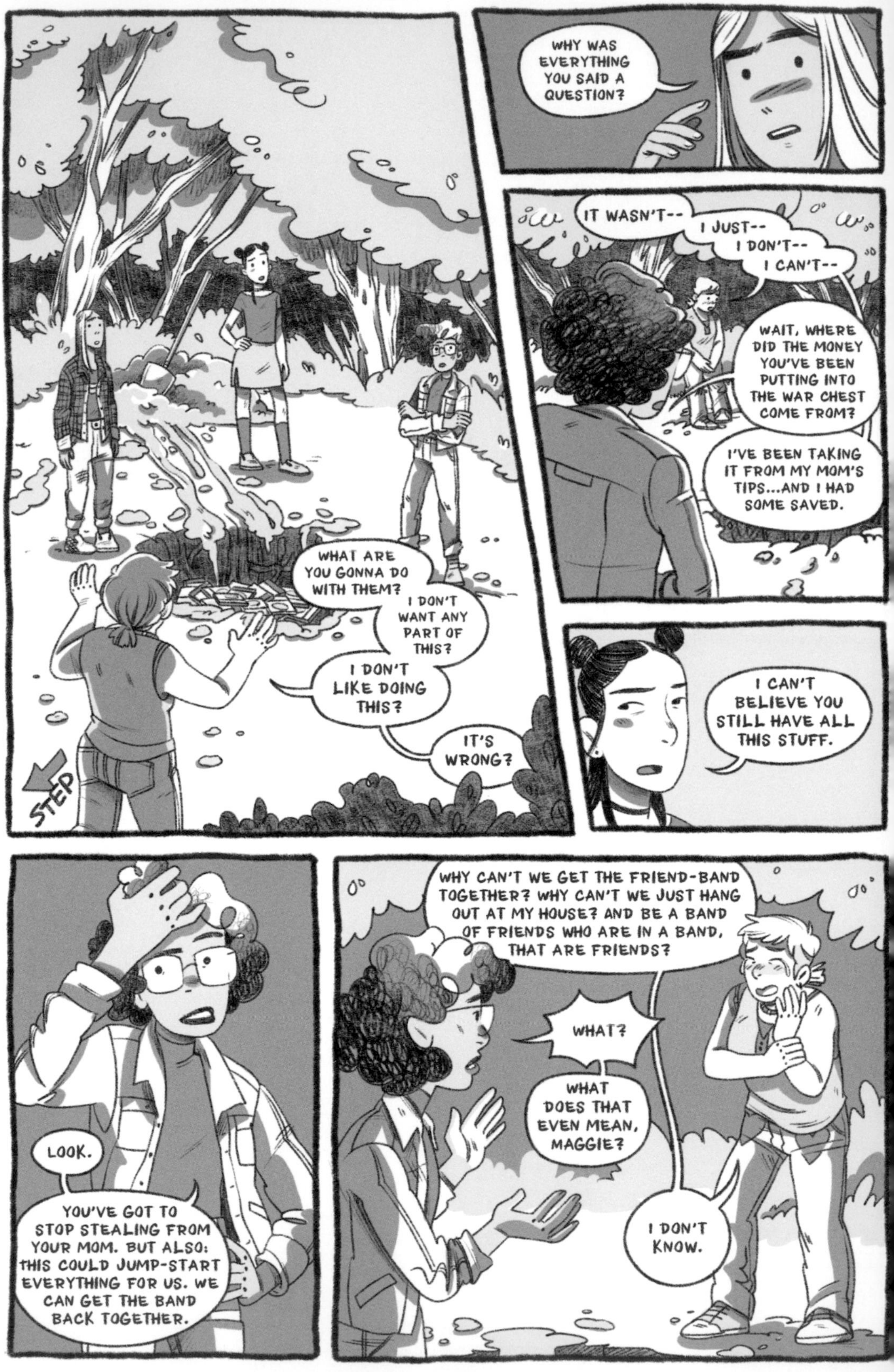
WHAT ARE YOU GONNA DO WITH THEM?
I DON'T WANT ANY PART OF THIS?
I DON'T LIKE DOING THIS?
IT'S WRONG?
STEP
WHY WAS EVERYTHING YOU SAID A QUESTION?
IT WASN'T--
I JUST--
I DON'T--
I CAN'T--
WAIT, WHERE DID THE MONEY YOU'VE BEEN PUTTING INTO THE WAR CHEST COME FROM?
I'VE BEEN TAKING IT FROM MY MOM'S TIPS...AND I HAD SOME SAVED.
I CAN'T BELIEVE YOU STILL HAVE ALL THIS STUFF.
LOOK.
YOU'VE GOT TO STOP STEALING FROM YOUR MOM. BUT ALSO: THIS COULD JUMP-START EVERYTHING FOR US. WE CAN GET THE BAND BACK TOGETHER.
WHY CAN'T WE GET THE FRIEND-BAND TOGETHER? WHY CAN'T WE JUST HANG OUT AT MY HOUSE? AND BE A BAND OF FRIENDS WHO ARE IN A BAND, THAT ARE FRIENDS?
WHAT?
WHAT DOES THAT EVEN MEAN, MAGGIE?
I DON'T KNOW.

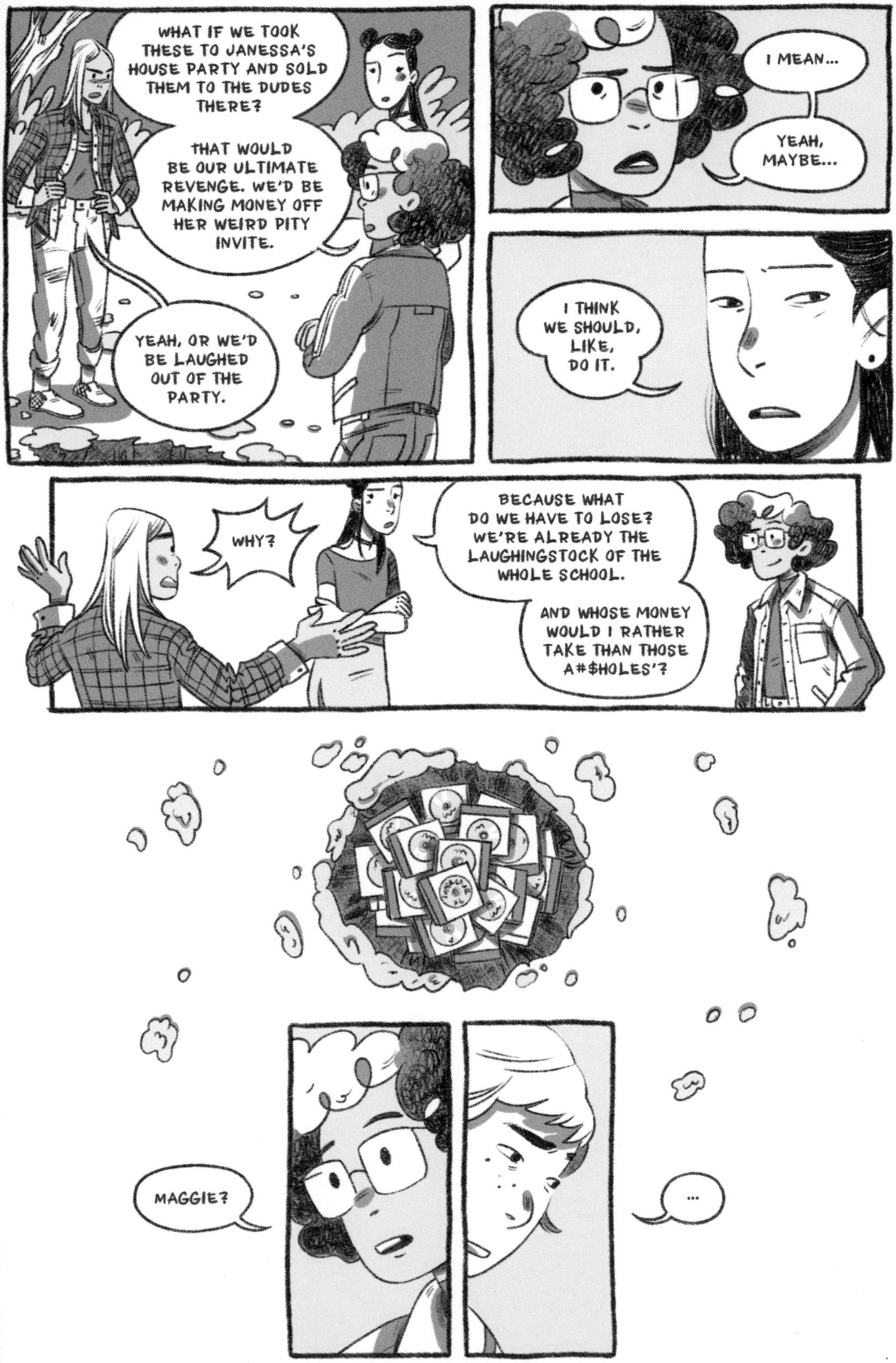
WHAT IF WE TOOK THESE TO JANESSA'S HOUSE PARTY AND SOLD THEM TO THE DUDES THERE?
THAT WOULD BE OUR ULTIMATE REVENGE. WE'D BE MAKING MONEY OFF HER WEIRD PITY INVITE.
YEAH, OR WE'D BE LAUGHED OUT OF THE PARTY.
I MEAN...
YEAH, MAYBE...
I THINK WE SHOULD, LIKE, DO IT.
WHY?
BECAUSE WHAT DO WE HAVE TO LOSE? WE'RE ALREADY THE LAUGHINGSTOCK OF THE WHOLE SCHOOL.
AND WHOSE MONEY WOULD I RATHER TAKE THAN THOSE A#$HOLES'?
MAGGIE?
...

A BRIEF HISTORY OF THE FOREST HILLS BOOTLEG SOCIETY

MAGGIE HILCOT HAS STRUGGLED WITH LONELINESS HER ENTIRE LIFE. IT'S SOMETHING SHE'S GROWN ACCUSTOMED TO. HOWEVER, WHEN SHE MET BROOKE TWO YEARS AGO, EVERYTHING CHANGED.

MAGGIE WAS SITTING BY HERSELF OUTSIDE THE SHIVER ME BURGERS WHEN THIS HAPPENED:

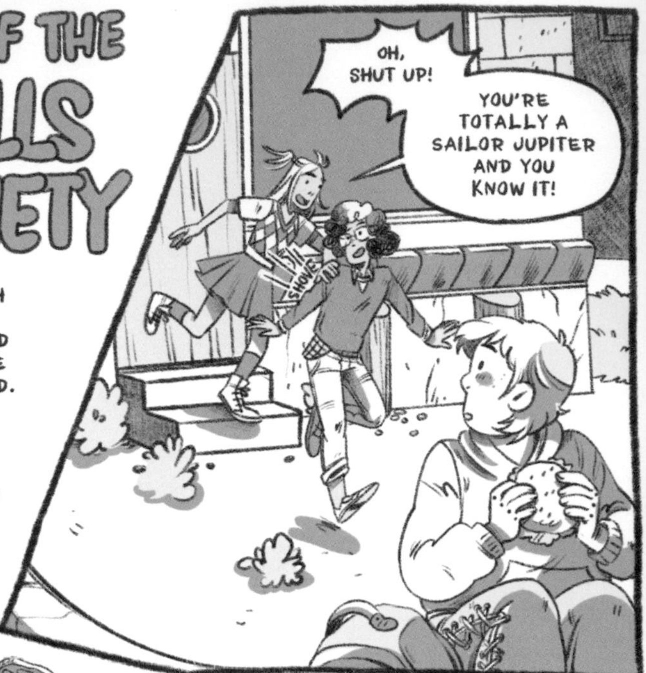
OH, SHUT UP!
YOU'RE TOTALLY A SAILOR JUPITER AND YOU KNOW IT!
SHOVE

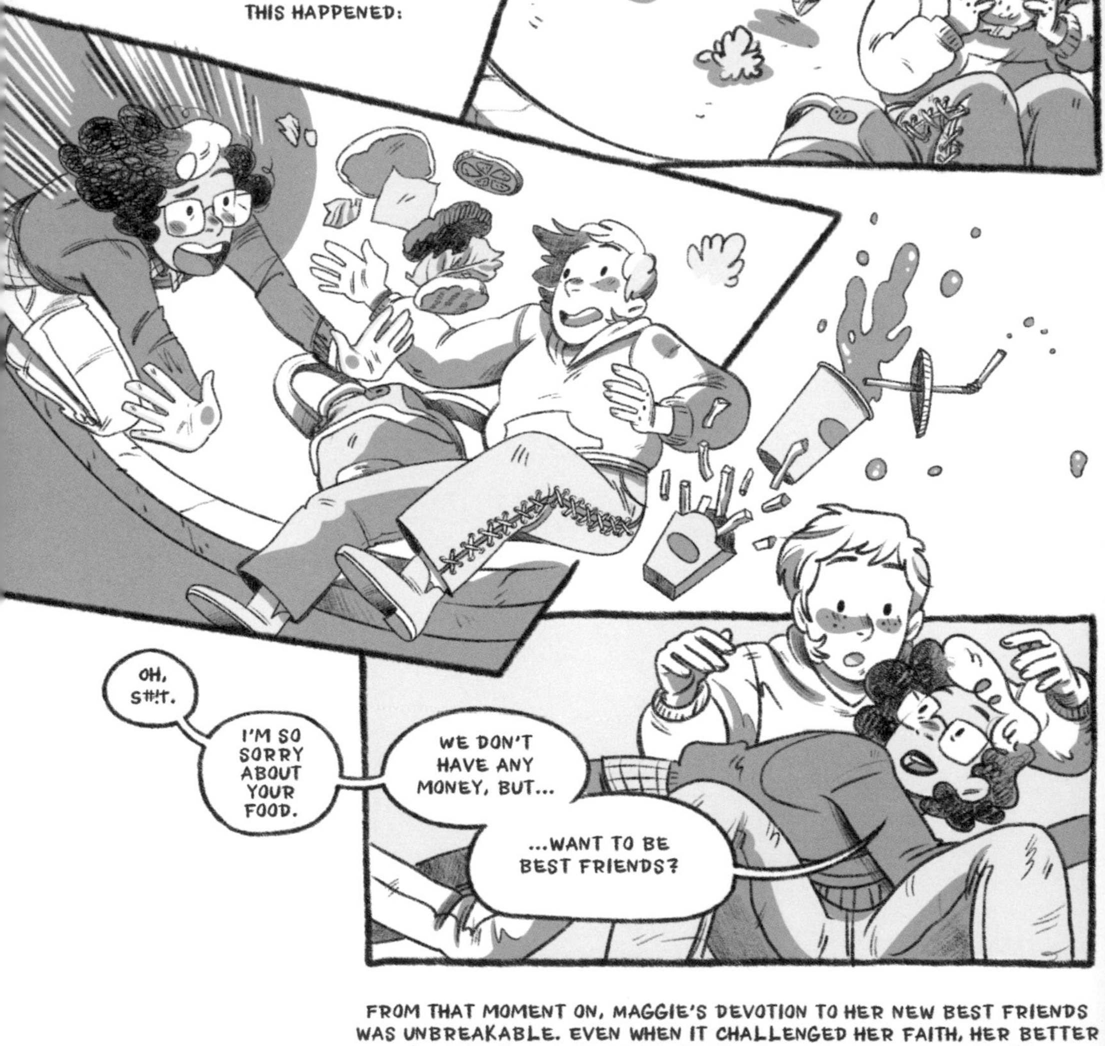
OH, S#!T.
I'M SO SORRY ABOUT YOUR FOOD.
WE DON'T HAVE ANY MONEY, BUT...
...WANT TO BE BEST FRIENDS?

FROM THAT MOMENT ON, MAGGIE'S DEVOTION TO HER NEW BEST FRIENDS WAS UNBREAKABLE. EVEN WHEN IT CHALLENGED HER FAITH, HER BETTER JUDGMENT, AND HER GOOD TASTE. IN A NORMAL SCENARIO, THIS STEADFASTNESS WOULD BE A QUALITY TO BE PRAISED. HOWEVER, MAGGIE WOULD SOON COME TO REGRET THE DECISION SHE WAS ABOUT TO MAKE...

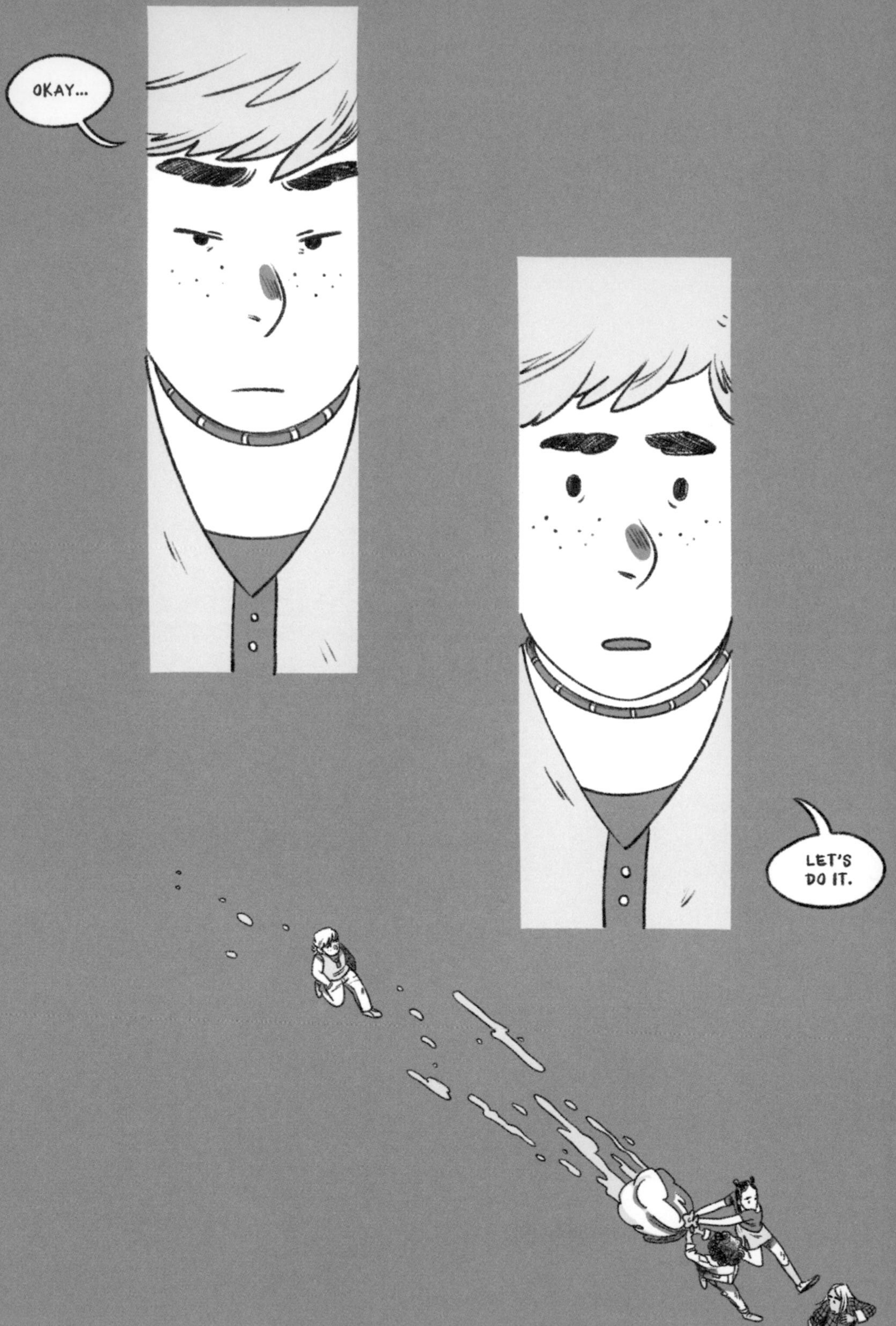
OKAY...
LET'S DO IT.

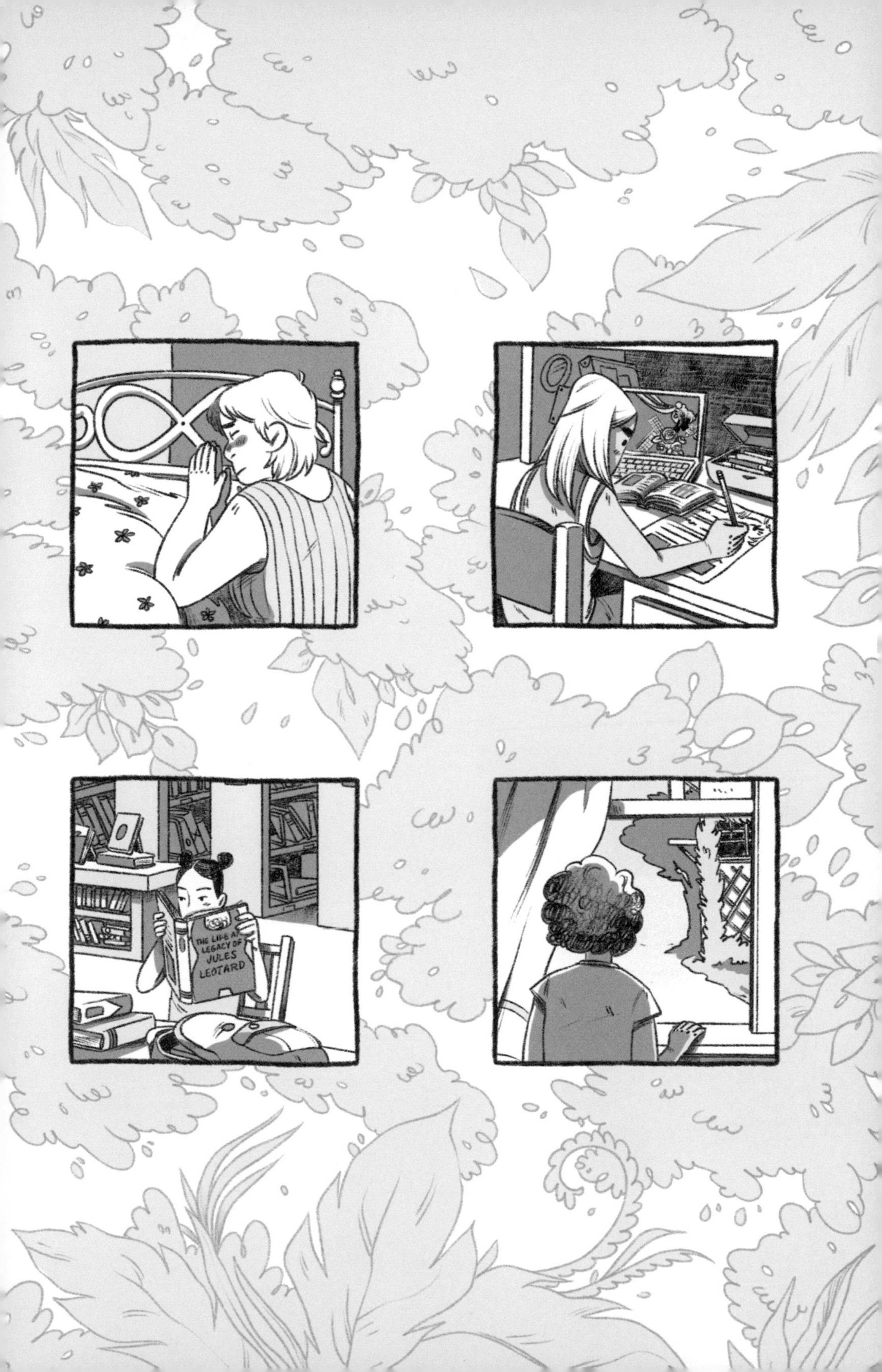
THE LIFE A
LEGACY OF
JULES
LEOTARD

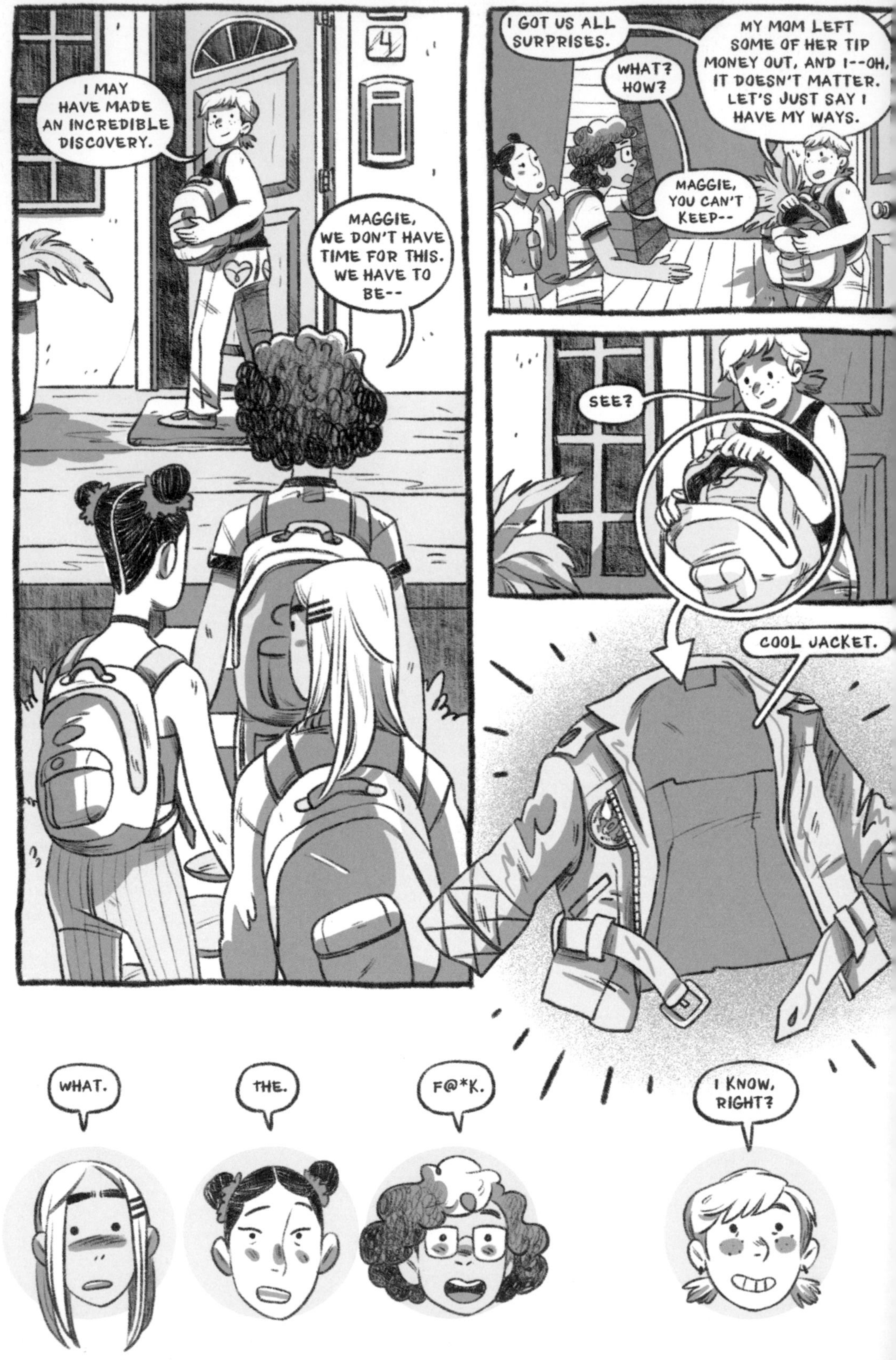
I MAY HAVE MADE AN INCREDIBLE DISCOVERY.
MAGGIE, WE DON'T HAVE TIME FOR THIS. WE HAVE TO BE--
I GOT US ALL SURPRISES.
WHAT? HOW?
MY MOM LEFT SOME OF HER TIP MONEY OUT, AND I--OH, IT DOESN'T MATTER. LET'S JUST SAY I HAVE MY WAYS.
MAGGIE, YOU CAN'T KEEP--
SEE?
COOL JACKET.
WHAT.
THE.
F@*K.
I KNOW, RIGHT?

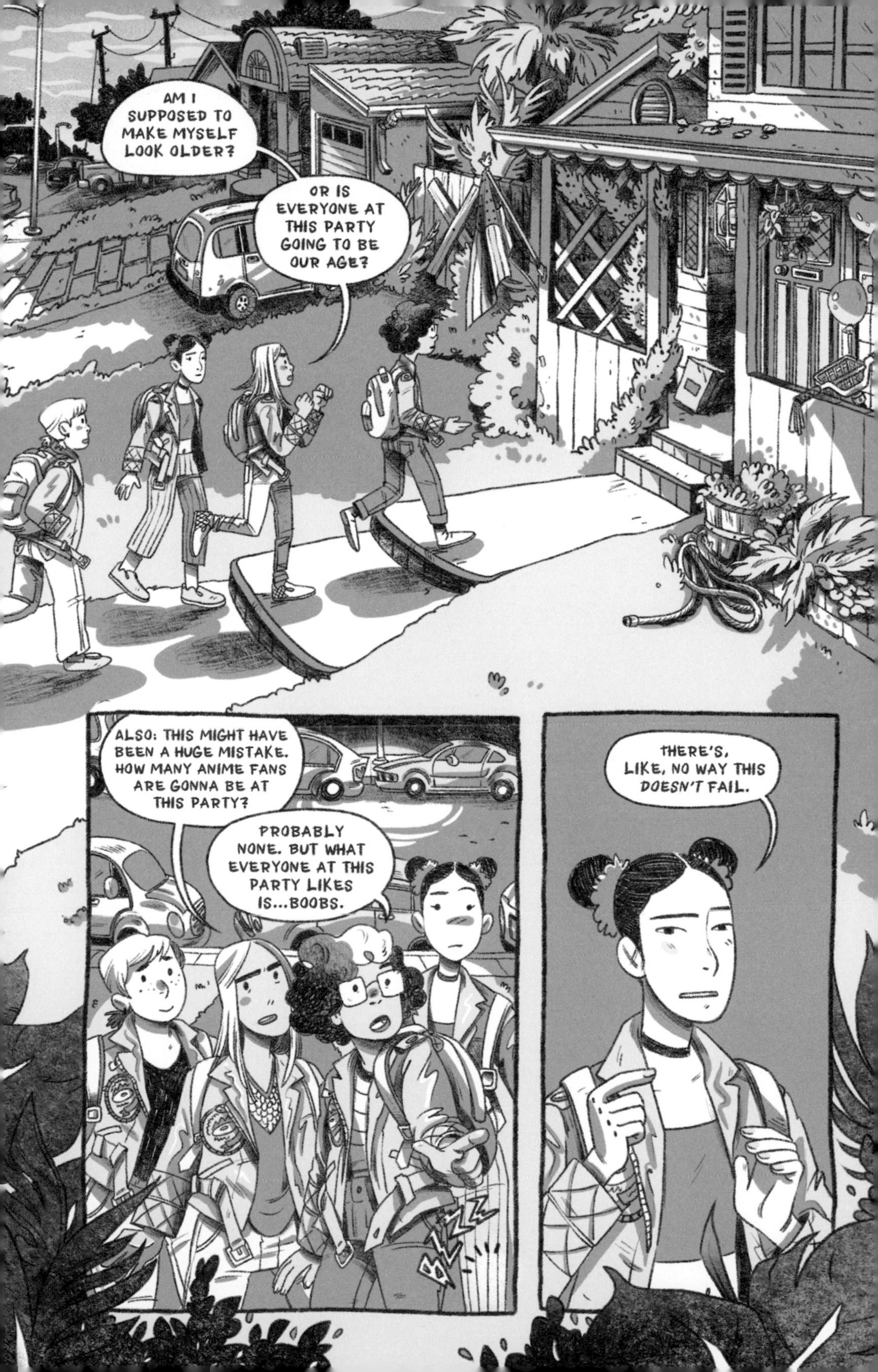
AM I SUPPOSED TO MAKE MYSELF LOOK OLDER?
OR IS EVERYONE AT THIS PARTY GOING TO BE OUR AGE?
ALSO: THIS MIGHT HAVE BEEN A HUGE MISTAKE. HOW MANY ANIME FANS ARE GONNA BE AT THIS PARTY?
PROBABLY NONE. BUT WHAT EVERYONE AT THIS PARTY LIKES IS...BOOBS.
THERE'S, LIKE, NO WAY THIS *DOESN'T* FAIL.

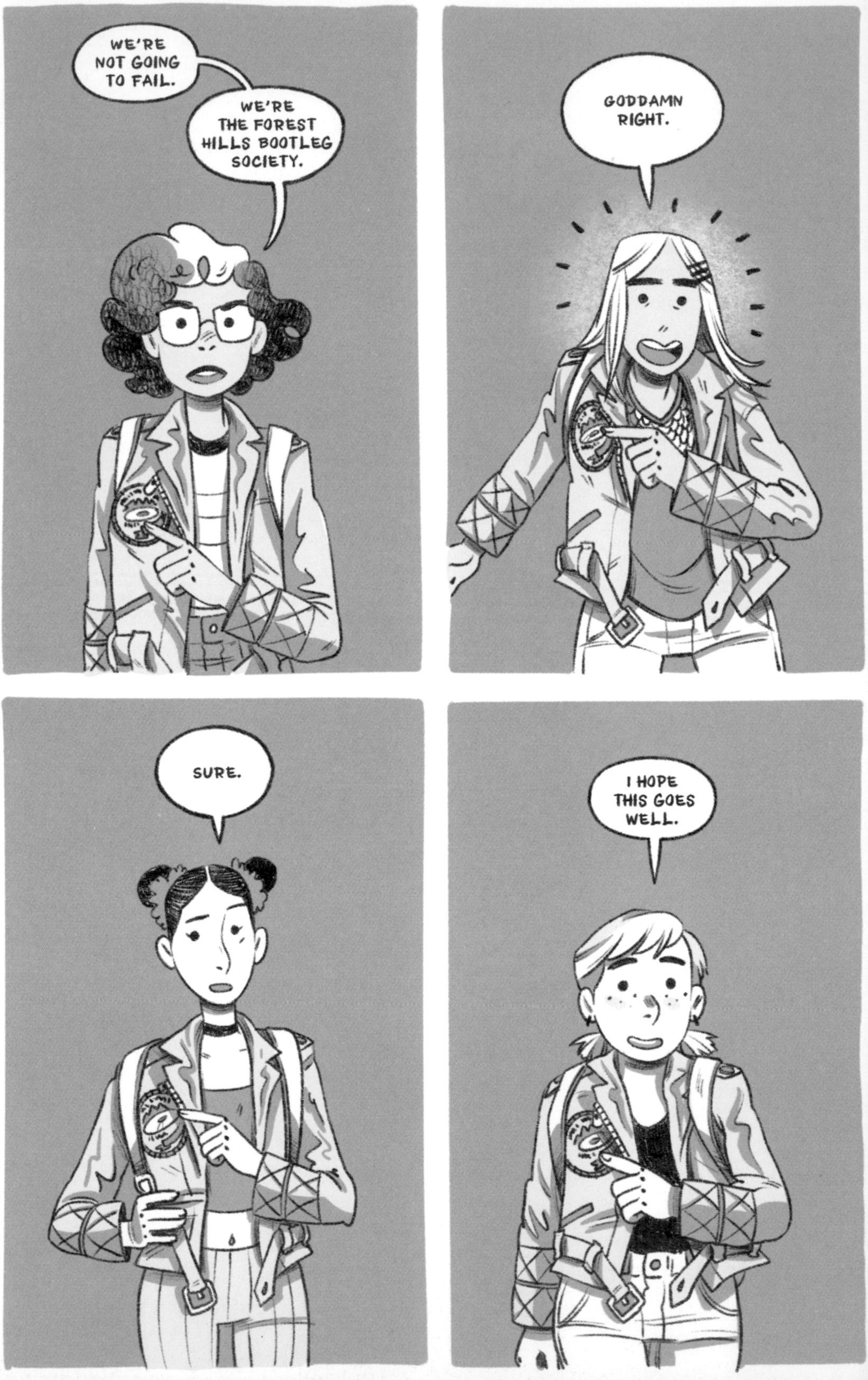
WE'RE NOT GOING TO FAIL.
WE'RE THE FOREST HILLS BOOTLEG SOCIETY.
GODDAMN RIGHT.
SURE.
I HOPE THIS GOES WELL.

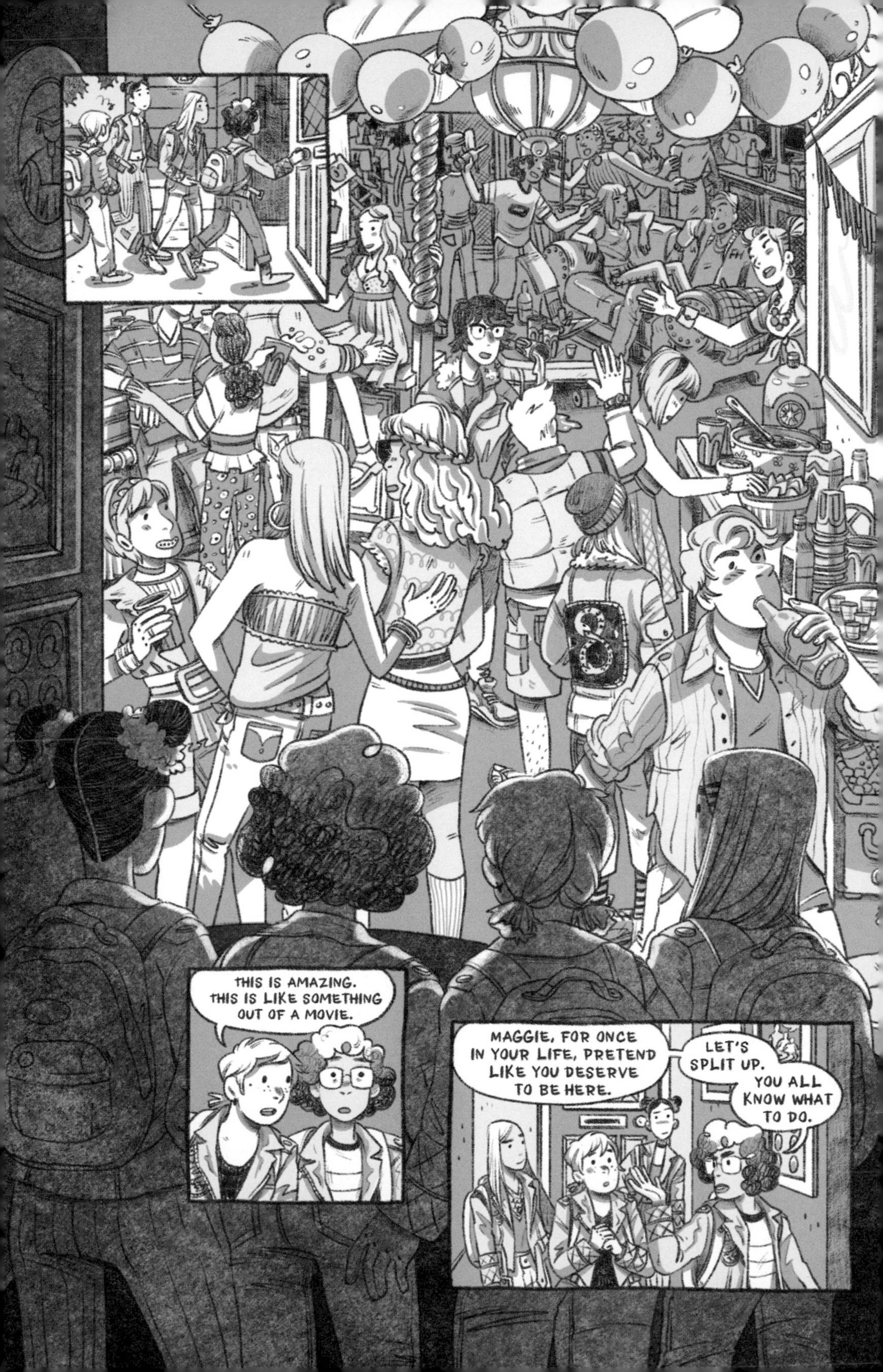
THIS IS AMAZING. THIS IS LIKE SOMETHING OUT OF A MOVIE.
MAGGIE, FOR ONCE IN YOUR LIFE, PRETEND LIKE YOU DESERVE TO BE HERE.
LET'S SPLIT UP. YOU ALL KNOW WHAT TO DO.

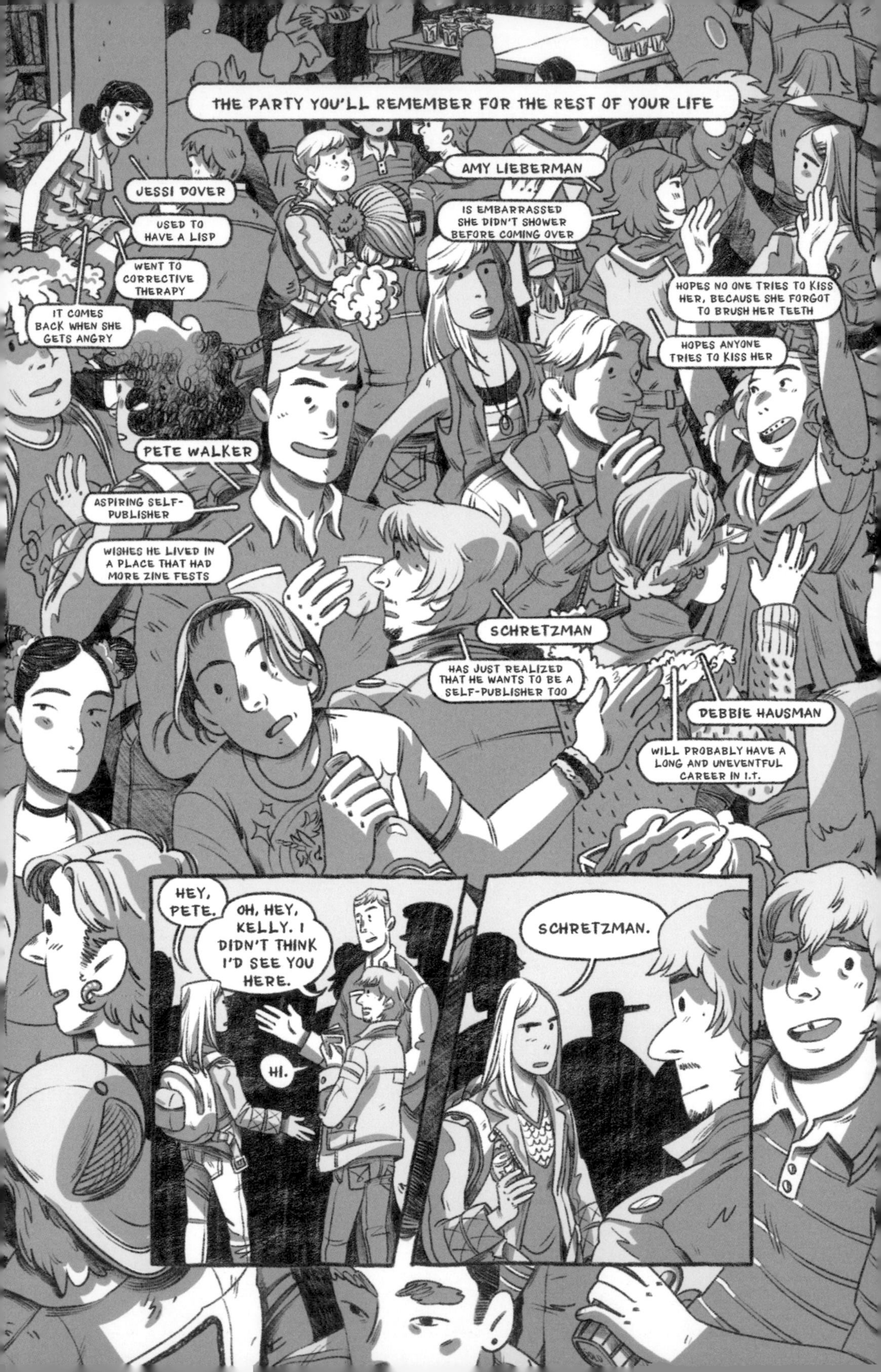
THE PARTY YOU'LL REMEMBER FOR THE REST OF YOUR LIFE
JESSI DOVER
USED TO HAVE A LISP
WENT TO CORRECTIVE THERAPY
IT COMES BACK WHEN SHE GETS ANGRY
AMY LIEBERMAN
IS EMBARRASSED SHE DIDN'T SHOWER BEFORE COMING OVER
HOPES NO ONE TRIES TO KISS HER, BECAUSE SHE FORGOT TO BRUSH HER TEETH
HOPES ANYONE TRIES TO KISS HER
PETE WALKER
ASPIRING SELF-PUBLISHER
WISHES HE LIVED IN A PLACE THAT HAD MORE ZINE FESTS
SCHRETZMAN
HAS JUST REALIZED THAT HE WANTS TO BE A SELF-PUBLISHER TOO
DEBBIE HAUSMAN
WILL PROBABLY HAVE A LONG AND UNEVENTFUL CAREER IN I.T.
HEY, PETE.
OH, HEY, KELLY. I DIDN'T THINK I'D SEE YOU HERE.
HI.
SCHRETZMAN.

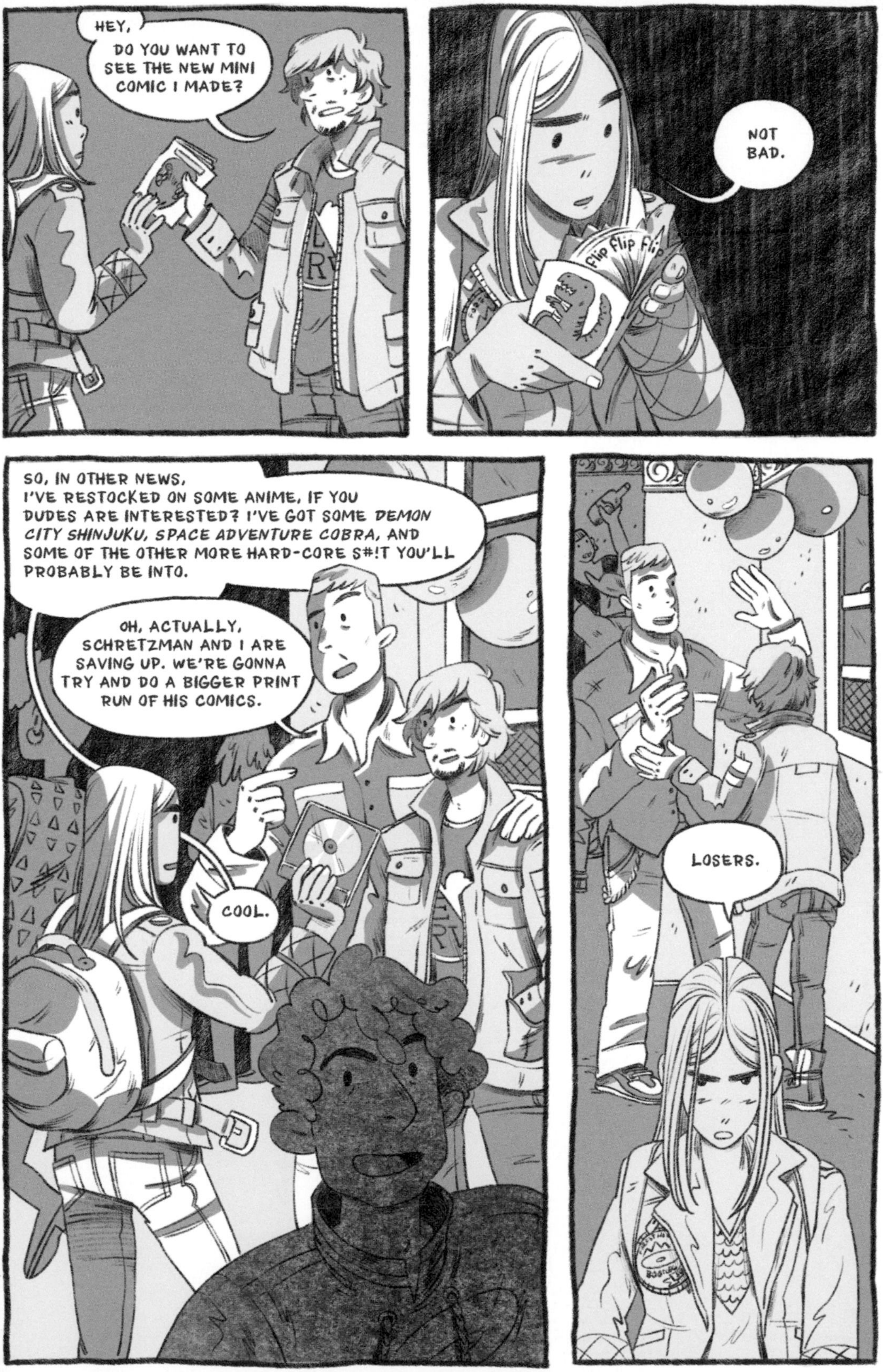
HEY,
DO YOU WANT TO SEE THE NEW MINI COMIC I MADE?
NOT BAD.
flip flip flip
SO, IN OTHER NEWS, I'VE RESTOCKED ON SOME ANIME, IF YOU DUDES ARE INTERESTED? I'VE GOT SOME DEMON CITY SHINJUKU, SPACE ADVENTURE COBRA, AND SOME OF THE OTHER MORE HARD-CORE S#!T YOU'LL PROBABLY BE INTO.
OH, ACTUALLY, SCHRETZMAN AND I ARE SAVING UP. WE'RE GONNA TRY AND DO A BIGGER PRINT RUN OF HIS COMICS.
COOL.
LOSERS.

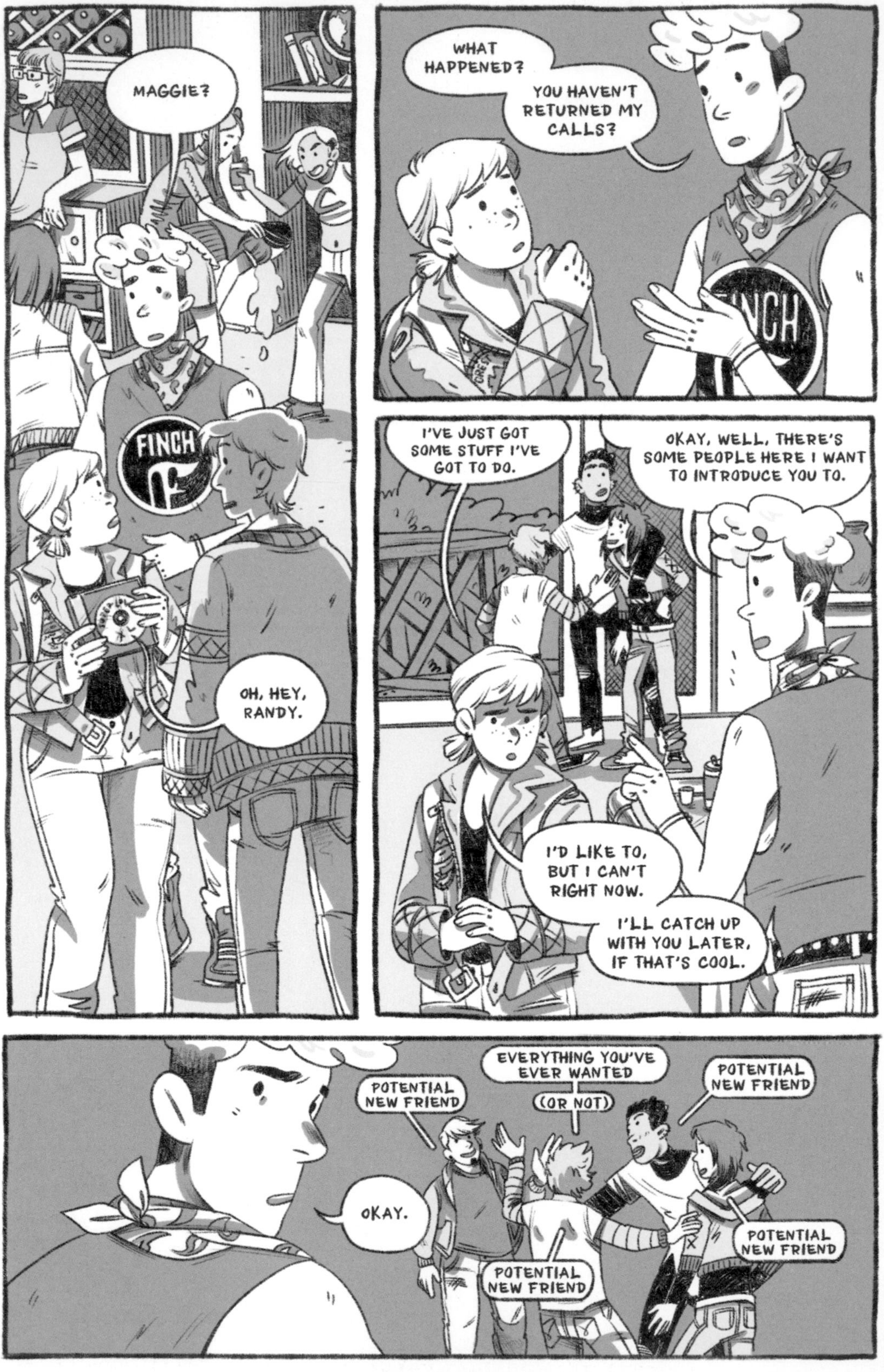
MAGGIE?
OH, HEY, RANDY.
WHAT HAPPENED?
YOU HAVEN'T RETURNED MY CALLS?
I'VE JUST GOT SOME STUFF I'VE GOT TO DO.
OKAY, WELL, THERE'S SOME PEOPLE HERE I WANT TO INTRODUCE YOU TO.
I'D LIKE TO, BUT I CAN'T RIGHT NOW.
I'LL CATCH UP WITH YOU LATER, IF THAT'S COOL.
OKAY.
POTENTIAL NEW FRIEND
EVERYTHING YOU'VE EVER WANTED
(OR NOT)
POTENTIAL NEW FRIEND
POTENTIAL NEW FRIEND
POTENTIAL NEW FRIEND
FINCH

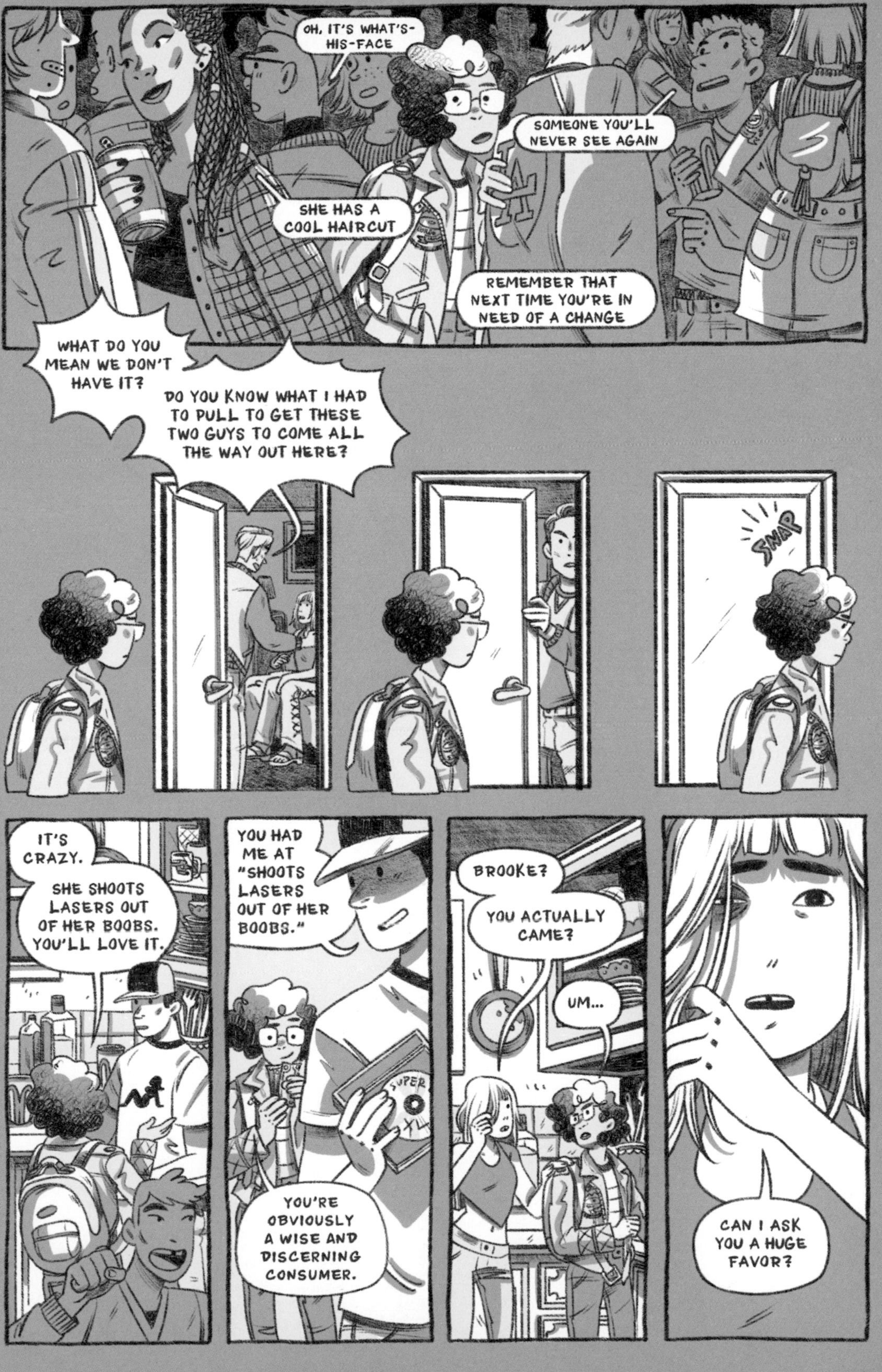
OH, IT'S WHAT'S-HIS-FACE
SOMEONE YOU'LL NEVER SEE AGAIN
SHE HAS A COOL HAIRCUT
REMEMBER THAT NEXT TIME YOU'RE IN NEED OF A CHANGE
WHAT DO YOU MEAN WE DON'T HAVE IT?
DO YOU KNOW WHAT I HAD TO PULL TO GET THESE TWO GUYS TO COME ALL THE WAY OUT HERE?
SNAP
IT'S CRAZY.
SHE SHOOTS LASERS OUT OF HER BOOBS. YOU'LL LOVE IT.
YOU HAD ME AT "SHOOTS LASERS OUT OF HER BOOBS."
SUPER
XL
YOU'RE OBVIOUSLY A WISE AND DISCERNING CONSUMER.
BROOKE?
YOU ACTUALLY CAME?
UM...
CAN I ASK YOU A HUGE FAVOR?

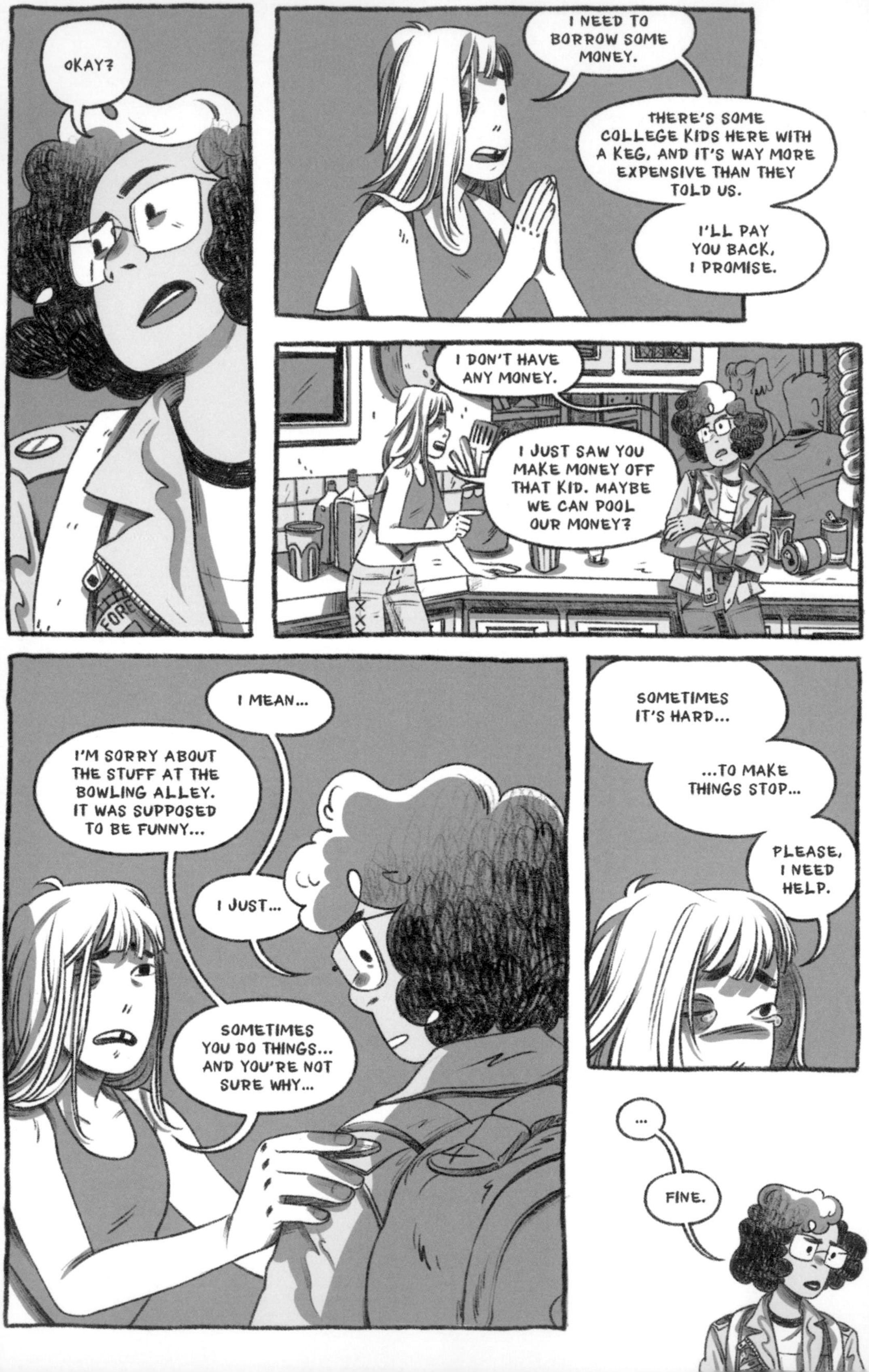
OKAY?
I NEED TO BORROW SOME MONEY.
THERE'S SOME COLLEGE KIDS HERE WITH A KEG, AND IT'S WAY MORE EXPENSIVE THAN THEY TOLD US.
I'LL PAY YOU BACK, I PROMISE.
I DON'T HAVE ANY MONEY.
I JUST SAW YOU MAKE MONEY OFF THAT KID. MAYBE WE CAN POOL OUR MONEY?
I MEAN...
I'M SORRY ABOUT THE STUFF AT THE BOWLING ALLEY. IT WAS SUPPOSED TO BE FUNNY...
I JUST...
SOMETIMES YOU DO THINGS... AND YOU'RE NOT SURE WHY...
SOMETIMES IT'S HARD...
...TO MAKE THINGS STOP...
PLEASE, I NEED HELP.
...
FINE.

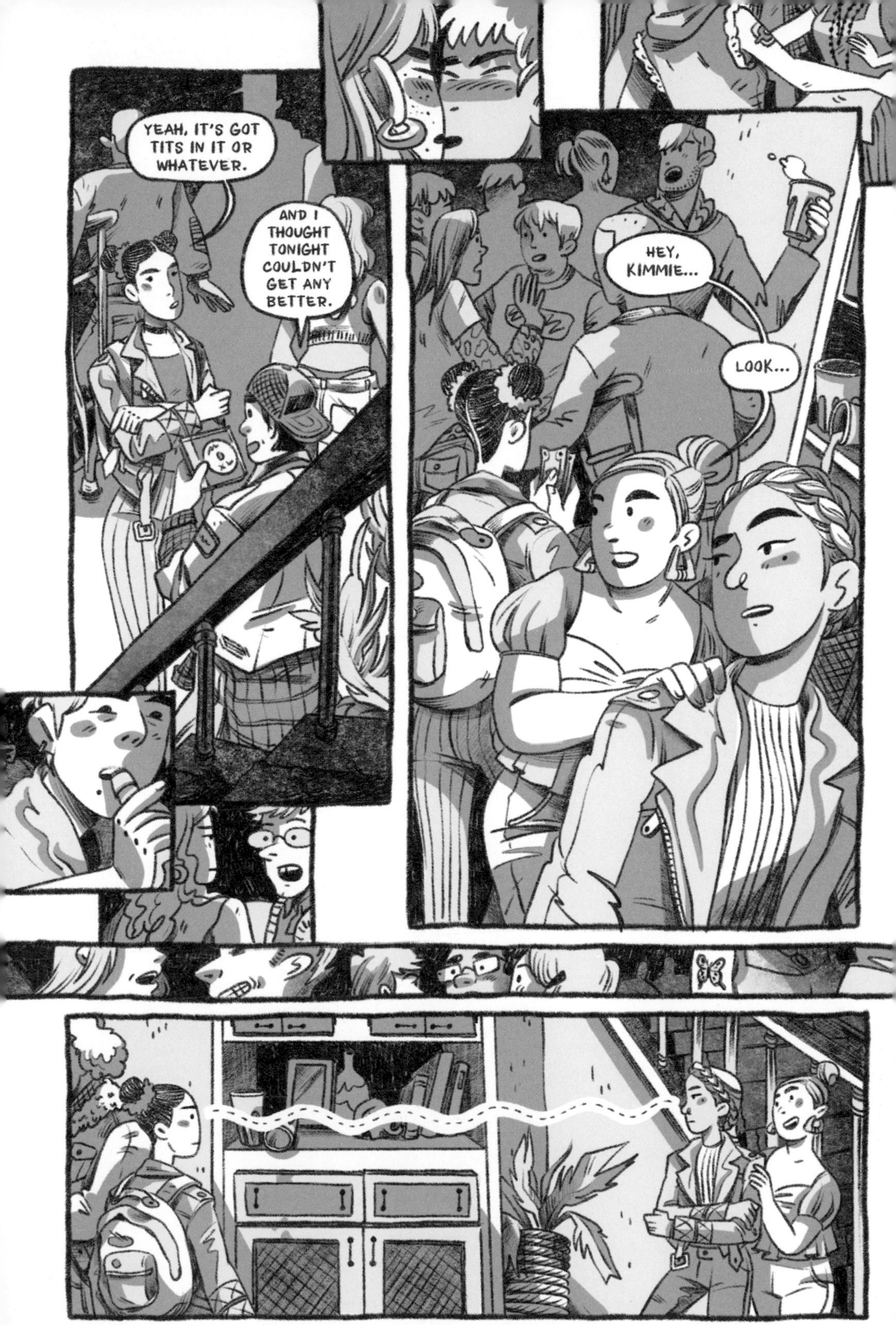
YEAH, IT'S GOT TITS IN IT OR WHATEVER.
AND I THOUGHT TONIGHT COULDN'T GET ANY BETTER.
HEY, KIMMIE...
LOOK...

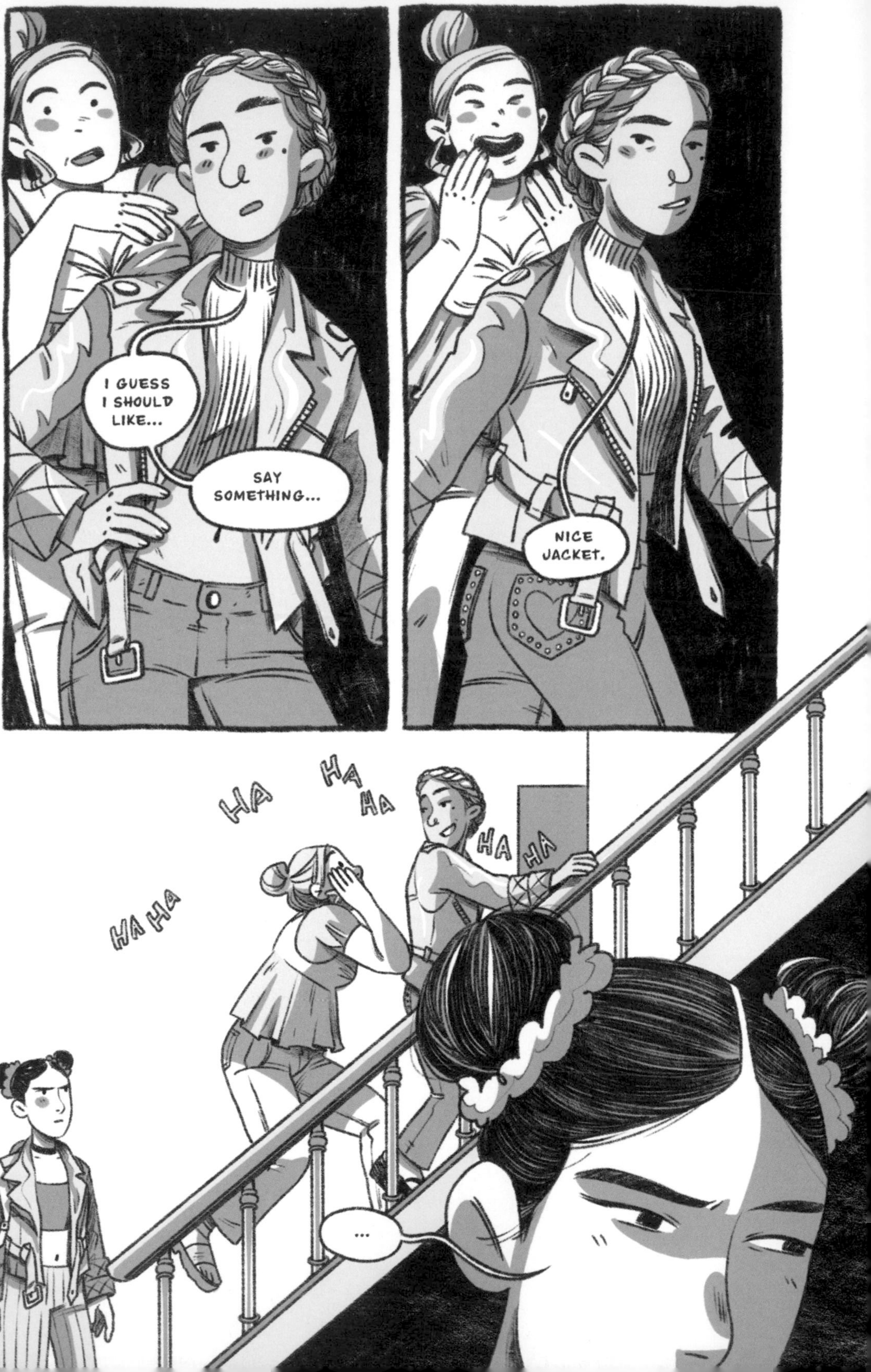
I GUESS I SHOULD LIKE...
SAY SOMETHING...
NICE JACKET.
HA
HA HA
HA HA
HA HA
...

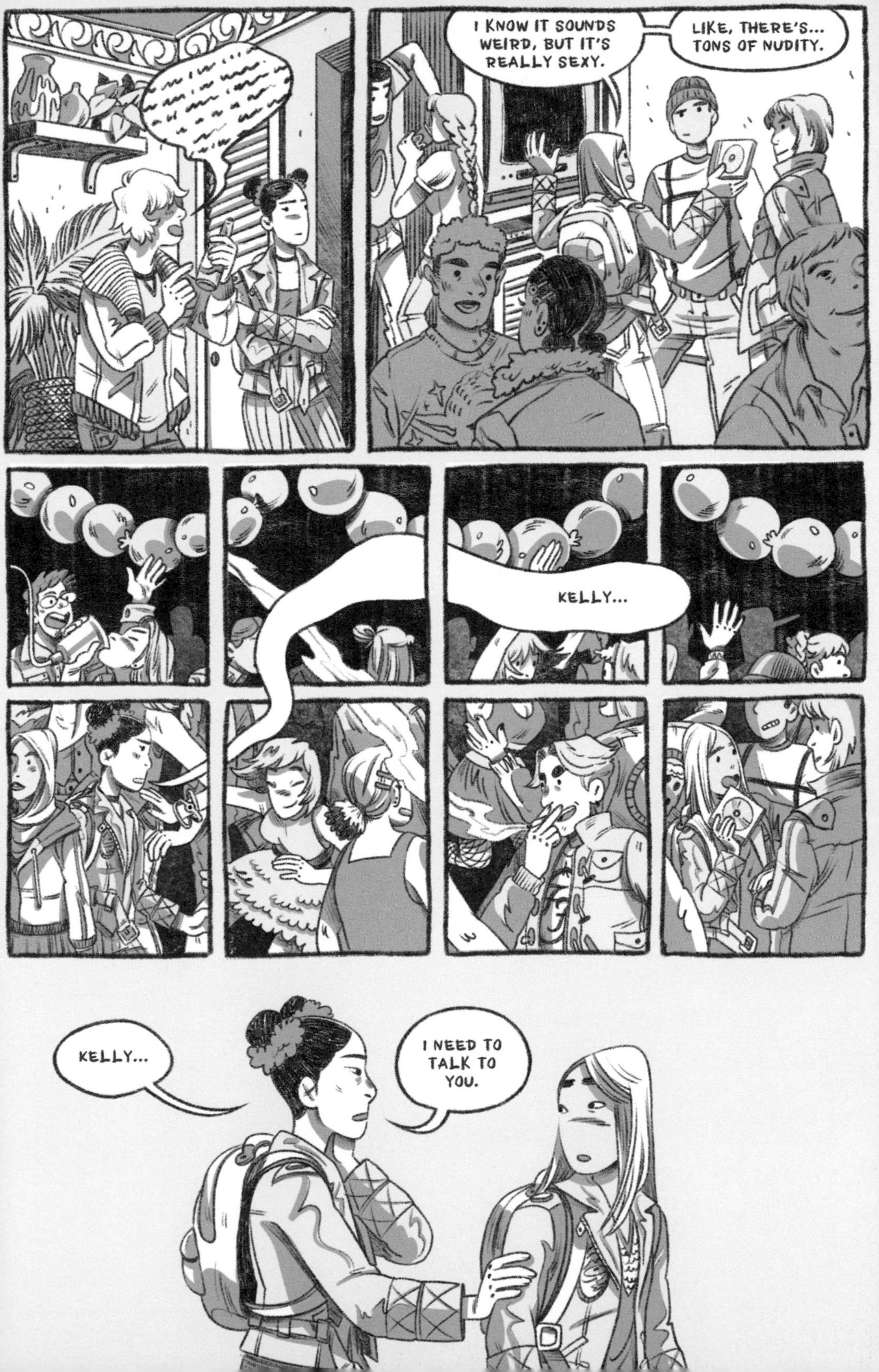
I KNOW IT SOUNDS WEIRD, BUT IT'S REALLY SEXY.
LIKE, THERE'S... TONS OF NUDITY.
KELLY...
KELLY...
I NEED TO TALK TO YOU.

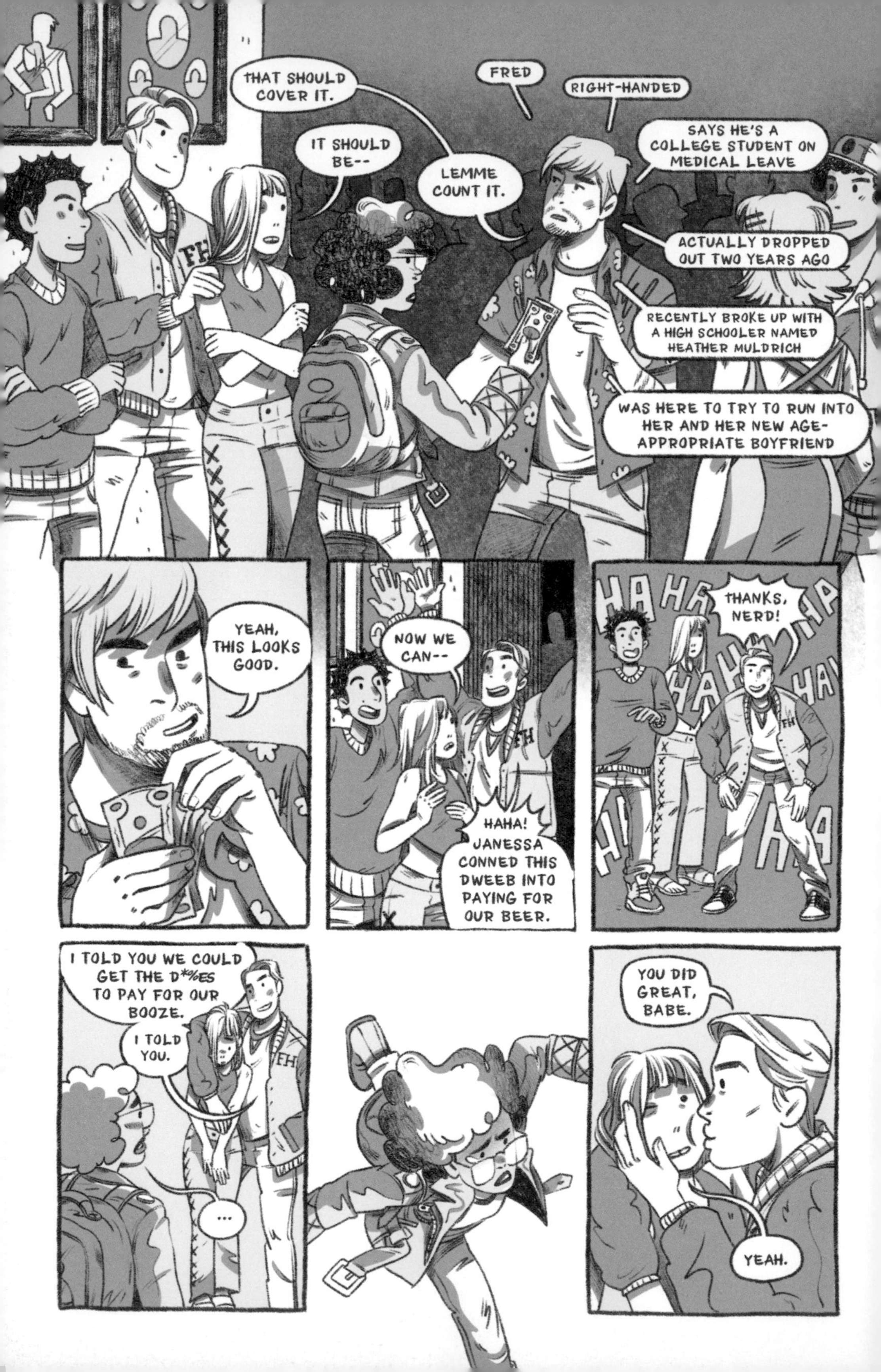
THAT SHOULD COVER IT.
IT SHOULD BE--
LEMME COUNT IT.
FRED
RIGHT-HANDED
SAYS HE'S A COLLEGE STUDENT ON MEDICAL LEAVE
ACTUALLY DROPPED OUT TWO YEARS AGO
RECENTLY BROKE UP WITH A HIGH SCHOOLER NAMED HEATHER MULDRICH
WAS HERE TO TRY TO RUN INTO HER AND HER NEW AGE-APPROPRIATE BOYFRIEND
YEAH, THIS LOOKS GOOD.
NOW WE CAN--
HAHA! JANESSA CONNED THIS DWEEB INTO PAYING FOR OUR BEER.
HAHA
THANKS, NERD!
I TOLD YOU WE COULD GET THE D*%ES TO PAY FOR OUR BOOZE.
I TOLD YOU.
...
YOU DID GREAT, BABE.
YEAH.

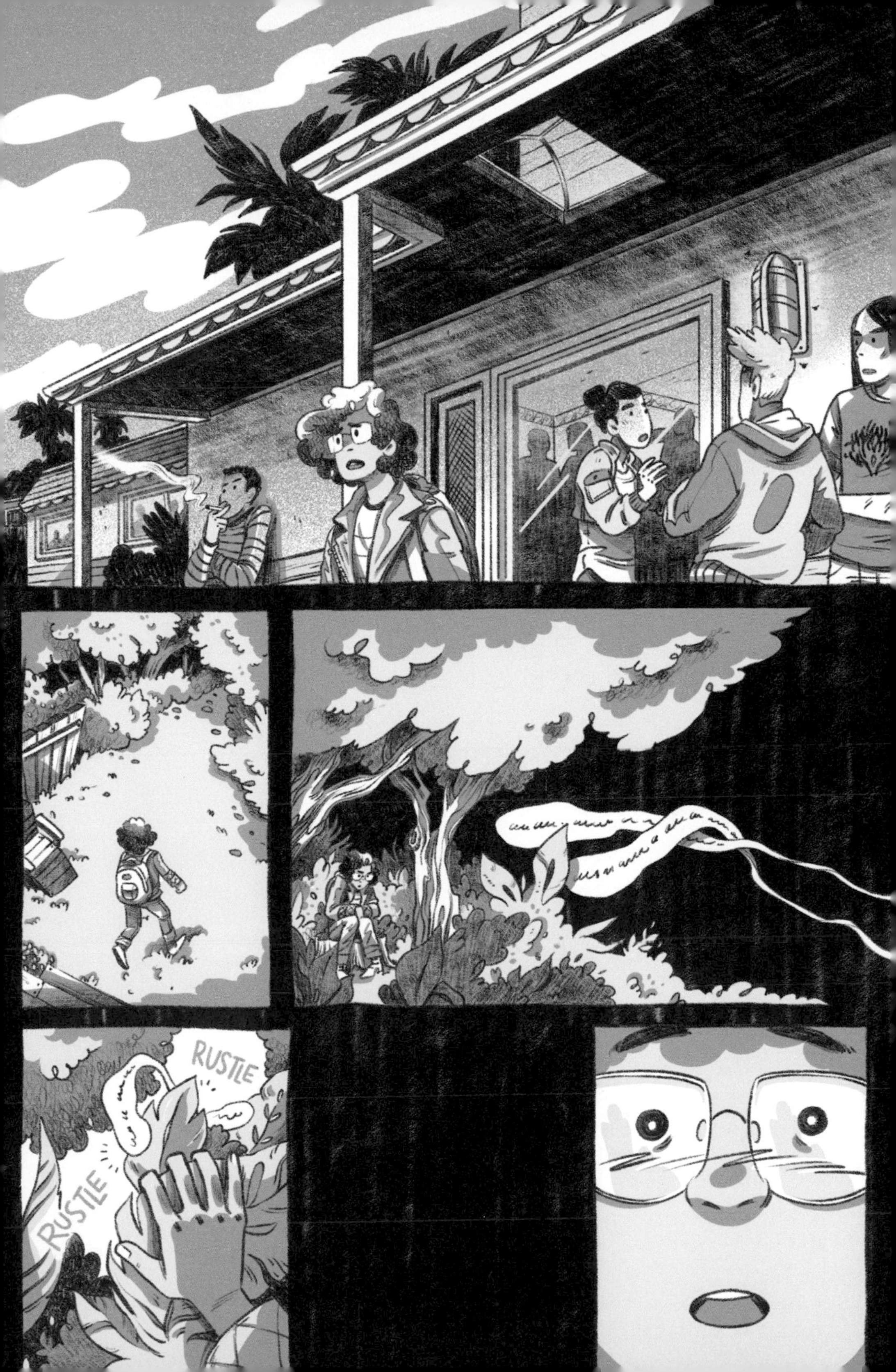
RUSTLE
RUSTLE

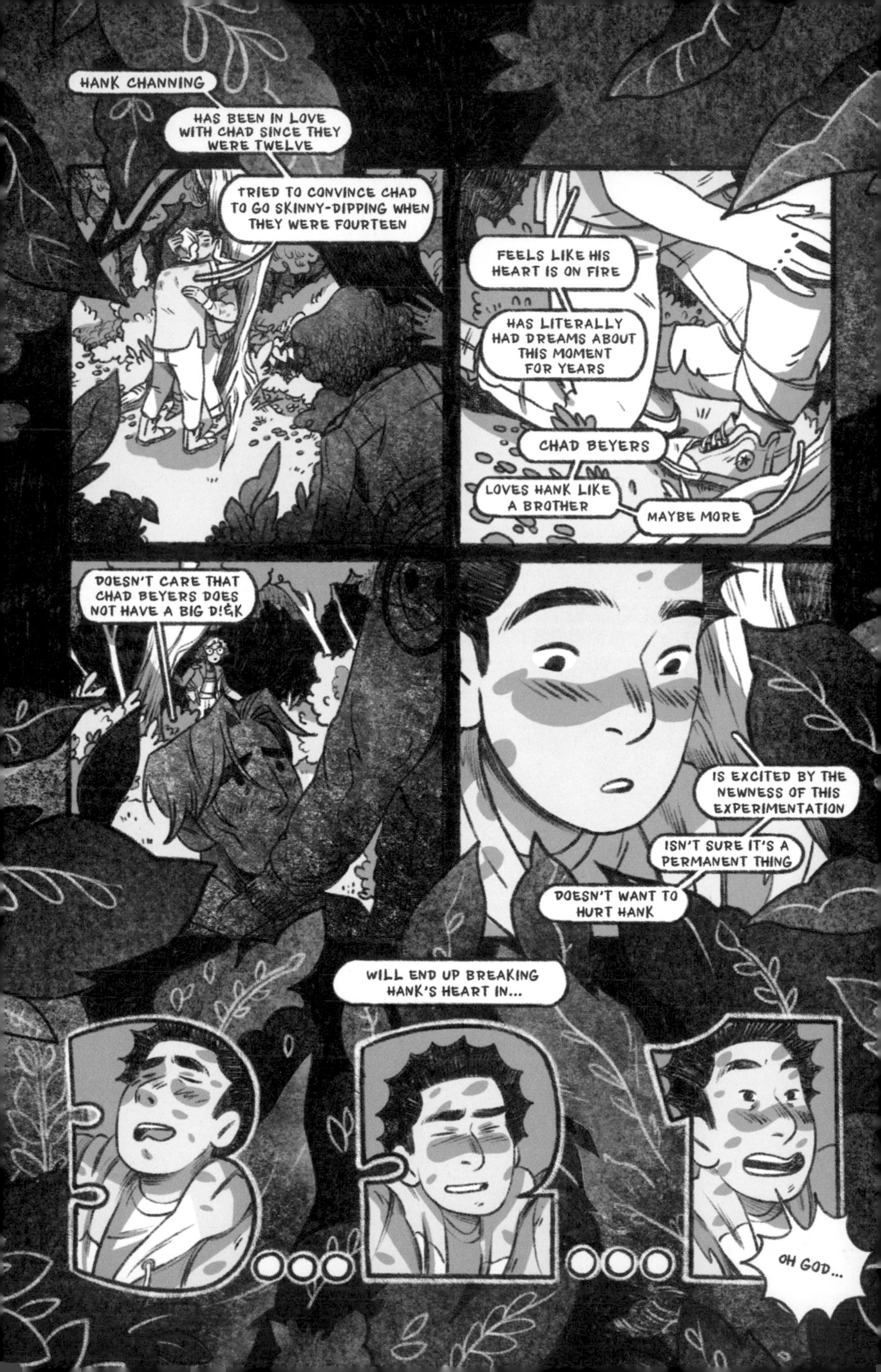
HANK CHANNING
HAS BEEN IN LOVE WITH CHAD SINCE THEY WERE TWELVE
TRIED TO CONVINCE CHAD TO GO SKINNY-DIPPING WHEN THEY WERE FOURTEEN
FEELS LIKE HIS HEART IS ON FIRE
HAS LITERALLY HAD DREAMS ABOUT THIS MOMENT FOR YEARS
CHAD BEYERS
LOVES HANK LIKE A BROTHER
MAYBE MORE
DOESN'T CARE THAT CHAD BEYERS DOES NOT HAVE A BIG D!€K
IS EXCITED BY THE NEWNESS OF THIS EXPERIMENTATION
ISN'T SURE IT'S A PERMANENT THING
DOESN'T WANT TO HURT HANK
WILL END UP BREAKING HANK'S HEART IN...
OH GOD...

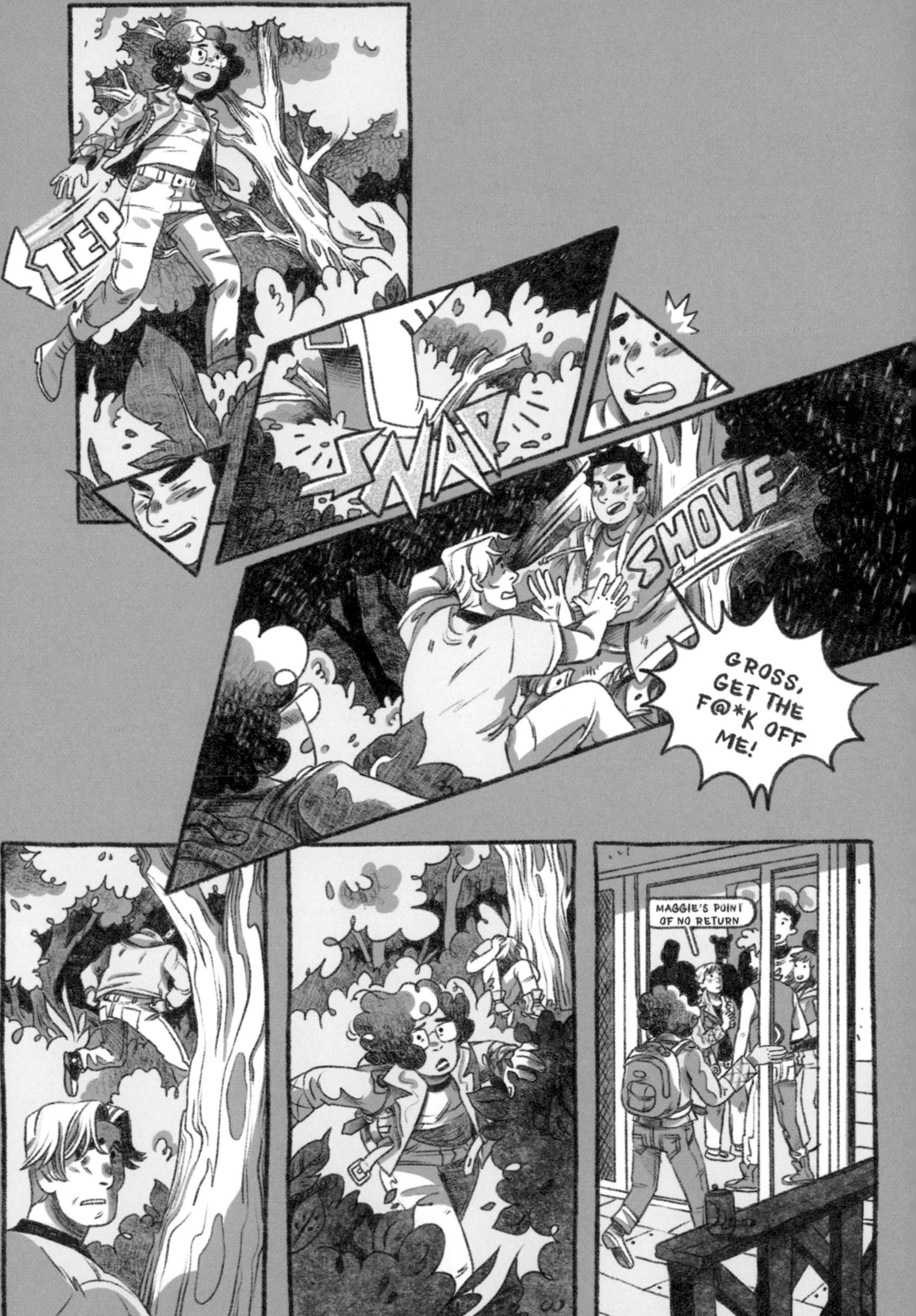
TEP
SNAP
SHOVE
GROSS, GET THE F@*K OFF ME!
MAGGIE'S POINT OF NO RETURN

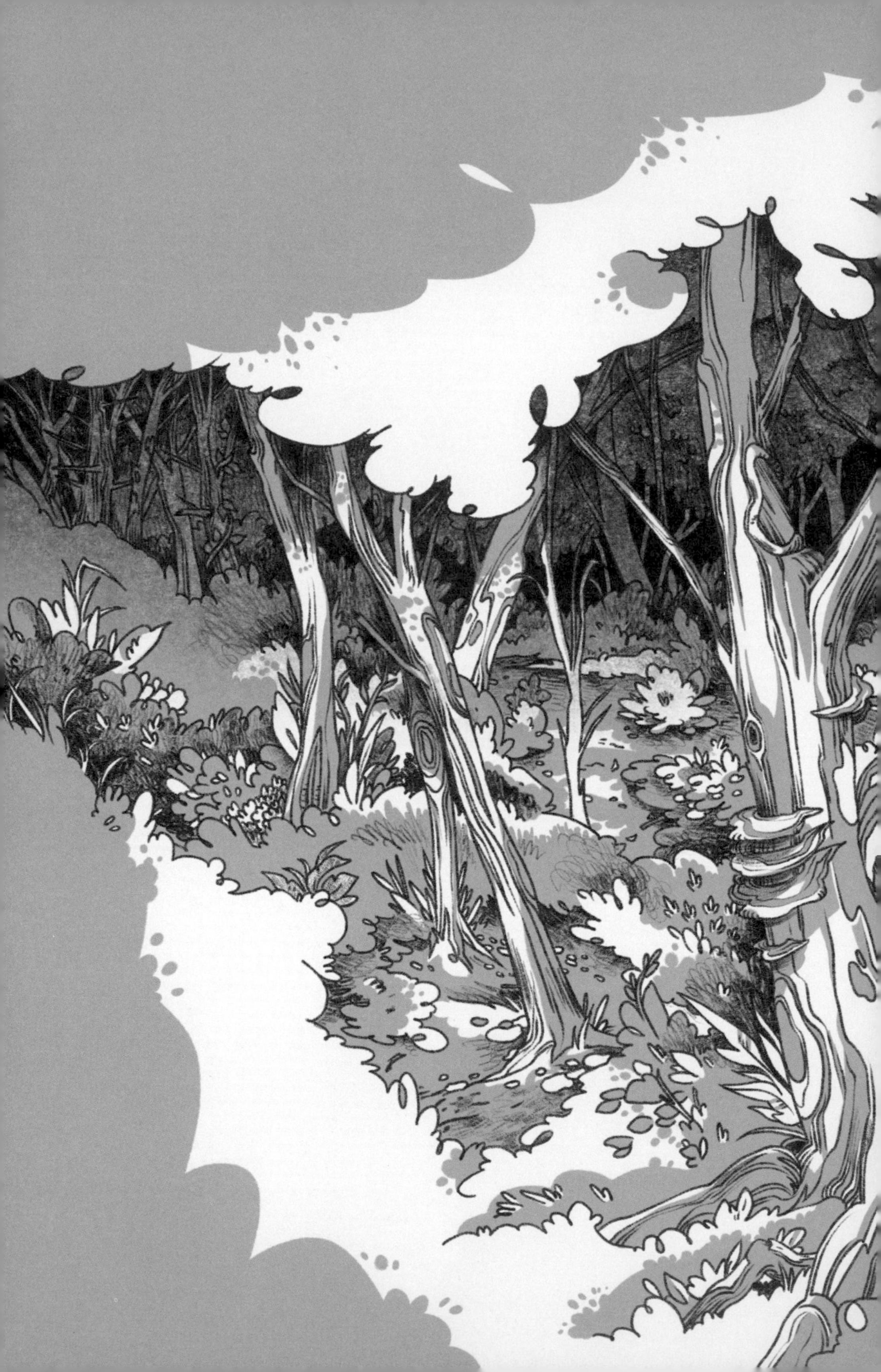

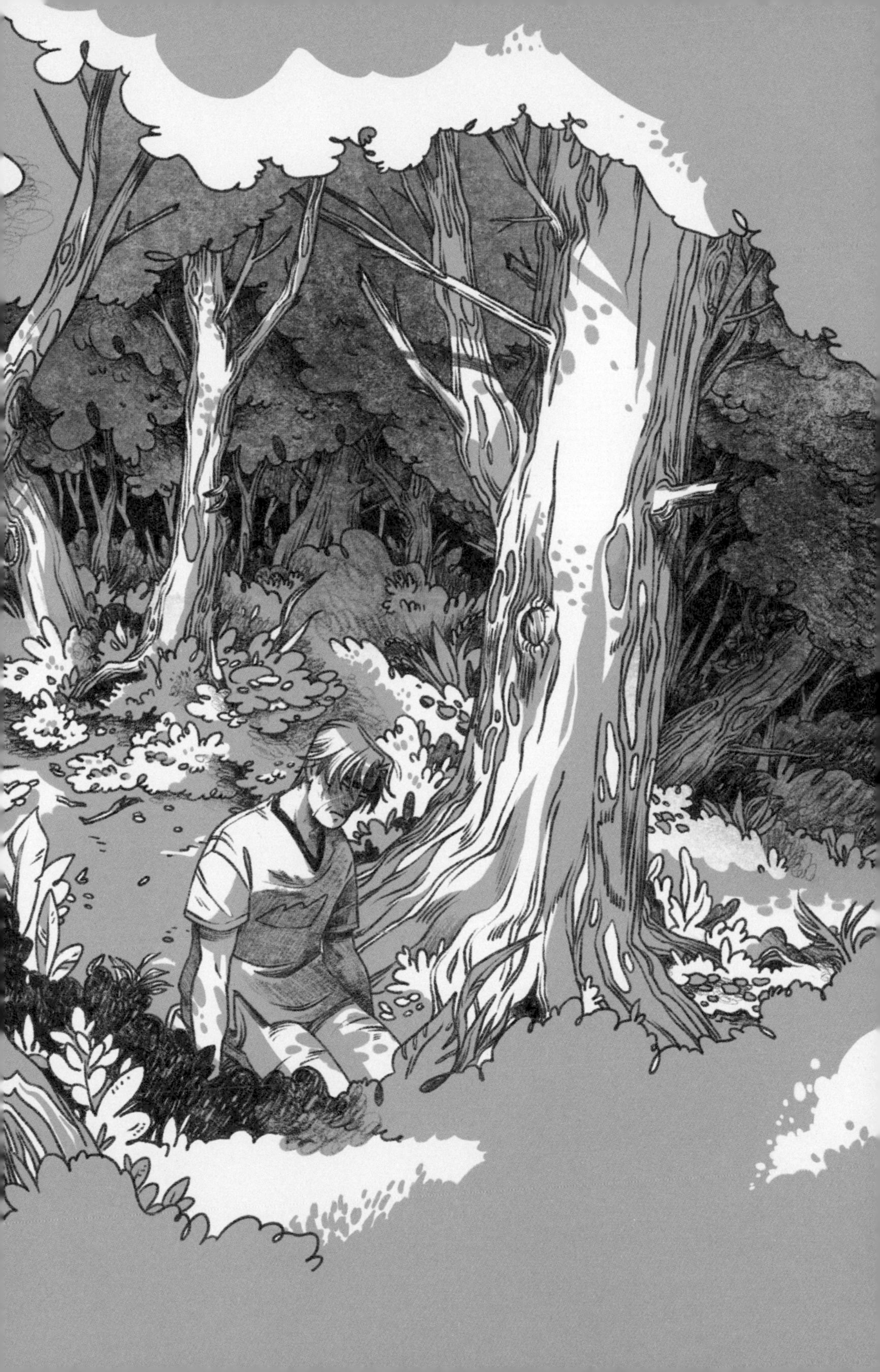

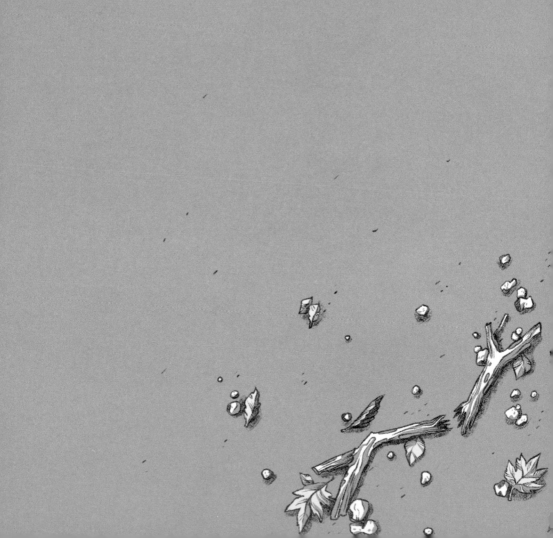

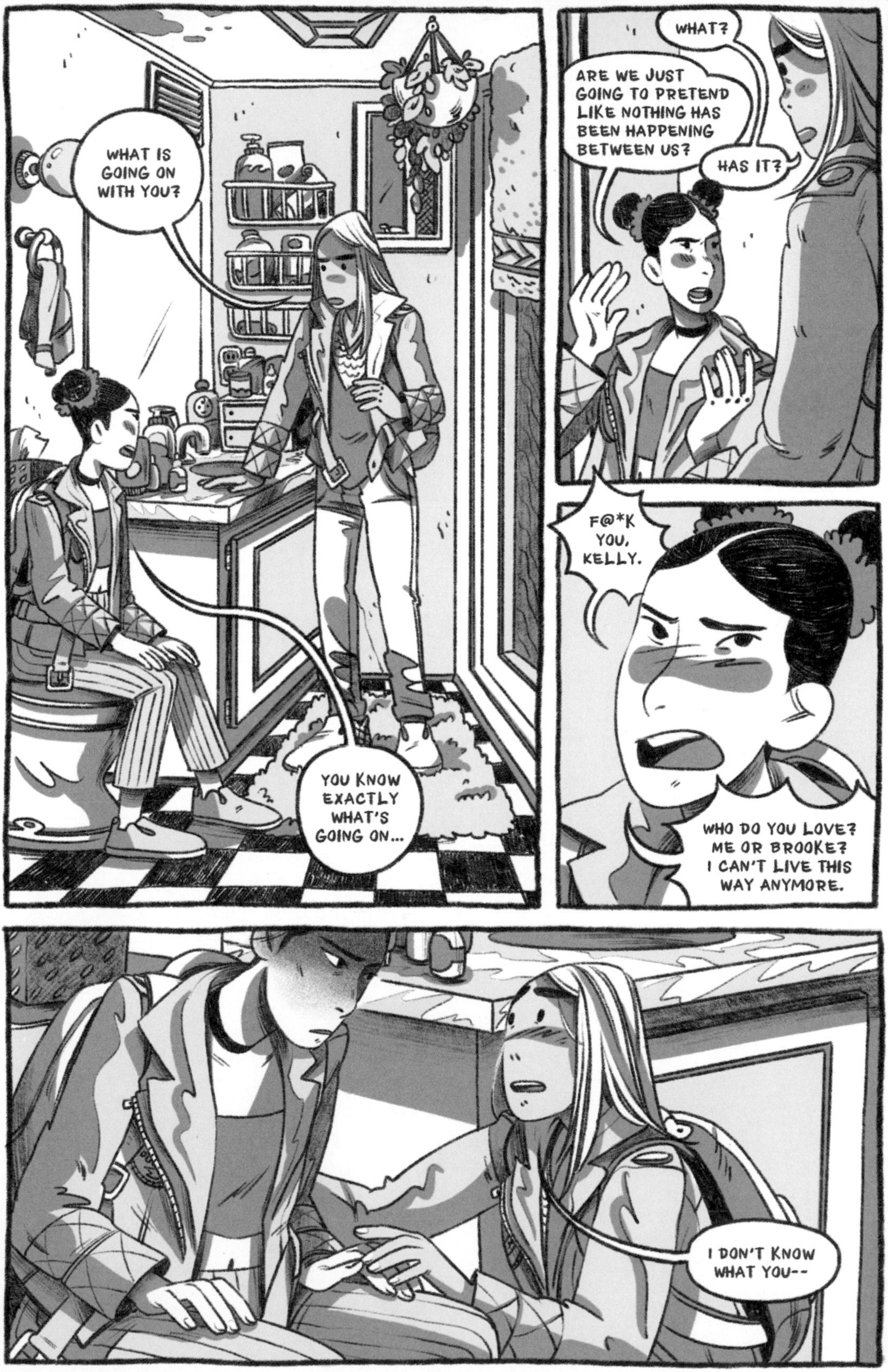
WHAT IS GOING ON WITH YOU?
YOU KNOW EXACTLY WHAT'S GOING ON...
WHAT?
ARE WE JUST GOING TO PRETEND LIKE NOTHING HAS BEEN HAPPENING BETWEEN US?
HAS IT?
F@*K YOU, KELLY.
WHO DO YOU LOVE? ME OR BROOKE? I CAN'T LIVE THIS WAY ANYMORE.
I DON'T KNOW WHAT YOU--

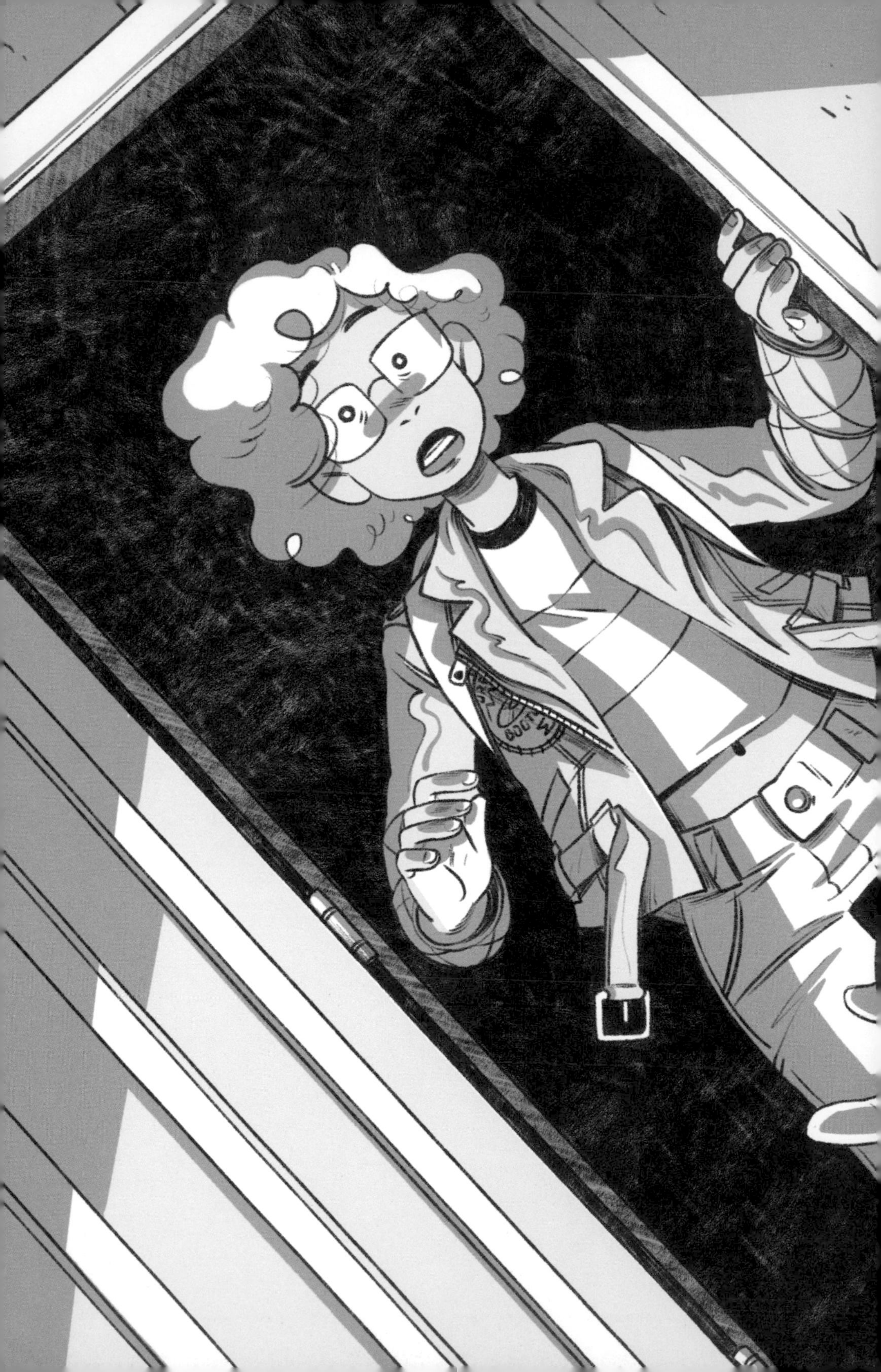

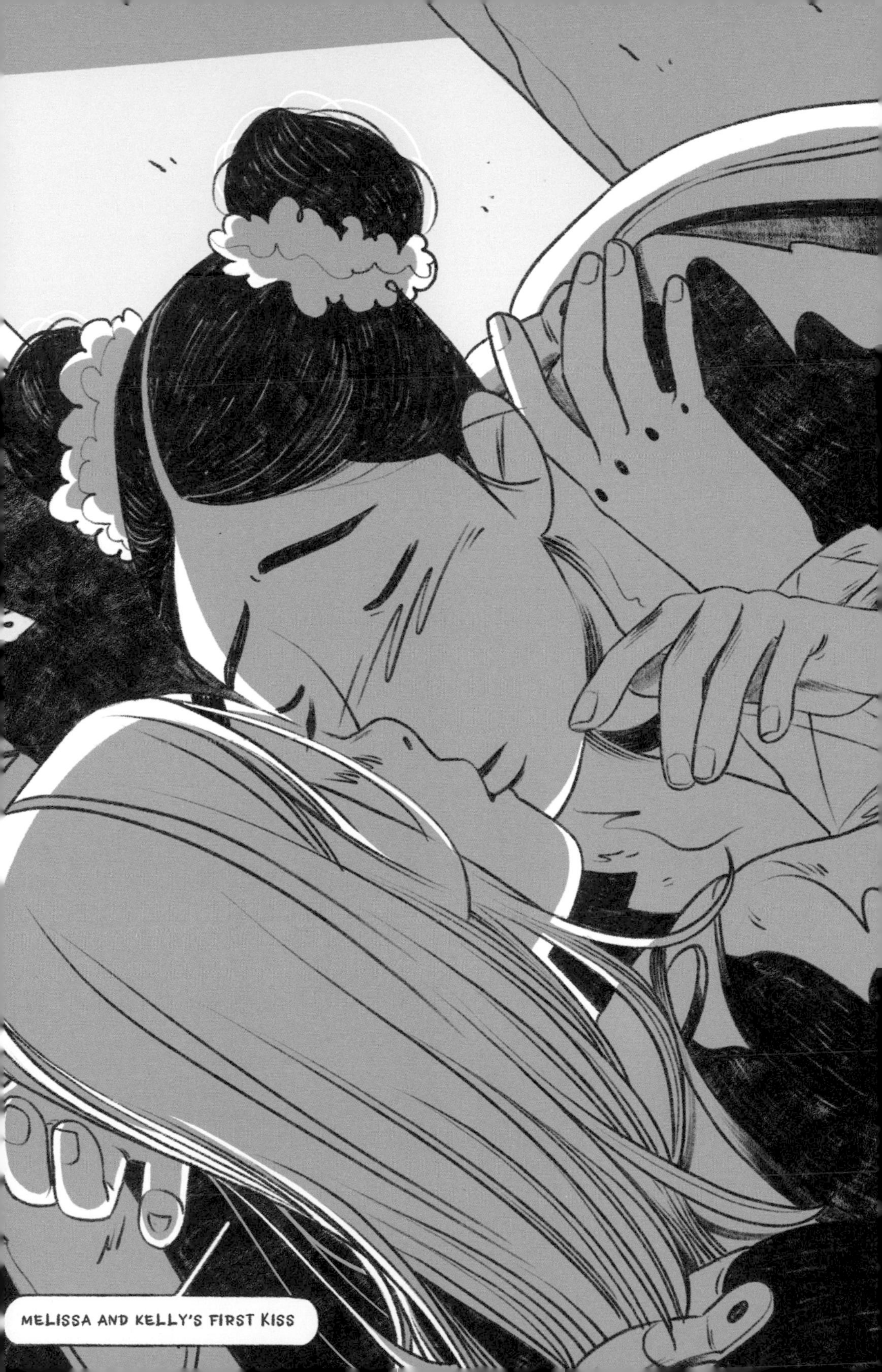
MELISSA AND KELLY'S FIRST KISS

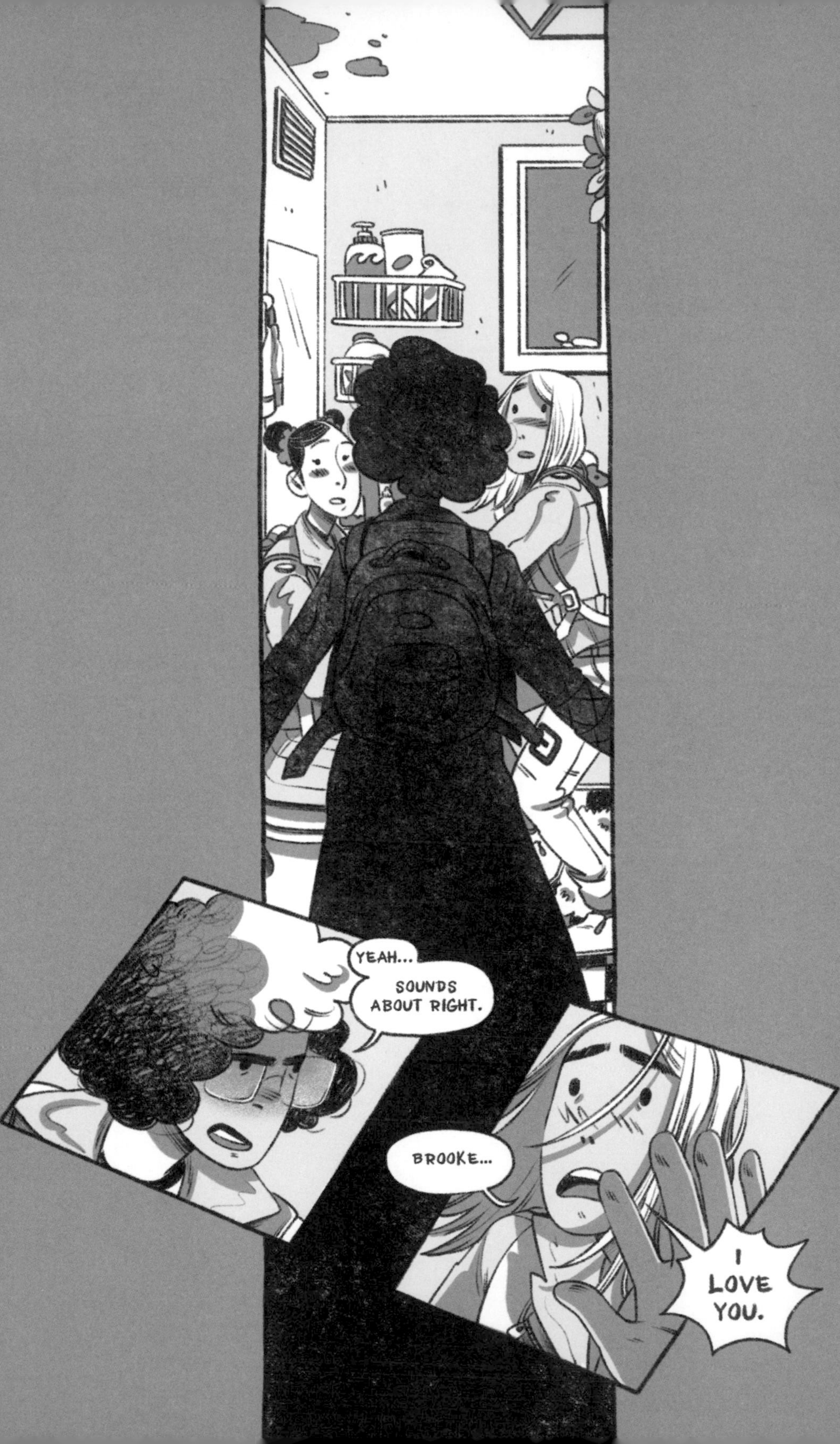
YEAH...
SOUNDS ABOUT RIGHT.
BROOKE...
I LOVE YOU.

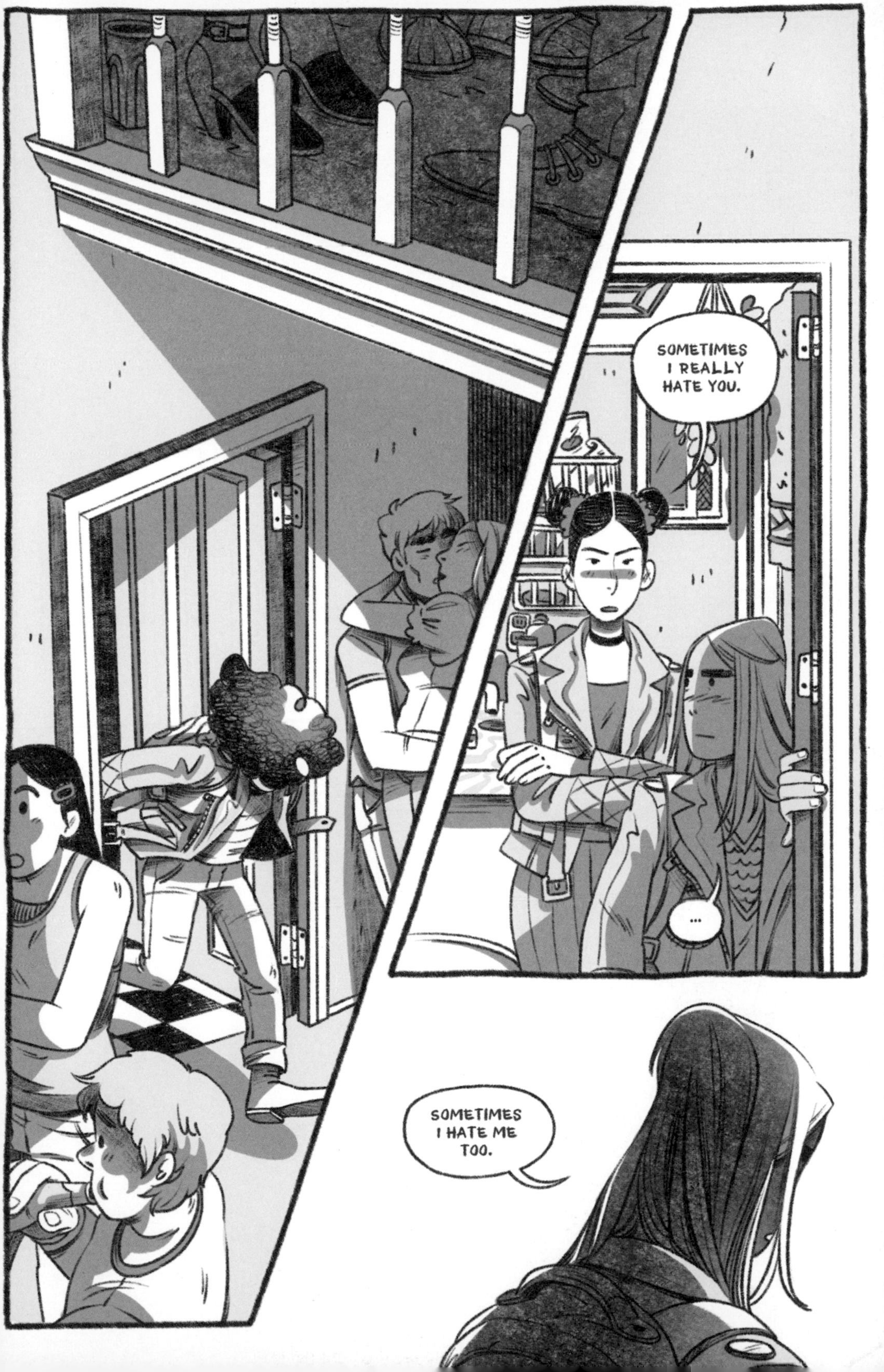
SOMETIMES I REALLY HATE YOU.
...
SOMETIMES I HATE ME TOO.

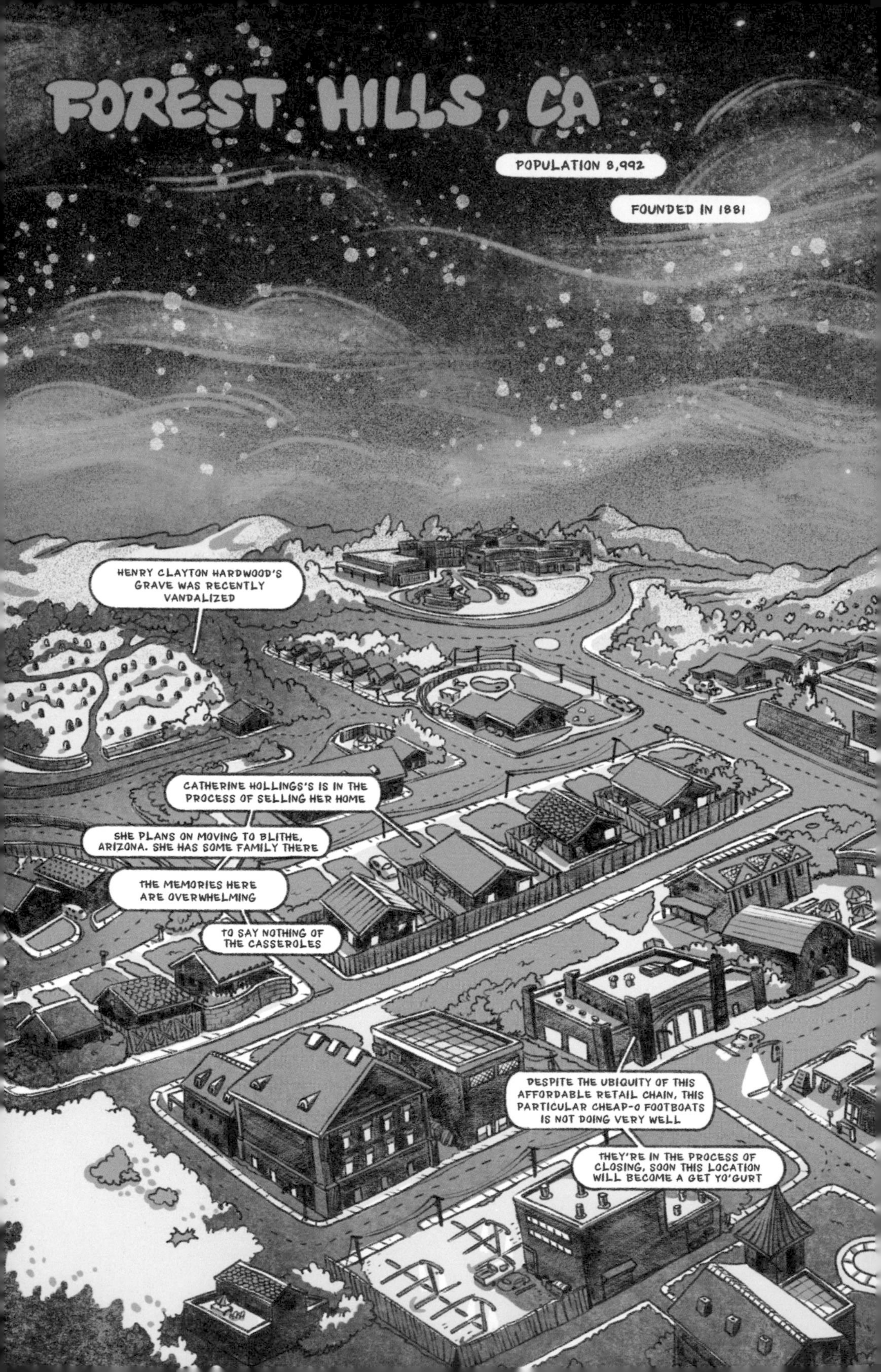
FOREST HILLS, CA
POPULATION 8,992
FOUNDED IN 1881
HENRY CLAYTON HARDWOOD'S GRAVE WAS RECENTLY VANDALIZED
CATHERINE HOLLINGS'S IS IN THE PROCESS OF SELLING HER HOME
SHE PLANS ON MOVING TO BLITHE, ARIZONA. SHE HAS SOME FAMILY THERE
THE MEMORIES HERE ARE OVERWHELMING
TO SAY NOTHING OF THE CASSEROLES
DESPITE THE UBIQUITY OF THIS AFFORDABLE RETAIL CHAIN, THIS PARTICULAR CHEAP-O FOOTBOATS IS NOT DOING VERY WELL
THEY'RE IN THE PROCESS OF CLOSING, SOON THIS LOCATION WILL BECOME A GET YO'GURT

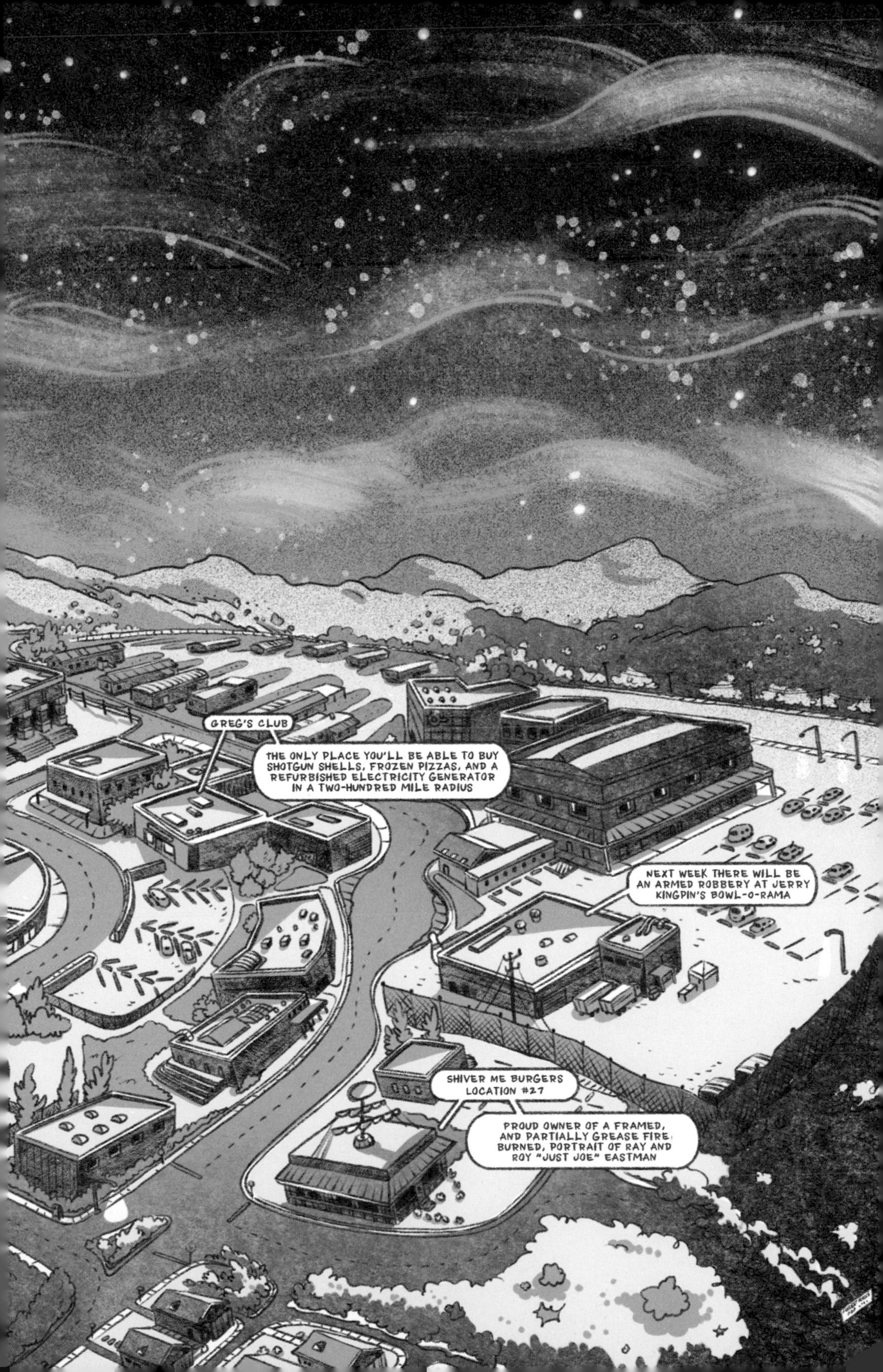
GREG'S CLUB
THE ONLY PLACE YOU'LL BE ABLE TO BUY SHOTGUN SHELLS, FROZEN PIZZAS, AND A REFURBISHED ELECTRICITY GENERATOR IN A TWO-HUNDRED MILE RADIUS
NEXT WEEK THERE WILL BE AN ARMED ROBBERY AT JERRY KINGPIN'S BOWL-O-RAMA
SHIVER ME BURGERS LOCATION #27
PROUD OWNER OF A FRAMED, AND PARTIALLY GREASE FIRE BURNED, PORTRAIT OF RAY AND ROY "JUST JOE" EASTMAN

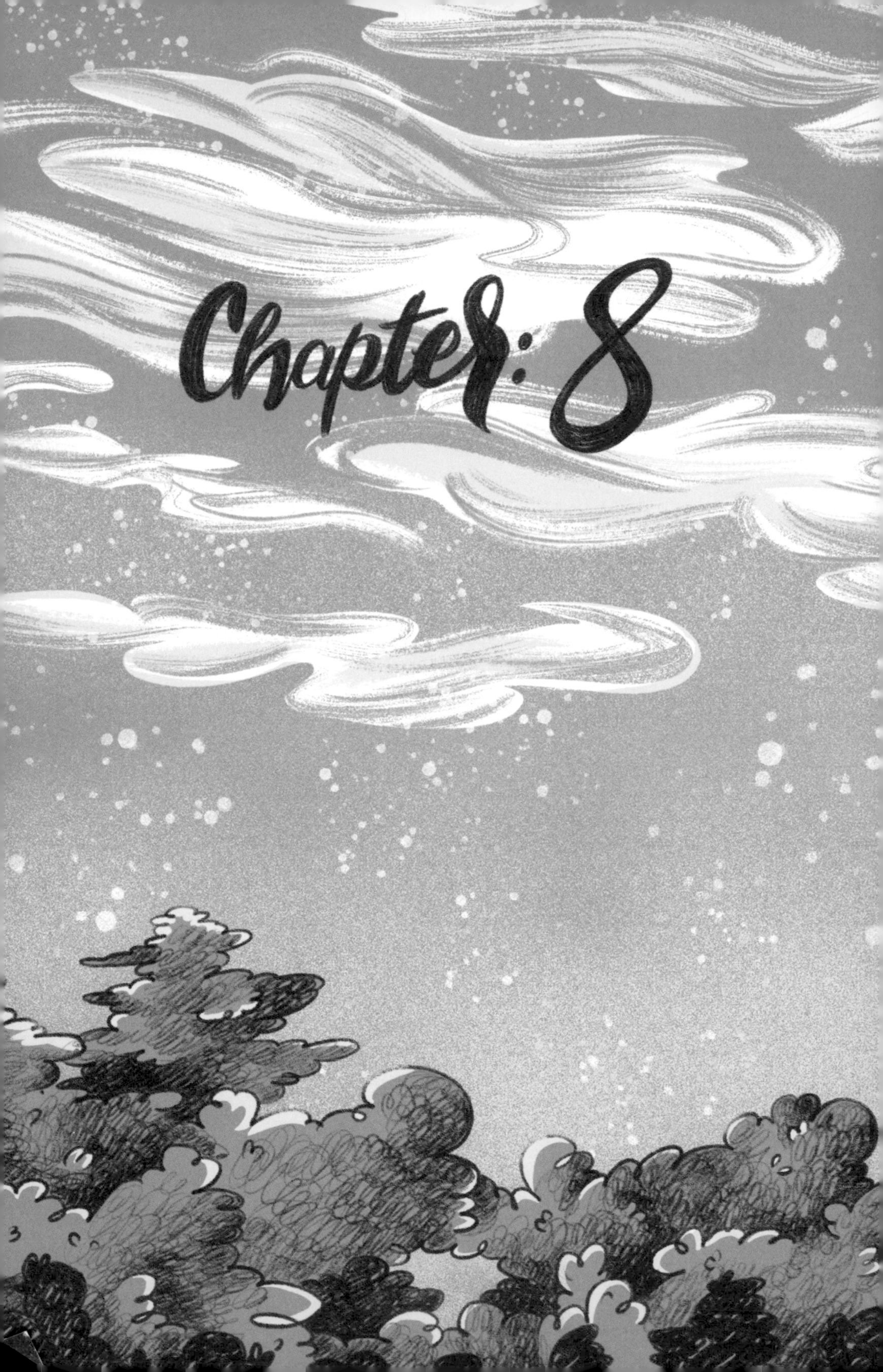
Chapter: 8

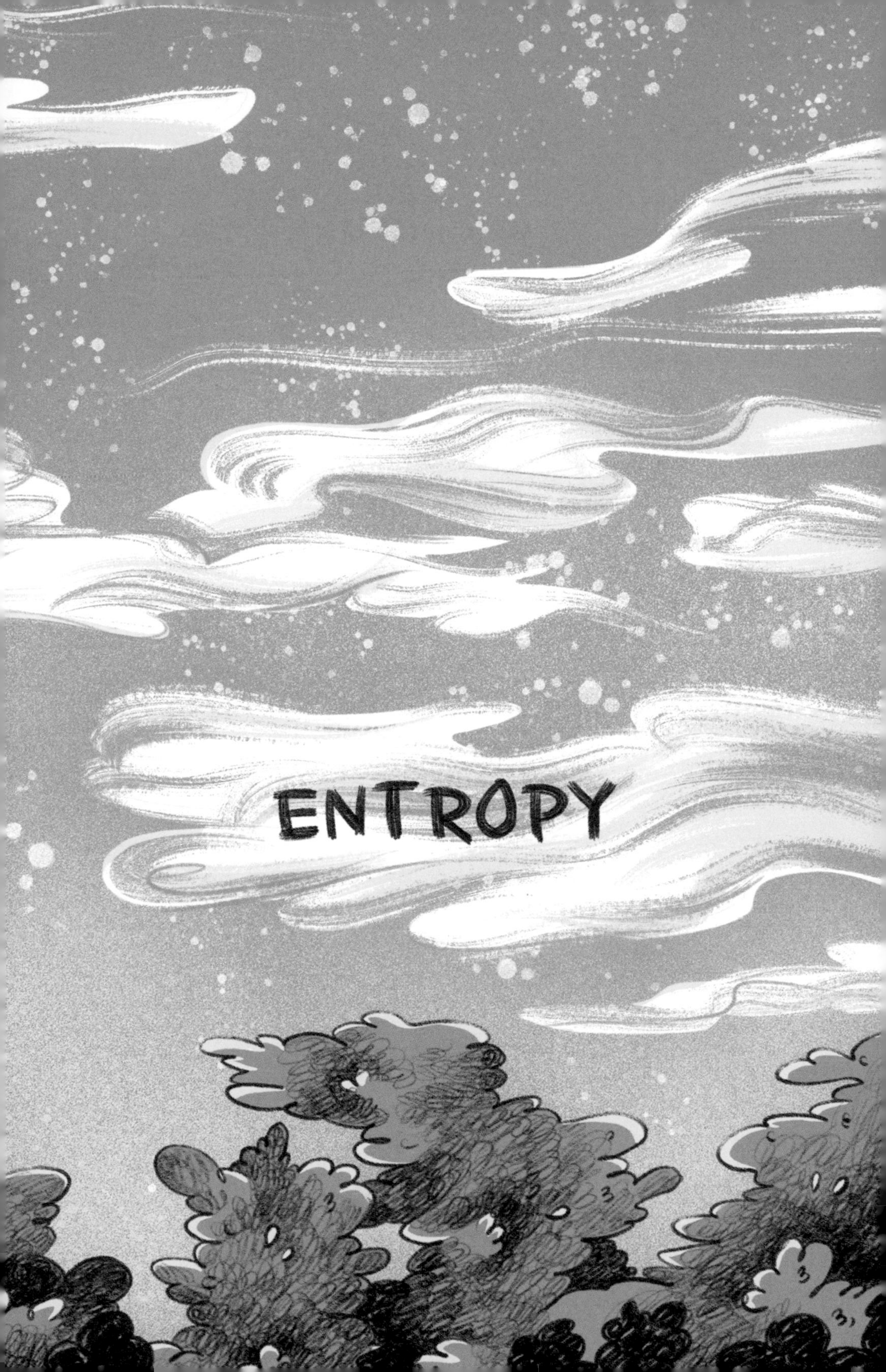
ENTROPY

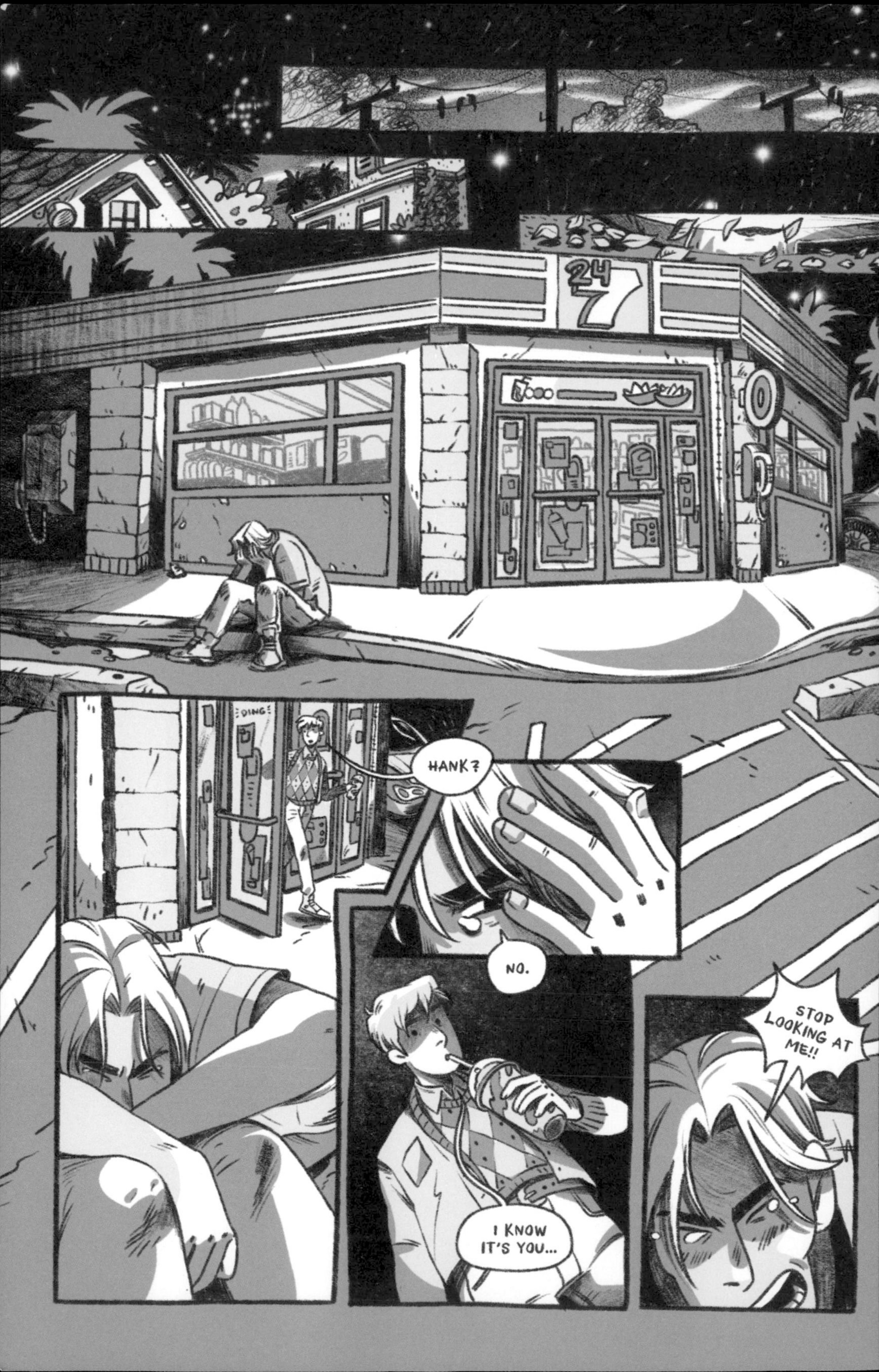
24 7
DING
HANK?
NO.
I KNOW IT'S YOU...
STOP LOOKING AT ME!!

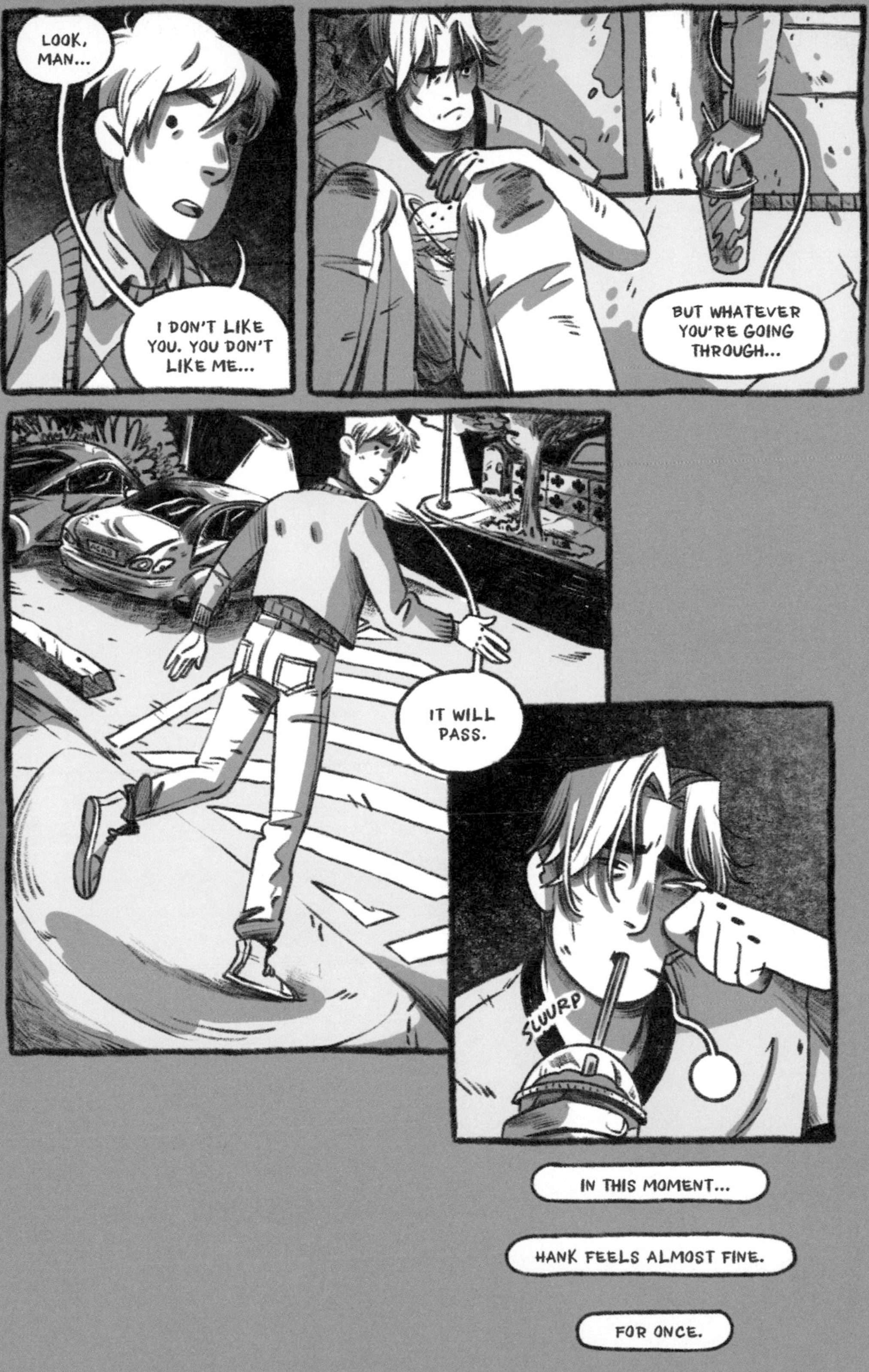
LOOK, MAN...
I DON'T LIKE YOU. YOU DON'T LIKE ME...
BUT WHATEVER YOU'RE GOING THROUGH...
IT WILL PASS.
SLUURP
IN THIS MOMENT...
HANK FEELS ALMOST FINE.
FOR ONCE.

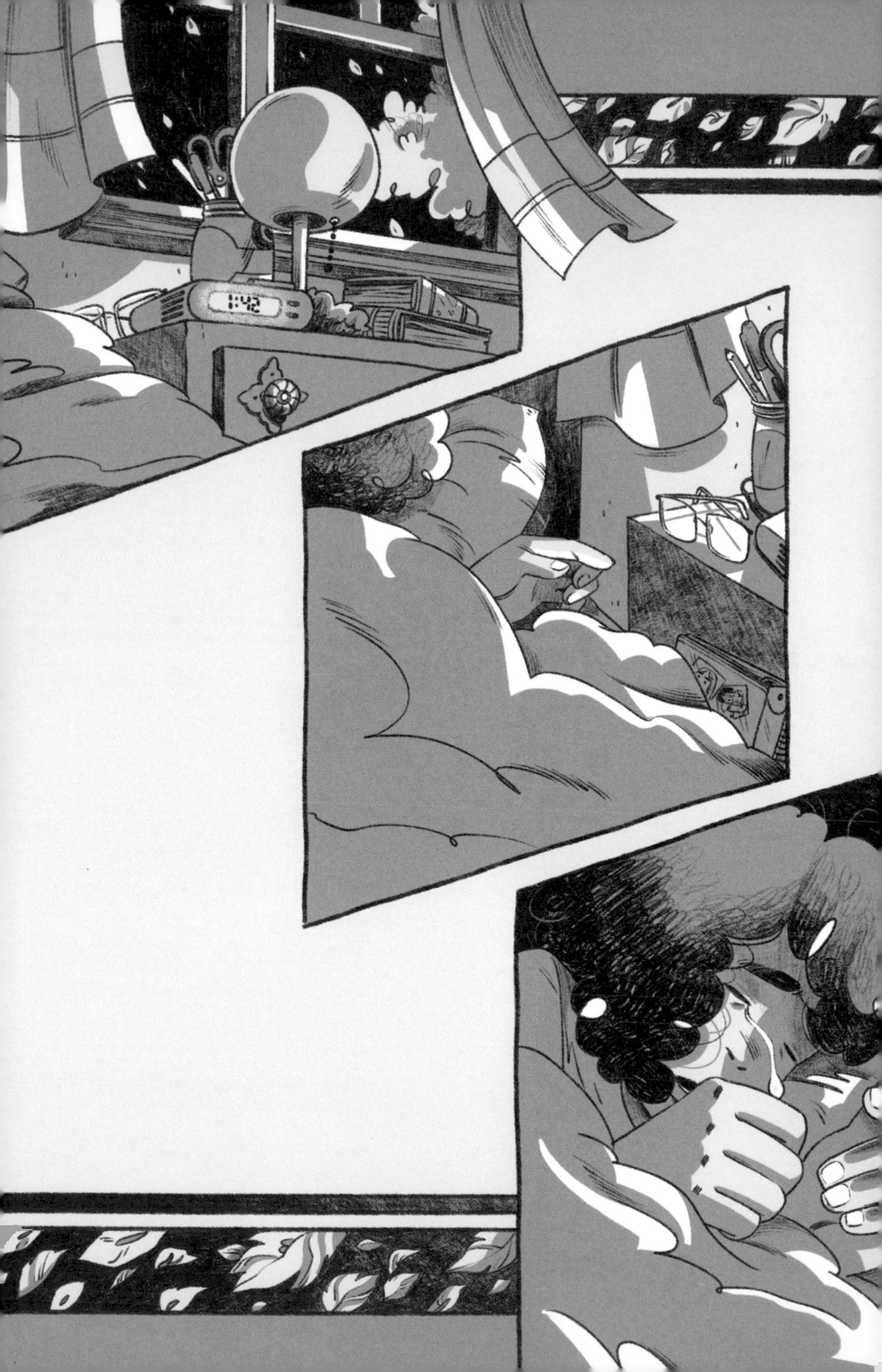
1:42

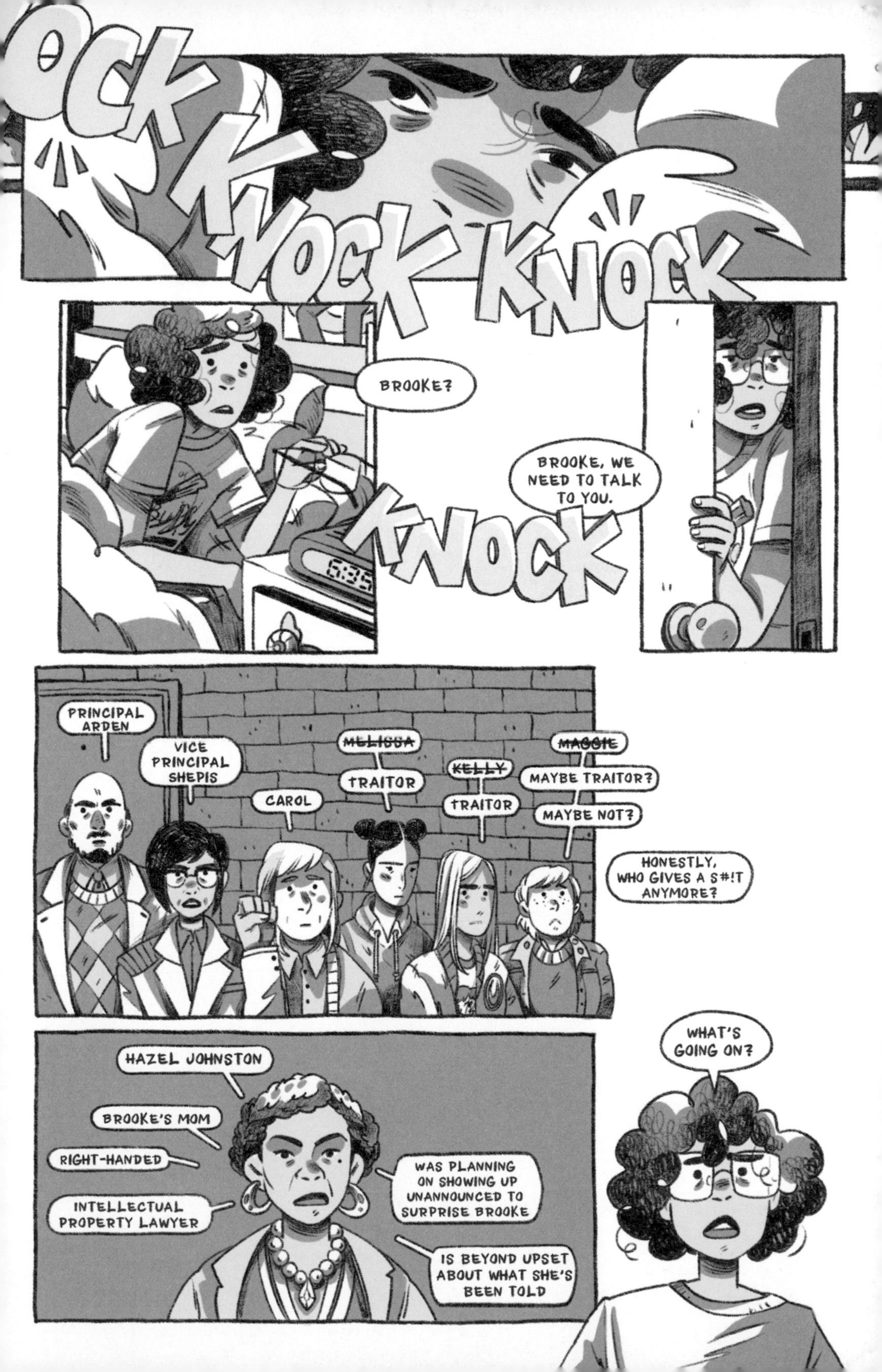
OCK
KNOCK KNOCK
BROOKE?
BROOKE, WE NEED TO TALK TO YOU.
KNOCK
PRINCIPAL ARDEN
VICE PRINCIPAL SHEPIS
CAROL
~~MELISSA~~
TRAITOR
~~KELLY~~
TRAITOR
~~MAGGIE~~
MAYBE TRAITOR?
MAYBE NOT?
HONESTLY, WHO GIVES A S#!T ANYMORE?
HAZEL JOHNSTON
BROOKE'S MOM
RIGHT-HANDED
INTELLECTUAL PROPERTY LAWYER
WAS PLANNING ON SHOWING UP UNANNOUNCED TO SURPRISE BROOKE
IS BEYOND UPSET ABOUT WHAT SHE'S BEEN TOLD
WHAT'S GOING ON?

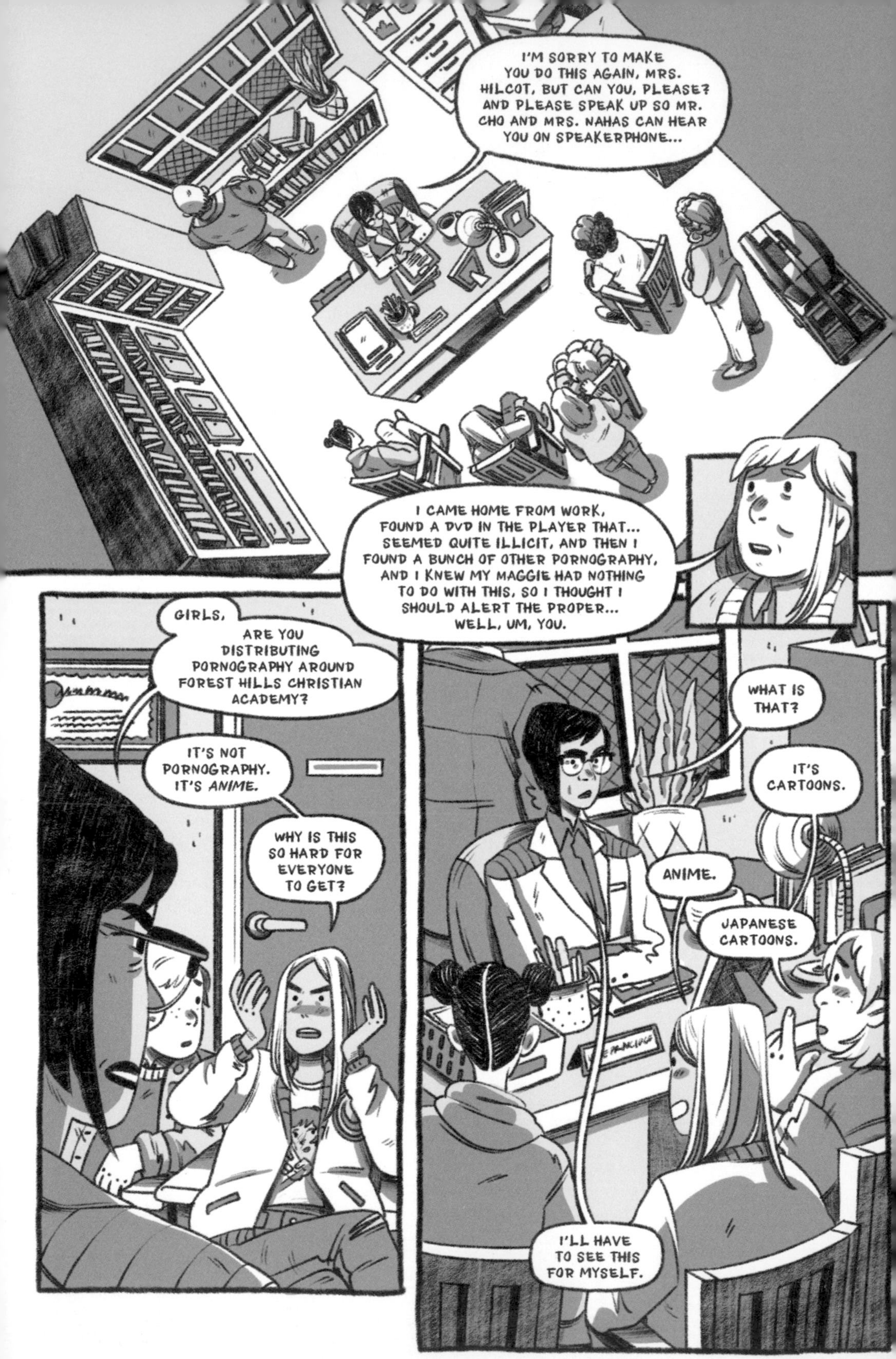
I'M SORRY TO MAKE YOU DO THIS AGAIN, MRS. HILCOT, BUT CAN YOU, PLEASE? AND PLEASE SPEAK UP SO MR. CHO AND MRS. NAHAS CAN HEAR YOU ON SPEAKERPHONE...
I CAME HOME FROM WORK, FOUND A DVD IN THE PLAYER THAT... SEEMED QUITE ILLICIT, AND THEN I FOUND A BUNCH OF OTHER PORNOGRAPHY, AND I KNEW MY MAGGIE HAD NOTHING TO DO WITH THIS, SO I THOUGHT I SHOULD ALERT THE PROPER... WELL, UM, YOU.
GIRLS,
ARE YOU DISTRIBUTING PORNOGRAPHY AROUND FOREST HILLS CHRISTIAN ACADEMY?
IT'S NOT PORNOGRAPHY. IT'S *ANIME.*
WHY IS THIS SO HARD FOR EVERYONE TO GET?
WHAT IS THAT?
IT'S CARTOONS.
ANIME.
JAPANESE CARTOONS.
I'LL HAVE TO SEE THIS FOR MYSELF.

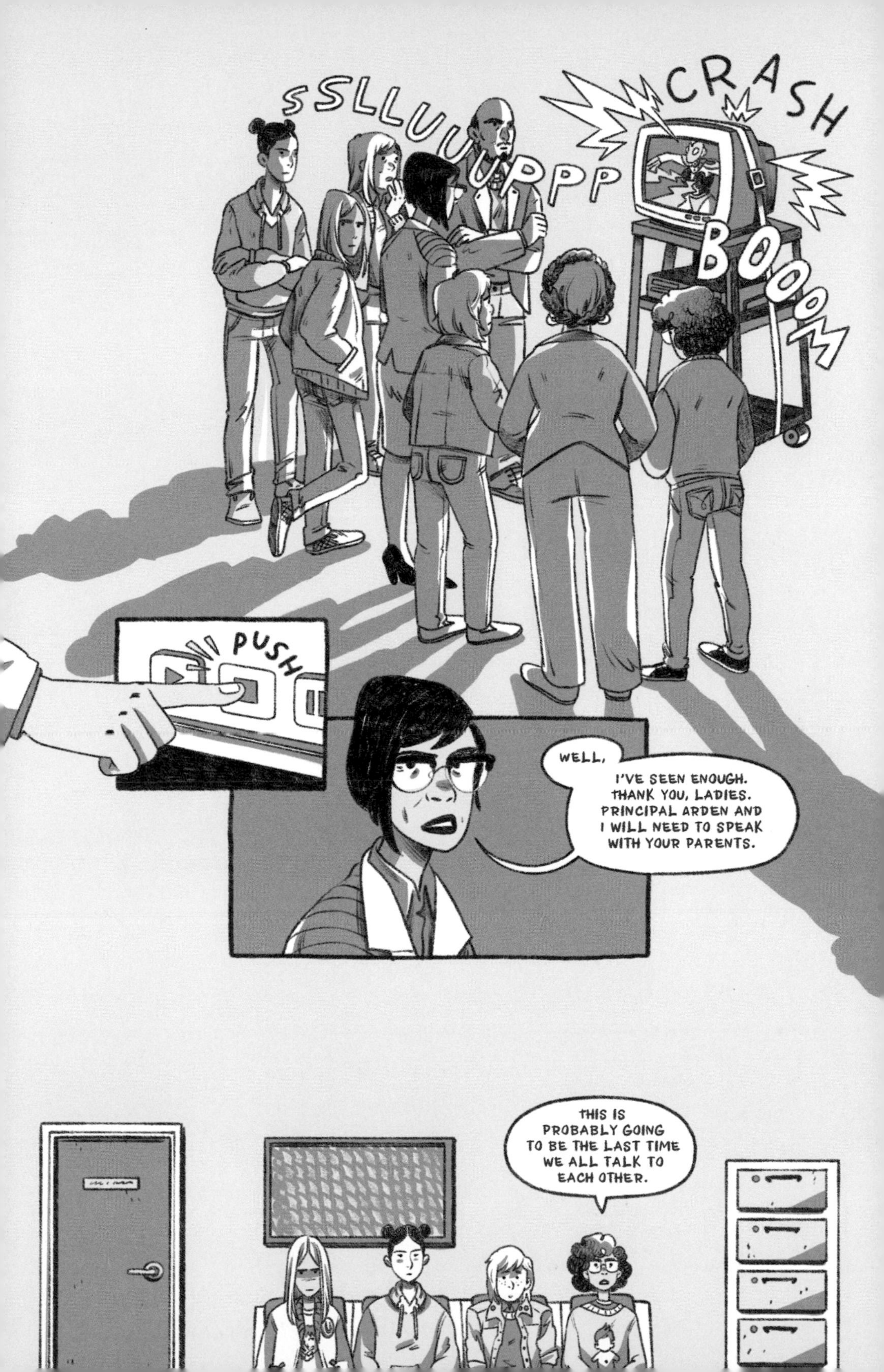
SSLLUUUPPP
CRASH
BOOOM
PUSH
WELL,
I'VE SEEN ENOUGH. THANK YOU, LADIES. PRINCIPAL ARDEN AND I WILL NEED TO SPEAK WITH YOUR PARENTS.
THIS IS PROBABLY GOING TO BE THE LAST TIME WE ALL TALK TO EACH OTHER.

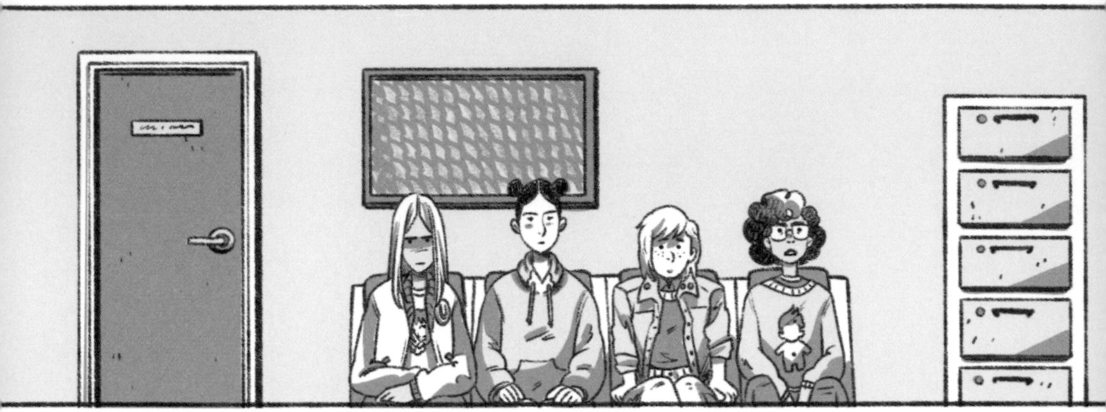

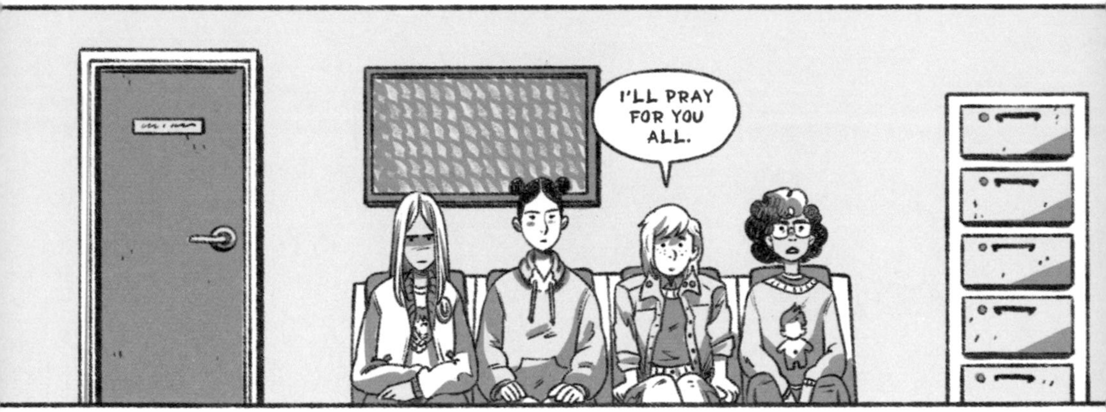
I'LL PRAY FOR YOU ALL.

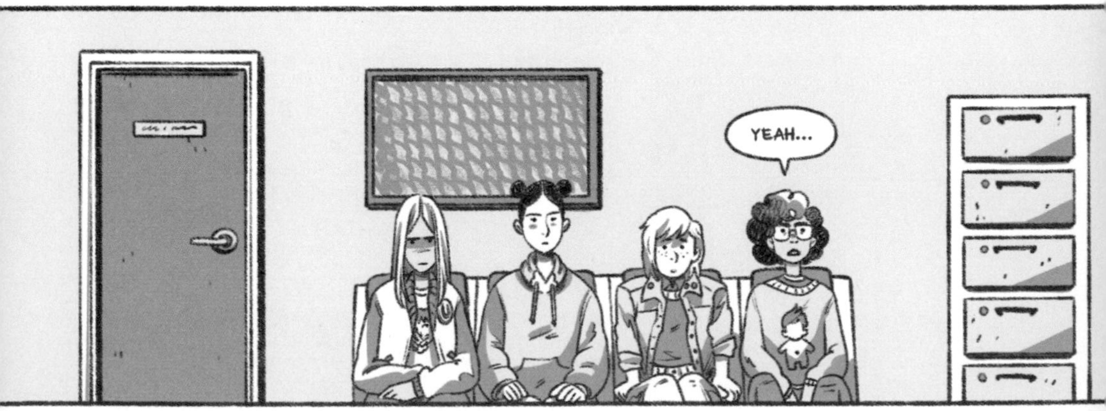
YEAH...

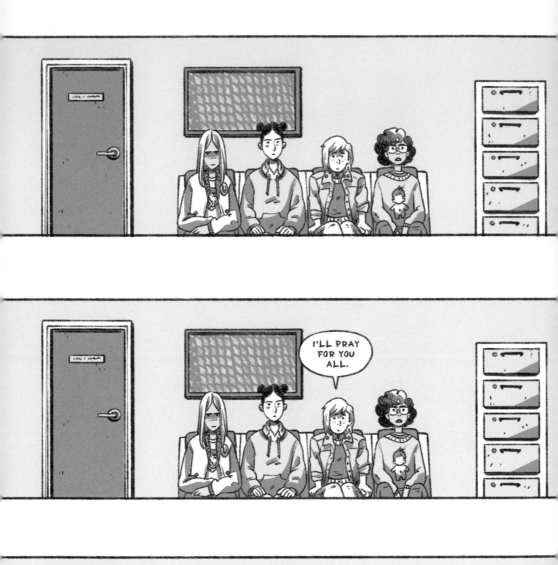

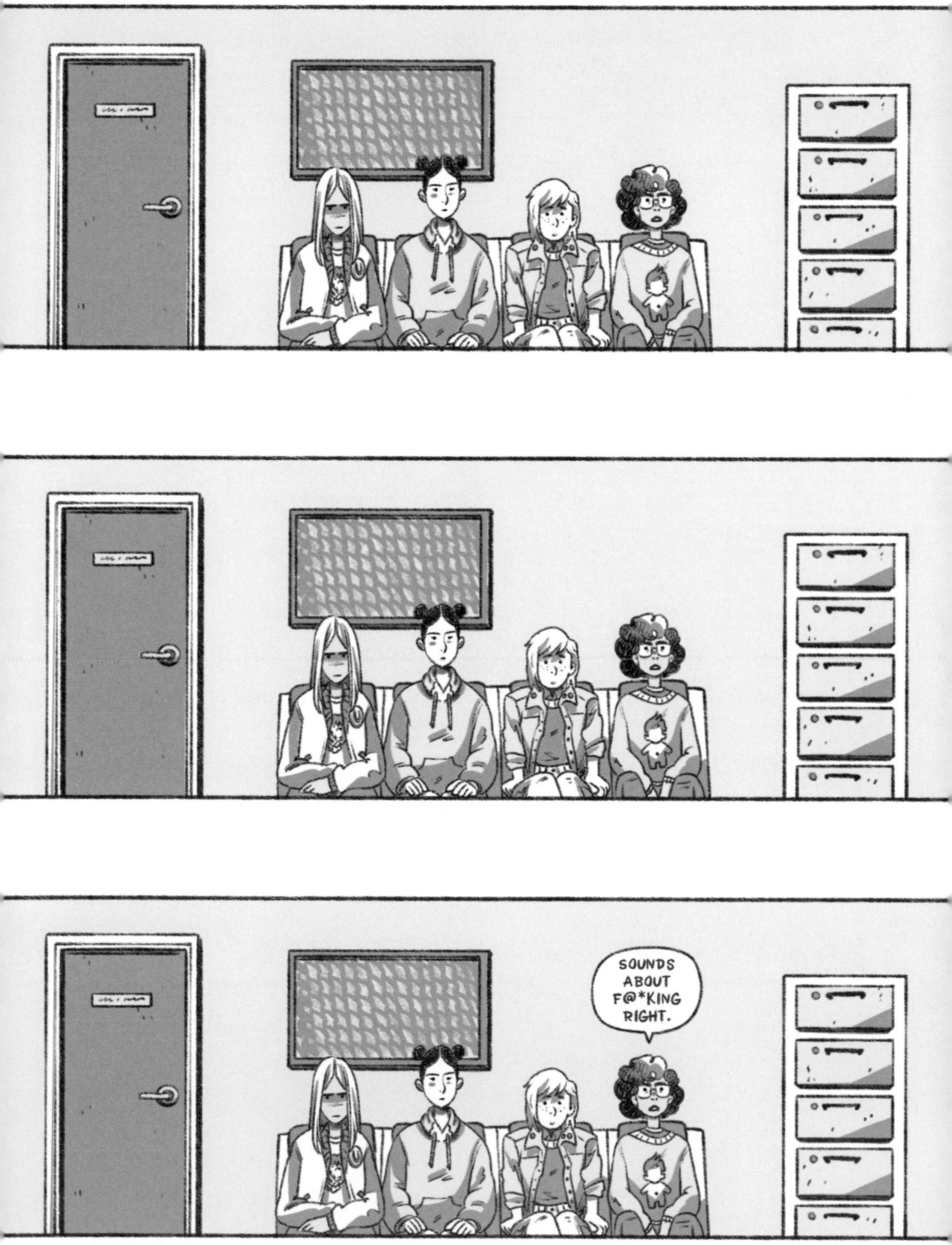
SOUNDS ABOUT F@*KING RIGHT.

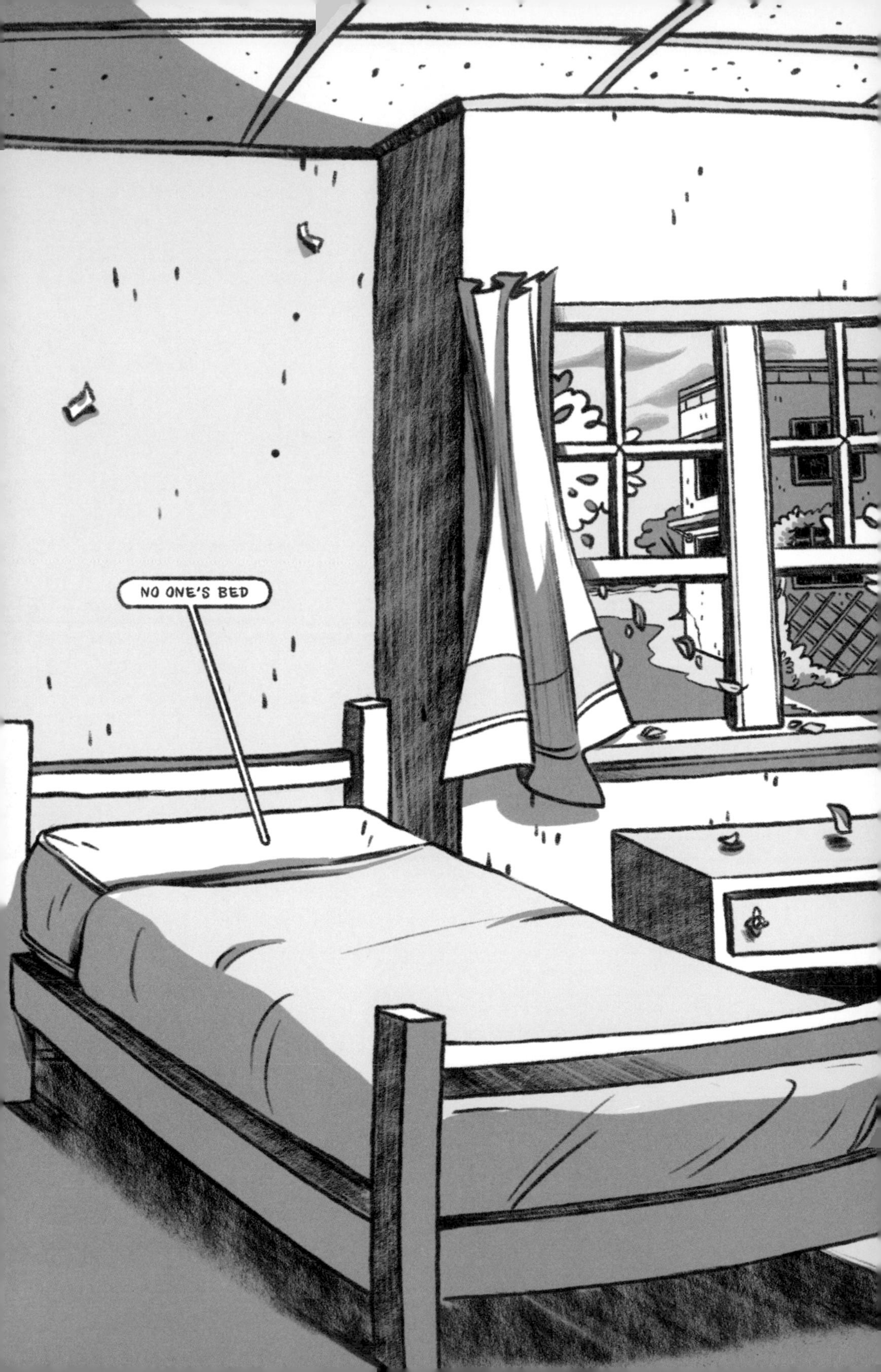
NO ONE'S BED

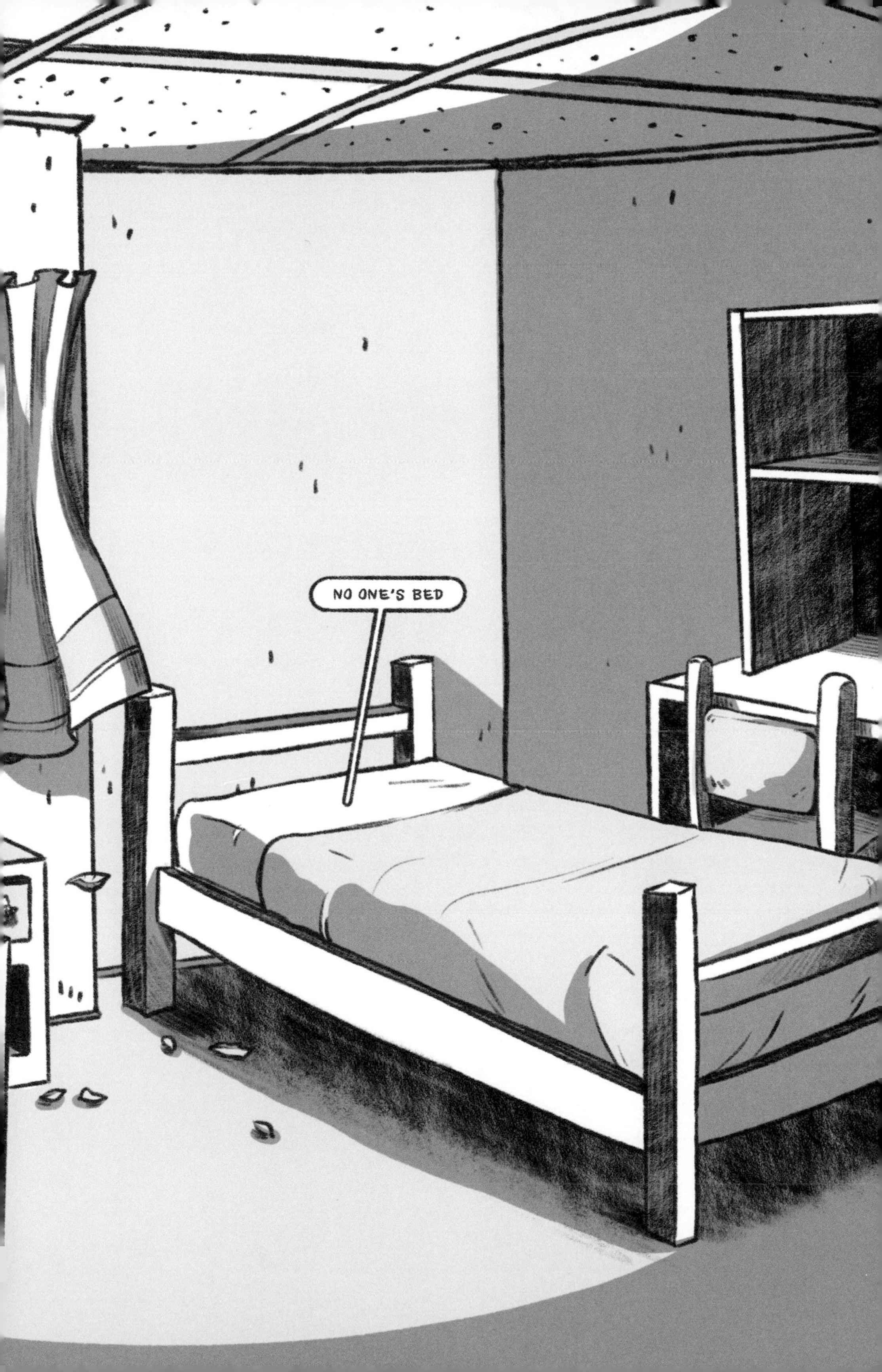
NO ONE'S BED

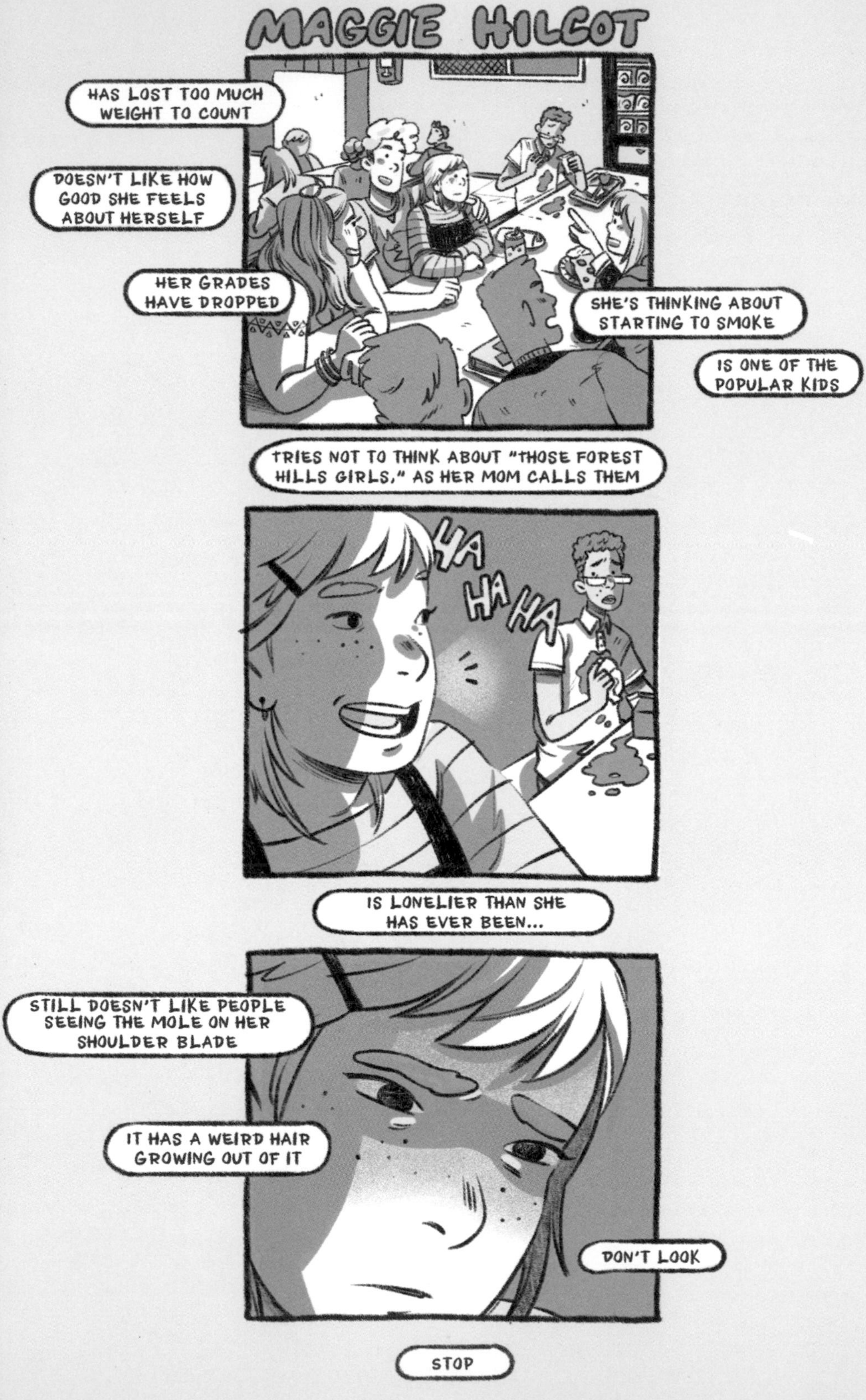
MAGGIE HILCOT
HAS LOST TOO MUCH WEIGHT TO COUNT
DOESN'T LIKE HOW GOOD SHE FEELS ABOUT HERSELF
HER GRADES HAVE DROPPED
SHE'S THINKING ABOUT STARTING TO SMOKE
IS ONE OF THE POPULAR KIDS
TRIES NOT TO THINK ABOUT "THOSE FOREST HILLS GIRLS," AS HER MOM CALLS THEM
HA HA HA
IS LONELIER THAN SHE HAS EVER BEEN...
STILL DOESN'T LIKE PEOPLE SEEING THE MOLE ON HER SHOULDER BLADE
IT HAS A WEIRD HAIR GROWING OUT OF IT
DON'T LOOK
STOP

MELISSA CHO

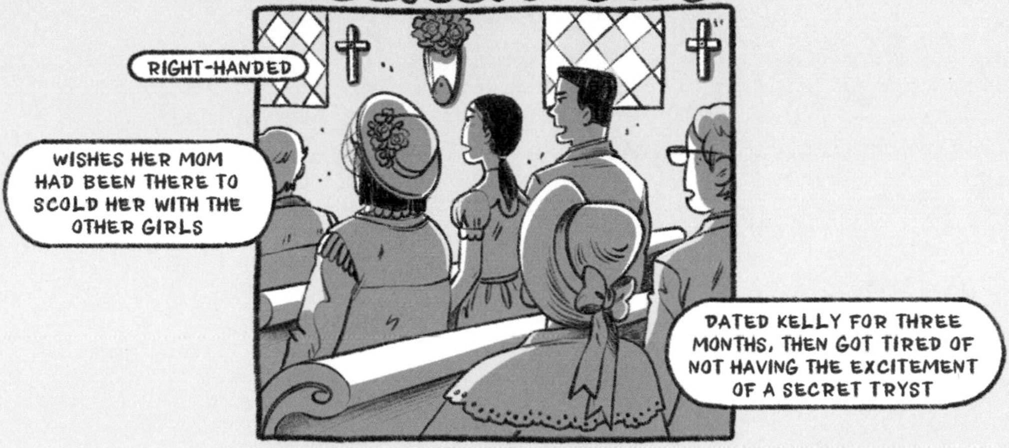
RIGHT-HANDED
WISHES HER MOM HAD BEEN THERE TO SCOLD HER WITH THE OTHER GIRLS
DATED KELLY FOR THREE MONTHS, THEN GOT TIRED OF NOT HAVING THE EXCITEMENT OF A SECRET TRYST

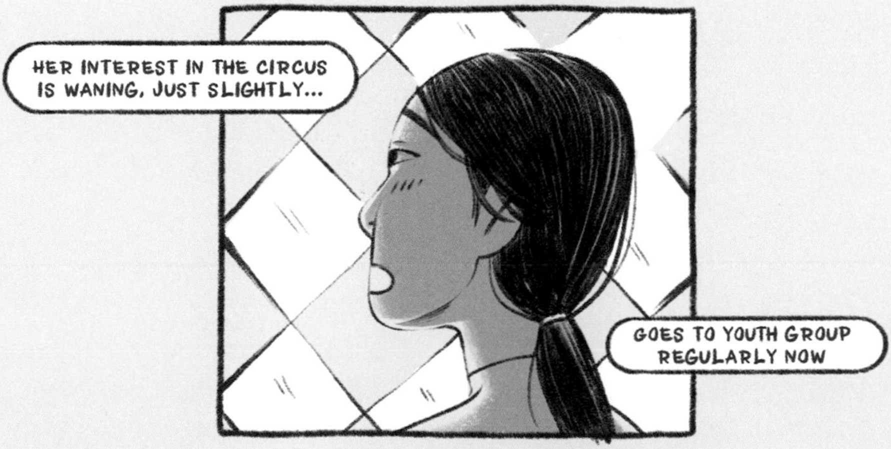
HER INTEREST IN THE CIRCUS IS WANING, JUST SLIGHTLY...
GOES TO YOUTH GROUP REGULARLY NOW

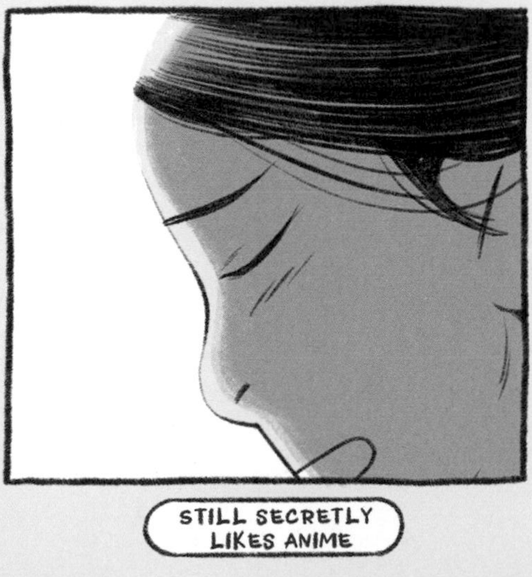
STILL SECRETLY LIKES ANIME

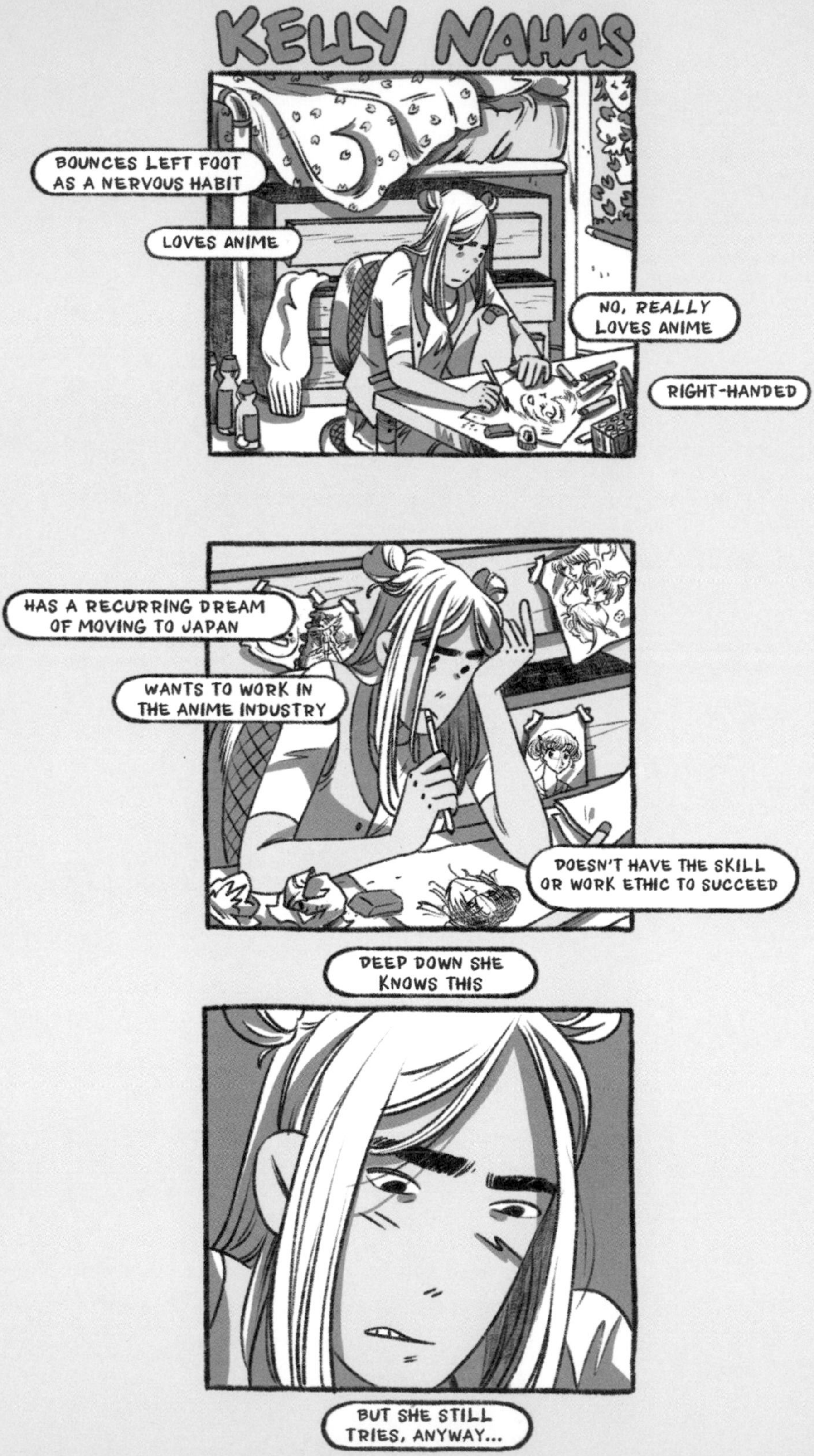
KELLY NAHAS
BOUNCES LEFT FOOT AS A NERVOUS HABIT
LOVES ANIME
NO, REALLY LOVES ANIME
RIGHT-HANDED
HAS A RECURRING DREAM OF MOVING TO JAPAN
WANTS TO WORK IN THE ANIME INDUSTRY
DOESN'T HAVE THE SKILL OR WORK ETHIC TO SUCCEED
DEEP DOWN SHE KNOWS THIS
BUT SHE STILL TRIES, ANYWAY...

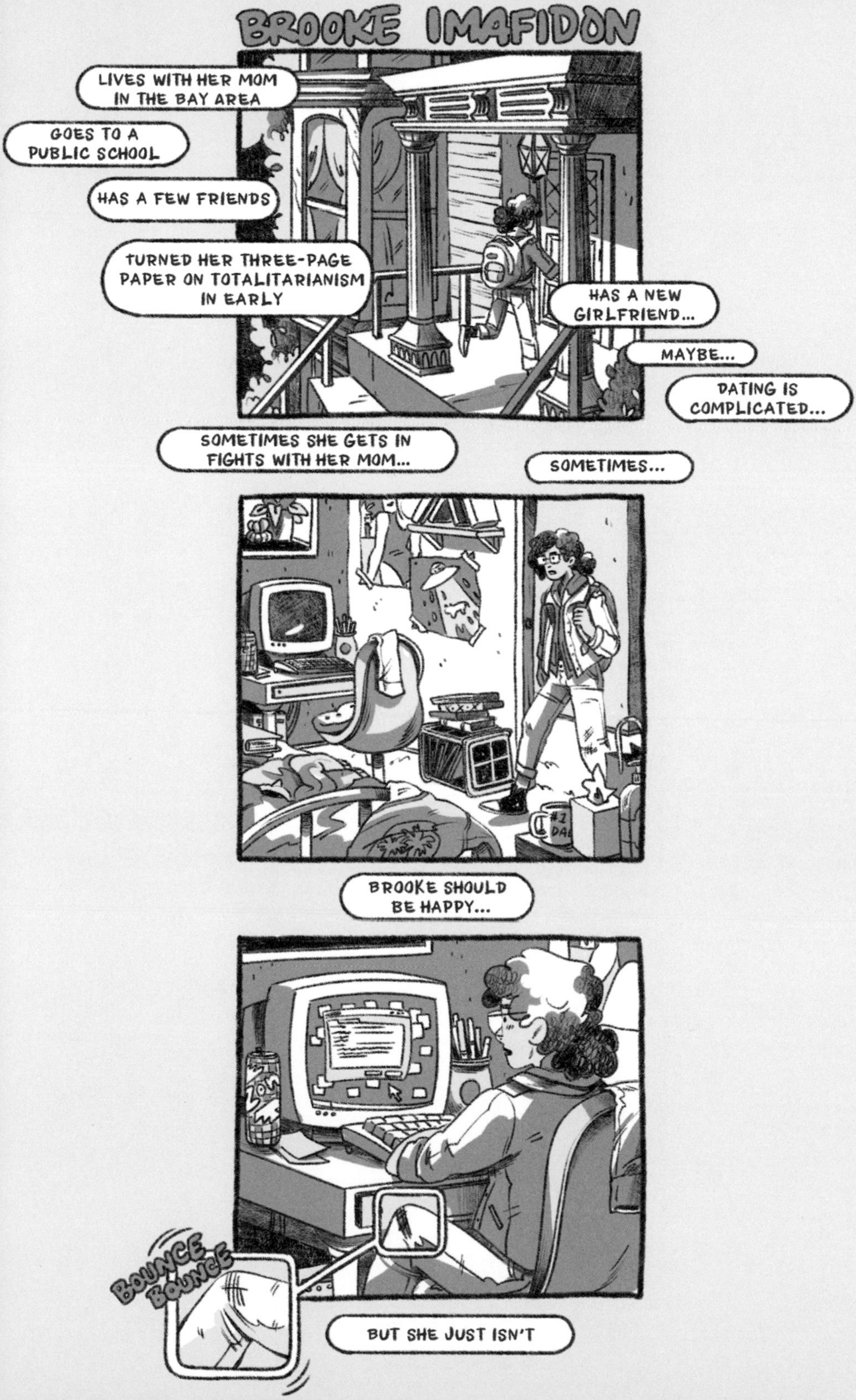
BROOKE IMAFIDON
LIVES WITH HER MOM IN THE BAY AREA
GOES TO A PUBLIC SCHOOL
HAS A FEW FRIENDS
TURNED HER THREE-PAGE PAPER ON TOTALITARIANISM IN EARLY
HAS A NEW GIRLFRIEND...
MAYBE...
DATING IS COMPLICATED...
SOMETIMES SHE GETS IN FIGHTS WITH HER MOM...
SOMETIMES...
BROOKE SHOULD BE HAPPY...
BOUNCE BOUNCE
BUT SHE JUST ISN'T

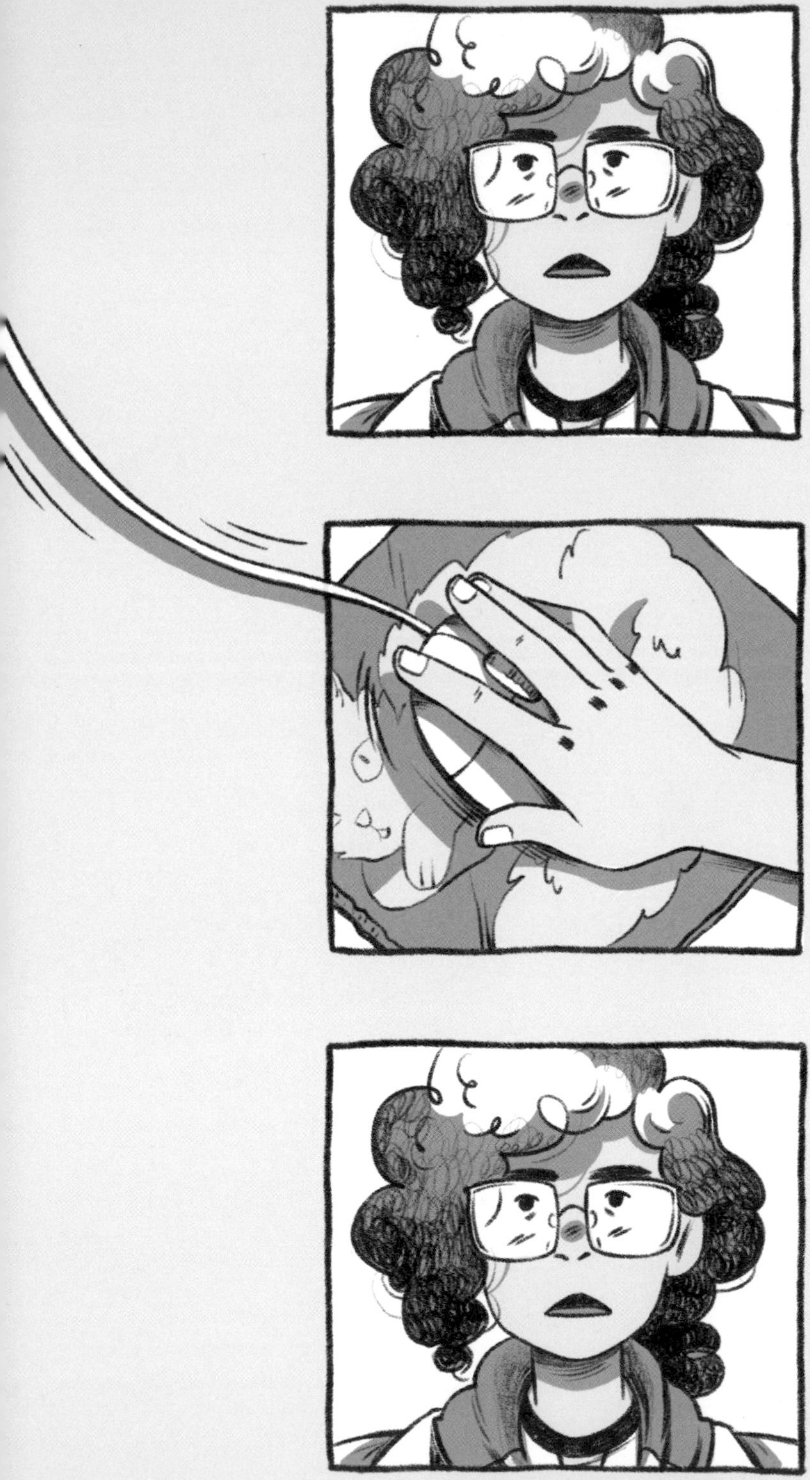

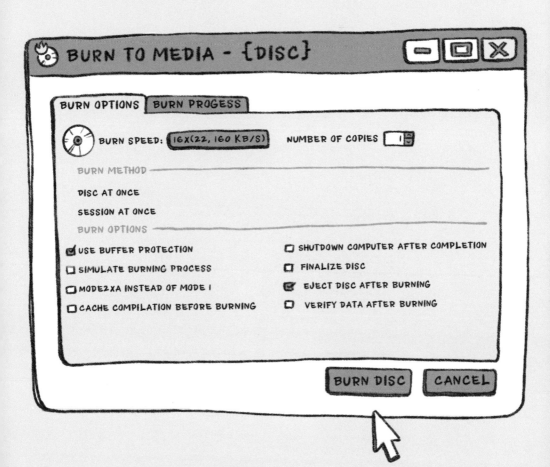

BURN TO MEDIA - {DISC}

BURN OPTIONS | **BURN PROGESS**

BURN SPEED: 16X(22,160 KB/S)   NUMBER OF COPIES [1]

BURN METHOD

DISC AT ONCE

SESSION AT ONCE

BURN OPTIONS

☑ USE BUFFER PROTECTION   ☐ SHUTDOWN COMPUTER AFTER COMPLETION

☐ SIMULATE BURNING PROCESS   ☐ FINALIZE DISC

☐ MODE2XA INSTEAD OF MODE 1   ☑ EJECT DISC AFTER BURNING

☐ CACHE COMPILATION BEFORE BURNING   ☐ VERIFY DATA AFTER BURNING

[BURN DISC]   [CANCEL]

BURN DISC

EVOLVE OR DIE

WELL, YOU'VE FINISHED OUR BOOK. Thank you. From the bottom of my heart, thank you. You don't know what it means to me that our book has found you. Nicole and I have been working on it for longer than I care to remember, and harder than I want to admit. There have been literal years of labor put into the pages that you've just read. Hopefully it shows. I'm exceedingly proud of the work Nicole and I have produced in this volume. I think it's a pretty accurate reflection of who we are and what we believe.

And that right there is the end goal.

I believe different art forms have different aims. For me, I think the goal of creating comics is to produce a record of who I am, who I was, or who I hope to be. And that's the thing with art—and being a human—you're always evolving. So, it's important to have a record so you can remind yourself where you've come from.

As I sit here, in my apartment, typing this essay, I find myself thinking about how much my perspective on the work has shifted and changed over time. And how, with any luck, it will be a book that people can have a relationship with and make their own drifting connections to.

All good art evolves. Both in a literal sense and metaphorical. When you first start to build an idea that will eventually become a book, you have this vision of what it will be. It's a hazy view. But there's something that pushes you forward it. And as you refine it and hone it . . . it evolves.

Then, after you've made it, the work is theoretically inert, but the way you think about it evolves as you come to terms with its flaws or its shortcomings. And then it goes out into the world . . . and people find a sense of connection to it . . . and it changes again.

At this point, *Forest Hills Bootleg Society* has evolved so many times that I'm a little reticent to tell you what we initially set out to do. I don't know that it matches what we have now.

For Nicole and me, that's what comics are. Or at least that's what they aspire to be: evolutionary reflections of a collective dream we've had. Not documents or records of actual happenings, but a shimmering doppelganger comprised of our joint hallucination.

I find it somewhat sad to think about the biographies of projects. About how many books go unpublished and about the struggle and length of time it takes to finally see your work put out into the world.

But that's part of the process of creating. If it were easy, everyone would do it and it wouldn't mean anything. The inherent difficulty involved in producing the close to 230 pages you've just read are a testament to that. They're a witness to the commitment that Nicole and I have to the greatest artistic medium of all time: comics.

When we started talking about the book that would eventually become *Forest Hills Bootleg Society*, we talked a lot about our respective high school experiences, our maturing, and our formative moments. When I was in high school, I ended up buying bootleg anime from a smelly kid named Max, burned onto a DVD. I remember secreting it away and using a portable DVD player to watch it late into the night. There's something about finding your own emotional pocket dimension at that age that has a magic and a safety to it that doesn't exist at almost any other point in life. That feeling became the root emotion and guiding light for the process of creating this book. I wanted to try to replicate that tangibly interior feeling of finding something that's exclusively yours.

To be frank, I wanted our book to function like that for someone else. To be their secret. To be their dog-eared friend that they repeatedly escaped into when the world proved too tough.

My experience discovering bootleg DVDs led me to a simple and yet profound realization. Art is something that can save you. It can be used as a standard for your hopes, dreams, and beliefs. For some people, that art can become a trap. It can devour your identity. It can become an overwhelming and crushing weight. Or it can be a conduit to making friends and developing lifelong relationships. It all depends on how you use the power that art can give us all.

Nicole and I wanted to create something that both reflected our experiences and worked as a call to arms. A rallying cry for people who needed it. A beam of light in the darkness that said, "You're not alone.... And also: anime is pretty cool, I guess."

We have worked on quite a few projects together. If you liked this book, please check out our other books *F**k Off Squad* and *Everyone Is Tulip*. We approach each of our books with a unique vision or goal. We want to make work that transcends the boundaries of the page, and hopefully really connects with people. We think of ourselves as a band. Only we don't make music. We make comics. Comics that can, for the right person, save their life.

Our ultimate goal was to create the book that, had we found it in high school, would have changed our lives. It's not really up to us to say if that's happened or not, but that was the mission. We set out to tell a story that had a tangible sense of vulnerability and was about how hard it can be to attempt to grow and change. And how sometimes that growth comes in unexpected or less-than-healthy ways. We wanted to explore the traumas of infidelity and organized religion. And how the former feels like it will follow you for the rest of your days, while, in reality, it's the latter that will more often than not prove inescapable.

Just like the characters in our book try and fail and stumble forward into adulthood, I think *Forest Hills Bootleg Society* is a perfect sense-memory document of Nicole's and my personal evolution. I look at the pages, and I can immediately remember where we were when we had specific ideas or conversations. I can remember which subplots we deleted or altered. But that's my personal connection to the work—and now the work has found you. And you will create your own history and connection with it. If we've done our jobs right, this book will play a role in your personal evolution... which is all any artist can hope for.

YOUR FRIEND,
DAVEY
LOS ANGELES, 2022

atheneum

An imprint of Simon & Schuster Children's Publishing Division
1230 Avenue of the Americas, New York, New York 10020
This book is a work of fiction. Any references to historical events, real people, or real places
are used fictitiously. Other names, characters, places, and events are products of the author's
imagination, and any resemblance to actual events or places or persons, living or dead, is
entirely coincidental.
© 2022 by Dave Baker and Nicole Goux
Book design by Rebecca Syracuse © 2022 by Simon & Schuster, Inc.
For information about special discounts for bulk purchases, please contact Simon & Schuster
Special Sales at 1-866-506-1949 or business@simonandschuster.com.
The Simon & Schuster Speakers Bureau can bring authors to your live event. For more
information or to book an event, contact the Simon & Schuster Speakers Bureau at
1-866-248-3049 or visit our website at www.simonspeakers.com.
The illustrations for this book were rendered digitally.
Manufactured in China
First Edition
1 2 3 4 5 6 7 8 9 10
CIP data for this book is available from the Library of Congress.
ISBN 9781534469488 (pbk)
ISBN 9781534469495 (hc)
ISBN 9781534469501 (ebook)

FOREST HILLS BOOTLEG SOCIETY

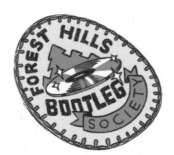